HIDDEN SOURCES

Tale of a Scoop

John Jessop

Published by New Generation Publishing in 2024

Copyright © John Jessop 2024

First Edition

The author asserts the moral right under the Copyright, Designs and Patents Act 1988 to be identified as the author of this work.

All Rights reserved. No part of this publication may be reproduced, stored in a retrieval system or transmitted, in any form or by any means without the prior consent of the author, nor be otherwise circulated in any form of binding or cover other than that which it is published and without a similar condition being imposed on the subsequent purchaser.

This book is a work of fiction.

All characters, other than those clearly in the public domain, and place names, other than those well-established such as towns and cities, are fictitious and any resemblance is purely coincidental.

Paperback ISBN: 978-1-83563-062-4
Hardback ISBN: 978-1-83563-063-1
eBook ISBN: 978-1-83563-064-8

www.newgeneration-publishing.com

ACKNOWLEDGEMENTS

This book was inspired by a television script I wrote for Dover Street Entertainment. I must thank Dover Street's directors, Graeme A Scott and Kathy A LoPrimo; first, for coming up with the initial idea, and second, for kindly permitting me to turn it into a novel.

I am also grateful to Denis Lyons, an old friend and professional colleague, who proof-read the text and provided useful advice in sundry other ways, notably an invaluable contribution to the chapter dealing with the complexities of United States securities law.

Above all, I thank my dear wife Martha for spotting various errors and omissions and for her many other helpful suggestions. We're still talking.

For Martha

PART ONE

The Reporter

Chapter 1

Nigel Harper woke up with a start in an unfamiliar bed. Through eyes not yet fully opened, he saw a large studio apartment, nicely furnished in the modern style, and somewhere in London, judging by the traffic noise outside the window. How he'd got there wasn't yet clear. The why was more easily explained by the woman still sleeping soundly under the sheet next to him. Late twenties, he guessed, an attractive redhead, lightly freckled, pre-Raphaelite curls cascading across the pillow.

Easing himself out of bed, he realized that he was fully dressed, minus only his jacket, tie and shoes. His head throbbed in time with a pile-driver thudding into the ground somewhere in the neighbourhood. Slowly, his brain began to function. Dim recollections began to accumulate. He'd spent the previous afternoon at a former colleague's memorial function in some dreary and obscure part of North London he had never been to before – one of those elusive places you only know from the front of buses, like Chalk Farm and Friern Barnet. After that, he and a couple of mates had extended the celebration trawling a variety of pubs on a southerly route that eventually guided them, some time before midnight, to Proud Mary's, his favourite Mayfair nightclub.

Glancing at the comatose woman in the bed, his memory placed her as the girl at the bar who'd been the object of his amorous attention. Obviously, it had paid off. Or had it? Among the many questions he now asked himself was why he'd woken up in his daytime clothes. He could think of several explanations, none of them reassuring. Noticing the open bathroom door, he tiptoed over and sloshed cold water over his face, which stared back at him from the mirror with an expression of disapproval mingled with shock. He wiped toothpaste over his teeth with a finger. Those cursory ablutions completed, he emerged to look for his jacket and tie. He found them neatly draped over a chair, his shoes underneath. Preparing to leave quietly, he put them on, feeling slightly ridiculous and vaguely uneasy.

The woman stirred. "What time is it?" The voice was sleepy, husky and even from those four short words could be identified as distinctly Home Counties.

Nigel checked his watch. "Ten o'clock. Good morning, by the way."

Propping herself up, she looked at him with an expression that suggested her own state of mind was no less confused than his. "And good morning to you," she said. "Nigel, isn't it?"

"It is."

"Ace political reporter with the *Morning Post*, as I recall."

"Well remembered," he mumbled. He didn't add her name because he couldn't remember it. "I must go. I was about to leave you a note."

"Don't bother." She sounded peeved. "But leave some money on the dresser if you don't mind."

"Money?" He looked startled.

"For the taxi fare. What the fuck did you think I meant? I'm a working girl, but not *that* kind."

"How much do I owe you?"

"You don't *owe* me, but our Uber last night cost a small fortune, which I can't afford. The driver was Romanian and seemed to think that Fulham is south of the river. I wasn't paying attention and by the time we'd crossed Wandsworth Bridge you were fast asleep."

He left a couple of twenties. "Look, I'd just like to say, by way of apology…"

"No apology required. I brought you here of my own free will. Oh, and in case you were wondering, nothing happened last night."

"Nothing?"

"We didn't *do* anything."

"We didn't?" He sounded more confused than ashamed.

She laughed at his discomfiture. "We came here for a nightcap. That, by the way, was the last thing either of us needed. And then you passed out on me. I didn't bother to undress you, as you probably noticed. Couldn't have if I'd wanted to. Anyway, there seemed no point."

"I'm terribly sorry," was all he could think to say, trying hard to conceal his embarrassment. "I'm so…"

"Don't be sorry," she interrupted. "Just be gone. I don't know about you, but I need to get to work." She worked at Sotheby's, he now remembered, in the Oriental department. Ming vases and all that.

4

"So do I," he said, grateful for the excuse to get out. "My managing editor wants to see me. I'm probably in for a bollocking, though God knows for what."

"I've no doubt you'll think of something between now and then, if he doesn't." She got out of bed herself, tied up her hair and pulled on a top that covered her black silk panties. Stumbling over to the kitchen area she poured a large orange juice. She offered him one. "I'm sure you could use it. Coffee you'll have to take care of yourself as I don't have time to make it. But there's a Starbucks on the next corner."

He declined the juice. "Where are we, by the way? I heard you mention Fulham."

"Parsons Green, just off the King's Road."

Nigel was relieved that it was at least in a civilised part of town. "Well, let me just say… er… I'm sorry, your name has…"

"Cynthia. Cynthia Fordham."

"Of course. And you, as I recall, are related to…"

"He's my father. Number two at the Ministry of Trade and Industry. But you ought to know that. You were deep in conversation with the man only a few hours ago."

"I was? At Mary's?"

"Yes. Where else? You spent half an hour hectoring him for an interview and then made a rather indelicate play for his new girlfriend. My stepmother-to-be, apparently."

"I did? That wasn't cool."

"Cool, no. Amusing, yes. My dear Papa gave you quite an earful before he left. I don't think you'll be interviewing him any time soon." She laughed. "After that, in a last desperate throw of the dice, you latched on to me. Still, you were entertaining company for a while, regaling me with tales from the exciting world of journalism.*"* She illustrated the point with a yawn.

"And then?"

"We left. But as you seemed unable to tell the taxi driver where you lived, I decided on the spur of the moment to bring you here. God knows what I was thinking."

He knew exactly what she'd been thinking. "I really don't know what to say."

"Goodbye will do."

"Or shall we say *a bientot*?"

"I think goodbye would be better."

Reaching the door, he paused before opening it. "Well, thanks again for taking care of me. Er, do I have your number?"

"No. But I have yours, though in an entirely different sense." She smiled at her play on words. "Let's just leave it at that, shall we?"

"Once again, I..."

"No more apologies, please. I'm late. Just go."

"Alright, alright, I'm going."

"No, Nigel, that's the wardrobe."

"Oops. Sorry."

* * *

The managing editor of the *Daily Post* emerged from his glass-walled office with a rare spring in his step. Duncan Erskine, a dour lowland Scot, could be a brooding, even menacing newsroom presence, but today his mood chimed with the balmy late-April weather. Setting off on his customary Friday morning walkabout, he was soon to be observed shaking hands with unusual vigour and greeting every limp witticism with intemperate laughter, his shoulders rocking in the much-derided manner of a certain former prime minister.

If his reporters seemed more perplexed than pleased, it was because he'd been known to use these promenades to deliver a public tongue-lashing *pour encourager les autres*. The view from the shop floor was that these outbursts demeaned him rather than his victims. Not that anyone had ever summoned the nerve to tell him so. It might have happened back in Fleet Street's more flamboyant days, when alcohol flowed more freely than ink, and senior reporters with bloated expenses treated a favoured watering hole as an extension of the newsroom. A tale from that time was still told about the popular *Post* columnist who once returned from an epic stand-up lunch to tell his editor what he thought of him in the kind of language that the paper couldn't have printed, safe in the knowledge that, should he be fired for his impertinence, another paper would snap him up before he'd time to rejoin his companions at the bar. As it happened, the columnist survived and the editor was fired. Such was the power of the celebrity journalist back in those dimly remembered days.

But the newsroom pecking order had long since been reversed. Editors now reigned supreme, like monarchs of old invoking the privilege of Divine Right. Their kingdoms might be battling for survival with proliferating on-line rivals, but the monarchs prevailed because their subjects knew that decent jobs in the print industry were becoming scarcer by the year. Many of those rivals were actively hiring, but few paid a living wage, and most were as ethically unsound as their finances. Nor did many of them engage in journalism in any accepted definition of the word.

As for Fleet Street, that once fabled enclave of the national press now existed only in the nostalgic recollections of a few survivors, themselves on the verge of extinction. The Great Diaspora of 1986, led by the titles owned by the much-reviled antipodean interloper Rupert Murdoch, had scattered newsrooms all over the city, often to its less civilized parts. Journalists now worked in hermetically sealed tower blocks, seldom venturing outside except for a few furtive puffs on a cigarette. Where they had once spent extended lunchtimes in bars exchanging war stories with colleagues or supposed 'sources' they now lunched at their desks on sandwiches and soft drinks, eyes glued to a computer screen that demanded their unwavering attention. The Street's once legendary taverns were now as eerily bereft of patrons as a main-line station after the last train had left. Quiet enough for that mythological character Lunchtime O'Booze, the invention of a satirical magazine, to be heard turning in his grave. Fleet Street still looked much as it always had but was now just another traffic-clogged thoroughfare of no discernible character, the only residual clues to its former glory a few newspaper titles inerasably etched into the walls of listed buildings. Few of them were noticed.

The *Post*'s newsroom on the equally unlovely Gray's Inn Road, less than a mile away, was no less sterile than others of its kind. Some observers would say that its joyless ambience was reflected in much of the copy it produced. The reporters rarely thought about it that way because they'd never known anything different. Even Duncan, by some distance the *Post*'s oldest editorial employee, had no memory of Fleet Street's halcyon days of typewriters, hot metal presses, front-page scoops and legendary drinking marathons. As for the profession's once renowned affinity with alcohol, he was curtly dismissive: "All booze, no news." These days the aphorism could be reversed.

If Duncan's calculated newsroom eruptions had become less frequent of late it was probably because management had found a more effective sanction in the form of staff redundancies. In truth, only a dozen 'inessential' administrative employees had been laid off. But the so-called 'Friday night massacre' had caused fearful rumblings throughout the building, and nowhere more loudly than in the newsroom, always the epicenter of such tremors. Doomsayers lurking at the coffee machine now claimed daily to have seen ominous writing on metaphorical walls. Duncan responded to these jeremiads with his own brand of sardonic wit: "Some of you graffiti-spotters would have been useful to Victorian archeologists on tomb-raiding expeditions to Egypt."

But the message from management was plainer than ancient hieroglyphics. At the *Post*, no less than at every other print publication, advertising revenue, commercial and classified, was under growing pressure from the Internet. Or in Duncan's scornful words, "That intellectual desert we laughingly call social media." The *Post*'s website had clawed back some of the lost revenue, and even established itself as a reliable profit-maker. But the urge to cut costs elsewhere was becoming irresistible. For all the managing editor's bonhomie this morning, his reporters were convinced that the Human Resources department was busy assembling tumbrels for the inevitable editorial cull. Nor, on the evidence, were the rumours entirely unfounded. Only a week earlier, Charles Waugh, the paper's Home Affairs editor, an award-winning Fleet Street veteran, had left Duncan's office ashen faced after being summarily pensioned off. Even his colleagues conceded that he had spent more time of late indulging his thirst for a drink than his hunger for a story, but after three decades of distinguished service, he'd surely earned the dignity of a valedictory lunch in a decent restaurant.

Today, though, the managing editor's ebullience precluded angry confrontations or cruel dismissals. It was also proving to be infectious. Junior reporters who normally kept their heads down to avoid being noticed were thrusting themselves forward like classroom children straining to be recognized by a teacher. Even their more cynical senior colleagues offered welcoming smiles. Journalists were a strange breed, Duncan silently reflected. Interrogating others they could be bold and assertive, but when the tables were turned, they often became timid and tongue-tied. It failed to occur to him that a Presbyterian editor on an evangelical mission was a sight to reduce even the most hardened newsman to a state of simpering servility.

To be fair, the managing editor's fierce public demeanour masked genuine empathy. Early in his career, as a junior reporter on provincial newspapers, Duncan had often suffered a confidence-sapping fear of failure. Twice he'd been fired for reasons unrelated to either his competence or his behaviour. Arbitrary dismissals had always been an occupational hazard in the news business, but that made them no less unnerving. Since then, of course, Duncan had done rather well for himself. But even during his climb to the summit there had been times when he'd despaired of ever earning a living as a journalist, much less as a widely admired and generously paid editorial supremo on a national broadsheet.

As his tour progressed, Duncan recognized that he commanded the full attention of the newsroom, if not its universal admiration. Dozens of keyboards had stopped clacking. Telephone calls were being cut off with a curt "I'll get back to you." For a moment he considered clambering onto a desk to deliver a morale-boosting speech in the manner of Henry V before Agincourt, but almost immediately thought better of it. A rousing call to imitate the action of the tiger might ring hollow in the light of recent and possible future redundancies. He decided that casual banter better suited his purpose than high-flown oratory, a skill which, by his own admission, he'd never really mastered. In truth, banter was hardly his forte either, as convinced as he may have been that it was.

"You're looking a bit glum this fine morning, Eddie."

Eddie Shaver, a senior reporter on the Home Desk, was a disheveled and rather morose individual. Known for his bellyaches, both literal and figurative, he claimed to be troubled by ulcers. Most of his colleagues regarded this as a manifestation of incipient hypochondria. Even when his ulcers weren't playing up, Eddie had a standby checklist of complaints, from the censorious brutality of the copy editors to the newsroom's harsh strip lighting which he was convinced was slowly destroying his eyesight and might soon be cooking his brain.

"Truth be told, I'm feeling a bit under the weather this morning," he told Duncan. "The old gut's been giving me gyp again."

"Probably something you've written," Duncan said, and then quickly moved away to avoid hearing another litany of Eddie's current problems, medical or otherwise.

"Morning, Jimmy!"

Duncan had made a point of stopping to chat to the most junior reporter on the floor, Jimmy Slaughter, an acne-riddled lad from the East End, who tended to write in the strange argot of that place. "Liked your piece yesterday on that big cat on the loose in Devon," Duncan gushed.

Sightings of mysterious creatures on the moors had been a staple of summer coverage all the way back to Arthur Conan Doyle's tale of the fictional Baskerville hound, but this one was a little early in the season. Duncan silently wondered why the *Post* bothered to run such nonsense at any time, but today he was content to let monsters, real or imagined, run wild and free - like the flights of fancy of those who claimed to have seen them.

"Well done, laddie," he chirped. "And keep up the good work."

Wee Jimmy beamed with the pride of someone who'd just been named Britain's Journalist of the Year.

Duncan glided away, pleased that his morale-boosting pronouncement had been so gratefully received. If only, he mused, some of his other reporters would take their cue from Jimmy.

"Morning, Annie, what's this you're working on?"

Annie Goldman was an ardent advocate of whatever happened to be the prevailing expression of feminist 'empowerment' - a word that Duncan hated - and seemed disinclined to tell him. He had to peer over her shoulder to find out. "The PM's new young wife, eh?" The prime minister had recently married an attractive campaign aide fifteen years his junior. A godsend to the tabloids, but hardly worthy material for a serious paper like the *Post*. "Beats me why anyone should be interested in what the woman eats for breakfast, or where she buys her clothes," he huffed, oblivious to the slight. Or perhaps, as Annie chose to believe, intent on provocation. "Personally, I couldn't care less about such trivia, but I suppose we have an obligation to please some of our readers some of the time."

Annie, on cue, found the observation profoundly condescending. "We do have a great many female readers, Mr Erskine, in case you hadn't noticed."

"And most grateful I am for their support," Duncan declared. "And for yours, Annie, in case *you* hadn't noticed."

"Then you'll also know that women represent about forty percent of our readership. Frankly, if we paid half as much attention to them as we do to those puerile football fans we dote on in our ever-expanding sports pages, we might gain considerably more."

She had a point, Duncan silently admitted, but he had no desire to get involved in a debate about reader demographics or gender politics, least of all with a fierce New Age suffragette like Annie Goldman. He admired Annie's work. He even liked Annie herself - once she'd descended from her pulpit - but for now, in the interest of sustaining the cheery mood, he'd head off in search of friendlier company. Annie's despised sports desk would be a good place to find it, he reckoned.

"Morning, George. How about those Scousers then?" George Crockett, the sports editor, a feisty Lancastrian, had just devoted six pages to the triumph of the Liverpool football team in coming back from a two-goal deficit to defeat a much-fancied Spanish side in a European Cup tie. Duncan feigned elation. "Talk about nerve-wracking! Never thought we'd pull it off."

The sports editor's broad grin camouflaged deep contempt. His managing editor always used 'we' after a victory and 'you' after a defeat. The joke was that Duncan was a rugby man through and through and cared little for football, even less for what F. Scott Fitzgerald in another context had called the 'foul dust that floated in its wake'. He was constantly pushing George to expanded coverage of 'the real game played by real men', but to no avail. The sports editor, an ardent Manchester United fan, and so secretly envious of Liverpool's success, was always ready to defend his turf against all comers. These included an overbearing managing editor.

"You'll find no better coverage in print, Duncan, not even in the tabloids. And, judging by some of the responses we're getting from our readers, they agree with me."

Normally, Duncan would have lingered to debate the point, if only for the rhetorical exercise. But that would have been to risk a mood-changing note of disharmony. "Well, congratulations," was all he said, "for the result… and for the coverage."

George smiled. Privately he regarded his editor as an unreconstructed snob. Worse, a snob from north of the border, where men, real or otherwise, rarely provided anything worth writing about in either sport. George was careful to keep such opinions to himself, of course, but as soon as Duncan had left, Mancunian eyeballs were rolling in unaffected scorn.

Even without Duncan's infusion of goodwill, the newsroom would have been a relatively relaxed place, as it usually was on Fridays with only a news-light Saturday edition to worry about. And with a three-day bank holiday coming up hard news would be even more scarce. Barring a natural disaster or a celebrity death, the front page would no doubt be given over to pictures of sun-deprived Brits gaily stripping off their clothes on packed beaches. Or, more likely, given the spiteful vagaries of the English climate, huddled dolefully in seafront bus shelters lashed by unpredicted squalls.

Duncan had no interest in the weather one way or the other. His weekend would be spent toiling over a speech to be delivered the following Tuesday to a prestigious media conference at which he'd be the keynote speaker. His topic, "Does Print Journalism Have a Future in the Internet Age?" posed a question that many industry observers believed, and Duncan privately admitted, might in any other context provoke a terse and less than reassuring answer. But for this occasion, he had no trouble deciding that his tone would be cautiously optimistic. Whatever his private views, no editor of a national newspaper would be admired for publicly predicting the industry's demise, much less by his own proprietor. Besides, as he reminded himself, London could still boast eight national dailies. Even New York City, the world's most lucrative media market, could boast only three. Many American cities only had one, and some not even that. He made a mental note to include those statistics in his talk.

* * *

Duncan could be pleased with professional life for other reasons.

He usually lunched on Fridays at the Savoy Grill, his favourite restaurant. More to the point, he'd just been given encouraging news about circulation. According to a closely followed readership survey, the *Post* had broken a string of quarterly declines with a small rise. The figures were far from exhilarating, or even statistically significant, but any rise, however small, made a welcome change these days. Even more gratifyingly, they had pushed the *Post* a place higher in the readership rankings at the expense of the *Daily Record,* the *Post's* rival for the early-morning affections of toast-munching Middle England. Duncan made another mental note to ask the news editor to carry a self-promoting piece on the front page of Monday's paper.

The circulation news was welcome for a more superficial reason: it might elicit a rare compliment from the proprietor, Lord Goodfriend, who usually called Duncan on Fridays for a chat. The former Anton Gutfreund, whose Austrian parents had fled the country days before the Anschluss, was a man not easily pleased, or much inclined to show it even when he was. Still, the circulation news could only improve his mood and Duncan could look forward with confidence to the owner's weekly call.

"How's our paper doing?" was His Lordship's invariable opening line. The enquiry was directed more to the *Post*'s financial health than to its editorial performance. Duncan often wondered why the proprietor seemed to place a greater value on the managing editor's opinion of financial matters than that of the finance director. Probably, he reflected, because that dreary fellow always talked in complex riddles laced with jargon, the result of having earned an advanced economics degree from one of America's prestigious business schools.

Lord Goodfriend affected to admire anyone who spoke plainly, but few were given the chance to exploit this liberal generosity. As His Lordship liked to joke, what was the point of being a media mogul if one constantly had to subject oneself to interrogation by people whose salaries one paid?

That lesser breed included the directors of the *Post Group* holding company, most of them appointed more for their political connections than for their superior intellects. His two sons, David and Simon, both in their late thirties, served on the board as the only two members who could aspire to replace him as head of the family's diversified media group. But neither was yet ready to do so, and few of their boardroom colleagues saw the slightest evidence that they ever would be. No less aware of their shortcomings than his directors, Lord Goodfriend maintained for public consumption the fiction that his sons merely had "a lot more to learn". His daughter Zoe, demonstrably brighter than both of her younger siblings, would have been a much better bet for the succession, but much to his disappointment she had never shown the slightest interest in the family business. Instead, as if to proclaim her independence, she'd carved out a career in public relations. Perhaps that was for the best anyway as her political views were a bit too left wing for her father's liking, and by extension for those of the *Post*'s middle-class readership.

The patriarch was well into his seventies, but according to his doctors he was in decent health, so the succession was not yet a pressing issue. But there would come a time…

Duncan usually lunched on Fridays with friends from outside the media industry, who provided a welcome relief from interminable, and these days invariably depressing, shop talk. Today, though, he'd booked a table for two rather than the usual six. He was planning a working lunch with Nigel Harper, the *Post*'s chief political reporter, a sometime protégé and frequent protagonist. Despite their obvious differences in politics and temperament, it promised to be a pleasant affair. Duncan disapproved of what he saw as Nigel's dissolute lifestyle, not to mention his casual working practices, a throwback, he felt, to earlier discredited journalistic habits. But he was happy to admit that the man was damned good at his job. And when in the right frame of mind - and sober - Nigel could be diverting and stimulating company.

But today's lunch had a singular and more serious purpose. Duncan would be offering Nigel Harper, his chief political reporter, the position of White House correspondent. The plum editorial assignment on any serious newspaper, it was one that demanded energy, imagination and chutzpah. As it happened, Nigel Harper possessed all three and well in excess of requirements. That put him in an entirely different category altogether from the long-serving incumbent, Graham Welbeck, who for all his virtues of reliability and grammatical rectitude, rarely produced copy lively enough to prevent *Post* readers from nodding off within an hour of rising from their beds.

Duncan was looking forward to lunch, but with just one nagging cause for concern: Mr Harper had so far failed to appear in the office. At eleven o'clock there was still no sign of the wretched man. He was usually in the newsroom on Fridays, Westminster having decanted most of its professional residents to the provinces for the weekend, but no one had seen him for two days. Back from his newsroom tour, convinced that it had been a diplomatic triumph, Duncan began to fret. His chief concern was that Nigel might already have decamped for the weekend, to some rock concert in Gloucestershire, or a rugby club reunion in Prague, or some other event at which strong liquor flowed in oceanic quantities.

He was uneasy for another reason. Having briefed the head of Human Resources, he faced the very real prospect that the appointment would be leaked. HR was supposed to be a safe repository of confidential information but in Duncan's experience it was the department most susceptible to the spilling of beans. Rarely did HR memoranda serve any more useful function than to confirm what everyone inside the organization already knew - and often a great many outside it. Fleet Street's days as the physical hub of the newspaper industry may have been consigned to history but somehow its intelligence network had remained in excellent working order. Duncan found that irritating but also reassuring, evidence that his reporters still had a nose for a story. Still, it would be awkward if Nigel Harper were to find out about his appointment on the grapevine before Duncan had informed Graham of his impending retirement.

The only other person aware of Nigel's appointment was the proprietor. When he'd first acquired the paper, His Lordship had publicly pledged never to interfere in editorial affairs. Privately, he demanded to be informed in advance of all top-level editorial appointments and in extreme circumstances might even exercise an unwritten power of veto. But as it happened, Goodfriend was an admirer of Nigel Harper's journalism, if not always his politics, and had readily given the appointment his blessing.

To avoid security breaches elsewhere, Duncan had taken all the usual precautions. That meant above all keeping his personal assistant in the dark. Elsa Moreton was a paragon of efficiency and unswervingly loyal to her boss, but also a compulsive tattler. He'd once put her to the test by feeding her false information "in the strictest confidence", and within the hour had received a call from the New York bureau asking him to confirm the story. Any other editor might have fired her, but Duncan had an understandable, if not commendable, reason for keeping her on. He and Elsa were involved in what the paper would have decorously called a "romantic relationship". The *Post*'s editorial staff, universally aware of the liaison, deployed considerably earthier descriptions.

Elsa was a South Londoner with a strong urban accent, which Duncan - as fond of her as he was - found as grating as her appetite for a well-directed expletive. Everyone else, including Nigel Harper, regarded it as part of her ineffable allure. But then he found everything else about Elsa Moreton alluring, and not so ineffably. Elsa was thirty-something and still single. She was tall, slim, occasionally blonde and, in a word beloved of the tabloids, curvaceous. Though far from a classic beauty, she might be described in the common vernacular as "a bit of alright". Or as Nigel had sometimes been heard to express it: "You would, wouldn't you?"

Duncan was convinced that their affair was a well-kept secret. But there are no secrets in a newsroom, as he of all people must have known. Even so, he insisted on certain time-worn and pointless precautions, like arriving in the office ten minutes apart, and only meeting at venues some distance from the *Post*'s office. These juvenile ploys fooled no one. Elsa went along with them only because they made her boss feel more comfortable. She herself couldn't have cared less who knew of their affair. Anyway, their cover had been blown months earlier by a former employee, fired by Duncan himself, who'd spotted them holding hands on a quiet street in Chelsea where Duncan owned a pied-a-terre. The informant, only too glad of the opportunity to exact his revenge, had wasted no time reporting the 'sighting' to his former colleagues. On being told that it was stale news, his disappointment was palpable.

Duncan was more worried about the impact of the affair on his professional reputation than on his marriage. He and his wife Caroline had lived apart for three years, and their two sons had long since left the family home to go to university, so eliminating the imperative to stay together "for the sake of the children". Neither he, a son of the manse, nor Caroline, who had been raised Catholic, were excessively devoted to their respective faiths, but shared an ingrained distaste for the breaking of marital vows. They spoke regularly by telephone and occasionally met for dinner. Caroline, as far as he could tell, knew nothing of his dalliance with Elsa, and he was keen to keep it that way, if only to keep the marital franchise alive.

Elsa, for her part, had no such scruples, religious or otherwise. As she elegantly put it: "Why would God, if such a thing exists, give a flying rat's arse who I choose to fuck?" Nor did she entertain any expectation that the affair represented any more than an office fling. Both of them wondered from time to time whether the affair could last, and both secretly suspected that it had already run its course - or at least was now on the back straight.

On this Friday morning, after a night of passion at Duncan's flat, they'd arrived in the newsroom the mandatory ten minutes apart. The reporters no longer even bothered to exchange knowing looks. Duncan was immediately all business.

"Dare I enquire," he barked at Elsa, sitting at the desk outside his office, "where our elusive Mr Harper is this morning? I need to see him right away. And for the avoidance of doubt that means the moment he arrives."

Elsa was aware that Nigel was "missing in action". Or as Duncan put it, "missing in inaction".

"No one's seen hide nor hair of him," she reported unhelpfully after returning from a brief scouting mission that included both the men's and ladies' lavatories.

"Well, try and get hold of him. And when you do, tell him to drag his sorry arse into my office. And I mean pronto."

"Yes, sir," she replied with a mock military salute.

Realising that this exchange may well have been loud enough to penetrate the newsroom ether Duncan appeared at Elsa's desk to deliver further instructions, this time in a quieter voice. "And if he's still sleeping off the mother of all hangovers, as I've no doubt he is, then get him out of bed. If necessary, go round there yourself and tip him out of it."

Elsa's lascivious grin was that of a woman who might welcome any excuse to pop round to Nigel's flat, which was less than a mile away, but for the purpose of tipping herself *into* his bed rather than him *out* of it.

Duncan, noticing Elsa's smirk, retracted the remark. "Just kidding, of course. But keep calling…" He went back into his office feeling somewhat aggrieved, his buoyant mood in danger of being deflated.

Nigel Harper was a divorced man and a notorious night-owl. Reverting to the customs of an earlier editorial generation, he often showed up to work closer to eleven than eight. And sometimes in no fit state to work, although Nigel had his own interpretation of what "no fit state" meant. He liked to boast that some of his most inspired work had been done while nursing a hangover. Duncan tolerated Nigel's erratic timekeeping, and the intemperate drinking, because the man was an editorial asset. He was also a marketable commodity, as evinced in the frequent attempts by rival papers to poach him, which Nigel seldom missed an opportunity to bring to his editor's attention. His managing editor, in turn, seldom missed an opportunity to remind him that nobody was indispensable. But there were limits to an editor's patience and Duncan's, Elsa could tell, was now being rudely tested.

"He's bound to ask what it's regarding," she observed, as usual angling for marketable gossip. "What do you want me to tell him?"

Duncan was wise to that trick. "Just tell him that his managing editor - if he can actually remember he has one - would like him to stop by for a chat." Noting that Elsa's antennae were already disturbing the dust motes, he quickly added, "You know, it's not at all unusual for an editor to wish to speak to his chief political correspondent, in case you were wondering."

Elsa was indeed wondering. The managing editor's summons might not be unusual, but she was canny enough to know that *something* was afoot. She could tell by the nervous tension in his voice.

Dialling Nigel's mobile number and then his home number, she was greeted by a perfunctory recording on both. '*I'm busy but leave a message.*' Not even so much, she noted, as a 'please' or a 'thank you'. Typical of the man, she was thinking, though not critically.

"I keep getting voice mail," she yelled at Duncan through his open office door, again loudly enough to be heard across the newsroom. The wheels of the rumour mill would soon be turning.

"Well, try again," Duncan insisted irritably. "And keep trying."

"I've left a message, mobile and home."

"Well, keep leaving them. And make them sound urgent. Better still, mysterious. Perhaps if we drive him mad with curiosity, he'll respond."

"Roger that," Elsa said, oblivious to the inapt choice of phrase.

She'd always nursed a soft spot for Nigel. She found him handsome, dashing and witty, and always good for a laugh at company events, sometimes for an entertaining 'scene'. Once, at a company function, he'd got involved in a scuffle with the deputy finance editor and they'd come to blows. Few real punches had been thrown and fewer still landed, but one of the *Post*'s directors had witnessed the incident. Fortunately, he was a former Fleet Street carouser himself and so he refrained from reporting it. Had Duncan been present he wouldn't have been so tolerant.

Even Elsa was left reflecting that one of these days Mr Harper would push his luck too far. "This time you were lucky, darlin', but next time…"

It saddened her that a man of such a superior education and glittering professional accomplishments should be reduced to living in one of London's poorest boroughs, and in a building that from the outside looked like a rather seedy block of council flats, which is what it had once been. She'd often thought about how she might convert her secret erotic fantasies into something more real, but sensibly concluded that it wouldn't be worth jeopardizing either her job or his. Nigel fancied her just as much in return, but in that respect the field was crowded. And he had no enthusiasm for risking a clash with his managing editor, least of all in such a marginal cause.

Duncan Erskine and Nigel Harper were a study in contrasts, physically, temperamentally and politically.

Duncan, now well into his fifties, was tall and thin. A rugged crofter's face was topped by a wiry shock of coppery hair, which of late seemed undecided whether to turn grey or fall out. His appearance and manner were those of an ascetic, reflecting either his Presbyterian upbringing or the gloomy climate that God had seen fit to inflict on the island's more northerly provinces. He was serious to a fault, high-strung, and forever worrying about his job, the health of the paper and the future of the country - not always in that order.

Nigel was in his late thirties, above medium height and of sturdy build. He had a debonair manner and a permanent twinkle in the eye, at least when sober. Elsa was far from alone of her gender in finding him attractive, and he was as much drawn to women, although these days consummations were few and far between. That alone might have explained why he drank so much. He liked a flutter on the ponies during the flat season, even though he knew little of horses and cared less. On winter evenings he could often be found at the blackjack tables in exclusive Mayfair casinos, where occasionally he'd win enough to keep him going back. That would be more difficult from now on as two of them had recently seen fit to eject him for ungentlemanly behaviour. "The home secretary will hear of this," he'd yelled manically as he was escorted to the door of one of them. Outwardly he was sociable and assured but like most journalists was secretly afflicted by insecurity and self-doubt. A suitable case for therapy, some would have said. He himself had thought about it from time to time, but not since the immediate aftermath of his divorce from Sarah.

Politically they parted company, too. Duncan was a middle-of-the road Tory, a stance reflected in the paper's editorials, which occasionally, to keep his hand in, he wrote himself. Nigel's politics were well to the left of Duncan's, although he was less the revolutionary firebrand he was reputed to be than a "champagne socialist". Nigel found that ironic, as he disliked the stuff.

For all their differences in style and temperament, they had certain things in common. By a curious coincidence they were both the sons of clerics. Duncan's father had been a Presbyterian minister in the South Lanarkshire town of Biggar; Nigel's still mounted the pulpit every Sunday as the vicar of a rural parish church in Norfolk. Both sons had gone to Oxford, Duncan to Magdalen to read philosophy, Nigel to Pembroke to read modern history, and both had graduated with respectable seconds. They'd both played rugby for their respective colleges - Duncan as a rather stringy back row forward, Nigel as a burly center - but neither had earned a blue. Each had experienced a broken marriage, but only Nigel had taken the irrevocable legal step of ending his.

What they shared above all was a passion for journalism. If Duncan's was the more cerebral, and Nigel's the more visceral, the contrast failed to pit them against each other in mortal combat. If anything, it brought them together. Duncan played the natural, some would say overly punctilious, role of editor. Nigel was the ace reporter, always alert to the prospect of a scoop. Some colleagues thought them an odd couple. In many respects they were. But as George Crockett once observed, so were Laurel and Hardy, and that pairing had endured for decades. And no newsroom performed effectively without what show-business people liked to call artistic differences. Over the years Duncan and Nigel had engaged in many a loud newsroom squabble but had always resolved it with a measure of decorum born of mutual respect.

Both men fancied themselves as oenophiles. In Duncan's case it represented a betrayal of his religious upbringing, but he placated his God by drinking wine only as a complement to food. Nigel could polish off a bottle of red while watching television. They'd discovered this mutual interest at their very first lunch four years earlier - at the Grill of course - when Duncan had lured Nigel away from the *Daily Record*. He'd used the occasion to challenge Nigel's appreciation of fine claret, and the test had been passed with flying colours. Duncan remembered with a touch of shame the three bottles of *Chateau Margaux* of excellent vintage they'd consumed that day - and with a touch of regret the exorbitant price he had paid for them. And that was before several rounds of vintage Armagnac had elevated the bill from the realms of the formidable to the legendary.

"This had better be worth it, laddie," Duncan had snapped at Nigel as he handed the waiter his credit card.

"Don't worry, it will be," Nigel had replied forcefully.

And so, by and large, it had been.

* * *

For all the messages Elsa had left on Nigel's answering machine - she'd now lost count - at noon there was still no word from the man. Duncan was starting to worry that he might have to cancel their lunch date, an intolerable insult and an unbearable sacrifice, especially as it was now too late to call friends to replace him.

"Nothing yet from Harper?" he asked Elsa for the umpteenth time. Surnames were now the order of the day.

"Not a dicky bird," came the reply. Even Elsa was becoming irritated after dialing both numbers again and still getting nothing but that rude recording.

Then she spotted him, sauntering across the newsroom - somewhat unsteadily she thought - pausing every few paces to chat with a colleague. Elsa was miffed. If he'd picked up her messages and ignored them, it was disrespectful. Watching his tentative progress across the newsroom floor, she decided that he deserved whatever book Duncan was about to throw at him. But then she scurried across the newsroom to warn him of the impending danger.

"The man's been desperate to get hold of you," she whispered in his ear while he was swapping jokes with George Crockett. "Do I want to know where the fuck you've been for the past two days?"

"My dear Elsa, that's for me to know and for you to find out - as I've no doubt you will. Good morning, by the way."

"Good afternoon, actually."

Nigel checked his watch. "So it is. How time flies when one is comatose."

"I'd get in there right away if I were you," she said, cocking a thumb in the direction of Duncan's office. "And I suggest you come up with a more plausible excuse than a hangover. You know how his moods can swing. First thing this morning he was as breezy as an elephant's fart, but now I'm not so sure. And for God's sake comb your hair. And tuck your fucking shirt in. You look as if you've been in a street brawl. At least show a little respect for the man. He is, after all, the managing editor of the fucking paper."

"Or the fucking managing editor of the paper."

"Ha, ha."

"Anyway, I don't dread a peevish master," Nigel responded, quoting a line from some vaguely remembered song. "But tell me, my dear perceptive, ever-watchful, hear-no-evil bard of Battersea, what kind of face is our esteemed leader wearing this morning? Are we 'cleansing the temple' or 'suffering little children'?"

"Right now, I'd say it's his 'where the fuck is that good-for-nothing Nigel Harper look'."

Duncan, as if he'd heard his name mentioned, suddenly materialized. Elsa had been right about the face.

"Ah, the ego has landed! How kind of you to grace us with your presence, Mr Harper."

"Good morning, chief."

"A good night, was it?" Since the evidence was plain to see, the question was redundant. "I'd say it was a long one, judging by your disheveled appearance and those deliquescent eyes. Tell me, did you even make it home to bed last night?"

"I think I was in bed by three, or maybe four."

"I don't know how you keep it up at your age."

"Sadly, I didn't," said Nigel. "Keep it up, that is."

Duncan snorted. "The less said about that aspect of your nocturnal activities the better. And was there a special reason for this celebration?"

"It was a leaving do for old Percy Montgomery from Accounts. Decent chap. Always prompt with my expenses. You must remember him."

"I do. I also remember that he left the paper three months ago. I went to his farewell party, at El Vino's if memory serves."

"That was the first one," Nigel said, grinning. "We've had several more since then."

"Several more?"

"Four at least. But last night's was the last."

"Oh, why's that, pray tell?"

"Because yesterday was his funeral. He died two weeks ago."

"Oh, I'm sorry to hear that. I didn't know." Duncan paused, looking puzzled. "But let me get this straight: you were at a funeral that lasted until three in the morning? Where?"

"Willesden."

"Willesden!"

"Yes, that's where he lived, poor chap. Never been there before. Ghastly place."

"And the ceremony lasted several hours."

"No. The service was over by three in the afternoon and the reception by five. But then a few of us thought we'd give him one final send-off, somewhere more appealing. He'd have liked that, old Percy. I hope to do the same for you one day, Duncan. No time soon, of course."

Duncan grunted. "And where did the rest of this macabre celebration take place?"

Nigel bit his lip, as if trying to remember. Then it came to him. "We ended up at Proud Mary's for a nightcap."

Proud Mary's, housed in the basement of a Georgian house in Mayfair, was London's most exclusive night-club, named for the owner's daughter. For three decades it had been the haunt of

Conservative politicians, television pundits and assorted celebrities. Even visiting Hollywood stars were sometimes seen there. What Proud Mary's was most proud of was the discretion of its staff, which allowed patrons to exhibit all manner of bad behaviour, confident that it would never find its way into the tabloids. Duncan disliked the place, not so much for reasons of taste or morality as for the price it charged for drinks, which matched what he normally paid for an entire meal.

"Mayfair, if memory serves, is nowhere near Willesden," Duncan observed accurately. "Nor is it on your way home. Anyway, I don't know how you can afford places like that, even on your inflated salary."

"You may not approve of it," Nigel countered, "but it's a great place to make contacts. Last night I ran into a senior member of the cabinet. Soon, I'm hearing, to be a former member. We had a good chat. Not a very long one, mind, as he was there with his latest mistress, but long enough for me to secure the promise of an exclusive interview."

"Oh, is that right? And may I ask the identity of this adulterous, high-living minister of the Crown?"

"I'd prefer not to say just now," said Nigel, tapping the side of his nose. "Not until I've called his office to confirm the appointment."

"Aha! I see what your game is. This nonsense is just an excuse to put the whole misbegotten expedition on expenses."

Nigel's response had a mocking tone. "Come now, Duncan, you of all people should know how scrupulous I am about my exes."

"Scrupulously inventive, I'd say."

A hovering Elsa had been eavesdropping on this exchange. She enjoyed the banter, finding it entertaining, and more importantly, reassuring. Whenever newsroom banter dried up it was a sign that trouble was brewing. Duncan, as if reading her mind, threw her a look of disapproval. "I dare say, Miss Moreton, you've a great deal of work to do. May I therefore strongly recommend that you attend to it?" Then, turning to Nigel, and maintaining his head-masterly manner, he said, "As for you, Mr Harper, be so kind as to accompany me to the conference room. We need to have a chat."

"Sounds ominous," said Nigel, flippantly, with a wink at the departing Elsa. He also gave her a gentle smack on the behind, hoping that Duncan had not seen it.

Elsa gave the game away. "Naughty!" she cried, plainly not meaning it.

"And we'll have none of that," Duncan snapped. "For pity's sake, HR has made our position on harassment quite clear. The least I can expect, Mr Harper, is that my own senior reporters observe the rules. That goes for you, too, Miss Moreton. You want to land us with a lawsuit?"

"You won't get any trouble from me," Elsa said cheekily over her shoulder. "A Friday slap on the bum from Nigel Harper is one of the highlights of my week."

Duncan's fury was now untamed. "That's quite enough! It's just not appropriate behaviour. Not in my newsroom. Or anywhere else. Don't you people read the papers? Our own paper, indeed. We just can't have that kind of thing anymore. Apart from anything else, it's wrong, just plain wrong."

Nigel cast a sly glance at his editor, thinking, *'There speaks someone who's acquainted with a great deal more of Elsa Moreton than her rear end.'*

Duncan was already heading for the glass-walled conference room. Nigel followed but far enough behind him to avoid giving watching eyes the impression that he was being led there. Duncan, still seething, settled into one of the Swedish-designed ergonomic chairs around the long mahogany table. He beckoned Nigel to sit across from him. An awkward silence followed.

It was breached by the buzzer on the telephone console in the middle of the table.

"I need to take this," Duncan said. "Give me a minute."

"You want me to leave?" Nigel rose from his chair.

"No. Sit down. But don't say a word."

It was Lord Goodfriend on the line, a little late with his regular Friday morning call. Nigel failed to catch the words, but the booming voice and Teutonic cadences came through loud and clear. Duncan wasted no time giving his proprietor the circulation news, which, judging by the editor's smile, was well received. The call went on for several more minutes, Lord Goodfriend doing most of the talking, Duncan repeatedly saying, "Yes, sir." Nigel expected at any moment to hear, "Up to a point, Lord Copper." Distractedly, he peered out at the newsroom, and saw fifty pairs of eyes trained on them, curiosity mingled with alarm. In truth, he was becoming a little concerned himself, especially when he heard Duncan say, "Yes, he's in my office as we speak."

Nigel was suddenly all ears.

But now Duncan was saying goodbye. "Yes, I'll keep you posted." He hung up. "That was Lord Goodfriend," he said needlessly, drawing quiet satisfaction from Nigel's quizzical expression.

"Since I heard you mention my name," Nigel said, "may I ask what our esteemed proprietor had to say that concerns me?"

"I'll to get to that. But not here. These walls have ears, you know. And there are several lip-readers out there. I'll explain everything over lunch. You *are* free for lunch, I take it? Or perhaps I should ask: are you up to lunch?"

Nigel was in fact famished, having eaten nothing the day before but a couple of sausage rolls at the funeral. He nodded vigorously. "Rather."

"Good. Then we'll grab a taxi and pop down to the Grill. I'm sure you'll recall the first time we met there, you and I."

Nigel remembered it well. "Yes. A coup for you and the beginning of a fruitful career for me. Today it must be something important if you're forsaking your friends from the halls of academia."

"Yes, it *is* important, and as much for you as for me. But I'm going to make you wait to find out why. That's your punishment for being late, and for behaving badly." Evidently Duncan was still fuming over the bottom-smacking. "Look, why don't you meet me in the lobby in half an hour. I usually walk to the Grill, especially on a day like this, but since I'm not sure you'd be able to make it that far we'll grab a taxi."

"A taxi does sound better, to be honest. Meanwhile, can't you give me at least an inkling about what's on the agenda? Obviously, it's something sensitive."

Duncan peered nervously across the newsroom. Elsa, he noticed, was watching them as intently as everyone else, desperately pretending not to. "I'll say just this much, if only to put your mind at rest. It's nothing bad. On the contrary, I'd say it's something good." After delivering this tantalizing assurance, he stood up. "Half an hour, then. Oh, and you might want to tidy yourself up a bit in the meantime. A shave might be in order."

Nigel was barely back at his desk before he was ambushed again by Elsa. "Everything alright, Nige darlin'?"

"Everything's fine," he said. "Your boss has obviously got something he wants to get off his chest but means to keep me waiting to find out what. He can be a sadistic bastard. Well, I don't have to tell you that. Do you know anything?"

"No. Nor would I tell you if I did. But whatever it is, good luck."

Nigel responded with a grin. "Luck, it seems, is the one thing I'm *not* going to need. But I'll say no more."

He didn't have to. The hint that he wasn't in the kind of trouble that had finished the career of poor old Charlie Waugh was enough to allow her to respond to the questions that a dozen people would be asking her as soon as he and Duncan had left the office.

* * *

"Always had a soft spot for this place," Duncan declared, gazing approvingly around the Savoy Grill as they followed the maître d' to a small corner table.

"I'd noticed," said Nigel.

"Even after the recent, and in my opinion, quite unnecessary refurbishment. Beats me why they can't leave well alone. I liked it as it was, as it had always been."

"Everything needs a makeover from time to time," Nigel said distractedly. "Even the *Post*."

Duncan, ignoring the prompt, said nothing. Nigel was not that fond of the place himself. "Never eat in hotel restaurants," a colleague had once advised him. "Food's usually crap, and the prices crazy." The Savoy Grill, Nigel thought, qualified on both counts. But if his boss thought otherwise, who was he to argue the point?

"The food here's actually quite decent," Duncan said, as if tuned in to Nigel's train of thought. "And the clientele is always interesting." He gazed around at their fellow diners, mostly gentlemen in dark suits, though with an ominous sprinkling of casually dressed tourists. "It's the kind of place where business deals are done. Or used to be, back in the day. You'll recall we had one ourselves. That worked out well enough, I think you'll agree."

"I have no complaints. Do you?"

"No. But now I have another one for you."

"Deal or complaint?"

At that pregnant moment, with the unfortunate timing for which members of his trade were apparently trained, the waiter arrived to hand out superfluous menus. "Anything to drink before lunch, sir?"

Without waiting for his host, Nigel blurted out, "I'll have a Bloody Mary. No ice."

"I'll wait for the wine list," Duncan said. "Can't stand that dreadful tomato concoction. Ruins the taste buds. But I dare say you're in need of a more vigorous pick-me-up."

"Yes, I am, rather," Nigel confessed.

Duncan pointlessly flipped open a menu. "I suggest we get our order in right away. That way we can talk without interruption."

Nigel snapped his shut decisively. "I'll have the mixed grill."

"Quite right, laddie. Me too."

The waiter scooped up the menus. "Very good choice, sir, if I may say so." He sounded like Jeeves.

A brief silence followed. Duncan filled it by pouring water with great concentration. Nigel was thinking, '*The bastard is enjoying all this manufactured tension.*'

"So…" said Duncan eventually, now intently studying the wine list, "… a quiet week in Westminster, I gather."

"Relatively speaking. Usual panic about a more severe economic downturn than we've been expecting. Not helped, of course, by the Bank of England coming out with a thinly veiled warning of an approaching Armageddon. I think someone over there on Threadneedle Street secretly enjoys spooking the markets."

"It's not the Bank of England I worry about, it's the government."

"And me, actually. This Chancellor doesn't seem to have the faintest idea what to do next, except of course to impose yet more austerity. That's this government's reflexive response to everything. No clue. No balls. No imagination."

"Imagination," Duncan pronounced, "is hard to exercise when the numbers refuse to add up. Anyway, austerity tends to be the default position of all chancellors, Tory and Labour. No doubt you'd be in favour of a tax and spend solution."

"Probably. But I'm no economist. But I suppose we're all economists these days."

"Yes, we are. That's what affluence has done for us. I'm old enough to remember when we used to worry about stretching the wages to pay the rent or putting enough food on the table. Now we discuss which market we're going to invest in, and whether we'll take our holiday in Thailand or Antigua. Say what you like, there's still a lot of money sloshing around out there."

"Well, it doesn't seem to have sloshed my way," Nigel said.

That was Nigel's second jibe about compensation, Duncan noted, but ignored it. Especially as it came from someone who could afford to spend his evenings at Proud Mary's. "I agree with you on one thing: this government is weak. Adrift in a sea of public debt and no idea what course to set. Clearly, this Chancellor isn't up to the job. Allows the PM to walk all over him."

"Not so much the PM, perhaps, as that sinister Rasputin of his in Downing Street."

"I'm told that whenever the Chancellor speaks at cabinet everyone pretends to fall asleep."

"Some of them aren't pretending," Nigel said. "And, yes, it's time for him to go. Well, the lot of them, for that matter."

"There seems to be increasing chatter about a snap election. Failing that, I suppose, we can expect a cabinet reshuffle."

Nigel dismissed both notions. "Talk of an election is just corridor scuttlebutt. Nothing to it, in my opinion. Just Rasputin at work again. The idea, apparently, is to provoke the Opposition leader. And it usually works. But calling an election wouldn't be a wise move right now. It's always a risk, even when it's a chump running against you. Look what happened last time. The Tories got it completely wrong. As for a reshuffle, that's always the last refuge of a doomed premiership. But who knows anymore? We live in strange, unpredictable times. And nothing is stranger or less predictable than this prime minister."

"Yes, one who seems to spend more time watching his popularity ratings than running the country."

"Well, don't they all? And with a Commons majority barely into double figures, wouldn't you?"

The waiter reappeared with the Bloody Mary. Nigel finished it in two gulps.

"Feel better for that?" Duncan enquired, sneeringly.

"It certainly helped."

Duncan tugged at the departing waiter's arm. "And we'll have a bottle of the *Lynch Bages*. Number 58, I believe." Turning to Nigel, he asked, "Is that alright with you?"

"You're the man in the chair," Nigel said, rather brusquely.

"Very drinkable, the old *Lynch Bages*. Always dependable. And less expensive than some of the other top clarets."

Nigel agreed, if only because it was always a good idea to reassure Duncan that he was getting good value for money. He also made a note of the downgrade from the *Chateau Margaux*.

"And so, to business…" Duncan said, so abruptly that it made Nigel jump. Even now, though, his editor failed to come to the point. "You've done a good job over there in Westminster, I must say."

"I'm not so sure about that 'must say'. It implies a reluctance to say it."

"Just an expression, laddie. Don't start getting your knickers in a twist."

"You can take some of the credit yourself, you know."

"Oh? How's that?"

"For hiring me in the first place." Nigel thought about saying more but decided not to. As much as he liked to butter up a man who enjoyed being flattered, he was anxious to get to the point of the lunch.

Duncan adopted a self-deprecating look. "Well, I like to think I've a good eye for talent. Let me also say, at the risk of further inflating your already swollen ego, that your best work has been beyond even my lofty expectations. We'll overlook some of your wilder prognostications, although even those have often been entertaining."

"They'll all come true one day, mark my words."

Duncan ventured deeper into the digression. "The proprietor himself thinks highly of your work, as I'm sure you know. Doesn't always agree with your opinions but admires your prose style. Now, that's high praise coming from a man who rarely offers it."

"I suppose it doesn't do any harm to have the approval of the man who owns the paper," Nigel said airily. He fell silent, determined to discourage any further conversational diversions. Duncan began to speak but was again interrupted by the waiter, who'd picked the moment to show up with the wine. Duncan tasted it. "Very good," he declared. "But we'll pour it ourselves, if you don't mind, give it a few minutes to open up." The waiter left the bottle and departed. "You'll have some of this, I presume?"

"Of course."

Duncan poured and raised his wine glass to the toasting position. "Well, cheers," he cried. "To happy days and no lonely nights."

Nigel responded with what Duncan recognized as a knowing smile. "Amen to both. And I can only hope, in my case, that both come true."

Putting his glass down, Duncan adopted a solemn expression. "Now, where were we…?"

"You were about to get down to business. Nigel pretended to be nonchalant but found himself leaning forward expectantly.

"Ah, yes. The point is, I'm thinking of a new assignment," Duncan said. "For you, that is, not for me. I'm going nowhere at my time of life."

Nigel suddenly felt concerned. His heart jumped. *'Just what could the man have in mind? Film reviews? Not among the Post's most popular features. Surely not obituaries. An editorial dead-end, so to speak. Nor sport, as George was a fixture there, irreplaceable. But Duncan had mentioned "good news". What could that possibly be, and when is he going to stop beating about the fucking bush and tell me?'*

"Oh, I know what's going through your mind," Duncan said, noting Nigel's pained expression. "You think I'm about to put you out to pasture."

"The thought had occurred, for all those earlier compliments."

"Well, laddie, you couldn't be more wrong." Duncan chuckled, with a self-satisfied look. "What I have in mind is something even *you'll* appreciate. A complete change of pace and scenery - and a promotion to boot." Pausing to let those last words sink in, Duncan took an appreciative sip of Mr Lynch's ruby elixir. "Very pleasant this. A good year."

"If you say so," Nigel said, not bothering to hide his anxiety.

Putting his glass down, Duncan assumed a solemn look, that of a judge about to pronounce a severe sentence. "How would you feel about going to Washington? And I don't mean for a visit."

If nothing else the man had the timing of a stand-up comic. Taken by surprise, Nigel was momentarily at a loss for words. "Oh, really? Do tell more."

Duncan was disappointed by the muted reaction but carried on. "Here's my thinking. We need some help in DC, and we need it now more than ever. There's too much going on over there to be complacent about it. We simply must beef up the coverage. Put some oomph into it. But I think you know all that, since you've been telling me as much at least once a week for the past three years."

"Yes, and so far with no result."

"Well, Mr Harper, you now have a result. Our Mr Welbeck has been over there fourteen years. It seems more like forty, but that's neither here nor there. Here's what I have in mind. You take over from him as White House correspondent. Best job on the paper. None more important, I'd say. You'd report directly to me." Duncan sat back with a smug expression that seemed to say: '*I bet you weren't expecting that, were you, my friend.*'

He was right, and Nigel was again momentarily lost for words. Eventually, he filled the void, but only to play for time while he collected his thoughts. "And what about Graham? What happens to him?" Nigel had no interest in a man he regarded as a journalistic lightweight but asking bought time. Inwardly, he was excited. He could feel his pulse quickening. But he didn't want Duncan to know that. Not yet. Two could play the managing editor's little mind games.

Across the table, Duncan looked genuinely astonished. Raising his voice, he said, "What happens to Graham Welbeck doesn't concern you. Now, if you're expressing concern for a colleague that's very noble of you, but it's *you* we're here to talk about. So, what do you have to say?"

"Well, I'm intrigued," Nigel said, still stalling, but also perversely enjoying the experience of putting his boss on the spot.

This provoked another outburst from across the table. "Is that all you can say? Intrigued! Here am I offering you the best position on the paper, a job for which most reporters would give their right arm, and all you can manage is… Well, all I can say is that I'm a little disappointed by your apparent lack of enthusiasm. Make that mystified."

"I'm sorry, Duncan, it's just that I was a bit taken aback."

"Well, I agree that it's not every day you get such a marvelous offer. Even so…"

Nigel decided to come clean. He looked squarely at Duncan, assumed his most ardent expression, and uttered the magic words. "To be honest, I'm flabbergasted. I'm also honoured and flattered. I'm also genuinely excited. Of course I accept the appointment: unequivocally, enthusiastically and, as hard as this may be for you to believe, humbly. In short, as we say at the tables, cut me in." He raised his glass in a confirmatory gesture.

Duncan didn't raise his own glass. Instead, he leaned back in his chair and exhaled a deep sigh, evidently of relief. "Well, thank the good Lord for small mercies."

"Why do you say that?"

"Because, my friend, for one moment I had an awful feeling that you were about to turn me down." He raised his own glass and took a large draught of *Lynch Bages*.

But Nigel hadn't yet finished playing hard-to-get. "Let me ask you another question - and please don't take this the wrong way. Why me?"

"Well, that's an odd question. I'd have thought the answer self-evident, even if I hadn't explained it already."

"I'm asking only because I'm curious about the thought process. Right now, I'm one of the most respected Westminster reporters in the country. An asset to the paper, as you said yourself. Even the proprietor seems to think so."

"All perfectly true, not to flatter you too much. But I'm not sure I see your point."

"My point is this: in Westminster I'm well established and well respected. I'm on speaking terms with most of the cabinet. Downing Street often calls me to find out what's going on. That didn't happen overnight, it took years. What I'm saying is that in Washington I'll be starting from scratch. Going from knowing everything and everybody to knowing fuck all and nobody. Over here I'm an ace correspondent. There I'll be a cub reporter."

Duncan again looked perplexed. "I still don't see…"

"Look, I'm not saying it's a bad move, least of all that I don't want it. But isn't it a case of robbing Peter to pay Paul? Our Washington coverage will improve, but at the expense of the Westminster file."

"Nobody's irreplaceable," Duncan said huffily. "Not even you. As a matter of fact, I already have someone in mind for your job."

"Oh! May I ask who?" Now it was Nigel who sounded offended.

"This may surprise you. Annie Goldman."

Nigel thought about it and then, though still vaguely upset by how dispensable Duncan had made him feel, pursed his lips and nodded his approval. "That makes sense, I must admit. Does she know yet?"

"No. And I don't want her to find out before I've talked to her. She may, of course, turn it down. You know how stubborn the woman can be. But never mind her. Let me respond to what you just said. It's all nonsense. Yes, you'll have to learn the ropes over there, but you're a smart journalist and a fast learner. You'll be doing over there exactly what you've been doing here. Tangling with a different cast of characters, it's true. But politicians are all the same everywhere, whatever the system."

"I suppose that's true."

"And you'll have a free hand over there. Your managing editor will be three thousand miles away and five hours adrift. I'd have thought you'd like that."

"I do." But Nigel had one more question, one that he knew would further test his editor's patience. "I think what I was also asking was whether there's an agenda of some kind here. Is the proprietor behind the move? I only ask because I've heard he's really in tight with this president. And an hour ago I heard you talking to him about me. So, I was just wondering whether…"

"Well, stop wondering and start listening." Duncan now made no attempt to hide his irritation. "Yes, Lord Goodfriend knows about the appointment. He readily approved it. This, I might add, was entirely my idea, not his. And, since you ask, he has no agenda at all. But *I* do. My agenda - my solemn mission if you like - is to get the *Post* a bigger bang for its buck in the biggest news market in the world. That's it. Period, end of story, as the Americans say."

"I see…"

"Sure, Lord Goodfriend knows President Jameson. He also knows just about every other head of state, including our own prime minister. And since you seem to have joined the ranks of conspiracy theorists, let me add this: in all the years I've worked for him he's never once attempted to influence the paper's coverage, or its editorial appointments. I wouldn't stand for it if he did. He's not Rupert Murdoch, you know."

"I'm glad to hear that," Nigel said, impressed by Duncan's sudden vehemence.

"Let me put it another way…" Duncan steepled his hands, a gesture that usual signaled the onset of a homily. "… as managing editor of the paper, it's one of my primary functions to allocate editorial resources as I see fit. You're doing a great job in Westminster, but you've been doing it for a long time. Nearly five years with the *Post* and five with that other paper. A man can get stale doing the same job day in and day out. It invites complacency, and I happen to think you're the type who might one day might get a bad dose of it."

"Well, I haven't so far," Nigel interjected testily.

"Frankly, I wouldn't blame you if you had." Duncan's tone suddenly became gentler. "Look, we can all experience boredom doing the same thing day in and day out. Even I sometimes wake up thinking about what might be next up for me." He laughed. "What do you reckon? Director-general of the BBC? Chairman of the Press Commission?" Duncan laughed again. "I don't think so."

"I don't see why not."

"Oh, and by the way, if you've entertained thoughts about stepping into my shoes one day, think again. I'm only fifty-five, I enjoy the job and also, so far as I can tell, the confidence of the proprietor. Taking over from me would be a long-term project. Still, if you do a good job in DC, I suppose anything's possible."

"Believe me, I'm not remotely interested in your job," Nigel, said casually. "I may be a born reporter, but I'm no editor, as I'm sure you'd be the first to agree."

"In which case, Washington should suit you down to the ground. You'll be a reporter in the purest sense of the word. No one will be looking over your shoulder. Look, a change like this can recharge a man's batteries. The whole idea of replacing dear old Graham is that he doesn't have any batteries to recharge. Besides, he wants to retire. Bought himself a place down in Florida, I understand." Nigel said nothing, happy to wait for more. "Look, I don't expect you single-handedly to bring down this administration; I think we can safely leave that to the *Washington Post* or the *New York Times*. I just want to put the *Post* - our *Post,* that is - on the map, which is where it belongs. It's also where it needs to be if we're to survive." Duncan again exhaled, as if exhausted.

Nigel reached for the wine bottle and topped up both glasses. "Forgive me, Duncan, I didn't mean to sound so diffident just now. It's just that all this has been very sudden."

"What did you expect, two years advance notice?" Nigel's manner had put him off his stroke, and Duncan never took kindly to that. "I must say you made this hard work. I seem to have been making a pitch that you ought to have been making to me. I expected you to lean over and kiss me."

"No offence, but you're not remotely my type."

"Well, that's a relief," Duncan said. They both laughed, relieving the tension.

Nigel, invigorated by the infusion of alcohol, and relieved that he was not being reassigned to Obituaries or Film Reviews, was now truly excited. He said so again, with as much effusion as he could muster. "I can't wait."

"Splendid," cried Duncan. "Now, before we both get too carried away, we ought to discuss some practical, administrative matters. I'm sure you have a host of questions."

Nigel had none and was forced to think of some. "First, I suppose I should ask when you want me there. And for how long."

"To the first part of your question, as soon as possible. As for how long, I've no idea. You may never come back. Graham didn't."

"That's because everyone forgot he was there."

"That's true. But I've a feeling we won't be forgetting *you're* there. At least, I hope not since that would defeat the purpose. Meanwhile, as a working premise, let's think in terms of four years."

"Why four?"

"Oh, I don't know, one to find your way around the Beltway and two more for doing the job."

"And the fourth?"

"Reserved for fending off all those lucrative offers you'll be getting from the American network news shows."

"Four years. A presidential term."

"Maybe you'll get to serve two terms. Is four years a problem, by the way? I know you've got two kids at school here."

"Yes, and frankly I see little enough of them as it is." Nigel suddenly felt sad at the prospect of even less contact.

"Well, you'll be entitled to home leave from time to time," Duncan said brightly. "You might even end up seeing them more often. How about your flat? Do you own it?"

"No. I'm renting. Who can afford to buy a flat in central London these days?"

"And what about your ex-wife? Will she present any problems?"

"Sarah? She won't give a damn. The farther away I am the better, as far as she's concerned. Just so long as I keep up the payments."

"Alimony?"

"Mainly school fees."

"Good Lord! She's the editor-in-chief of *MODE* magazine and married to that hedge fund billionaire who's richer than Croesus. Between them they must be raking it in."

"They're not married yet. Even if they were, our divorce settlement stipulated my paying the school fees. And Sarah's not the type who'd allow them to lapse, whatever my circumstances. Nor, for that matter, her boyfriend, who hates me. I don't want to get into a pissing contest over it and start paying legal fees as well." Thinking about the school fees made Nigel wince.

Duncan noticed. "I know how you feel." Duncan was thinking about his own marital situation and how his own wife might have reacted in a similar situation. "What about the kids - Jack and Ellie, if I remember correctly - are they going to be upset?"

"Kids of their age don't get too bothered about these things," Nigel said and then fell silent. There was something else he was supposed to ask, but it was lodged inaccessibly at the back of his mind.

Duncan supplied the answer. "I've had HR draw up an agreement. I don't think you'll find anything in it you don't like. No hidden terms and conditions or anything like that. If there are, come and see me." Duncan looked across the table. "Meanwhile, isn't there something else you'd like to ask me? Something rather important."

"Like what?"

"The package, laddie, the package. In other words, how much I'm prepared to pay to get rid of you. Or, if you prefer, how much *you're* prepared to take to get away from *me*."

"Ah, yes, I was going to get to that," Nigel fibbed. "Since you mention it, just what do you have in mind?" Nigel put on a resolute face.

Duncan could only laugh and shake his head in wonder. Nigel Harper might be a tough-as-nails interviewer, but as a business negotiator he was a pussycat. Saying nothing, Duncan took out a pen and wrote something on his napkin. Folding it, he pushed it across the table, with furtive sidelong glances, as if he were passing a document to a secret agent in a Moscow restaurant.

Nigel opened it, nodded, and put it into his jacket pocket. "Thank you. I'm pleased to confirm that the number is satisfactory. Generous, even."

"Well, there's no point in sending you over there and then having you call once a week to complain that you don't have enough to live on. This is an important assignment, and you deserve to be paid accordingly. By the way, the figure I just showed you doesn't include the housing allowance. Your pension will remain intact, of course."

Nigel suddenly looked thoughtful. "One last question: what if, for some reason, things don't work out?"

"That's not a problem I'm prepared to discuss. It's no way to start."

"But if something should go wrong, I don't know what, anything?"

"I've no idea what that might be. Unless, of course, you get yourself arrested for making a pass at the first lady. In that case I won't even have to fire you. The Federal Bureau of Investigation would take care of that."

"Fair enough."

"Anything else?"

Nigel was embarrassed. "Nothing that you'd want to hear from someone who doesn't even think to ask what he's going to be paid."

They both laughed. Duncan wrapped things up. "Good. Meanwhile, first thing Monday, I suggest you get yourself over to the US embassy and sort out a visa. You'll need what they call an 'I' visa. That's one they issue to media professionals. HR will help you fill in the forms. Were you ever a member of the Communist Party?"

"No. Does it still exist?"

"There's just one more thing, a nagging concern I feel needs to be addressed."

"Oh, what's that?"

It was now Duncan's turn to feel uncomfortable. "Your drinking habit. You asked me what might go wrong. Well, that's something that could go *very* wrong. I mention it because over there they take a more puritanical view of these things than we do. And, let's face it, you do have a bit of form in that department."

Nigel bristled. "It's never been a problem. Nor will it be. You have my assurance on that. I've already cut down my consumption."

"Except at funerals."

"I don't know what else to tell you…"

"I want you to tell me that it's under control. If it isn't, then do something about it. Your assurance is noted, for the record. But for God's sake, laddie, watch your step. And that goes for that breezy social manner of yours. No more slapping backsides in the office. Over there, puritanism still rules. If someone complained, they could put you away for ten years."

"Point taken," Nigel said emphatically. His tone made clear that he wanted a change of subject.

Duncan took the hint. He turned to look for the waiter, who, true to form, had disappeared. "I'm trying to order another bottle. Up for it?"

"After everything you've just said about drinking…?"

"Another point taken. But my excuse is that I make an exception for special occasions - and this, I think you'll agree, is one of them."

Nigel was suddenly feeling light-hearted, even a little light-headed. "First, you'd better call Elsa, tell her you won't be back... in the office, I mean."

"I know what you meant," Duncan snapped.

* * * * *

Chapter 2

The next day, a Saturday, Nigel rang Sarah, his former wife, to give her the news of his appointment. He called her house phone, hoping that one of his kids, Jack or Ellie, would pick up, as they sometimes did. He ran the risk of having to talk to her boyfriend, Vincent Marchetti, instead, but they would have little to say to each other, so it was a chance worth taking. In the event, it was Sarah herself who answered. They had not spoken for several weeks. It was also that long since he'd called the kids, so he could expect a lecture on parental neglect. He'd have preferred to meet her face-to-face, but those encounters had become rare events, all too often ending with one of them stalking off in high dudgeon. The telephone calls often ended badly, too, but hanging up was much less stressful than a public scene.

Even on a bank-holiday weekend she was reluctant to tear herself away from business. "Let's make this quick," she snapped. He'd called at the worst possible time, she said accusingly, noting that *MODE* magazine's special summer edition was about to go to the printer, and she was swamped with last-minute changes.

"I'd have thought a person of your elevated status would have dozens of people to do the running around."

"I do," she replied tartly. "But as editor-in-chief, I'm the one who has to sign off on everything."

There was a click on the line and for a moment Nigel thought she'd hung up. Or that someone else had hung up. Vincent Marchetti, perhaps. Nigel often wondered whether he listened in on their calls. He wouldn't have put it past him. The man thrived on malicious gossip, especially if it involved his predecessor in Sarah's affections. Not that Nigel, if he was honest, was above doing the same thing.

"Hello?" he said. "Hello?"

"Yes, I'm still here." Sarah deduced from the background noise of clinking glasses and hearty laughter that her former husband was calling from a bar, as indeed he was. "It's terribly noisy, though. I can barely hear you."

"I'll go outside," he said, and found himself on a sweltering, crowded pavement.

"That's better," she said, "but now I'm hearing traffic."

"Well, I've tried inside, and now outside, so I'm all out of options."

"Are you celebrating something or drowning sorrows? Or just drinking for the sake of it?"

"The first one. In fact, it's the reason for my call."

"Is this about money?" Sarah always expected his calls to be about money, even though they never were. Her obsession with accumulating wealth, Nigel thought, had become all-consuming. Never a religious person, she now worshipped devoutly at the temple of Mammon. He had once asked her if she'd built a shrine to her new deity in one of the many spare bedrooms in Marchetti's substantial Chelsea house. "If you're going to insult me, I'll hang up," she'd replied. But then Sarah always seemed to be looking for an excuse to end his calls.

Bearing that in mind, he moved straight to the point of his call. "I'm going to be working in the United States for a while. I thought you ought to know before you read it in the papers."

"Your going to America is a story?" The sniping had started.

"Only because of what I'll be doing. The *Post* is sending me to Washington to be their White House correspondent."

"Oh, really?" she replied in a bored tone, anxious to avoid saying anything that might smack of congratulations. Nigel sensed the stifling of a manufactured yawn. "And when will you be leaving?"

"A month. Maybe sooner. I plan to call the kids, too, but you'll probably be seeing them before I get the chance. I'd like to see them before I go, just to say that while I'll be a long way from home, I'll be just as close in spirit as I am now."

"Oh, please, don't go all fucking lyrical on me." Then she paused, as if trying to think of something even more hurtful to say. It came to her soon enough. "I hope this won't affect your paying their school fees. We do have a contract, you know. And I'm sure it's valid wherever you are in the world."

How typical, Nigel thought. "I'm sure it is, too. But why would you even think I'd break our agreement? In all these years I've never missed a payment, and I never will. They're my kids, too, you know."

"Yes, sometimes I forget that."

"Well, I don't. I'm a man of my word. You should know that, or you would if that bloody husband of yours wasn't constantly winding you up."

"He doesn't wind me up, as you put it. But you do, every time we speak."

Forking over £40,000 a year for school fees rankled. Sarah's boyfriend, partner, fiancé, or whatever he was these days, was worth countless millions. For Vincent Marchetti school fees would be chump change, but for Nigel they were a serious financial burden. The irony was that Nigel had been against sending the kids to private schools in the first place, mainly for egalitarian reasons, but also mindful of the cost. It was Sarah who had insisted on it. "They can only benefit from mingling with children from a better class of family." How far, he thought, the woman had strayed from the ardent idealism which he had so admired during their days at Oxford.

He bit back. "I'm sure Vincent is most grateful for my regular donations to the household budget."

"Let's leave Vincent out of this. *He* didn't sign the fucking divorce settlement, *you* did."

"As you seem compelled to remind me every time we talk. Anyway, I've no problem leaving Vincent out of this - or anything else. I'll happily make a promise to that effect."

"Yes, well, we all know what your promises are worth, don't we?"

He didn't bother to ask her to specify what promises had been broken because he couldn't think of any. Other than the marriage vow, of course. But they had both broken that one, and she'd been the one to insist on it. But this relentless winding up went on whenever they spoke, bile compulsively inserted into every sentence, as vital a component as a verb.

For his part, he found her calculated bellicosity more baffling than upsetting. She lacked for nothing, materially or financially, or even emotionally since she liked to proclaim that her relationship with Marchetti was founded on their mutual and enduring adoration. He could believe it, too, since they both had the same insatiable monetary appetites. *'Love conquers all,'* he mused cynically, *'but especially when accompanied by a multi-million-dollar bank account.'* Even deprived of Marchetti's fortune she wouldn't be short of money. She had one of the best-paid jobs in publishing, and a salary which he guessed wasn't far short of the magic million. And if the rumours were true, that *MODE's* elderly French owner was thinking of rewarding his sundry heirs by taking the property public, then stock options would add millions to the ever-expanding pile. But still her greed couldn't be satisfied. Her diligently accumulated fortune may have put her on level pegging with her new friends, but now she was determined to leave them floundering in her dollar-strewn wake. Few of her peers doubted that she would accomplish it.

If wealth had been her initial obsession, status now competed for her affections. Her job meant that she had become deeply immersed in that strange and rarified biosphere called celebrity. To her it was a joy rather than a duty. She was delighted that her black book contained the private telephone numbers of a host of fashion and show business stars, and she was in many of theirs. She was invited to all the parties that mattered, and *MODE* magazine threw quite a few of its own, highlighted by a star-studded, black-tie annual event that alternated between London and Paris. (New York was "that other woman's turf", a reference to a long-standing rival named Susan Winter). Then there were the various fashion, film and music award ceremonies, of which there were now so many that even the most assiduous stargazers could scarcely keep up with the acronyms. Such was her status in this glittering world that she could look forward with confidence to receiving an imperial-sounding award of the kind bestowed in the Palace. To enhance the prospect, she made a point of inviting minor royals to her 'soirees', as she called them. Some even came. In her even wilder fantasies, she could see Hollywood making a movie about her meteoric rise from gutter to firmament, and not even caring that it might cast her in an unflattering light.

But there was one black cloud looming on this otherwise sun-drenched horizon - an irrational conviction that sinister forces were conspiring to bring her down. Nigel featured in one of the plots - Cassius, if not Brutus - though how he was supposed to bring it about she was no more able to imagine than he could have done. In fact, the thought had never occurred to him. He didn't resent her wealth or her status, and a part of him was rather proud of what she had accomplished. What saddened him was how corrosively it had affected her personality and altered her view of the world. Worse, it nauseated him.

The change in the woman he had once adored was perplexing. Like so many failed marriages, theirs had not so much collapsed as imploded, a process with no identifiable beginning but a sickeningly abrupt end. There had been no infidelity on either side - not on his, at any rate - just years of bickering which shaded over time from the usual marital tiffs to screaming, door-slamming rows. The arguments were usually over money, but also, now that he cast his mind back, the disintegration of her enlightened values. In truth, he had himself come to nurse certain doubts about the radical idealism of their undergraduate days, but at least he had retained a few residual principles. She had simply abandoned hers, suddenly and irrevocably, like a snake shedding a skin.

When the marriage ended, she told friends that he was the one who had walked out, creating the narrative of a distraught woman left penniless with two children to bring up alone. The truth is that she was the one who had instigated divorce proceedings and had done so without even consulting him. The first he knew of the impending breakup was when she casually informed him over breakfast one morning that she had been in touch with a lawyer. Shocked, he tried to talk her out of it, but the effort left him so pained and exhausted that in the end he went along with her, at first with regret, especially when he thought about the children, but before long with an overpowering sense of relief.

"Well, I suppose congratulations are in order," Sarah finally and reluctantly croaked into the telephone. That reluctant concession to protocol was nullified by her next utterance. "You're aware, of course, that Vincent went to school with President Jameson."

"I know that. Everyone knows that."

"The two of them still talk, you know. Quite often, he tells me. Not that it will be of much to help you, I'm afraid." That last remark came out with more glee than regret.

"Vincent's help is the last thing I'd expect," he said angrily. "I'm not writing for some celebrity-besotted, empty-headed periodical that writes whatever its advertisers demand."

That jibe hit the mark, judging by the angry snort at the end of the line, making him feel all the better for having delivered it.

Vincent was a presidential groupie of long standing. He was always in the papers, in the financial sections as a self-proclaimed guru of Wall Street, and in the gossip columns as an 'available' man-about-town. Television was a less prominent vehicle for his self-promotion, but only because he was always traveling. Once a year he mingled with the great and the good from the worlds of politics and finance at Davos, sometimes as a guest speaker. To Nigel, the

Alpine pronouncements that followed the event only confirmed in his eyes that an already corrupt and uncaring global elite was becoming more corrupt and less caring by the day. Not to mention crazier.

He switched the conversation to domestic matters. "How are the kids doing at school?"

"How kind of you to ask. Jack's doing quite well, or at least holding his own. He seems, though, to pay more attention to games than to his studies. Reserves most of his energies for the rugby field - and we know who to thank for that."

Nigel knew and was gratified. If rugby distracted the boy from being groomed by Marchetti for a career in one of the shadier fields of finance where Vincent himself plied his trade, and regulators seemed loath to venture, so much the better.

"Ellie's doing okay, too," Sarah was saying. "She's not at the top of her class either, but she tries hard. She really does. You really ought to pay more attention to them, you know, and I mean Ellie as well as Jack."

"I do my best," he said lamely.

"Somehow, you're best is never quite enough."

"I'll see them next week, if that's alright with you." Nigel realized that he sounded as if he were making last-minute amends, but what else could he say? "I'll take them out for a slap-up meal, and perhaps a trip to the theatre afterwards."

"By all means. But don't go feeding them junk food. Oh, and take them to see something appropriate."

"An Ibsen play, perhaps."

"Don't be an idiot. And don't do any of this because you're feeling guilty. Children can tell, you know. I always could."

"I don't feel in the least bit guilty," Nigel replied indignantly.

He adored both children, although it was Jack who exerted the greater gravitational pull. For a fourteen-year-old, he was a down-to-earth lad, with few delusions of grandeur; not even on the playing field where he excelled. Ellie, on the other hand, was starting to show, at twelve, disturbing signs of taking after her mother, throwing tantrums whenever denied money to buy fancy clothes or shockingly expensive riding gear. Not that she had to resort to such tactics very often: Sarah seemed only too glad to sponsor her developing taste for the high life. Both children found much to like in their supposedly missing father - Jack more avidly than Ellie, and for different reasons. Jack thought of his father as mischievous, always ready for a secret don't-tell-your-mother escapade. Elie found him intelligent and, as she put it, "switched on", but some of her mother's disapproval had rubbed off on her.

As for Vincent, the kids went so far as to agree, a rare occurrence, that they 'sort of' liked him but were also prepared to admit that he was "never much fun". Having been too young to comprehend the unpleasantness that preceded the divorce, they now recognized what had happened and were less confused than curious. Many of their classmates, as Jack mentioned, perhaps to make his father feel better, had divorced parents. "It's no big deal." But then nothing was a Big Deal to Jack, unless it was England beating the All Blacks.

"I'll call them both today to arrange something," Nigel said.

"I'm sure they'll appreciate it," Sarah said in a matter-of-fact tone, though whether it was born of resignation or sarcasm, Jack couldn't tell. He guessed the latter.

The conversation was already petering out when Sarah ended it in a faux regretful tone. "I must run, I'm afraid. As I told you, I have a magazine to put out."

"Well, far be it for me to deprive an anxious world of the next issue of *MODE*."

"Goodbye, Nigel. Oh, and good luck. I've a feeling you're going to need it."

* * *

That evening, sitting at the tiny kitchen table in his inadequate, damp-smelling flat, after a fart-inducing dinner of baked beans on toast, Nigel reflected forlornly on what had gone wrong with their marriage. More to the point, what had gone wrong with Sarah. She'd changed a great deal from the bubbly, petite, socially concerned girl he had once hopelessly fallen for and was now a different person. She still looked good, thanks to several interventions by a well-known Harley Street miracle-worker, but her elfin looks were now more those of a troll, her once fetchingly demure pout now more often a rancid scowl.

They'd become soulmates in their first year at Oxford, drawn together by a shared idealism that found its outlet in progressive politics, various social causes and the performing arts. They were serious students of 'cinema', which they regarded more as an art form than a means of passing a couple of hours in popcorn-crunching limbo. He recalled how impressed they had been by the 'social realism' of their first Visconti film, discussing it for hours in a pub over the half-pints that meager pocket-money allowed. They soon graduated to Antonioni, whose obscure plots and limpid style they found even more convoluted than his name. Their musical tastes settled on the classical. They adored 'serious' theatre, the more avant-garde the better. For several months after they first met, they had continued to live in their respective halls of residence, which were shabby, though no shabbier than most of the other edifices in the Victorian poet's City of Dreaming Spires. Socially they were inseparable and were soon a familiar couple at student marches against poverty, war and other supposedly government-sponsored offences against the downtrodden.

When Nigel persuaded her that they should move in together, they took digs in a dreary semi-detached on the outskirts of town, after persuading the elderly landlady that she shouldn't feel complicit in undermining the moral fibre of the nation by admitting an unwed couple. It was there, one rain-drenched Sunday morning, with Nigel and the newspapers spread over the bed, that Sarah had emerged from the bathroom to announce that she was probably pregnant, a diagnosis confirmed by her doctor the next day. Neither of them had been ecstatic, to say the least, but nor for a moment did they consider a termination. By the time Jack was born, they had both graduated. Within weeks, they motored down to London, babe in arms, in Nigel's rust-encrusted Ford Fiesta. Already intent on a career in journalism, motivated as much by the chance to change the world as earning a living, he took a junior reporting job with a provincial paper in Hertfordshire. The pay was derisory, and world-changing opportunities elusive, but it just about covered the rent on a studio flat in Tring. Sarah would also have to work to supply the food, though her income mostly went on paying for a child-minder. She fancied publishing, too, and found a job in London as a gal Friday with a fashion-cum-music magazine. Within months it had folded, though, putting them under even more financial strain. Further tension was added months later when they learned that a second child was on the way, an inconvenience for which each blamed the other. If they'd decided to marry for the sake of the children, it was also for some lingering old-fashioned notion of enduring love.

The five-minute wedding ceremony took place at the registry office in Tring, attended by just five guests, excluding one-year old Jack. Even Nigel's widowed father came, though scarcely bothering to disguise his anger that Nigel hadn't seen fit to marry in his own parish church. Nigel's Anglicanism, never robust, had long since shaded into atheism - an intellectual journey less arduous than he had expected it to be, and which he had never confided to his father. Sarah's parents, a worthy but rather gloomy couple, drove down from their village in some anonymous Midlands town. They left shortly after the ceremony, apparently to beat the evening rush hour traffic. Nigel's father made his apologies, too, claiming that he had a sermon to write. The other two guests were Nigel's work colleagues who had agreed to act as witnesses with a promise of a free meal and as much as they could drink. They joined the couple for lunch at a local pub. By late afternoon Nigel and his companions were as drunk as lords. This led to the first serious marital row, and Sarah walking out in the kind of huff with which he was to become familiar over the years.

Looking back, Nigel wondered whether the marriage had started to crumble from that very first day, although the disintegration took several years to ratchet up enough force to propel them into the wood-paneled offices of her divorce lawyer.

By then, Nigel was making his way in journalism as the chief political reporter at the left-leaning *Daily Record*, where the editor gave him his head in peddling his opinions in a weekly column called 'Westminster Notes'. Sarah, meanwhile, had become a rising star at *MODE,* working her way up to a senior editorial position. Along the way she acquired a reputation for ruthless efficiency. She was 'someone to be watched', which was meant in both the negative and positive senses. Her lucky break came when her boss, the deputy editor, was hired by a rival publication. Sarah took over from her with a remit to 'save' the magazine. And save it she did. Or so she believed, even if others didn't. More importantly, the corporate owners believed it. From that point, taking the editor's chair was only a matter of time, especially as the incumbent was a gentle soul, unskilled in the dark arts of office politics that Sarah had now perfected. Two years, to be precise.

And then she met Vincent Marchetti.

Marchetti had been born and raised in a poor Italian neighborhood in Trenton, New Jersey, the youngest of four sons. His father was a waiter. His mother worked as a seamstress to supplement her husband's erratic paychecks. Vincent, the runt of the litter, was short, skinny and short-sighted. By grade school he was wearing spectacles, earning the nickname 'Squint'. He was an introverted boy but a born student, which wasn't an endearing quality in an earthy working-class district. Much to his father's dismay, if not his mother's, he felt more comfortable swotting at home than hanging out with his classmates. He was awkward with girls, too, which perhaps explained his early affinity for figures of a different kind. In his final high school year, he won a coveted prize for excellence in mathematics, paving the way for a scholarship to Penn State University. There he gained a Bachelor of Science degree in economics. He followed this up with a master's in business administration from the prestigious Barton Business School.

In his final year there, he had fallen in with a fellow student named Martin Jameson, the son of a wealthy Manhattan property developer. It was a fateful meeting, for him if not for Jameson. His new friend was no academic, to put it politely, and he had a feckless history that was camouflaged by arrogance and bombast. In physical contrast to Marchetti, he was tall, broad shouldered and decent looking. He walked with a swagger and his manner was cocky, evidence of a vainglorious streak. Another point of difference was that he felt more at home with girls than with books - he liked to boast that he'd never read one. He might have struggled to graduate, but his father's generous donations to the college ensured that he left with a respectable degree.

After college, Jameson introduced the late-blooming but fast-learning Vincent to a hedonistic lifestyle, paid for entirely by Jameson. A world that featured executive jets, improbably large yachts, and parties on private islands attended by an unending stream of starlets and models. Unusually for their milieu, neither Jameson nor Marchetti touched alcohol or drugs. Instead, they obtained their jollies by dating beautiful, promiscuous and usually vacuous women. Marchetti had little money of his own, but his friendship with Jameson gave him access to just about anything that money could buy, all the while observing Jameson carefully, picking up tips on how to dress and how to impress his friend's business associates with bullshit. Above all, though, how to assume an effortless ease with powerful men and desirable women. If girls had never warmed to Marchetti, they now swarmed about him like birds at a feeder. He no longer had to wonder why.

All this time, it had hardly occurred to him that he ought to find a proper job. But after several years as his friend's 'financial adviser', and co-investor in several lucrative property deals, he began to feel uneasy about the dependency. For the first time, his confidence was rooted in fertile soil. The time had come to acquire a fortune of his own, by his own efforts. Given his aptitude for numbers, he considered accountancy, but that would have entailed acquiring yet another degree. Besides, there was little money, and less satisfaction in cooking another company's books. A better option, he decided, was to cook one's own company books. He joined a boutique private equity firm that specialized in breaking up struggling companies and selling off the profitable parts. Readily adapting to this world - and given more leeway in deal-making by his employer than his junior position warranted - he made a fair amount of money, both for the firm and for himself. For a change of pace, he joined a hedge fund group, a fast-growing firm in a new and exciting branch of the investment business. It focused on the defence industry, where lucrative government contracts were always up for grabs. Within two years, after adding considerably to his now respectable personal wealth, he left to start his own fund management company. In a roaring bull market, the business expanded rapidly, and before long he was running a diversified stable of investment funds. Along with his fortune, he acquired a reputation as something of a sage, often adorning the cover of glossy investment magazines. One of them devoted a cover article to Vincent Marchetti as 'Investment Manager of the Year'.

Marchetti had been wildly successful in finance, but his old college pal Martin Jameson had accomplished even more - unexpectedly and to many quite absurdly - in politics. After years of losing money in assorted and ill-conceived real estate developments, Jameson exploited his inherited wealth, and campaign financing of questionable legality, to obtain the Republican Party's nomination for the presidency. It had seemed a remote prospect when he faced several better-known and infinitely more qualified rivals in a television debate, but he proceeded to reduce each of them in turn to stuttering incoherence. Among the shocked were many of the grandees of his own party. Most of them soon got over it and rallied behind him. And in the presidential election that followed he once more prevailed over the odds against a competent but unloved Democratic candidate, shocking the American political establishment all over again.

If the political world was stunned, so was Jameson himself, who'd run only to satisfy a large debt with a Russian oligarch willing to relinquish repayment for influence. Above all, though, just for a laugh. "Can you fucking believe it," Jameson had gloated to his equally disbelieving wife Samantha, as he sat for the first time with his feet on the desk in the Oval Office and giggling like a schoolboy. "This is going to be so much fun."

What he really meant was that it would be extraordinarily profitable.

Vincent Marchetti of course had contributed financially to the Jameson campaign, payments which he regarded as debts repaid to a mentor. They were also, of course, a deposit on future favours. Like many in the Republican Party, he secretly doubted Jameson's suitability for the job. But friends in high places meant opportunity and having one in the highest place of all meant unlimited opportunities. Vincent had been among the first to call the president-elect to congratulate him. "I'm always here for you," he'd told him. And so he would be, though not in ways that he could talk about publicly. Or even privately for that matter.

Then, weeks after the Inauguration, which he'd attended as an honoured guest on the platform, Marchetti went to London. It was no more than a stopover between a speaking engagement in Zurich and a shareholder meeting in New York, and he'd be spending only one evening in town. He had just one meeting scheduled, with Patrick Moreau, a wealthy French fashion tycoon, who'd just ploughed millions into one of Vincent's new European equity funds. Moreau invited Marchetti to join him later that evening at a glitzy reception at the Dorchester. Marchetti rarely enjoyed such occasions, and anyway was committed to attending a business dinner. Pop in just for an hour, Patrick suggested, mentioning as a further inducement that the party would be swarming with glamorous models and actresses. Given the size of Moreau's investment, which produced an income of millions of dollars in management fees, Vincent decided that he had no choice but to go. The party, Moreau mentioned, was being given by *MODE* magazine.

He met her as soon as he arrived. Sarah was at the entrance to the Dorchester's grand ballroom, greeting arriving guests. It was early in the evening but already the ballroom was a heaving mass, everyone dressed to the nines, and many into considerably higher figures. A white-suited band was playing Cole Porter tunes, to which some people were dancing. Vincent joined what he took to be a receiving line.

Moments later he found himself face to face with the hostess, the editor-in-chief of *MODE* magazine. She was wearing a fetching black gown - donated for the occasion by one of the magazine's prominent advertisers - which revealed considerable décolletage. She was also festooned with jewellery, none of it faux, and likewise borrowed for the evening.

Sarah introduced herself with a regal nod of the head and a smile. "Good evening and welcome, sir. I'm Sarah Harper. *MODE* magazine. So glad you could attend our little soiree."

"Hello," he said, rather stiffly. "I'm Vincent Marchetti."

"I don't think we've had the pleasure. What is it that you do, Mr Marchetti?"

"I run a hedge fund."

"Oh," she said, not bothering to hide her surprise but was thinking. *"Since I scarcely knew what hedge funds do, what on earth is he doing here?'*

"I was invited by a client," he explained, noting her puzzled expression. "Patrick Moreau. You may not have heard of me, but I'm sure you've heard of him."

"Oh, yes, I know Patrick very well. Where is he, by the way?"

Vincent turned to introduce him, but Patrick had already melted into the jitterbugging throng. "All I can say is thank you so much for having me."

"We don't often get City people at an event like this," Sarah said cheerily. "But welcome. You may find some of our guests interesting. Some of them are fabulously wealthy, so you might even find yourself drumming up some business. Enjoy." Smiling, she turned away to great another guest.

That was the extent of their first conversation, but it was enough to leave a strong impression on them both.

'*Very attractive*', Vincent was thinking as he skirted the perimeter of the ballroom, '*and obviously well-connected in her world'.*

Watching him walk away, Sarah had precisely the same thoughts.

The next time they met was when he was leaving. Sarah spotted him heading for the door. She hurried over. "Ah, Mr Marchetti. Not leaving so soon? Why?"

Pleased that she'd remembered his name, he offered his apologies with a slight bow. "I'm afraid I have a prior engagement. I'd much rather stay here, really. It's a truly fabulous party." In fact, he could hardly wait to leave the tumult and the crowd. She alone was a reason to stay - and he nearly did for that reason.

"And it's hardly just begun," she was saying. "Many of our more illustrious guests haven't even arrived."

"I'd love to stay, I really would, but I have a business dinner. Can't be helped."

"Well, perhaps you'll consider coming back *after* your dinner," she gushed. "We'll all still be here. These things do go on until the wee small hours."

"Well, I'll try." Vincent said, just to be polite. "Susan, is it?"

"My close friends call me Sarah - if they know what's good for them."

"I'm sorry. Sarah. Perhaps I'll pop back later. But I can't promise anything."

"That's the spirit. Now, off you go to your silly dinner, and get back here as soon as you can. By the way, do you like the Rolling Stones?"

"I do. Why?"

"Because Mick and Ronnie are in town and promised to drop in."

"In that case, I'll see what I can do." Vincent failed to reveal that his passion for the Rolling Stones was in his intense dislike of them. "But for now, goodnight and, again, thank you."

Sarah's press officer, a young man named Trevor, sidled up to her. "You're not mingling, Sarah," he scolded, half-jokingly.

She bridled at his impertinence. How dare he! She'd been planning to fire the silly man anyway. Now she had yet another reason to do it. "Trevor, dear, please don't presume to tell me how to behave at my own fucking party. But you can redeem yourself. Find out who that man is." She pointed at Vincent's departing figure. "Vincent Marchetti's the name. He's in hedge funds, apparently. Came with another guest."

Trevor, peering after him, broke into a relieved smile. "Oh, I know who Vincent Marchetti is alright. He's a big name in finance, and I mean BIG. Can't think why he'd be here, though, at an event like this." Trevor, it seemed, had joined *MODE* from an investment bank and was familiar with Marchetti and his works. Sarah looked at him doubtingly, affronted that Trevor might know anyone important, much less someone she'd never heard of. "I don't know him personally, of course, but in the City of London everyone knows of him. My partner Bob works for an investment firm and brings home financial magazines. I sometimes flip through them, just to see who's doing what. Vincent Marchetti's often in them, sometimes on the cover. Worth billions. Well-connected politically, too. An old college buddy of President Jameson. There's talk that he could one day be something important in government, like secretary of the treasury. Not ours, of course."

"Well, well…" Sarah muttered, more to herself than to Trevor, whom she dismissed from her presence with an airy wave.

* * *

Three hours later, she spotted Vincent across the packed ballroom. He *had* come back. She felt a surge of relief. Almost excited, she made her way over to him.

"Vincent! I'm so-o-o glad you decided to come back to us. Your dinner must have been boring."

"Worse than that, a complete waste of time. I left after the main course. This looks like much more fun." He didn't look like a man having fun.

"Let me fetch you a glass of champagne," Sarah purred, batting away a stray balloon. "That is, if I can find a waiter who's not carrying empties. These people could drink for Britain. Well, I suppose in a way they *are* drinking for Britain."

"Thanks for the offer," said Marchetti, "but I don't drink."

"Not at all?"

"Never."

"I'm sure we can find you something non-alcoholic. Tell me - and I hope you won't think me rude for asking - are you teetotal from choice or because it's not an option?"

"I've never been a drinker. Just never took to it. Tried it a few times but never much liked it. And I've seen what it can do to people."

"Like this lot," said Sarah, sweeping a hand across the sea of manic, pulsating figures, where decorum was disintegrating fast. "And my former husband."

Vincent perked up at the mention of her marital status. "Was he an alcoholic?"

"No. But he was, still is, a journalist. Consuming large quantities of alcohol goes with the territory. The booze could make him quite unreasonable. Offensive even. Mind you, he started out that way."

"I'm sorry to hear that. Have you replaced him yet?"

"Oh, no. Never found the time. Or more to the point, the right man. My job keeps me busy. That and two children. Mercifully they're both away at boarding school most of the time."

"Kids need a father," Vincent pronounced, having read it somewhere.

"How about you, Vincent? Married? Children?"

"Single. No partner. Not even a girlfriend. No ex-wife. And obviously no children. Oh, and not gay."

"Too busy making money to have time for love, I suppose." That sounded rude, she decided, so quickly added, "Just like me."

With that essential intelligence out of the way, they lapsed into a momentary silence, each turning over what they had just learned about the other. It was Vincent who broke it. "Look, I know you're on duty, so please don't let me keep you from your obligations as hostess. I'm perfectly able to look after myself."

Sarah put on a coquettish look. "Thank you, kind sir. Yes, I suppose I ought to be mingling with my guests. But, please, before you leave this time, make sure you come and find me."

He refrained from asking for what purpose, but said, "I will. But in case we miss each other, here's my business card."

She studied it closely, as if looking for clues, but only saw a company name and a midtown Manhattan office address.

"You run an investment group."

"Actually, several groups," he corrected her, looking to impress. "This is just one of my business cards. I have many." An idea came to him. "Look, perhaps we could have lunch soon. I'd like to learn more about the magazine business. Who knows, we might even end up investing in it, if we're not already. I'll have to check on what's in our portfolios."

"You could do worse. Fashion is booming. Show business is booming. The magazine is booming. *MODE* is privately held, of course. A French entrepreneur. But you never know what might happen. But as he's close to ninety, and not quite as mentally robust as he once was - that's strictly off the record, of course - you never know."

"Don't worry, I won't be quoting you. In my line of work, discretion rules."

"I'd be happy to tell you whatever you'd like to know about the group's business, and the politics." Sarah realized she was saying too much. "Not that we're in immediate need of cash, you understand. In our branch of publishing, unlike everyone else in the print world, advertising revenue is growing nicely. At *MODE* especially. We're on a roll, right now. Cash rich."

"Cash is king." Vincent paused before saying anything else. "Look, I'm off to New York tomorrow. I'll be there for about a week, but perhaps when I get back…"

"You live in New York, I take it?"

"I have an apartment there, on Park Avenue, but I'm spending more and more time in London these days. I have a home in Chelsea Village."

Sarah was duly impressed, but also a little panicked by his imminent departure. "What time is your flight tomorrow? Perhaps you'd have time for an early lunch. It's short notice, I know, but..."

"I suppose I could put off leaving until Sunday," Vincent said. "I'll have to juggle my schedule, but I'm sure it can be done." He laughed. "But what am I saying? I'm the boss. I can do what I want."

And that, as she would often say in retelling the story of the encounter, was that. The easiest deal either of them had ever transacted.

* * *

Two days before he was due to fly out on his great adventure, Nigel arranged to meet a reluctant Sarah for a drink.

"It'll have to be a quick one," she told him. "Vincent and I have theatre tickets."

"Well, we could meet early, say six o'clock. How about the American Bar at the Savoy Hotel? It's bound to be close to whatever theatre you're going to."

"As it happens, it's right across the street."

Nigel, arriving first, ordered a dry martini, thinking that he might as well get used to what Americans called highballs. Or was that a word only used in old movies? Sarah, true to form, showed up forty minutes late. Worse, she'd brought Vincent along. He'd met Vincent twice now and their mutual dislike had seemed to blossom on each occasion. The meeting that now followed merely served to confirm their mutual antipathy, which neither bothered to disguise.

"I must say you're looking very smart this evening, Sassie."

"I always look smart when I'm out on the town with my man," she said, before adding snappily, "and please don't call me that. You know how I hate it."

"He knows," said Vincent over her shoulder. "Why do you think he does it?"

"It never bothered you that much," Nigel said, "but I suppose you're moving in more sophisticated circles these days. Oh, hello, Vincent. I didn't see you there."

They shook hands coldly, avoiding eye contact. Vincent nodded but said nothing.

"What can I get you?" Nigel asked Sarah. "White wine?" She nodded. "And what about you, Vincent?"

"Mineral water," Vincent said. "I prefer still, if you don't mind."

There was waiter service, but Nigel went to the bar to vent his irritation. Returning with the drinks, he sat opposite the two lovebirds. "I thought the kids were in fine form last week." Nigel had, as promised, taken them out, on an expedition that included a dinner of hamburgers and ice cream and theatre.

"They usually are these days." There was an emphasis on 'these days'.

"I know they're sad to see me go, but at the same time they're happy for me. I must say they've taken my news rather well."

"Yes, they're quite the little grown-ups now. And thanks to the fine schools they go to, they've learnt their manners."

"You know," said Nigel wistfully, "all things considered, we've raised two very nice children."

Sarah snorted. "Yes, well, I've done a good job. And so have you, Vincent." Vincent smiled wanly.

Nigel, ignoring the slight, decided to get down to business. "Excuse me, Vincent, but a brief conversation between Sarah and me on financial matters is in order, if you don't mind." He turned to face Sarah with his back to Vincent. "It might interest you to know that I've had my solicitor draw up a letter of comfort, or some such thing, just to make sure I don't suspend my school fee payments. Or in case one day I disappear into the American hinterland, never to be seen again." Neither Sarah nor Vincent smiled. "I'll maintain a bank account here, of course, so the payments will keep coming automatically, direct debit, just as they do now."

"I would hope so," said Sarah, as matter-of-factly as she could, although Nigel noted the implied warning.

"I can't give you my contact details yet because I don't have any. I'll keep my UK mobile alive for the time being, but as of now I'm both homeless and stateless." He giggled nervously.

"Ah, yes," Vincent suddenly put in. "I hear congratulations are in order." The tone was strictly neutral. Any compliment from Vincent could sound like a reproof.

"Thanks," said Nigel said, equally off-handedly.

"White House correspondent... that sounds impressive, even if it is for a left-wing tabloid."

"Clearly you don't know what you're talking about," said Nigel heatedly. "The *Post* is politically somewhat to the right of centre. And it's not a tabloid. It's a broadsheet. But then I dare say you don't know the difference." Nigel realized that to Vincent anything to the left of the American alt-right was outright socialism. Now on a roll, he decided to try a little provocation. "We live, politically speaking, in the worst of times. The loonies of the hard right are trying to destroy our democratic institutions and then they'll start on the rest of us, the ordinary people. They're already in power in some southern and western states."

"Oh, and how exactly are we trying to destroy those institutions?" Vincent asked, rising to the bait. Nigel noticed the 'we'. Vincent ploughed on without an answer. "If you're referring to the government of the United States, let me remind you that it was democratically elected, and with a strong mandate for change. The people, in short, have spoken. That is the very essence of democracy."

"Well, more fool the people," Nigel snapped. "As far as I can see, America's in a total mess, and in a dangerous place. The right likes to exploit chaos. Mind you, we're not far behind here in Britain. Both countries are run by incompetent right-wing governments. The difference is that yours is led by people with despotic tendencies."

"I can't agree with your assessment at all," Vincent said, clearly trying to control his temper, but failing. "At least not about the United States. Nobody believes all that liberal crap you people put out. Jameson's right. Fake news, all of it. The reality is very different. The American economy, in case you hadn't noticed, is booming. Employment's at record levels, corporate profits are soaring, the stock market's flying. There's no gloom on Wall Street, I can assure you. Or on Main Street. Only you media people spread gloom and doom. You don't want to give our man credit for anything. Never have and never will. The truth just doesn't suit your agenda."

"And what agenda might that be?" Nigel asked, now bracing for an argument, without quite realising that he was already in one.

"That's obvious. You want to take a democratically elected president down, and by whatever means that comes to hand. The trouble with the liberal elite is that it can't abide a winner. You just can't stand that our man has the support of the working people you think ought to have voted the other way. Well, my friend, times have changed, and you need to get over it. What have you got against him, anyway?"

"That would take all evening and most of the night."

Sarah, increasingly irritated, now had had enough. "Gentlemen, gentlemen... I didn't come here to listen to a bad-tempered political debate. Cut it out, both of you, before things turn even nastier, and someone says something he'll regret."

Nigel, shooting her a defiant glance, carried on regardless. "Frankly, there's nothing I can say about his man in the White House that I would regret. Let me tell you, Vincent, what I've got against him. The man's a fucking disgrace. He's a blight on normal, well-mannered political discourse. He's scarcely literate. Can't even bother to read his briefing paper. He's not remotely qualified for the job. What's more, he's a born liar. He's almost certainly a crook, too, and driven solely by ego and greed. His narcissism, as any psychiatrist will tell you, means that he's incapable of making rational decisions. That, in my opinion, makes him doubly dangerous. Every time he opens his mouth or sends out one of those puerile tweets of his, he demeans his office, and us. On top all that – and I should have started with this – he's a bigot, a misogynist and a racist. How's that for the time being?"

"Quite finished?" Vincent said.

"Not by a long chalk," Nigel replied. Then he noticed that people at adjoining tables were listening with intense interest, some with amusement. "But Sarah's right: this is neither the time nor the place."

"You might have said that to begin with," Sarah snapped. Checking her watch, she gave Vincent a signaling look. "We need to be making a move, darling. I hate to be late for the theatre... all those people having to stand up while we get to our seats."

Nigel thought about reminding her that they only had to cross the Strand to get there, and had at least half an hour to kill, but he knew that she was merely seizing an excuse to leave.

"Well," said Sarah, "this was all a waste of time. And far from elevating."

Vincent glared, frustrated that he wouldn't have time for a rebuttal. Even so, like the president he so greatly admired, he insisted on having the last word. "This nonsense is what they call objective reporting, Sarah. And he's only a part of the whole damn media-driven feeding frenzy."

"At *MODE,* we always insist on objectivity," Sarah put in perkily.

Nigel looked at her with disdain. "Well, objectivity is hardly a burning issue when you're writing about the latest trend in ladies' underwear."

"This conversation is over," declared Vincent, as if wrapping up a board meeting. He stood up. "All I can tell you, Mr Hot Shit White House correspondent, is that I'm well connected in political circles. Not only did I go to school with the president, but I'm also an old friend of his press secretary, Frank Hoffman. We go back a long way, the three of us." Vincent's lip curled. "Well, I look forward to seeing how much cooperation you get from this White House. Frank on his own can make your life extremely difficult. And if I have anything to do with it, he'll do just that."

As if fleeing the scene of a crime, Sarah and Vincent moved swiftly towards the exit.

"Goodnight, Nigel," she said coldly over her shoulder. "And good luck. Somehow, I think you're going to need it."

As Nigel watched them go, he regretted suggesting meeting in the first place. But how was he supposed to know she would bring that vile boyfriend of hers? They deserved each other, he concluded. He conjured up the dreadful Buchanans from his favourite book, *The Great Gatsby.* He knew the passage by heart: '*They were careless people, Tom and Daisy – they smashed up things and creatures, and then retreated into their money or their vast carelessness, or whatever it was that kept them together, and left other people to clean up the mess they had made…*'

He looked at his watch. Just after seven o'clock. Ordering another nerve-soothing martini, he wondered what he could do for the rest of the evening. He took out his mobile and called the *Post* newsroom, hoping to persuade Duncan - or someone - to join him for a drink. Surprisingly, it was Elsa who picked up. "Hello, Duncan Erskine's office."

"What are you doing in the office so late, and on a Friday, too? Has a major story broken? Has something happened that I should know about?"

"Nothing of the kind. I had a backlog of work, that's all, stuff I've been putting off for a week. I was just getting ready to leave, as it happens."

"Is Duncan still there?"

"No. He's gone up to Scotland for the weekend. A family birthday, or something like that."

"I see. Does that mean you've nothing on tonight?"

"Actually, I'm wearing a rather fetching ensemble in blue."

"Very funny. What I meant was, do you have a date or an appointment?"

"Neither. I was planning a quiet evening at home watching telly. A rare event for me, but frankly, after this week, a welcome one."

"That sounds tragic. Why don't you meet me for a drink? I could use a little company right now."

"I don't know about that..."

"Just a drink, that's all."

"There's no such thing as 'just a drink' where you're concerned. We'll finish up in one of your fancy late-night Mayfair fleshpots. And then I'll have a splitting headache for two days."

"I promise to be good."

"Ha! Pull the other one. Where are you, anyway?"

"I'm calling from the Savoy bar, but I don't much like it here. I was thinking we might meet somewhere more convivial, more comfortable."

"I'm not sure about that. Being comfortable isn't a requirement for a quick drink."

"How about El Vino's on Fleet Street? No one ever called that place comfortable."

"Mmm, I don't know."

"Come on, just the one. I promise. Scout's honour."

"Mmm..."

She was still obviously debating with herself. A good sign, Nigel thought.

"Alright then, Nige. First, though, I need to freshen up a bit. I'll see you at El Vino's in half an hour. Remind where it is."

"Fleet Street, bottom of Fetter Lane. Best take a taxi."

* * *

El Vino - always El Vino's even to its regular patrons - was a wine bar. Back in the day it had enjoyed legendary status, not so much for the quality of its service - and least of all for its antiquated décor, unchanged since the Second Word War - as for the literary status of its clientele. It was there that the mythical Lunchtime O'Booze, the invention of a satirical magazine called *Private Eye*, had spent his afternoons. The 1986 exodus had deprived the place of most of its regulars, some of them honoured by little brass plaques set into the nicotine-stained walls, and the few that remained were rapidly diminishing in number. Popular it may have been, but El Vino had never been the most welcoming of the Street's taverns. Even in its heyday, when it was packed daily with hard-drinking scribes from the classier papers, the manager, a large, florid man given to wearing multi-colored waistcoats, took pleasure in ejecting people, often for no better reason than his taking a dislike to a haircut or the colour of a tie. Such was El Vino's standing that many of the victims regarded their treatment less as an insult than a badge of honour. Nowadays, El Vino could no longer afford to be rude to its patrons, though it hardly mattered since there were so few of them left.

Nigel entered the place half expecting a heaving noisy crowd, but it was almost empty. A few drinkers at the bar looked as if they hadn't moved in thirty years. The place was dimly lit and comfortably tatty. Nigel took the one remaining barstool. His nods to his fellow patrons earned a couple of desultory nods back. Anticipating Elsa's choice of tipple, he ordered a bottle of Macon-Villages.

She appeared half an hour later. She looked, Nigel thought, quite ravishing. She also turned the heads of the other customers, he noticed.

"Sorry I'm late," she said, somewhat breathlessly. "Just as I was leaving, Duncan called. From the bloody train. Kept me on for twenty minutes with a lecture."

"On what?"

"Get this: to tell me to go home. He was worried that I might be working too hard. What a joke! I didn't tell him I was meeting you. Blimey, he'd have thrown a fit."

Nigel didn't ask why but it pleased him to speculate. "I just got here myself," he fibbed, before realizing that the depleted bottle suggested otherwise. He emptied it by pouring her a full glass. "I hope I guessed right."

"Perfect," she purred. "My favourite."

She hoisted herself onto the adjoining barstool, in the process revealing a lengthy and shapely expanse of leg, and a momentary flash of knickers. She caught him looking.

"Very nice, too," he said brazenly, but quickly diverted her attention from his prurience by raising another topic. "Elsa Moreton working late on a Friday... I mean, what *is* the world coming to?"

"I'm quite dedicated to my job, you know, despite whatever you might hear to the contrary. Haven't seen you all week, by the way. I hear you and Duncan had quite a session last Friday."

"Did *he* tell you that?"

"He didn't have to. He called me at about six o-clock to say he wouldn't be back. As if I didn't know. He could hardly get the words out. He slept on the sofa that night, I can tell you. Not that I want to give away any boudoir secrets."

"Nor do I wish to hear them. He's always enjoyed his lunches at the Grill on Fridays. God knows why. Food's awful."

"Yes, he has. But he's usually with the kind of friends who wouldn't dream of getting pissed. He was always religiously back by three."

"You like him, don't you?" Nigel said, stating the blindingly obvious.

"Well, obviously. And I could have a worse boss. Why do you ask?"

Nigel grinned. "I'm not fishing, my dear Elsa. And you don't have to be coy. Nobody even talks about you two anymore."

"And I'm one of them."

"Ha! That's rich coming from the *Post*'s very own town crier. You thrive on gossip."

"Not when it's about me." Elsa sipped her wine delicately, holding the glass by the stem, remembering that she had been told that was the correct way. "This is delicious, Nige, and just what the doctor ordered. It's been a long day. A long week. I'm knackered."

"A long week for me, too, or at least it seems that way."

"You sounded a bit down on the phone. Has something happened?"

"Only that I made the mistake of meeting Sarah for a drink. That would have been bad enough, but she brought along that obnoxious boyfriend of hers. It didn't go well, to put it mildly. Vincent and I had words, and so they left. I suppose you could say they stormed out."

"Are you telling me that if he hadn't been there, it might have been a sweetly nostalgic evening?"

"God, no! Too late for that. No, I just thought I ought to see her before I left for Washington. Let her know I wouldn't be disappearing off the face of the earth. That I'd still be supporting the kids, paying the bills. I should have known better. She despises me, I'm sad to say. And hates me."

"It seems to be mutual, to be honest."

"That's also true, I suppose. But I don't really hate her. I feel sorry for her. She's no longer the woman I once knew and, God help me, once adored. All she cares about now is money and status. What galls is that vile boyfriend of hers has more money than even she would know how to spend."

"Remind me who he is."

"Vincent Marchetti. Big shot in hedge funds. Complete cunt. Bad reputation on the Street. Boasts constantly that he went to school with President Jameson. They're still pals.

"Sounds delightful. But why should you care about either of them?"

"Because, my dear Elsa, it can't be good for me where I'm going. And Vincent is also, apparently, a mate of the White House press secretary. I'll be a marked man."

"I'm sure you'll handle the situation with your usual competence and flair."

"Well, I'm going to try. It won't be easy. I'll be the new kid in school. And these are powerful people I'm talking about. They don't take prisoners. They kill them."

Elsa put on a pantomime act of being desperately concerned. "Poor little Nigel, alone in a strange country, surrounded by ruthless enemies. How on earth will he cope?"

"Now you're just taking the piss."

"Well, you deserve it. And if I didn't, then you'd just get yourself depressed, drink yourself silly, and fall apart. Lighten up, for God's sake. Be the Nigel Harper that we all know and love. The Nigel Harper that Downing Street fears. I heard Duncan say that last bit earlier today, by the way. It seems that you've offended the prime minister. I'm not sure how or when."

"Good. Offending prime ministers is part of my job."

"Well, it hardly matters now. In a few days you'll have scarpered."

"I'm afraid so."

"Afraid? You're about to take the best job on the newspaper. Enjoy it, for fuck's sake… and that's an order." She emptied her glass. Nigel, afraid that she might be about to leave, responded to the barman's enquiring look by nodding his assent to a second bottle.

Elsa hadn't yet finished her cheerleading. "I for one have every confidence in the future success of Nigel Harper. So does Duncan, or he wouldn't be sending you. I see a brilliant future for you over there, and I'm going to raise a glass to it. So, cheers, mate, and the best of British luck."

Nigel was deeply touched. "You always were a very present help in trouble, Elsa Moreton. Talking to you always lifts my spirits."

"You make me sound like your shrink."

"Something I'm often told I could use. But you've been a most able substitute, and without charging a fee. For that I'll always be grateful."

"For the service, or for not charging a fee? This wine is very nice, by the way. You always did have good taste… in wine if nothing else."

Two hours and two bottles later they were still there. They'd now moved to a table in the rear, largely because attempting to descend from their barstools to go to the lavatory had become a hazardous enterprise. Elsa was no stranger to drink, but she looked slightly flushed. Her words were becoming slurred. Nigel, with a head start on her, was in no better condition. But they chatted merrily on, covering a range of topics, reducing the serious ones to nonsense, their conversation punctuated by roars of childish laughter. By now they were the only customers in the place. The manager, having sent the only waiter home, looked anxious to close.

Nigel hiccupped. "Oops!"

"You're rat-arsed," she accused, chortling.

"Not at all. I'm just hungry. Haven't eaten a thing all day." His hand was on her thigh, just above her left knee.

"I'm not sure that's a good idea," she protested, but didn't remove the hand.

"That's not the same as saying it's a bad one," Nigel replied. "We should grab something to eat. Drinking on an empty stomach isn't good." He gestured to the barman. "Any chance of a cheese sandwich?"

"Sorry, sir, kitchen's closed, I'm afraid."

"You don't need a fucking kitchen to make a sandwich."

The barman looked less than pleased. "There's a coffee shop three doors along the street. They sell snacks."

"Perhaps," said Nigel to Elsa, "we should head for the Grill. It'll be quiet there, at least until the post-theatre crowd turns out."

"Sorry, Nigel, but it's a bit late for that. And I told you quite clearly I was just going to stay for one. I'm way past that." She checked her watch. "As a matter of fact, I really ought to think about getting home."

"I have an idea," Nigel said brightly, anxious not to lose her. "What do you say we combine the two?"

"How's that?"

"I buy a bottle of wine, then we go to your place, and you rustle up a little something to eat. Cheese on toast will do. You do have some cheese, don't you?"

Elsa gave him a disapproving look. "What did I tell you when you called? One drink, I said, and you agreed. I've already had the best part of two bottles. And now, just as I'd feared, you're starting to misbehave. I thought I'd made myself clear. I thought we had an understanding."

The hand on her thigh still hadn't moved. Or been removed.

Nigel adopted a plaintive tone. "Let me just say, my sweet girl, that in two days I'm leaving the country. You won't see me for months. Perhaps years. Who knows, we may never see each other again."

"Rubbish! That's just the wine talking."

"No, it's all me. All I'm saying is this: the least you can do to give me a decent send-off."

"You're a menace to women, Nigel Harper, and no mistake."

She checked her watch again, and this time stood up, somewhat unsteadily. "Time to go, I think. There's a nine-twenty from Waterloo. I can catch it if I hurry."

Elsa lived, he recalled, in Battersea, south of the river and so to Nigel, as to all north Londoners, part of a strange foreign country with a dark interior to which even drivers of black taxis were loath to venture. Seeing that Nigel suddenly looked downcast, Elsa placed a consoling arm around his shoulder. Mistaking the gesture, he responded by kissing her. To his surprise, there was no resistance. They stayed in the docked position for several minutes. Finally, the manager came over, coughed loudly, and announced rather definitively that he'd be closing the bar in five minutes.

They finished off the bottle.

Then Elsa looked at him and said with a smile: "As it so happens, Nige, I do have a large slab of mature cheddar in the fridge."

* * *

An hour or so after Nigel and Elsa had left El Vino, Sarah glanced at Vincent with a look of some concern. They were on their way home in a taxi. He seemed to have been in a funk all evening. All Nigel Harper's fault, of course. And the play had provided no relief. Vincent had found it depressing, and at times incomprehensible.

"You didn't like the play at all, did you," Sarah said, reading his thoughts.

"No, I didn't." Vincent spat out. He opened the window. It's so damned hot in here. And why the hell aren't we moving?" The traffic was snarled as usual around Trafalgar Square. "Take the Mall," he snapped at the driver.

"What other way would I go?" the man said testily.

"Well, I'm sorry you didn't enjoy the play," Sarah said. "I thought it was thought-provoking, if nothing else."

"Well, it didn't provoke any thoughts from me, except that it was lousy. Look, I just don't go in for this life-is-hell-when-you're-poor stuff. I was reading about the playwright in the programme. He's a strange man by all accounts."

"He's from up north if that's what you mean. They *can* be a bit different up there, I admit."

"Well, you're a northerner, and you're not strange."

"I'm from Warwickshire. That's not up north. It's barely in the midlands."

"Well, wherever the fuck he's from, it must be a miserable kind of place. If he hated it so much why didn't he just get out?"

"He did. He lives in London. He was originally from Leeds. Not everyone's favourite part of the country, I'll give you that."

"Never heard of the place. Must have been sheer hell if it made him write that kind of crap. And I hear he's not just left-wing, that he's also a poofter."

"So what? He's not the first gay playwright, you know. Think Wilde, Coward, Rattigan…even your own Tennessee Williams."

"They all probably wrote crap, too."

"I'm surrounded by gay men every day and it doesn't bother me one bit. In fact, you could say that they're the driving force in our industry."

"Well, I don't like them, wherever they show up."

"Why not? If they don't offend me, why should they bother you? But tonight, my darling, everything seems to be bothering you."

"It all started with that awful shit-shoveling Commie ex-husband of yours…"

Sarah changed the subject, not because Nigel was under attack but because she wanted to lift the mood. "Never mind, my love, we'll soon be home. Then we can relax. Have a nightcap. Forget about lousy plays and former husbands. And after that…"

Vincent ignored the promise, failed even to acknowledge the hand stroking his thigh. "Just where does the little fuck get off talking to me like that? I make in an hour what he makes in a year, so what's he got to be so damned cocky about?"

"The plain fact, darling, is that you just don't like each other. Let's leave it at that, because it really, really doesn't matter anymore. He no longer means anything to me. That means he shouldn't mean anything to you either. Anyway, he'll soon be off to America. And then, as you said, your friends in Washington can take care of him."

"As I'm sure they will," Vincent snarled. "I'll personally see to it. The little bastard won't know what's hit him." The repeated use of the diminutive was odd, since Vincent was at least three inches shorter than Nigel. "First thing tomorrow I'll call Frank Hoffman. Brief him on this little shit. Believe me, by the time we're through with him your man's life won't be worth living."

"*You're* my man now, Vincent, darling. And I know you'll do what you think is best."

"You bet your sweet ass I will."

"Well, if nothing else, I'm delighted you still think my ass is still sweet."

* * * * *

Chapter 3

Nigel's taxi edged onto the cantilevered 59th Street bridge, otherwise known as the Queensborough Bridge. Through the girders of that unlovely span, he caught his first glimpse of the Manhattan skyline. Whenever Nigel approached that vast concrete stockade on the Hudson, from whatever direction, the sight never failed to inspire in him an acute sense of anticipation - a promise that something interesting and perhaps even life-changing was bound to occur. And the city that famously never sleeps usually delivered.

His two previous visits, some years back, had both yielded minor scoops. On the first occasion, at a cocktail party at the United Nations, he'd found himself in conversation with Russia's deputy foreign secretary. After several glasses of wine, the man blurted out some ill-advised remarks to the effect that Russia had indeed secretly helped the Republican Party win the American election, failing to mention that he was speaking off the record. Nigel therefore felt free, under the recognized rules of engagement, to file a story. It was only a minor coup, though, as it was universally assumed, if not by Republicans, that Russia had been up to no good. But after a White House factotum derided it as fake news - the invention of a sensation-seeking foreign left-wing journalist - the story received more attention than it deserved. And on a subsequent visit, he had been in a Brooklyn bar and fallen in with a group of fire-fighters who had survived the collapse of the World Trade Center towers. Most of them had long since retired but all were still suffering from survivor's guilt over an event in which hundreds of their comrades had been killed. In several cases their marriages had collapsed. Nigel spoke to many of them in turn and then wrote a poignant article, which Duncan ran on the front page under the headline, '*The Hidden Casualties of 9/11*'.

"Guess we've hit the rush hour," Nigel said to the driver, absently.

"Mister, it's rush hour all day every day in this city," the driver complained over his shoulder. "This trip could take us another hour."

In the event, it took forty-five minutes - fifteen to cross the bridge and another thirty to negotiate the perpetually snarled East Side traffic. The city was humid, the air filled with almost enough moisture to muffle the sounds of horns blaring and drivers cursing.

After checking into the Norfolk Hotel - a converted midtown apartment house in which Cary Grant, and for a time the Beatles, were said to have lived - Nigel took a shower and changed into a smart-casual ensemble of blazer and slacks. Feeling better, he called Bill Palmer, the *Post*'s long-standing New York correspondent. They had arranged to meet for drinks and dinner, the reason why Nigel had stopped over in New York on his way to Washington. They had met only a few times, but Bill, a Londoner by birth and upbringing, was someone Nigel regarded as a kindred spirit: a journalist from the old school who rarely bowed to editorial authority. He also enjoyed exchanging gossip over a few jars. In his younger days he had been something of a man-about-town. Now in his late fifties, and married to a woman twenty years his junior, he was said to have mellowed into a devoted family man.

Bill had been sent to Washington two decades earlier, spending the first one there and the second in New York. Knowing his way around America's two most influential cities made him a useful source of diversified intelligence. In four presidential elections, he had crossed America from sea to shining sea on rickety planes and rancid press buses. Recognized as a zealous but even-handed reporter, he had interviewed four of the successful candidates and had often appeared on television news to offer a foreign perspective on domestic issues. In New York, he had become the doyen of correspondents, with useful contacts in institutions ranging from the United Nations to the Metropolitan Museum of Art.

Nigel was anxious to pick his brain about what, in British if not American eyes, appeared to be a dangerously fractious state of the union. Bill would also be able to deliver advice on what Nigel should do to thrive in the capital's notoriously dog-eat-dog media environment, especially as the new boy in school could expect to be on the menu.

Bill suggested they meet at the Norfolk hotel bar, Rudolph's, in an hour. That would give him time, he said, time to file what he dismissed as a 'non-story' about a Russian display of intransigence at the United Nations during a debate on the latest Middle East crisis. "This week's Levantine eruption," as he called it.

With an hour to kill, Nigel decided to go out for a stroll to savour the city's restless tempo. He headed east to Fifth Avenue, one block away. Nothing seemed to have changed since his previous visits. The sidewalks were jammed with gawping tourists, American and foreign, all ambling along as if trying to re-create the Easter Parade of yesteryear, perhaps in the hope of bumping into Astaire or Garland, or more likely these days, a famous rapper. The traffic inching its way downtown was dominated as usual by taxis, a great yellow snake, horns blaring as pointlessly as ever. In any other city the cacophony would have turned heads but here it went unnoticed. The air was still slightly dank, shimmering from a cocktail of exhaust fumes that mingled with oily blasts from subway grills, the spirals of steam rising from vents in the side streets, and the unidentifiable odours emanating from the convenience food stands that occupied every cross-street corner.

Nigel reached Rockefeller Center, but by then he was tired of being jostled by people with nowhere to go but still disinclined to give way to those who did. He decided to head back to the hotel to wait for Bill in the hotel's air-conditioned ground-floor bar. Rudolph's was crowded, too, not so much with tourists as dark-suited office workers relaxing after sundry exertions on what had been an unseasonably warm day. Parking himself on a barstool, he ordered a large Bushmill's Irish whiskey. Nigel had once favoured the Jameson's brand but switched brands as a symbolic gesture of protest when the presidency was taken over by someone of that name. Illogical, but it made him feel better.

A few minutes later, he spotted Bill elbowing his way through the crowd. Tall and slim, with thinning hair, carefully slicked down with brilliantine, or some other oily substance, he stood head and shoulders above everyone else. He spotted Nigel right away and waved.

"Hello, my old son," he gushed in a residual cockney accent that seemed hardly unaltered since his time as the *Post*'s political editor, one of Nigel's predecessors. "You're looking uncommonly well, old son. Decent flight?"

"Blessedly uneventful," Nigel replied. "You're not looking so bad yourself. You seem to look younger every time I see you."

"Don't be fucking daft. But thank you. And since you mention it, I *am* feeling quite spry."

Bill asked for a Bushmill's as well and Nigel ordered a second for himself. "It's always good to be back in New York," Nigel said, watching the bartender pour two very generous measures. "At least here you get a decent drink. Not like those pathetic thimblefuls we get back home."

"Why do you think I've been here for so long?" Bill replied, laughing.

"How long *has* it been? I've lost track."

Bill, like most expatriates, knew how long to the day. "On the fifteenth of this month, it'll be twenty-one years."

"Half an adult lifetime."

"I've never thought of it that way, but yes. Too long, some would say."

"Would you?"

"Nah. I'm part of the scenery here now, like the Empire State building."

"Ever think about going back?"

"Never," said Bill with no hesitation. "Not anymore. Truth is, I don't think much about the old country. Anyway, I've never asked to go back. As far as the *Post*'s concerned, I'm a fixture here, forgotten but also somehow irreplaceable."

"I wouldn't say forgotten. I might agree with irreplaceable."

"Being here suits me just fine. And what, I ask you, would a man of my advanced years do back in London?"

"Edit the paper, perhaps."

"Fat fuckin' chance of that."

"Well, you're obviously happy here."

"For which I can thank my young wife," Bill said with a wink. Bill's second wife was from South America, or so Nigel seemed to recall from once meeting her on a previous visit. Bill called her Holly, for a reason that Nigel had forgotten. Her real name, as Bill now reminded him, was Juanita.

"Do give Juanita, I mean Holly, my best," said Nigel. "She's a bonny lass, as Duncan would say."

"I will. Speaking of Mr Erskine, how is that old Presbyterian skinflint these days?"

"Still skinning flints."

Bill suddenly turned serious. "I've got a good thing going here. But the city isn't the same as it used to be. Same goes for the country."

"Tell me more."

"America is in serious trouble - and that's not just my opinion. Lost its way and fast losing its confidence. The brilliant future that every American once believed in is no long as assured as it once one. Fear stalks the land, as the cheap novelists would say."

"Yes, so we keep hearing. How much trouble, would you say?"

"Hard to say, but the old swagger, the boundless optimism, that innate sense of superiority – it's all crumbling. It doesn't help that we've got a certifiable lunatic in the White House."

"One who's going to restore America's greatness..."

"Don't make me laugh. It wasn't hope that put him there; it was desperation. The man couldn't run a scout troop, let alone the country. Everyone knows it, of course, but the politicians made such a hash of things he came across as a political messiah - at least out there in the boonies, where the so-called forgotten Americans live. They said, 'Fuck the politicians; what have they ever done for us? Why don't we try someone different? Someone who at least talks our language.'

"Well, they got something different alright, but that's not to say better."

"Damned sight worse, in fact. The state of the Union right now? I'd say the Union's in a state. You hear the word 'disintegration' bandied about. Remember the time when Americans felt so confident about everything that the world resented them for it? Well, now they're afraid, and the world's starting to pity them for it. Tell the truth, I'm a bit nervous myself."

"You can always get out. Go back to London. Anywhere."

"At my age! After twenty-odd years! We ex-pats are like religious converts, more native than the natives. Sure, I could fuck off somewhere else. My pension pot's big enough that I can do what I like. But now I've got an American passport, an American wife, and two American boys, both born here; wouldn't know a cricket bat from a stick of rock. We're all rabid Mets fans and we've got season tickets to the Jets." He chuckled, nudging Nigel in the ribs. "It's all a far cry from standing on the terraces at Queens Park Rangers in the pissing rain with numb feet. Blimey, those Saturday afternoons could be grim. You're too young to remember."

"I am. But things have changed a bit. Now we have seats, and under cover." Like most Britons abroad, or at least Englishmen, Nigel felt a primal urge to stick up for the old country, without being able to explain why, and not altogether believing it.

"Don't get me wrong, mate. I love London, but I don't miss it. Can't imagine ever living there again. The last time we went back, Holly and me, the damp got to both of us. Me especially. Here it's freezing fucking cold in winter and stinking hot in summer, but at least it's predictable - and usually dry. But it's not just the weather."

"What then?"

"I live in Westchester County in a six-bedroom house. I have a swimming pool out back and an acre of land. I couldn't afford a place like that within fifty miles of London. I've already paid off the mortgage and both boys are at university. I spend the summers sailing my forty-five-foot sloop on the Sound. I may not be fabulously wealthy, but I don't have to worry about the moolah. No, sir, you wouldn't get me back to Blighty now. Not even as managing editor… and that's never going to happen."

"You *have* gone native," Nigel observed gently.

"It'll happen to you, as well, mate. Look at Graham Welbeck."

"I'd rather not."

"Yeah, I know what you mean. Hardly a bundle of laughs, is he. But look, he's bought himself a nice place in Boca Raton and plans to spend the rest of his days down there. The old country may be doing okay, but few of us Brits ever think about going back."

"We'll see," was all Nigel could think of saying.

"But changing tack, as we mariners say, how's the newspaper business doing over there? Hardly anyone reads newspapers over here."

"Strangely enough, holding its own, though admittedly by the skin of our teeth. But somehow, we all seem to survive. How, though, remains a mystery. It's all about the websites these days; a case of feeding the hand that bites you, you might say. How about here?"

"Dire. New York City still has two papers: one for people who read all the news that's fit to print, and the other for people who can't read. That's to exclude the *Post*. That's Murdoch's rag, of course, the closest we come to a tabloid, minus the tits and bums. Anyway, who needs them? We've got instant news on our cell phones and 24-hour news on television. And we don't need newspapers to wrap up the fish and chips."

"I don't trust news on a phone," Nigel said emphatically. "Where's it from? Could be anywhere… Russia, China, some maniac in a loony bin. But at least we no longer have access to Fox News – that's something to be thankful for."

"Also owned by the Dirty Digger, of course. The man who killed Fleet Street."

"Or saved it, as some believe."

"Well, he's not my idea of a saviour. But neither is Jesus Christ. Rupert's close to ninety now, and still peddling insane right-wing propaganda. Some of his presenters are completely deranged but they still top the ratings. That tells you something. He's got this president in his pocket, of course, just as he did Blair and Thatcher years ago. Jameson's on Fox so often some people think he's a news anchor."

"Objectivity and good taste were never Murdoch's strong suits."

"Objectivity! Now there's a quaint, old-fashioned concept. We now have top White House people talking about 'alternative facts' – and people believe it."

"Well, at least it made the rest of us laugh."

"Laughing can be hard sometimes. Don't get me wrong: I still love my job, but I can't shake the feeling that I'm better off being closer to the end of my career than the beginning. I never used to feel that way."

"Look, it may make your skin crawl and your balls ache to write it, but this president is nothing if good copy."

"Sadly, all too true. So, when are you heading down to DC? And before I forget, congratulations on the appointment. I was very glad to hear about it. Long overdue as far as I'm concerned."

"Thanks. Tomorrow afternoon, to answer your question. I stopped here overnight to pick up a few useful tips, catch up on the latest scandal." Bill was renowned equally as a dispenser of sage advice and as a purveyor of gossip.

Bill laughed. "Frankly, there's not much of a market for wisdom these days. As for gossip, I'm no longer in the loop."

"You know about Duncan and Elsa…"

"My Aunt Mabel in Torquay knows about Duncan and Elsa."

Bill drained his glass and then laid a restraining hand on Nigel's raised arm to stop him ordering another. "What do you say we get out of here? I'm not hearing too well. The old shell-likes don't function quite as well as they used to, with all this ambient noise. We'll have an early dinner at Starks, one of my favorite restaurants. Best steak in town. Great wine list, too. It'll give us a chance of a proper chinwag."

"You don't have to dash home?"

"I'll take an eleven something from Grand Central. Starks is four blocks away. That'll give us plenty of time."

Paying the bill, Nigel understood why the drinks were so generous.

***

Early as it was, Starks was already crowded and even noisier than Rudolph's. Their fellow diners, Nigel noticed, were overwhelmingly male and white - expensively suited - and advertising men by the look of them. He was struck by the sumptuous décor, the mahogany paneling and red velvet banquettes, the landscape paintings on the walls. All discreetly lit but somehow both tasteful and tasteless. The ancient waiter who showed them to a table struck Nigel as a dead ringer for Abe Vigoda from *The Godfather*.

"Quite a place, huh?" Bill said, as they were seated. He lowered his voice. "Used to be owned by some interesting fellas with lots of vowels in their surnames. Probably still is."

"You mean the…"

"Yeah, them. Back in the eighties, someone named Paul Allesandro was whacked right outside the front door that we just came through. For days you could still see traces of the chalk outline on the sidewalk where the body had been – or so I've been told."

"So, it's a Mafia hangout," said Nigel, gazing around.

Bill hushed him with a finger to his lip. "Best not to use that word in a place like this. You never know who's listening. You'll have the same problem in Washington, my son, but for different reasons… well, maybe not so different."

Bill ordered a pricey bottle of Brunello. When the waiter arrived with it, they asked him to stand by while they gave him an order for a pair of T-bone steaks. Nigel suddenly felt hungry.

Sliding into interrogation mode, he said, "You were telling me how bad things are over here. How bad? Seems to us back home that it's falling apart at the seams, dividing into two warring tribes, both ready to start a new Civil War. But is it really that bad?"

"Not far off. But it depends on which channel you watch. CNN says things are going downhill rapidly and with no end in sight; Fox News says everything's fine and that this president's doing a great job. Take your pick."

"You watch Fox News?"

"Only when I feel like winding myself up into a rage. My wife usually turns it off. Says it's bad for my blood pressure. I don't watch much television myself, and only to stay in touch. Mostly CNBC. I read the *New York Times*, of course, and the *Washington*

Post. They're no friends of the administration, of course. Jameson says they're enemies of the people. Well, I suppose he's right if he means enemies of *his* people."

"How, then, would you judge the national mood right now?"

"Do you want bromides or Bill Palmer's patented apocalyptic version?"

"Bad as that, is it?"

"In medical terms you might say the patient's condition is terminal, verging on serious."

"In other words, situation hopeless but not serious."

"That's it. This president says he'll come up with a cure, but that's like expecting a child to build a hadron collider. The stock market's flying, if that means anything. So are corporate profits. But to state the obvious, Wall Street ain't Main Street. The reason the market's running is low interest rates and low inflation. When they both go in the other direction - and that's bound to happen the way this administration is spending - so will the market. All of which supposes that Jameson hasn't by then provoked a war with China - and I'm not necessarily talking trade war."

"You don't get that impression reading Graham Welbeck's stuff."

"Well, what can I tell you…?"

"Everything that Graham can't, I'm hoping."

"Well, he's the reason you're here, my old son. Poor old Graham was never up to the job; I knew that when he took over from me. Should have said so at the time. Come to think of it, I did say so at the time. The man should have been pensioned off some time ago. I've been telling Duncan that for years, by the way."

"As have I. But at least he's finally listened."

But Bill's baleful disquisition had yet to run its course. "This president is clueless: economically, socially and ethically. He's a racist and a misogynist, and almost certainly a crook. Above all, he's dangerous."

"Dangerous? In what way?"

"He has despotic instincts. He's a would-be dictator, just waiting for his chance."

"And you're speaking as a fully paid-up member of the privileged elite."

"They - we - don't count for much right now. Anyway, I don't count myself as a member of the elite. I worked my way up to where I am today. No education to speak of, unlike you Oxbridge types, but at least I can still use my brain. The sad truth is that most Americans can't. We've become an unthinking society. Millions of voters - nearly half of them, it seems - are convinced that Jameson will restore the country to its former glory - whatever that means. But then it doesn't mean anything, as most of his supporters are as ignorant and illiterate as he is."

"He didn't win the popular vote."

"So what? It's the Electoral College that counts. Dreamed up by supposedly thoughtful men, the beloved Founding Fathers, the kind of people who spent all their spare time writing constitutions. What the fuck could they have been thinking?"

"What do you think will happen at the next election?"

"Too early to tell. According to most polls Jameson would win hands down. But voters are fickle - or to put it another way, totally confused. They're like sheep being herded by dogs, first to the left, then to the right, and then back again. But if a week's a long time in politics, two years is an eternity. In other words, anything can happen."

"Maybe Jameson will have been found out by then."

"What does that mean - 'found out'?"

"They'll realize that he's clueless, divisive and ignorant. I mean, how could such a man even stand a chance being re-elected?"

Bill peered across the table at Nigel as a teacher might at a student who's just submitted an inadequate thesis. "You might say the same of our recent prime ministers. Look, Jameson made it once, against all the odds, so he could well do it again. But let me take those objections of yours one by one, and there's an element of devil's advocacy here, so don't go busting my balls at the end of it."

Nigel gave the three-fingered scout salute.

"First, being clueless is no handicap. Half the presidents in our two-hundred-year-old history have been clueless. Take some recent examples. Look at Harry Truman. Not a bad president, but before he took office, nobody even bothered to tell him that America had the A-bomb - and he was the vice-president! More recently there was Bush junior, a complete numbskull, who only wanted the job to prove himself to his father. As soon he got in, he left Cheney to run the show. Result? That stupid Gulf War, nothing but a profit-making exercise for Cheney's business interests. And then they're outraged when Arabs come over and blow up the World Trade Center. Truman of course went on to get re-elected in his own right and Bush got a second term. And I didn't even mention Nixon."

"Nixon was smart, though."

"Yah, so smart that he got himself impeached for covering up a burglary committed by halfwits." Bill resumed his countdown. "As to the second point, dividing the nation is, almost by definition, what politics is all about. Most politicians get elected by pinching a few voters from the half of the country who think he's God's gift from the other half who think he's a fool. That's how it always worked. What changed is that the two sides now hate each other so much they can't bear to talk to each other. Even Congress can't have a civil conversation, which is the whole fucking point of it."

Nigel kept nodding, if only to show that he was still listening. Jet lag was creeping up on him.

"And third, this president may be ignorant, but if the people rooting for him are just as ignorant then it's a perfect marriage."

"Well, this is all very reassuring, I must say." Nigel stifled a yawn.

But Bill, failing to notice, was still on a roll. "There's something else I should say about this president - and you should take it as a piece of advice: don't listen to what he says, watch what he does. What he says is usually just to divert attention from what he's doing. While we're all getting our knickers in a twist over some stupid tweet he's sent out, there's usually something going on that we don't even know about. He's like one of those magicians hired for parties: you're so interested in what he's saying, you don't notice that he's picking your pocket."

"And meanwhile American society is slowly disintegrating… is that what you're saying?"

"He doesn't give a toss about what we laughingly call society. Nor does the Republican Party, which is fast becoming a crypto-fascist organisation. In my opinion, it may be the most dangerous political institution in the western world. Make that the whole fucking world."

"And the object of this crypto-fascist organisation is what?"

"To gain power. What else? And then to keep power. Permanently."

"A dictatorship, you mean."

"Yes, exactly that. Jameson uses the Oval Office as corporate headquarters for his business interests. The Republicans are happy to go along because it represents their interests, too."

"And Congress does nothing…"

Bill sniggered. "Congress! It's hopeless. Irrelevant. Permanently deadlocked but not talking. In that sense it reflects the electorate. And then there's the Supreme Court. Jameson's busy reshaping it for the next thirty years. Look at his four recent appointments: second-rate jurists, all of them, but first-rate arse-lickers. That lot will take us back to the fifties. No more civil rights. No more women's choice. No more progress."

"And this is the country where you want to spend the rest of your life?"

"Well, it's home now. Home, my old son, is defined as where you happen to live. I grew up on a council estate in north London. Bloody awful place: juvenile delinquents running wild; half the neighbours in jail and the other half headed there. But it was still home. Westchester County is now home."

"Is there a relief column in sight?"

"Not as far as I can see. The danger, as I see it, is that the warring factions will take up arms. There are right-wing loonies everywhere. They may not have brains, but they have weapons. If they start shooting, the government will have a perfect excuse to send in the troops. Then we'd truly have a Second Civil War, this one fought on the streets instead of the battlefields."

"It all sounds quite frightful," said Nigel, sounding genuinely alarmed. "But surely talk of Civil War is a bit extreme."

"Is it? Certain state governors have been overheard muttering in private about seceding from the Union. It may sound far-fetched, but not as much as it used to."

"That's just bravado. Bar talk."

"Maybe. But most civil wars start with bravado in bars. The Nazis began with bravado in a beer cellar. Then came the rallies, and the violence, and… well, you know the rest."

"If your nightmare scenario should come about, what would you do?"

"I'd sell up. Probably move down to the Caribbean. We have friends in Antigua, so I might go there." Bill suddenly realized that he'd been painting a frightful picture. "But you're right: we shouldn't get carried away. Yet."

That was rich, Nigel was thinking, since his friend had allowed himself to do just that for twenty minutes. "Maybe the Democrats will get their shit together."

"The Democrats? Don't make me laugh. Whenever opportunity beckons, the Democrats fall apart. Happens every time. Then they'll put up some far-left whack job who couldn't win an election in Venezuela."

"Speaking of which, what does Holly think about all this?"

"What do you think? She was born Juanita Dominguez. Her parents were illegal immigrants from Venezuela. Came up through Mexico. That means Holly and my sons are the kind of people this president casually calls murderers, rapists, drug dealers and lazy good-for-nothings. How do you think she feels?"

"Disturbed, I'm sure."

"She's light-skinned, so some people don't realize she's Latino. She hears terrible things in the checkout line at the supermarket. We even hear it at cocktail parties in Westchester, from people who ought to know better."

"But Jameson takes a terrible pasting in the media," said Nigel, vainly searching for some way to inject a note of sanity. "That must have an impact in the long run."

"You're joking. His people hate us. We represent the elite and peddle fake news. Anyway, do you think those working stiffs out there in the Jameson heartlands read the *New York Times* or the *Washington Post?* No, they watch that brain-rotting poison on Fox News, night after night. Can't get enough of it."

Nigel fell silent. He had heard enough talk of looming chaos and disintegration, of civil war and coups. Time, now, for something more frivolous. "What do you think about Samantha Jameson? What's she like? Not your normal first lady. Much brighter than he is, I'm told. Not bad looking, either... but don't quote me on that."

"Brighter wouldn't take much doing. She's also a closet liberal. And, yes, good looking. Makes you wonder what she ever saw in him."

"His bank account, would be my guess."

"I don't think so. She's worth millions in her own right. To be honest, I can't quite work her out. Intelligent and beautiful, but at the same time remote and mysterious. Washington's very own Greta Garbo."

"You've met them both, I take it."

"Her and Garbo?"

"No, Mr and Mrs Jameson."

"Him several times, her just twice. To quote Mort Sahl in another context, 'hated him, loved her'. And there's one obvious point in her favour."

"Oh, what's that?"

"She can't stand her husband. It's the worst-kept secret in Washington. She has her own bedroom in the White House. He, of course, has bedrooms in many places. That's the second worst-kept secret in Washington."

"And after all this, the man still has a shot at re-election. Baffling."

"All I know is that the more bizarre his statements, the more reckless his behaviour, the more his core voters adore him. They don't just tolerate it, they love it. The mystery to me is why some poor jerk working in a mid-west plant on the verge of closing thinks he'll somehow be saved by a billionaire property developer from New York."

Bill, too, now seemed to have tired of talking politics. "How's Sarah?" he asked brightly. "Happy as Larry, I bet, now that she's hooked up with that human cash machine."

"You'd think so, wouldn't you. But for some reason she feels hard done by. Not that I care. I've seen very little of her of late. I think about her even less often. I'll miss the kids, though."

"Yeah, that'll be rough. When you get yourself a decent place to live you can bring them over."

"I intend to."

"But watch your step with that Marchetti fellow," Bill warned darkly, casting a wary eye around the restaurant. "I know all about him. He's not just a bastard, he's a clever bastard. Wouldn't trust him with my grandmother's dentures. I take it he's aware of your posting."

"Oh, more than aware: he's made a solemn promise to fuck me over."

"And he's capable of doing it. You know how he'll get at you? Through Frank Hoffman, the White House press secretary. He and Frank were at college together... along with Jameson. But I'm sure you knew all that."

"I did, and if I didn't, he made a point of reminding me. You know Frank?"

"Not really. Came in after my time. Strikes me as a decent kind of guy, though, and relatively normal. That makes him something of a freak in this administration. You know there are rumours that he's in the closet?"

"I didn't. Should I care?"

"Not at all. But it would be ironic, wouldn't it, him working for a homophobic bigot like Jameson." Bill took a long swig of Brunello and ordered another bottle. "Good stuff this, don't you think?"

"Very fine," Nigel said distractedly. "So, Bill, let me ask you how you'd approach my job. A short, pithy answer preferred. A clever epigram, maybe."

Bill failed to answer immediately, failing to think of an epigram, and evidently excavating memories of his own experience in Washington. "You don't really need my advice, old chum. First things first: settle in, learn the ropes, and watch your ass. What more can I tell you?"

"Things will be very different from what I'm used to."

"Nah, I don't think so. Is Washington essentially that much different from Westminster? Just bigger and richer, and for those reasons, even nastier. Just one tip: never believe anything they tell you up on the Hill. They love feeding shit to journalists. Hucksters and liars the lot of them. I'll give you a list of my contacts. It's much shorter than it used to be, but I can still call a few people…"

"Thanks. Anything else?"

"Just one more other thing. Clever and well-read Brits like you can easily get up American noses, especially in the press room. Over here they take their jobs much more seriously than we do. They're on a mission to right wrongs, cleanse the body politic, change the world."

"Quite right, too."

"If you say so." Bill needed a break. Eating would provide it. "Where's that fucking steak we ordered half an hour ago?"

By the time they parted company, with mutual promises to stay in close touch, it was close to eleven. They shook hands outside Starks and walked together for a block or two. Then Nigel stood for a while watching Bill striding briskly down Lexington Avenue on his way to Grand Central.

Nigel was starting to feel the time change but didn't want to go to bed just yet. Better to stay up late and adjust to the local timezone. A nightcap seemed in order. He wandered uptown in search of a bar. There was no shortage of them, but as he peered through windows into stygian gloom, he saw surly bartenders serving solitary, glum-looking figures from an Edward Hopper painting. He decided to return to the hotel. At least Randolph's might still be buzzing. He wandered through Rockefeller Center again. Most of the tourists had gone, leaving smart-looking, uniformed attendants to clear up the mess they had left. For a few minutes he watched a man on a small tractor, apparently called a Zamboni, resurfacing the ice, endlessly circling the skating rink. The place had a dispiriting aura, like a sporting arena after the spectators had left. He suddenly became aware that it was raining, a light drizzle but from a darkening sky that promised worse.

He left, quickening his step to beat the threatened downpour.

* * *

Rudolph's *was* buzzing, although the business crowd had largely given way to hotel guests. The bartender who had been there earlier in the evening, welcomed him back with a grin of recognition, as if greeting one of his regulars.

"The usual is it, sir?" The 'sir' came out as 'sor'. He introduced himself as Joe.

"Hi, Joe. I'm Nigel." He took a seat at the bar. "Well, set 'em up, Joe. I've got a little story I think you should know…"

"Ah, I love that song," Joe said, suddenly looking misty-eyed. Leaning back to retrieve the Bushmill's bottle he gave a passable rendition of a mellow Mr Sinatra. '*It's quarter to three, there's no one in the place except you and me...*'

Nigel gazed distractedly at the television above the bar. It was on silent but showing the aftermath of a Yankee game. The Yankees, it seems, had just beaten the Boston Red Sox in extra innings.

"How about those Yankees?" Nigel said, anxious to reciprocate Joe's friendly manner.

"You a baseball fan?" Joe said with an incredulous grin. "Now *that* I wouldn't have figured, sor, not with an accent like yours."

"Always have been," Nigel fibbed, praying that he would not be put to the test.

"I'd have thought cricket would be more your style," Joe said, pouring Nigel's drink. "We get quite a few Brits in here. I've heard them talking about the game. It's all Greek to me. They tell me a cricket game can go on for five days."

"One of our many little island eccentricities, my friend. I won't bore you trying to explain it."

"Thanks. Wouldn't understand it anyway."

"Nor do we, if truth be told."

Joe shuffled along the bar to serve someone else, and Nigel swung around on his barstool to survey his fellow patrons. Every table was taken. In contrast to the solitary men in grim saloons he had just observed, they exuded the contentment of people who more enjoyed a drink than needed one. His gaze settled on the window looking out onto Sixth Avenue, where he saw the same slow-moving yellow snake that he had seen on Fifth, still honking pointlessly, this one moving uptown. No wonder the city never slept. His eye was drawn to one of the window tables. It was occupied by two young women, an ash blonde and a brunette, both attractive. The blonde spotted him looking and said something to her companion. Office workers, Nigel guessed. He wondered how they might react if he offered to buy them a drink. He turned to ask Joe if he knew them.

"Been in a couple of times this week," Joe said. "One works at the United Nations is all I know. Heard her talking about it."

Nigel wondered whether using Joe as a go-between might be more agreeable than a direct approach. "Is one allowed to buy drinks for ladies in bars these days?"

"It's a free country, bud. I could send the waiter over."

At that moment, the blonde stood up and approached the bar close to where Nigel was sitting. She spoke to Joe. "Excuse me, but can you remind me where the restrooms are?" Joe, serving someone, had not heard her.

"You need a rest?" Nigel interjected with a smile.

"No, something more urgent," she said, in no way put out by the feeble joke.

"Well, go through the lobby, then turn right at the front desk and head up the stairs."

"Thanks awfully," said the blonde, affecting an English accent.

"Nicely done," Joe said, winking.

Both watched her go, admiring the view. The woman was in her mid-thirties, Nigel guessed. Tallish. Handsome rather than stunning. Tastefully dressed, apparently for work. Good figure and shapely legs. He noticed that other eyes were following her progress across the bar.

"That's one classy broad," Joe said, wiping the counter. Nigel couldn't have expressed it better. Height and hair colour aside, she vaguely put him in mind of Jean Simmons, one of his favourite Hollywood actresses from yesteryear, formerly of north London.

A few minutes later, she returned. On her way back to the table, she paused and addressed Nigel. "Thank you again for your directions, kind sir."

"Always ready to help a lady in distress," he said lightly. "I take it you're not a hotel guest."

"No, I'm visiting my friend, the lady sitting over there." The friend, seeing them looking, waved discreetly. "She works at the UN. I'm just visiting and I'm staying with her. I live in Washington."

Nigel seized the opening. "What a coincidence. I'm heading for Washington tomorrow morning. I'll be working there for a while."

"Oh, really! Are you a diplomat?"

"God, no. Journalist. London *Daily Post*. I'll be covering the White House."

"How interesting. Can't say I'm a regular reader of the *Post*, but I always enjoy meeting writers."

"I'm a reporter, not a writer."

"What's the difference?"

"A reporter writes what he sees, a writer writes what he feels."

"Who said that?"

"I did. And what do you do in DC?"

"I work for the State Department. I'm an analyst."

"And what do you analyse?"

"The Middle East."

"You must be busy, then. My name's Nigel, by the way. Nigel Harper."

"Jane Hockley."

They shook hands. Encouraged, Nigel pressed on. "I flew in from London just this afternoon."

"You seem to have ended up in the wrong city."

"Oh, I'm just passing through. Just had dinner with a colleague."

She looked over her shoulder at her friend. "Well, Nigel, it's been nice meeting you, but I ought to be getting back to my friend."

"May I buy you a drink? Both of you, I mean."

"No thanks, but I'd be happy to buy you one. At least you've earned it."

"So, it's not okay for a lady to accept a drink from a stranger, but alright to offer one?"

She laughed. "Only as a reward for a kind act."

"Well, in that case I'll be glad to accept." He nodded at Joe, who refilled his glass. "And now that we've introduced ourselves, I'm no longer a stranger."

Jane gave him a far from subtle look of appraisal, before uttering the magic words, "Well, since you're alone in a strange town, why don't you join us at our table? I'm sure Maria won't mind - that's my friend. We're just chilling out. But we won't be staying too much longer. She's got to get up early even if I don't."

"Are you sure I'm not intruding?" Nigel said, in his most deferential English manner, although she noticed that he had already descended from his perch.

"If you were, I wouldn't have asked you."

Nigel followed her across to the table, discreetly studying her figure. He was also calculating, from sheer force of habit, the chances of Maria leaving early. But since they were lodging together, that was unlikely to happen.

"You're English!" declared Maria, as they were introduced. She was not bad looking herself, small, dark and perky. Sally Fields, Nigel decided.

"You're working in New York?" Maria asked.

Jane answered for him. "Nigel's heading for Washington. He's a journalist for a London newspaper. He'll be covering the White House. I've already told him what I do."

Nigel looked at Maria. He already knew from Joe that she worked at the UN but asked anyway.

"I work at the UN."

"Something important, I imagine."

"Not at all. I'm the one who makes sure our representative is where she's supposed to be, organize her schedules and sometimes deal with the press… that sort of thing. Nothing terribly important. Oh, I'm sorry, I didn't mean to imply that the press isn't important."

"She's being modest as usual," Jane put in. "She practically runs the place. Knows it inside out. Speaks four languages. Or is it five?"

Maria dismissed the compliment with a downward drop of the hand. She was tipsy enough to be indiscreet. "Nothing we do up here is important to the people down there where you're going. At least not to this administration. They see us as babbling idiots who do nothing but get in the way. There are times when I think they may be right. This president would just as soon withdraw from the organisation. But you didn't hear *me* say that."

Nigel nodded in sympathy. "Yes, he doesn't seem to care much about the UN. Or, for that matter, about any other form of international cooperation."

"We meet a lot of Brits in our line of work," Maria said, somewhat absently. "Especially journalists. They drink rather a lot, in my experience. My friend here is always getting invited to cocktail parties at the British embassy. Same for me at the British consulate. I must say you Brits know how to throw a good party. I don't see too many stiff upper lips, just dry ones." Jane nodded by way of confirmation. "Jane does far more important work than I do. She's trying to sort out the Middle East."

"A lifetime's employment, then. And what have you concluded about the sad and untidy situation there?"

"That it's a sad and untidy situation. I do my best to shed some light. That means writing endless position papers, all carefully researched, none of which are read by the people who are supposed to read them. I'm supposed to be something of an expert, but that's no big deal. I'm just one of hundreds of Middle East experts in the world, and none of us have come up with a solution. That, I'm afraid, would take someone far more intelligent than I am."

Nigel took issue with her modesty. "Clever people have been trying to do it for decades and they haven't come up with a solution either. Some would say the clever people have only made a bad situation worse. So, perhaps you shouldn't feel so bad."

"Thank you for that consoling thought," Jane said brightly. "Yes, it's a bloody tangle right now, and that's the truth."

"But it always has been."

"It has. But I must say your Foreign Office people seem to understand the region better than we do. We're often asking them for help. Me in particular. They're always very cooperative."

"But do they give you any answers?"

"No." She laughed. "But that's hardly their fault."

"I wouldn't be so sure about that," ventured Nigel, who had written a paper on the Middle East for his degree in modern history. "Unlike the State Department, which cleared out its Arabists years ago, our Foreign Office is still packed with them, still acting as if nothing has changed from the century before last. Let's not forget that it was the British, with a little help from the French, who buggered it all up in the first place. We've always meddled in Arab affairs, stirring up tribal rivalries, drawing arbitrary lines in the sand. I'm thinking here of Mr Sykes and Monsieur Picot, carving the place up into so-called spheres of influence. Then there were all those other mysterious imperial characters: Lawrence, Clayton, Allenby, Gertrude Bell, always plotting and scheming to protect Britain's so-called vital interests. In those days it was the Suez Canal. Then it was oil. I've no idea what it is now."

Jane was impressed. "Still oil. I must say, you seem remarkably well informed."

He mentioned his degree.

"More impressive still. Most Americans, even in DC, even at State, couldn't point to a Middle East country if you gave them a map."

"Nor, to be fair, could most Brits."

"Anyway, you don't need to apologize for the past sins of the British. Even if you'd never sent a single soldier out there the locals would still have been fighting each other. They've been going at it for centuries, tribe against tribe, Sunni against Shia, this kingdom against that one. Since the so-called experts in the West haven't come up with solutions, perhaps there aren't any." Suddenly she looked alarmed. "That's strictly off the record, of course. I wouldn't want to see such comments in print, even anonymously."

"Don't worry, I'm not working right now. Look, no notepad or tape recorder." He opened his jacket to demonstrate the fact. "We can turn our noses up at warring tribes, but Europe was no better." Nigel was now in tutorial mode. "For centuries, right up to the last one, it was one war after another: most of them about religion, of course, but then Communism and Fascism. That's why I was against my country leaving the European Union. The EU, if nothing else, ended all that. Sadly, no one seems to care about history these days."

"Good point," Jane said, adding rather abruptly. "But now we're getting rather deep into the geo-political stuff. I don't know about you, but I came here for a relaxing drink."

"Me, too," said Maria, feeling somewhat left out.

Nigel turned to Jane. "Well, I must say it's odd, our meeting like this, two soon-to-be fellow Washingtonians. You must both give me your business cards. You never know…" Observing that the women had exchanged knowing glances, he quickly added, "My motives are strictly professional. I mean, you may both turn out to be useful contacts. We journos collect business cards as schoolboys used to collect stamps."

He gave each of them an old London card, apologizing that it was out of date. "I'll give you my new card when I get one. Jane handed him hers. "Sorry, I don't have one with me," said Maria. But Nigel had the one he wanted.

"Will your family be joining you in Washington, Nigel?" Jane asked him coyly.

"No. I'm divorced. No current partner, either. But I do have two kids back in England, both at boarding school. And you two ladies?" He had already noted the absence of wedding rings.

"Both single," Jane said, more promptly than she had intended. "And for better or worse, unattached."

"And I for one intend to keep it that way," Maria said. "Not that I don't like men, but I just don't want to be tied down. Not yet anyway. I'm having far too much fun in New York."

"Maria's a party girl," Jane explained. "You wouldn't know it looking at her, but she can't stay home in the evenings. Wears me out, I can tell you."

"You're staying here at the hotel?" she asked, again regretting that she might be giving him the wrong idea.

"I am. Not a bad place. Room's a bit poky, but I'm only here for one night. Speaking of rooms, where do you think I should look for a flat - sorry, apartment - in DC? I haven't a clue where to start."

"That would depend on a number of things," Jane said. "Your budget, for a start. Then there are other factors: lifestyle, tolerance for commuting, that kind of thing. Some people prefer to live across the Potomac in Virginia. It's not that far in miles but the traffic can be awful. I like to be able to walk to work. We do, of course, have a metro system, which widens the choices. I can't think what else to tell you."

"Where do *you* live?"

"Georgetown. Near the university. Not quite what it used to be, but still quite a lively place. Lots of bars, restaurants and funky stores. A bit expensive for someone on a government salary, but I happen to know my landlord. He's an old family friend. Gave me a sweetheart deal on the rent."

"Is that because you're his sweetheart?" Nigel enquired slyly.

"Oh, nothing like that. He's gay, in fact. He once lived next door to my family back in Wilkes Barre, Pennsylvania, and when I first went to Washington, he helped to find me a place. He owns several apartments. I could call him if you like."

"I'd appreciate that," Nigel said, hardly believing his luck. "And for that favour, I owe you a drink. Same again?"

"Yes, please," they cried in unison.

"We must seem like alcoholics," Jane said.

"Well, *you* are," Maria retorted.

"No, I'm not. I just like a nice glass of wine when I'm with nice people." She blushed.

Maria looked across at Nigel. "All I can say is she must know an awful lot of nice people."

They both laughed, although Jane looked slightly put out.

Nigel said, "You may say so, Maria, but I couldn't possibly comment."

"That sounds familiar," Jane said.

"It's from a British television series," Nigel told her. "I can't remember the name offhand."

"I like programmes about political life," Jane said. "Have you seen *The West Wing*?"

"Yes, I'm a big fan," Nigel said. It was true. He had been watching it recently to pick up some tips about how the White House worked. It looked chaotic. "I bet you wish you had a real president like that one right now."

"Since I work for the government, I couldn't possibly comment. I have an opinion, of course, but not one that I'm prepared to reveal to a stranger, least of all a journalist. I'm sure you're perfectly trustworthy, but we've only just met. And DC these days is a hotbed of intrigue. That man in the White House calls it a swamp, which he intends to drain. These days, though, it's more a breeding ground for paranoiacs than mosquitoes."

"My colleague has just been telling me that," Nigel said. "But things aren't much different back home, believe me. Brexit has turned us all against each other."

"Politicians…" Maria said with a sigh, again feeling a bit neglected. "They're the same the world over. I see it all the time."

"See what all the time?" asked Nigel, ever the journalist, looking for something juicy.

"Oh, you know, the plotting, the manipulating, the double-dealing, the breaking of promises… and, of course, mischief of all kinds. Half the delegates at the UN seem to have a mistress - or in some cases master. I could tell you a tale or two… but not if they're going to end up on the front page of your newspaper."

"The *Post* doesn't really go in for that kind of stuff," said Nigel. "We're not a tabloid. We're a serious paper – or so we like to think."

Acutely aware that they were talking to a reporter, Jane turned the conversation to more personal topics. Maria mentioned that she had been born and raised in Brooklyn, studied at Harvard, and graduated with a degree in modern languages. "We lived in the safest neighbourhood in New York. No burglaries. No muggings. No trouble of any kind. Too many of the residents had 'connections' with the kind of people you wouldn't want to cross, if you know what I mean."

Thanks to Bill, Nigel knew exactly what she meant. He was not sure what to say next and settled for, "Brooklyn to Harvard, that's very impressive."

Jane had gone to Penn State, as had Marchetti, Nigel noted, but he didn't want to ask whether she had known him. She had left with a degree in political science, the better to facilitate her ambition to work in government. 'For the people' as she put it. "Sounds old-fashioned doesn't it, a devotion to public service, but that's what I always wanted to do."

"Someone has to do it," Nigel said. Then, worried that the remark could be misinterpreted, he quickly added, "Most people would say it's more commendable than what I do."

"Oh, not at all! We need a free press. Now more than ever."

There was a brief silence as they sipped their drinks and looked around the bar. The conversation was in danger of petering out.

"Well, I must say this is a unique experience," Nigel said, rather desperately.

"How so?" Jane asked.

"Well, it's not every day one walks into a bar in New York and by chance encounters people with so much in common, with so much erudition."

"You haven't told us much about yourself," Maria said, almost accusingly.

He told them something of his own background, leaving out the more sordid parts.

"A vicar's son!" exclaimed Maria, sounding more surprised than good manners permitted. "Are your parents still alive?"

Nigel wondered why she had asked the question. Did he look so old that it seemed unlikely his parents could still be living? "My father is alive and well but now retired. My mother died some years ago. Cancer. She was a remarkable woman. Very bright. A modern thinker, way ahead of her generation. I suppose I inherited my liberal political instincts from her. I still miss her wise counsel."

The ladies reflexively adopted sorrowful expressions, as if she had died a week earlier. The wine must be making him mawkish, he suddenly thought, and switched back to the safer ground of current politics. "Tell me, is your man in the White House going to be re-elected?"

"He's not *my* man," Maria said, rather too abruptly. "But yes, I think he might be."

"Nor mine," Jane put in. "But he's got the money and a solid voter base. He also has a message that some Americans find compelling. They call themselves the Forgotten Americans - the ones Nixon used to call the Silent Majority. Well, they're back. Frankly, I wish some of them had stayed forgotten and silent." She suddenly clammed up, the government employee conscious of saying too much.

Nigel was left to deliver the summing-up. "So, what you're saying is, we can all look forward to four more years of a man who may be mentally unhinged, can't string together a decent sentence, divides the country and is despised by every elected world leader. Something to look forward to…"

He knew he had gone too far. As if to prove the point, the ladies said nothing. Too many indiscretions had been uttered already.

Jane looked at her watch. "Oh my God, it's well past eleven. We should be going, Maria. You've got an early start, and I've got an early flight."

Nigel himself was suddenly feeling the effects of the time change and the alcohol. On cue, he yawned. "I suppose I should turn in, too. It's been a long day." Then he added, "But I must say, it's one that ended most delightfully."

Maria stood up first. "Thank you so much for the drinks, Nigel. And, of course, the company, which was as entertaining as it was unexpected."

Jane endorsed the sentiment. "It was a pleasure to meet you, Mr Harper."

"Nigel, please."

"And who knows, perhaps we'll bump into each other in DC. It's a small town."

"The pleasure was all mine," Nigel said, before turning to Jane and adding. "And I'm sure we'll meet again. I certainly hope so."

"Well, by all means get in touch," she reaffirmed. "You have my office number. Perhaps I can help you sort out that apartment."

"I appreciate the offer, I really do. You're very kind. Goodnight to you both, and sweet dreams."

Like Sir Walter Raleigh at court, he made a sweeping bow, making them smile. As he watched them leave, he hoped that Jane would look back. She did.

* * * * *

Chapter 4

Nigel's plane banked sharply for its final approach into Ronald Reagan airport. How odd, he was thinking, this American custom of naming airports after presidents. He couldn't imagine Heathrow being renamed after a prime minister. Which one? Thatcher? More likely Churchill. He would have chosen Clement Attlee, Britain's post-war Labour prime minister, a personal hero - but any of them would have sounded ridiculous to British ears.

From his starboard window, Washington presented an impressive spectacle. The great neoclassical dome of the Capitol building, a secular cathedral, gleamed in the late-morning sun, dwarfing the nearby White House, merely an executive mansion. And beyond them both, dotted along the National Mall, were the white basilicas dedicated to presidents too esteemed to lend their names to airports, and the assorted granite blocks of vast federal government buildings, all nestled in neatly manicured parkland. The place was crawling with tourists which from a couple of thousand feet up looked like a colony of ants in a disturbed nest moving in slow motion. Nigel found it incongruous that a nascent Republic freed from an imperial yoke should have seen fit to build a grand imperial capital. Bill Palmer had come up with a more down-to-earth description: "A movie set for a Roman epic built in a ramshackle southern town."

Nigel could see what Bill meant as his eye travelled beyond the great marble edifices to the endless tracts of red-brick houses radiating out in every direction. In Washington the contrast between imperial magnificence and abject poverty was more evident than in any of the grand capitals of Europe. Here the Roman palaces, surrounded by shaded brownstone streets redolent of the Gilded Age, were only a bus stop or two away from run-down inner-city neighborhoods. The difference, as everyone knew but few mentioned, was defined by race. Washington was a black city with a white heart.

Unlike most capitals, Washington had not sprung organically from a vital strategic location on a great river but from a small trading post on an insignificant one, which the indigenous residents had named the Potomac. America's early political leaders had selected the site more as a defensive redoubt than a commercial centre - a necessary precaution after soldiers demanding payment for services in the Revolutionary War attacked the then seat of government, Independence Hall in Philadelphia. The first president readily approved the plan, not because it was named after him but because it was only a few miles up-river from his Virginia plantation at Mount Vernon. As it happened, he never did take up residence in the new capital. Later, the neighbouring states of Maryland and Virginia ceded considerable land for an area soon to be designated the District of Columbia, an administrative entity rather than a state, with no representation in either of the congressional chambers. But for that spot of bother in Philadelphia, Washington might have remained what it had been from the start, a sleepy village of no great commercial or political importance.

Nigel had been to Washington several times but never for more than a couple of days at a time. And like most occasional visitors he had seen little of the city beyond the downtown tourist attractions. It would be different this time. He was about to become a resident, working in that great colonial residence which he had just seen from the air. As part of his due diligence, Nigel had searched in vain for literary quotes about the city, hoping to find one that captured its essential character. The most noteworthy was John F. Kennedy's ironic remark that Washington "perfectly combines southern efficiency with northern charm". The one other interesting observation he came across was a definition of what an anonymous politician had called the 'Washington Lie' - a conversation in which 'the other person knows you're lying and knows that you know he knows.' Nigel made a note of it, thinking it might come in handy as a conversation piece at cocktail parties.

Graham Welbeck had booked him into a modest but comfortable downtown hotel, inaptly named the Capitol since it couldn't have contrasted more starkly with the great edifice that loomed over it. Not quite seedy but with a tired look and a vaguely musty smell that Nigel had no desire to identify.

After leaving his bags in his room, he set off to meet his soon-to-be predecessor for a welcoming lunch. A welcome one, too, as he'd declined before leaving New York to spend fifty dollars on a hotel breakfast of toast and coffee. The venue Graham had selected was a short walk from the hotel. Called, somewhat incongruously given its location, the *Happy Heifer*, it was a popular venue for politicians from the western, cattle-breeding states. Hardly, Nigel would have thought, Graham's line of country. After lunch they would call in at the *Post*'s tiny outpost on H Street NW, a blandly functional address with an office to match, but having the practical advantage of being within walking distance of both the White House and the Capitol.

The *Happy Heifer* was decorated in the style of the Old West. The mock-adobe walls were adorned with Remington-inspired murals of cowboys roping steers or sitting round flickering campfires, dominated by a crudely drawn centerpiece depicting a cow grinning insanely. Even the coat-hooks were made from horns. Duncan Erskine would have been appalled by the brazen vulgarity of the place. Nigel chuckled at the thought. The restaurant was crowded but subdued. In New York there would have been a cacophony of lively chatter - about the Yankees or the Giants, and fashion or the movies - but in Washington lunchtime conversations tended to be more about the hatching of plots and the preservation of secrets. Where Manhattanites looked around the room to see who they might wish to join their table, Beltway insiders looked around to see if there was anyone they needed to avoid.

Graham was already there, sitting at a table in the middle of the restaurant, sipping a beer and unravelling anagrams in the margin of the London *Times* crossword. Rising to greet his successor, he shook Nigel's hand effusively. "Awfully good to see you again, my dear fellow. It's been quite a while…"

"Far too long," Nigel fibbed.

"Two years at least," Graham said gravely, as if the matter carried some importance. Never short of a cliché, he added, "My, how the time flies."

"Yes, it does," mumbled Nigel absently.

"Permit me, sir, to be the first formally to welcome you to Washington."

No one talked like that anymore, Nigel was thinking uncharitably, especially in that studied avoidance of the split infinitive. The man spoke the way he wrote, in the style of a pedantic schoolteacher.

"Permit me formally to thank you," Nigel replied in a parody of the style. "It's kind of you to take the time to see me in the middle of what I'm sure is a busy day."

"It's not busy at all right now," Graham confessed, beckoning a waiter. "There's a long weekend coming up. Memorial Day. That means the usual exodus from the city. Only the tourists will be left.

There will be a parade, of course. How about a cold beer to start with? It's rather a warm day, as I'm sure you've noticed."

Nigel had indeed noticed. From the short walk from the hotel to the restaurant he was perspiring freely. It didn't help that he was wearing a suit of a rather thick English fabric.

Nigel examined the label on Graham's beer bottle. Rolling Rock, a Pittsburgh beer, of which he'd vaguely heard. He'd rather have had a pint of good English ale, but for now - and who could say for how long - such delights were beyond reach. "I'll have the same," he said with an expression of mild distaste.

Graham noticed. "You'll get used to American beer."

"Well, at least it'll be cold."

"I'd have thought you'd like your beer warm."

"Not warm, old chap, cellar temperature. But over here, the beer tastes so bad it needs to be ice-cold. I'm going to miss my pint of good English ale, which, I might add, tastes good at cellar temperature." Graham ignored the dig but was thinking, '*Yes, and you've got a lot of other adjustments to make.*'

Nigel found himself silently sizing up his colleague. They had met several times, but on the flight down from New York he had struggled to remember what Graham looked like. Graham Welbeck was that kind of person. He was sixty-something, of medium height and average build. Everything about him was middling. His face was as bland as his copy. His thinning sandy hair had grey roots, and what remained of it was arranged in a swirl across his head to disguise the recession.

Nigel became aware that Graham was appraising him, too, no doubt concluding that his successor was a cocky arriviste with a fragile ego.

Graham was still English enough to turn the conversation to the weather. "You must be boiling." Nigel was indeed very hot, aware that rivulets of sweat were running down his face. "You might consider getting yourself some lighter clothes. The summers here can be brutal. Wait until July and August; then you'll find out what humidity means."

"But you're retiring to Florida. It's even hotter and more humid down there."

"But I'll be living in shorts and a T-shirt. Besides, my place in Boca is right on the ocean and we get the Atlantic breezes. And air conditioned, of course. You must come down and visit us some time."

The plural presumably meant a wife or partner, though Nigel had no idea which, or of what gender, or whether he had children. "How's the family?" he asked, by way of finding out.

"Oh, Cynthia's just fine," said Graham, filling in one of the blanks. "Like me, can't wait to get out of Washington. As for the kids, both boys flew the nest years ago. The older one is in Silicon Valley working for some high-tech outfit that recently went public. No revenue to speak of, let alone profit, but the offering made him a fortune. The younger one, last I heard, was in Rome, pursuing some Italian girl he met when she was working over here as a waitress. Kids... you just never know how they'll turn out."

"I was in Boca once," Nigel said. "I went to a conference at the Boca Raton Club. Big sprawling pink building, as I recall - you must know the place." Graham mentioned that he lived not far from it. "The reason I remember it," Nigel said, "is because one evening before dinner I was taking a stroll around the grounds when the garden sprinklers came on. I got drenched. As I had only one suit with me, I had to sit through dinner soaked to the skin. Several people asked if it was raining. I nearly froze to death in the air-conditioning."

Graham smiled faintly. "I've played golf there. But where we'll be living, we have our own course. Beautiful place, although you need to keep an eye on the alligators at the pond near the tenth hole."

"That sounds alarming," Nigel said.

"Oh, not really. We have an understanding: we ignore them, and they ignore us. And anyway, they're asleep most of the time."

"I can't say Florida's my kind of place," Nigel declared abruptly. "You know what the comedian said about it?"

"No, but I'm guessing you're about to tell me."

"Everything in Florida is in the eighties - the temperature, the median age, and the average IQ."

"Very funny," Graham said, without mirth. "At least I'll be changing two of those statistics - reducing the median age and raising the IQ."

"Exactly how old *are* you, if you don't mind my asking?"

"Not at all. Coming up to sixty-five."

As if in deference to his colleague's advancing years - and as a former president had once prescribed - Nigel adopted a kinder, gentler tone. "Well, I must say you don't look it. And I'm sure you've many more good years ahead of you. Just make sure you can outrun those reptiles. I'm told they can be lightning fast."

Graham, studying the menu, didn't seem to be listening. "Fancy a steak? That's what most people order here, as I'm sure you've figured out."

"What else?" Having decided what to eat, Nigel scanned the panoramic prairie murals. "Odd sort of joint. Seems out of place, all this cowboy stuff in the middle of Washington. I was rather hoping you'd take me to Sans Souci. Isn't that where the high and the mighty go to be spotted?"

"Not anymore. It closed back in the eighties. It's an office block now, or a parking lot."

"What a terrible fate."

"Well, time marches on."

"Where do the so-called thought leaders go now? Is there an equivalent of Wilton's in London, where the Tories used to break bread and hatch plots?"

"I've no idea. Those long boozy power lunches are a thing of the past. They were never my scene anyway, not even on Fleet Street." He was still scanning the menu, though he must have known it by heart. "I recommend the filet mignon, by the way. That's what I'm having. A bit pricey, but easier to handle than those great rib-eyes and T-bones that take up half the table."

"Good idea," Nigel said chirpily, still recovering from his carnivorous experience at Starks.

"So, Graham, when are you planning to leave? Pass the torch to a new generation, as JFK once put it."

"I'll stick around for as long as you need me. You can decide when you're ready to take over. That's what Duncan said." '*How about right now?*' Nigel was thinking.

"And how is our esteemed managing editor? I haven't seen him here for quite a while."

"Same as ever," Nigel said off-handedly. "Showing commendable grace under pressure after the recent layoffs. As you know, our Scottish friend is hardly the most sensitive soul in those situations. Not that they've fired any editorial staff yet, other than one or two for cause. You know, of course, that poor old Charlie Waugh got the chop."

"I heard."

"In the end it was the booze that did for him." He told the story of Charlie's public execution. "No redundancies pending here, I take it?"

"You must be joking. We don't have enough people to dispose of. Unless, of course, it's you and me - and you've just got here and I'm leaving anyway."

"Remind me, how many of us are there?"

"A junior reporter, local lad name of Joe Hart. Writes well. Not much imagination but always dependable." Graham might have been describing himself. "Then there are the two ladies. Helen's an editorial assistant. She's a rather vapid type, you'll find, but a decent researcher. Then there's an ancient monument named Gloria, the part-time office manager. She takes care of the administration, such as it is. I think she was here when Eisenhower was president. We used to have more people. We could certainly *use* more… but that's going to be your problem now."

"I'll look into it. Meanwhile, I can always call on Bill Palmer if I need help. He knows his way around this town as well as anyone."

"He can be a bit grumpy I find."

"Can't we all? He's already offered his services. I had dinner with him last night in New York. Sends his best, by the way."

"I'm sure he did."

"I think he's quietly pondering retirement, too. Sounds as if we're going to have a complete changing of the guard over here."

"Well," said Graham, cliché at the ready, "all good things must come to an end. I've had a good run. Eighteen years at the *Post*, fourteen of them here in DC. I've seen a few changes I can tell you. On the political scene, especially. Few of them for the better, I might add. It's become a bad-tempered place."

"Would you by chance be speaking of the right-wing resurgence as represented by the current occupant of the Oval Office?"

"Well, he's certainly a change from your usual politician. Whether for good or ill is debatable."

"Not by me."

"Yes, I gather you're not a fan."

"What person with half a brain could be? "

"That would describe the millions of Americans who voted for him."

"Well, shame on them."

"That's democracy."

"But what do *you* think of him?" Nigel suddenly realized that he had no idea what Graham's politics were. You wouldn't know from reading his copy. Graham may not have embraced the alt-right, but neither had he conspicuously denounced it. Graham's turgid dispatches gave the impression that his primary objection to the president was not so much his despicable policies as his mangling of the English language and his manners.

Graham must have read Nigel's mind. "I don't much care for his style, to be perfectly honest. He can be crude, childish, petulant. Still, love him or loathe him, he knows what he wants to achieve, even if he has a clumsy way of going about it."

"Oh, really?" Nigel's scorn was now unleashed. "If this president has a strategic plan - other than feathering his own nest - it seems to have escaped my attention."

"Actually," Graham said, taking the hook, "he *does* have an agenda; it's just not to your taste."

"Restoring America's greatness, you mean? That's not an agenda, it's a slogan." When was the last time Congress debated, let alone passed, a major act? They must be drawing unemployment benefits up on the Hill."

"Look, I understand that you can't stand the man," Graham said feebly. "I'm not too keen myself. But he was elected, fair and square, and many Americans adore him." Nigel was beginning to suspect that Graham might secretly be one of them.

"I find that profoundly dispiriting."

"I'll say this for him. He promised to shake this town up and he's doing just that." Graham almost sounded like an admirer. "His methods may be rough, but perhaps that's no bad thing. Anyway, we might have to get used to him. He's stolen the blue-collar vote which the Democrats used to claim by right, and I don't see it switching back any time soon."

"Well, shaking things up - whatever that means - is hardly an adequate substitute for constructive policies. Herr Hitler shook things up…"

"Come on, that's hardly a fair comparison." Graham looked genuinely affronted.

"Isn't it? This president is a despot in the making - and who's there to stop him. Not the fucking Republican Party, that's for sure. Meanwhile, so far as I can tell, his overriding mandate seems to be to promote his own business interests."

"There were the tax cuts. They really helped people."

"Yeah, mostly the people who didn't need them."

"And let's face it, unrestricted immigration *is* a problem. He's only responding to what most Americans are thinking."

"Which is what?"

"That everything has got out of control."

All attempts at empathy forgotten, Nigel sneered openly. "The country was founded on immigration. You're an immigrant yourself, by the way, even if you did fly in on business class." Graham merely shrugged. Nigel was now livid. "Picking on immigrants is cruel. Ask Bill Palmer's Hispanic wife. I was happy to read, incidentally, that his popularity may be sliding."

"Well, it's true he may be given a black eye in the mid-terms, but that happens to every sitting president. He still has plenty of time before the next election to bounce back. Don't underestimate him. The Democrats made that mistake and paid for it. The fact is, he strikes a chord with the voters."

"Yeah, but all the wrong notes. Two years is plenty of time to fuck up the economy - and the country. If he loses, his successor will inherit the biggest budget deficit in history. All that money he's put into defense industry is making his friends in the military happy, but everyone else will pay the price."

Graham winced, probably, Nigel thought, at the rising tide of expletives. "He's going to be a hard man to beat, is all I'm saying. Ordinary people were sick and tired of being ignored by their government. His brand of populism may not be the wave of the future, but it's certainly the wave of the present."

"And how would you explain that 'wave', as you call it?"

"Well, we live in a time of universal disillusionment. People now hate the institutions they once respected. Most of all, they hate the politicians. People feel let down. This president may not be your normal politician, but that's his appeal. He promised change, and so he's delivering it."

"Change that takes the country backwards, not forwards."

"That's your opinion. Look, he does nothing by the book, it's true, but that's precisely what his supporter love about him."

"Sounds as if you don't much object to it either," Nigel sniffed, his irritation still rising.

"At the end of the day, it isn't my place to object, or endorse," Graham protested. "I'm here to report what's happening, not why. Opinions I leave to the leader writers."

"That's an arguable point," Nigel countered, "and I'm one of those who's prepared to argue it."

"That's your privilege, of course. It's not necessarily your remit."

"My remit..." Nigel's sentence stopped there. He had thought better of saying what he had been about to say, which was that his remit was to do everything that Graham had failed to do.

"Most Republicans on the Hill secretly despise him - or so I've been told."

"Some. But for most he's their meal-ticket. He's what'll keep many of them in office. They go along because they know he's a winner."

"Which in my book makes them nothing but gutless cowards. The Republican Party would be a joke if it weren't so dangerous."

"You may think so. But it's hard to argue when the economy is booming and unemployment dropping. No politician up for re-election wants to rock the boat. Look, you may despise the man - and I'll admit I have my own reservations - but even you'll have to admit that he's effective."

"Effective but in an unworthy cause - and I'd question 'effective'."

"He gets a rough ride from the media. You seem to be proving it."

"Really!" Nigel was genuinely astonished by that last remark, uncertain whether Graham really meant it or was merely trying to provoke him. Sadly, he concluded the former. "I'm appalled that you could even think that. That man's a threat to democracy, an affront to common decency, and probably a crook. The media shouldn't hesitate to say so. We have a duty to say so."

"That's your opinion. Millions of Americans wouldn't agree."

"We're not in the business of writing what would be popular. Do you honestly think that pandering to the more bovine elements in society is commendable? Is that really what this troubled country needs? Is that the message you think the *Post* ought to be conveying to its readers, that the president of the United States may be an awful shit, but it doesn't matter because he's a popular shit."

Graham continued to push back. "I told you: I don't have a message. I'm a reporter, not an advocate."

"What the fuck does that mean?"

"It means that my job, as I see it, is to set out the facts. My own opinions are irrelevant. Remember what we learnt when we were cub reporters? 'You're not the story, so keep yourself out of it'."

"I'm afraid that's precisely the opposite of how I see my job. There are still millions of Americans - and billions around the world - who see this president for what he is. It's something we should confront, not ignore. Red-necked morons may be content to live in a moral vacuum, but the rest of us shouldn't have to. And we in the media have a higher duty to recognize it."

Nigel believed what he was saying, but he also relished the opportunity to goad someone who apparently didn't believe the debate was even worth having.

"We're not historians," Graham said, grumpily.

"But as someone once said, we *are* the first witnesses to history. The *Post* should be out in front as an interpreter of serious events. If we're not, what's the fucking point of us?"

If Nigel was an irresistible force, Graham was happy to play the immovable object. "It doesn't always do to take sides, you know. If you go out on a limb with that kind of talk, you'll find your job here more difficult. Perhaps next to impossible."

Nigel was starting to tire of the game, but he kept playing. "Nonsense. The news agencies break the news - and they do it very well - but the rest of us have an obligation to do more than that. Any fool can lift agency copy and tart it up with a few adjectives. That's not journalism." This was a clear dig at Graham, who was renowned as a 'cut and paste man'. "You and I may be reporters first, but we're also opinion-makers. If that involves a degree of subjective observation, it's what we columnists do."

"I'm not a columnist, I'm a reporter."

"That's bollocks! You're both. For God's sake, you write a weekly 'Letter from Washington'. It's supposed to be informed analysis. Our readers already know the news when they read it; what they want is explanations. They don't all read *The Economist,* you know."

"Nor do I, for that matter."

"Well, maybe you should."

But trying to steer Graham away from the path of true righteousness - the slavish devotion to objectivity - was a lost cause. Enough was enough, he decided. Time to switch to more practical matters. After a momentary silence, he said: "What do you make of Frank Hoffman?"

Graham seemed relieved to be off the interrogatory hook. "Oh, he's a wily old bird, our press secretary. Keep an eye on him. He'll certainly be keeping an eye on you."

Graham didn't know how true that was. Or did he?

"But tell me," Nigel said, "what's he like as a person?"

"A charmer when the mood takes him. But watch your step when it doesn't. He promotes the party line, but I sometimes get the impression that his heart isn't in it. He's a deep one, our Frank. Some say he's a closet liberal. Wouldn't surprise me."

"I'm told that may not be the only closet he occupies."

"Well, I don't know about that. Nor do I care." Graham seemed offended. "Do you?"

"Not at all."

"Then why mention it?"

"Because if he's standing up at the lectern every morning and spouting on about the virtues of Christian Values, that would make him a hypocrite. Republican senators can fuck their interns until their dicks fall off for all I care, but if all the time they're preaching that adultery is an abomination, then they should be exposed… so to speak."

Graham didn't smile. "That's the excuse the tabloids always use."

"I wouldn't expose anyone's private life unless the public had a right to know."

"And who should decide that?"

"Me. Or my editor. It's called editorial judgement."

"I just happen to believe," Graham said airily, "that private lives should be just that. I'm surprised that you, of all people, don't seem to think so."

"Well, here's a curious reversal," said Nigel with a grin, hoping to lighten the mood. "I'm supposed to be the progressive, and you the traditionalist. Now we seem to have switched sides."

But if he was confused about that, he was in no doubt about the journalist's obligation to illuminate an unfolding story with more than cold facts. Graham's embrace of objectivity was commendable as far as it went, but newspapers were no longer mere bulletin boards. Graham was being replaced not because he was unreliable but because he was unreadable. He had never demonstrated the slightest interest in rocking boats, which might be considered unique in a trade that was supposed to thrive on provocation. Graham had spent two decades polishing his prose and buffing his platitudes. In the process he had become a kind of literary computer. His articles were verbal algorithms.

"Another beer?" Graham enquired, hoping to persuade Nigel Harper to descend from his pulpit.

"I think a hunk of all-American beef calls for a robust American red."

"I'm staying with beer if you don't mind. Wine at lunchtime always sends me to sleep in the afternoon."

That would explain the soporific quality of his copy, Nigel thought.

"Are you an American citizen?" he asked, apropos of nothing.

"Yes. For some years now."

"You and Bill Palmer both. So, you're a registered voter."

"Of course."

"Republican or Democrat, if you don't mind my asking." Nigel knew what was coming.

"Neither. I'm an independent."

"From political choice or by professional obligation?"

"Both, I suppose."

Back home, Nigel reckoned, Graham would have been a 'floating' voter, one of those fence-sitters who could find no merit in either of the two parties with a chance of winning, happy instead to vote for any well-meaning but mediocre third-party candidate with no hope of being elected.

The food arrived, a welcome distraction. Nigel ordered a glass of one of the countless California cabernet sauvignons on the wine list.

"Good choice," he said, chewing his filet mignon with a pleasing lack of effort.

"I knew you'd like the place. They do a good job here. By the way, have you given any thought about where you want to live?"

"No idea. But last night in New York I met this woman who lives in Georgetown. She offered to have a word with her landlord. I was planning to call her this afternoon."

"Georgetown's very nice, but I prefer to live across the Potomac. The drive into town can be gruelling, but it's quiet and pleasant out there. Mind you, a young single man like you might prefer somewhere livelier… closer to the 'action', as you probably call it." Graham grinned. "I must say, you didn't waste much time."

"Doing what?"

"Picking up a girl on your first night in the country."

"I didn't pick her up, as you put it. If anything, she picked me up. And, by the way, only misogynists say 'girl' these days. See, I'm learning."

"And I'm happy to stand corrected. What does she do?

"She works at the State Department. Middle East analyst. Perhaps you've met her. Her name's Jane Hockley. Good looker."

"Doesn't ring any bells... but she obviously rang yours. 'Good looker', by the way, is also verboten these days."

"I too stand corrected."

Ignoring Graham's persistent smirk, Nigel said: "Getting back to Frank Hoffman, I'd like to know what rings his chimes. You hinted at something more complex, perhaps even dialectically treasonous."

"The truth is, I don't know. He's a hard man to read."

"That should make him stand out in a house of the simple-minded."

"You know his background, of course, his association with..."

"Yes, yes, I know all that."

"What else can I tell you. He seems to enjoy a wide range of interests outside politics... now *that's* unusual in this town. They tell me he has a serious art collection. Buys stuff in Europe. He also likes to cook. Sometimes he announces from the lectern that he's got some new recipe. Oh, and he adores movies. Fancies he's an expert there, too. You're a film buff, I seem to remember. Well, if you want to get on his good side, get him talking about old films."

There seemed little else to say about Hoffman.

"Any political scandals brewing?" Nigel said, picking at errant peas. "Of the sexual variety, I mean. Given this president's history, it would be surprising if there weren't. We hear all kinds of things back home."

"Does anyone really care about political sex scandals these days? There are, of course, stories..."

Nigel was suddenly all ears. "Stories? Do tell."

"You really want to know about that stuff?"

"Yes. Duncan didn't send me over here just to cover trade disputes and budget negotiations."

"Since you mention it, why *did* he send you? Sorry, what I meant to say was, why you? You were the star turn in Westminster. Sold papers on the back of it, Duncan always said."

"Why *not* me? I know politics and politicians and how it all operates."

"Yes, I know. I make a point of reading your column myself. It's lively stuff sometimes."

Nigel put his knife and fork down. "Forgive me for being blunt, Graham, but you asked, 'Why me?" Well, the plain fact of the matter is that I'm here to do the same thing - enliven the coverage. Please don't infer from that comment any criticism of your performance. You've done good, solid, reliable work here."

"That sounds like damning with faint praise," Graham interjected with a glum expression.

"No, I mean it. You've guided the ship through some rocky shoals." Nigel winced as he was saying it. "But look, these are weird times, unprecedented times, unpredictable. And now we've got a president who's never been an elected politician and who breaks all the rules. None of the old political orthodoxies seem to apply now. We may now - forgive me - be at an inflexion point. The future of the Republic may be at stake. The *Post*'s coverage needs to be hard-hitting. That, with respect, has never been your style. Having said that, you're not being fired. You're retiring. And you'll be leaving with your reputation intact. I mean it. So does Duncan, by the way."

"What kind of reputation is that? Spell it out, if you don't mind."

"You're accurate and dependable. Your literary style puts the rest of us to shame. Those are legacies, I'd say." Nigel didn't believe a word of what he was saying, but what was the point of further denigrating a man about to ride into the sunset? He concentrated on his steak.

Graham smiled wearily. "Look, I know I'm a steady Eddy, but my style is what it is. I deal in cold facts. They're the best kind. In fact, the only kind."

"Ah, but what about those 'alternative' facts?"

Ignoring the question as rhetorical, Graham finally felt the need to go on the offensive. "I know you, Nigel Harper, you're looking for drama. The scoop of the decade. Well, with respect, there *are* no scoops anymore, least of all for us old-fashioned print Johnnies. Unless, of course, you have access to the investigative resources of the *Washington Post* or the *New York Times.* Even they struggle nowadays. Know why there are no more scoops?"

"No. But do tell me."

"It's obvious. Social media. This president scoops the newspapers. He even scoops the television channels. Every morning. His pre-breakfast tweets reach an audience of countless millions. Those are numbers we can't even dream about. If anyone's going to leak something these days, they think first and foremost about the internet. By the time our presses are running, or the television programming has been interrupted, those damn tweets have been around the world several times and back."

"Sounds as if you think newspapers are redundant. We do, of course, have a website of our own."

"Yes, but I'm sure many of our older readers struggle with technology. To some of them it's science fiction."

"Well, all I can say, then, is that you're retiring at the right time." Nigel's tone was scornful. "Before the rest of us old-fashioned 'print Johnnies' join you down there in alligator heaven."

Graham exhaled the sigh of a tired man. "Look, I know your style will be markedly different from mine. That's fair enough. But let me give you a word of advice."

"I'm listening," said Nigel, wolfing down his food.

"Don't go chasing after headlines at the expense of the routine stuff. You find out what's going on in DC - what's *really* going on - through good, solid field work. It may sound dull and old-fashioned, but it works. You make contacts up on the Hill, and in the agencies, and you work hard to nurture them. Digging for dirt is best left to tabloids and gardeners." Graham smiled at his little epigram.

And that, in a nutshell, was Graham's fundamental and, in Nigel's view, disqualifying defect: he came, he saw, he concurred. He didn't go after the news; he waited for it to come to him. He had never missed a major story, as far as Nigel could remember, but nor had he ever broken one. Obsessed with objective facts, Graham was suspicious of anything that smacked of speculation, even of the intelligent kind. And Graham, bless him, just didn't relish the thrill of the chase, preferring to follow the pack at a discreet distance. Nigel had no idea what made Graham's adrenaline flow faster, but whatever it was didn't include getting his teeth into a juicy story.

* * *

Unnoticed by either of them, a man had sidled up to the table.

Nigel spotted him first. He was in his sixties, tall, with a sun-leathered face and a silvery mane swept back in well-tended waves. He was impeccably dressed, except for the big-heeled cowboy boots. His smile was that of a man accustomed to smiling for votes. In every aspect he was Nigel's idea of a United States senator, which is precisely what he turned out to be.

As soon as Graham became aware of the man's presence, he leapt from his chair. "Senator Pitman, how good to see you. How have you been?"

"I've been just fine, Graham, mighty fine. And how about you, my friend?" The voice was southern. Or perhaps western. Either way, it was treacly.

"Oh, I can't complain. No one listens anyway." Graham took Nigel's arm. "Allow me, Senator, to introduce you to a colleague of mine, Nigel Harper. My successor. He'll be taking over from me at the White House. Nigel, meet Senator Charles Pitman from the great state of New Mexico."

They shook hands, eyeing each other warily. Pitman had served, Graham was saying, four terms in the Senate, winning each election with an increased majority. In political circles he was 'a force to be reckoned with', despite the insignificance of the state he represented.

Nigel could well believe it. "Pleased to meet you, Senator," he said, though less than warmly. "I've heard a great deal about you."

"All good, I hope."

"Nothing bad, anyway." Which was true, as Nigel had only vaguely heard of the man.

"Well, young fella, all I can say is you've got yourself a big pair of boots to fill. I hope you're up to it."

"I hope so, too."

"Graham and I go back aways, isn't that right, my friend?"

"We do indeed," Graham agreed. "For more years than I care to remember." He turned to Nigel. "The senator here is ranking member of the Senate Defense Appropriations Committee, among several other important bodies. He's a man worth knowing in this town."

Nigel had taken an instant dislike to the man, but he nodded dutifully, trying to give the impression that he was impressed.

"Senator Pitman has been a reliable source to me over the years, and a good friend of the *Post*," Graham was intoning. "Knows this town the way he knows his own ranch back home - and there we're talking several million acres."

Nigel could well believe that too. The senator looked like a man who roped steers for fun, or felled trees, or hunted things and skinned them himself. He presented a figure who might have stepped out of one of the murals on the wall behind him.

"You two should get to know each other," Graham gushed, "as I'm sure you will."

"I'll be grateful for all the help I can get," Nigel said, again dutifully.

"Well, y'all just pick up the telephone any time and I'll see what I can do to help. If I'm out of town, why, you just talk to my people. They'll always get word to me."

Unction, Nigel was thinking, oozed from every pore... if there were any pores left in that leathered skin. That 'y'all' seemed a little contrived, too. Nigel had been silently reaching for a word to describe the senator's manner, and the one that came to him was oleaginous. "That's a kind offer, Senator. And I'm sure I'll be taking you up on it."

"Always happy to cooperate with the media... even if the media doesn't always see fit to cooperate with me." He gave Graham a knowing wink. The senator's antipathy towards journalists was well known, expressed in dozens of interviews on Fox News, and shared, of course, by Martin Jameson. "Not only that, my friend, I'll be happy to show you around the place. Give you a few pointers. And I mean that sincerely."

Sincerity was the last quality that Nigel would have ascribed to such a figure, but the senatorial grin was still firmly in place. "That's really most kind of you," Nigel repeated.

Graham was patting the back of an empty chair. "Won't you join us, Senator, at least for a quick drink."

"I'd love to, my friend, but duty calls." He rolled his eyes in resignation. "I have a committee to chair this afternoon. One more drink and I'd be nodding off. I might anyway, especially if those Democrats get a burr under the saddle, as they usually do." He laughed at his down-home witticism. "Some other time, maybe. Meanwhile... Nigel, is it?... you feel free to call me. Any time."

Then, as silently as he had arrived, the senator glided away, stopping twice on the way out to greet acquaintances at other tables.

"A smooth operator," was Nigel's polite verdict.

"Yes, but a powerful figure in Washington," Graham said. His eyes were deliquescent with admiration. "He's the kind of man you need to be on the right side of in this town. Cross him at your peril." Nigel refrained from pointing out that crossing powerful figures, perilously or otherwise, was a necessary part of the journalist's job.

"Immensely rich, too," Graham felt compelled to add. "Owns half the state of New Mexico. Well, not quite. He lives in a big white mansion on a prairie, miles from anywhere. Remember that movie *Giant?* Rock Hudson. Elizabeth Taylor. Well, his house reminded me of that."

"You've been there?" Nigel asked, incredulously.

"A few of us stayed overnight once, after some campaign rally. He hosted a barbecue. My bedroom was bigger than the ground floor of my house."

Nigel was shocked that a fellow journalist should be impressed by such trappings of wealth, much of it probably accumulated by dumb luck or sordid business deals. "You two make an odd couple, I must say, the humble English scribbler and the billionaire senator from cowboy country. What could you two possibly have in common? Nigel's suspicions had suddenly been aroused.

"That's easy to answer," Graham said. "I once did him a small favour." Nigel waited for elaboration, but Graham offered only that it was nothing significant. "If truth be told, I've forgotten what it was. Still, there's a lesson there."

"Oh, what's that?"

"Nobody in this town ever forgets a favour, however small."

"Unless it suits them to ignore it."

"Play the cynic if you like, but people like Senator Pitman can get you into all kinds of places you'd never get into, introduce you to people you'd otherwise never have a chance to meet. He's one of the president's confidants, too, one of his key allies on the Hill. And let me tell you, he likes to talk."

Nigel found himself disliking the Senator more with each succeeding plaudit. "I'll call him, if only to remind him who I am."

"Oh, he'll remember," Graham assured him.

Nigel, tired of discussing the merits of Senator Pitman, steered the conversation in another direction. "Let me ask you about the first lady. What is it we call her these days, FLOTUS?" What's the story on her? She and the president are not exactly love birds, are they?"

"Nobody *really* knows her. Samantha Jameson's very much her own person. Seldom speaks in public and then sticks rigidly to whatever script she's been given. If she's ever expressed a spontaneous opinion, I must have missed it. She does have her favourite charities, most of them to do with children. Other than that, she seems to spend most of her time riding or playing golf, her two pet hobbies. And yes, you could say they lead separate lives."

"Like Franklin and Eleanor..."

"I hadn't thought of it that way, but now that you mention it…"

Nigel knew remarkably little about the first lady, but he was sure there was much more to know that he would find interesting. She came across, both in speech and manner, as elegant, refined and understated - everything, in short, that her husband was not. Her upbringing had been as privileged as her husband's, with the crucial difference that she had come from 'old' money. She'd been raised, he had read, in a big colonial pile in the back country above Greenwich, Connecticut, and been educated in exclusive private schools. She had a degree in philosophy from Cornell. She had travelled extensively in Europe, including a year on a post-graduate course at the Sorbonne in Paris and another at University College London. She spoke fluent French and Spanish.

That much he knew. And so far, so impressive. But who was she?

Within her circle of friends, her romance with the president had caused shock and despair. It was said that she had considered seeking office in her own right, but marriage and the demands of their two children - a boy and a girl now in their teens - had put paid to that ambition. The children were rarely seen in public. Unlike her husband's daughter from his first wife, and two sons from his second, who seemed to be on the front pages all the time, courtesy of activities undertaken on behalf of the White House but which few had been able to define.

"What about those rumours of a presidential mistress?" Nigel asked.

"Too numerous to be worth mentioning," Graham said airily.

"The rumours or the mistresses?"

"Both."

"I understand some supermarket tabloid says he's involved with some Russian woman. Anastasia, I think is the name." Nigel had spotted this on the cover of the magazine at a newsstand, under the headline 'President Jameson's Mysterious Russian Lady-friend'.

Graham snorted derisively. "*Skandal* magazine! A pathetic rag. No credibility. Anastasia! Now, there's a clue, Sherlock. Anastasia, as in one of those women who used to claim to be the Tsar's long-lost daughter. All imposters of course."

"It's not a happy coincidence, I agree." Nigel had to laugh.

"Well, then..." said Graham blankly.

"It doesn't mean the story isn't true..."

"True or not, I don't care. *Skandal* may be read by celebrity-obsessed freaks, but the *Post* isn't. We write for serious readers... as you never tire of pointing out."

"But a sitting president in a dalliance with a KGB agent... now that would be news in any paper."

"Look, it's well known that this president is no saint, but so far all attempts to expose him have come to nothing."

"Perhaps he's too clever to be caught."

"Or that there's nothing to be caught at. Either way, I'm not interested."

"You've made a few good points," Nigel conceded, trying not to sound too amiable. "But if you think I'm too concerned with the seamier aspects of political life in order to boost circulation you'd be wrong. I just happen to think the American public is entitled to know if their president, with a base of voters strongly represented by evangelical Christians, is playing away from home."

"Talk to me when the story breaks," Graham said dismissively. "And I mean in a respectable publication."

"That's the whole point," Nigel said. "It won't happen until someone reports it."

"Well, I wish you the best of luck with that." Graham's tone was icy. "Anyway, *Skandal* seems to have got there first. And so far, there have been no public eruptions of righteous outrage. As for me, I prefer the French attitude to these things. There, as you know, the sexual adventures of politicians are almost mandatory, and so usually ignored."

"You surprise me," Nigel said laughing. "I'd have put you down as some kind of puritan."

"I'm a Methodist, if that's what you mean. In fact, I'm a lay preacher."

Nigel realized that the flogged horse was now so battered as to be barely recognizable as a horse. He invited Graham to change the subject.

"Good idea," Graham said. "But first, how about dessert? They do a fabulous cheesecake here - as good as anything in New York."

"My brain says no, but my heart says yes," Nigel said.

"And it's our hearts we should be worrying about, I suppose. So maybe that should be a no." It was the first attempt at wit Nigel had heard from him.

"I'll have another glass of red instead," Nigel said, finding his glass empty.

But Graham was checking his watch, conscious of the housekeeping chores ahead of them. "We should think about heading over to the office. Find you a desk. Meet the staff. After that, I suggest we check in at the White House, make sure your credentials have been sorted out. I'll show you the press room. We might even run into Frank Hoffman. Then, if there's time, we'll head over to the Capitol."

"Sounds like a good plan, "Nigel said brightly, though in truth he dreaded the prospect of spending the rest of the day with a droning Methodist lay preacher. He was also thinking about when he might get the chance to call Jane Hockley, who had been on his mind all day.

"If we're skipping the cheesecake, I'll get the check," Graham said. "Lunch is on me, of course. Look, this could be my last expense claim."

"We could make it my first," Nigel offered.

"I couldn't possibly," Graham said with finality. "You're the honoured guest today."

"And the guest feels duly honoured," Nigel said, smile fixed in place, trying to sound grateful but not quite making it.

* * * * *

Chapter 5

It was well after seven when Nigel finally escaped Graham's didactic clutches. After the *Happy Heifer* lunch, they had set out on a tour that took up the intervening four hours: first to the Capitol, almost exclusively populated by bands of chirruping, selfie-snapping tourists, and then, after a brisk walk along Pennsylvania Avenue to the White House, also largely deserted by the working inhabitants although its perimeter was ringed by milling, gawping crowds. Graham had a 'hard' pass that allowed him to come and go at will. Nigel's papers were still being processed, he explained to the guard at the security post, who let them through without undue fuss.

Once inside, Nigel enjoyed two special moments. In the West Wing press room, he sat for the first time in the 'bullpen' that would be his working space for the next four years. Not much care had been put into it, but it was as comfortable as journalists needed it to be. And then Graham had persuaded a reluctant junior press officer to give them a peek into the Oval Office, which by Nigel's quick calculation was no more than thirty feet away from where they were standing. Even unoccupied, it struck Nigel as somewhat smaller than the impression he had formed from countless photographs and newsreel footage. All the same, he found it profoundly evocative. He pictured feisty little Harry Truman wrestling with the decision to drop two atom bombs on Japan. Then, glancing out the window at the colonnaded terrace, he fancied he spotted the Kennedy brothers in ardent conversation, Jack puffing on an inappropriate Havana, as they waited for the next Russian move in the Cuban missile crisis. Then he heard the distinctive drawl of Lyndon Johnson, on the telephone to recalcitrant southerners, urging them to push his civil rights legislation through Congress.

But then the sense of history was rudely dispelled by the spectacle of the present incumbent, Martin Jameson, lounging on a sofa watching television game shows, lunching on hamburgers and endless diet Cokes, and tapping out inane tweets designed to generate meaningless controversy, reducing the most famous office in the world to the status of a playboy's playpen. Nigel swept the spoiling image from his mind.

Graham had revelled in the role of tour guide. Although undoubtedly knowledgeable, he was relentlessly didactic. At first, Nigel had found his observations cogent and informative, but the longer the afternoon wore on, the more the novelty wore thin. Given the chance, Graham would have added yet more venues to the itinerary, but as the evening shadows lengthened, Nigel felt that he had been subjected to more than enough enlightenment for one day. His feet ached from the miles they had trudged, his head from Graham's unceasing drone. Turning down Graham's suggestion that they close out the day with a nightcap, and perhaps dinner to follow, he mumbled his apologies about having a prior engagement. Graham was too polite to ask who Nigel could possibly be meeting on his first day in town but guessed that it was the woman he had met in New York. In a way it was true: Nigel had been silently anxious to find a moment to call her and get the search for an apartment underway... and for other reasons.

Back in the drab but welcoming refuge of his hotel room, Nigel kicked off his shoes, took a beer from the minibar and flopped down on the bed. He switched on the television, hoping to empty his head by watching something diverting. He found a quiz show in which a contestant with tens of thousands of dollars at stake was having a hard time trying to recall the capital of Sweden. He would probably, Nigel thought, have had a hard time remembering the capital of the United States. Flipping channels in search of intelligent life, and finding none, he switched off the television and took a shower.

Afterwards, feeling greatly refreshed, and fortified by a couple of whiskies, he took Jane's business card out of his wallet. For a few moments he stared at it, pondering whether to call or not. If he did, he half expected to be given the brush-off. *"Well, Nigel, I'm afraid I'm a little tied up right now..."* But if he didn't call, he might regret it, especially as her offer to help him find an apartment had sounded genuine... and she *was* uncommonly attractive, there was no doubt about that. He flipped the card over to the personal number she had scribbled on the back. With some trepidation he dialled it. When it kept ringing, he guessed that she was probably out to dinner. Then, as he was about to hang up, someone picked up. It was a female voice, but not Jane's, or at least not the voice he remembered as Jane's. "Hello?"

"Oh, hello. I'm ringing to speak to Jane Hockley. Is she there? This is Nigel. Nigel Harper. She'll know who I am... I hope."

"She will," the voice declared emphatically, which meant, encouragingly, that Jane must have mentioned him. "This is Fran Powell, a friend of hers. She's in the kitchen destroying dinner, but please hold while I see if she can come to the phone." Then he heard her say loudly, "Jane, darling, there's a charming English-sounding gentleman on the phone. Name of Nigel. Claims you know him." All this was said, he assumed, for his benefit.

There was a brief silence. Then he heard Jane's voice, the soft and slightly husky purr that he remembered. "Why, hello. Nice to hear from you."

"I'm sorry, have I caught you at a bad time?"

"Not at all. Anything that drags me away from the kitchen is a welcome diversion. Cooking isn't really my thing, as my friends would tell you, but tonight it's my turn to play hostess."

"If it's not convenient, I can call back tomorrow."

"No, it's quite alright. Really. And the guests have yet to arrive, other than Fran who thinks she lives here anyway."

"Well, I won't keep you. I'm calling to take you up on your offer to help me find an apartment. That is, if you recall making it."

"Yes, of course I do," she said, slightly affronted that he might have thought otherwise. He could hear her shooing away Fran, whom he guessed was leaning over her shoulder trying to listen in.

"I was hoping that we could make a date. I mean an appointment. Next week, perhaps."

"That would be fine."

"What day would suit you?"

"Well, I'm a working girl so a weekend would be better than a weekday." There was an extended pause. Then, as if the thought had suddenly occurred to her, Jane said, "What are you doing tomorrow? I mean, if you need a place to live, the sooner you start looking the better. As it happens, I have no plans until the evening, and it's Memorial Day weekend, so the city will be quiet."

Nigel was happily taken aback. "Are you sure? In fact, tomorrow works fine for me, too. My social calendar isn't exactly overflowing, as you can probably imagine."

"Tomorrow morning it is, then. But, please, not too early. Tonight's likely to be a late one. My friend Fran likes to stay up and talk well into the wee small hours." Jane suggested they meet at eleven. "Let's say outside Luigi's. It's a restaurant in Georgetown."

She gave him the address. "It happens to be close to where I live, which means I can sleep in for an extra half-hour."

"I'm really grateful," Nigel said, the intimidating dread of trudging the streets apartment-hunting replaced by the pleasing prospect of seeing her again. "I'll try not to take up too much of your time. Just point me in a certain direction. I'll do the rest."

"It's really no problem at all. I've already put in a call to my landlord. He's the family friend I think I told you about."

"Sounds perfect. I appreciate your taking the trouble, I really do."

"It's no trouble at all. But now I'd better get back to my beef stroganoff. Luigi's at eleven. There's a big Italian flag outside, so you can't miss it. See you then."

"Goodnight and thank you. Oh, and Jane…"

"Yes?"

"… enjoy your dinner party."

Hanging up, he felt disappointed that he hadn't been invited to join it. No matter. He would put on some casual clothes, such as he had brought, and take a walk, perhaps find a friendly neighborhood bar that served snacks. First, though, he would do a little homework on Georgetown.

Sitting on the bed, he propped his back against the headboard and took out his laptop. Perusing a map of the area, the first thing he noticed was that the area was close enough to his office to walk to work. He googled on, not sure what he was looking for, but after twenty minutes or so the time-change and the day's exertions finally caught up with him. He fell into a deep sleep, dead to the world.

When he woke up, the sun was streaming through the window. He looked at the digital bedside clock. Nearly ten. In something of a panic, he leapt from the bed, took another shower, shaved, and put on an ensemble of slacks, blazer and loafers, looking every inch a preppy model from a Tommy Hilfiger catalogue, though a little too old for the role, and more than a little too flabby. As luck would have it, he walked out of the hotel as a taxi pulled up delivering arriving guests. The cabbie knew Luigi's, and with traffic unusually light, delivered him there a few minutes early.

Nigel was studying the menu in Luigi's window when Jane Hockley materialized as a ghostly reflection. Before he could turn round, a breathless voice was muttering in his ear. "Sorry I'm a bit late. I've been in slow motion all morning. The dinner guests left at midnight, but then Fran kept me up until three in the morning. I've left her fast asleep, on the sofa."

They shook hands rather formally, each rather unsubtly studying the other, as if to confirm that they were indeed the couple who had met in New York two days earlier. The result, as far as he was concerned, was most satisfactory.

"Fran's a good friend, I take it."

"My best friend," Jane said. "We were college roommates."

"No secrets, then."

"Not many." She laughed. "She's a hoot. Always was. I love her dearly, but she does like to drink and stay up late. You'd like her. She's very bright. One of these days perhaps you'll get to meet her."

Nigel was pleased to note that there might be more days to come. "What does she do for a living?"

"You'll never guess."

"Well, I wouldn't know where to start."

"She works for the first lady. She's Samantha Jameson's deputy director of communications."

Nigel's eyes brightened. "Oh, is she!"

Jane knew what he was thinking. "Yes, I agree, she could turn out to be a valuable contact."

"That was exactly my thought, I must confess."

Second encounters sometimes disappoint, but not this one. Jane may have been nursing a hangover and suffering from a lack of sleep but to Nigel she looked if anything more attractive than he remembered from their first meeting. She was dressed in jeans and a white blouse, a pale blue angora sweater draped over her shoulders. She might have been on her way to a college lecture at Yale. It was if they had agreed to coordinate.

"Well, now that I'm here," she said, why don't we go find you an apartment? Or at least take a stroll round the neighbourhood. See if you like what you see."

As they stood waiting for a traffic light to change, her attention was momentarily diverted. He slyly took the opportunity to reappraise her physical attributes. He liked what he saw. She turned and caught him doing it. To cover his embarrassment, he said, "I was just thinking how fresh you look this morning, considering your late night."

"Thanks to the miraculous properties of modern cosmetics," she said, blushing slightly. "You're not looking so bad yourself."

"As well I might. After calling you I fell asleep on the bed, fully clothed. I didn't wake up till ten this morning."

"Jet lag, I'm sure," Jane said. "Always gets you in the end."

Nigel took in the surroundings. "Where are we, by the way? And where are we heading?"

They were on a pavement - or sidewalk as he must now call it - that was narrowed by the tables of outdoor cafes. It was further constricted by crowds of strolling pedestrians enjoying the fine weather. The area had the feel of a college town - which is exactly what it was, of course.

"First, I thought I'd give you a taste of Georgetown. Give you a feel for the place. I quite like the atmosphere. There's something of a village about it." She pointed ahead of them. "I live three blocks over there, by the way."

"From what I've seen so far," he said, "I like it very much."

She touched his elbow to guide him into a tree-lined side-street. Mistaking the gesture, he hooked her arm in his. She left it there.

"This area is one of the fancier parts. As I've already mentioned, very nice but a tad expensive. I can afford it only because my friend gave me a deal."

She suddenly stopped. "How rude of me. I haven't even asked what your budget is."

"That, within reason, won't be a problem. My paper has given me a generous housing allowance."

"Well, aren't you the lucky one."

They turned into a tree shaded street of old, terraced brownstones with stoops. "This is pretty much like the street I live on. I like these turn-of-the-century houses. They're spacious inside: big rooms and high ceilings. Does something like this interest you?" Suddenly she stopped again, as though remembering something else. "But I've no idea know what you like. I apologize for not asking. Perhaps you'd prefer a modern high-rise with a doorman. There are plenty of those, too, though not so many around here."

"I suppose a doorman would come in handy, but since I've never had one it's not something I've thought about. Anyway, I'm a bit old-fashioned. I prefer older houses like these. High-rise apartment blocks have all the advantages of modernity but none of the charm. This street puts me in mind how Washington must have looked in the days of Henry James. Are you a fan of his?"

"Now there's a question no one has ever asked me." She laughed easily. "I read him once in high school, but I can't say I enjoyed him much; just did a good job pretending to. Gore Vidal is more to my taste."

Nigel was not a fan of James either, or Vidal for that matter, but he found himself being transported back a century, to the so-called Gilded Age, when carriages dropped off gentlemen in top hats and tails and ladies in bonnets, on their way to lavish dinner parties or music recitals. He told her what he was thinking.

"Below that cynical exterior of yours there apparently lurks a secret romantic," she said.

"I can't remember the last time I was called a romantic. If ever. Maybe there's hope for me."

Arms still linked, and chatting comfortably about this and that, they walked on.

Jane got down to practical matters. "I spoke to my landlord friend, by the way. He lives not far from here. It so happens he has an apartment available, not yet on the market. Ground floor. One bedroom. Furnished. Want to see it? His brother Joe, who lives on the top floor, has been told we might stop by. As I said before, I live three blocks from here."

"Let's do it," Nigel said, with a faux Humphrey Bogart lisp which he thought he had got down pat.

Jane agreeably disagreed. "I'm afraid that accent of yours needs a little work. I think I'd prefer Colin Firth."

Brother Joe answered on the intercom but took several minutes to get downstairs to open the door. He was unshaven and his hair was tousled. He was wearing shorts and a T-shirt but no shoes.

"I'm Joe," he said sleepily. Having been aroused from his bed he looked none too pleased. "Lew called last night to say you might show up," he mumbled, fumbling with a set of keys before ushering them into the ground-floor apartment.

Then and there - startling himself as much as Jane - Nigel made a bold decision. "It's perfect. I love it."

Anything would be better than the dreary Islington bedsit he had lived in for the past three years, and this place had genuine charm. In that instant, he felt at home, as if fate had somehow brought them there. The main living space ran from the front of the house to the rear - the front section the living room, the back part the dining room. Adjoining it was a small kitchen, no more than adequate. But as Nigel explained, he wouldn't be spending more time there than was necessary to make toast. The front windows had shutters. Nigel liked that; curtains could be so dreary. French doors at the rear opened onto a small patio, seldom used judging by the weeds growing through the paving cracks. It was shaded by an ancient sprawling magnolia that badly needed pruning to let in more light. The bedroom was unnecessarily large, with an en suite bathroom, recently refurbished. The furnishings were a bit old-fashioned, but of high quality and in good condition. The place had been well taken care of. The previous tenant, Joe mentioned, had been a French travel writer who he explained unnecessarily had spent most of his time travelling.

"Only one bedroom," Jane pointed out. "Is that a problem?"

"No," Nigel said. "I don't suppose I'll be having too many houseguests. If I do, they can sleep on the sofa."

"Is this really the kind of place you had in mind?" The tone was querulous. "It's the first one we've looked at. Do you want to see more? You must tell me."

"This one seems just about perfect for my purposes. In which case, what's the point of looking any further? I'll take it."

Jane looked puzzled. Also slightly alarmed. He hadn't even asked what the rent was. In fact, she was thinking, he seemed to be taking the whole exercise less than seriously.

Seeing the concern on her face he said, "Look, I like the area and I love the flat. So why waste time trying to find something better?" He turned to Joe, who was leaning against a wall, evidently trying hard not to fall asleep standing up. "Do you happen to know what the rent is?"

"Four grand a month, I believe," Joe said. Jane whistled.

Joe looked slightly offended. "What can I tell you? That's what these places are fetching now, often much more."

"That sounds fine," said Nigel, without batting an eye. The rent did seem steep, but he had no comparisons to make. Anyway, his remuneration package would take care of it. And perhaps there was room to negotiate. Not with Joe, however. "Who do I have to talk to?"

"That'll be my friend Lewis," Jane said, still astonished by Nigel's hasty decision. "I happen to know that he's in this morning. We could go and see him right now if you like."

"Let's do it," Nigel said, again in his silly Bogie accent. Turning to sleepy Joe, who looked as though he might sink to the floor, exhausted, at any moment, he said, "Well, it looks as though we may soon be neighbours." Joe didn't make his enthusiasm at the prospect immediately apparent.

Fifteen minutes later, in Lewis's office in the living room of a similar house, they concluded the formalities. There were surprisingly few. Lewis - "Please call me Lew" - seemed very casual about the whole transaction. He asked for neither references nor bank details.

"I don't even have a bank account here yet," Nigel felt obliged to mention.

Lewis seemed unfazed. "I understand. But then I'll be asking for a three-month deposit. Anyway, you're a friend of Jane's, and that's good enough for me. We'll work out the other details on Monday, and meanwhile I'll prepare the paperwork."

Did he know, Nigel wondered, that he and Jane had only just met?

Anyway, as of now, it seemed that he had a Washington home.

After they left Lewis, he turned to Jane and said brightly, "Well, since my accommodation issue is settled, the least I can do is buy you lunch."

"For five minutes work? You don't owe me a thing." He had half expected her to say that she was already booked. He was relieved when, after some hesitation, she said, "Lunch would be very welcome, in fact. I sure could use a hair of the dog."

"I know the feeling."

"There's a place I know. It's right on the canal. Very pleasant. Not far from here. The weather's nice, so we can sit outside."

"Canal?"

"Yes. It runs right through Georgetown. Used to be an industrial waterway, the Chesapeake and Ohio. Now it's a kind of residential park. Popular with joggers. Are you a jogger?"

"Not if I can help it. Are you?"

"Now and then, but I prefer Pilates and yoga." Nigel winced. Jane smiled. "I'm guessing that the exercise you enjoy most is bending that right elbow."

"You got that in one."

A few minutes later they entered the restaurant, which was not yet busy, and were guided to an outside table. All the tables were covered by an awning and most overlooked the canal. The building had once been a warehouse, Jane explained. The waterway was lined in both directions with houses painted in different pastel colours. The view was more European than American, Nigel was thinking, more Amsterdam than Washington. "Charming," he said with surprised delight. When a waiter appeared, Jane asked for a glass of Chardonnay. Nigel overruled her by ordering a bottle.

"As much as I ate last night," she said, "I'm famished. I didn't have breakfast."

"Me, too," Nigel said. "I missed dinner *and* breakfast." He picked up a menu.

"I hope you've made the right decision about the apartment," she said, again looking concerned. "To be honest, I'd expected to spend the entire day looking. I must say you're very decisive. I wish I could be like that. I'd have been dithering for days."

"You think I made a mistake?"

"Not at all."

"Good, because I like the flat and I like the location. I also like the idea that it's not far from you."

"I hope that's not the basis for your decision," she said, her tone suddenly guarded. In fact, she found the remark a little presumptuous. After all, they had only just met, and she had no idea where this brief acquaintance of theirs might lead, if anywhere. But she also knew that she liked him - or at least had enjoyed his company so far.

"Tell me more about your work at State," Nigel said, putting the menu down. "Oh, and please explain why it's called Foggy Bottom. I seem to have forgotten."

"The original office was built on a swamp, where there was an almost permanent fog. Nowadays, the fog's usually *inside* the building."

"You're referring, I presume, to the confused state of American foreign policy."

"If you can call it that..."

"Tell me more."

"Well, nothing about it seems clear right now, at least not in my area of expertise. We never want to get involved in the Middle East, but then we always seem to get sucked in anyway. Especially if the Russians are making mischief, as they usually are. And like all the western powers, once we're there we can never decide exactly what the endgame is supposed to be."

"Peace, I would have thought."

"Of course, but as usual the devil is in the detail, and the details here are as complex as you can imagine. Putin usually makes the short-term decisions for us - and for others. To be fair, this administration is probably no more clueless than its predecessors, but this president seems to make every policy decision on the hoof. By the time I get to the office on a Monday, our position has often changed over the weekend. All this I'm expressing as a personal view, of course, and strictly off the record."

Nigel assumed a pained look. "As I said the last time we met, I'm not talking to you as a working journalist. And even if I *were*, I'd always respect a source."

Jane affected to be offended. "A source? Is that what I am?"

"I didn't mean it quite that way," Nigel said with some feeling. "You're a friend who's just helped someone." He looked her in the eye. "We *are* friends, aren't we?"

"Well, not quite yet." She said this rather abruptly, he thought. "I mean, this is only our second meeting. But perhaps we'll become friends in time."

"I'd like that," Nigel said softly. "I'd like that very much."

The waiter arrived with the wine. After a toast to Henry James, Nigel downed most of his glass in one.

"You like to drink, don't you?" Jane's voice had just a hint of censure.

"It goes with the territory," he said. "I feel obliged to live up to the popular image of my trade."

"You drink because you think you ought to?"

"No, because I enjoy it. Always have."

"Me, too, to be honest. Some drink to drown sorrows - a painful past, perhaps, or to get over a lost love or some tragedy. Are you one of those?"

"You mean like Rick in *Casablanca*?"

"Well, you did have a wife, you mentioned, and presumably once the love of your life."

"She was. But that was a long time ago… or seems that way. Anyhow, I'm over it now. Sarah - that's my ex - is no longer the woman I once knew. She's become hard and spiteful." He sighed, but lightened the mood, again by putting on that awful, lisping Humphrey Bogart voice: "But we'll always have Oxford."

"Oxford?"

"That's where we first met, as students. And courted, if that's not too old-fashioned a word."

"You read modern history there, I think you said." This was hardly relevant to his early love life, but he was grateful to be steered away from the subject of Sarah.

"I did. You have a good memory."

"It was only two days ago. What made you become a journalist?"

"What do you do with a degree in modern history? Academia? Diplomacy? It's not much use in the business world. I could always write a decent sentence. Other than rugby, it was the only thing I was ever good at in school. Journalism somehow seemed a natural fit. Perhaps even a true vocation. Mind you, some would question that."

"But obviously not your editor, or he wouldn't have sent you here."

"I suppose. I once had this idealistic notion that honest journalism would help change the world for the better. Deep down, I suppose I still do. The truth will set you free, and all that. Of course, that's what all journalists tell themselves at the start, and then they see that a mad world carries on getting madder regardless of what they write. Still, some of us keep trying..."

"And I hope you'll keep trying," Jane said with some force. "It may sound like a cliché, but we need a free and honest press, and now more than ever - whatever this president and the Republican Party might say about you."

"You're right. But enough of me. I'd like to hear more about you. All I know - apart from your job - is that you're from Wilkes Barre, Pennsylvania."

"Did I mention that?"

"Yes."

"Nice place?"

"Nothing special, that's for sure. It went downhill a bit along with the steel industry. A lot of local businesses died. That made it Martin Jameson country. The whole state went for him last time out. But not my parents. While they've always been Republicans, they can't stand the man. My father worked for a small steel extruding company. Rose through the ranks to a senior management position. My mother taught school. They're both approaching their seventies and so far, touch wood, in good health."

"Do you see them often?"

"Not often enough, as they're always quick to point out. As an only child, it makes my extended absences worse. We get along fine, though, and for some reason they're both proud of me."

"As well they should be."

"Well, I don't know about that..."

The waiter arrived to take their food order. Nigel settled for a hamburger. Jane selected a salad with several exotic ingredients that Nigel failed to recognize.

"And university?" he asked. He remembered that she had gone to Penn State. "Did you enjoy it?"

"I did. I got a decent degree. I majored in political science. Then, like you, I asked myself, 'where do I go with a degree like this'? The answer seemed obvious: where else but government. And so, here I am, trying to make some sense out of the Middle East... so far with no great success."

"But you enjoy your job. That's a question, by the way."

"Not quite as much as I once did. It's not so much the job but the politicians - our masters. Many of those people in Congress - especially from the midwestern states - are perfectly ignorant about what happens in the rest of the world. In an earlier age we called them isolationists, or America Firsters, or something like that. Some of them, I swear, think Damascus is a cloth. They manage to make those of us who work down in the boiler-room feel somewhat superfluous to requirements."

"Really? How so?"

"Well, I spend countless hours delving into complex situations, and then produce reports that no one bothers to read. Including, I might add, my boss, the Secretary of State. He comes from the oil industry, so you'd think he'd know a thing or two about the region."

"I'm sure he knows about the oil, if not the politics."

"The point is that they're inseparable."

"Does writing what no one reads - dispiriting as it may be - at least pay well?"

"You're joking. No government job pays well. Not at my level anyway. No one goes into public service for the money. We're motivated by job satisfaction, and a sense that we're serving our country... as naïve as that might seem."

"It's not naïve at all," Nigel said, sympathetically. "After university, I thought about taking a job in government myself. The Foreign Office, would you believe. Even got so far as a preliminary interview. I didn't follow through, though, because the mindless bureaucracy was obvious from the start: endless forms to fill in, strange questions about whether I'd spent any time in Moscow, and whether my father had been a Communist... that kind of thing. The FO is renowned, of course, for being a hotbed of Arabists. They're not anti-Semitic, but in the corridors of Whitehall, Israel doesn't get much of a look in. For what it's worth, my view is that the Palestinians have got a raw deal." He paused. "But I don't want to get too political; not on our second meeting. Anyway, journalism is much more exciting than diplomacy. At least we're allowed opinions, even if my predecessor doesn't seem to think so."

"At least your FO people seem to know what they're talking about. Even educated Americans know too little of the world. What's worse, we don't seem anxious to learn. That's inexcusable in a country claiming to be the leader of the Free World."

"Have you travelled much in the Middle East?"

"Enough to know where everything is. I've also read quite a bit of history. The other night you mentioned Sykes and Picot: most people here, if you asked them, would guess that they're the Nationals' first base-shortstop combination. Sometimes I feel as though I'm teaching children with learning disabilities. I know that sounds terribly arrogant, but it's the way most of us feel."

"If you don't think much of *your* boss, what do you think of *his*?"

She gave him an old-fashioned look. "I think I said too much the other evening, but since you've asked again, let me put it this way: I've always been a Republican but, like my Lutheran upbringing, it's more by inheritance than conviction. Now I'm lapsed in both. More often I now find myself voting for the other ticket. That's strictly between us, of course."

"You a Republican! I must say I'm disappointed." He laughed to hide his disapproval.

"Perhaps I never was a true believer. And the Grand Old Party, so-called, has changed. Right now, it's in the hands of people who scare the hell out of me. We seem to have forgotten that some of the most reform-minded presidents of the past were Republicans. I'm thinking Lincoln. And Teddy, of course. Perhaps even the late unlamented Nixon - at least before he went power-mad and neurotic."

"I think he was probably both of those things all along."

"The truth is, I'm not really all that political. I can't say what I am, in politics or religion. How about you - as if I couldn't guess?"

"Then I can confirm that I'm left of centre. That's after growing up in a Tory-voting household. My father - a humble man of the cloth - professed to be apolitical, but the Conservative Party and the Church of England have always been a double act. Frankly, I don't have much time for either of them. The Conservative Party spent its early years building that vast Empire of ours and the dear old C of E was founded on a divorce. Hardly the most commendable origins in either case. At Oxford, hating the Tories was almost an extension of the curriculum. We spent more time marching against something or other than on our studies. I'm also a republican, but that's with a small 'r'. And an atheist, thank God."

"Ha, ha," Jane said.

All these revelations, major and minor, had come so quick and fast that they both needed a little time to digest them. The digestive process was shortly transferred to the food, which the waiter had placed in front of them.

"I could eat a horse," said Jane, eyeing nothing more substantial than a prettily arranged salad.

"Over the past two days I've already eaten half a cow," Nigel rejoined. "Graham - my predecessor - took me to the Happy Heifer."

"Oh, you poor soul. I went there just once, years ago. Vowed never to go again. I'm not a vegetarian, but that restaurant could push me in that direction... all that blood and gore and grease."

Jane tucked into her mysterious organic, multi-hued salad. He was meanwhile trying to decide how to tackle a multi-layered hamburger, which soared skyward from the plate like a half-demolished pagoda. Should he use a knife and fork, or pick it up by hand? He decided on the cutlery-free option but immediately regretted it, as blood, fat and a viscous red and yellow substance trickled over his hand and down his arm. Jane laughed at the spectacle. Nigel was embarrassed. "It's not that I've never eaten a hamburger, of course, but our typical British equivalent is about a fifth the size of this one." Exasperated, he picked up his knife and fork. "I know it's un-American, but if I don't use these then I'll have to head back to the hotel to change clothes."

"You'll soon get the hang of it," she said, still chortling. Despite the awkward moment Nigel derived great satisfaction from his ability to amuse her.

"Grappling with giant hamburgers aside," she said, "how do you think you're going to like living here in the United States?"

"If everyone here is as nice as you," he mumbled through a mouth stuffed to capacity, "I think I'm going to like it just fine."

She ignored the fulsome compliment, looking slightly uneasy. "I'm sure you're going to find it a little different. Let's face it, it *is* different. I remember how I first felt when I first went to London. It seemed, I don't know, primitive, somehow alien. Back then we Americans used to find that quaint."

"A much-abused word," Nigel observed. "But deep down the Brits kind of like it that way. We hanker for the nineteenth century. Why? Because that's when we ruled the world. Mind you, the two

Brits who work here for the *Post* have both gone native, and I'm told the same thing will happen to me. Which means I'll also have to learn to curb some of my ingrained anti-American attitudes. Let me add that I've always found you Americans on a personal level to be generous and open, but when it comes to politics you seem to be a negative print of both. But then maybe we Brits are a bit too buttoned up for our own good."

"Well, if that's the rule, you seem to be an exception."

"It's all that rain and grey skies. It gets to us. Just as the daytime darkness gets to the Scandinavians. Here, the weather is better and so the optimism is infectious. It's the enthusiasm of a young country, which you still have by our standards. Having said that, my colleague Bill in New York seems to think you're experiencing a dark night of the soul. Britain is, too, for that matter. Countries are like people: they get old and tired. Instead of looking forward, we spend too much of our time looking back, yearning for the Good Old Days. I still often wonder, though, why the richest country in the world can't afford a decent state health system - socialized medicine, as you call it."

"We *can* afford it, but the politicians don't want it. There's too much profit in health care."

"Now you're sounding liked a card-carryings socialist."

"You'll find that word something of a pejorative here."

"Yes, I've heard."

"What do you think you're going to miss most about England?"

"I'm not sure. Rugby and cricket, I suppose. Also, our peculiar sense of humour. Britain may be a spent force in world affairs, but at least we can still laugh at ourselves. You Americans, with respect, don't do self-deprecation. As for everything else I'll have to deal with, I'm sure I'll cope."

"I once had a boyfriend who played rugby," Jane said, but not ruefully. "I didn't see much of him at weekends, and even when he did come home, he was often none too sober. Sometimes he looked as if he'd just been mugged."

"He *had* been mugged," Nigel said, laughing. "That's what rugby is about: mugging people - within certain rules of course."

"It sounds frightful."

"How long ago did you know him?" Nigel was keen to learn something of Jane's romantic history. That 'come home' had suggested a live-in arrangement.

"Oh, some years now, maybe five. In the end, though, I was well shot of him."

"What happened? If you don't mind talking about it."

"Appropriately enough, I gave him the boot. The final straw was when I realized that some of the scratches across his back hadn't been inflicted on the rugby field."

"Oh dear. And since then?"

"A few boyfriends but nothing serious. None lasted more than a few weeks. As my friend Fran would happily tell you - at inordinate length and in gory detail - I've been unlucky in love. Always picked the wrong-uns. Says I'm too demanding. Well, I suppose I am. She's convinced I'm on the way to becoming an old maid. She calls me Calamity Jane - always happy but never attached. Sad, isn't it?"

"If it were true."

"And when I stop to think about it, it isn't true. I'm perfectly content with my life right now. Well, maybe not perfectly…" She suddenly frowned, uncomfortable with self-revelation. "My turn to ask a few questions about *your* romantic history."

Nigel emptied his mouth and cleared his throat. "How long do you have?"

"All the time in the world… although I do have to put a laundry in later."

"I was joking. We don't need any time at all. To be honest, I've had more scoops than affairs. Most of my attachments didn't last beyond the first date. I'm not always the easiest person to get on with, as my ex-wife keeps telling me. Since the divorce, my life has pretty much been my work. The trivial round, the common task, and so on That's from a hymn, by the way. Let's hope there's still time to save me. Perhaps I can enlist your help… and perhaps I could do the same for you."

Jane began to feel edgy again. She forced a laugh. "You make us sound like two orphans in a storm, huddled together for comfort."

"Well, the motto on the Statue of Liberty refers to huddled masses. And I'm all for a little huddling."

In this vein they cooed, like flirtatious but wary pigeons, for quite a while. Eventually, Nigel suggested dessert. Jane responded by looking at her watch. "Oh, my Lord and Taylor, do you know what time it is? It's gone three."

"You have to be somewhere?"

"No, but I have a few errands to run - clothes to wash, ironing, that sort of thing."

Nigel was suddenly panicked about losing her to the laundry. "Look I've got nothing on tonight. How about dinner?"

"We haven't even finished lunch."

"I know, but we do have to eat twice a day, or so my nutritionist tells me."

"You have a nutritionist?"

"No. Does this body look as if it were designed by a nutritionist?"

"Frankly, no. But I'm supposed to be seeing Fran for dinner. She's probably still hanging out at my place, wondering where I've got to."

"Didn't you just spend half the night gossiping?"

"Yes, and now I've spent half the afternoon doing the same with you," she said, undermining his point. "The fact is, we have a dinner date. An informal one, just the two of us, but I don't like to let her down."

Nigel suddenly thought of a solution. "We can kill two birds with one stone."

"How's that?"

"I take you *both* out for dinner. My treat."

Jane hesitated. She had enjoyed both encounters with Nigel, but she couldn't avoid the feeling that he was moving things along a little too fast. And Nigel, as soon as he had made the offer, found himself thinking the same thing. "Forget it," he said. "That was very presumptuous of me."

"That's alright," she replied, not quite knowing how to turn him down gently. "It's just that…" She didn't finish what she was about to say, because she realized that she didn't know what she'd been about to say. Then she surprised herself by blurting out, "I suppose it would be an opportunity for you two to meet." She knew that Fran would jump at the chance to appraise her new acquaintance, and her evaluations were always refreshingly candid.

"Well, there we are…"

"I'll have to call her first. Make sure she's up for it." Jane knew that she would be. "I'll call you later to confirm. We were going to Luigi's, where we met this morning."

"Sounds splendid," said a now unrepentant Nigel.

Forgetting that they were about to order dessert, Nigel asked for the bill. They parted with a rather formal and distracted handshake.

Nigel wondered if he hadn't pushed his luck too far.

Jane worried that she had given in to him too easily.

* * *

"I hear you're moving into the neighborhood," Fran Powell said, making conversation as they took their seats at Luigi's, having commandeered a coveted window table.

"News travels fast," Nigel said.

"It's the only thing that does in this town," Fran said, "as you're about to find out."

She had agreed to play gooseberry with enthusiasm. She felt protective of Jane, whose lack of male admirers she found baffling, and was anxious to meet this new man in her friend's life, this Brit, to whom Jane had by her own reluctant admission taken more than a passing fancy.

Fran was tall and slim, with short-cropped chestnut hair, striking looking rather than conventionally beautiful. Her manner was outgoing, and it came with a ready smile and a quick wit. Some found her to be outspoken to a fault, overly confident in her opinions and evaluations, which she was always ready to offer - invited or not - on a broad range of subjects. Those who knew her best, like Jane, found in her a staunch if sometimes unpredictable friend.

"I'm a lesbian," she announced early in the conversation, as if to measure Nigel's response. Nigel passed the test handily with a so-what shrug. "But I'm not the flamboyant kind. Nor am I an activist. Frankly, I don't really care for all this rainbow coalition stuff. All these marches and demonstrations do more harm than good. If we're now accepted in society as normal, why do we still need to keep waving banners around and dressing up in weird costumes? It's all self-defeating, in my humble opinion."

"None of your opinions are humble," Jane interjected.

"Au contraire, my darling girl. All my opinions are humble because they're invariably right."

"I agree with you on the demos," Nigel said, "but it'll all settle down eventually, you'll see. People just take time to get used to these things."

"That," Fran remarked, looking at Jane, "is a perfect example of British understatement. Keep calm and carry on, what?" The last sentence was uttered in an English accent as bad as Nigel's Bogart impression.

"I happen to approve of understatement," Nigel said, "even if I don't much practice it myself."

"I had noticed," Jane said.

"A point of view expressed quietly is so much more effective than one that's shouted. Not that it's much better these days in Britain. It's the evangelists I hate most. Crooks, the lot of them. They make a fortune from gullible people, and over here I understand the government gives them a tax break for doing it."

Fran nodded vigorously in agreement. "Well, you can't trust a government that keeps proclaiming that it's a secular institution but prints 'In God We Trust' on its dollar bills."

Nigel had taken an instant shine to her. He could see why, as he had read in preparation for this meeting, the first lady relied on this woman more than the job specifications demanded. She had become, in two short years, a close political adviser and personal confidante.

Fran had met Samantha Jameson at an early stage in the presidential campaign, while working, without enthusiasm, for a public relations agency the president had retained to evaluate polling numbers for the obligatory Committee to Elect the President. Fran had been hired to devise a communications strategy for the candidate's wife, largely in response to pressure from the president's advisers to show that she was committed to his campaign. In truth, the first lady had needed no help, having had no wish to contribute more to it than protocol demanded, either in time or in energy. Astute political observers picked this up. To them it was plain that she would rather be doing anything but acting out this charade of the candidate's loyal and dutiful wife. Nor, whenever questioned about it, had the first lady said much to disabuse them of the opinion.

She and Fran had hit it off at their first meeting. After that, they were rarely apart during working hours, acting as a pair of co-conspirators in search of a new scenario, while doing as little as possible to further the one in which they were already supposed to be involved; namely, to put Martin Jameson in the White House by hook or by crook. Or, as Fran had once joked, by crooks. In a Republican Party newly and slavishly devoted to the so-called alt-right, Fran's political views would have been viewed as more in keeping with those espoused by the other party. But then she had never made any bones about her progressive political views, which she applied with glee to a host of social issues denounced by the administration as subversive.

Some of this Nigel was now learning from Fran herself. She had wasted no time regaling him with her life history - unexpurgated as far as he could tell. Like Samantha Jameson, Nigel found himself drawn to a woman who was a force of nature. He could see her becoming a potentially useful source. Having listened to her monologue for fifteen uninterrupted minutes, accompanied by Jane's frequent objections, he gladly submitted to her intense interrogation of him.

"So, tell me, Nigel, how would you describe your politics, if you don't mind me asking? And I must insist that you tell me even if you do."

"In a British or American context?"

"What's the difference, would you say?"

"For a start, Britain's political spectrum is well to the left of yours. Our right wing is your centre-left. In party terms, I'd say our Conservative Party is the equivalent of your Democratic Party."

"And where does that leave the Labour Party, His Majesty's loyal opposition?"

"Labour thinks of itself as a socialist party, although some would argue it's no such thing. There's no socialist party of any consequence in America. In the public mind here, the word socialist seems to equate to communism."

"I'll rephrase the question, then. Where would you put yourself on the British spectrum?"

"Liberal but pragmatic. A progressive on most social issues, less so on economic ones, but in neither case tied to any ancient shibboleths."

Jane intervened, looking slightly aggrieved. "Pardon me for interrupting, but I hope we're not going to spend the entire evening talking politics. I listen to this stuff all week."

Fran looked peeved. "Look, girl, I'm just trying to find out what kind of man you've brought here. You did say you wanted my opinion of him, and that needs to include his political views. I know nothing about this stray Englishman of yours. Fuck all, as he would say. Nor, for that matter, do you. And I haven't even got to the private stuff yet."

"Perhaps you should hand me a questionnaire," Nigel offered, deploying the irony for which his countrymen were supposedly renowned, and which Americans called sarcasm. "I had to fill in several for the Department of Immigration and Naturalization before they'd let me in."

"They didn't ask about your politics," Fran said. "Or your religion... if you have one. Do you?"

"Anglican by upbringing - that's Episcopalian in your language - but long since abandoned. But your President Jameson seems to think that an immigrant's religion is important, as least as it applies to Muslims."

"You make a good point," Fran agreed dolefully. "The man is a shameless bigot... I didn't say that, of course."

Nigel laughed. "Your secrets are safe with me."

"I'm beginning to feel like a moderator at a political debate," Jane put in with a weary sigh.

Fran took advantage of a lull in the interview to twirl spaghetti round her fork. It kept coming. "You know, I adore Italian food, but I've never found a lady-like way to eat spaghetti. I should have ordered the veal scaloppini."

"Since when were you worried about being lady-like," Jane twitted.

"I try to, at least when I'm meeting someone for the first time," Fran said, writhing lengths of tomato-drenched spaghetti dangling from her lips before slowly disappearing with a slurp. Nigel watched the performance with amusement, remembering his lunchtime contest with a hamburger.

"My turn," he said. "For a few questions, I mean."

"I hadn't even got warmed up," Fran said poutingly. "But fire away."

"What do you like about working for the first lady? Or FLOTUS if you prefer."

"I don't prefer. It's just a silly anagram for lazy people. POTUS and FLOTUS make them sound like a comedy team. Some, of course, would say that's exactly what they are. But to answer your question, I enjoy my job immensely. I like what I'm doing because I like Samantha personally. She's thoughtful and kind, bright and well-educated. Not like that band of unscrupulous gangsters who've taken over the other wing of the White House - including that dreadful husband of hers. I didn't say that, either, but I sure mean it."

"Unlike them, she seems to prefer to stay in the shadows."

"She does, although that makes her sound vaguely sinister. There's nothing sinister about her. Look, I think we all know the lie of the land here. First ladies are not elected, so they must go along, playing the devoted spouse. Some go along more than others. This one falls into the 'other' category. She's a private person, and that's not such a bad thing to be. She does good work but does it in her own way and without the usual fanfare. She ought to take more credit. I've even suggested it, but that's just not her style."

"Hence the Woman of Mystery tag..."

"I don't find her in the least mysterious. Merely modest. And a little shy."

"I'd like to understand better what makes her tick, as I understand many others would."

"There's not a whole lot to understand that isn't obvious to those who take the trouble to look. She has her own interests and her own circle of friends, neither of which coincide with her husband's. His only interests seem to be golf and chasing women. Incidentally, Samantha's a keen golfer, too, though I can't recall them ever playing together. He probably thinks she's too good for him - and we all know how he hates to lose. She also likes horse-riding, as is well known, and she's lately taken up bridge. I'm not sure what else I can tell you."

"It seems she hasn't quite come to terms with the role of first lady. Some of her predecessors couldn't wait to share their husband's limelight. Others came to think of themselves as the main attraction. A few even had political ambitions of their own."

"For example…"

"Of recent vintage, there's Hillary Clinton. Her problem, as far as I could tell, was that she got ahead of herself. So confident she'd win the presidency in her own right that she forgot the basic campaign rules… like going to the swing states."

"Who else?"

Nigel was starting to feel like someone sitting a history examination. "Eleanor Roosevelt. She was almost as popular as her husband, and more so in some circles. Could have run for the office herself and won."

"She had too much private baggage for that - and I think you know what I'm talking about."

"I do. So, where do you think Samantha Jameson will stand in the pantheon of first ladies?"

"I've no idea. She's only been in the job two years. Anyway, that husband of hers doesn't want her going around shooting her mouth off. She'd contradict him and his policies and show him up as less articulate or caring. She does go on foreign trips with him, as required, and attends White House social events. Not that there are many of those these days. Camelot, this ain't. Can you imagine her husband sitting through a cello concert? She supports several charities, but most don't fit in with this administration's agenda. I can tell you this much: as solemn and self-conscious as she seems in public, when the cameras are flashing and people are thrusting microphones up her nose, in private social settings she's a joy to be with."

"And the marriage?"

"I think you already know the answer to that, Mr Harper. You and everyone else on Planet Earth. First off, what goes on inside any marriage is a mystery - sometimes even to the two people in it. We speak on a variety of other subjects of an intimate nature, but on that one we have an understanding: she doesn't tell, and I don't ask. That's how it should be. He was the one elected to do the job, not her. There, how's that for a diplomatic response?"

"Very impressive," said Nigel. "Perhaps I should top up your glass more often."

"Don't waste your time," Jane said, chuckling. "She can drink us all under the table."

Nigel looked around for a waiter. "Speaking of which, I'm going to order another bottle anyway."

They left the restaurant three hours later, pretty much talked out. Even Fran seemed to have run out of conversational steam, although in Jane's experience, whenever that happened, she was merely resting for a renewed onslaught. For now, Jane thought, Fran and Nigel had fought each other to a standstill, an honourable tie.

* * *

They stood outside the restaurant saying awkward goodnights, each not sure what was supposed to happen next. It was Fran who resolved their dilemma. Suddenly, she leapt into the street, arms waving madly, and hailed a taxi. Fran lived across town in the Capitol district, not far from Nigel's hotel, but she made no effort to offer him a lift. Ducking into the taxi as if making an escape, she gave them a thumbs up sign. "Goodnight, you love-birds."

From that hasty departure and the inappropriate remark, Nigel inferred a clear indication of Fran's approval of him. He and Jane watched, smiling, as the taxi disappeared, Fran's arm waving frantically from the window.

"Sometimes she can be *so* embarrassing," Jane sputtered.

"I can believe it," Nigel said.

They began walking in the direction of her apartment, wordlessly, but with the implicit understanding that this was their destination. This time she thrust *her* arm through *his*. With luck, Nigel was thinking he'd be invited in for a nightcap, although his expectations after that were modest.

"So, what did you really think of my friend Fran?" she asked.

"I like her. She's a straight shooter, that's for sure. A bit of a hoot, as you called her earlier. She must be wild when the mood takes her."

"And the mood takes her quite often, I can tell you. Not so much tonight, though. She was in investigative mode."

"Yes, I noticed."

"She's very protective of me," Jane explained by way of apology. "Thinks I need looking after. Preferably by a man."

"Do you?"

"Of course not. I'm thirty-seven years old and perfectly capable of looking after myself. I've got a decent job, a nice circle of friends, and I enjoy my freedom... well, most of the time. Fran has been a wonderful, reliable friend. There have been times, I admit, when I wondered what I'd have done without her." Realizing how revealing that last remark sounded, she abruptly stopped talking.

Nigel took up the slack. "Some friend! She just took off in a taxi without a by-your-leave. Didn't even offer to drop me off. Or you, for that matter. Just left you alone on a dark street with a complete stranger."

"Which only shows that she trusts you. If she didn't, you'd be heading back to your hotel alone. I suppose she also thinks we already have something going."

"Do we?"

"You'll know as soon as I do," Jane said, rather diffidently, and quickly changed the subject. "What a lovely evening. That rain earlier cleaned the air. I think it'll be a nice day tomorrow. Look. It's so clear you can see the stars. That's something you can't often say in London."

"Now you're sounding English, talking about the weather."

"Now that you've mentioned it, why *do* you always talk about the weather?"

"Because we never know what it's going to do from one day to the next. Sometimes one hour to the next. It's also a conversational device when we're lost for words, which, given our natural reserve, is quite often."

"You don't often seem lost for words."

"Perhaps because I make a living from them, though most journalists I know feel more comfortable writing them than saying them." They fell silent. Then he said, "I take it, from the route we're taking, that I'm walking you home."

"I suppose you are. It's only two or three blocks away, if you remember from this morning's rather strange excursion."

"I lose track of distance in the dark." He was going to add, *'And when I'm with a beautiful woman',* but in the nick of time thought better of it.

Ten minutes later, they stopped outside a house much like the one in which he was about to live. She rummaged in her handbag for the key, and then uttered the magic words, "It's not too late. Fancy a coffee or something?"

"Define 'something'."

"I have wine, maybe even some whisky."

He followed her up the steps of the stoop. She opened the front door and stepped inside. "This is me, here on the right. It's just like yours."

"Remarkably so."

Her apartment was indeed very much like the one he'd rented that morning. That now seemed weeks ago. Hers was tastefully furnished in a vaguely early American style, with lots of fruitwood tables and muted floral patterns on covering fabrics. She noticed that he'd noticed. "I got some of the basic furniture from my parents. Most of the rest I bought at antique fairs. It's all a bit old-fashioned. A bit like me, I suppose."

"It's charming," he said, "… also a bit like you."

She removed her topcoat and helped him out of his. Neither of them had been needed.

She went to the small kitchen. He looked at books on a shelf. The first one he saw was *The Seven Pillars of Wisdom,* the supposed masterpiece of that shameless and unreadable old fraud T.E. Lawrence. Anywhere else he might have found its presence a little pretentious. Here, it was probably a textbook. There were other tomes on the Middle East, some by well-known writers, others by little-known diplomats.

Jane called out from the kitchen. "What'll you have? I don't have any whisky, it seems. There's some red wine, though."

He had moved away from the bookcase. "Red wine would be perfect. You don't mind me nosing around? I'm just comparing notes."

"Go ahead. The bedroom may be a mess. I didn't even make the bed this morning… and try not to trip over my underwear."

"There's nothing I'd like better," he said, immediately wishing he hadn't.

Returning to the living room, he found two glasses of red wine on the small dining table. Jane was selecting a radio station. Ella Fitzgerald permeated the ether. '*We'll take Manhattan, the Bronx and Staten Island, too…*'

"Do you like Ella?" she asked.

"One of my favourites," he said, which was true.

Sitting at the table, he suddenly felt light-headed, from the wine consumed earlier perhaps, but also from something else: her presence on the first occasion when they had been alone in an intimate setting. He felt exquisitely on edge. Jane did, too, he noticed.

"As she passed behind his chair to join him at the table, she paused and put her hands on his shoulders. "Your muscles are tight," she said, and started to knead them. "You have some knots here. I can feel them."

He felt his heart rate quicken. "Mm, that feels good," he murmured.

"You know," she replied, somewhat dreamily, still working at knots, "but for some reason I feel as though I've known you longer than our three brief encounters."

"Is it only three?"

"Tonight was the third," she confirmed.

"I hope we get to the point where we can stop counting."

He tilted his head up to see her reaction. She responded by leaning down and kissing him lightly on the mouth, before pulling away, as if embarrassed. "I'm sorry, I… "

He drew her back down, meeting no resistance, and they stayed locked in that position for some time, before parting to draw breath.

"Well, there's a surprise," he muttered.

"And, who knows, I may have a few more," she purred into his ear, moving from his shoulders to his chest.

* * * * *

Chapter 6

Nigel trailed Graham through the White House press room like a schoolboy being introduced by a teacher to new classmates.

"Meet my protégé," Graham announced chirpily to the few journalists present. "Nigel Harper. Taught him everything he knows."

"That shouldn't have taken too long," snapped a reporter from one of the Chicago papers, not bothering to look up from his laptop.

"Does this mean we're getting a new English instructor?" another sniped.

Graham seemed oblivious to the ribbing. Or perhaps, since he would soon be off to the land of golden sunsets and frozen daiquiris, he could find no reason to care. A few colleagues wandered over to wish him good luck, but most ignored him. They all but ignored Nigel, too, offering only cursory nods or silent handshakes.

"The natives seem none too friendly," Nigel muttered. He should not have been surprised. Journalists always put on a professional show of indifference when meeting a stranger, determined to show that no one should mistake them for someone easily impressed. Not even when, or perhaps especially when, meeting fellow scribblers.

"Oh, they're not so bad when you get to know them," Graham assured him, dipping into his bottomless sack of banalities.

"Well, I guess I'll just have to earn my stripes, like any new boy at school."

"Just as I did," said Graham, who, on the evidence Nigel had just seen, had not advanced beyond the rank of corporal.

"Thanks for getting my credentials in order so quickly," said Nigel, suddenly feeling sorry for his colleague. "You've obviously got some pull around here."

"Well, I *am* one of the longest-serving correspondents here, although the Reuters man seems to have been around since Calvin Coolidge."

"Speaking of Coolidge," said Nigel, "did you ever hear the story about his reputation for reticence?"

"No. But do tell."

"Two elderly ladies at a party attended by Mr Coolidge have a little wager. One bets the other that she can get a president known for his taciturnity to utter more than two words. Introducing herself to the president, she says, 'Mr Coolidge, I have a bet with my friend that I can get you to say more than two words.' 'Silent Cal' looks down at her from on high and says: 'You lose.'"

Graham managed to break a smile. "If only the present holder of the office would take a leaf out of his book."

Nigel returned to the question of Graham's longevity, again deploying flattery. "Your staying power is something of an achievement. You and Bill Palmer are both a pair of grizzled veterans. Hard shoes to fill." Graham smiled again, unsure whether 'grizzled' was a compliment or an insult. "Does that mean," Nigel asked, "that you get to say 'Thank you, Mr President' at press conferences. Like that woman, I forget her name, who always…"

Graham filled in the blank. "That would be Helen Thomas, United Press International. The first female White House correspondent, I believe. Had her own reserved seat in the front row of the briefing room. Hardly ever asked a question but as the senior reporter present, she always had the final word. I met her once. Nice woman, but tough as nails. Sadly, no longer with us. Nor is UPI, for that matter."

Nigel moved the conversation to more practical matters. "How many other Brits are there here?" He asked because he was keen to identify the competition. He'd met a few of his transatlantic colleagues and knew most of them by name or reputation. None, he'd decided, would cause him any headaches, at least not as rivals.

Graham began to count them off. "There's the BBC man of course, Ivan Brand, otherwise known as Ivan the Horrible, for reasons I'll leave you to work out. Then there's John Terrence from ITN, or whatever it's called these days, and Bill Jones from Sky. CNN has a couple of our compatriots, too. The London dailies are here - or at least the broadsheets - but you won't see many of them. The tabloids are here, too, but usually busy chasing celebrity scandals. You must know Kenny Brooks of the *Star*, and late of the *Post*."

"Ah, yes, the late and unlamented Mr Brooks. Lovely bloke but he wouldn't recognize a story if the King dropped dead in front of him."

Graham, a friend of Kenny's, ignored the jibe. "I don't see any of them here today. They're probably keeping their heads down. We

Brits are not flavour of the month right now, if you'll pardon the silly expression."

"Oh, why's that?"

"That bloody leaked embassy cable. President Jameson wasn't best pleased when he heard what His Majesty's ambassador secretly thought about him."

"All of it perfectly accurate, as I recall."

Graham pursed his lips. "You may well think so, but it got Jameson so hopping mad he banned him from the White House. Imagine that! A British ambassador persona non grata. Anyway, since then, Jameson has tarred all us Brits with the same brush." Graham seemed in no doubt that it was all the ambassador's fault. "You'd think Britain's senior diplomat would be able to temper his language."

"Why should he? He was reporting to London on a supposedly secure line. It's the ambassador's job to be blunt. How was he to know some resentful twerp in London would leak the stuff?"

"Everything seems to get leaked these days," Graham said, with evident regret.

"Splendid!" cried Nigel. "Indiscretions, deliberate or otherwise, are all grist to our mill. Leak on, O ship of state, leak on…"

"The president, of course, would like to see Nigel - that other one - in the embassy post."

"Well, in the immortal courtroom words of Miss Rice Davies, 'He would, wouldn't he?' And what the fuck does that soapbox blowhard know about diplomacy? About as much as this president knows how to be president. And since when do the Americans get to choose the British ambassador? Can you imagine the situation in reverse? It might explain why America always sends us nonentities whose only qualification is that they donated fortunes to the presidential election campaign. That goes for the current man, by the way."

"It's not just the cable leak," Graham continued. "The British media have given this administration an even harder time than the locals, and that's saying something. I'm afraid the so-called 'special relationship' isn't so special these days."

"Was it ever?" Nigel shot back.

"Why do you say that?" Graham seemed offended by the idea.

"Because it's a myth of our own creation. Goes back to the Second World War: Lend-Lease, the Atlantic Charter, and all that. That was the last time both countries sang from the same hymnal.

Remember Suez? Eisenhower humiliated us in front of the world. Not to mention the Falklands, when Thatcher had to practically beg Reagan to stay out of it. Even Obama, for all his cozying up to the royals, didn't like us that much. Never quite forgave us our imperial sins, especially in Kenya. The president who had most time for us was Dubya, thanks to that lickspittle Tony Blair... and look where that got us."

"Where?"

"Into an illegal fucking war."

"But not, one might argue, an unnecessary one."

"Don't get me started," Nigel replied waspishly, shocked that his colleague should seek to justify such a misbegotten enterprise.

Graham counterattacked: "You don't seem to care much for Americans, do you."

"My quarrel isn't with Americans, only with their government's arrogant world view. Their foreign policy has never been anything but self-serving."

"What about the Second World War? They saved our bacon, wouldn't you say?"

"Yes, but only up to a point, Lord Copper. They came in only when the Japanese bombed Pearl Harbor. If that hadn't happened, we'd have been left on our own. As for Lend Lease, we got fifty old destroyers already on their way to the scrapyard in return for all our best naval bases in the Caribbean. And the loans? We paid them back with interest. Nearly broke us. And then they made sure we dismantled the British Empire. Quite right, too, except that they only did it to make way for one of their own. Look, I'm not saying they're bad allies, just not quite the generous and selfless friends they're always painted to be. As for my loathing of this president, well, that puts me in the same company as more than half the population of the United States; not to mention most of the Free World."

"He's not universally loved, that's true," Graham conceded, in a tone which suggested that he thought he ought to be. He coughed, a signal that he was changing the subject to more mundane matters. "You remember there's going to be a press briefing today? Eleven o'clock. We're not expecting any sensations, but you never know... and at least we'll have a chance to have a quiet word with Frank Hoffman. If we can get to him."

"Is that so difficult?"

"He doesn't hang around long after briefings, especially if he's been given a hard time."

"You mean he storms out?"

"No, although he has been known to. He doesn't suffer fools gladly."

"You think the press corps is composed of fools?"

"No, but some of them go too far. I'll say one thing for Frank: he's not as bad as some in this White House. This president, as you know, doesn't always pick the right people. Frank is one of the exceptions."

"They're a bad lot because he picks cronies who'll be sure to agree with anything he says or does. The first time they contradict him he fires them. It doesn't say a lot for Frank Hoffman that he's still in post."

"At least he's read a few books - more than you can say for the rest of them."

"Or for their boss. I'm told he doesn't even bother to read his briefing papers. Probably wouldn't understand them even if he did."

"That may be true, as reluctant as I am to admit it."

A tall, dark man, unmistakably English both in appearance and manner, lurched towards them with a kind of sideways walk. Despite the warm weather he was sharply dressed in a three-piece suit, an ensemble of Savile Row quality. It included a bow tie, always in Nigel's mind grounds for suspicion, signifying a yearning for attention. The man announced himself with a slight bow, offering a hand at the end of what seemed a preternaturally long arm.

"Ivan Brand, BBC." The diction was as sharp as his suit. "You're Nigel Harper of the *Daily Post,* if I'm not mistaken."

"I am," Nigel confirmed. "Actually, we've met."

"Have we?"

"Yes. The last time, if memory serves, was a few years back, on the terrace at the House of Commons. A cocktail reception. I think it was when Obama was in town."

"Ah, yes, now I remember," Ivan said. "We had a discussion about England's problems with its middle-order batting."

"And an argument about it with the *Telegraph's* cricket correspondent, fellow named Benson. Pompous old fool. Can't think why he was there in the first place. I mean, what does cricket have to do with politics?"

"They both reduce us to despair," Ivan quipped. "I wouldn't say the American political establishment is any better than ours. All this populist nonsense is demagoguery for dimwits. God only knows where it's leading us..." The thought trailed off. "I enjoy your reporting, by the way."

"And I've been watching your performances on Newsnight," Nigel said, returning the compliment. Newsnight, as the title cleverly suggested, was a late-night news programme on the BBC. "I'm always impressed when you're on. You don't pull your punches, do you?" Ivan Brand had a well-earned reputation for being blunt about the shortcomings of politicians - with a special contempt reserved for the present incumbent, and often with a striking turn of phrase. Once, picking up a quip of Churchill's, he'd described the president as a "wolf in wolf's clothing".

"Ah, yes, the Emily Show," mused Ivan, referring to the presenter who often hosted the programme. "Smart as a whip. And not bad looking. You must have run into her from time to time."

"Once or twice," said Nigel. "I used to be an occasional guest myself. Then suddenly they stopped calling. I've no idea why. It was as if I'd been struck off the approved list."

"Happens all the time, old chap. There's never a good reason why you get on, and always a bad reason why you're chucked off. You probably offended some junior editor. The same rules apply in Washington right now. We Brits have been banished to the wilderness. And that includes the ambassador himself."

"Graham and I were just talking about it."

"It'll pass. He hates all of us media people in turn. Bashing the media is an essential component of his vote-winning strategy. Let's face it: he doesn't have much else to offer. The Brits have formed a new luncheon club, by the way. We call it the Confederacy of Dunces."

"After the book?"

"Yes, but not that one. Jonathan Swift." Ivan knew the line by heart, and as proof he recited it. "When a true genius appears in the world, you may know him by this sign, that the dunces are all in confederacy against him." The irony fits the current man perfectly, don't you think?"

Nigel thought so. Graham said nothing but displayed a disapproving look.

"How do I join?" Nigel asked.

"That's easy. There's only one qualification: you need to be personally and publicly insulted either by the president or his press secretary. Just ask a question you know will offend and you'll qualify on the spot."

Nigel laughed. He looked at Graham, who obviously found the conversation objectionable. "The way some of you behave, you provoke the man for sport. It plays into his hands. No wonder he bashes the media."

Ivan looked astonished. "My dear Graham, there's no avoiding it if we're doing our fucking jobs. But perhaps that's why you're not one of our members."

Graham shook his head. Nigel, enjoying the rebuke, stifled a chuckle.

Ivan checked the clock on the wall. "Well, I must be toddling off. I'm skipping today's briefing. I'm interviewing our long esteemed but currently despised ambassador, now under house arrest in the presidential doghouse, otherwise known as the British Embassy." He looked directly at Graham. "Come on, Graham, even you must admit it's all good knockabout stuff." He turned to Nigel. "Meanwhile, Mr Harper, welcome to the best comedy show in town. You won't be bored, that's for sure. Let's have a spot of lunch one of these days; swap notes, talk some cricket. We've still got a problem opening the batting."

"I'd like that. How does next week look?"

"Sounds fine, just so long as the president hasn't meanwhile declared war on a country he's never heard of. Call me." Ivan handed Nigel a business card.

"I like him," Nigel said after Ivan had left, apparently having forgiven him his taste in neckties.

Graham's lack of enthusiasm was manifest. "He's a bit flip for my taste. Too much of a smarty-pants. That brings me to a note of caution: mind who you hang out with around this place. They watch us all the time, you know, make note of who's friends with whom." He didn't have to identify the 'they'.

Nigel dismissed the warning angrily. "You know what? Fuck the White House. Fuck all of them. They're not paying my salary. Frankly, I wouldn't care if they were. My friends are whoever I choose them to be."

"Well, don't say I didn't warn you," Graham said primly.

Nigel felt like punching the man on the snout.

* * *

By eleven, the James S. Brady briefing room had filled up. It was named after President Reagan's press secretary, who was shot in the attempt on the president's life and had been confined to a wheelchair for life. Nigel counted about fifty attendees, and more were still trickling in. A few nodded in his direction. He and Graham took seats near the back, evidently Graham's regular place. The location was ideal for anonymity, Nigel was thinking, but hardly the place for a supposed doyen of the White House press corps. He would have liked to move closer to the front, but as Graham pointed out, the seating plan was determined by the Washington Correspondents Association according to a rigid pecking order: the front rows were reserved for the television networks and major American papers, the ones at the rear for lesser media mortals. "The *Post* is lucky to have a seat at all," Graham offered.

The Reuters man sitting in front of them turned around to greet them. Nigel recognized him as someone he had occasionally run into in London. "Welcome to the cuckoo's nest," the Reuters man said genially.

"Cuckoos don't have nests," Graham pointed out, pedantically.

"This cuckoo does," said the Reuters man, with a jerk of the head in the direction of the Oval Office, stage left about twenty-five paces away.

The briefing room was about the size of a school classroom and in some ways resembled one. The walls were windowless on three sides. On the fourth, tall windows overlooked an area shaded by trees. The room was dominated by a small platform and a podium adorned with a sign that read, somewhat redundantly, 'The White House'. In case anyone should be in any doubt about it, a similar but larger sign was affixed to the wall behind the stage, which for the avoidance of all doubt was framed by two large flags and, like every other structure in Washington, Roman columns. Several White House staffers, looking nervous, were standing in a line against the wall to the left. Some gazed expectantly at the discreet door through which the press secretary would arrive. Nigel expected them to snap to attention when he entered. The room was warm, reflecting the weather outside, but heated further by the television cameras arrayed along the back wall. Most of the reporters, now about seventy of them, were perspiring profusely.

Nigel turned to Graham. "Will you be asking a question this morning?" He wondered whether Graham had *ever* asked a question, making a mental note to ask him later.

"Not today," Graham said distractedly.

"What are we expecting?"

"No idea. The CNN man and the lady from Fox News usually dominate proceedings. The way it works is that the CNN man makes some contentious point, which the Fox lady helps Frank to knock down. It's a kind of double act. Since there's not much going on right now, I doubt we'll be here more than twenty minutes."

"And then we'll meet Frank?"

"If we can." Nigel was thinking that it might be difficult if only for physical reasons, since they would have to battle their way through bodies and chairs from the back of the room to the front.

Just then, the man himself walked in, carrying a small folder. Without so much as a glance at the reporters, he strode the few steps to the podium. From there he looked up for the first time, surveying the audience much as a headmaster might a morning school assembly. "Good morning, ladies and gentlemen."

A few perfunctory 'good mornings' were mumbled back.

"Ah, the usual enthusiastic welcome," said Frank, without the trace of a smile. "But I'm happy to see all of you, even if the reverse isn't true." He opened the folder. "I trust you all had a restful Memorial Day weekend; or, for those of you who never rest from calling this administration to account, a wasted one."

Between rows of heads, Nigel watched the press secretary intently. Frank Hoffman was a sallow, dapper man of medium height and slim build. For a man of his age, which was hard to guess, his face seemed curiously unlined. His hair was dark and starting to recede at the temples. Some women found him handsome, debonair. Some men, too, it was said. Nigel thought he looked shifty.

Frank opened proceedings with no evident enthusiasm of his own. "We haven't been together for some days now, but I have only a few small housekeeping matters. Then, I'll take a few questions."

He droned on for several minutes, the reporters looking bored and restive. Peering over the shoulder of the Reuters man, Nigel saw that he was doodling a very competent and unflattering caricature of the president. That afternoon, Frank intoned, President Jameson would be meeting senior members of the House Ways and Means Committee to iron out a few outstanding budgetary issues. Action was needed NOW, Frank stressed, parroting the official line by calling on the Democrats to "get behind the process" rather than "stalling, as usual, for partisan political reasons." Later that day the White House would be hosting a lunch for the Veterans of Foreign Wars, an organisation for which the president "has a deep and abiding affection." This line drew muted titters from the audience, who were all aware that the president had assiduously avoided the military draft by invoking an old football injury. And this evening, the president and the first lady - Frank seemed to emphasize the 'and' - would be attending a concert at the Kennedy Center, given by some Korean violin prodigy, whose name Nigel failed to catch. There were more titters; this president was known for his aversion to such cultural events. And in conclusion, Frank said, the president would be leaving the following morning for a few working days at his Florida home to prepare for the approaching meeting with the Chinese president. The administration, Frank said, was confident of resolving certain long-standing trade issues with China, although more work needed to be done on the finer points. Preparations for a mooted visit to Beijing, scheduled for later in the year, were "active and on-going".

"And that's about it from me," Frank concluded abruptly. "Questions?"

A man in the front row raised a hand. "Jack Williams, CNN."

"As if we don't know who you are," Frank said flippantly.

Williams ignored the jibe. "Will the first lady be going to China with her husband? I ask because certain published reports have questioned of late her absence from official functions, including President Jameson's recent trip to the G10 summit. There is also - if I may follow up - considerable speculation about her role in general, including her position regarding many of the administration's policies. Is there anything you can tell us in either regard?"

"I see you've been reading the gossip pages," Frank replied testily. "My response, as you won't be surprised to learn, is that I have no response. I can only respond to things which have occurred. In this case, nothing has occurred. You may feel free, of course, to enquire of the first lady herself... if you can find her."

All eyes turned to the Fox lady, but she continued to sit with a blank expression and said nothing.

Frank pointed to someone else. "Ben?"

"Ben Larkin, Washington Herald." Everyone knew who he was, too, but reporters always made a point of mentioning their affiliation for the benefit of the television news shows.

"Ah, yes, speaking of the more scurrilous elements of the media...."

"With respect, Frank, I don't think that remark was called for."

"A joke, Ben. A throwaway line. I happily withdraw it. My word, we do live in sensitive times..."

"How would this White House know," Ben snapped, to more ripples of laughter. "As I was about to say, sir, the White House chief of staff has been in place for three months now but is still called 'acting'. Why is that? Is it the president's intention to confirm Frank O'Malley in the post or is a search underway for someone else? It has been widely reported that the president would prefer to act as his own chief of staff, and that the job has been downgraded, or perhaps even eliminated. Can you enlighten us as to the official position?"

Frank put on his "I-don't-know-where-this-stuff-comes-from" look. "I can tell you this much: the chief of staff is performing his duties very efficiently and I can assure you that the president is more than pleased with his performance. Let me add, in response to all the nonsense I read and hear in the media, that the White House machine is running smoothly in the service of the American people. There is currently no - I repeat no - search going on to fill the role currently occupied by Mr O'Malley."

"In that case, Frank, why hasn't he been confirmed in the post?" Larkin, under the rules of engagement, was allowed a follow-up question.

"The president will do so at a time of his own choosing. You should read nothing into that... though I've no doubt that you will. I don't know what else to add, except to advise you to watch this space."

Nigel leaned over to mutter in Graham's ear. "Hardly riveting stuff, is it?"

"Sometimes these affairs are all fire and fury," Graham whispered back, "and sometimes everyone nods off. This one seems to fit the second category."

Frank, moving on, pointed to the Fox News lady, who seemed to have just woken up herself. "Yes, Andrea. Nice to see you, by the way."

"At the G10 meeting, when the president last met the Russian leader, there was some talk of a visit here by Mr Putin. The president said at the time that he was open to the idea. I quote: 'I have made it clear to Mr Putin that he would be welcome here any time he wishes to come', and that it's a – quote - 'standing invitation' - unquote. Since then, we've heard nothing. Are there any background discussions taking place regarding such a visit? Or, alternatively, are there plans for a meeting at some neutral venue? Especially in the light of Russian military exercises going on close to the Baltic states. Are you, Frank, in a position to clarify the situation regarding a visit? And, if I may add a further question, does the president view the Baltic exercises as a provocation, as some of our European allies seem to think. The president is on record as saying that any renewed military activity in that region would have - and again I quote - 'potentially serious consequences' - unquote. Are those potential consequences under active discussion?"

Frank wiped his brow in a mock gesture of bewilderment. "Phew! That was more a speech than a question. But I'll try to take each point in turn, if I can remember them. There are no immediate - and I stress the word 'immediate' - plans for a Putin visit. The president's invitation was open-ended. Having said that, I'd have to say that now might not be the most auspicious time for such a visit. It can never entirely be ruled out. As for allegations of heightened Russian activity in the Baltic, all I can say is that they are being closely monitored. I might add, in passing, that there is no hard evidence - as opposed to rampant media speculation - of threatening Russian behaviour. I should also point out that we and our NATO allies have ourselves been conducting similar exercises in the region. If the Russians are sending a message to us, then we are sending one back to them. Next..."

Frank took a sip from a glass of water as he pointed to a reporter in the second row. "Ah, Mr Jenkins of the apparently - I might say inexplicably - much-revered BBC. Where is our friend Ivan today?"

"Called away on an assignment," said Robert Jenkins, standing in for him.

Frank failed to resist a dig. "Ah, yes, to another debriefing at the British Embassy. You see, Robert, this White House is as well-informed as you are - even without the benefit of leaked cables." The remark provoked some laughter. There was more when Jenkins retorted, "The BBC was not responsible for the leaks, sir." He pressed on. "The president has recently had some harsh things to say about Britain's recent negotiations with the European Union - namely that the prime minister chose to ignore his advice. Can you tell us what form that advice took, and in what forum it was delivered?"

Frank looked exasperated. "Our position has already been stated. It is, I repeat, that Britain's relations with Europe are entirely a matter for the UK government, and Brussels. Nothing to do with us. The president and the new PM have established a close working relationship and have frequent telephone conversations on Europe as well as a great many other topics. I can only presume that the issue came up during one of those calls. I think it's fair to say - as the president himself has made clear- that he would have steered a somewhat different course from that pursued by the government of the United Kingdom. I've nothing useful to add to that."

Jenkins, apparently content with the answer, sat down.

A few more desultory enquiries followed, mainly about some agricultural controversy, something to do with farm subsidies, which Nigel neither understood nor cared about. Frank, who felt the same way, met them with the usual bromides: "I'll have to get back to you on that" and "Let me see what I can find out." Several other hands were raised, but Frank's folder was already in his hand, signalling that the briefing was over. "Now, if that's all, ladies and gentlemen, I think we should all go back to work. Good morning."

The reporters began to file out of the room, though whether disappointed or relieved Nigel found it difficult to tell. Graham tried to hustle Nigel towards the front, but by the time they reached the door at the side of the stage, Frank had already slipped through it. He left his administrative assistant, Cindy Adams, to answer routine questions, mainly from the agriculturalists.

Graham finally reached her. "Good morning, Cindy. Before you disappear, I'd like you to meet my successor, Nigel Harper. Treat him kindly. He's fresh off the boat from London."

"Nice to meet you, Mr Harper," she said with distracted formality. "We've been expecting you. Welcome to the White House." She was hard-looking, Nigel thought, and bristling with suppressed belligerence. She turned to Graham. "Frank's rather busy today. Full schedule, I'm afraid. Can it wait?"

"I just wanted him to meet Nigel before I depart."

"Ah, yes, you'll soon be leaving us, I hear. Please accept my belated congratulations." Then she turned to Nigel "And to you… Nigel, is it?" Then she spoke again to Graham. "You've been a credit to your profession - unlike some I could mention here. Good luck to you."

"I appreciate that, Cindy. But is there any chance of a quick word with the man? It won't take a moment." Graham braced for the usual excuse.

"I might be able to arrange it," Cindy said, unexpectedly, "seeing as you're leaving. But only for a minute."

Graham looked pleased with himself. *Yes, he did have some pull.*

"Why don't you both follow me?" Cindy said, pushing the door open.

"This is a first," Graham whispered to Nigel as she ushered them through.

Frank was sitting behind the desk in his office. Cindy put a finger to her lips and left. Frank was already on the telephone, evidently with his boss. "No, nothing about that other thing," he was saying. "A non-event, really, Mr President." Nigel wondered what the 'other thing' might be. "Yes, I agree with you... we shouldn't have to put up with it... yes, sir, I'm sure you will."

Frank put the phone down. "Come in, gentlemen, come in," he said, rather unnecessarily as they were already standing in front of his desk. He stood up and shook hands with both men. "Nigel Harper, I take it. Pleased to meet you. Your reputation precedes you."

"I'm not sure what I should make of that."

Frank grinned. "A reputation for writing good English - like your friend Graham here - like all you Brits. You seem to have an innate command of the language... even if it's often written in an unworthy cause."

Nigel bristled. "And what unworthy cause would that be, sir?"

"Well, I think we're all aware here that your paper is not particularly sympathetic to this president, or his policies. But then that goes for more than a few of your competitors."

"I'm glad to hear that someone over here reads the *Post*," Nigel said, making a point of not provoking an argument on his debut appearance.

"Oh, I take a great interest in the British press. Especially right now, with a State Visit to Britain in the works. Meanwhile, allow me to welcome you to the presidential mansion, even if you think the current occupant is a 'preening narcissist', as I think you recently described him."

"How thoughtful of you to point that out," Nigel said, matching Frank for sarcasm. "It seems that your reputation has preceded you, too."

"I'll take that observation in a positive light. How's Sarah, by the way?"

Nigel was a little taken aback by mention of his former wife, though perhaps he shouldn't have been in the light of Vincent Marchetti's recent threats. "She's fine as far as I know. I don't see too much of her these days. I wasn't aware that you knew her."

"Oh, we've met once or twice. As you know, I was at school with her husband for a time, as was the president."

"Have you heard from him lately? Vincent Marchetti, I mean."

"It so happens he was here a few days ago. He mentioned in passing that you were coming over. Of course, I knew that already, having just approved your credentials." Nigel could only imagine what Vincent had said about him. Frank seemed to read his mind. "I saw him for no more than a minute or two, so we had no time for a chat. He was on his way into the Oval Office, and I was just leaving."

"It's a small world, isn't it?" said Nigel, for want of anything more illuminating.

Frank meanwhile had turned his attention to Graham. "And you, my friend, are off to tropical climes for a well-earned retirement. We shall miss you." He turned to Nigel to explain. "Graham's our resident expert on the language. Sometimes I'd give him press releases to read, just to make sure there were no dangling participles or obvious tautologies. He's the Sherlock Holmes of grammarians." Nigel thought he would make a better Watson - plodding and slightly dim,

"You're too kind," Graham said obsequiously. "And may I extend my best wishes to you for a long and happy career."

"Thank you, but there are no long careers in my line of work. Four years. Eight if you're lucky... or a masochist." Frank suddenly looked distracted. "Now, gentlemen, I'm afraid duty calls. Good to meet you, Nigel. I'm sure we'll be seeing a lot of each other." They shook hands. "Cindy will show you out."

"I know the way," Graham said.

"Cindy needs to take you anyway. House rules."

Frank went back to his desk but before sitting down he addressed Nigel. "We must have lunch one of these days, Mr Harper. Or, at any rate, a glass of wine. I'm told you're something of an authority on the subject."

"I wouldn't go that far. I know my Bordeaux from my Burgundy."

"Spoken like a man of discernment. We Americans tend to stick to our Californian wines. We're quite proud of them, you know."

"As you should be," said Nigel, "even if they do originate from French vines."

"And, of course, vice versa," Frank shot back. "When phylloxera wiped out the French vines, they replaced theirs with ours. But I'm sure you knew that."

"I did, but only after you'd destroyed their vineyards in the first place. As I understand it, phylloxera was first introduced to France by American scientists doing research on vines that had built up a resistance."

Nigel wasn't sure that he was entirely correct, but he noted with satisfaction that Frank was trying hard not to be impressed. The press secretary looked him in the eye. "You and I are going to have some interesting cultural discussions and I look forward to comparing notes. You can drink a subtle French claret and I'll provide a hearty California Cabernet. Meanwhile, good luck to you in your new post."

"Thank you for that," Nigel said rather stiffly. "And thank you for taking a few precious minutes of your time."

Frank took note of the irony in that 'precious' as he picked up the ringing telephone.

As they left the building into the warm spring sunshine, Graham apologized for having to skip lunch. He needed to pick up some obscure piece of marine equipment that he had ordered. Nigel, in truth, was relieved to be free of him. Left to his own devices, he wandered off to the lobby, where several reporters had lingered to chat. One was Jack Williams, the CNN man who had asked the question about the first lady. Nigel walked over and introduced himself.

"Ah, the freshman," Williams said, in a friendly manner. "Settling in okay?"

"I have a desk and a computer. What more does an honest scribbler need?"

"Native intelligence, I'd say, and a sharp nose for a story. Not that you'll need either with this administration, which leaks like the proverbial sieve. Anything I can do to help?"

"I was interested in your question about the status of the first lady."

"Oh, that," said Jack, dismissively. "I only asked to keep the pot boiling. I never get a straight answer, and never expect one."

"This president's marriage seems far from conventional, to put it mildly."

"Well, there's a great deal of talk, as you know. And then there was that *Skandal* piece last week. It raised a few eyebrows. But not mine. *Skandal* is a sleazy rag and not to be taken seriously."

"I haven't read it. What did it say?"

"Oh, some nonsense about the president being involved with a Russian lady in New York."

"Do you think there's anything in it?"

"No idea. And I'm not sure I care. Where would you start? This president is less than wholeheartedly devoted to the old-fashioned concept of marriage, as everyone knows. Including, I might add, his wife. Three women have already made claims about him, and I've no doubt there'll be more. They're stacked up like landing aircraft. Frankly, I can't get too excited about any of it."

"I see," Nigel said, plainly disappointed.

"Look, this town is always alive with rumours of presidential infidelity. We used to thrive on them, back in the days of Bill Clinton. Nowadays, they're largely ignored. The world has changed. There *was* a time when a divorced man couldn't even run for president, let alone get himself elected. But if you're that interested, I suggest you call the people at *Skandal*. Why don't you take the editor to lunch. He loves talking to reporters and he's always desperate for attention, especially from people who know what they're doing. They validate his status – or so he believes."

"I may just do that," Nigel said. "Right now, how about I buy *you* lunch. I'd like to pick your brains on a few things."

"As it happened, my twelve o'clock just cancelled. I can't do a full lunch, though, just a quick sandwich. And no alcohol as I may have to go on the air later. That's something you print boys don't have to worry about. Meanwhile, you can fill me in on the dirt in Westminster. Your new prime minister seems a little cock-happy himself. Installed his mistress in No.10, I hear. He and the president should compare notes."

"I'm sure they have already."

"Now, those are transcripts I *would* like to read - an erotic version of the Pentagon Papers. Let's go. I know a decent sandwich bar around the corner."

"Lead on, Macduff," said Nigel.

Jack ordered a pastrami sandwich, and something called a Dr Pepper. Nigel did the same. He asked Jack what he thought about the trade dispute with China.

"Well, it's a risky business, what with all that American treasury paper in Chinese hands. And a complex issue, which means that this president struggles with it. The markets are already unsettled. Still, this administration seems to have convinced American workers that bashing China will be great for business. Some of them would stand and cheer if he punched Chairman Xi's lights out on prime-time television."

"He does have a point," Nigel ventured, "as much as I hate to say it. China has been ripping off America for decades: stealing industrial secrets, dumping steel at cut-rate prices, flooding the world with cheap goods. A lot of people think it's come-uppance time."

"They'd change their tune if the stock market fell out of bed. Punishing the Chinese is all well and good as a vote-winner, but not if it sends the price of everything through the roof. When disposable income takes a hit, patriotism is the first casualty." Jack changed the subject. "How's London these days? I spent a year there with the *Boston News*. I had a great time. London and New York know how to mix business with pleasure. Not DC, of course. Here it's all politics. There's nothing else. I happen to love the theatre. London has plenty of it. Not here."

"There's the Kennedy Center," Nigel pointed out.

"Oh, yeah, the one institution in town dedicated to high culture rather than low politics. And even that's used largely by people who aren't cultured but want to be seen as cultured. I've seen senators horse-trading during the interval. Sometimes even during the performance. Those days of Camelot are long gone, my friend."

"I understand some of you guys take a dim view of British print journalism," Nigel said, changing tack.

"I'm not one of them. Our American newspapers are dull as dishwater. But then who reads newspapers these days? No one under forty, anyway. No offence, friend."

"Londoners still read newspapers."

"Well, you Brits do love your muck-raking tabloids. They wouldn't sell over here. We're still puritans at heart. How's El Vino's, by the way. My British colleagues used to take me there sometimes. Treated it as if it were a kind of pilgrimage to a shrine."

"I was there not so long ago. Hardly changed except for the clientele. No more journalists. Just lawyers. That means very few customers."

"Ah, yes, Mr Murdoch kicked you all out of Fleet Street. Are you married?" Jack asked, lurching to yet another topic, conscious that he had little time.

"Divorced," said Nigel matter-of-factly. "Two kids at school."

"Me too," said Jack. "Divorced and two kids. My two boys will soon be heading off to university. The fees are killing me."

"Tell me about it," Nigel said. "Getting back to this Russian woman the president is supposedly...'

"You really have an obsession with this, don't you?" Jack's look was close to a sneer.

"Let's just say I'm intrigued."

"Look, I can't tell you how to do your job, but if you want my advice you'll move on. Talk of presidential girlfriends no longer gets anyone excited. Not even curious. Jack Kennedy used to have his girlfriends smuggled into the White House by the dozen. Everyone in political circles, his own included, knew what was going on, but no one talked. Not a word of it ever appeared in the press. I think we've gone back to those days, though perhaps for different reasons."

Jack's cell phone buzzed. He answered it and turned to Nigel. "Sorry, friend, it's back to work for me. It seems that I've been booked to interview a Republican senator who's desperate to show that he'll be supporting the president's latest Supreme Court nominee."

"Is the nomination in doubt?"

"Not at all. The Senator's just out to score a few brownie points."

"I should get cracking, too," Nigel countered, though in truth he had little to do.

After leaving Jack, he walked to the *Post*'s office on H Street. The least he could do was to stop by for a chat with the three members of staff, whose names he'd already forgotten. On the way, he stopped at a news stand to pick up a copy of *Skandal* magazine. The cover showed the president at a party, drink in hand, leering at an attractive unidentified woman dancing. Nigel sat on a bench and read the article. It was poorly written and poorly sourced. The writer had merely referred to 'rumours widely circulating in Washington'. The entire piece, as Nigel recognized, was founded on nothing more than hearsay, but he still wondered whether there was anything to it. After making a note of the writer's name, he tossed the magazine into a trash can.

In the office, he was greeted by Joe Hart, the junior reporter, and Helen, the administrator. The other employee, the editorial assistant, was out. Joe was tapping furiously on his computer keyboard.

"What are you working on?" Nigel asked. Joe stood up as a mark of respect. He was a gangling six-footer, all skin and bone, probably in his late twenties but looking no more than eighteen.

"Graham asked me to do some research on the China trade talks. Nothing exciting. Do you happen to know where he is? I have a couple of questions."

"He went shopping," said Nigel, not bothering to hide his disdain. "You can drop the China project. I have something else I'd like you to do. I have here the name of a writer at *Skandal* magazine, Eli Cohen. Do you know him?"

"Only of him. We've never met."

"I'd like you to find out what you can about him, and how I can reach him. Then I may call him for a chat."

"Sure thing. May I know why?"

"Oh, I just want to pick his brains."

"About the Russian lady? I should say alleged Russian lady."

"That's the one. Just want to know if there's anything in it."

"I'm sure there is, knowing this president."

"Meanwhile, I'll be in my office for an hour or so, clearing up a few loose ends. Then maybe we'll go out and grab a beer. You must know some place around here where we can get a decent draft ale."

"That would be Slattery's. It's an Irish bar, about five minutes' walk from here."

"Sounds perfect. Let's go there and figure out who should be doing what around here. And I'd like to hear what you've been working on. Then we can discuss where we go from here, how best we can work together."

"Yes, sir," young Joe said, earnestly, hoping he would now finally be working for a boss who'd treat him as more of an equal, or at least someone with promise.

"And don't call me 'sir', Nigel commanded, settling into Graham's - now his - rather dilapidated faux leather chair behind a battered old partner's desk.

* * * * *

Chapter 7

Preparing for dinner guests, Jane fussed in the kitchen preparing a dessert, a process to which Nigel had contributed by opening a bottle of white wine, half of which he had already consumed. From her living-room sofa he was holding forth in an expletive-laden diatribe against the *Post*'s London sub-editors, who it seemed had 'butchered' his latest dispatch. Adding insult to injury, the editor had buried the story on page eight in a catch-all section called 'Other Foreign News'. Admittedly, the president's sabre-rattling remarks to the VFW dinner had contained nothing new, but considering the present tense state of international relations, any presidential pronouncement, however innocuous-sounding, commanded attention: at least three times the column inches allotted, if not a byline. This was no way to raise the *Post*'s Washington profile, he fumed. First thing Monday morning he would have a word with Duncan Erskine.

"Did you just say something?" Jane yelled from the kitchen, where Mozart on a classical radio station competed with the harsh grind of a blender.

"I was just wondering out loud," he barked back, "why those London subs destroyed my piece." Wolfgang Amadeus and the blender went silent. A disheveled Jane, hair pomaded white with icing sugar, emerged from the kitchen, irritated by the disruption. "I'm sorry, I still couldn't hear you."

He held aloft a crumpled newspaper and shook it. "What I said was that those bloody subs of ours seem to get their jollies ripping the guts out of a story. Especially, it seems, when my name is on it. If you gave them *War and Peace* to edit, they'd reduce it to a novella."

"At least then I might get round to reading it," she said, trying to lighten his mood. She returned to the kitchen and Wolfgang Amadeus and the blender resumed their discordant concert.

"What really pisses me off is that those boring bastards have more sacred cows than India. Graham Welbeck was one of them. I've known them devote half a page to his platitudinous crap. You don't need half a page to say fuck all!" He suddenly remembered what a parliamentary correspondent had once written about a loquacious MP: 'He rose with nothing to say but managed to spend the next two hours saying it' - or words to that effect. "Someone over there has it in for me."

"Oh, really?" said a querulous voice from the kitchen. "Who?"

"Well, I happen to know that my appointment was resented in some quarters. I could name names."

Jane briefly reappeared. "Nonsense! You're the one who keeps telling me that conspiracy theorists are idiots. Now you're sounding like one."

"I suspend all belief when it comes to newspaper politics. This editorial emasculation will become a pattern unless I nip it in the bud. Just wait till I get hold of Duncan..."

"You want my advice? Give yourself a little more time in the job. With this president and his gang, you know there'll be no shortage of sensations to come... and I mean real ones."

"Well, things had better change soon," Nigel said, tossing the paper aside in disgust, "or I'm on the next bloody plane home."

"Oh, really!" Jane said in a hurt tone. "And where would that leave me? If I thought for one moment you were serious, I'd be asking myself what I'm doing here. And what you're doing here, in my apartment, sharing my life... not to mention my bed."

He suddenly felt contrite, which required another large glass of wine. "You know, one of the things I like about you, Jane, is that you always bring me down to earth from my more egregious flights of fancy."

"Well, someone has to..."

"Remind me again who's coming tonight. And tell me, is getting rat-arsed permitted? At London dinner parties it's pretty much de rigueur. Keeps the conversation lively."

"I'm sure you'll have no trouble on either score." For the third time that day she recited the guest list. "There are two couples. I went to school with both ladies. Betsy's in corporate public relations. She's married to Brad, who's with the Defense Department, something to do with procurement." Jane ignored the groan from the sofa. "Elizabeth is an academic at Georgetown University - government affairs, of course - and married to Jules, who's an economist with a well-known think-tank."

"Sounds like a fun crowd." Nigel's voice oozed sarcasm. "Public relations, defense procurement, political theory and voodoo economics... what the fuck are we going to talk about?"

"Cricket, if you like." Jane sounded slightly aggrieved. "At least it would send the guests home at a reasonable hour." She suddenly adopted a concerned expression. "Seriously, though, will you be going out of your way to let your silly sub-editors ruin a nice evening?" She didn't bother to wait for the response.

With some effort, accompanied by physiological sound effects, Nigel hauled himself off the sofa and joined her in the kitchen. He planted a conciliarity kiss on the nape of her neck. "That, my sweet girl, would be downright rude and is not something I'd ever do in your home, least of all at our very first dinner party. Rest assured, I shall be the soul of diplomacy and discretion."

"I should live to see it," she said, thinking that they already sounded like an old married couple… and that he already sounded a little drunk.

The outside doorbell rang. Jane pushed a buzzer to let the visitors in.

"I'll get it," said Nigel, eager to show willing. He placed his glass on the counter, but not before topping it up.

"Good, and I'll leave you to introduce yourself," Jane said.

"As what?"

"A 'friend'. Or whatever you like. I'm sure to get a fierce grilling later anyway."

Brad and Betsy presented themselves at the door. Brad handed Nigel the mandatory bottle of supermarket wine. He was a large, florid man with an earnest face that Nigel thought otherwise rather blank - a Republican face, he decided. He enjoyed matching faces with political opinions and fancied he had become rather good at it. Betsy was a petite and bouncy brunette, vaguely attractive in a cheer-leaderish sort of way. A Democrat, he guessed, without knowing why. He imagined them having stand-up political arguments in the kitchen, Brad taking it much too seriously, Betsy not seriously at all.

He invited them in. "I'm Nigel. I'm a friend of Jane's. She's in the kitchen. I'm helping."

"Not so that I'd noticed," came a voice from within.

"You're British!" Brad exclaimed, as if he'd made a startling discovery. "Betsy and I love London, don't we, honey, even if it always seems to rain when we're there."

Nigel was mildly irritated, not by the slur on his city but by the triteness of the observation. "Well, the tourists expect rain, so we always lay it on, just to give the tourists proper value for money. Sorry about the fogs, though."

"Fogs?"

"We used to lay on fogs as well, but it's not allowed anymore. Bad for the health, you see."

Brad looked perplexed.

Betsy laughed at her husband's expense. "Do you live in London, Nigel?" Clearly, Jane had failed to brief her.

"Until a few weeks ago, yes, but I'll be working in DC for the next few years." He told them why.

"How exciting," cried Betsy. "I mean, what a marvellous time to be in Washington. So much happening in the political world these days."

"I'm with Defense," Brad announced, self-importantly. "Procurement officer. I purchase materials used for advanced weapons systems."

"How interesting," Nigel said, lying badly. Brad noticed.

"It has never been *more* interesting than now," he pronounced.

"Yes, you must be a busy man with this administration on a military spending spree. A missile in every pot, a bomb in every garage - to misquote another of your less successful presidents."

"Yes, I'm extremely busy," Brad confirmed, ignoring the joke, but for the first time showing a glimmer of enthusiasm. "He's raised defence spending by a third. A third! We're all hopping around like mad right now I can tell you. Just can't procure enough. I spend half my working life in California, begging firms to raise production levels."

"And have they?"

"You bet. Only too willing."

"Well, that's wonderful," Nigel said. "Now, for the icing on the cake, all you need is a war."

Brad looked at him strangely, not sure whether the remark was serious or flippant. You could never tell with these Brits, he was thinking.

Jane intervened to deliver welcoming air kisses. "Now, you guys, let's not get into politics before we've even sat down."

"We *are* in Washington," said Nigel. "What else is there to talk about? And I am a political journalist."

"Then I'd better mind what I say." Brad turned to his wife. "I think it's fair to say that Betsy and I have slightly divergent views on politics. Isn't that true, honey?" Nigel had been right on the money. He was the Republican, and she a Democrat, or at least a liberal. He was glad to see that his identification system still worked, even in a foreign land.

Betsy insisted on explaining their political differences, which Nigel assumed probably extended to a great many other topics. "Our divergences are more than slight, I'd say. He's an ardent Republican. Me, I'm more of an independent. Always vote for the man I think will do the better job, regardless of party." She seemed proud of her even-handed approach. *Another Graham*, Nigel was thinking. "And, of course, on character. That's why I couldn't bring myself to vote for the man we've got now. Terrible man, in my opinion, though Brad for some reason likes him. We argue about it all the time, don't we, honey?" She paused to sigh. "Still, the marriage seems to have survived..." she laughed nervously. "... so far." Brad scowled.

"Well, you've only got another two years to get through - assuming the American voters finally see sense and throw him out, which for reasons I frankly find inexplicable, not to say disgraceful, still seems to be in some doubt."

Encouraged by Nigel's bold declaration of allegiance to the moderate liberal cause – little did she know! - Betsy looked at her husband with an expression of resigned forbearance. "I'm afraid Brad and I part company on most of the burning social issues of the day. I'm a feminist. Brad, well, I'm not quite sure what he is… a masculinist, perhaps. Is there such a word?"

"If there isn't, then there ought to be," said Nigel, smiling benignly. "Perhaps you've coined a new one." The words came out slightly slurred, Jane observed, with a gathering feeling of foreboding.

Brad set his jaw in the manner of Richard Nixon trying to convey resolute sincerity. "Don't get me wrong, Nigel, I'm not against the feminist movement. There's a great deal to be said for it. But some of these women go too far. That's the trouble with supposedly worthy causes: they all begin well and then fall into the hands of the extremists. Look at the African Americans. I'm not saying they haven't had a tough time of it but burning down cities and looting doesn't help their case. I don't hold with that kind of behaviour, whatever the reason."

"Even if the reason is the Republican Party," Nigel countered provocatively. Brad was going to be an uncomfortable dinner companion. The choice boiled down to humouring him or confronting him. Confrontation, he decided, would at least be more entertaining.

The front door buzzed again. "Excuse me," Nigel said, glad of the diversion. "Let me get this. And then, I promise, I'll fix some drinks." His own, they noticed, was still in his hand.

"Saved by the buzzer," Brad said, predictably.

Nigel introduced himself to Jules and Elizabeth, who proffered another bottle of doubtful pedigree. "Do come in. You know Brad and Betsy, I believe."

"Oh, yes," Jules confirmed. "And for quite a few years." And to Jane, who had just appeared, he said: "Hello, dear girl. I must say you're looking very well."

"You needn't sound so surprised," she said, affecting to be offended.

Nigel finally took drink orders. Everyone opted for white wine, the default choice at social gatherings these days, as sherry had been in an earlier age. The group drifted toward the tiny kitchen, as if to make sure a bottle was opened.

Nigel opened a California Chardonnay, apparently ubiquitous, but mercifully a screw top. "I understand, Jules, that you work for a think-tank. Tell me more."

"It's called the Institute for Advanced Economic Studies," Jules said.

"Catchy," Nigel said with undisguised irony. "And what have your studies concluded?"

"That we need far more studies."

They both laughed.

Nigel stole a glance across the counter at Jane, whose eyebrows had formed querulous arches, like a couple of advancing caterpillars. The expression said, *'Is this going to be a lively evening or merely a long one? And are you getting pissed already?'*

The men drifted into the living room. Betsy and Elizabeth stayed in the kitchen, ostensibly to offer help, but also to pump Jane for the dirt on her new boyfriend.

Elizabeth wasted no time opening the interrogation. "Now, tell me, Jane darling, how did you two first meet? And when? Do tell all."

"In a New York bar, a few weeks ago. It seems longer, though, and I mean that in the positive sense."

Betsy weighed in. "So, he's a journalist. Dangerous types, I've heard. None too reliable. He's obviously bright, if a little too intent on showing it. Not bad looking though. I must say he seems to be very much at home here, Janey dear, I mean opening the door for your guests, offering drinks. If you don't mind me asking, does that mean he has a toothbrush here?"

"I don't mind at all," Jane said with a condescending smile. "And since you ask, the answer is yes. A toothbrush and much else besides."

"Well, you didn't waste much time, did you, my girl?"

"No. In fact, this is only our fourth or fifth public appearance. And yes, before you ask, we've also had sex. And, yes, it was marvellous. I've never tried so many new positions in one night."

Betsy's jaw dropped.

Elizabeth, giggling, asked, pointedly. "And where does he live, this young man?"

"Three blocks away. Close enough for convenience, far enough for independence."

Sensing the imminence of sage sisterly advice, Jane headed it off. "Look, you two nosey parkers, we happened to hit it off from the start. Since then, we've gotten along well. I can't tell you where we're going with this, but I'm enjoying the ride - no pun intended. He's a kind man and, as you'll soon find out, an interesting one. You do need to get used to his humour, and he does come out with some odd remarks, but then he's English. And he makes me laugh all the time. Will that do for now?"

The intended finality of that last remark failed to halt the cross-examination, though, and Jane was relieved when it was time to announce that dinner was ready. "Please, will everyone please sit. There's no seating plan. Just leave me the chair nearest the kitchen."

Nigel managed to manoeuvre himself into a place between the husband-and-wife academics, although it hardly mattered, since the table, apart from being small, was also round. Wherever Brad chose to sit, Nigel was thinking, he'd be within range.

"So, Nigel, do please tell us something about yourself," Elizabeth said, delving into a salad bowl with wooden tongs. "First, where did you go to university?"

He told her.

"And what was your subject?"

"Modern history… and in case you were wondering, a second."

"What a coincidence. I'm teaching American political history at Georgetown, not far from where we're sitting." Elizabeth paused with lettuce-laden tongs suspended in mid-air. "We live, do we not, in those interesting times the Chinese apparently wished upon us."

Nigel spotted an opportunity to enliven the evening. "I'm not sure 'interesting' is the word I'd choose. All times are interesting. Right now, things seem to be going beyond interesting into some other realm."

"And how would you define that realm?" Elizabeth asked.

"A dark one, for a start. A time, if we're not careful, of social disintegration."

Jane, holding a steaming salver in oven gloves, shot Nigel another admonishing look, which he noted but ignored. "You must have a view of the present administration," he said to Elizabeth, but for general consumption, "and what it means for the future of American democracy - not to mention the future of the planet, which happens to be a particular hobbyhorse of mine. Both are endangered, I'd say."

Elizabeth had noticed Jane's look, too, but like Nigel she failed to take the hint. "I have very pronounced views on this administration, and even more to say about the man who leads it. I realize, though, that I'm at dinner with friends. Suffice to say, this administration would not regard me as a friend. If I were more important, I'd be one of the despised liberal elites that he goes on about. Probably on the White House 'enemies list'. Shades of Nixon... but now may not be the time to go into all that."

"It's never stopped you before," her husband chided gently.

"Well, alright then," she said, as if invited to make further pronouncements. "I have profound fears, Nigel, that this country, as we've known it, and this precious democracy of ours, may be in some peril. Progress isn't just being retarded but reversed. That Man – she didn't have to identify who - is taking us back decades. We're heading back to the 1950s; to a time before we had civil rights legislation; before the social and professional emancipation of women; before we'd learned to respect sexual orientation. At the rate we're going, we won't be living in Washington DC but in Washington BC."

"All too true," Nigel inserted, making a mental note of the pun, happy to stir the conversational pot.

But Elizabeth had not quite finished. "If truth be told, I'm distraught about it all. But sadly, while my view is shared by many, it's by no means shared by all. America was in a sour, resentful mood during the last presidential election and this president seems intent on keeping it that way, for no better reason than his own political agenda - though God only knows what that is. Lincoln appealed to the 'better angels of our nature'. This man only seeks to exploit the worst." Elizabeth sat back in her chair as if spent from her peroration.

"Well said, Elizabeth," cried Nigel, raising a glass. "Couldn't have expressed it better myself."

Jules weighed in. "I've met the man, several times, and he's no charmer. But then I'm not a statuesque blonde with large breasts."

Brad, forcing a grin, jumped in to offer an opinion. "In the interest of balance, and at the risk of being controversial, I'd say this president, for all his undeniable flaws, gets a rough ride from you liberals. And the media, which amounts to the same thing. He's made some brave decisions, in my view, and some of them long overdue. Washington, I can tell you from personal experience, needed shaking up." He turned to address Nigel, as if a foreigner couldn't possibly know, let alone comprehend, what was happening on this side of the Atlantic. "The voters may be sour and resentful, as you put it Elizabeth, but that's because they've good reason to be. Their government is always letting them down. For years Congress has been wasting its time, and the taxpayer's money, on nonsense like social cohesion, wealth redistribution, racial equality and what have you. The voters want an end to it all. Unlike his predecessor - make that predecessors plural - this president is responding to their needs. At least he makes things happen. You privileged liberals on two coasts may not like it, but for the millions who live in between he's obviously struck a chord."

Brad's trite little speech had the effect of bringing conversation to a halt. Jane, armed with a ladle, seized the opportunity to ask for plates.

"Beef stroganoff!" someone exclaimed. "My favourite." And apparently Jane's go-to dish, Nigel noted silently.

He was upset by Brad's little address - which resembled the Gettysburg address only in length - and felt obliged to exercise the right of response. "Am I to understand you correctly, Brad, that saying things that are plainly untrue - which we used to call lies - is now to be the approved mode of political discourse in this country?"

Brad reddened but kept control, though the effort expended in doing so was evident. "All I'm saying is that, agree with him or not, a lot of what he stands for responds to what many citizens are thinking. And what they elected him for. If you want my honest opinion, that makes a great deal of sense."

"He doesn't represent the majority," Nigel pointed out. "He was three million votes short of that in the popular vote, so he hardly has a strong mandate.

"He still won the election. That's all that counts."

"Everyone served?" asked Jane, somewhat desperately, less concerned about whether the food had been distributed than whether she was about to host an unseemly political brawl.

"Tell us, Nigel," said Elizabeth, ostensibly keen to avoid conflict but also adept at creating one, "what's the view in Britain on the present state of American politics. I'd be interested to know - from the horse's mouth as it were."

Nigel lowered his cutlery. "Most of us in Britain are repelled, and I use the word advisedly. The view is that Martin Jameson's pandering to bigotry, his pathological lying, the vile self-obsessed nature of the man, is dangerous. As you so eloquently pointed out, Elizabeth, he's taking us back to the days of the Cold War and McCarthyism. Back then hate objects were Communists and negroes; now it's liberals and Hispanics. Building a thousand-mile wall to keep Mexicans out hardly represents enlightenment. I seem to remember that one of your presidents - a Republican one at that - saying, 'Mr Gorbachev, tear down this wall.' Well, this president wants to erect one."

Brad snorted. "Different context altogether, pal. Anyway, I seem to have read that you guys have your own problems with unrestricted immigration."

"Our problems are not so much with immigrants as with our loony right-wing political fringe, which seems intent on emulating yours. On any objective level, immigration has been as advantageous for my country as it has been for yours. I didn't catch your surname, Brad, but I venture to guess that *your* forebears came here from somewhere else."

"It's Kammerer. My grandparents came here from Germany."

"Well, there you are then…"

"Your point being…?"

"Only that every provocative and deliberately misleading utterance about immigrants coming out of the Oval Office takes the world a step in the wrong direction. Do I speak for Britain? Of course not. Do I speak for the majority? I've no idea. But even if I don't, I'm not inclined to join an ill-informed consensus whipped up by racists. That way lies mob rule and fascism. That's what happened in Germany in the thirties, when some brown-shirted thug in a beer hall did precisely what I'm talking about. And look what happened next."

"Well said yourself!" cried Elizabeth, exuberantly, raising her glass. As did all the others, except Brad, whose corrugated brow betrayed a mind trying to work up a suitably vigorous response. "That reference to Germany is way off the mark, my friend, and quite shameful. This country has fought for freedom all over the world, including baling out your own country against the man you've just been talking about."

"For which," Nigel snapped, "I'm sure we'll be eternally grateful."

"Sneer if you like, but your country has as many problems as ours. What do I read about these days? Brexit dividing the country; neighbours no longer talking to each other; knife crime rampant in London; immigration out of control… and more. Scotland wants to get out, and who the hell can blame them? My point is that the UK doesn't sound to me like a particularly happy place, either."

"You're right there, Brad, I must admit. But in my view, Brexit was a tragic mistake. It may well precipitate the break-up of the United Kingdom. But telling me I've got a shit government is no excuse for yours to be shittier. Governments should learn from the mistakes of their predecessors, not copy them. Let me also say that on balance I'd rather live in a country that attempts to solve its problems for the right reasons than one that tries to ignore them for the wrong reasons. I'm not here to defend Britain, or to attack America, but more than ever we need that old-fashioned virtue we used to call leadership. Or, if you prefer, statesmanship. Yes, on both sides of the pond."

"The fact is," said Brad, now working up a head of steam, "you can't seem to survive any longer without your famous bloody Empire." Brad tried to avoid sneering but failed. "I mean, talk about oppressing the downtrodden. We can't be tarred with that brush because we never had an empire to maintain."

"Ah, but with respect, you did! You had an empire, too."

"No, we didn't. That's crap."

"You did, though. The only difference is that ours stretched across oceans while yours was land-based. Yes, we exploited the indigenous population in the name of greed and Christianity, but so did you. Ours was called Pax Britannica; you called yours Manifest

Destiny. I'd say you were just as devoted to your empire as we were to ours. Oh, and we dismantled ours. You didn't. You call it America."

"He has a point," Betsy piped up, anxious to record a contribution, and without feeling obliged to defend her husband. His disapproving, non-egalitarian glare said, '*And what the fuck do you know about it, anyway.*'

Jules, the economist, pitched in with a different concern. "As flimsy as this president's grasp of history may be," he said with a professorial air, "I'm more concerned with his ignorance of economics. This rise in defense spending and those outrageous tax cuts are all well and good for trickle-down theorists but, in case anyone hasn't noticed, the national debt is soaring. Three trillion dollars, the last time I looked. That, I submit, is unsustainable. And not just over the long term. Chickens will be coming home to roost soon. I guarantee it. This president doesn't seem concerned in the slightest. God only knows who he's listening to."

"Wall Street investment bankers would be my guess," Nigel suggested. "Military spending and tax cuts always push the market higher. That's all bankers care about."

"But the markets can't keep pushing higher forever," Jules declared with authority. "They never do. We seem to forget that every time."

"This is all getting a bit profound," Jane said brightly, but despairingly. "How's the food everyone? Any one for more?"

"It's delicious," Nigel proclaimed, and stood somewhat unsteadily. "Which seems a good moment to toast our hostess, for providing a wonderful meal." Glasses were raised again, this time by everyone. "And, I might add, for being so enchantingly beautiful." He sat down, wishing he'd left out the afterthought.

"Leave room for some dessert," Jane said, ignoring the muttered accolades.

The conversation switched to more mundane matters, starting with the Washington Nationals, which Nigel now learnt was the name of the local baseball team. But the small talk, lacking controversy, soon fell flat. Nigel was looking tired, if not emotional. Brad had gone into a funk. After that, the rest of the evening seemed to proceed interminably.

At eleven, Brad conveniently remembered that he had an early-morning flight to catch. "California again, of course." He and Betsy rose from the table, apologizing more profusely than was necessary to support the fiction.

"A wonderful evening, Jane," said Betsy, before adding in a whisper, "And I do think your boyfriend is rather dishy. Nor do I mind his politics. But don't tell Brad I said that. It'll just set him off again."

Brad and Betsy said their goodnights, trying to look reluctant to leave.

"I didn't know Brad was such a staunch right-winger," said Elizabeth as soon as the coast was clear. "But then, I can't say I really know the man." Her distaste, though, was evident.

"I hope I didn't go at him too hard," Nigel said, apologetically, mostly for Jane's benefit.

"Well, let me put it this way," Jane said, sounding more relieved than angry, "I don't think he'll be back for more any time soon. How Betsy copes with him I simply can't imagine. She was one of the brighter students at college. Always so vivacious. Now, she's just so, I don't know, browbeaten. What's the female equivalent of henpecked?"

"Cockpecked," Nigel offered.

Shortly, after further pained discussion about the state of the union, and Brad's rampant misogyny, the academics left, too. On the way out, Elizabeth gave Nigel a big hug, and whispered in his ear a grateful, "Bless you."

"For what?"

"For facing down a bully."

After they too had left, Nigel sheepishly offered to help with the clearing up. "A lovely evening," he said. "The meal was superb, darling. I do hope the politics didn't spoil it. I mean, I hope I didn't ruffle too many feathers."

"An appropriate expression, since you went on at some length about the plight of Native Americans."

That made Nigel laugh. "All I'm saying is that I hope I didn't go too far. But I do have to say that your friend Brad comes across as a complete tosser."

"Tosser? That's a new one on me, although I can guess what it means."

"British English for wanker, or in American, asshole." Now it was Jane's turn to laugh. "I'm beginning to understand, Nigel Harper, that your entire social existence is devoted to the proposition that going too far is never quite far enough."

"That's been said before, I have to admit."

"And will be again, I've no doubt, and probably by me."

"Meanwhile, let me give you a big hug and a wet kiss to show my gratitude."

"Gratitude? For what exactly?"

"For an excellent meal. For putting up with me. And, above all, just for being you."

She turned to reciprocate his affection. "If you help clear the table, I'll think about letting you stay the night."

"Consider it done."

* * *

Meanwhile, across town, in a small townhouse in the Capitol district, another dinner party was about to get under way.

Curiously enough, it would follow a similar pattern to the one given by Jane, starting politely and rapidly shading into conflict. The hosts were Frank Hoffman and his wife Marian. The guests were Vincent Marchetti and Sarah Harper, recently arrived from London on what he called a 'flying visit'.

"Hello, good evening and welcome," Frank said, imitating with a nasal British accent a late television interrogator of presidents past as he welcomed the couple to his Washington townhouse. "Of course, you're both too young to remember David Frost."

"So are you, Frank," Sarah said, allowing him to take her jacket.

Vincent looked puzzled. "Frost? Isn't he a poet?"

"That's *Robert* Frost," Frank said. "But no matter. How are you both?"

"We're both well, Frank," Sarah said. "And you're looking in fine fettle yourself. How's Marian?"

Marian chose that moment to appear from the kitchen and spoke for herself. "I'm very well, too, thank you. Welcome to our home. Your first visit, isn't it?"

"Yes," Sarah confirmed, "and it's perfectly lovely. I like that you can see the Capitol."

"Someone has to keep an eye on the bastards," Frank said, leading them into the living room. He headed for the drinks table, and a glistening array of crystal glasses. "What can I get you both?"

Sarah settled for white wine. Vincent asked for mineral water. Frank poured himself a whisky. Marian retreated to the kitchen to continue fixing dinner.

Vincent wandered round the room peering at photographs on the wall. He paused as he recognized himself in one, a college snap of a dozen or so white-tied students. Frank was in it, too, he noticed, and, though barely recognizable, the president. "That was quite a class, wasn't it? I'm standing here looking at the leader of the Free World, the White House press secretary and at least four important corporate chief executives. And then, of course, there's little old me."

"You've done rather well yourself, darling," Sarah chirped from the sofa.

"Speaking of our esteemed alumnus," Frank said. "I understand you saw him a few days ago."

"All too briefly," said Vincent. "He was diverted by some new eruption in the Middle East, so I got all of five minutes."

"That's more than I get most of the time," Frank said.

"We talked about getting a round of golf in, down at Palm Beach, but I can't spare the time. At least not on this trip."

"What could possibly be so important to keep you from a round of golf with the President of the United States?"

"Making money," said Vincent, without smiling.

Sarah, sensing that the two men might have something to talk about, wandered off to the kitchen. "I'll go see if Marion needs some help."

Vincent watched her go before asking, casually, "By the way, seen anything of Nigel Harper?"

"Funny you should ask," Frank said. "He came to see me a week or so back. We had a short chat after a press briefing. Just an introductory meeting, really."

"And…?"

"Seemed like a pleasant enough fellow."

"Clearly, you didn't have time to form a proper opinion."

"You've made it clear that you don't like him."

"That's putting it mildly. The man's a complete fucking waste as a human being, and dangerous as a journalist. He's your typical left-wing media agitator. And a sworn enemy of this administration. As I told you when we last spoke, keep an eye on him. In fact, I hope you'll do more than that. He needs to be put in his place, and you have all the means at your disposal to do it. I'm counting on you, Frank. The president agrees with me, of course."

"You had a five-minute conversation and that's what you discussed?"

"Only for a few seconds. Not that I needed more time. I'm surprised he hasn't mentioned it to you, or perhaps he has."

"He hasn't. And as much as he likes and admires you, Vincent, I think he's got enough on his plate right now to put your personal vendetta with Mr Harper well down on his priority list."

"Which is precisely why," Vincent said, "I've mentioned it to *you*. You're our designated 'hit man' in this project."

Frank paused before responding, mulling over the word 'project'. While he rarely missed a sporting opportunity to give 'unfriendly' reporters a working over, there was a line to be drawn before it shaded from banter into outright persecution. He had once been a political correspondent himself and often on the receiving end of the sniping from government functionaries. Even Martin Jameson had described him as a 'softie'. Without saying so, Frank had taken that as a compliment. "Just leave Mr Harper to me," he told Vincent, a remark intended to terminate this line of conversation. Vincent took it to mean that the persecution and ultimate destruction of Nigel Harper was in safe hands, and about to begin.

Frank had never been able to decide whether he liked Vincent or merely tolerated him, but with each encounter he found himself leaning to active dislike. For all Vincent Marchetti's wealth, and the influential friends in high places, the man lacked grace. Awkward in social situations to the point of embarrassment, he had no interests beyond making money, and more than was good for any man. But the kind of returns he made for his investors - including, Frank happened to know, several prominent members of Congress - gave him a great deal of political clout. He exercised it in the shadows, of course, given what Frank suspected was the dubious nature of the transactions. At least three Republican senators of high standing had received from Vincent large and probably illegal campaign donations. Vincent also seemed to be embedded with the military and intelligence people across the river in McLean.

"The economy's looking good," said Vincent, suddenly breaking Frank's wandering trains of thought. "Not that our mutual friend gets much credit for it. The Democrats seem to think these things happen by accident. Unless they're in office, of course, in which case they're only too happy to claim the credit."

"That's politics," Frank said sardonically. "It was ever thus, I'm afraid. Always will be."

"Well, it's high time we changed all that. Especially now that we finally have an unashamedly business-friendly administration. High employment, lower taxes, soaring profits, stock market at record levels... I'd say our friend Martin Jameson has set things up very nicely. He's even bringing those cheating Chinese back into line. Come the next election we'll see who gets the credit."

"Yes, we shall see," Frank said distractedly, sounding far from convinced, or even, as far as Vincent could tell, very much interested. In truth, Frank was far from convinced that giving Martin Jameson the credit, or a free rein to do whatever he wanted, was the result he desired, or that the country needed. But that, as he had resolved long ago, would remain his dirty little secret.

Vincent picked up on his host's apparent lack of enthusiasm. "You seem to have doubts..."

"Not at all," Frank lied crisply, "but in this crazy world, things can change in an instant. We've got nearly two years left."

"All the more reason to make hay while the sun shines," Marchetti corrected him. "I think he's a cinch for re-election. You for one should be happy about that. You'll get to keep your job for another six years."

"My job is the least of it. All I'm saying is that I'm not counting chickens yet."

"I must say you're not exactly brimming with confidence."

"We'll see," Frank said again, absently, refilling his own glass.

A distant voice called out that they should be seated. Frank guided his guests into the dining room. "I've decanted a very decent wine. I'm only sorry you won't be able to appreciate it, Vincent, but I promise you I'll be enjoying it. And the food, it goes without saying, will be excellent." Marion was a brilliant cook - "even better than I am," as Frank liked to say. Vincent didn't bother to look at what was being served. Instead, he found himself wondering why Frank seemed so lukewarm about a brilliant administration intent on reinvigorating, indeed cleansing, an America badly in need of both.

Sarah, who had not been privy to their conversation, turned the dinner conversation back to politics. "What do you think, Frank, about the border wall, and all this other stuff about immigration? You know, in England we have our own problems with immigrants. All over Europe, in fact. I have nothing against them, you understand, but there are just too many to be absorbed. And once you open the gates, the trickle becomes a flood."

"I agree," added Vincent, enthusiastically. "The president's got it exactly right. He's properly in sync with the American public on this, as with so much else. The immigration issue alone will probably get him re-elected. Don't you agree, Frank?"

"Maybe."

Marchetti was again put out by his host's lack of enthusiasm. "Maybe?"

"You know, Vincent, I was a newsman once, a long time ago, and as a result I suppose I tend to see things more objectively than some. Can't help it, I'm afraid. Apart from that, I'm not convinced that the wall will work. Determined immigrants will always find a way through."

Vincent grunted. "Well, we need to do *something*. The point is that these Mexicans and what have you, pouring into the country, contribute nothing to the economy."

"Perhaps not immediately," Frank said, the closest he had come to outright disagreement with Vincent. "But they will, ten or twenty years from now."

"They won't," Vincent said with vehemence. "They're too lazy, too busy dealing drugs. And worse."

"I'm remembering that my great grandparents were immigrants," Frank said softly. "Yours too, Vincent, in case you'd forgotten."

"Yes," Vincent said, "but they were the right kind of immigrants, hard-working, grateful to be free."

Now it was Frank's turn to bristle. His heritage was an unusual combination of Jewish and Irish, but he had never felt any special allegiance to either tribe. His father, the Jew, had not been a religious man. Nor had his mother instilled into her son, or her two daughters, the sort of devotion to spiritual matters that her Catholic faith requires of its blessed mothers. Having grown up without an imposed religion - and exposed while reading history at college to the impact of all religions through the ages - Frank was comfortable in his agnosticism in matters of faith and of politics. His wife, he was grateful to know, felt the same way.

"I remember," Frank said, "my grandfather telling me about his father's early days in New York. After being 'processed', as they called it, on Ellis Island, he went looking for a place to live, and found only squalor and disease, and signs everywhere saying, 'No Jews' or 'No Irish'. Or both. Can you imagine how he must have felt?"

"That was then, Frank, a long time ago. Things have changed."

"Have they?" Frank recognized that he and Vincent were now verging on having a full-blooded argument. "Back then, the Jews were accused of secretly running the world. Some still believe it. My grandfather was thrown out of his own country and landed in this one with no more than the clothes he stood up in. Then he had to tramp the streets to find some rat-infested hovel to live in. Doesn't sound to me like a member of some secret cabal bent on running the world. As for the Irish," he said, looking at Marian, whose maiden name was Kelly, "they were considered lazy, drunken brawlers. Hispanics are now getting the same misguided rap. Some attitudes never seem to change, no matter how enlightened we think we are. Instead of Jews and Irish, think Hispanics and Muslims."

Sarah perked up before Vincent could respond. "I'm sure, gentlemen, we can think of something to talk about besides politics."

"I can agree with that," said Marian, without much conviction. "And we might start, Mr Hoffman, with your passing the decanter down to this end of the table."

"All I'm saying," Vincent said, passing the decanter with evident distaste, "is that we now have an administration that puts America and Americans first. And quite rightly, in my opinion."

"Think so?" Frank said, raising a quizzical eyebrow. "I'd like to hear a Republican president – and, yes, even this one - saying once, just once, that humanity always trumps profitability."

Vincent looked genuinely shocked. "My God, you're starting to sound like an editorial in the *Washington Post.*"

"Ah, yes," said Frank, "another media company to add to the growing number of enemies of the people."

"Well, isn't it?"

"No," Frank said flatly. "I don't always agree with the *Washington Post*, or the *New York Times*, but there are occasions when I find it hard to argue with them. I don't believe in absolutes. The world is too complex a place for anyone to be right all the time. And that includes Martin Jameson, even if he can't admit it. He may not like what the media write - he wouldn't be the first in that respect - but 'enemies of the people' is the kind of language that takes me back to my point about the supposedly sinister, all-powerful Jews, who throughout history have been served up as scapegoats for everything that's wrong with the world."

"Both of those papers, by the way, are run by Jews," Vincent said, revealing more of himself than he'd intended. Or perhaps not.

Frank was shocked. The remark hung in the air like an acrid cloud of ectoplasm. Picking up the decanter on the pretext of refilling it, he left the table. It had been as much as he could do to refrain from hitting Vincent over the head with it. A closet bigot spouting bile under Frank's own roof, and a Jewish roof, at that, or at least half a Jewish roof.

Sarah, to break the tension, leaned across the table and spoke quietly to her husband, but for all to hear. "Vincent, I may agree with much of what you've said, but I think we've had quite enough political talk for one evening." Frank, she noticed, was still seething.

Marian said nothing but she was thinking a great deal about what had just been said, and she didn't care for it one bit.

From then on, the evening was consumed by casual chit-chat, but the strain was evident, the conversation forced. The hosts, having decided with mutual glances that asking their guests to leave would have contravened the norms of social behaviour, could only wait for the evening to run its painful course. Later, they would regret their cowardice.

Finally, the evening petered out. It was not yet eleven when Vincent rose from the table, and without a trace of a smile, said, "And now, Frank, I really think we must be going. Long day tomorrow for some of us. Thank you for a lovely dinner, Marion."

After their guests had left, Frank made a rapid beeline for the kitchen, where Marion was clearing up. "Good God, I think I need a stiff drink." He poured himself a generous whisky.

"I think I'll join you," his wife said.

Frank put his arm around her. "That was excruciating. But I rather think we won't be seeing much more of our guests, at least not socially."

"After that appalling display of shameless bigotry, I can't say I'll be sorry."

"Nor me. But I may be sorry in other ways," Frank added, ruefully.

"Oh, how?"

"A report of this evening is bound to get back to our mutual friend, who just happens to be my employer. Could be my job, you know. Others have been fired by this administration for much less. I know because I made most of the announcements myself."

"Well, so be it," Marian said. "But integrity is everything. And the fact is, my darling, that you have it, and Mr Marchetti, as is painfully obvious, does not."

"If I had integrity, dear, I would have resigned. Wouldn't have taken the damned job in the first place."

"I'd happily drink to your resignation," Marion said, "but let's not be quite so hasty. Given what you recently told me, you can get more done from the inside than from the outside - at least for the time being."

* * * * *

Chapter 8

In the White House press room, Nigel distractedly checked his emails, none of them of more than passing interest. He looked up to find Ivan Brand peering down at him. "I was looking for Graham," the BBC man said. "I just wanted to say goodbye and wish the old chap good luck."

"I'm sure he'd appreciate it, but he's gone. Left for Florida this very morning."

"Ah, well, never mind. I dare say you're quite relieved to be in sole charge now."

"Frankly, yes. Graham, bless him, could be hard work."

"I know what you mean. Not a lot stored in that attic, I'd say. Still, let's not speak ill of the dearly departed. Going to the briefing?"

"Can't wait," said Nigel. "My first solo flight. Are we expecting stormy weather?"

"No approaching hurricanes as far as I know. Mind you, that's tempting fate with this administration. And you never know, there's always a chance that some fool will ask a question that gets up Frank's nose."

Nigel glanced at the clock on the wall. "Speaking of which, it's time to go."

The briefing room was filled with the usual conversational hum, but with none of the excitement of anticipation that used to precede them in what now seemed a bygone age. Once regular events, briefings had become less and less frequent of late and they were rarely more interesting than a school assembly, the press secretary seldom venturing beyond routine scheduling announcements. He was acting on instructions. The president had told him to avoid the spirited exchanges that had once made briefings at least entertaining. The view from the Oval Office was that they merely fed red meat to the liberal media, and that his morning tweets had a much wider audience. He had gone so far as to propose suspending these sessions altogether, but Frank Hoffman had successfully fought against this degradation of his role, in the process probably earning himself a black mark. The briefings would continue,

Jameson had agreed, but from now on they were to serve no other purpose than announcing routine housekeeping matters. Questions about more substantive matters would from now on be stonewalled, especially those that might cast the administration in a bad light. Hoffman was a good stonewaller but a reluctant one; he had enjoyed the briefing room banter and fancied that he had become rather adept at swatting aside awkward customers. The subterfuge had worked: fewer and fewer network 'stars' bothered to show up these days, not even the lady from Fox.

Nigel took the same allotted seat he had occupied since his first visit - the Graham Welbeck memorial chair, as he called it. Frank shortly entered the room from the mysterious door stage right, sundry staffers forming the customary guard of honour. Nigel was certain that one of them had bowed.

"Good morning, ladies and gentlemen," Frank said, unsmiling, from the podium. He was not, Nigel noticed, carrying his usual folder, a sure sign that the briefing was going to be short and uneventful. Frank confirmed it. "I have just one brief announcement. President Jameson this morning is delighted to confirm Liam O'Malley as his permanent chief of staff. Liam has been in the post for several months, as you know. As I told you at the last briefing, the president is well pleased with the job that he's been doing, and Mr O'Malley thoroughly deserves his appointment. We wish him well. And with that, are there any questions?"

Several hands went up, though none earnestly. A heavily accented reporter, whose affiliation Nigel failed to catch, asked the now almost obligatory question about Russian mischief-making in the Middle East. Frank dismissed the topic with the usual bromide about 'watching the situation carefully' More questions on the same subject followed, each unanswerable since, as Frank pointed out, it was the Russians who were asserting themselves in the region, not the United States. "Your question, sir, would therefore best be directed at the Kremlin. And good luck with that." Nigel groaned. The region had been in turmoil for centuries, and this administration was the least likely in history to contribute to a solution. His thoughts turned to Jane, ferreting away in the bowels of the State Department, trying to make sense of it all. The problem, in his mind, was that there were no easy answers because there were no easy questions.

Frank looked as bored as most of his audience obviously were. Nor did his mood lighten when the back-of-the-room agricultural correspondents started asking yet more questions about farming subsidies, or the lack of them - Nigel couldn't tell - although this time Frank had evidently done enough homework to be able to respond with a new-found authority. Nigel whiled away the time doodling on his notepad. Most of the other attendees were doing the same, or quietly checking their cell phones. Nigel thought he heard a snore coming from the Reuters man in front of him.

Having exhausted his new-found knowledge of soybeans and winter wheat, Frank was about to call a halt to proceedings with his signature paper-straightening gesture when a hand shot up at the back of the room. To reporters sitting nearby it seemed like an almost reflexive, involuntary motion. Heads swivelled to find out what damned fool was trying to extend the briefing beyond its natural life. It was the new Brit from the *Pos*t who had risen from his seat. He now had the room's attention.

"Good morning, Frank," said Nigel.

"Ah, our debutant from London. Good morning, Mr Harper. And welcome."

"Frank, I keep reading published reports, which I'm sure you've read, alleging that the president is, er, romantically involved with a Russian woman. Some of these reports have gone so far as to imply that she may constitute a threat to national security. I know you've dealt with this at previous briefings, but I understand that one of the publications in question has since come up with some fresh revelations."

There was a momentary silence in the room followed by a chorus of audible groans and a few titters. Nigel, instantly regretting his impulse, quickly sat down. Judging by the old-fashioned looks he was getting, including one from the podium, he had breached some sacred protocol. "Is there a question somewhere on the horizon, Mr Harper?"

Reluctantly, Nigel stood up again. Now he had no option but to press on. "My question, Mr Press Secretary, is whether the White House would care to comment on these reports, which have now appeared in several other publications." That much was true. The initial report in *Skandal* had been picked up by a few other tabloids of similar low repute, though none had taken the story any further than the airy speculation that had driven the original. And *Skandal'*s own 'new revelations' were nothing more than a rehash of the original. The *Washington Post* and the *New York Times* had carried nothing.

Frank's baleful stare was that of a man who had just been asked if he beat his wife. Several dozen heads had turned to determine the identity of this interloper intent on a suicide mission. They then turned back again, back in the direction of the press secretary, anticipating the explosion.

But Frank was calm. "Mr Harper, all I can suggest to you, if I may be so bold, is that you consider changing your reading habits. You might try something more plausible. Science fiction perhaps. Or if that's too much for you, some of Mr Marvel's comic books." The riposte was greeted with laughter. "Both, I venture, would be considerably more informative than what you're reading now." More laughter swept the room.

"Is that your response, sir?"

Frank's calm demeanour gave way to one of impatience. "You ask for a response? I'll give you a response. My response, sir, is the same one I gave when the subject was last raised. It is that I have *no* response. For the avoidance of doubt, that means no comment. You may ask the question daily for the rest of your tenure here, and the answer will be the same every time. For the record, this White House does not pander to the mendacious, irresponsible and laughable falsehoods that appear with monotonous regularity in disreputable and frankly sordid publications of the kind to which you refer. The fact that you've seen fit to dignify them with a question suggests to me that you yourself may be equally mendacious, irresponsible and laughable. Up to now I'd been under the impression that the *Daily Post* was a serious newspaper, and that you were a serious journalist. Clearly, I was misinformed on both counts. Now, if there are no further questions - that is, of a sensible nature - this briefing is concluded."

There were none, and Frank was in any event halfway through the door.

As the reporters filed out of the briefing room, some of them stared at Nigel with looks ranging from contempt to pity. He remained in his seat. Obviously, he'd committed an offence of some kind, if only against convention, though what that convention was he had no idea. He had not, as far as he knew, broken any rules of engagement. At an earlier briefing, he'd been told, a reporter had asked pretty much the same question without being openly mocked. Nigel may have been guilty of a freshman's naiveté, but that was hardly a criminal act.

Feeling uncomfortable, Nigel made his way back to the press room. There, he sat at his desk and silently fumed.

"What the fuck were you thinking, anyway?"

The question was posed by a stocky, red-haired man who Nigel failed to recognize. He was fifty something, with the knowing hard-as-nails demeanour of a news veteran. Resting his arms on the top of the partition, he followed up on his initial comment. "You weren't expecting Frank to answer your question, were you? Frankly, I'm surprised the vitriol from the podium was as mild as it was."

Nigel felt peeved being dressed down by a perfect stranger. "I don't think we've met."

"I'm Harrison Wojciechowski, *Pittsburgh Herald*." They shook hands. "Don't try to remember the name." he said. "It's impossible to spell and harder to pronounce. People call me Sonny." His manner was friendly.

Ivan Brand strolled past, stopping long enough to say, "Well played, old chap," as if Nigel had just completed a gritty innings for England in a Test Match.

"I'm not sure what came over me," Nigel replied plaintively. "The briefing was such a non-event. I don't know… I just decided to liven it up."

"Well, clearly you failed," Ivan said brusquely. "Unless your sole objective was to annoy the hell out of Frank Hoffman, in which case you were wildly successful."

"Have *you* done anything on the story?"

"Fuck all," Ivan said emphatically. "It's a non-story in my opinion. This president is a serial philanderer - everyone knows that, including his wife - so one more alleged dalliance is neither here nor there. For all I know, he's fucking the vice-president's wife. Wouldn't put it past him." Ivan wandered off, chuckling to himself.

Sonny whatever-his-bloody-name-was had remained, apparently bent on imparting wisdom. "Look, take a tip from an old-timer. I don't know how you guys operate in London, but over here we never ask a question about a published article unless it's from a respectable publication. That means one that you can be sure has checked the facts and quoted solid sources. *Skandal* magazine hardly qualifies on either count. And the story's been doing the rounds for weeks. Little wonder Hoffman reacted as he did. I think I'd have probably done the same." He laughed to show that he was offering advice, not a reprimand.

Nigel could only admit that Sonny was right. "Well, I guess I fucked up."

"Yeah, but not royally, as you might say. It's just that you sounded like a schoolboy asking his teacher a silly question to which the rest of the class already knows the answer."

"Oh, dear," Nigel said, sounding like that schoolboy.

"Hey, look, we've all done it, had a sudden rush of shit to the brain. You'll survive the experience. At least you asked a question, which is more than your friend Graham ever managed to do in all the years he was here." Perhaps, Nigel reflected, his impulse had been motivated by an unconscious desire not to be tarred with the same brush.

Sonny's expression turned serious. "Got time for a beer? There's something I'd like to share with you. I think you'll find it will be worth your while because, guess what, it's on this very topic."

Intrigued, Nigel had no hesitation in accepting the invitation. "Sure, why not? I'm a bit short of drinking companions these days."

"We'll go to one of my regular hangouts. Slattery's."

"I've been there only once." Nigel made a face while saying it.

"Then you'll know that it's a dump. As Yogi Berra might have said, 'Nobody goes there anymore, it's too popular.' You know who Yogi Berra was, I take it." Nigel knew the name, and the baseball connection, but not much else. Sonny enlightened him. "Catcher, New York Yankees. Later their manager. And always a fount of pearls of philosophical wisdom."

* * *

Conforming to Mr Berra's epigram, Slattery's was almost deserted. Only three barstools were occupied, two by men in working clothes eating hamburgers, the other by the house drunk, who eyed them expectantly from his permanent spot at the far end of the bar. The counter ran almost the entire length of the place, leaving just enough room for a row of booths along the opposite wall. There were also a few tables in a gloomy area in the back, which is where they took a table.

Sonny went to the bar. "They do a decent draft ale here." Nigel said that would be fine.

The bartender, whose name was Declan, nodded absently, the most effusive welcome he could muster for any customer. He was chewing a matchstick, his tongue working it unceasingly from one side of the mouth to the other. Nigel found this irritating. The pocked mirror behind the bar was ringed by the mandatory border of shamrocks.

"Real classy joint, huh?" said Sonny, returning with the beers. No sooner had they sat down than the drunk ambled over, looking for a handout. Sonny waved him away. "Beats me why Declan lets the guy in, but he's here every day." *As, therefore, you must be*, Nigel was thinking.

"Cheers," said Nigel, raising his glass. The draft beer was drinkable. "So, tell me something about yourself. Been covering the White House long?"

"About ten years now. I'm from Pittsburgh. Fifty-three years old. Irish on my mother's side, Polish on my father's. Some combination, huh! I just wish it had been the other way around."

"Oh, why's that?"

"Her maiden name was Flynn, which would have been easier to remember than my father's."

Nigel laughed. "It *is* something of a tongue-twister."

"Pittsburgh, as I'm sure you know, used to be a steel town. Now it's more famous as the home of the Steelers. That's football, in case you didn't know. My father worked in the steel industry, straight from school. Stayed in it until he retired. Died a year later. That happens a lot. I'm the eldest of five children. I've got four daughters, twenty to twenty-seven, all at college or working. We'd probably have ended up with more, but I got myself snipped - which a good Catholic boy isn't supposed to do. My wife Jane teaches at an inner-city grade school in Washington. How about you?"

Nigel reciprocated with his own potted history.

Sonny, impressed, emitted a whistle. "Oxford, eh? I guess that makes you a clever man."

"Who right now isn't feeling so clever." The tone was self-pitying. Nigel quickly changed the subject. "What about the *Pittsburgh Herald?* Can't say I know the paper. Good, bad, indifferent? Liberal? Conservative?"

"Your typical metropolitan paper. We can never decide whether local or national news comes first. As for international news, you've got to look inside with a magnifying glass. Politically, the ink runs Republican red. Our editorials sometimes make the *Washington Post*'s read like Pravda in the old Soviet days. My weekly column - called *Washington Insider* - doesn't always toe the party line. I get away with it because I'm regarded as a useful idiot - useful because many of our readers are Democrats. The owner used to be Jack O'Herlihy. Made a fortune in steel, then bought the paper as a vanity project. When he died, a few years back, his son Dan took over. He's more liberal than his dad, but only a tad. What we're big on is sport. Especially football, of course. I'm a big Steelers fan, by the way. Most of our readers probably read the paper back to front: sport first, politics second. I once told the editor we ought to put sport at the front, politics at the back. It didn't happen, but I think he was tempted."

"Where does the paper stand on this president? And you, for that matter."

"Oh, we're so Republican we'd support a gorilla if he stood for the GOP. Come to think of it, we've got a gorilla anyway. What I think of him, in case you haven't figured it out, can't be written in a family newspaper. He's stupid, morally unfit and maybe unhinged. That combination ought to be enough to hand the White House to the Democrats, of course, but we live in strange times. The Democrats can't decide whether to swing to the right or veer to the left, and as usual end up in no man's land, where you get shot at from both sides. That's no place to be when you're looking for votes. What I think will happen is that the hard left will prevail and push a candidate who's so off-the-wall they'll scare off the voters. Like the Republicans did on the right with Goldwater back in the Sixties."

"Sounds a bit like the Labour Party back home. So, you think Martin Jameson's a shoo-in for a second term?"

"I'm pretty sure of it. Whenever Americans are asked to choose between extreme left or hard right, they invariably go right. That's certainly the mood now, especially out there in the fly-over states. And in the South, of course. Moderates don't get a lot of respect these days… in either party."

The conversation rambled along this path for several minutes. Nigel soon lost interest, silently wondering what Sonny wanted to tell him; why he was sitting here now in a less than salubrious bar. Finally, he broached the subject that Sonny seemed to be avoiding. "You mentioned there was something you wanted to tell me…"

"There is." Sonny glanced around the bar before proceeding. "I'm going to tell you a story. It's a strange one, I think you'll agree, but it also happens to be true."

"And it has something to do with my question this morning?"

"Yes."

Nigel leaned forward eagerly. "Tell me more."

"I've already told you what I thought of your question. What I didn't tell you is that *Skandal* were on to something."

"Really!" Nigel was all ears now.

"Yeah. On the right track but on the wrong train."

Nigel looked puzzled. "What the fuck does that mean?"

"I'm about to tell you," Sonny paused, shifting uncomfortably in his chair. "I have a daughter, Sally. She's my eldest. Works for a well-known advertising agency in New York. She's a bright, personable kid, and I love her to bits. Anyway, a couple of years back she had this brief… er… friendship… a fling of some kind."

"I think it's called an affair. Is she married?"

"No, she was single then. Still is. But let me continue. The point is that the object of her affection was a woman. What they had going I can't say. It's not something a father likes to ask a daughter. Let's just say that for a while they seemed to have been close."

"Did you have any inkling…?"

"… that she was a lesbian. No. And I don't think she is. She has a boyfriend now. They plan to get engaged she tells me. Decent enough fella."

Nigel wondered where this was going. He drummed his fingers on the table, a signal for Sonny to get on with the story. "So far, all very interesting, but what's the point."

"I'm getting there. Sally, as I said, met this woman at a bridge tournament, of all places. Sally's gotten into bridge and apparently this friend of hers was a decent player. Quite well-known in bridge circles. Anyway, she became Sally's tutor… at bridge, I mean."

"Who is this woman?" Nigel asked impatiently.

"I'm about to tell you that, and why it's relevant to what we're talking about. She's a Russian émigré. A real good looker, apparently. I've seen a picture, and I can tell you that she is, and then some."

A penny suddenly dropped. Nigel leaned across the table and said in a low voice, "And would I be right in guessing she's the Russian lady in the *Skandal* piece?"

"You got it in one. Her name, as *Skandal* reported, is Anastasia, but she prefers to be known as Anna."

"But here's the thing. She's hardly a party girl, and she's not having an affair with the president. I know that for a fact. Sally told me the real story."

"Which is?"

"She's not having an affair with the president; she's having an affair with the president's wife."

Nigel's jaw dropped. He uttered the name just to make sure that he had heard correctly. "Samantha Jameson?"

"Yes. It seems that she and Anastasia - sorry, Anna - have been romantically involved for some time."

"Wow," was all that Nigel could manage. Then, quickly recovering from the shock of this revelation, he slipped into the role of inquisitor. "Is Sally your only source on this?"

"Yes, but they don't come more reliable than her. She had no reason to tell me anything. But we're very close and she tells me everything. She may not have wanted to, but she dropped a hint and I kind of dragged the rest out of her - acting more like a journalist than a father, I'm ashamed to say. And what she told me authenticates the story as far as I'm concerned."

"A father *would* say that, of course," Nigel said, flatly.

"True enough. But Sally wouldn't lie to me. She's not the kind of person who makes things up."

"And how did Sally come to learn about the affair with Samantha Jameson?"

"Sheer chance. She was having dinner at Anna's place - somewhere on the Upper East Side I believe. Anna went to the kitchen and left her phone on the table. It rang and the caller's name appeared. Sally saw it. She asked how come Anna knew the president's wife and Anna told her. Everything. Well, maybe not everything, but enough. Why, I've no idea. The wine talking, perhaps. That was the evening Sally's little fling ended, by mutual consent. Apparently, it wasn't going anywhere anyway, and now she knew why. They've stayed in touch, though, and still talk from time to time."

"Has Sally told anyone else about this?"

"She assures me that she hasn't. I believe her. Neither have I - not even my wife. She's quite progressive in these matters, but I couldn't think of any good reason why she needed to know."

"Why did Sally tell you? I mean, she could have kept quiet about it."

"As I said, she tells me everything. Probably just wanted to get it off her chest."

"You mentioned a photograph…"

"Yes. But to anticipate your next question, it's not compromising. Just the two of them holding drinks at some social event. A bridge thing, I think."

"How did it come to light?"

"Sally had it. It's a clipping from some obscure bridge magazine."

"So, if a reporter, say from *Skandal,* were to do some digging in bridge circles…"

"I'd say that's unlikely. *Skandal'*s good for repeating rumours but not for sifting facts. And what would it prove, anyway?"

"Nothing, I suppose. How did *Skandal* get on to it, even if they *were* barking up the wrong tree?"

"No idea. And, yes, it's worrying that *someone* out there knows something. But obviously they didn't know enough. Even so, when the article came out, Sally went apeshit. Thought she'd be exposed at some point. That's when she called me for advice."

"Why haven't you investigated the story yourself? Or perhaps you have?"

"I haven't."

"Why not?"

"Because, my friend, in this town we have an unwritten code. We leave private lives private - unless of course they involve an elected politician, and then only if he's a 'family values' man. Look, dozens of members of Congress are known to be fucking secretaries or interns, and we don't report it. Samantha Jameson isn't an elected politician, so there's no compelling reason why I should want to expose her."

"Unless, of course, this Russian woman *is* a KGB agent. It would make Samantha Jameson a potential threat to national security. Now, that would be a story."

"I agree. But there's another reason I don't want to work on it. Tell me how a father could write a story like that using his own daughter as a source… and she told me in strictest confidence."

"You wouldn't have to name her."

"I don't want to involve Sally in any way, anonymously or peripherally."

"Some other reporter could find out about her."

"Well, it's a risk, but in my opinion a very small one. And at least my conscience would be clear."

"You could dig around and find another source and leave Sally out of it altogether."

"I could. But the bottom line here is that I just don't have the stomach for it."

Nigel had one final question. "Why, then, are you telling *me* all this? A fellow journalist of all people. And one that you've only just met."

"Cards on the table. When I heard you'd been sniffing around, I was afraid that sooner or later you'd stumble across Sally's name. You're no tabloid hack; you're a good investigative reporter. I checked you out, you see. I figured I'd rather tell you myself than have you find out from someone else."

"But since I probably wouldn't have come across Sally's name, why give me the story on a platter? And what am I supposed to do now?"

"I'm hoping I can persuade you to stop digging. I'm also hoping you'll agree with me that there's no story."

"Well, I'm not so sure about that. Anyway, you can't give me what some would regard as the scoop of the year and then sit there and tell me not to write it."

"I'm not telling you. I'm asking you. In the end you'll do as you see fit. I understand that."

"What if *Skandal* should surprise us all and figure all this out for themselves?"

"*Skandal* doesn't do investigative reporting. They rely almost entirely on tip-offs. They came out with a follow-up piece last week, as you know, but it added nothing to the first one. That tells me they found nothing else, which is why they tucked it away on an inside page. I'm guessing they've already moved on. Last week's front page was devoted to a married actor who's having an affair with his married co-star. And this week's is about some pop idol explaining why he's never had a girlfriend. I'm betting they've already lost interest in our Russian lady."

"And you've told no one else about all this..."

Sonny shifted uncomfortably in his chair. "Well, there was just one other person..."

Nigel's heart sank. "Who?"

"Frank Hoffman."

"Frank Hoffman!" Nigel spat a mouthful of beer across the table.

"I know what you're thinking: him of all people. But look, Frank and I go back a long way. He started out on a paper in Scranton, Pennsylvania when I was there, just before I left to join the *Herald*. For a short time, I was his mentor. Anyway, we were having a drink recently and this Anastasia thing came up and... well, I told him what I knew."

"Fuck!"

"Now don't get all bent out of shape. He's hardly likely to tell anyone, is he? Anyway, I got the feeling he knew already."

"From whom?"

"Samantha herself would be my bet. They're very close, you know."

"I didn't know. No chance that he's told the president...?"

Sonny snorted. "No way. Frank would never betray her. And he can't stand *him*. That's between you and me, too."

"Maybe the president knows anyway."

"Possible. But I doubt it. He's so self-absorbed he wouldn't notice if his wife were running an escort service from the East Wing."

"He might, though, have become aware of his wife's sexual predilection, even it's only lately been manifested. I mean, they *are* married."

Sonny snorted again. "Yes, but in name only. They have separate bedrooms. Frank told me that. They also lead separate lives. That, of course, is pretty much common knowledge."

"What about the children? Do you think they know?"

"How? Who'd tell them? Although they probably know about the *Skandal* story because their classmates told them. You know how cruel kids can be."

They sat in silence for a minute. Sonny had run out of revelations. Nigel was busy trying to make sense of them. He was also wondering what he should do with what he'd just learnt. He noticed that the drunk at the bar was eyeing them intently, hoping that his rheumy glare might provoke the offer of a drink. It occurred to Nigel that the man could have overheard something. But they had been talking in hushed tones, and anyway an hour from now the poor wretch would scarcely remember having been there.

It was Nigel who broke the silence. "So, tell me, Sonny, what's supposed to happen next?"

Sonny shrugged. "Beats me."

"That's not exactly helpful. What's to stop me leaving here right now and working on the story?"

"Nothing at all. But I don't think you will."

"And why do you think that?"

"I just don't think you're so desperate for a story that you'd rat out a colleague, even one you've only just met."

"Someone I met less than one hour ago..."

"Or betray a confidence.

"...from someone who didn't bother to say he was speaking off the record."

"I may have got you all wrong, of course. You could leave here right now and start working on your story, but I'm reliably informed you're a man who can be trusted."

"Reliably informed? By whom? I don't know a soul in this town."

"Well, I'm not going to reveal my source."

"Fair enough. But ruthless isn't my style, even in pursuit of a scoop - although this is a story that could break at any time. And what then if our femme fatale turns out to be a Russian agent?"

"Doesn't bear thinking about. But from everything Sally's told me, this Anastasia is no more a Russian spy than I am."

Nigel laughed. "How do I know *you're* not a spy? I mean, who's being naïve now? Spies never admit to being spies, not even to lovers. Then again, you could be a CIA asset and me an MI6 agent."

Sonny laughed too, but nervously. "I wouldn't have told you the story if I were a spy. And if we're both spies, we can write a story about each other. That might be fun."

"Would Sally be prepared to give me Anastasia's address, or other contact details?"

"Then you *are* going to work on a story?"

"I don't know yet. But as you said yourself, better me than someone else."

"Frankly, I'm hoping you'll drop it, and not put me on the spot. If you go ahead, then I'll have to react."

Nigel bridled. "That sounds like a threat."

"No, it's just a fact. I'd have no choice."

Nigel was angry now. "This is a bit rich, *me* putting *you* on the spot. It's the other way round, mate. And let me tell you something else: I just don't work this way."

"I understand, believe me."

Nigel continued to put the boot in. "You knew my interest in the story, but you didn't bother to say when we sat down that you were speaking off the record, or on deep background. Just what are my ethical obligations here? None, I'd say."

"I agree." Sonny looked forlorn, and then turned thoughtful. "Maybe, thinking about it, I should have just called *Skandal*. Told them everything I know. Done a deal: a story in exchange for a promise to leave Sally out of it. That would have been better than getting fucked over by a fellow journalist."

"Well, I'm sorry you feel I'm going to fuck you over," Nigel said, standing up. He had heard enough, and he'd had more than enough of Sonny's company. He threw a twenty on the table. "Do whatever you see fit. As I will. Meanwhile, I'll see you around."

Sonny reached up to grab Nigel's arm and gripped it firmly. "Wait. Let's just talk this thing through. Maybe..."

Nigel shook his arm free and sat down again, if only to avoid causing a scene. "If you're assuming that I've already decided what I'm going to do you'd be wrong. The fact is, I've no fucking idea what I'm going to do. Not a clue. But *Skandal* has already put this story in play, and neither of us knows what might come out next, let alone doing something to stop it. That goes for me, too."

"I can't stop you doing whatever you decide to do, I know that."

"Well, whatever I do, it won't include ratting you out, as you put it."

"Sure sounds that way to me." Sonny sounded bitter. But then he tried a softer approach. "Listen, I've been thinking - and this is right out of left field, I admit - but maybe we could work on the story together. Gather the facts, and then decide what to do. I'd be happy to give you the byline."

"That's ridiculous. I don't know how you work at the *Herald*, but I can tell you that the *Post* doesn't operate that way. Nor do I. If my editor got wind of such a thing, he'd fire me. I couldn't blame him."

"You're right. I'm not thinking straight."

"That makes two of us," Nigel said. He stood up again. "Frankly, I need to think this through... in my own time, if you don't mind."

Sonny looked solemn. "I'm sorry I sprang all this on you."

"Well, you did, and you've put me in a bind. And, frankly, that's not a place I like to be."

Sonny drained his glass and looked at his watch. "Let's talk again, maybe early next week. Meanwhile, I must go, too. I've got a late afternoon flight." His face brightened. "I'm heading up to New York to see Sally. She wants me to have dinner with her and her boyfriend."

"Then she's returned from her brief Sapphic adventure."

"I don't think there was much to it anyway." Sonny stood up. "Let's talk some more when we've both had time to think things through."

Nigel watched Sonny leave and then went to the bar to order a whisky. He needed to ponder what he'd just heard. For a start, ask himself why a fellow journalist would go out of his way to tell him a story he couldn't bring himself to write. A story that would make headlines around the world, and not just in the tabloids. Sonny's desire to protect his daughter was understandable, but Nigel couldn't shake the suspicion that someone else might be involved in this strange situation. Sonny's 'reliable source', perhaps. Someone with an agenda of some kind. He ought to make finding out who his first order of business. But where to start...?

He ordered another whisky. And while he was at it, on a whim he bought one for the drunk as well.

In the taxi on the way home, one name kept worming its way into his thoughts. Fran Powell.

* * *

Two days later, a Saturday, Nigel had a lunch date with Jane. She'd mentioned, annoyingly, that Fran might be joining them. He would have liked some time alone with Jane. But then he found himself wondering, not for the first time, what Fran knew about her boss's affair, and he took little time concluding that, given their close personal relationship, it was likely that she knew everything. Lunch would provide an opportunity to raise the subject. Discretion being the better part of valour, he'd have to work out how.

He arrived at the bistro on Wisconsin Avenue twenty minutes late. The ladies were already two-thirds of the way into a bottle of white wine. "My apologies. I had to make a couple of calls. One was to my editor in London. He just wouldn't stop talking." In truth, he'd simply lost track of time.

He gave Jane a prolonged kiss and then shook hands with Fran, a cold gesture that he'd have been hard put to explain. "It's nice to see you again, Miss Powell."

"Likewise, Mr Harper. My, my, we are being formal today. I'll put that down to your English reserve. You're just in time to order a second bottle of wine. That, my boy, is your penance for keeping us ladies waiting."

"Oh, it's going to be that kind of lunch, is it?"

Nigel reached across the table for the wine bottle and poured what was left into his glass. He needed the hair of the dog. And, for that matter, the company. Jane had been tied up the previous evening at some State Department function, so he'd spent it in his apartment alone with a bottle of single malt, the alcohol twisting whatever potential plans of action he'd formulated into grotesque fantasies, which became stranger and more complex with each succeeding tumbler. He glanced across at Fran. What did she know? And was she herself wondering, at that moment, what *he* knew? He thought of the fabled Washington Lie. Since Fran was the first lady's friend and working confidante, was it even remotely plausible that she knew nothing about Samantha Jameson's affair? Fran, as if sensing what he was thinking, averted her eyes from his gaze. "Clever as a snake," was how one of his colleagues had described her. He could see why; she always seemed poised to strike. But was it one of the venomous species? More likely a constrictor, he decided.

"You seem rather preoccupied this morning," Jane said, placing a soothing hand on his forearm. "I don't know how. Somehow distant. Is everything alright?"

"Yes, all's fine," he said brightly. "And much the better for seeing you, my dear girl."

"How sweet," said Fran, beaming. "Are you two sure you wouldn't prefer to have lunch *a deux*? I have plenty to do, believe me."

"Nonsense," Nigel said, casting a sidelong glance at Jane in case she wanted to accept the offer, but she gave no hint of it. The pleasure of seeing you again, Fran, is more than I could have hoped for. A real bonus. Now, you stay right where you are."

"Well, I feel honoured, sir," she said. "And although this is only our second meeting, I feel as if I've known you much longer. That, by the way, is a compliment."

"And I took it as such," Nigel said, forcing a smile. "So, tell me, Fran, how was your week? Mine, by the way, was dreadful."

"I'm sorry to hear that, although I must confess that I'm praying you'll spare us the gory details. Look at it this way: things can only get better."

"Sadly, I suspect they might get even worse," he said, but made no attempt to explain why. "How's Samantha?"

"She's in very good form. Keeping us all busy, as usual - well, everyone in the East Wing. We always seem to be working much harder than that lazy bunch over in the other wing. You'd think, in these troubled times, it would be the other way round."

"Yes, you would." Nigel wondered what 'busy' meant, given the first lady's studious adherence to maintaining a low profile. But perhaps keeping a low profile requires as much effort as a high one.

"Speaking of Samantha," Fran said, "There's something I've been meaning to ask you, Nigel. It's the Year of the Children, and she's putting on a little reception for kids from deprived local neighbourhoods. You know the kind of thing: a few brief speeches, a presentation or two, general milling around. Next Tuesday afternoon in the Rose Garden. If the weather's bad, then in the Big

House. I'm coordinating the event and wondered whether you'd like to attend. It'll be a low-key affair. Hardly front-page stuff, of course, but it could be a perfect opportunity for you to meet the first lady in person. She doesn't get involved in too many of these things, as you know, but she always makes an exception for kids. It may not be your cup of Earl Grey, but the whole thing probably won't last more than an hour. What do you say?"

"I'd say that's a kind invitation," Nigel said graciously, aware that he was a last-minute addition to the cast. "And I'll be delighted to accept."

"I'll put you on the list then."

"Will Frank Hoffman be there, by chance?"

"Now there's an odd question. No, of course not. He works for the Opposition on the other side of the building. Why do you ask?"

"Oh, no particular reason."

She knew better and persisted. "Do you ask because you wish to meet him, or because you wish to avoid him?"

Nigel sensed that Fran may have been referring to the briefing incident. "Neither. But why would you think I might want to avoid him?"

"Just curious, that's all. Ah, but you'll get to meet his counterpart, the first lady's own press secretary, the redoubtable Beate Sanders. She'll be happy to meet you - though whether you'll be pleased to meet her may be another matter."

"Oh, why's that?"

"Well, she can be – how shall I put this - a bit Teutonic, and not just in manner. Compared to her, Frank's cotton candy."

"Yes, it sounds lovely," Nigel said, smiling. "By the way, Fran, do you by chance know a reporter named Harrison... I seem to have forgotten his surname... at the *Pittsburgh Herald*? Calls himself Sonny." He was watching Fran's face intently, trying not to show it.

"Yes, I do. But not that well. I'm told he's a good man, even if he does work for that alt-right, shit-shoveling rag in Pittsburgh. Why do you ask?"

"I happened to run into him yesterday. We had a few beers. He seems remarkably well-informed." Nigel was still watching Fran carefully but detected no sign of alarm, or even more than passing curiosity.

"Informed about what, exactly?"

"We were talking, as it happened, about Samantha."

"And what about her?" Fran's tone was still casual. Perhaps too casual, Nigel was thinking.

"Oh, the usual things, mostly about how sad she seems sometimes, out of place in her role and…"

"… and in her marriage, I suspect you were about to say."

"I may have been thinking that. But then so is everyone else in this town."

"Well, all I can say is, I'm with the woman just about every day, and she seems perfectly happy to me."

"I'm glad to hear it," Nigel said dispassionately. In truth, he hadn't expected any other response from a woman who had no doubt become adept at keeping a straight face. "Anyway, I look forward to meeting her. She's obviously an interesting woman. And, if I may also say so, if it's still permitted in these gender sensitive times, a fine-looking one."

"She's both, I agree. She's also, I might add, a very much misunderstood one."

Nigel wanted to ask why but just then the waiter showed up with menus, and a new bottle. He doubted very much that he would get anything out of Fran Powell, no matter how he tried, and even though his instinct told him there was a great deal to get. And sitting next to Jane, he had no wish to embarrass her by playing the kind of cat-and-mouse tricks he used to deploy in Westminster to persuade senior officials into saying things they didn't want to say.

"Now that you're finally here," Fran barked at Nigel in a matronly manner, "let's order some food. I don't know about you, but I'm starving."

* * * * *

Chapter 9

Arriving a few minutes early for Samantha Jameson's White House reception, Nigel took a stroll in the rose garden. He immediately felt at home there, the brief expanse of lawn and shaded borders vaguely reminding him of the formal rear garden of his childhood home in Norfolk. There he used to sit and read under an ancient willow while his mother, a keen gardener, pottered among the roses, sniffing, pruning and occasionally pricking a finger with a genteel cry of 'bother'. The memory of it set off a sudden surge of nostalgia. His reverie was interrupted when he noticed a uniformed security guard eyeing him with evident suspicion while muttering into a walkie-talkie. We live in a curious age, Nigel thought, when admiring a garden can arouse concern. Slightly unnerved by the man's attention, real or imagined, Nigel joined the growing swell of visitors, scanning the crowd looking for someone to engage in conversation. Anything to ward off that evil eye.

Many of the guests promenading in the spring sunshine were mothers with children. Most of them were black, he noticed, and all immaculately dressed for the occasion, the children in their Sunday best, and on their best behaviour. There seemed to be as many photographers present as guests, most of them congregated around a lectern at the foot of a set of steps leading to the famous colonnade that ran from the Oval Office to the private residence. A dozen rows of folding chairs had been placed in front of the lectern. Obviously, there were going to be speeches, although there seemed to be very few reporters present. Nigel approached a mother holding the hand of a boy of about eleven. "What a beautiful day," he said awkwardly, "and what a splendid occasion. And a very good cause, too."

"Yes, and a great honour to be invited," the woman said deferentially. She introduced herself as Janine Brown. "I've lived in DC all my life and I've always wanted to see inside the White House. Never thought that day would come. And now, here we are." She glowed with pride. "A day to remember. Something to tell my grandchildren."

"Yes, we're all very lucky," Nigel said, a little desperately. And the weather has been kind."

The woman smiled. "Yes, thank the Lord. I take it from your accent, sir, that you're not from these parts."

"I'm not. I work for a London newspaper, the *Daily Post*."

"I've never been to London. Are you just visiting DC, sir, or do you work here?"

"I cover the White House, Mrs Brown. "And I live in Georgetown."

"Oh, such a nice part of town. But too expensive for the likes of me, I'm afraid. My husband drives a bus."

"A very essential occupation, I'd say."

"Well, I suppose so. It pays the rent, if not much else."

He was already running out of small talk, at which he had never been very adept. At political gatherings, he could hold forth ad infinitum on the issues of the day, happy to tear a strip off the government for its waste and incompetence, but this was a non-political event and politics would be out of place. He was relieved of further conversational obligations by the arrival of the hostess, who had just emerged from the colonnade with an entourage of aides. They included, he was relieved to observe, Fran Powell.

Samantha Jameson's appearance was greeted by 'oohs' and 'aahs' and scattered applause. A rather burly Germanic blonde, who from Fran's description he took to be Beate Sanders, the first lady's press secretary, was attempting to guide her boss to the lectern. Samantha was having none of it, though, stopping along the way to chat to parents and children. She looked, Nigel thought, thoroughly at ease – and even more handsome than in her photographs. She was dressed in a deep blue suit. Taller than he had imagined, she looked fit and tanned. She carried herself with the bearing of a royal personage or a film star. Grace Kelly - who had been both - came to mind. The first lady lit up the sun-dappled garden with a radiant smile that belied her reputation as a distant and aloof figure. Nigel was smitten at first sight. And so, he suspected, was everyone else there.

"Told you she was in great shape." Fran had sidled up to him unnoticed. She was wearing an ensemble that comprised a purple above-the-knee skirt, which showed off shapely legs, and a jacket and blouse, each in some shade of blue, presumably coordinated with her boss. She looked both efficient and fetching. "I'm so glad you could make it, Nigel. And what a nice day. Made for the occasion. After the speeches - which I assure you will be short - I'll try to get you an audience with Samantha."

"I'd appreciate that," Nigel said. "And thanks again for thinking of me."

"You're welcome. I felt I owed you."

"For what?"

"For being a good friend to my friend Jane. But now forgive me, I must get back to my duties, which I'm afraid include trying to keep Miss Sanders from offending the guests."

Fran bustled back to the entourage behind Samantha, who had finally reached the lectern. Flanking her was a row of guests, each one standing in a photographic pose, with hands crossed awkwardly in front of them. They included a beaming Mayor of Washington, a short black man wearing a lurid bow tie, and by several women who looked and acted like watchful schoolmarms, as indeed most of them were.

Samantha reached for the microphone and began to speak. Her voice was soft but clear, redolent of the New England private academies that she had attended, and the confidence of someone who had mingled from an early age with people representing the moneyed class of that region. She spoke for only a few minutes, mainly about the need to protect and nurture a rising generation, the need for a good education, and the possibilities that life offered in having one. It was all boilerplate, taken from a prepared script, but she still managed to invest it with feeling, speaking without once referring to the notes in front of her. Nigel scribbled a few of his own, already thinking about a headline for the short piece he would write: *'A Breath of Fresh Air'* was the first one that occurred to him. After two or three other dignitaries had finished speaking - the mayor, seizing his moment in the spotlight, going on at some length - Samantha left the podium to mingle with the crowd. Fran came over again to Nigel and whispered her apologies. "I'm still on duty, but I'll be back."

Samantha's conversational pleasantries seemed both informal and informed, although Nigel noticed that Fran, at her elbow, was discreetly briefing her from a crib sheet. The retinue seemed to expand as she did the rounds. It now included, at a respectful distance, two bulky men, obviously Secret Service agents, the fabric of their dark suits stretched to the limit and looking quite out of place in the gay surroundings. At one point the procession passed within a few yards of him, the agents eyeing him warily - but then they eyed everyone warily. Cameras clicked and whirred. Samantha fixed Nigel with a brief and unexpected glance that he guessed was her way of saying, *"Yes, I know you're there."*

After half an hour, the party started to break up. Mothers and children, with a sprinkling of fathers, were being shepherded back into the White House, apparently for a short tour. Cameramen and photographers, having shot what they had come for, drifted away. Nigel bumped into one whom he recognized from White House briefings, and for a while they chatted about this and that. After he, too, had left, Nigel again felt a little lost, but then he sensed a presence behind him. Turning round, he found himself face-to-face with Samantha Jameson.

Fran, still at her side, said, "May I introduce you, Mrs Jameson, to Nigel Harper of the London *Daily Post*. He's now with the White House Press corps. He's only been in the city a few weeks, but in that short time we've got to know each other quite well." They had, in fact, met only three or four times.

Samantha, offering her hand, smiled. The handshake was firm. Luminous green eyes bored unblinkingly into his dull brown ones. "Welcome to America, Mr Harper, and to the White House. Fran has spoken to me about you, so the least I could do was come over to meet you. And thank you so much for coming. I greatly appreciate your interest in our cause."

Nigel was trying to imagine what Fran had told her. "It's a pleasure to meet you, Ma'am," he said, silently thinking *'Does one call a first lady Ma'am, or is that just for a queen*? "And thank you for inviting me. It's a cause that I heartily endorse."

"You have children of your own?"

"Two. Both back in England, with their mother." He didn't mention their stepfather. "We're divorced."

"I'm sorry to hear that. I do agree with you about the cause. I'm glad to know that you share our concern about the children of this country. Children everywhere, of course. They represent the future, and I can't think of a worthier cause than to take good care of them. It may surprise you to know, Mr Harper, that I'm acquainted with your newspaper."

Nigel's look expressed surprise. "Oh, really? Why? I suppose I mean how come."

"I spent a year in London, as you probably know, and became a regular reader during that time. I even sometimes read your Westminster column. You write well, and if I may say so, with a candour and wit that nowadays seems all too rare on this side of the pond."

"I'm both flattered and honoured," Nigel said, not entirely believing anything she had said to be remotely true. He found himself in the throes of a bow, before straightening up to avoid looking ridiculous.

"By the way, how is my good friend Lord Goodfriend?"

"You know him?"

"But of course. *Everyone* knows Lord Goodfriend. We've met on several occasions. An interesting man with an interesting background. I can't say that I'm always in sympathy with his politics, but that's strictly *entre nous*." She looked around with a feigned conspiratorial air. "Whatever his politics, he's a man of culture, a modern thinker and, beneath the public bombast designed to appeal to his conservative advertisers, a social progressive. The *Post* is in good hands."

"I don't always see eye-to-eye with him, either, if truth be told."

"I had noticed. Fran tells me you're living in Georgetown. Such a friendly, accessible and civilized part of town. Lively, too. Lots of young people. I wish I could enjoy it myself more often, but you know how it is... I trust you've settled in. Fran tells me you're almost a native already."

It was plain that Fran had briefed her. He was less impressed by that than by her boss's ability to remember what she'd been told - always the mark of a politician, though not necessarily of a politician's wife.

"I still have a great deal to learn about Washington and America. And even more about the job. I'm still something of a fish out of water here." He wondered whether she'd been told about the question he'd asked at the recent press briefing.

"Well, since we're on aquatic analogies, you *have* rather been thrown in at the deep end. My advice - still in that watery vein - is that you watch out for those sharks up on Capitol Hill." Everyone around her laughed dutifully. "There are quite a few of them swimming about here in this White House, too." She chuckled at her own little indiscretion. "You know what they say about sharks: they do nothing all day but swim, eat and make little sharks. I think the comparison with our friends on the Hill is perfectly apt."

"Forgive me for asking, Mrs Jameson - and I know this isn't the proper occasion - but I'd very much appreciate an interview. Your husband is on the front pages every day, but I think the *Post*'s readers would like to know as much about the first lady as the first gentleman." He had nearly said 'mysterious first lady'. "What are the chances?"

"Oh, I dare say something can be arranged, but I'll have to defer to my press secretary. I don't give many interviews, but we'll see what Miss Sanders has to say."

Beate Sanders, standing close by, looked none too pleased with Nigel's direct approach. "It can be arranged, of course, within certain agreed parameters, of course."

"Then arrange it, if you please, with the usual parameters, whatever they are."

Samantha turned back to Nigel. "Beate will discuss the rules of engagement, as she calls them. As you know, nothing is straightforward anymore. If I don't watch what I say, then you can be sure someone will make a note of it. And heaven forbid I should say anything that the politicians don't like." The smile remained in place, but she sighed deeply. "Now, I'm afraid, I must return to my guests. It has been a pleasure meeting you, Mr Harper ... and someone will be in touch, I promise."

Nigel responded with a gesture that fell between Sir Walter's bow and a slow nod. The entourage moved on, heading back into the White House by the same route that it had come out.

He had taken an instant liking to Samantha Jameson, but for all her easy charm, he felt that below the surface there lurked an ineffable melancholia. She had engaged him, a stranger, as if talking to a long-lost friend, but the soulful eyes had given the game away. This only served to feed his curiosity to know more about the real person as opposed to the reticent public person. As they filed into the building, he noticed Beate Sanders looking back at him with an expression of disapproval that carried an underlying threat of retribution.

Fran glanced back, too, but with a reassuring smile and a none too subtle wink.

* * *

A few days later, over breakfast at his dining-room table, Nigel was still trying to decide what to do about Sonny's startling revelations. If anything. He had yet to make up his mind, but a nagging voice in his head, every journalistic instinct he possessed, urged him to find out more, in case the story should start to build a head of steam. An inner voice kept telling him that *Skandal*, deficient as its editorial standards and skills undoubtedly were, had not been so far off the mark and this could have set editorial wheels in motion in any number of obscure and shady publications, perhaps even a few respectable ones as well. And while the source of *Skandal*'s story had put two and two together and made three, who could say that he might not check the figures again and this time come up with the right number. Anyway, there was little else going on in DC to command his attention right now.

Nigel put in two calls to New York. One was to Bill Palmer. Bill didn't pick up, so Nigel responded to the recorded message by asking Bill to call him back. He hoped to persuade his colleague to do some quiet sniffing around the Russian delegation at the United Nations, where he was well connected, to see if mention of the name Anastasia, or Anna, elicited any kind of reaction. The second call, for the same purpose, was to an organization called the World Bridge Federation.

After a great many rings, a querulous female voice finally answered. "Hello?"

"Hello, my name is Nigel Harper. I'm with the London *Daily Post*."

"Oh! And how may I help you, Mr Harper?" The voice, that of an elderly woman, was tinged with suspicion. The WBF, Nigel imagined, did not receive too many unsolicited calls from the media.

"I'm working on a feature about bridge. My paper has a regular bridge column, you see, and our readers are always asking for more coverage."

"Yes …?"

"With that in mind, I'm thinking of doing a piece on how popular bridge has become. What the latest trends are. Who the reigning champions are, that sort of thing."

"I see…" The voice was still wary, or perhaps puzzled.

"I'm told that one of the rising stars in the bridge world is a Russian lady named Anastasia. I don't know her surname, but I think she resides here in Manhattan. I'd be interested in interviewing her. I was wondering if by chance you knew her and could tell me how I might contact her. Incidentally, I was put in touch with you by Kate McPhee, who I understand writes a column in the *New York Chronicle*." The first part of this was a fib, the second true.

Another brief silence followed. "Yes, I know Kate. Would you mind holding on, Mr… forgive me, but I've forgotten the name."

"Harper. Nigel Harper. Yes, I'll be happy to hold."

After a minute or so another woman came on the line, a younger voice. "Hello, this is Olga Pelikan. I'm assistant secretary of the Bridge Federation. How may I help you, Mr Harris?"

"Harper. Nigel Harper. I'm with the London *Daily Post*. As I mentioned to your colleague, I'm doing an article on bridge, and in that context I'm trying to track down one of your members. At least I'm assuming she's a member. A Russian lady. Name of Anastasia. Anna as I believe she's sometimes known. I'm not sure about…"

"Anna Litovka?"

"Yes, that's her." This was an unexpected slice of luck, assuming of course that this was indeed the Anastasia he was looking for. It seemed a reasonable bet. "Would you mind spelling that for me."

"L-I-T-O-V-K-A. "She's not a member, I should tell you Mr Harper, but as it happens, I do know her."

"Oh, good. I don't seem to have her contact details. Would you happen to have an email address? Better still, a phone number?"

"I'm not sure I do. And I'm sure you'll understand, Mr Harper, that I couldn't possibly give out such personal details on the telephone without …"

"I understand perfectly. I wouldn't want you to do anything like that. But do you have any suggestions as to how I might reach her?"

"Well, you might ask Kate McPhee. They've been bridge partners from time to time, and I believe they're also friends."

"That's most helpful. I will call her. And thank you very much for your assistance."

Nigel dialled the *Chronicle*'s main number. McPhee was not a full-time employee, so he doubted that she would have an office number, but a switchboard voice said, "I'll put you through to her line now." After a few rings, a recorded female voice asked him to leave a number and promised to return his call.

It was several hours before she called back. "This is Kate McPhee."

"Oh, hello. Thanks for returning my call."

"I'm sorry it took so long, but I was in Chicago at a tournament. We get quite wrapped up in these things, as I'm sure you can imagine."

"I understand," said Nigel.

"Now, what can I do for you, Mr… Harper, is it?" Nigel went through his well-practised routine. "Oh, I see. Well, I'd be glad to help if I could, especially since you're a fellow scribbler. But the fact is, I haven't seen Anna for some time. At least a year, I'd say. She was once an active player, but in recent months she seems to have faded from the scene. I'm not sure why. Do you know her?"

"No. Do you by chance have any idea how I can reach her? An email address, telephone number?"

"Well, obviously I can't give you those details. And to be honest I'm not even sure I even have them."

"I'm told she lives somewhere on the Upper East Side."

"Well, last I heard she did. She and I met a few times in a restaurant called *Fredo's*. I mention it because I seem to remember she lived not far away. A couple of blocks, I think."

"Well, thank you, Kate. You've been most helpful. And I'm sorry to have bothered you."

"No bother at all. And look, if there's anything else I can do to help you with your article feel free to call me. We bridge types are always looking to expand our press coverage, and you're not a rival of the *Chronicle*. You have my number."

"Yes, I do. And thank you for your time." He hung up.

Now he had a surname - which Sonny hadn't been able to remember - and if not an address an approximate location. He looked up *Fredo's* website and found it. A photograph showed a small, bistro-style restaurant – Louie's in *The Godfather* came to mind - on Madison Avenue in the seventies. He'd first try *Fredo's*, on the chance that someone working there might know her, and if that failed, fly to New York and check the apartment buildings in the immediate area. He had already come up with a plan. Hoping that she lived in a high rise where there would be a porter, he would ask for her at the front desk on the pretext of delivering a package, for the appearance of authenticity a book in brown paper. If the porter agreed to take the delivery, he had the right location. But what next? He could hardly leave the package. And as curious as he was to see her, or even talk to her, he didn't want to meet her in the lobby of her own apartment building where she could turn tail and escape upstairs. The solution he worked out was to ask the porter to call up to her apartment and while he was doing that pretend to take a phone call and then vanish. The plan was far from foolproof, but he'd found elusive people under more difficult circumstances - like the disgraced former government minister whom he had famously tracked down after a week-long search that took him to a remote fishing village in Scotland.

His cell phone buzzed. It was Bill Palmer. "Sorry I missed your call, my old son. What's up?"

"I have a small favour to ask."

"Shoot."

"Could you, very discreetly, ask some of your Russian contacts at the UN, or the consulate, if they know anything about a woman named Anna Litovka, real name Anastasia. It's got to do with a story I'm kind of working on."

"What kind of story?"

"I'd rather not say at the moment."

"Well, I'll need *something* to go on, old bean." A bell rang in Bill's head. "You're not talking about the woman mentioned in that shitty tabloid?"

"Well, yes, it so happens that I am."

Bill groaned. "Frankly, I wouldn't be wasting my bloody time if I were you."

"Yes, so everyone keeps telling me."

"Well, they're right. The gutter press has gone over all that and come up with fuck all. Look, the man probably has a dozen mistresses. We know of several, as it is. Nobody cares. Don't you have anything more important in the works - like when Congress is going to get off its ass and finally pass a budget bill?"

"I can do more than one thing at a time." Nigel was not going to tell him anything about the conversation with Sonny. He liked and admired Bill, but the man did a roaring trade in gossip, especially after a few drinks, and Bill Palmer was a man known to like a few drinks. And if his Russian friends did by chance come up with something, Bill might try to muscle in on the story. "Indulge me, that's all I'm asking. I'd do it myself but you're the man with all the contacts. Tread gently, though, I can't stress..."

"Teach your grandmother to suck eggs," Bill interrupted irritably. Nigel thought he was about to hang up, but after a brief silence, Bill said: "Alright, whatever makes you happy. But don't expect me to drop everything else. Wild goose chasing aside, how's it going down there? Are you coping? Floundering like a beached whale without Graham, I'm sure." He laughed.

"Everything's fine. I'm still in the on-the-job-training phase but starting to find my feet. Give me a few weeks more and I'll be the talk of the town."

Bill was in the mood to talk but Nigel cut him off. "I'm sorry, Bill, but I must fly. Duncan Erskine has been after me. But I'll be in touch in a day or so." He refrained from repeating the need for discretion, which would only put Bill on alert.

* * *

The next day, a Saturday, he took an early morning shuttle flight to New York.

At La Guardia, his taxi driver turned out to be a Russian - a good omen, Nigel thought. He gave the driver the address of *Fredo's*. The restaurant was not yet open, and seeing no movement inside, he set off on his round of apartment buildings. He would start on 70th Street and would work his way uptown block by block. On each of the first three cross streets there was one high-rise, each with a reception desk. At the first one, a parked delivery truck outside was unloading furniture, blocking the street, setting off a chorus of honking. The harassed doorman was busy remonstrating with the driver in Spanish, and after looking at the name on the piece of paper Nigel had given him, turned away. "No one of that name at this address, mister." Nigel headed for the next block, and then the next. Two more apartment buildings were strikeouts. Passing several brownstones and walk-ups, it occurred to him that if she lived in one of those his plan would fall apart. Three more high-rise buildings yielded nothing.

By lunchtime, he was hungry and no longer sure that he was spending his time wisely. He slipped into a sandwich bar to consider his next move. He bought a bagel with lox and cream cheese and a black coffee and settled on a stool at the plastic counter that ran along the front window. After lunch, he'd try three more blocks and, if they produced nothing, call it a day; perhaps call Bill and head out to Scarsdale. From his window perch, he watched the flow of pedestrian traffic with idle curiosity.

Everyone passing by seemed to be in a hurry, an immutable feature of life in this city. Many of them looked anxious or angry. Curiously, there seemed to be far more women than men, and mostly middle-aged to elderly. Some were evidently returning from the beauty salon, judging by the immaculately coiffed hair and glowing faces. Others seemed to be exercising absurdly miniature poodles or chihuahuas. Widows and divorcees, he reckoned, and judging by the expensive clothes, all very comfortably off. Downing the last of his coffee, uncertain what to do next, he watched casually as a younger woman crossed the avenue in his direction. She was casually dressed in jeans and a blouse and wore a headscarf and dark glasses. Draped over one shoulder was what appeared to be a suit-carrier. The sun was in his eyes, forcing him to shade them with his hand, but there seemed to be something vaguely familiar about her. As she strode past the deli, not ten feet from where he was sitting, the sense of the familiar turned to the shock of recognition.

The face behind the shades was unmistakably that of Fran Powell.

He prepared to dash outside to greet her, but then changed his mind. He decided instead to follow her. He didn't have to walk far. Two blocks down Madison she turned a corner, and halfway along the block she entered a modern high-rise fronted by a small circular driveway fringed by ornamental shrubs. He peered through the front window and saw Fran chatting to the porter. Both were laughing. Obviously, she was known to him. He watched as she headed for the elevator bank.

Minutes later, he entered the lobby, package in hand. The porter looked up as he approached the front desk. "Good morning, sir. Can I help you?" The tag on the porter's uniform revealed his name as Lou.

"I have a delivery for Miss Litovka," said Nigel, adopting a thick East European accent, one that the lady in question would have seen through in an instant. "I think this is right address..." He pretended to examine the label he had stuck on the package.

"It is," the porter said. "You can leave it with me. Do you need me to sign for it?"

"No, I don't need a signature."

At that moment, an elderly, rather regal woman, armed with shopping bags with famous brand names on them, appeared at the desk. Ignoring Nigel, she asked Lou to fetch her dry-cleaning from the small office behind the desk. By the time Lou came back, Nigel had disappeared. Puzzled, Lou picked up the telephone.

"Ah, Miss Powell, were you or Miss Litovka expecting a package?"

"I don't think so." He heard her ask someone else the same question. The answer is no. Why do you ask?"

"Because some delivery guy just came in. Said he had a package for Miss Litovka..."

"I'll come down shortly."

"Don't bother."

"Why not?"

"Well, there's no package. A strange thing happened. I got distracted for a moment and the man disappeared. Didn't leave the package. One minute he was there, at the desk, then he was gone. That's why I'm calling. I found it a bit odd. I thought you ought to know, that's all."

"What was the name of the delivery company?"

"I can't say, Miss Powell. He wasn't wearing a uniform."

"Very strange, I agree. Well, thanks, Lou. I'll mention it to Anna."

Nigel, having fled the scene, was already in a taxi heading back to La Guardia. He sat back, pleased that he had located the object of his search, but perplexed by Fran's unexpected appearance. What was she doing there? And why the suit carrier? Dry cleaning? An overnight bag? Either way, it seemed that Fran and Anna - and there was now no doubt that he had found the right Russian - were obviously known to each other and had more than a casual acquaintance.

On the plane, Nigel went over the situation, from the meeting with Sonny to his New York expedition. Scribbling on a notepad, he reminded himself what he'd discovered so far. The fragments, like jigsaw pieces, began to form an emerging picture, though far from complete.

"Start at the beginning," he muttered to himself, and began writing a chronology.

Skandal. President & Russian woman. Sources unknown.
Question at WH annoys Frank Hoffman.
Sonny tells 'real story' - source Sally.
Sonny tells Frank H. Why?
"AND WHY TELL ME?"
Fran/Anna. Friends? Something else?
Anna. KGB?
WH garden party to meet FLOTUS. Coincidence?
SET-UP??? Why? Who?

Nigel stopped scribbling and went through the list. It made for an interesting sequence of apparently random events. But were they random? Journalists, like policemen, are trained to mistrust coincidences, and right now they seemed to be forming a queue. What was his next move to be? "Aye, there's the rub," he said to himself aloud, attracting the attention of the middle-aged matron in the adjacent seat. She, he now observed, was squinting at the scrawls on his pad. He put it in his pocket

"Been in New York on business?" she asked, slightly embarrassed at being caught in the act.

"Yes, just for the day," Nigel replied.

"You a banker?"

"No, I'm an *honest* working man."

"What field, if you don't mind me asking?"

"Communications technology," he lied, hoping it would be a conversation killer.

"I've been in New York for three days," the woman said. "Family business. Glad to be going home. Three days in that place is about as much as I can stand these days. All that noise, all those fumes, everyone rushing about... I'm exhausted already."

"I know what you mean," Nigel agreed, picking up the in-flight magazine to signal the end of the conversation.

He resumed his silent deliberations, all of which seemed to be leading to an unsettling conclusion.

When coincidences start to accumulate, they are usually something else. But if his list of incidents formed a pattern, what was behind it? Or was he simply allowing his imagination to run wild? His ruminations were interrupted by an announcement from the captain that seatbelts should be 'securely fastened' for landing.

Under the circumstances, he found the instruction preternaturally apposite.

* * *

On a brilliant early morning in the gently rolling northern Virginia hills - perfect horse country - Samantha Jameson was putting Geronimo, a silky black stallion, through its paces. Three times she had taken him round the white-fenced track, the first lap at a canter, the second at a trot and finally at an exhilarating gallop. Patting the perspiring horse, she headed back to the stable block.

The farm, owned by a long-standing friend of hers, had white clapboard out-buildings in the same style as the rambling, porticoed colonial-style house nearby. The setting was decorative enough to warrant the cover of a coffee-table book. The farm was isolated - several miles from the nearest highway - and accessible only by a long winding drive that led from black high-security gates set into a stone wall. The entrance was scanned by cameras. Visitors were asked to announce themselves via an intercom in one of the gateposts. A secret service agent sat in a parked car across the road.

Another one was stationed at the stables. He greeted Samantha with a nod and a trace of a smile as she dismounted.

She handed the reins to a stable girl named Meredith. "Not bad," the girl said admiringly, "I was watching you all the way round the paddock. I think Geronimo enjoyed that exercise as much as you did."

Samantha, clad in jodhpurs and polished riding boots, thanked her. Walking past the tack rooms, she paused to pat Gambling Man, a handsome red chestnut colt being groomed by Candace, another stable hand. Gambling Man greeted her with a snort and a swish of the tail. As Meredith followed, taking Geronimo off for a thorough wash-down and grooming, Samantha looked at Gambling Man and then spoke gently to Candace, who was new to the job. "Pretty good for a rookie, but one suggestion: always comb in the same direction as the coat. There, see how he likes it. Look, he's leaning against you. He wants more, you can tell."

Candace said, "Yes, I see what you mean. Thank you so much, Mrs Jameson."

"He's not so keen when you brush against the coat. Use nice easy sweeping motions, varying the pressure. He'll be your friend for life."

Samantha checked her watch. Not yet ten o'clock, and already the sun was beating down from a faultless blue sky. Even with the doors wide open, the stables were hot and airless. Outside, the secret service man, a member of the first lady's permanent protection unit, scanned the horizon with binoculars as if expecting an arrival. Samantha went into the house. Forty minutes later, the rural silence was broken by the unmistakable whir of helicopter blades. The security man, watching a distant speck getting larger, adopted a full-alert posture, largely by doing nothing except tightening a few muscles. The chopper was soon a recognizable object as it descended onto a nearby helipad. The pilot left the engine running. Some of the horses, slightly alarmed, pawed at the ground.

Samantha emerged from the main house, showered and changed. She wore dark designer slacks and a fetching peach coloured blouse. Her hair, still wet, glinted in the sun.

"Ready when you are Ma'am," the agent told her.

"Thanks, Mike," she said. "I'm all set to go. Phew, it's a warm one."

"They say it's going to get even hotter, Ma'am."

She called over to the stable girls. "Thank you, Meredith. Thank you, Candace. You've looked after me very well as usual. Now you take care of those horses. Tell them I'll be back when I can."

She headed for the helicopter at a trot, instinctively ducking under the rotating blades. Standing by the lowered steps, a hand extended to help her aboard, was Fran Powell. "Hi, Fran, thanks for picking me up."

As soon as they were both belted in, the helicopter seemed to hover uncertainly for a few seconds, and then reluctantly lurched into the air as if yanked by an unseen hand.

"What's new?" Samantha asked, raising her voice to counteract the noise from the blades. "How was our friend in New York?"

"She's fine. Looking forward to seeing you tonight." Fran briefed Samantha on various matters, none of them pressing. She then paused, as if trying to think of how to broach the next subject. "I suppose I ought to tell you something else. There was an odd incident in New York. A minor one, and probably nothing, but I thought I ought to mention it."

"An incident? What kind of incident?" Samantha looked and sounded concerned.

"Yesterday, about lunchtime, a delivery man showed up at the apartment building with a package for Anna. Lou, who was on the desk that day, said he had to pop into his office for something and when he came back the delivery man had disappeared. Took the package with him. Lou thought it odd and called to tell me."

"Odd, I agree, but maybe the delivery man suddenly realized he'd got the wrong address."

"No, he mentioned Anna's name."

"I see. What was the name of the delivery company?"

"The man didn't say, and Lou didn't ask. He wasn't wearing a uniform. Lou mentioned that he had a thick foreign accent, possibly Russian he thought. A little strange, don't you think?"

"Oh, I'm sure there's a reasonable explanation."

"But it could have been a reporter," Fran said, "trying to find out if Anna was in. *Skandal* maybe. I wouldn't put it past them. That's the only thing I can think of."

"That would be worrying. But so far, they've been barking up the wrong tree."

"That doesn't mean they haven't suddenly found the right one."

"True. But you know what, there's nothing we can do about it. We just need to stay vigilant. And stick to the plan."

*\ *\ *

That afternoon, on Manhattan's East Side, Samantha's taxi pulled up outside a gray, vaguely art-deco building on Park Avenue. It was raining hard, and a doorman ran over with an umbrella. She took an elevator to the fifth floor and entered an office with a small vestibule. A receptionist greeted her with a smile of recognition. "Dr Wexler will be with you in five minutes," she said. "Please take a seat."

Samantha sat on the only one available, picked up a copy of *Psychology Today* from a side table and flipped through the pages rather aimlessly. The promised five minutes later, Aaron Wexler appeared and, after shaking hands, ushered her into his office. It was furnished like a study, two of the walls lined with books. Wexler guided Samantha to a comfortable faux leather armchair, and parked himself in its twin, separated by a low table, on which more books were stacked up. The blinds were closed, and the only light in the room came from a table lamp that cast a gentle, suffused glow. Everything - the soft furnishings, the dim lighting - had all been arranged to create a serene atmosphere that would put patients at their ease. Wexler himself, a man in his fifties, was dressed casually in slacks and an open-necked shirt.

"Pity about the weather," Wexler said. "I was looking forward to one of our walk-and-talk sessions." Occasionally, weather permitting, he would conduct a consultation in Central Park, between strenuous intervals of jogging or exercising. Starting as an experiment, these al fresco appointments had become something of a fad. They had not proved to be suitable for Samantha Jameson, as they forced her to adopt some form of disguise, and required the attendance of a secret service agent, although Wexler had never noticed one.

"So, what would you like to talk about today?" he asked, leaning back in his chair, folding his hands in his lap. On the table lay a pen and a yellow legal pad, but Wexler rarely took notes in the presence of a patient. Some found it intimidating, as if they were being interrogated by a journalist or a detective.

"I don't know," said Samantha rather dreamily. "Anything and everything."

"Well, where would *you* like to start?"

"If we start at the beginning, we might be here all night, and I have a dinner date. Anyway, we went over much of my early life at our last session."

Wexler sat back in his chair, steepled his fingers, and placed a foot on the edge of the table, a position designed to contribute to a relaxed mood. "Well then, why don't we start with the current situation? I'd like to hear more of your life in the White House. And why you find it so... I think the word you used was 'excruciating'."

"I don't remember using it, but excruciating will do. I can think of less polite terms."

"Why do you find it such an ordeal?" Aaron's voice was soft, emollient.

"Where to begin...? Let me put it in theatrical terms: I'm performing a bit part in a stage play, but I'm under scrutiny as if I were the lead. I wasn't elected and I don't participate in the political process. So why am I the one in the spotlight?"

"That kind of attention goes with the territory," Wexler said. "Or so some would say."

"That may be so. But it gets to me sometimes...make that all the time. I'm supposed to play the role of dutiful first lady when the last thing I feel is dutiful. It will come as no surprise when I tell you that I'm not in sympathy with the policies of this administration. I'm also supposed to be a dutiful wife, and the same thing applies. Everyone knows the score, of course, including my own children, as much as I try to shield them from the realities. The plain truth is, I'm living a lie - about my marriage and about my social views. My whole personality has been subsumed into this lie. And all the while I'm watched by people who seem to be waiting for me - daring me - to break down, or forget my lines, or rush from the stage in tears. I'm constantly having to smile when all I feel like doing is crying. It's... I don't know what word to use... demeaning. It's also, I might add, exhausting."

Aaron nodded. "Go on."

"It also won't surprise you to know that my husband doesn't even notice. Even if he did, he wouldn't care. Oddly enough, it works to my advantage. I no longer need or want his attention. I've come to realize that his indifference is the one useful contribution he makes to our marriage. As you've no doubt picked up in the media, we have little to do with each other these days, professionally or socially. Or, I might add, intimately." She paused to take a handkerchief from her bag. Dr Wexler assumed a professional look of concern, but she assured him with a wave of the hand that she was fine. "It's alright, Aaron, I'm not going to cry here. I'm just blowing my nose. I think I may have a cold coming on."

"Crying can be a release sometimes. Like opening a valve."

"Oh, this valve is switched to open most of the time." She smiled mirthlessly. "Never in public, of course. That, as the English might say, would never do."

"You can do and say what you like in this office. You can cry. You can even shout. You're here because you can be yourself. I'm here to allow you to be yourself."

"I know. I think it's the lack of personal freedom that gets to me as much as anything. The only time I feel free is when I'm out riding. I'm doing more of that these days than public duty or good manners allow. At this rate I'll become bow-legged." She paused to reflect on the matter of what might happen to her legs.

Dr Wexler said nothing himself for a few moments and then quietly said, "Do you feel like going on?"

"Yes. Then there are the ever-present bodyguards, the need always to announce in advance where I'm going and what I'm doing. Worse is the pretense that my energies are being expended to some useful purpose. I hate to sound so plaintive, Aaron, but that's how I feel. When I'm with the president in public I'm merely a decorative appendage. When I'm supposed to represent him, I can only do it through gritted teeth. Thank God I have a good dentist."

"You must have anticipated what public life would be like." Aaron's tone was again gentle enough not to sound critical. "And you're probably not the first to experience these conflicts."

"I had no idea when I married him that he'd run for office, let alone the highest office in the land. He was a businessman, and I'd never heard him utter a word about politics. And when he did run, not in my wildest dreams - sleeping and waking - did I expect him to win. Nor did he, although he'd be the last to admit it. By the way, he's still a businessman first and a politician second. Business expands his wealth; politics swells his ego. People say he's an unusual president. Don't make me laugh. He's not a president; he's the head of a commercial enterprise that operates from the Oval Office. He ran for president to boost his brand. I still haven't recovered from the shock of his election. Sadly, it seems, the country has."

"You're not the first presidential wife to go through this... ordeal."

"Well, apparently they handled it better than I have."

"Not all of them. Betty Ford didn't."

"She's the exception that proves the rule. Some first ladies, I'm told, enjoyed the role, only too glad and proud to serve their husbands. I don't fall into that category. Nor do I wish to end up, like poor Mrs Ford, in a drying-out clinic."

"Have you thought about taking up a worthy cause? Something you could really get stuck into. Something to put your stamp on. Most first ladies have. The last time we met you mentioned certain favourite charities…"

Samantha accepted the implied criticism. "You make a good point, Aaron, and there are several charities that are close to my heart. But there's one overriding problem: most of them would bring me into direct conflict with the ethos of this administration. They're considered subversive, even treasonable." She smiled, wanly.

"What's amusing?"

"I realized, as I was saying it, that I used the words 'ethos' and 'administration' in the same sentence. This administration has no ethos. Except, of course, greed. Can greed be an ethos?"

Dr Wexler, a registered Democrat, was no admirer of the president himself and silently agreed with her with the slightest of sympathetic nods. "I see the nature of the problem."

"But what about the solution?"

"I don't have one, I'm afraid. I'll give the matter further thought. We both will."

"Forgive me, Aaron, if I find that statement a trifle disappointing."

"I'm sorry about that. But I can't solve problems that lie outside my professional domain. I think you understand that. All I can do is listen, and then help put you in the right frame of mind that allows you to think your way through them with clarity and confidence."

Samantha exhaled a sigh of resignation. "I know, I know…"

"Meanwhile, let's go back to an earlier stage of your life. I'd like to hear more about your childhood."

"Didn't we go over all that the last time I was here?"

"Briefly. But tell me more. Something fresh may occur to you that might stimulate you and interest me. Something we both missed. Would you say it was a happy childhood?"

"A perfectly pleasant one. Also, a very privileged one. There were no juvenile traumas. No abuse. Nothing of that kind. A few temper tantrums, perhaps. I can't help thinking that I'd be a very different person if there *had* been some trauma. I was an only child, of course. Does that give you something to chew on?" Samantha sounded testy.

"I'm not sure why you'd think that."

"Don't you have something called the only-child syndrome?"

"That's a myth," Wexler said. "Something the Victorians believed in. We now see more complexity in these matters than they did, but thanks for the tip. Now, do continue."

"I grew up, as you know, on a horse farm in Connecticut. A big spread, fifty acres or more, in the back country, a few miles outside Greenwich. Oddly enough, neither of my parents had much interest in horses."

"Then why buy a horse farm?"

"They loved the property, which at the time was a working farm. My mother was an academic, a serious and intelligent woman, and at her happiest teaching class. My father was an investment banker, and a very successful one, so his principal interest was in making money. They couldn't have been more different."

"Did they get along?"

"Yes, but at a distance. Most days, my father went to Wall Street early in the morning before I was up and came back late in the evening - if at all - after I'd gone to bed. He also travelled a great deal. I'm not complaining about that, you understand, but I can't help thinking sometimes that *their* marriage in many ways finds echoes in my own, only much more so."

"But for all the differences in style and temperament, would you say it was a happy marriage. Theirs, not yours."

"I suppose so, although I've often wondered why. I rarely saw any displays of affection between them. I was closer to my mother, perhaps because I saw more of her. He was a somewhat remote figure, often absent at crucial times. I suspect now - even if I didn't at the time - that he had affairs. If he did, my mother seemed unaware of them. Or perhaps she just put up with them. A child has no way of knowing these things. And I was probably too busy with my horses to notice. At seven or eight I was taking riding lessons just about every day. I was proficient at an alarmingly precocious age. Tell the truth, I had more horses than friends. That may still be true. Unlike people, horses never give me a hard time."

For the first time, she noticed, Wexler was writing something on his pad.

"Ah, I've said something revealing," Samantha deduced. "The stuff about horses and friends, no doubt."

Wexler smiled. "You just keep talking and leave me to take the notes. That's how this works. What about school?"

"I went to the best. Two of them. Both private, both very exclusive, and both no doubt terribly expensive. They were the kind of schools that like to call themselves Academies."

"You were a good student, or indifferent?"

"I was always in the top ten in my class, sometimes the top five. I loved languages. I spoke fluent French and Spanish before I was out of my teens. Polished them up later in Europe. I was also into sports. Mainly hockey. Soccer, too. Much later golf, which I still love. The academic skills I suppose I inherited from my mother, who taught at UConn, and sport from my dad, who played football at Yale and rowed."

"Both are deceased, you mentioned."

"My father had a fatal heart attack at the office, fifteen years ago this year. My mother died just last year. Ovarian cancer. Anyway, in summary, they gave me a happy childhood that lacked for nothing, least of all materially. You could call it idyllic: horses, golf, pool parties, tennis weekends at the Round Hill Club, winter trips to the Caribbean, ski trips to Aspen. What child wouldn't be happy with all that?"

"You might be surprised."

"Well, I can't speak for others, but I was happy. But the more I look back at my life, the more it seems like a wasted one: all that unearned privilege in a world quite unrelated to real existence."

She looked at Wexler, expecting a reaction, but his face was expressionless. "And after school…?"

"I went to university. Ivy League, of course. Cornell. I thrived there, too, and even enjoyed it, though the winters can be severe up there in the frozen tundra of upstate New York. I graduated with a bachelor's degree in history. After that, I took off for Europe and took a post-grad at UCL in London. Modern history. I also spent a year at the Sorbonne in Paris, which if nothing else allowed me to perfect my French, not that I've done anything with it. I sometimes wish I had, but somehow never got around to deciding what. You could have called me a playgirl."

"Did you ever have any ambition? For anything? Make that the present tense if you like."

"Ambition, now there's a much-reviled word. Show too much and you're ruthless, show too little and you're lazy. I suppose, if I'm honest, I was too busy swanning around Europe, having fun, dating interesting men - and women - to take anything seriously. See, I *was* a playgirl."

"I would never have guessed," Wexler said, and immediately regretted it. "I didn't mean…"

"Oh, you can say what you're thinking, Aaron. I don't mind. And it's only fair since that's exactly what I'm doing."

"We're here to talk about what *you're* thinking, not me. Now, where were we…?"

"I was talking about my lost years as playgirl of the western world."

"Lost years?"

"Well, they weren't exactly productive."

"But you enjoyed them all the same, it seems."

"At the time, yes. But you can have only so much fun. Then it starts to pall. Takes a physical toll. Well, it did for me."

"And when that happened…?"

"I came home. The prodigal daughter returned. I'd had enough of frivolity. Time, I thought, to do something serious with my life. But what that might be I had no idea. Another was that, financially, I didn't have to work. Then, of course, I met *him*." The 'him' came out underlined.

"So, you never had a yen to pursue a serious career… in business, or law, or politics, or whatever?"

"Well, I wasn't interested in making money. There was plenty of that in my trust funds. I'd have been hopeless in business anyway. The law didn't appeal to me. Lawyers are now coming off a production line that Honda would be proud of. As for power, my ego wasn't big enough."

"So, what happened in the period between your coming home and arriving in this office?"

"Well, marriage and kids. Sadly, not much else to shout about."

"Do you consider yourself a good mother? A good wife?"

"A good mother, I think. We know the answer to the second question."

"What interests did you pursue outside marriage? Or perhaps I should say wished you'd pursued?"

"All too few. I'm always interested in the challenging social issues of the day. I still am, more than ever. I don't think of myself as a feminist, but I regret the seriously under-represented role women play in the higher reaches of society. Also, I worry about America's racial tensions, and their impact on the underprivileged. Somehow, though, I allowed myself to be sidetracked. Those early years swanning about Europe were a blast. I thought about staying there permanently. I seem to have a greater affinity with Europeans than with Americans. Despite all the wars and revolutions - or perhaps because of them - Europeans seem to have a more balanced view of history. We Americans always seem to feel we've got more of a point to prove. We spend our lives trying to figure out how to achieve the American Dream, which may be translated as getting filthy rich. If you're not rich in this world, you're a failure. The European men I dated were more sophisticated. More sensitive. And more subtly macho - except for the Italians. All those qualities I've mostly found lacking in the American male.

"Yet you finished up marrying one…"

"Yes, to my everlasting regret."

"What was it that attracted you to him in the first place?"

"Damned if I can remember. We met at a cocktail party in DC. A Republican Party fund-raiser, would you believe. Funny thing is, I only went to keep a friend company. Some friend!"

"But something must have attracted you to him at that time."

"Well, he had an earthy kind of charm. He was lively and outgoing. He introduced me to a great many aspects of life with which, for all my privileged upbringing, I'd been unfamiliar. He had oodles of money, of course, and for a while we had a life of uninterrupted fun. I think I became corrupted by our hedonistic lifestyle. Thinking back on it now, it was entirely out of character. Meanwhile I got pregnant. And then we got married. And then another child came along a couple of years later. Children changed me. My social conscience returned from purdah. He didn't change, of course. He'll never change."

"Was he… is he, a good father?"

"Yes. To the extent that he can spare the time, he dotes on them."

"Those lost ideals you mentioned: obviously you've now found them. That means there's still time to make up for lost time."

"I'm thinking about it, believe me. Every day."

"Even hobbies might help."

"Funny you should mention it. I took up bridge a few months ago. I have a great teacher. She lives in New York… just a few blocks from here, as it happens."

"Can we talk about a subject we haven't mentioned? I mean sex."

Samantha shifted uncomfortably in her chair. "Nothing going on there, at least not in *our* bed. And before you ask, he doesn't have a problem in that department. Far from it. I'm told by people who know about these things that he puts it about all over the place."

"That must be difficult for you …"

"Not anymore. The only inconvenience now is pretending that I care."

"Where does that leave the marriage?"

"On the rocks, I'd say."

"Is divorce an option?"

"Ah, now there's a question. I don't have a ready answer. It wouldn't be pretty, given that he's President of the United States. Nor would it be easy since he's got his re-election prospects to consider. He's a powerful and wealthy man. He has an ego more active than his Johnson. He won't just roll over." She stared at Wexler with a searching look. "Quite a pickle I'm in, wouldn't you say?"

"Well, we just have to figure a way for you to get out of it, don't we."

Samantha grunted.

"Getting back to sex… We know, or at least suspect, that he's been exercising his libido. But how about you?"

Samantha, for the first time, felt embarrassed.

"I believe that what you're asking, Aaron, in plain English, is whether I've had affairs?"

"Have you?"

She paused to gather her thoughts. "Yes. But affair singular. And current. I have a lover. Here in New York."

"Is he unattached?"

"Yes. But I must modify the pronoun. It's a 'she'."

"I see. And is this romance going anywhere, do you think?"

"I like to think so, although we've already touched on a few of the obstacles."

"What can you tell me about her."

"She's Russian, in my age bracket, clever and beautiful. She's also warm and caring, genuinely interested in me as a person, as I am in her." Samantha laughed out loud. "You're the first person I've told. Well, the fourth, now that I think about it. Thanks to you, Aaron, I'm now out of the closet, as we now say of the love that dare not speak its name."

"Well, not quite out. You see, I can't tell anyone under the rules of patient confidentiality."

"Good point."

"And does this person return your obvious affections in full measure?"

"I believe she does. I know she does."

"I have no judgment to make in such matters, of course, but since you're married to a prominent public figure, I can only presume that this relationship is a carefully guarded secret, from your husband but also from others."

"Yes, to both."

"Does maintaining this secrecy contribute to your emotional stress?"

"Yes, of course."

"And how well do you think you're coping with it?"

"As well as can be expected, which is to say not terribly well."

"That might well explain a great deal about your present level of anxiety. We need to talk about this aspect of your life at greater length. A matter of the heart is, if you'll forgive the quip, often the heart of the matter. But not now, because I'm afraid we've no time left…." Aaron stood up. "We should talk again soon."

"I'd appreciate that," said Samantha, who had also stood up and now slipped into the raincoat he held for her. "I do feel a measure of relief being able to talk this through with another human being."

"Which is precisely what I'm here for, Samantha." Wexler opened his desk diary. "When would be convenient for you? I have a couple of openings next week. Tuesday or Thursday would be best, I see."

"I'll be in New York next Tuesday. Late afternoon would be better."

"Four, if that suits you."

"It does," she said, standing. "And thank you, Aaron. As ever. I look forward to seeing you then."

* * * * *

Chapter 10

Back home after his interesting expedition to New York, Nigel poured a stiff drink and sat down at the dining room table. Opening his laptop, he typed the notes he'd scribbled on the plane. Adding fresh comments as he went along, he started to write a story about what he'd learnt, just to see how it might look in cold print. He failed to get much beyond a couple of opening paragraphs - and only then after several attempts. The more he reflected on what he was writing the less enthusiasm he had for the task. He had the framework of a story, but no solid peg to hang it on. The first lady's adultery might excite public prurience, but that was more the province of a supermarket tabloid, unworthy of a quality broadsheet. A threat to national security, real or potential, would be a peg, but he had no proof that Anastasia was a Russian agent; she might be nothing more than one of millions of American citizens of Russian extraction going about their legitimate business. Nor did the moral angle appeal to him, least of all that it would draw a frenzied censure from the alt-righters and evangelists, the voters who made up a large proportion of Martin Jameson's electoral base. Nigel Harper basked in his righteous objections: he was neither the kind of man nor the kind of journalist to stir up a scandal for no better motives than titillation or stirring outrage from the kind of people he despised. And even if there were more to this tale than met the eye, as he suspected there might be, he had no evidence for it, much less proof.

Unable to continue, and feeling tired, Nigel snapped the laptop shut. That left one unresolved decision: what to do next. The first option was to do nothing and forget the whole sorry business. But he still had a nagging feeling that someone had been playing him like the proverbial fiddle, and the fact that he couldn't work out who or why only kept it alive. After much thought, and two tumblers of whisky, the immediate way forward became clear. He needed to find out who knew what, and what the game was. And the only way to do that, if only for his own peace of mind, was to wheedle it out of one of the three characters in the drama. But which one? Not Samantha Jameson, who was, after all, the first lady and unlikely to be wheedled. Fran Powell, then, or Frank Hoffman, or his new friend Sonny whatever-his-name-was.

The obvious candidate was Fran Powell. She was the person closest to Samantha Jameson and she liked to talk. She also liked to drink. That combination, in Nigel's experience, usually produced unguarded responses, even in hardened professionals and seasoned drinkers. He resolved to call her first thing in the morning.

One remaining question bothered him. What, if anything, did Jane know?

If Fran had told anyone it would have been her best friend. That would make Jane a co-conspirator, if only an unwitting one. But Jane wasn't the kind of person who'd betray a confidence, even under torture, so that ruled her out as a source. And Fran had no doubt reminded her that she was consorting with a journalist. *'They can be tricky and ruthless in pursuit of a story. They can't help it. It's in their bones, you see.'*

Sure enough, Nigel was already trying to work out how he might deploy some of the tricks of his trade to get Jane to cough up information without her realizing that she was doing it. He paused, though, to consider the consequences for their relationship if she were to discover what he was up to. Better, then, to ask her point blank even if it meant telling her everything. But he'd rather keep her out of whatever it was that he'd got himself into, at least for the time being. Nigel, in short, was a man in a quandary. But he needed to resolve it quickly because he and Jane had a dinner date that evening. Meanwhile, he decided on a safer course: pour another drink.

His cell phone buzzed. It was Bill Palmer. He had nothing substantive to report, he said, but he'd picked up a 'few morsels' over drinks with one of his contacts at the Russian consulate.

"Is it wise to talk on the phone?" Nigel asked.

Bill chortled. "You've been reading too much John Le Carré, my old son. But if you're that paranoid, we can talk in person. As it happens, I'm going to be in DC tonight for a dinner date. I'm on my way in from the airport right now. I could meet you for a quick drink. Or since I'm staying overnight, we could have breakfast tomorrow. Take your pick."

"Where's dinner?"

"At a restaurant in Georgetown, the French Table."

"Ah, that's only a ten-minute walk from my apartment. You could pop into my place on the way there." Nigel gave him the address.

"I'll be there at about six-thirty, traffic permitting," Bill said, and hung up.

He arrived on time. "Very nice," Bill said, looking around the apartment. "Didn't know you had such refined tastes."

"I don't. I can thank Jane for the decor."

"Jane?"

"My girlfriend."

"Girlfriend! Blimey, you don't waste much time, do you."

"I met her in New York, and funnily enough on the evening you and I had dinner. Anyway, she helped me decorate the place. I had my art shipped over, what little was left to me after the divorce settlement. At least I managed to hang on to my Japanese woodblock prints, but only because Sarah hates them." Several adorned the living room wall in a cluster. "They look good there, don't you think?" Bill had no interest in Japanese art and surveyed the prints with sightless incuriosity.

"Where does she live, this Jane? And what does she do?"

"She lives a few blocks from here. She's an analyst with the State Department. Middle East section."

"That could be useful," Bill observed, on cue.

Nigel filled two glasses with Bushmill's. "So, what have you got for me?"

"We're all business, aren't we." Bill took from his pocket a couple of stained napkins and flattened them on the table. "I took some notes."

"You've been busy, then," Nigel said.

"Not really. Just a couple of phone calls. But yesterday I met my friend Dimitri for a drink, as I often do. He's a cultural attaché at the Russian consulate. When it comes to gossip, he's always good value. A bit like me in that respect. Anyway, as it turns out he knows two Anastasias."

"Oh really!"

"Now, don't get excited yet. One's a middle-aged clerk at the consulate. Apparently looks like one of those rotund political wives from the Soviet era. The other might be a possibility, though. She's well known in New York's Russian community, but with no known government connections, and Dimitri would know if she had. She's in her thirties, and by all accounts a bit tasty. Name of Markova, or something like that... Sorry, I can't read my own handwriting."

"Litovka?"

"Yeah, that could be it."

"This Dimitri, I presume he's some kind of agent?"

"Of course. You're not in New York as a cultural attaché to arrange art shows, or museum swaps. Dimitri's an old hand at this game and experienced enough even when he's in his cups not to talk freely to the likes of you and me."

"You trust him?"

"Yeah, as far as I can throw him, though to be fair, he's never given me any duff info."

"Go on..."

"He ran into this woman at a couple of diplomatic functions. She didn't strike him as a swinger. A bit prim, he thought. After one event, he told me, he dropped her off at her apartment. Made a move on her in the taxi but she brushed him off."

"How long ago was this?"

"Couple of years back, I think. The fact is, old son, there's nothing unusual going on here as far as I can see. But in case you think I've been doing nothing I also put a few calls into..."

"Sorry to interrupt again, but I presume Dimitri would know if this Anastasia was an agent."

"Yes, of course. But then he wouldn't be telling me that, would he."

"Was he at all curious why you were asking about her?"

"Not very. I told him a friend of mine had met her and wanted to get in touch. Look, if she's a spy, I think he might have been more curious about my interest than he was. Then again, he may just be clever enough not to seem curious at all."

"Did the *Skandal* article come up?"

"I mentioned it in passing. He thought it was crap. Didn't think it could possibly refer to the woman he dropped off in the taxi."

"Oh, why's that?"

"She just didn't seem the femme fatale type."

"Isn't that the whole point of the femme fatale?"

"True enough."

"Does he know *anything* about her background?"

"No. But as I was about to say when you interrupted, I spoke to another Russian contact of mine who knows of her. Says she's the daughter of a minor industrialist in Moscow." Bill peered at his battered napkin. "Agricultural machinery. Name's Sergei. Now retired. Wealthy, but not one of your oligarchs. Not rich enough to be a pal of Putin's."

"Any suggestion of government connections at a lower level?"

"No idea." Bill put the rancid napkin back in his pocket. "That's about it. Disappointed?"

"Not at all," Nigel fibbed.

"Oh, I nearly forgot. Dimitri said our girl mentioned she'd been to NYU.

"So…"

"So, a contact I have there checked her out for me. She left with a degree."

"Did he mention in what?"

"Philosophy. Is that relevant?"

"Just curious," Nigel said.

Bill checked his watch and held out his glass. "I've time for one more drink, my old son. You know, I was thinking: if Dimitri's Anastasia *does* know the president - and that's a big if in my mind - chances are they met at some diplomatic reception. Jameson used to go to those things when he lived in New York. It's where he did a lot of his real estate business: selling expensive properties to Russians. Otherwise known as money-laundering. He and Vlad are as thick as thieves, as we now know. Could be that once Jameson leaves the White House, he and Vlad will go into business together, if they're not already. Build hotels, casinos, resorts down on the Black Sea. There's too much pristine coastline down there to go wasted."

Bill drained his glass and stood, ready to leave.

"Anything else?" Nigel asked, knowing that there wasn't.

"What were you expecting, a fifty-page dossier marked 'Top Secret'?"

"No. But thanks anyway, Bill. I'm grateful for your help. Truly. Dinner on me next time. And soon, I hope."

"You're on." Bill was already at the door, but he hesitated before opening it, apparently remembering something. "Oh, I nearly forgot one last observation. Dimitri said he dropped Anastasia off at a flashy apartment building on the Upper East Side. Somewhere near the Met, he mentioned."

"And…?"

"It's an expensive neighbourhood up there, which suggests to me that she's not short of a few roubles. And that makes me wonder what she does for a living. High-class escort was my first thought. Our friend in the White House has been known to avail himself of such services. But I'm just thinking out loud." Bill had one more parting shot. "If it turns out there really *is* a deeply imbedded Russian spy ring here, with the President of the United States as its main target, you're sitting on a big story. I wouldn't hold your breath, mind. But then you know my opinion on the matter."

"Yes, you've made it clear. Which amplifies my gratitude even more."

Bill checked his watch again. "Sorry, but now I really do have to make a move."

"You're okay for time, Bill. The restaurant's a ten-minute walk away. Turn left out of here, left again at the end of the street and keep going."

"I'll keep sniffing around," said Bill, without enthusiasm, "but only because you're convinced there's a time-bomb waiting to be detonated. God knows why. Unless, of course, there's something you're not telling me…"

"There isn't," said Nigel, surprised by how easily the lie tripped off the tongue.

Nigel was momentarily tempted to tell Bill what he knew but thought better of it. As much as he liked his colleague, he didn't trust him entirely, least of all when it came to journalistic ethics. Nigel remembered once being told a story by a reporter from another paper that he'd told Bill over drinks what he was working on, only to read the story in the *Post* two days later under Bill's byline. Confronted with the betrayal, Bill had told him, "All's fair in love and journalism, old cock."

"Keep me posted," Nigel said, his brief crisis of conscience already over.

"I will. Meanwhile, my old son, I suggest that you get on with some real reporting. You might start on the federal budget thing."

"Point taken," said Nigel. "Look, this Anastasia thing isn't consuming g me. It's just a sideline. A hobby if you like."

"Well, maybe you should switch to stamp-collecting," Bill said, gently closing the door behind him.

* * *

Nigel met Jane at Luigi's. The weather had suddenly turned chilly. It matched the mood at the table. Jane sensed it as soon as they sat down. "You seem a little off colour tonight, honey. Have you been drinking?"

"I had a couple with a colleague." Giving her what he intended to be a reassuring smile, he wished he hadn't drunk four large whiskies.

"I get the feeling," said Jane still in a concerned tone, "that there's something you'd like to tell me but can't bring yourself to do it. I can't explain why I think that. Call it female intuition."

Her powers of perception always astonished him. "Look, here's the thing. I'm working on a story and the pieces just won't fit into place. That's all. It happens sometimes. All the time, in fact. And when it does, we journalists tend to get a bit distracted." He was tempted to come right out and ask her what she knew, but having thought about it on the walk over, he was as certain as anyone could be in a town of secrets that she was completely in the dark. For one thing, she lacked guile. In the short time that he had known her, she'd been open about everything: her personal demons; the trail of broken romances; her professional disappointments; above all her dread of making romantic commitments. "I don't know where this thing of ours is going," she'd told him one evening, "but for now I'm enjoying your company, we're getting along fine, and the sex is fun. Let's just leave it at that for now."

He felt the same way. Or did he?

Their acquaintance had now moved beyond mere friendship, that much was clear, but into what further emotional realms he couldn't define. 'Affair' sounded both sordid and impermanent. 'Courtship' and 'romance' both seemed terribly old-fashioned. As for 'relationship', he regarded the word as meaningless without an explanatory modifier. It occurred to him that he might be in love, but then he realized with something approaching alarm that he didn't know the symptoms, which sadly suggested that he'd never experienced them with Sarah. What he did know without question was that, whatever the future had in store for him, he'd be perfectly happy if it included this woman.

That thought, and its sundry implications, he was mulling over when Jane reached across the table and gently took his hands in hers. "Look, if you don't want to talk about whatever it is that's bothering you, let's talk about something positive. We might start with what we should do this weekend."

Nigel brightened. "Good idea. Let's do something diverting." He thought about what for a moment. "You know where I've never been in Washington? The Smithsonian. I hear they've got the Apollo capsule there, the one that went to the moon. I'd love to see that. And, of course, there's a lot more to see."

"What a good idea," she responded with genuine enthusiasm. "I haven't been there myself since high school."

"Did you know that this grand American institution was founded by an Englishman? Martin Smithson."

"You Brits do get around. But if you'll forgive me for saying so, I'm glad you didn't *all* stick around, otherwise we wouldn't have a White House. Or even the State Department. I'll get onto the website tonight. Do you care if Fran joins us?"

"Yes, I do," said Nigel with some force. The woman was becoming too ubiquitous for comfort.

"I thought you liked her."

"I do. It's just that she seems to be around us rather a lot lately." Mention of Fran's name was annoying, but it had the redeeming virtue of giving him an excuse to open his reluctant line of enquiry.

"Since her name keeps coming up, why don't you tell me something about her. You were roommates at college, so you must know her better than anyone."

"I've told you most of it. And what I haven't, I'm sure she has."

"I'd like to hear more. Was she a good student? Was she political? I picture her as a perpetual rebel with a cause, leading protest marches, facing down the police on the steps of the faculty building, that kind of thing. I can picture her being carried off by the cops and loaded into a van, waving triumphantly to her cheering followers – and the next day being fined for contempt for swearing at the judge in court."

Jane laughed. But she was puzzled by this sudden outbreak of curiosity. "Fran was an excellent student - much cleverer than I was and without trying too hard. No, she wasn't a campus agitator – and we had plenty of those - but she was usually involved in some campaign or other: trying to help the oppressed of the world; women's rights, gay rights, some environmental cause or other. She was good company, always the life and soul of the party. We drank a lot in those days, gallons of the stuff, gut-rot most of it, specially brewed for students, I suspect. Pot, too, of course."

"*You* smoked pot?" Nigel sounded more astonished than he'd wanted to.

"Is that so hard to imagine? Do I come across as Little Miss Prude?"

"I didn't mean it that way."

"Yes, of course I smoked pot. Everyone did then. Many still do. Didn't you?"

"Sure. But in England we were a little behind the curve on illicit substances, as on everything else. Mind you, we soon caught up. We always catch up with America eventually, especially when it comes to the bad stuff. Booze was more my scene in those days. Still is… as I'm sure you've noticed."

"I have. Anyway, pot is off limits now. Especially for government workers like me. They do spot tests, you know. Fail one and you're out, and that pretty much means forever."

"Getting back to Fran, just how political was she back then?"

"More than most. Less than some. She was no power-to-the-people radical if that's what you're getting at. Still, we had plenty of worthy causes to support, and did. I've forgotten most of them. I was a registered Republican then. Republicans didn't do riots and demonstrations."

"They do now…"

"Yes, but only because the Republican asylum has been taken over by its more dangerous inmates."

"Are you still a registered Republican? Frankly, I'm kind of shocked that you ever were such a thing."

"Well, it's a bit like religion: you inherit your politics from your parents. But I'm apolitical now, at least in public, though I'm not high enough on the pay scale to be a political appointee. Anyway, when it comes to my subject, the Middle East, both parties are equally clueless. But at least as a registered Republican I get to vote in the primaries against right-wing loonies. But most of the time, between you and me, I vote for the other ticket. I went for Obama twice. I certainly didn't vote for this one." She didn't have to define who 'this one' was. "Truth be known, I've lost my appetite for party politics. It's all so brutal now - partisan, spiteful and ugly, personalities rather than policies."

"For which we can thank the current occupant of the Oval Office."

"Yes, but be fair, it was just as bad during the Nixon years. He had a list of 'enemies', too, with the media at the top of the list. Just like now."

"Let's hope this presidency ends the same way as Nixon's. I'd love to see Jameson waving goodbye from a helicopter from the South Lawn."

"I think they all leave that way."

"You know what I mean."

The conversation seemed to have strayed from the subject of Fran. Nigel took it back there again, though with some hesitation. "Let me ask you something: do you trust Fran?"

"My, that one came out of left field."

"I mean, has she ever given you any reason to doubt her loyalty, let you down so badly it might have jeopardized your friendship?"

She looked him squarely in the face. "Never. I'm surprised by the question. Just what are you trying to get at?"

Nigel squirmed without moving. He had long earned a living by eviscerating politicians, and now he was the one on the receiving end. She was watching him intently. The way forward was now clear, time to come clean. "Actually, there *is* something on my mind," he said in a confessional tone. "It's something I've been wanting to share with you but didn't know how."

Jane looked baffled. "And it involves Fran?"

"Yes."

He proceeded, in a quiet voice, to lay out the whole sequence of events: Sonny's revelations about Samantha Jameson; his discovery of Anna's identity; spotting Fran in New York; his suspicion that someone might be trying to set him up. On the last point, he went so far as to name Fran as a possible suspect. He delivered a concluding remark rather in the manner of a prosecuting attorney addressing a jury. "These revelations and coincidences seem nothing if not remarkable."

From Jane's horrified expression he was relieved to conclude that she'd been completely in the dark. "I can see why you had a hard time telling me - but I'm glad you did."

"Fran has said nothing, not even a hint?"

"Not a word. But now I know why you were pumping me for information about her. You can be quite duplicitous, can't you, Nigel Harper? It's a side of you I'm seeing for the first time."

"Old journalistic habits die hard, I'm afraid."

"Well, I didn't fall off my chair, did I?"

"No. But what do you think?"

"Well, Fran is Samantha Jameson's confidante, and she can't be that without knowing a few intimate secrets. Samantha's behaviour surprises me a little, not because she's gay but because adultery seems more her husband's line of country. Not that I blame her, poor woman. If I were married to that dreadful man, I'd be... well, it's beyond my imagination, so I can't say what I'd do."

Nigel reached across the table and took her hands in his. "Look, I'm sorry to have dumped all this on you, but I couldn't bear to think about keeping it to myself and then have you find out from someone else. It's been giving me stomach cramps over the last twenty-four hours."

Jane bridled. "So that's why you told me all this, to relieve your gut?"

"No. But holding back would have put an unthinkable strain on more than my gut. On us. What we have between us."

"And now your revelations are out of the way, what are you going to do?"

"I honestly don't know," he said, rather feebly, she thought.

"Well, the first question is the obvious one: are you going for the story or not?"

"I don't know. I swing from one side to the other, depending on my mood, and how much I've had to drink."

What she said next surprised him. "I'm playing devil's advocate here, which isn't my usual instinct, but how can you *not* write it? Isn't a journalist supposed to tell the truth, whatever the consequences? Isn't that what the media call serving the public interest?"

"Let me put it to you as the angel's advocate. Does exposing Samantha Jameson as an adulteress, and a lesbian - shock, horror - in any way serve the public interest? Unless, of course, she's a Russian agent, in which case all bets are off. But I've heard nothing to suggest that she is. Samantha is not an elected politician. She hasn't broken any promises to voters. Only to her husband. Now, if *he* were involved it would be entirely another matter."

"Why?"

"Because he rode the moral high horse when he ran for office, and he's still in the saddle - no pun intended. I'd have no hesitation outing him as a hypocrite. She may be deceiving him, but he lies to her all the time. He also lies to the rest of us, whenever he opens his mouth, which is every day of the week. And the evangelicals readily forgive her husband's flouting of their beloved Commandments."

"They'd forgive him anything to get a tax cut, which is the only thing this president has delivered."

"Churches don't pay taxes."

"No, but their congregants do."

"So, what are you saying? Publish and be damned? Is that your considered recommendation?"

"Not at all. I told you I was speaking for the Devil."

"So, what is your view, considered or otherwise?"

"I'm not a journalist, so I can't argue the finer ethical points with any authority…" She paused to gather more thoughts. "Forgive the clichés, but I believe in a free press and that the media plays an essential role in any democracy. There are far too many secrets in this town as it is. We all make fine judgments on those that ought to be revealed and those that should remain hidden. That said, I think Samantha Jameson's love life falls into the second category. So, I say don't publish, though you may be damned anyway."

"Good." Nigel was grinning from ear to ear. "Because what we have here has nothing to do with politics. Just an unhappy woman, married to a shit, and who decided to have a fling."

But he still wanted to talk to Fran, he told her. If someone was playing a game, he sure as hell wanted to know why. Why, for a start, she had put Sonny what's-his-name onto him.

"You don't know that she did. But I agree that Fran would be a good place to start."

"Meanwhile, please don't say anything to her. Let me handle it."

"Can you?" asked Jane.

"Can I what?"

"Handle her."

"I think so. Right now, I'm thinking she may be a damn sight more nervous than I am."

Jane laughed. "That woman nervous! She's never been nervous in her life. But rest assured that my lips are sealed." She made the pledge by covering them with both hands.

"I know a better way to seal those lovely lips," Nigel said, suddenly feeling as if a burden had been lifted from his shoulders, but also because the alcohol was starting to kick in.

"I agree," she said, "but before we say, or do, anything else, let's enjoy dinner and then we can go home and play some naughty games ourselves."

* * *

Two days later, in the press room, Sonny stopped by Nigel's desk. "Hey, buddy, how they hangin'?"

Sonny hadn't called him since their meeting in Slattery's. Right now, he was the last person Nigel wanted to see. Sonny, for his part, seemed unusually chirpy, as if he, too, had been relieved of a burden. Nigel wondered if there had been some new development.

"What are you working on?" Sonny asked casually.

"I'm having a hard time making a budget story comprehensible for British readers. It's not the financial stuff I'm struggling with, but all the political skullduggery that's been going on in the background - who decides what goes in and what comes out - the process seems endless."

"Oh, they'll come up with a budget eventually, and it'll leave no one happy. That's how the folks on Capitol Hill keep themselves busy all year, negotiating which pork-barrel projects will get their states or districts the most votes. They call it 'government in action'. The rest of us call it government inaction, one word. The more pork they can load in, the more votes they garner back home. It's all about pork."

"Don't tell the Jewish voters."

"I finished my own budget piece this morning," Sonny said, ignoring the quip. "It's hardly front-page stuff. Belongs more in the business section, which hardly anyone reads."

Guessing that Sonny hadn't stopped by to chat about the budget, Nigel raised the unmentionable topic himself. "By the way, I've pretty much decided not to spend my time chasing mysterious Russian socialites. As my reverend father used to sing at Evensong, 'The common round, the trivial task, should furnish all we need to ask…' That's an English hymn, by the way."

"You've decided to drop it then…" Sonny repeated, as if to confirm the decision.

"Yes, subject to… come to think of it, I don't know what it *is* subject to. I just don't feel at ease doing it."

"Well, whatever it is, I'm happy to hear it. But then, I always knew you'd do what's right." Sonny seemed at a loss to say more. "Well, I guess I'll see you around." He began to move away.

"Where are you off to in such a hurry, and all dressed up?" Sonny, not the nattiest dresser, seemed rather smartly turned out for a regular working day.

"Frank Hoffman invited me to lunch. In the White House, no less. I've no idea why, but it's a rare honour. Incidentally, I don't know if you've seen the latest edition of *Skandal* magazine…" Nigel's heart skipped a beat.

"No, there's nothing about you-know-what. Zilch. But that's the whole point." Sonny again turned to leave. "I'll be seeing you. Maybe later, for a beer? I could fill you in on the Frank lunch. He's usually good for some unprintable gossip."

"Not today, thanks. Nothing personal, but I don't think I'm ready for any more revelations, much less from you. Besides, I've got this bloody budget piece to finish."

Just then Frank's personal assistant, Maryam Tekin, by reputation a formidable guardian of Frank's gate, appeared. "Ready, Sonny? The man is waiting for you."

Nigel watched them as they headed for the press secretary's office. He was in two minds about Sonny. He liked the man, but for all his hail-fellow-well-met performances there was something unfathomable about him. Nigel couldn't decide what.

Reluctantly, he turned back to his budget story, which even more than Sonny's was destined for the *Post*'s unexplored dark interior, if it ran at all. A new river crossing in Manchester, New Hampshire was hardly going to set pulses racing in Manchester, England.

***

Jane, sitting at her desk in the bowels of the State Department, took a call from Fran. "I'm bored," her friend announced. "How about a quick lunch? Samantha's gone off riding, bless her. Again. For three days. That leaves me with a rare break in my otherwise frantic schedule."

Jane smiled at the remark. Fran was in a perpetual state of agitation, even when she was doing the laundry or shopping for shoes. Jane was tempted to excuse herself on the grounds that she was too busy working on a position paper for the Secretary of State himself. She had been, in fact, but it was now finished, and well ahead of deadline. But Fran's quick lunches were usually anything but, and the paper could probably use a little last-minute polishing. On the other hand, her conversation with Nigel the previous evening had piqued her curiosity about the first lady's act of marital betrayal, and if anyone could provide elucidation it was Fran. She would not mention the subject, as she had agreed with Nigel, but a glass of wine or two might well loosen her friend's tongue.

"Sure," she heard herself saying. "Why not?"

"How's our boy," was Fran's opening gambit.

"If you mean Nigel," replied Jane, "he's a bit preoccupied of late."

"With what?"

"Work. Other than that, I've no idea. He doesn't tell me what he's writing, and I don't ask. Some story is giving him problems. He mentioned a crisis of conscience… if you can believe that."

"It's not easy. But I thought you two lovebirds shared everything."

"Sometimes he asks for my opinion. On this occasion, though, he seems to be fighting a lone battle." Jane, playing the journalist herself, thought she might goad Fran into a revelation. "It seems he's grappling with a decision to publish a story or not. Apparently, it's a big one. It's not unusual for journalists to go through these agonizing bouts of soul-searching, he tells me. Tells me I shouldn't worry."

"What kind of story?" asked Fran, examining the menu with what Jane imagined was unwarranted fascination.

"He didn't say." Jane lied effortlessly. "It's something that he says could be a major scoop. You know how reporters are: they can go from elated to depressed and back in minutes." Jane was in a venturesome mood. "I think it might have something to do with Samantha Jameson." Jane was watching her friend for a reaction - if only a raised eyebrow - but her face remained impassive. "But that's a guess. He was quite taken with her, you know, after their brief White House meeting."

"Interesting," said Fran, in a tone that suggested that she found it far from that. "Anything I can help with?"

"If there were, I'm sure he'd have called you himself by now. Maybe he's prepping for his upcoming interview with her."

"It hasn't even been scheduled yet." Fran had a distracted look. She changed the subject. "Someone in the shopping mall this morning put a dent in my new car. Drove off without reporting it. Some people, I tell you…"

"It has happened to all of us," Jane said. "Always very annoying. How big is the dent?"

"Small enough not to warrant a trip to the body shop but big enough to be obvious. Isn't that always the way?"

Jane had only one ploy left. "Was there anything in particular you wanted to talk about today, Fran?"

"Do old friends need a reason to get together?"

Jane offered a reassuring smile. "Of course not. I'm delighted to see you, as always. So, by the way, is Nigel. He was asking about you only last night. I gather he rather admires you, too. Thinks you're a straight shooter."

"Really? I rather got the impression he views me rather warily, as if I'm concealing something, or that I'm out to thwart him."

"Are you?" asked Jane, pointedly.

"That often comes with the job, but on this occasion, I can't think of anything. Nothing, anyway, that I feel compelled to share with you."

Jane laughed, disguising annoyance. Was it her imagination, or had Fran's remark seemed taunting? "Where are you?" she suddenly asked.

"Right here."

"You're not here, Fran. You're somewhere else. I can sense it."

Fran pulled a face. "You mentioned that Nigel was asking about me. Did he give a reason?"

"Oh, he was asking what you were like in college, what we got up to, that kind of thing."

"What did he want to know, especially?"

"Whether we were political activists. What kind of social life we led... nothing heavy. I think he was curious, that's all. Just casual dinner conversation."

"And what did you tell him? Anything that he'd find fascinating?"

"I told him how it was. He didn't seem to find it all that interesting."

"Well, looking back now, it wasn't nearly as interesting as what we both do now. My, how we've changed since those carefree days."

Jane wondered how Fran thought they had changed. "Have we? In what way?"

"In so many ways. My coming out, for a start."

"That's not so remarkable these days."

"It is if *you're* the one in the closet. I'll never forget the day I told my parents. They were mortified. Something of a trauma for all concerned. I'm sure they still worry about what the neighbours would think if they were to find out. And then there's you, and *your* romantic entanglements. Speaking of which, how are you and Nigel... progressing?"

"You make it sound like a business project. But to answer your question, we're doing fine. Getting along better than I'd expected to, if truth be told."

"What were you expecting?"

"Oh, I don't know. But based on past experiences I suppose I was afraid that he wouldn't turn out to be the man I thought he was."

"And did he?"

"Yes. At first, I found his direct manner disconcerting - a bit like yours, come to think of it - but now I find it refreshing. I'm sure he has his secrets…but don't we all? That story he mentioned, for one." She looked across at Fran. Still no evident reaction. She found herself wondering how she might have handled Nigel if it had been Fran who had told her about the Samantha Jameson business. "Why do you keep asking about us?"

"Because I can, Janey. And probably because I've always been a little suspicious about whirlwind romances. This one clearly falls into that category. And, let's face it, you've been bowled over a few times before with dire results."

"Well, all I can say is, so far, so good."

"Well, let's pray it stays that way."

"You know, I think it will," said Jane brightly. "I like him. A lot. He's kind and considerate… most of the time. A little eccentric, perhaps, but then he's English. Above all, though, he's always interesting. That's more than you can say about most of my earlier boyfriends. We enjoy each other's company very much. I couldn't ask for much more."

"I disagree. There's much more you can ask," Fran said.

"Such as?"

"The word commitment comes to mind."

"It's a little early for that." Jane suddenly found herself on the defensive.

"Just good friends, then…"

"Yes, just good friends. At least for now. Speaking of love-life, how's yours?"

"Non-existent." Fran sighed but then perked up. "But there's a girl in my office I've had my eye on. Whether she's had her eye on me I can't tell. She's not one to readily reveal her feelings. I may have to be a little more assertive."

"You've never had any trouble with that."

"True. But back to Nigel. You're still paying two rents. Any thought of cutting them down to one?"

"My word, Nigel was right. You *are* the Grand Inquisitor."

"No, I'm your friend. That means I like to know you're being taken care of - and not just in the bedroom. That's what friends are for you know."

Tiring of the small talk, and especially these Oprah Winfrey couch exchanges, Jane made one last attempt to draw Fran out, feeling that she would at least be fulfilling a duty. "I hear you were in New York last week."

"Oh! Who told you that?"

"I, er, called your office, looking for you. They told me."

"My office is telling people on the phone where I am! I'll have to have a word with someone."

"Well, were you?" Jane persisted.

"Yes, as it happens. Just for the day. A minor errand for Samantha. She'd forgotten something."

"And how *is* Samantha these days?"

"Samantha's just fine." That, as Jane now knew, was far from true. "Does a lot of riding these days. Finds it liberating. But then she was riding before she could walk, so I shouldn't be surprised."

"I can see how riding in good clean country air would make a change from the oppressive atmosphere of Washington. Of the White House. Not to mention that awful marriage of hers."

"You got that right," Fran said, revealing nothing that was not already widely known.

"We know that husband of hers strays," Jane said coyly. "You know, I've often wondered whether she herself has ever been tempted..."

"I wouldn't tell you even if I knew," Fran said casually. "Anyway, I'd probably be the last to know. This is a strange line of questioning, I must say." She suddenly looked uncomfortable, Jane thought, perhaps sensing that she was being drawn into turbulent waters.

Fran looked at her watch. "Look, my darling Jane, I'd love to stay and chat some more, but there's something I've got to do this afternoon that simply can't be put off. I hope you don't mind. I'm sorry."

Jane didn't mind in the least. If anything, she was relieved. "I need to get back, too."

Fran kissed her on both cheeks, European style. "If I can leave you to pick up the tab..."

Watching her go, Jane thought about a remark Nigel had made over dinner. *She's a deep one, your friend Fran, for all her public effervescence.'* Now she knew it was true, not that there had ever been much doubt about it. Jane liked her no less for it, but now, after Nigel's startling revelations, she was more ready to believe it.

* * * * *

Chapter 11

Nigel woke up with a hangover, the result of a long session at a local tavern the previous evening with a group of students from Georgetown University. His delicate condition was exacerbated by a stifling apartment. Overnight, the weather had turned muggy, and he had yet to work out how to switch on the air conditioning. Either that or it was broken. He felt better after taking a shower and gulping down several black coffees. Then he foolishly undid all the good work by electing to stroll the mile or so to work. The sky was leaden, the air heavy, a storm in the making. Despite walking at a leisurely pace, he arrived at the White House perspiring as profusely as if he had run a cross-country race. Thunder rolled across an area to the south of the city, where an ominous confederation of bruise-black clouds had gathered, as if preparing for an assault on the capital - as indeed they were.

The White House press room was as oppressive as his apartment. Gratefully, he removed his jacket. West Wing staffers enjoyed no such privilege and could be seen discreetly dabbing as rivulets of sweat trickled down brows and necks. He felt especially sorry for the uniformed guards, who couldn't even do that, although on closer inspection he noticed that they seemed sweatless, as oblivious to the heat as they were intent on everything else happening around them.

Nigel had hated thunderstorms since childhood. Angry storm gods had symbolically attended some of the significant moments of his life. He could still remember vividly his first day at grammar school, when a violent electrical storm had caught him unawares as he was cycling home. Terrified, he had taken shelter under a tree; the least sensible thing that he could have done, as his father reminded him in a sermon more terrifying than the storm itself. A few years later, a thunderstorm had broken during the closing moments of his mother's funeral, scattering the mourners at the gravesite, leaving the presiding minister to complete the final words of committal to a congregation reduced to three. Then there had been the day of his formal divorce from Sarah, which he remembered less for the execution of the final act of his marriage than for the lightning flashes and the torrential rain lashing at the windows of his solicitor's office, as if the proceedings had been singled out for divine wrath. What form of retribution might the gods have in store for him today?

After hours of toil trying to fathom the complexities of the American legislative process, he put the finishing touches to the infernal budget story, which Republicans and Democrats from both houses had finally thrashed out after months of Byzantine negotiations, producing a compromise bill that pleased no one. Least of all the president, who had called for draconian spending cuts across the board - the military excluded - and been given only a few minor exclusions, mainly of projects he had vigorously opposed. Universal dissatisfaction follows most legislative acts, as Nigel knew from his experience in Westminster, and this one was no exception. He doubted that his efforts would be appreciated. The *Post*'s subs, in their impeccable insularity, would no doubt cut his story down to a few mid-paper paragraphs. As he idly flipped through the New York and Washington papers to make sure that he hadn't missed anything, Frank Hoffman suddenly appeared at his shoulder. His arrival was heralded by a loud clap of thunder that startled them both.

"Perfect timing," Nigel said, looking up. "A Valkyrie riding in on the storm."

Frank, obviously in a pedantic frame of mind, corrected him. "The Valkyries, I feel bound to remind you, were women. I don't think I qualify."

"Whatever their gender, they were harbingers of doom. Are you?"

"Not at all. But I was wondering if you could give me a few moments. Good morning, by the way."

"And good morning to you, Mr Press Secretary. What can I do for you?" Nigel had an ominous feeling, despite Frank's assurance, that storm clouds might be looming inside the building as well as outside.

"Let's go through to my office," Frank said, acknowledging several other reporters with cursory nods. "We'll have fewer eavesdroppers there."

No sooner had they reached his office than a red phone on Frank's desk rang. "Excuse me, but I need to take this."

Nigel took the opportunity to look around the room. What struck him immediately was that it was preternaturally tidy, with none of the paperweights, photographs and other desk-top clutter that Nigel would have expected to see. Both the in-tray and out-tray were empty. It looked as though the occupant had cleared it out in preparation for leaving. Even the walls were bare, except for a couple of framed photographs behind Frank's desk. In one, Frank and the president were both grinning for the camera, like a pair of sixth formers on a school outing. In the other, Frank was in a group that included several familiar faces, posing drinks in hand beside a palm-fringed swimming pool, which Nigel presumed was at the president's Florida retreat. One of the faces was Fran Powell's.

After several minutes, Frank put the phone down. He looked exasperated. "I'm surrounded by fucking idiots," he snapped, and then bit his lip, having no desire to leave Nigel with the impression that this White House was anything but an efficient well-oiled machine, even if they both knew it was far from the case. Frank wiped his face with his handkerchief. "Damned hot in here, isn't it? You'd think the leader of the Free World would be able to afford air conditioning. What do you say we take a walk outside?"

Nigel winced. "Are you serious? There's a storm coming in." Still damp from his earlier walk, he was far from keen to venture outside again.

"Oh, don't worry about a few storm clouds," Frank said blithely. "They're down there in Virginia, I see, but they'll pass us by, believe me. You know, my father was an amateur meteorologist. Studying weather patterns became one of my more unusual childhood passions."

"Really? I think of you more as an artist than a scientist."

"The two often converge. The weather has always inspired artists, from Caravaggio to van Gogh. These days, human intervention seems to be changing that order."

"I wouldn't have put you down as an environmentalist either."

"Aren't we all these days?"

"Not, apparently, this president."

"Yes, well, I'm working on that. I'm as concerned as the next man about the future of the planet."

Frank had indeed raised the issue with the president on several occasions without getting far. Martin Jameson's position - if it could be called that - was that climate change - if such a thing existed - was an entirely natural phenomenon. "Weather patterns have been changing for centuries," he had told Frank dismissively. "First one way, then the other. So, don't listen to those panic-mongers who'd happily wreck the economy to prove their point." Frank had learnt to live with that, along with many other administration positions with which he privately disagreed. All press secretaries submerged opinions that conflicted with those of their employer, even when doing so involved a great deal of grinding teeth. Frank's teeth ought by now to have been worn to stubs, he liked to joke, but only to his wife Marion.

Frank ushered Nigel out of the office. "By the way, speaking of mythical women, are you still obsessed with Slavic sirens luring our unwary warriors to their doom?"

Nigel was caught off guard. "If you're referring to recent published allegations, I think I'm over it now, thanks to you working me over in the briefing room."

"Well, let's face it, my scolding was no more than you deserved." Frank sounded like a parent confronting an errant child. "I'm not usually in the business of teaching reporters how to do their job, but I must admit I found your embarrassment quite gratifying."

"You and apparently a great many others."

"You'll get over it, and I've no doubt you've suffered worse humiliations."

"I have. I once incurred the wrath of a British prime minister. It doesn't matter which one, but he was sufficiently pissed off that the home secretary was ordered to call me in for a personal bollocking. But I even wrote a story about that. And guess what, next thing I know I've received a personal letter of apology from the PM himself, under his own signature."

"Well, good for him. Just don't expect one from me, much less from the president. Apologies don't figure prominently in his repertoire, as I'm sure you've worked out."

"No apology needed."

As they strolled out of the gates, Nigel cast an apprehensive glance at the heavens, which looked not so much threatening as cataclysmic. Frank looked up, too, but seemed unconcerned. "Don't worry, we'll be fine," he said.

"I'm not so sure the weather will be," Nigel shot back. "And I've no coat. Not even an umbrella."

"Coming from a country where it rains incessantly you should know better." Frank suggested that they head for the Lincoln Memorial. "I always find it a source of inspiration. Lincoln is one of my personal heroes." On the way, he chatted amiably, on subjects ranging from the American Civil War to movies. "You like movies, I hear."

"I do. But, you know, I never could bring myself to use the word 'movie'." Nigel realized how pompous he sounded but pressed on. "To me, it reduces what should be an art form to banal, time-killing entertainment for the masses. That probably strikes you as pretentious."

"It does. I hate to state the obvious, my friend, but that's exactly what movies are: entertainment for the masses. And even if most of them are no better than that, we can appreciate the exceptions. Sure, most people wouldn't know a Hawks from a Hitchcock, but I do, which is all that matters. And you know what: if your brow is higher than that, then go to an art gallery instead of the movie theatre."

"Point taken," said Nigel.

On reaching Abe, majestically enthroned like a God in a Roman temple, they paused to admire the great marble figure. It was milled about with hundreds of selfie-snapping tourists. After a few minutes of silent contemplation, Frank pointed to a shaded path running alongside the nearby reflecting pool. Finding an empty bench to sit on, they watched the passing tourists who, as Nigel pointed out, seemed less interested in the monuments themselves than having their picture taken in front of them. "History on a stick, I call it," he observed.

Frank declined to reply, anxious to avoid agreeing with Nigel Harper too many times in one morning.

"Honest Abe is a true national hero," Frank offered. The giant figure seated in front of them provided an impressive embodiment of the opinion. Nigel regarded the monument, like all the others, as ostentatious to a fault. What, he wondered out loud, would a self-effacing president raised in a humble log cabin have thought of it? "How different you are from us Brits in these matters," he said, remembering Bill's crack about DC as a movie set. "If London, with its two thousand years of history, were to treat its heroes with all this magnificence it would look more like ancient Rome than ancient Rome itself. Most of our former prime ministers get at best a small statue, and usually in a place where no one notices it."

"We do go overboard, I agree, but that's the American way. Someone worth remembering deserves to be remembered on a grand scale. But, come now, you must agree that it's an imposing sight."

"As was the man, by all accounts. But a flawed hero, wouldn't you say?"

"Flawed?" Frank was evidently affronted by the idea. "In what way?"

"He may have emancipated the slaves, but he didn't really care for them. He himself was a segregationist. He was convinced that mingling the races couldn't work and did nothing to encourage it. I believe his preferred solution - which understandably he kept quiet once he was elected - was to repatriate the slaves back to Africa. Might have done it, too, if he could have found a way. Nowadays, when *your* boss says something similar about Mexicans, he's called a racist. I'm quite sure he is, but then so perhaps was that man over there."

"But he genuinely believed that all men should be free."

"Free, yes, but not equal."

"Well, he had politics to consider, which was just as much the art of the practical as it is now. In persuading Congress to free the slaves, he also managed to save the Union. That surely counts as an impressive accomplishment if he achieved nothing else. Anyway, aren't all great men flawed? Our Abe was the man for that hour, and so was your Winston Churchill, a Victorian imperialist with no interest in social issues. When their time came, they rose to the occasion, saved their respective countries."

Nigel looked at Frank with new-found respect. "If we keep agreeing, Frank, we're going to have to stop meeting like this."

Frank Hoffman didn't present the appearance of a man who commanded respect. Before leaving the White House, he had put on a battered over-large trilby that rested on his ears. His suit was shiny with age and badly needed pressing. And the ensemble was hardly enhanced by the scuffed, unpolished loafers. He was wearing sunglasses, now redundant under a lowering sky. Nigel could only suppose that they were a form of disguise. Frank saw Nigel eyeing the trilby. "Yes, it's awful, I know, but I've grown fond of it over the years. Bought it in London as a matter of fact. It's my own fashion statement, which is that I don't give a damn for fashion."

"I thought perhaps you were trying to look like George Smiley."

"Ah, a John le Carré fan. Me, too."

"I'm not a fan, but a colleague of mine recently told me I'm showing the paranoid tendencies of one of his characters."

"He could be right if you're spending your time hunting for imaginary Russian agents. But then you Brits were always more into that stuff than we are. Maybe it says something about our respective countries. Yours anyway."

"Especially at Cambridge," Nigel said.

Frank laughed. "Well, thank God you went to Oxford. That must put you above suspicion."

"It doesn't, but our esteemed rival seems to have been as much a breeding ground for double agents as for Nobel prizes. And for the record, I've done nothing to arouse suspicion."

"I'll make a note of that." Frank changed the subject. "How are you finding the job?"

"Other than reading too many tabloids, so far so good. Still finding my way around, of course. Capitol Hill and Westminster, I'm finding, *are* quite different. For a start, there's so much going on here, it's hard to keep up with it all - and we're in the quiet season."

"Our politicians and yours share one characteristic: both make solemn promises to garner votes and then freely break them to suit their own political ends. Or pocketbooks."

"But surely not when they get to the White House?" Nigel's tone was sardonic.

"*Especially* when they get to the White House."

If Nigel had expected a stout defence of the president, he was not about to get one.

"The Oval Office," Frank said, "tends to bring out the best in good people and the worst in the bad ones. In the end, some occupants rise to the occasion, others sink below it. But that, I suppose, applies to anyone in high office, anywhere in the world."

"And to the present occupant…?"

"Now, you wouldn't expect me to comment on that, would you. Not for another two years anyway…or maybe it'll be six."

"Ah, I sniff a memoir in the works."

"That'll be the day, as a movie character used to say." Frank challenged Nigel to name him.

"Ethan Edwards. *The Searchers*."

"Directed by …?

"John Ford, of course."

"Top marks, old chap," said Frank, once more in the tone of Hollywood's idea of a supercilious Brit. After a pause he said, "Changing the topic, there's something I've been meaning to ask you. It has to do with the question you asked at the briefing, the one that I so rudely but justifiably derided."

He now had Nigel's full attention. "What about it?" Nigel braced for yet another scolding.

"I'm still trying to work out what possessed you to ask it."

"To be honest, I'm not sure myself. Call it a rush of blood to the brain."

"The point is, I've been wondering whether there's something you know - or think you know - that the rest of us don't. If so, I'd sure like to be in on it."

As Nigel looked at Frank, he thought again about the 'Washington Lie'. *Did Frank know that Nigel knew something...?* But as it was the press secretary who had initiated the discussion, he was the one who ought to show his hand first. "Do go on..."

"Whatever you say, of course, will be strictly between us. It won't go beyond the bench we're sitting on."

Nigel thought carefully before replying. "Let me just say, Frank, that I'm prepared to believe - and, yes, may have reason to believe - that *Skandal* was on to something."

"And what exactly is it that makes you think so?"

"I'd rather not go into it right now. My information may be incomplete but it's quite compelling."

"I can tell you categorically that the *Skandal* story is inaccurate," Frank said flatly.

"Yes, you've made that clear. Which means you must be in possession of alternative facts, if I may borrow from one of your esteemed White House colleagues."

"What makes you say that?" Frank looked puzzled.

"Pure logic. If you know something is categorically untrue you must, by definition, know what *is* true."

"Now we're entering the realms of semantics and philosophy."

"Or the world of George Smiley."

"Either way, we seem to be at a conversational impasse," Frank said with a sigh. "You're the one who seems to be withholding something. If you have evidence of this alleged affair, or whatever it is, then all I can say is produce it. Do you have pictures? Witnesses? Reputable sources? If you think you do, I can assure you that they're all fakes."

"Ah, my first encounter with the Fake News Syndrome. Look, if I had all the evidence I needed, I wouldn't be sitting here on a park bench discussing it with the White House press secretary. I'd have written the story. In other words, it's still a work in progress."

"And are you, may I ask, satisfied with that progress?"

Nigel was about to respond when a deep and loud roll of thunder caused them both to look at the sky. It had darkened considerably. They noticed that the tourists were already scampering in all directions looking for shelter. Frank and Nigel stood up themselves and started walking back to the White House at a brisk pace.

"I thought you said the storm would miss the city," Nigel said.

"Well, I'm sometimes wrong," Frank admitted cheerfully, pulling down the brim of his trilby. "But getting back to what we were just discussing, may I offer a suggestion?"

"All contributions gratefully received," Nigel said brightly.

"Have a chat with Fran Powell. I understand that you two have become what you Brits would call mates."

"And why should I do that?"

"Just talk to her, and I'm sure certain things will become clear." Frank glanced at him with a steely look. "Some of it you may already know. For now, I'd rather not say more. Perhaps we'll talk at some later date..."

Nigel was more perplexed than annoyed. He found it odd that Frank, who was aware of Nigel's conversation with Sonny - and knew that Nigel knew that he knew - would hold back. But that seemed to be the way the game was played in this town. Not that it mattered much. He had already decided to talk to Fran anyway. Clearly, though, conversations had been going on, and Fran had been designated as the one to provide enlightenment. Or obfuscation. "If that's the way you want to play it, Frank, I'll call her."

"Let's just say that I think you'll find it informative."

They had quickened their pace in response to the black mass of cloud above them. No sooner had they entered the West Wing than the rain duly began to fall, cutting diagonal sheets across the White House lawns, bending trees to its will.

"Perfect timing," said Frank with a grin as they entered the lobby.

"I've underestimated you," Nigel said. "Clearly, you're a man of many talents, timing being one of them."

They shook hands and parted, if not as friends, then as men who had forged a bond in the form of an unutterable secret. That, and apparently a shared admiration for John Ford.

* * *

Nigel called Fran that afternoon.

"What a coincidence," she said gaily. "*I've* been meaning to call *you*, but since you've beaten me to it, what can I do for you?"

"We need to chat."

"Fire away."

"Not on the phone. In person. Perhaps over a drink. Preferably somewhere quiet."

"I'll be free about five. Does that work?"

"Perfect. Where?"

"The *Blue Orchid*. It's in the Capitol district."

"Sounds terribly exotic," Nigel said. "Is it a nightclub?"

"It's a gay bar, which amounts to the same thing." Fran's tone was amused. "But you'll be safe with me. I'm well known there."

"I'm sure I'd be quite safe even if you weren't. See you there at five."

The *Blue Orchid* was a basement bar of the kind that seems glamorous and exciting when strobe lights enfilade a packed field of swaying silhouettes, but grungy in daytime when the threadbare carpeting and fittings are exposed. Maroon velvet curtains framed false windows, through which could be seen murals of cavorting Greek nymphs, presumably on the Isle of Lesbos. The fabric and colour were matched on recessed banquettes that ran along three walls. The other wall was taken up by a long bar, its entire length backed by a mirror. In the middle of the room, a small dance floor was underlit by twinkling stars. Nigel was ten minutes late but the first to arrive. His entry attracted a few curious glances, but none that made him feel uncomfortable. He perched on a bar stool and beckoned the barmaid, a blowsy blonde of indeterminate age who might have been more attractive if her make-up had not been applied with a trowel. "Good evening, sir. Meeting someone, I presume?"

"Yes, a friend. I'll have a large Bushmill's while I'm waiting. That's on the rocks." He had always disapproved of the practice of diluting good liquor with ice, but in America it somehow seemed the natural thing to do. As the barmaid was pouring the drink, Fran arrived, looking damp, windswept and slightly out of breath. "God, it's grim out there." She took the stool next to Nigel's and spoke to the barmaid. "Good evening, Joyce. I hope you've been entertaining my friend here. Oh, and I'll have whatever he had."

"Sure thing, Fran. How's it going, babe?"

"You look as if you could use a drink," Nigel said.

"Stiffer the better if that's not intruding on the male preserve. This humidity got to me today." From a dripping brow she wiped off water mingled with sweat. "I must look like a drowned rat. If you'll excuse me, I'll just pop to the powder-room to freshen up."

"Don't bother on my account," Nigel said. "You look just fine. The wet and wild look suits you."

Ignoring the compliment, Fran downed her drink in one. "Ah, I feel better already. But give me another of those and I'll feel even better."

She returned looking, Nigel had to admit, far less bedraggled.

"How's Jane?" Fran asked, pointlessly, since she had lunched with her the previous day.

"She's fine."

"Glad to hear it. Now, what's cookin', good lookin'? You sounded somewhat mysterious on the phone."

"That's because there's a mystery afoot... and I can't help feeling I'm in the middle of it. You, too."

"Me? Do tell me about it. I love a good mystery story."

"I was with Frank Hoffman this morning. We went for a walk - his daft idea, not mine. We avoided getting drenched by seconds."

"Yes, it was quite a storm, wasn't it."

"A meteorological metaphor for something else, perhaps."

Fran didn't ask what that meant. "How *is* Frank? And how are you two getting along, anyhow?"

"I like him," said Nigel, "although I'm not sure I could tell you why."

"I like him, too," Fran broke in, "and I *can* tell you why."

"As I'm sure you will. But first let me get to the point."

"The point?"

"The point of this meeting."

"Oh, is that what it is? A meeting?"

"Your friend Frank turned it into that. He seemed to be on the brink of telling me something but then he stopped. He suggested I talk to you instead, said you were the one who could 'fill me in', whatever that meant."

"And what, if I may ask, is the mystery topic we're supposed to be discussing?"

"Samantha Jameson."

Fran's face, for once, registered mild surprise, perhaps feigned. "Well, I can't think what it is he wants me to tell you."

"I think you do, Fran" Nigel said, as gently as he could.

Fran suddenly stood up. "If we're about to drop recognizable names, perhaps we should retire to a booth. We can talk more freely there."

Nigel was again in two minds about the tactics he should employ. Drop a few hints and see how she responded? Or, as he had done with Jane, come right out and say what was on his mind? He still hadn't decided even as he began talking. "I've been taking an interest in a story doing the rounds that President Jameson is having an affair..."

"Yes, I know. But there's nothing new there, as I'm sure you know."

"According to a certain nefarious periodical I won't bother to mention, the woman is a Russian, name of Anastasia." He paused to examine Fran's reaction, but her expression was unreadable. "Shall I go on?"

"Please do. But so far what you've told me I can read at the checkout of my local supermarket."

"As can I. But I've reason to believe that *Skandal* was on to something, but that it got hold of the wrong end of the stick. Or, as someone put it: right train, wrong track."

"As these tabloids do most of the time." Fran idly swirled the ice in her glass.

Since she was obviously determined to play hard-to-get, he switched to the more direct approach. "My sources tell me that there *is* an affair, and that it involves the White House... but not the president."

Fran remained expressionless. "Then who?"

"His wife. Samantha Jameson. Your boss."

"Oh, really! And how, may I ask, did you come by such information?"

"I won't reveal my source, of course, though I suspect you know exactly who it is. First, though, I'd like you to comment."

"Now, what made you think I'd be prepared to do that?"

"I didn't assume that you would. I'm just hoping you will."

"Good. In that case, for the record, I have no comment."

His irritation apparent, Nigel resolved to put cards on the table. "Let's not waste time playing cat-and-mouse. You know damned well what I'm talking about. Frank Hoffman knows, too, but he told me to talk to you. And you know who my source is." His tone startled her. "So why don't we stop dancing round the mulberry bush. You know that I've discovered the affair. We'll call it alleged affair, for the sake of appearances, but it's one that I have every reason to believe is true."

Fran looked slightly put out. She said nothing, thinking about her next response. Then she said, "Alright. You win. I'll come clean. Off the record, naturally. But first, tell me what you know, or think you know, and then I'll tell you whether you're barking up the wrong tree. Or just barking mad."

"I know about Samantha's affair. I know who the Russian lady is. I know where she lives. I even know something about her background."

"My, you *have* been busy. And how do you know all this?"

"First, from my source - *our* source, I should say - who we know is of the reliable variety. Second, from some digging around I did on my own. One of the things I also found out was that you and the lady in question know each other well. Apparently, you're a regular visitor to her apartment in New York."

"Now, how could you possibly know that?" Fran sounded less surprised than playful. She was, Nigel felt, still toying with him.

"Because, my dear Fran, I saw you - with my own eyes - going into her building. I watched you chatting with the doorman, which suggested, even to this dim Dr Watson, that you'd been there many times before. The doorman's name, as I recall, is Lou."

Fran suddenly looked angry. "So, you've been watching me. Following me."

"Yes and no."

"What the fuck does that mean?"

"I was in New York trying to find out where Anastasia - or Anna - lives when, out of the blue, you showed up. I was as surprised to see you as you'd have been to see me. I did follow you, it's true, but only for one block. You led me straight to her."

"Ah, so you must be the mysterious delivery man who disappeared without leaving a package."

"Guilty as charged."

"And how did you know where the lady lived?"

"A source gave me an approximate location. Someone in the bridge world, of all places. The rest was legwork and luck. You were the luck."

She sighed. "Well, I must say, this is all very cloak-and-dagger. And how far has your investigation progressed since then?"

"It hasn't. It came to a halt up there on the East Side. Not because I ran out of steam but because my instincts told me to hold fire. I'm hoping, one way or another, that you'll save me considerable further effort."

"Not quite how Woodward and Bernstein would have played it. So, what next?"

"I'd like you to do some talking."

Fran sighed again. "Okay, okay. The gig is up, as they say. And the ground rules? Is this on 'deep background' - as you journos like to say - and am I being taped?"

"Background. No attribution. No tape. But you're aware that I'm a reporter, and that I've announced my intentions. I always observe the ground rules. Now, if you still don't want to talk, you can say nothing and just walk away. That's my offer: talk or walk."

Fran knew the game. She also knew the game was up. She had known it from the moment Nigel had called her. "Okay, I'll talk. But only because you're someone I believe I can trust. But first, be a darling and fetch two more drinks. What I have to say may take some time."

He went to the bar and returned with refills. Fran finished hers before saying another word. "You seem to know most of the story already. You know that it started with Sonny's daughter Sally telling her father about Anna. Sonny had already confided all this to me. He was thoroughly confused, poor man, so anxious to protect his daughter that he didn't know what to do. He called me for advice. We're old friends, by the way... but I'm sure you've gathered that. Then *Skandal* magazine came out with that silly piece. I've no idea where they got it. The source, I suspect, may even have been Sonny himself; he's been known to shoot his mouth off when he's had a few. Anyway, Sonny's discovery, and then that bloody *Skandal* piece, combined to set alarm bells ringing. Then, just as the hue and cry seemed to have died down, you asked your silly question at the briefing. That set off more bells. *Skandal* wouldn't recognize a story if someone fire-bombed their building, but someone like you sniffing around was another matter. Take that as a compliment, by the way. Anyway, we decided to - I don't know - adopt you."

"We? Adopt? What the fuck are you talking about?"

"I'm sure you've already worked out who's on stage in this little drama. Four of us: Samantha herself, Frank Hoffman, me, and in a walk-on part, Sonny. Oh, and Anna makes five. So far, that's the entire cast."

"So, we have the cast. But what's the play?"

"I'll tell you - or at least tell you what I know. I've been aware of Samantha's liaison with Anna for some time. How could someone in my position not know? But I'm sure you worked that out. She told Frank because they're old friends and, believe it or not, political soulmates. Sonny made his appearance after Sally started talking. Her relationship with Anna, by the way, was affectionate but entirely platonic. So, then we put our heads together - Samantha, Frank, and me - to figure out how to contain the thing. Sonny wanted nothing further to do with us, or the story, terrified his daughter's name would come up. But then we persuaded him to approach you, to find out what you knew. And, if possible, to talk you out of writing something. Well, you know that part. And now you've joined the cast."

"I've often been recruited to write something, but never *not* to write something."

"You surprise me. Journalists are asked to sit on stories all the time."

"Not this journalist."

"I knew you were a man of integrity."

"Anyway, here we are because of that silly question. By the way, when I asked it, I knew fuck all."

"Well, we couldn't know that, could we. The point is - the reason we're here, I suppose - is that we wanted someone we could rely on to do the right thing."

"The right thing?"

"To protect the innocent. The ideal scenario was that, since the president wasn't involved, you could be persuaded not to pursue it. If that didn't work, we figured we'd give you the chance to do it but with us helping to - how can I put it - guide the narrative."

"Guide the narrative!"

"A naïve idea, perhaps. And I suppose, looking back, the whole thing sounds silly."

"I would say so."

"So now, here I am, sitting in a gay bar, chatting with the sixth member of our little troupe..."

"There's a seventh," Nigel said casually.

Fran looked horrified. "You've told someone else? Who, for God's sake?"

"Jane."

Fran exhaled a relieved sigh. "Well, I suppose I ought to have known you'd tell her. We can trust her, of course, but a word of caution: the more people who know about this, the less likely it'll stay under wraps."

"And you're hoping I'll go along with the wrapping?"

"Frankly, I've no idea what you're going to do."

"Frankly, nor do I. But I know you'll understand that I can't be part of a conspiracy to contain a story of this magnitude. It would be a conflict of interest, a dereliction of duty. Call it what you will, but I'm not in the habit of negotiating terms for what I write, much less what someone doesn't want me to write."

"Yes, yes, I get all that," Fran said. "But first, if you'll stop talking while I'm interrupting, let me finish what I was going to say, and then we'll exchange notes."

Nigel put a mocking finger to his lips.

"We're six, now seven, people in possession of a secret which, if exposed, would have startling repercussions... on many levels. I'm sure I don't have to spell them out. Now we just need to decide what to do with it. Your advice about how to manage the process would be greatly appreciated."

"I don't know what 'process' means, but as a journalist I'm the last person to give such advice. And why me, anyway, a relative newcomer from a foreign paper that most Americans have never heard of? Why not someone from the *Washington Post* or the *New York Times?* You must know people at both papers."

"Two reasons. First, but not necessarily the best, is that Samantha Jameson doesn't like either paper - largely because they don't seem to like her. Second, you seemed the reporter most likely to break the story. Third, using an American media outlet, we felt we'd lose all control." Fran noted Nigel's arched eyebrow. "I'm not saying we think we can control you, but if the story broke in the American media, the pack would spare no effort trying to top it. There would be a pissing contest for the next sensation. We decided instead to break the story - if it had to be broken at all - in a gentler way, through a publication hardly anyone over here reads. No offence intended, by the way."

Nigel looked incredulous. "That, if I may say so, is also a rather naïve view. The story will be a sensation however it breaks, and whoever breaks it. I don't have to tell you that."

"Well," Fran added, "perhaps we got it all wrong. I'm only telling you what we were thinking. Now I'd like to ask what *you're* thinking."

"I'm thinking that I'm not comfortable with any of this. I've never been told what to write, or not to write, and never will. I need you to know that."

"And I do know it. But there's something else you should." Fran paused to think. "It's something I haven't mentioned."

"I had a suspicion there might be…"

"There's something bigger going on in the background. Now, this will give you even more to ponder. What we're thinking is that we might persuade you to sit on the story of the Samantha affair by offering you some kind of… let me find the right word here… incentive."

"Are you talking about a bribe?"

"That's an ugly word. Let's call it a trade. I'm talking about you killing that story in exchange for an even bigger one. I can't say too much more but it doesn't involve sex."

"Then what does it involve?"

"I can't tell you. But it would be big, and it would be exclusive to the *Post*. There would, though, be certain conditions."

"There you go again with terms and conditions. I told you, none of this is negotiable. I'll make the decision. Me. Alone. On its merits. And I can't evaluate the merits because I don't know what the alternative story is."

"Only Samantha Jameson can tell you that. And she will. She wants to meet you."

"When?"

"Soon. She's already offered you an interview, at your request; now, she'd like to grant one, at her request. You wanted something from her; now she wants something from you. All I can tell you meanwhile is that she has more to talk to you about than an extramarital affair. Much more."

"How soon is 'soon'?"

"Probably in the next day or so."

Nigel's glass was as empty as his imagination, but he was loath to interrupt the flow of disclosures by walking to the bar. "And during this interview, or whatever it now is, she'll tell all, presumably on the record? Whatever the fuck 'all' is."

"I don't want to second-guess her, but I believe so."

Nigel seemed more doubtful than ever, but there seemed little more to be said. "Can we backtrack for a moment to this Anastasia story, which happens to be the only tangible one we've got going right now. What can you tell me about this Anna? You obviously know her well. What do you make of her?"

"Before I get to answer that, why don't you get us two more drinks. Same again for me. I'm in the mood for it, I can tell you."

Reluctantly, Nigel again went to the bar. The *Blue Orchid* was starting to fill up, most of the patrons obviously out for drinks after work. He returned with two more whiskies, attracting a few curious glances on the way. He felt no embarrassment, having been in many a gay bar in his time.

"I'd normally drink champagne here," Fran said when he returned, "but I think this is more a whisky moment. Champagne is for celebrations. This isn't a celebration. Yet."

"To be honest, I wish I knew what it was," said Nigel, picking up from the 'yet' that a celebration might be the outcome of whatever it was that Samantha Jameson was going to tell him.

Fran tried to pick up the conversational thread. "Now, where was I…?

"You were going to give me your evaluation of Anna."

"Ah, yes. I should start by telling you that she's no Russian agent. Neither is she some empty-headed, headline-grabbing socialite on the make. Quite the opposite. She's quiet and reserved, doesn't even like parties. And she's no gold-digger, I assure you, because she's quite wealthy in her own right. An inheritance from her father."

Nigel was looking skeptical.

"Oh, I know what you're thinking. Before I met her, I shared your doubts. But since then, I've been converted. In any other circumstances I'd rather fancy her myself, as you Brits say."

"When I saw you in New York, you had an overnight bag, and I started to think…"

"I do stay over sometimes, but not in that way."

Nigel continued to prod. "What about Anna's affair with Sonny's daughter?"

"That was before Samantha came on the scene. Anyway, as I told you, it was no more than a casual friendship. Of that much I'm certain. Sally's not remotely Anna's type."

"How did Samantha meet Anna?"

"At a charity event. In the Metropolitan Museum, I believe."

"The ladies who don't enjoy parties…"

"We all find ourselves at charity events from time to time."

"I'd still like to meet this Anna," Nigel said.

"Why?"

"Because if I'm to be completely in the picture, I'd like to make my own assessment of her."

"Funny you should mention it," Fran said, grinning from ear to ear.

"Oh, why's that?"

"Because she'll be arriving shortly."

Nigel was caught off guard. "Here?"

"Yes," Fran said. "Here. In the flesh, as it were. You see, I've anticipated your every need."

"I'm starting to worry about that," Nigel said, reflexively straightening his tie and brushing his hair back.

They both laughed, and the mood lightened a little.

* * *

Nigel knew it was her the moment she walked in.

Her handsome looks had not been exaggerated. She was a brunette, tall and slender, with sculpted Slavic cheekbones, a vaguely oriental look. She could have been a model. She had obviously dressed for anonymity. Her hair was tied back into a rather severe bun, and she was dressed casually in slacks and jacket, both in sombre colours. She looked less the voluptuous siren than a little girl lost. Even so, Nigel's was not the only head that turned.

Anna approached the booth with a discreet below-the-waist wave at Fran and returned Nigel's evaluating look with one of her own. After kissing Anna on both cheeks three times, European style, Fran introduced her. In the moment before shaking her hand, Nigel was as flummoxed as a schoolboy.

Fran slid across the banquette to make room, in the process separating her from Nigel. "What will you have to drink?" he asked. "We're on Irish whiskey."

"I'll have a diet Coke," Anna said quietly. "I'm not much of a drinker." The voice was soft and lightly accented, not quite a seductive purr but warm and welcoming. Nigel left to get her drink. Coming back, he noticed that the two women were in conversation, apparently about him, since it ended abruptly as soon as he came within earshot.

Fran spoke first. "I was just saying to Anna that this is a very strange situation we find ourselves in."

"You might say so," said Nigel, looking directly at Anna, who smiled enigmatically, no more at ease than he was. "Do you prefer Anastasia or Anna?"

"Always Anna," she said. The smile was still faintly in place. "I'm American now, and Americans seem to struggle with foreign names. I'm not sure why, as many of them have difficult foreign names themselves, including Russian ones." She paused.

"True," said Nigel, to fill the gap.

Anna looked at him directly, with a serious expression. "I understand, Mr Harper, that you have a package for me. Now you can give it to me in person."

They all laughed.

Nigel above all, pleased to know that she had a sense of humour, impressed that she could deploy it while under a great strain.

"I'm afraid I forgot to bring it," he replied, causing more merriment. "But it was only a second-hand copy of *Gone with the Wind*. I'm sure you've read it already."

More laughter. Then he looked at Fran for guidance in her role as mistress of ceremonies.

Fran rose to the occasion. "Well, now that the formalities are out of the way, perhaps we can chat."

"Alright," said Anna, whose smile now faded. Her look was that of a Tolstoy heroine after learning that Napoleon's army was outside Moscow.

Fran led off. "Nigel's now completely in the picture, Anna, at least as far as you're concerned. He'll be meeting Samantha in a few days. She'll have more to say than I've been able to tell him. And then… well, it's not yet clear what will happen after that. Let me just say, Anna, that I can vouch for this man. He's dating - is that the word, Nigel? - another dear friend of mine. She'll keep him in line if he misbehaves." Fran laughed nervously. "She, by the way, knows pretty much what he knows." Anna looked startled. "Oh, don't worry, I'll vouch for her."

Anna looked less than reassured. "But I *am* worried. Not for myself, you understand, but for Samantha. I know the pressure she's under. I'm not sure how much more she can take. She's already seeing a therapist." Nigel had not known that and made a mental note of it. Yet another interesting sub-plot in a tale that was becoming as dense as a Chinese menu.

"We'll see her through this, Anna, don't you worry."

Fran glanced at Nigel, as if to give Anna the impression that he was a member of the rehabilitation team. Nigel looked blank. He had no idea what his role in this process was supposed to be. Process? Is that what it was? He had never been in a situation quite like it. Sailors in uncharted waters refrain from advancing with every sail unfurled. The same principle of caution, he concluded, should apply in this case.

Fran spoke again. "Anna, why don't you tell Nigel something about yourself." Anna gave her a look as if whatever she said, he wouldn't believe it.

"I was born in Moscow. I am only child. My parents were wealthy. My mother died when I was still at school, so my father raised me. And, of course, there were nannies. I studied politics at Moscow University. After that, I went to Paris, to Sorbonne - as Samantha did. Later, I lived in London for a while, also like Samantha. So, you see, we have much in common. In London I learnt to play bridge. Is very big there. Also, here. I am quite good player. Then I moved to New York. I studied at NYU." She paused, as if her educational record was all that she was obliged to recount.

Anxious to cut to the chase, but with polite reluctance, Nigel asked: "Were you, while in New York or anywhere else, ever asked to give information about America to Russia?"

Anna looked horrified. "You mean, am I Russian spy?"

"Since you put it that way, yes."

"No. That is stupid talk. Americans seem to think all Russians are spies."

"You're right," Nigel said, smiling, "but when you're secretly involved with the wife of the President of the United States..."

"I am good American citizen. Now I shall stay here in America for the rest of my life. I have passport, too, thanks to my former husband."

"Husband!" Nigel almost spat it out.

"Yes, I once married fellow NYU student. How do you say? Nice Jewish boy from Brooklyn. Only for one year. Then he found other woman. So, maybe not so nice after all."

"But I thought you were..."

"I know what you're about to say. Yes, I am."

Nigel pushed on. "Forgive me for asking, but did you marry the nice Jewish boy to get a passport?"

"That is rude question. No. I married him because I like him. But then…."

"I'm divorced, too," Nigel said, thinking it might make them fellow sufferers. "What happened after that?"

"One year ago, I met Samantha at party. We talked. We made dinner date. Soon, we fell in love. What more to tell you?" Anna now appeared to be agitated. "May I have another Coke? And I must go to rest room."

While she was gone, Fran spoke sternly. "I think you should ease up on the third-degree stuff. She's not a KGB agent, you know, trained to resist interrogation. And that question about the passport... The last thing I want is to tip her over the edge."

"I'll try," Nigel said, without empathy. Now he had some bones to his story, and from the horse's mouth. What he was supposed to do with it he didn't want to think about, pending his meeting with Samantha Jameson.

When Anna returned, Nigel pushed a fresh drink in her direction. "I'm sorry if I sounded too direct, Anna, but I'm a journalist, you see, and I'm afraid it's ingrained. Forgive me." He looked across at Fran for approval. "And I want to stress that *you're* not the story here. I can see that now."

"I'm happy to hear it," said Anna, brightening a little.

After that, she became almost chatty. She described her childhood, a privileged and happy one, apparently, despite the early loss of her mother. Of life in general, she was more emphatic. "The Communists have gone, but what replaced them is worse. Now we have Putin. A gangster. Now is even less freedom. I was glad to leave. I will never go back... perhaps to see my papa before he dies." Her voice tailed off. "Now, Mr Harper, let me ask you questions. You are English journalist in Washington. You like it better here than London?"

"No... well, I don't really know yet. I've only been here a few weeks. Ask me again in a year."

More questions followed, to most of which Nigel responded with a potted, light-hearted history of his own life, lacing facts with witty asides. Fran laughed at some, despite having heard them before. Even Anna smiled at those few that didn't sail over her head. When he had finished, Anna delivered her verdict: "Fran told me you were interesting man. I think she was right."

Nigel found himself disarmed by the woman's appealingly gauche manner. Either she was the innocent that she appeared to be, or she was a consummate actor. But then, just as they seemed to be getting along, Anna suddenly stood up. "I have to go now."

"Where are you off to?" Fran asked, startled.

"Maryland."

Fran nodded, understanding why. "Ah. Then please tell Samantha that I'll call her first thing in the morning."

Anna rose, kissed Fran, and then, much to Nigel's surprise, kissed him too. He stood and watched her leave. So again did many others, he noticed.

Fran sat down again. "Phew, that was a close call. For a moment there I thought she was going to lose the plot. Thank you, by the way, for being so gentle. She's a rather delicate thing, isn't she? What did you think of her?"

Nigel thought about it before responding. "Well, she's beautiful and obviously intelligent. Terribly sensitive. As for whether she's everything she says she is, my editorial instinct tells me to keep an open mind, but I have to say my gut feel is that what you see is what you get."

"Mine too. But I didn't know about the husband."

"Really? So, she does have secrets."

"Don't we all. Now, what say we get snockered, unless you have to rush back to your beloved."

"I called her. When I told her I was meeting you she said, 'See you in the morning'."

"She knows me too well."

"But before we both lose it, I do have a few more questions… and more than a few observations."

"In that case, you'll have to feed me. Let's get out of here. I know a place not far from here."

* * * * *

PART TWO

The First Lady

Chapter 12

Nigel was home alone on a Friday evening watching television when his cell phone buzzed. Jane had gone to Wilkes Barre for the weekend for a family occasion to which he had not been invited. "It's not something I'd want to put you through," she'd told him. "You'll meet my parents soon enough, I promise." In truth, it was something he anticipated more as a duty than a treat.

The caller was Fran Powell, speaking loudly enough to be heard above the sound of music and laughter. "Sorry about the background noise, but I'm at the *Orchid* with some friends. I'm calling to invite you for a drive in the country."

"When?

"Tomorrow morning."

"Where are we going?"

"Maryland. Eastern Shore. To Frank Hoffman's weekend place. It's about an hour and a half from here. I'll be driving. I'll pick you up."

"Why are we going to see Frank?"

"We're not. He's at Camp David with the president. We're meeting Samantha Jameson."

"I take it this is for the interview that we discussed?"

"No, something else."

"What?"

"She wants to chat."

"Chat?"

"Her word, not mine, so I'll leave her to explain it."

"Why can't *you* explain it?"

"Because I can't. And that's 'can't' rather than 'won't'. Do you play golf, by the way?"

"After a fashion. Why?"

"Because she's bound to invite you to join her for a round. She's golf mad. After horses it's her favourite thing. I'm told she plays as well as she rides. I wouldn't know. I hate golf."

"She'll change her mind when she sees me play. I'm a once-a-year hacker."

"Don't worry, you'll probably be more hack than hacker. No doubt she'll have more on her mind than golf."

"Like what?"

"You're all questions today."

"That's because it all sounds very mysterious."

"Well, you're a writer. You figure it out. Meanwhile, I'll be at your place at eight. Sharp." Nigel said he would prefer nine. "No, eight," Fran insisted. "She's an early riser. And be ready. We wouldn't want to keep her waiting."

"Dress code?"

"Smart casual. Do you have any golf gear?"

"No."

"Well, I'm sure all that can be arranged. See you at eight." She hung up.

Arriving at Nigel's place a few minutes early, Fran sat in her car, listening to the radio. On the stroke of eight, she honked the horn twice. Nigel emerged from his apartment in jeans, a leather jacket in one hand, a half-eaten slice of toast and marmalade in the other. He slid into the front seat looking mildly irritated. You're very prompt. I was just finishing breakfast."

"Well, I did warn you." As he wiped a crumb from his upper lip she chuckled at his disheveled appearance. "I like your idea of smart casual. You look as if you're heading for an outdoor rock concert."

"It's called shabby chic."

"I'd call it just shabby."

She was still giggling as she pulled away from the kerb. He didn't tell her that his mode of dress was calculated to get him out of playing golf. Fran was a good driver, he noticed immediately. He was inept behind the wheel. Some would say a potential menace. He marvelled at Fran's skill as she negotiated her way through the heavy traffic with the dexterity of a cab driver on an incentive. He was usually a nervous passenger, especially with someone he'd never driven with before, but today he felt unusually relaxed.

"I must say you drive very well," he said, failing to keep the surprise out of his voice.

"For a woman, you mean?"

"That's not what I meant at all."

"I bet you did, she said, laughing." She was in an amiable and talkative mood. "I like driving. My Dad taught me before I was in my teens. He used to take me to a local school at weekends and have me drive round the playground, using the basketball poles as traffic lights. One day a police car showed up for a routine security check and ordered us to stop, although they seemed quite amused. By then I was something of an ace behind the wheel."

"You still are," Nigel said, genuinely impressed. He glanced at the sat-nav screen, but it made no more sense to him than an X-ray picture of an eyeball. "How far is it, where we're going?"

"About seventy miles. Close to a town called Easton if that means anything. Beautiful area, the Eastern Shore. A lot of people have second homes down there. It's one of Washington's summer playgrounds. Frank's house is on the water."

"So, who's going to be there?"

"Just the three of us, not counting the housekeeper. Samantha uses the place from time to time. And it so happens it's close to one of her favourite golf courses. Speaking of Frank, I understand you're missing a White House briefing this morning."

"I've sent the junior reporter from our office. I don't think we're expecting any major announcements."

"Maybe a date for the president's State Visit to Britain, although I'm sure you know all about that already."

"I do. The BBC man told me."

"Ivan Brand, that pompous old blowhard..."

"Well, he *does* work for the BBC."

"Ah, yes, the British Blowhard Corporation."

"I don't know why Jameson thinks it's a good idea. We Brits certainly don't want him there. He'll get a warm reception in London. The demonstrators will be out in force. Not the kind of reception an American president usually expects."

"This one will probably think they've come to cheer him on."

"And why he barred the British ambassador from the White House on the eve of a State Visit is beyond me."

"In retaliation to the Speaker's recent remark that he won't be invited to address Parliament. That's a slap in the face, especially as his predecessor went there and got a standing ovation. Good for Mr Speaker, I say." Fran deftly overtook a slow-moving truck, giving Nigel the first nervous moment of the journey.

"First decent thing the little shit's done since he's been in the chair," said Nigel, recovering.

"Will you go over to cover it?"

"Maybe. That's up to my editor. If I do, I'd like to take Jane with me."

"She'd like that, I'm sure."

"Samantha will be joining her husband, I take it."

"Yes. She doesn't want to, but duty demands it. She also knows that staying away would raise yet more questions about the state of their marriage. Anyway, how could she miss an opportunity for a sleepover at the Palace?"

"That could be ruled out as well."

"I doubt it. It's kind of mandatory for a State Visit, however unpopular the president. Not inviting him would be seen as a calculated insult."

"Will you be going?"

"No. Samantha wanted me there, but I told her I'd rather sit this one out. We had a bit of an argument about it."

"You two argue?"

"All the time. Sometimes we go at it like a couple of hellcats in heat."

"Really! I thought you two were close."

"We are, but like sisters who love each other but also can't stand each other. We're quite different in many ways, though in one respect we're not different at all, as you now know. She's terribly sensitive. I can be rather brutal. Where she suffers fools gladly, or pretends to, I'd just as soon knock their fucking heads off. She can also be taciturn to a fault, a trait that no one has ever ascribed to me."

"That last assertion is open to contradiction, I'd say, based on recent events."

"That's only because I've been talking to a nosy foreign journalist."

Nigel laughed. His relationship with Fran had indeed been prickly at times, but he was getting used to her direct manner. He admired her dedication to protecting the woman she served, and Samantha plainly thought highly of her in return. Which meant, he presumed, that whatever lay in store for him in Maryland, they had planned it together, despite Fran's denial. The thought set him wondering again why he was allowing himself to be drawn into a Faustian pact to suppress a news story of some importance for the promise of a bigger one yet to be identified. He hoped to learn more today - no, he expected to learn everything today. The first lady wouldn't have summoned him to her country retreat as a mere courtesy, or even for an interview, so he could only guess that she had something important to say. And Fran had promised as much.

"You've suddenly gone quiet," she said, disturbing his reverie. "What were you thinking about?"

"Oh, I was just mulling over the rather odd situation in which I find myself."

"Odd would be one word for it," said Fran. "I can think of stronger ones."

"Me, too, and none of them comforting."

"Well, let's not allow our imaginations to run away with us."

Fran said nothing more, and for the next few miles they drove on in contemplative silence. They had been driving for a little under an hour. Nigel saw that they were now on a highway called Route 50, about to cross a vast bridge over Chesapeake Bay at a place called Kent Island. The Annapolis naval academy, which he'd always wanted to visit, was somewhere off to their right. A few miles farther on the highway swung east, urban sprawl giving way to a rolling landscape of small farms and clapboard houses nestling in groves of trees. Half an hour later they turned off onto a minor, rural road, passing an occasional roadside general store-cum diner, with pickup trucks parked diagonally out front, and small gas stations where attendants still filled up the cars. This, Nigel thought, was the real America, or at any rate the America of his childhood imagination. A Norman Rockwell America, of quiet sleepy towns where people went to village barbecues, held Fourth-of-July parties, and on Memorial Day stood on sidewalks waving flags to remember long departed sons and daughters. A lost America, some would say, though perhaps not so much lost as overlooked. Certainly, an America more typical than those towering canyons of Manhattan or the faux Roman temples of Washington. At one point they passed a vast high school campus, dominated by the biggest flag he'd ever seen, the modern glassed building behind it a monument to the propagation of the American dream. A far cry from the tiny village school Nigel had attended in rural Norfolk, or the ramshackle Georgian grammar school he'd gone to later.

"Not far now," said Fran, as they turned off onto a meandering single-lane road, heavily wooded on both sides. Clearly, she had taken this route many times before. Here the houses were progressively larger, less visible from the road, some separated from neighbours by hundreds of yards. "Just two more miles," Fran said shortly. Within minutes they were pulling into a gravel driveway. A burly man in a dark suit, obviously a secret service agent, appeared as if from nowhere. Fran rolled down the window.

"Hello, Joe," she said, flashing an identity card. "Beautiful day."

"Good morning, Miss Powell. Mrs Jameson is out on the golf course right now. Told me to tell you to go right in and make yourself at home."

"Joe, this is our guest, Nigel Harper. He's been cleared, I presume."

"Yes ma'am. He's on my list." He examined Nigel for a moment but - surprisingly, Nigel thought - failed to ask for any identification.

Fran eased into the drive. Ahead of them, hidden from the road by stands of hickory and tulip trees, stood a white clapboard colonial with a broad wrap-around verandah. For Nigel, it evoked old black-and white films featuring corn-fed Americans sitting in swing chairs with neighbours drinking lemonade on hot summer nights, as cicadas whirred in chorus on the soundtrack. The perfect place for a weekend hideaway. Fran parked behind a large black limousine, Samantha's official car. At the back of the house, Nigel glimpsed a terrace and a well laid-out garden that ran down to a large body of water, agitated by white caps, and dotted with sailboats heeled over in a gusty breeze.

The front door was opened by a black maid in uniform, who introduced herself as Ethel. She greeted Fran with a hug. "Coffee, ma'am? And for you, sir?"

"Oh, yes, please," they chirped, almost in unison.

Just minutes later, Samantha's grey BMW - actually Frank Hoffman's - pulled into the driveway. They went outside to meet her, each with coffee in hand. Samantha was wearing a slacks-and-blouse ensemble complete with an angora sweater draped over her shoulders. A picture of informal elegance, Nigel thought. The word radiant came to mind again. What Martin Jameson had seen in her was plain to see - but what could she possibly have seen in him?

"Good morning, both of you," Samantha proclaimed cheerily. "Perfect timing as usual. Easy drive? That Route 50 can be a real pain." She didn't wait for an answer. "So nice to see you again, Mr Harper." Samantha offered her hand, which he shook rather than kissed, his first impulse. She brought out the Walter Raleigh in him; if there had been a puddle, he'd had thrown his leather jacket over it

"The traffic was pretty light on 50," Fran said, answering the first question, and offered one of her own. How was your game?"

"Not good. My long game was all over the place. The ball seemed to be guided into the rough by some invisible hand. I could blame the wind, of course, but a more likely explanation would be my distracted state of mind." She turned to Nigel. "I'm reliably informed that you're a decent golfer, Mr Harper."

"Not so reliably," he replied flippantly, hoping the remark would get him off the hook. "Neither decent nor a golfer."

She smiled. "What a pity. I was looking forward to another round this afternoon. Golf, that is. But perhaps you'll indulge me anyway."

"I'm not exactly dressed for the part."

"We can take care of it," she said. And that was that. If the First Lady of the United States wanted to play golf, then golf it would be. "At least out there on the course we'll be able to talk without interruption." She gave Nigel what he took to be a knowing look. "Meanwhile, though, I think lunch might be in order."

It was not yet eleven, but Samantha, a compulsive early riser, invariably lunched at noon.

"Good," said Fran. "I skipped breakfast. But then in this job I skip breakfast most mornings." She turned to Nigel. "I work for a ruthless, hard-driving woman, you know. Breakfasts, even lunches, are luxuries."

"Now, don't you go blaming me," Samantha said, wagging a disapproving finger. "The White House chef is always available to you. Your problem is not me, just bad habits. You just can't be bothered to eat at regular times. Too many snacks. And, let's face it, too many hangovers." Samantha strode purposefully into the well-appointed kitchen and saw that Ethel was preparing something involving chicken and vast quantities of salad. Samantha nodded approval. "The kitchen is obviously in good hands, so perhaps I should tend bar instead. Lemonade, freshly squeezed, might go down well. It's a little early for anything stronger. For me, anyway."

Nigel would have preferred a beer but was too eager to create a good impression to say so. "That sounds perfect, Mrs Jameson."

"Out here you can call me Samantha. Be a darling, Fran, and fetch some ice. Oh, and tell Ethel we'll have lunch on the terrace. It's much too nice to stay indoors."

At noon, on the sun-dappled stone terrace, partly shaded by a pergola covered by a gnarled wisteria of some antiquity, they tucked into the chicken salads. Fran had quietly opened a bottle of white wine, which nestled in ice in a nearby cooler. Samantha noticed but said nothing. He was the only one drinking. "It's still a little too early for me," Samantha said. Fran also declined because she'd be driving later. The atmosphere was relaxed. Samantha had been rejuvenated by her round of golf and Fran was still in a chatty mood. They talked about this and that, mostly about the local cultural scene. The small talk, Nigel assumed, was a necessary preamble to more significant topics, or at least he hoped so. Sure enough, Samantha suddenly turned serious. The subject she raised was journalism, in which she claimed to have an 'abiding interest'. Nigel guessed that this was merely a lead-in to what she really wanted to talk about, the reason he'd been invited.

"You enjoy quite a stellar reputation in your profession, Nigel. I've been catching up on some of your recent pieces. You have a nice turn of phrase, I must say. I like the light, almost satirical touch, especially when you're writing about parliamentary debates. You let nobody off the hook."

"There's a great deal to satirize," said Nigel, ignoring the compliment." He wondered whether she had really been reading his copy or was just buttering him up. The latter, he concluded.

"Language," said Samantha, distractedly picking chicken pieces out of the salad, "has become so degraded. We talk in nothing but clichés, euphemisms and catch phrases. We fill sentences with pointless words like 'absolutely' and 'literally'. We don't seem to talk *to* each other anymore, only *at* each other. It's as if we've forgotten how to. Or worse, can no longer bear to. That's especially true in the political world. Do you agree?"

"Absolutely," Nigel said, deadpanning.

Samantha laughed. "It may surprise you to know that I once thought about going into journalism myself. It always appealed to me. The search for truth is a noble thing and never more vital than now. Only an alert media can keep those political scoundrels in line - and the rest of us safe."

"Safe from what?"

"From dark and dangerous forces, like certain political parties I could mention, and the dark forces that control them."

"In that case," Nigel remarked drily, "we in the media seem to have fallen short of our duty."

"I think you have, sad to say. Good investigative reporting is becoming a rare thing. It's just too labor-intensive for most editorial budgets. Then, of course, there are the legal risks. I don't know how it is in Britain these days - worse, I've always heard - but even here, if you get a few minor facts wrong, you can find yourself in court defending a libel suit that could destroy the paper."

"The *Post* used to have a special investigative unit, but it was disbanded two years ago. I wonder how many readers even noticed."

"Well, I think the best and brightest of you still do a marvellous job. And what, we must ask ourselves, is the alternative to a free and inquisitive press?"

"Apparently, getting your news from the political spin doctors, blogs, anonymous tweets and other social media sites."

"Less reliable sources of the truth it would be hard to imagine. But my husband, as you know, is convinced that all journalists are corrupt. Or at least that's his public stance. And his 'fake news' mantra sells well. He's managed to convince his voter base that the media are the enemy of the people. Well, as far as I'm concerned, *he's* the enemy of the people."

Nigel was momentarily taken aback by her frankness. Was all this off the record? She hadn't said so, and he hadn't asked. "A legendary British editor, C.P. Scott, once said, 'Comment is free, but facts are sacred.' That seems unimprovable. If ego and hubris sometimes send us off course, we're no less human than anyone else. We can only do our best. "I hope I'm not sounding too evangelical."

"Evangelism in pursuit of truth is no bad thing. Unlike those charlatans who make fortunes on television peddling lies in the name of tax-free religions they themselves have founded. You should take pride in being on the receiving end of this administration's media attacks; they can only mean one thing: you're doing your job. On a more personal note, you must be delighted to have been assigned to the White House. It doesn't get any better than that in your profession, does it."

"No, it doesn't."

"And please don't abandon that sense of mission. Honest citizens of the Free World, Americans especially, are depending on you, even if they don't know it. The future of democracy is at stake, if that doesn't sound too dramatic."

"It doesn't sound dramatic at all, not in these vexatious times."

Samantha laughed. "Only you Brits still use words like vexatious. I've no doubt you think my husband has something to do with the vexing."

"Many would say so."

"Would you say so?"

"Yes, since you ask."

"But I'll give him this: he gets his message out very effectively. Those tweets of his don't have an original thought in them, of course, but those 140 characters of pure fluff are as effective as any televised address to the nation. Come to think of it, I don't think he's ever given a televised address to the nation. He'd have trouble reading the teleprompter."

"A recent poll I saw found that only ten percent of people under twenty-five read a newspaper. The rest prefer taking their news from social media. Now, there's a frightening thought."

"Then print journalism must fight back," Samantha declared with Churchillian resolution. "Social media was supposed to bring us all closer together but does the opposite. So, keep producing those newspapers for as long as you can. Keep our literary digestive systems working. We need solid meals, not just fast-food snacks." She looked at Fran, who shrugged.

"We do our best," said Nigel, "but circulations keep falling, year on year. Our website has five times more readers than the paper, carries considerably more advertising, and the operating costs are marginal."

"Well, the delivery method is neither here nor there; it's the integrity of the source that matters. Personally, if perhaps illogically, I find a newspaper somehow more authentic than anything I read on a screen."

"Me, too. But then I'm a hack from the old Fleet Street mould."

"Well, we could talk about this for hours…" A change of subject seemed imminent and duly arrived. "You don't think much of my husband, do you?"

"I think you know the answer to that already."

Samantha smiled. "Yes, I do. But I'd still like to hear why. A foreigner's perspective. And please forget who you're talking to. Pretend you're in the pub talking to a mate. I won't be shocked by anything you say, I assure you."

Nigel knew he was being tested but relished the prospect of rising to the challenge. "It's hard to know where to start. Let's leave out that he's a vile human being. Worst of all, for me, is his ignorance. He doesn't know how to govern and doesn't seem to want to learn how. That makes him dangerous. He's also a narcissist, which means - or so the psychologists tell us - that he's incapable of objective judgment. That's even more dangerous. His approach to complex social issues - to the extent that he gives them any thought at all - is puerile. We talk about social division; to him it's a calculated policy position. It's also alarming that such a man has the world's biggest nuclear arsenal at his disposal. I suspect he's also a crook, though proving it might be difficult."

"Maybe not so difficult," said Samantha enigmatically. "But bravo! Honestly and succinctly put. You don't mince words, do you."

"You told me not to."

"Well, you didn't disappoint."

Nigel turned the tables. "But you know him better than anyone. Leaving aside all that I've said, does he, whatever his public statements, believe in anything?"

"Yes, his own bullshit."

"Sadly, so do seventy million Americans."

"What do you think should drive a political leader?"

"Humanity. What else? A desire to improve the human condition, to make the world a better place."

"Well said again, though somehow it sounds old-fashioned, doesn't it, even naïve."

"I'm sure your husband would say so."

"Yes, he would. You left out more of his deficiencies than you mentioned, but since it's an endless list, you're forgiven. We might think of some more out on the golf course. Speaking of which…"

He would have liked to discuss them now, but Samantha now seemed ready to move on from reciting her husband's manifest sins, leaving Nigel to marvel silently at how this woman of charm and intelligence managed to live under the same roof as a man who shared none of her values and cared no more for *her* hopes and aspirations than he did for the country's. His respect for her knew no bounds. Nor did his sadness. And yet… something else kept nagging at him: an insistent feeling that she might just be too good to be true. She had agreed with everything he had said, but it was nothing that millions of others wouldn't have happily endorsed. She was eminently believable, yet she had married the man she now despised, and had once reveled in the vacuous, careless life to which he had introduced her. What had she been thinking then? And what had happened to her since? Was her evident revulsion an exercise to expunge past sins, a search for redemption? Or was it for no better motive than revenge? And what did she plan to do about it other than talk?

Samantha seemed to sense his thoughts. "You must be anxious to know why I invited you here."

The question caught him off guard. "Well, yes, I was rather hoping for more than an interview that can never be published."

"Fair enough." She paused, as if wondering how to frame her response. "I understand that you've recently come to learn of certain aspects of my private life that aren't widely known, and which, for reasons too obvious to state, I wouldn't wish to be known."

"I have."

"The question now is what to do with that information." She paused again, apparently trying to strike the right tone. "Let me, as it were, put my cards on the table. If my extra-marital affair should become public knowledge, the consequences would be profound; for me personally, but also for the country. Having said that, I understand that the genie is now out of the bottle." As obvious as the statement was, it seemed to carry some hidden implication. Samantha didn't add to it, though, and seemed to be waiting for his reaction.

"The only genie is me, and I haven't written a story yet. I'm not even sure I will. Nor do I wish to."

"I'm glad to hear it."

"But allow me a peripheral observation."

"Go ahead."

"The world has changed over the past thirty years. Revelations of extramarital activities are no longer as shocking as they would have been a generation ago. Even same-sex relationships no longer have that power. Society has come a long way in that regard. In Britain, we recently elected a prime minister whose private life reads like a cheap paperback bodice-ripper."

"Well, you Brits, like the French, are more sophisticated in these matters than Americans. Many of my fellow citizens would see things rather differently. Out there in the American hinterland there are many who regard this country as the last bulwark against a sinister assault on Christian values; the kind of people who believe in original sin; the kind of people who still use words like fornication."

"But a rapidly shrinking minority…"

"Still, though, a substantial minority. And a potent political force. Revealing my private life would bring the wrath of God down on my head. God I can deal with, but one-hundred million righteous evangelicals would be something else."

"That would be richly ironic, given your husband's less than exemplary moral record, which, by the way, those same evangelicals seem perfectly happy to ignore."

"True. But while plastering my private life all over the tabloids would hurt me personally, it might also help my husband politically. That's not something I would wish to happen."

"How would it help him?"

"By generating sympathy for a cuckolded husband; one who's been not just betrayed but betrayed by a sexual deviant. It could help his re-election prospects." She laughed mirthlessly. "But now I'm going to tell you a story, and it's one that has nothing to do with my exotic love life."

Nigel leaned forward expectantly.

"Let me open by telling you that I've always been a Republican. But the party is a far cry from the one I thought I knew. It's been taken over by a band of neo-fascists - I use the term advisedly - who peddle hate and bigotry for the sole purpose of retaining power. They've persuaded millions of Americans to hate their fellow-Americans. Unless we stop it, the country will self-destruct. In short, the damage to my reputation is nothing compared with the damage America would suffer if this administration remained in office too long."

Nigel was gripping the arms of his chair, sensing that she was about to say something that would cause him to fall out of it. His pulse was racing. Should he be taking notes? Should he insist on taking notes? But the moment passed, and Samantha was still talking. "Democracy, like truth, is in grave danger. This president, if he wins next time around, could well attempt to replace it with something else. He must never be given the chance. Now, I'm not saying it should be done by violent means; there must be another way. There *is* another way. I have a plan. And that, Nigel, is what I want to talk to you about this afternoon. That's going to be your story."

Nigel's mouth was open. Fran, he noticed, was looking just as nonplussed as he was. She had no more idea what was coming next, Nigel now realized, than he did.

Samantha felt the rising tension and attempted to lighten the mood. "My, I have been going on a bit... and you're both still awake."

At that moment - of all moments - her cell phone buzzed. Samantha looked at it, sighed in irritation, and rose from the table.

"Excuse me, but I really need to take this." She headed for the kitchen.

Nigel cursed out loud. "Fuck." He strained to hear what Samantha was saying, but her voice was too muffled. From the few words he did manage to pick up, it was obvious that she was talking to a lawyer.

Fran slapped his arm. "Are you trying to listen in?"

"You bet I am," he said.

After a few minutes, Samantha came back, but didn't sit down. "Look, I'm sorry, Nigel. Something's come up, and I need to attend to it right away. Unfortunately, that means I must get back to Washington. Now."

"Do you want me to drive you?" asked Fran.

"No, Joe will take me. That way I can make some phone calls." She looked at Nigel. "I can only apologize. I know you were waiting for more; and there's more to come, believe me. But we're going to have to take a raincheck. We'll talk again, I promise. And soon. But now I really do have to go..."

Nigel's frustration was palpable. This situation was like the penultimate episode of a television serial that leaves viewers eagerly anticipating the final one but having to wait a week. In his experience final episodes almost invariably disappointed, although he doubted that this one would.

Samantha, observing his crestfallen expression, smiled encouragingly. "I've enjoyed meeting you again, Nigel. And again, I apologize for leaving you in the lurch, but I'm afraid it can't be helped. We'll rearrange another golf date. Soon."

"I understand," he said, for want of anything else to say.

"We'll catch up in a few days. By then I may have more to report. Meanwhile, it hardly needs saying that everything I've said was strictly off the record." Samantha had broken the cardinal rule of not saying so at the start, but that was a quibble.

"You can rely on me," he said rather limply.

"I hope so," she said, already opening the front door. "But the course of action I have in mind still has some unresolved issues. I can't say more. I can only ask for your patience. It will be well rewarded, I assure you."

With that remark hanging in the air, she was gone. They heard two car doors slam. By the time they reached the veranda to watch her go, the limousine was already moving, trailing dust... and much else besides.

Nigel turned to Fran. "Well, what the fuck are we to make of that?"

"Her leaving so suddenly?"

"No, that stuff about - tell me if I heard this right - removing the government."

"Your guess is as good as mine," Fran replied, "But I agree that something seems to be afoot. I have no more idea what that is than you. Even if I did know, I wouldn't tell you. Only she can do that."

This time, looking her in the eye, he believed it.

Nigel poured himself another glass of wine and went outside to the terrace. She joined him.

"You know what? I find her candour exhilarating, but right now I feel like kicking a door down. So, what the hell do we do now?"

"We drive back to Washington," she said flatly. "What else? But first, since we have unexpected time on our hands, let's take a relaxed drive down to the shore. I'm sure you'll find it quite beautiful."

* * *

Two days later, as he was turning in for the night, his cell phone rang. It was close to midnight. Jane, staying overnight, had been asleep for an hour, but now woke up with a start. "Who on earth could that be?" she muttered dreamily, "at this ungodly hour? It can't be London."

It was Fran. "Apologies for the late call, Nigel, but we're on call again. A repeat performance. Same place, same time. Tomorrow. I'll pick you up. I trust you're free. Oh, and bring an overnight bag; we'll be staying for the weekend. Sounds like it's game on."

Nigel could hardly wait. Since he had no idea what the next day would bring, he allowed himself to be unabashedly thrilled at the prospect of seeing Samantha Jameson again. There was more, much more, to this woman than he had ever imagined. She was no vacuous show wife, even if her husband thought of her that way. She exuded intelligence and class. She was also endowed, he suspected, with a resolve that would not easily be broken. Whatever course of action she had in mind, he had no doubt - not a scintilla of doubt - that it would have far-reaching consequences. Clearly, she meant business. But what business? He spent the rest of the night trying to work it out and failing. He fell asleep.

This time, Nigel dressed more appropriately, in blue blazer and gray slacks. Jane had insisted on it.

For much of the journey, Nigel and Fran were both too lost in their own thoughts - tinged with dread - to exchange much more than small talk. The subject of Samantha Jameson was carefully avoided. Neither of them could think of anything more to say on the subject.

Samantha had arrived before them. She greeted them warmly. "Welcome back, both of you, and this time I'm sure we won't be so rudely interrupted."

Fran asked, "Did you resolve whatever it was that needed resolving?"

"Yes," said Samantha decisively. "Everything is now clear to me. Well, as much as it ever will be."

She showed them to their rooms, which were small but comfortable. Nigel's was furnished in the classical New England style: Windsor chairs and an old-fashioned roll-top secretaire; the bed covered with a star-spangled quilt; the walls adorned with American primitive folk art in the manner of Grandma Moses. Marion Hoffman's taste, Nigel guessed. The decor seemed out of keeping with the situation. It was out of keeping with the century.

By the time he went back downstairs Samantha and Fran were already outside on the terrace, again drinking the ubiquitous lemonade. Passing the dining room table, he noticed that it had been set for five.

"Are we expecting company?" he asked, joining them at the table.

"Ah, ever the keen-eyed reporter," Samantha remarked breezily. "Yes, we'll be joined later by two mystery guests." Since she had not seen fit to mention their names, Nigel thought better than to ask.

Samantha filled his glass with lemonade, apparently a home recipe devised by Ethel, who he noticed, was suddenly nowhere to be seen. "Not your usual choice of beverage I dare say, Nigel."

"But perfect for such a warm day," he fibbed.

"If it's alright with you, Nigel, I thought we might get in that round of golf."

As she spoke, he noticed dark rainclouds approaching from the direction of the bay. He hoped they might yet arrive in time to save him.

"I did warn you how atrocious I am," he said.

"I know the course well and will be happy to guide you round it. What I can't predict is the wind. I think a storm's coming in."

"I'll be delighted to join you," Nigel said, not keen on the prospect of sporting embarrassment, but anxious to spend an uninterrupted hour or two with a woman who evidently had a lot left to say. "Is the club far from here?"

"Ten minutes away. It's a lovely course, one of my favourites. I just hope the rain holds off." She looked across Chesapeake Bay, still churned by whitecaps, this time under a threatening sky, and few sails in sight. "I think we should go now, to beat the weather."

The Hawkwood Golf Club professional provided Nigel with a pair of shoes, slightly too large for him but adequate for the occasion. A set of well-used clubs also appeared.

"Do you need a caddie, ma'am?" the pro asked.

"Not today, Jim, but thanks."

Walking through the clubhouse Samantha received a few cursory nods and smiles of recognition. Nigel attracted questioning looks. Most of the members had already completed their rounds, presumably in anticipation of the rain, and were heading for the bar or the restaurant.

"That's good," Samantha observed. "We'll have the course to ourselves." That proved to be the case.

Nigel had played some golf at Oxford, but only occasionally since then, and not seriously enough to have acquired a handicap. He was dreading the first drive off the tee, afraid to reduce his standing in the eyes of his partner. In the event, he took a decent shot; not powerfully hit but at least staying – just - on the fairway.

"I think you've been holding out on me."

"Beginner's luck," said Nigel, truthfully.

After a few practise swings, Samantha teed off with a well-struck drive that put the ball some fifty yards beyond his, and in the middle of the fairway. She had looked like a professional herself - the easy swing, the lazy arc of the follow-through.

"Very nice," Nigel said, bracing for a golfing humiliation.

As they walked up the fairway, Samantha started talking. "I apologize again for my sudden departure two days ago. You must have thought me awfully rude. It won't happen today, I promise."

"I'm sure you had a perfectly good reason."

"I did. An important legal matter." She sighed reflectively. "I must say, we live in strange times."

He wanted to ask what she meant but thought better of it. No doubt she would tell him in her own sweet time.

Nigel's second shot landed just short of the green, two feet away from an artfully placed sand-trap. "You see," Samantha exclaimed, "you're not as bad as you led me to believe. Either you're a con man, or Lady Luck's on your side." Then she added in an aside, "I just hope she'll serve me just as well in the coming weeks."

Nigel took this as an opening to resume the interrupted conversation of two days earlier. "Will it be luck you'll be needing, or judgment?"

"Both, I suppose. But luck may be a more reliable companion in this situation."

"Anything I can do to help?" He had nothing in mind, since he had no idea what *she* had in mind.

Samantha, ignoring the question, took her swing with an iron. It was another smoothly executed shot that put the ball on the green. A par for the hole beckoned. She slid the iron into her bag and started walking. "I'm sure you're anxious to hear the rest of the story I left in mid-sentence last week. We talked then about missions. Well, I find myself embarked on one, and an extremely dangerous one at that." She turned to him with an earnest look. "Once more, I must emphasize that everything I tell you today is strictly off the record. You may find some of it hard to believe. But for now, I'm asking you to suspend judgement as well as exercise restraint above and beyond the normal call of duty."

"You have my word as a scholar and a gentleman."

"I'd rather have it from a journalist."

"You have that, too."

"Good, because what I'm about to tell you is quite a story. It's one that you may have a hard time believing - even when you come to write it."

"Try me."

"I will. But before I proceed, you must be wondering why I'd prefer a foreigner and a stranger for the job. Well, it's precisely *because* you're a foreigner and a stranger. I was reluctant to assign it to one of our leading American media outlets for reasons… but I understand that Fran has already explained all that."

"She has."

"Did it make sense to you?"

"Frankly, no."

"Well, let's just say that I didn't want either of our two leading papers to get it. We have something of a history; I won't bore you with the details. Whoever writes it, the 'you-know-what' will hit the fan. You'll find yourself a media celebrity. Not, though, with the United States government; you'll come under severe attack from that quarter. And these are people who shouldn't be underestimated."

"Caveat emptor," he muttered.

Then she said, almost as an afterthought, "I understand your former wife is married to Vincent Marchetti."

"They're not married, just living together. But why do you mention it?"

"Because it turns out that our friend Mr Marchetti is one of the villains of the piece."

Nigel whistled. "I think I ought to know first what the play is."

"I'm going to tell you. In fact, I'm going to tell you everything... well, perhaps not quite everything." Samantha said nothing for a few moments, evidently thinking about how to start. "To begin, like the Welsh poet, at the beginning: certain sensitive financial documents have come into my possession; documents which, if publicly disclosed, would bring down this administration."

Nigel's eyes widened perceptibly.

Samantha said, "Yes, that would make quite a lead for a front-page story wouldn't it."

Nigel was standing stock still, all thought of golf forgotten. He would rather have had a notepad and pen in his hands than a club and a ball. He felt vulnerable, but he could do nothing about that now. He said nothing, waiting for more.

"As you will see, the situation goes way beyond my little affair. That may be a story, too, but one for another time and another place. This one is much more significant. As they say on the covers of cheap paperback novels, it's a sordid tale of corruption and greed. It would be no exaggeration to say that the amount of money involved is staggering."

Nigel found himself trembling with anticipation. The first drops of rain were falling, with the promise of reinforcements. "And what do these documents show?"

Samantha, ignoring the rain, turned to face him, chipper in hand. "They show a series of illegal stock market transactions spread over a period of months - no, years. Several political and military figures are involved, names that you'd immediately recognize." Samantha sighed. "They include, I'm sorry to say, the president of the United States. Also, I'm much less sorry to say, our friend Mr Marchetti."

"He's no friend of mine."

Samantha ignored the trite disclaimer. "But before I go on, I want to assure you of one thing: I had no prior knowledge of what they'd been up to... are still up to. What I saw in those documents, and what I've learnt since, has shocked me profoundly. And I'm not easily shocked."

"Have you told your husband what you've found?"

"Have I confronted him, I think you mean. No. I thought about it, long and hard. But I quickly decided that it was the very last thing I should do. I'll tell you why shortly."

"What makes these stock market transactions illegal?"

"They represent stock market manipulation on a grand scale. To be more specific, insider trading. You're familiar with the term, I take it."

"I am."

"Good. It's all part of a carefully constructed scheme. It involves shell companies set up offshore to avoid scrutiny by federal agencies, and to facilitate money laundering for the purposes of tax evasion. Much of the trading was in the shares of defence companies about to be awarded significant government contracts. Market regulators take a very dim view of that kind of thing. Over here, money crimes are taken even more seriously than acts of violence, and the men involved - they're all men - would face extensive prison terms if convicted. I'm talking decades rather than years. The perpetrators - I suppose I must say alleged perpetrators - include two senators, three congressmen and two generals. The documents I found, and others that I've seen since, show that the proceeds of the illicit trades were largely funneled into a bank account in the Cayman Islands."

"You've identified the Wall Street firm, or firms, involved?" Nigel already knew the answer.

"There are several, one of them a prominent hedge fund group..."

"... owned and managed by one Vincent Marchetti," Nigel said, completing the sentence.

"Correct."

The rain was becoming more persistent, ending any chance of completing a round of golf.

"There's a greenkeeper's shed over there," Samantha said, pointing to it. "We can take shelter there and continue talking."

They set off at a brisk pace, pulling their bags behind them. The shed - more a small barn - was filled with tractor-mowers and other green maintenance paraphernalia. Samantha spotted an old metal bench. "Let's sit on that." Fastidiously, she wiped it off with a towel from her golf bag. "One good thing about this place: we could hardly be more private."

Nigel resumed the discussion with a question. "How do you know these documents are genuine? I mean, did they come from a dependable source?"

"There *was* no source. I found them. Someone had carelessly dropped them. It happened quite by chance. Where, I'd rather not say. Just to be sure they were what I thought they were, I gave them to an investigative firm in DC that specializes in financial irregularities. They investigated them thoroughly and then uncovered additional incriminating data. They found a pattern of illicit trading: names, dates, times and so on. The evidence, they tell me, is irrefutable. In short, we have everything that a public prosecutor could possibly need for a conviction."

"Why didn't you alert the regulators - presumably in this case, the Securities and Exchange Commission?"

"Ah, now that takes us to the heart of the matter. Three reasons. First, I had to be sure that what I'd found was what it seemed to be. The investigators took care of that. Second, the current head of the SEC was appointed by my husband, an old crony of his from business school. I'm not suggesting that he's corrupt, but you know what a cozy place Washington is, and I didn't want to risk the agency tipping him off. Or, more likely, putting the documents in a filing cabinet and doing nothing. It may be that the case will end up with the regulators anyway, but until that day comes, I want to manage the process my way. Which brings me to a third and more vital reason for not reporting it. This one, frankly, has more to do with my personal agenda than the observance of legal niceties. I'll get to that, too."

Nigel interrupted. "I'm no attorney, but doesn't withholding that kind of information make you an accessory? Or something like that."

"I've talked to my lawyers about that. To be honest, it's unclear. It's complicated. We're still talking about it."

"If the evidence of illicit trading was clear to your investigators, why didn't the SEC pick it up? I understand they have experts who do nothing all day but look for unusual trading patterns."

"A good question. They may simply have missed them. Or, if you like conspiracy theories, they didn't miss them but were ordered to do nothing about it. The real reason, I suspect, is that the trades were cleverly executed to avoid detection. There are some smart people on Wall Street who know how to play the system."

"And the personal agenda you mentioned..."

Samantha seemed reluctant to reveal it, but then blurted it out. "I intend to use what I know to take this administration down."

Nigel was suitably dumbstruck. "So, you do intend to go to the SEC?"

"No, I don't. And let me explain why. If I were to go public, it would mean a scandal. The president would have to resign, of course, and would face impeachment and other criminal proceedings. It would mean prosecutions, endless investigations, enquiries, and of course the inevitable leaks. The thing could rumble on for months, years even. The government would be engulfed. The country would be plunged into chaos, with repercussions that would be unpredictable, socially as well as politically. I wouldn't want to be responsible for all that. And another thing: I have two children to think about. Do I really want them to know that their father is a crook and is going to jail?"

"What's the alternative?" Nigel couldn't see one.

"Ah, I have a plan, one that would spare the country the kind of turmoil I've just described." Samantha smiled with evident satisfaction. "I do indeed intend to confront my husband with his crimes. He'll deny everything, of course, I expect that. But when I tell him about the evidence that I've accumulated I'm hoping he'll realize he doesn't have a leg to stand on."

"But then he would have to resign, and the cat would be out of the bag."

"No. Under my plan he won't have to resign. That's the whole point. I won't ask him to resign; I'll demand instead that he announce publicly that he won't run for a second term, without giving the real reason. That way there'll be no public scandal, no prosecutions, no lawsuits, no turmoil. He'll get to stay in office, it's true, but only for another two years. He'll be a lame duck - I'll see to that. Then he'll be gone. If we do this my way, his criminality will be our dirty little secret."

Nigel could hardly grasp the sheer audacity of it. "Dear God."

"Is that your best response, to invoke divine intervention?"

"I'm just trying to take it all in."

"Yes, it's quite a story, isn't it. There, I said you wouldn't be disappointed."

"What story will I be breaking, then?"

"I would have thought it obvious: you'll simply write that he's decided not to seek a second term. That's your scoop."

"And what reason will he give?"

"We'll agree on something. Age, health, family concerns… you know the form."

"And if he doesn't go along with it? What if he decides to fight? He's a powerful man with powerful friends; not to mention clever lawyers. You're asking him to give up the most influential job in the world. Why would he do that without a fight?"

"Because if he fights me, I'll go public."

"Some would call that blackmail."

"Yes, some would. But they'll never know, will they. Anyway, I'm betting he'll want to avoid the disgrace of being removed from office. Doing it my way he'll leave with his honour and reputation, such as they are, intact. What would you do?"

"I can't answer that, because I'm not him."

"Pretend you're him."

"I'd call in my lawyers."

"Oh, he'll do that. They'll want to see the evidence, of course, and we can show them some of it. Then what can they do?"

"I can't begin to imagine. Has any sitting president ever declined, voluntarily, to run for a second term?"

"Yes. Lyndon Johnson. In 1968, he declined a second term, not because of a scandal, but because of public outrage over the Vietnam War. He was hounded from office. I've been reading up on it. He went on television one Sunday evening and at the end of a long rambling speech about Vietnam, and other things, he suddenly announced that he wouldn't run again. I can quote him verbatim: *'Accordingly, I shall not seek, and I will not accept, the nomination of my party for another term as your president.'* Nobody saw that coming; not even some of his closest associates. The nation was stunned. Well, I want my husband to do the same. The nation will be stunned again, but at least it won't explode."

"You seem to have thought of everything," said Nigel. "Or, for your sake, I hope you have."

"I've tried," Samantha said. "I'm still in talks with my personal lawyer, and other experts in the securities business. I have the bills to prove it."

"And do they consider your plan feasible?" Nigel failed to disguise his incredulity.

"Not yet. My lawyer's first words were, 'Not a chance in hell'. Others had similar initial responses. I could even be putting myself at risk, they told me. Judging by your expression right now, I'd say you pretty much agree with them."

"I'm no lawyer."

"But what do you think, as a non-legal person?"

"Right now, my mind's working overtime. My first reaction? Honestly? It's the most extraordinary story I've ever heard."

"I'm glad you said that."

"Why?"

"Because it means that when you come to write the story, you'll be so awestruck by the sheer magnitude of it that you'll take every precaution to get it right."

"Getting back to the president's resignation statement: whatever reason he gives, will the public buy it? Will the media?"

Samantha shrugged. "The public will have no reason not to believe it. Some reporters will be suspicious and start digging, I suppose, but where would they start? The incriminating documents will be locked away in a safe, as they are now. Forever. The president won't talk. His lawyers won't talk. His criminal associates obviously won't talk. I certainly won't talk. My investigators won't talk."

"How can you be sure of the investigators?"

"Because they earn their living keeping secrets. If they leaked it, they'd be out of business the next day."

"You want my honest opinion?"

"Of course."

"It all sounds too fantastic to stand a chance."

"I thought you'd say that. It would be my reaction, too. But let me assure that everything I've told you is true."

"I didn't mean to suggest otherwise."

"It's a lot to take in, I agree."

"The story I'll be writing won't have much substance. A five-word headline."

"So what? Most big stories are five-word headlines - some only two. The rest is always background, reactions, analysis. That kind of thing."

Nigel looked out across the golf course. The rain had stopped.

"Perhaps," said Samantha, standing up, "this would be a good time to head back to the clubhouse - before the next downpour."

"I think that's a good idea. Anything else while we're still alone?"

"Yes, one more thing, which you didn't ask me about. I'll also be asking my husband for a divorce. Make that demanding a divorce. It will be part of our 'understanding' on the other matter, although we might not announce it right away."

"So as not to cloud the issue?"

"Yes. One more thing before we go: do we have an understanding here? Everything I've said has been strictly off the record. I want no leaks."

"We have a deal," he said, flatly, "and I'll stick to it. You have my word on it." They shook hands rather solemnly. "But what happens next?"

"I'll be meeting my lawyers. Next week. I need to go through some things. Then, depending on what they say - or maybe not - I'll be making a final decision: go or no go."

"So, there may be no scoop after all."

"There's a risk of that, but I think it'll be a 'go'… whatever the lawyers say."

They tramped back to the clubhouse in silence, the rain getting heavier.

An hour later, after showering, Nigel sat on the terrace with Fran. Both nursed over-large whiskies. Samantha had gone upstairs to make phone calls. Few words were exchanged. He was silently mulling over everything he had just heard. She was afraid to ask.

A car door slammed, then another. He turned to see Samantha, hurrying downstairs to open the front door. "Ah, they're here already," she cried excitedly. Apparently, the two mystery guests had arrived.

From the terrace, Nigel and Fran could hear Samantha's voice of welcome. "I can't tell you how happy and relieved I am to see you. Both of you. Come in, come on in." Moments later, she came back in through the front door.

Behind her, carrying bags, were Frank Hoffman and Anna Litovka.

"Well, what a delightful surprise," said Frank, shaking Nigel's hand. Anna merely smiled and extended her own.

"I could use a drink," Frank said emphatically. He looked at Nigel's glass. "One of those will do just fine."

Not for the first time that day, nor the last, Nigel's mouth was slightly agape.

* * * * *

Chapter 13

Air Force One gently touched down at a Royal Air Force base fifty miles north of London, the landing watched by a herd of barely curious cud-munching cows. The British government had decreed a low-key arrival after protest groups threatened to disrupt the occasion with demonstrations. Despite the snub delivered by the British parliament, the president had insisted on making the trip, secure in the knowledge that His Majesty's Government - ever mindful of the economic power wielded by the United States and, as always, anxious to preserve the so-called 'special relationship' - could find no compelling reason to keep him away. What he hoped to achieve, other than an exercise in public relations, neither he nor the British government had made clear, and perhaps didn't even know.

Martin Jameson emerged from the giant plane with an enthusiastic wave to a non-existent crowd, rather ungallantly leaving his wife to make her own way down the steps. The onlookers were mainly cameramen, reinforced by the usual gaggle of unidentifiable dignitaries and minor military figures. His wife followed him with no more than a token wave, a smile fixed firmly in place. Samantha's decision to accompany her husband followed weeks of cajoling by White House and State Department advisers. In truth, she had always intended to make the trip, conscious of a first lady's duty to be seen at a president's side, but she had rather enjoyed the petulant reactions of the panjandrums when she told them otherwise. Her husband hadn't tried very hard to talk her into it, not caring much one way or the other, but perhaps knowing all along that she would come anyway. And now, as she gazed across a flat, hedge-veined vista of luminous green fields, she felt genuinely glad to be back in a country whose hospitality she had enjoyed in her younger, more carefree days.

At the bottom of the ramp her husband was already saluting and shaking hands with the United States Ambassador - a prominent donor to his election campaign - and various officials from both countries. A helicopter waited nearby, blades whirring, ready to whisk the presidential pair to the rear lawn of Buckingham Palace, there to be greeted by the King and the prime minister. Samantha noticed that soldiers armed with automatic weapons had formed a cordon around both aircraft. Not, she was thinking, the rather quaint and peaceful Britain of legend, back in her childhood days, when it had still been just possible to maintain the fiction that a few helmeted bobbies could do the job. '*How times had changed,*' she was thinking.

An hour later, just as the presidential helicopter was passing over Hyde Park, Nigel and Jane sat in a black taxi heading for their modest Bayswater hotel on its northern side. Unlike the first lady, Jane had needed no persuading to come. "What a lovely idea," she'd said immediately, "and I sure could use a break." But not that much of a break, as her boss at State, after learning of her plans, had found work for her to do, renewing contacts with Middle East experts at the Foreign Office. In return, the government had agreed to pay her travel expenses, and required her to attend a couple of official functions, including a grand affair at the United States Ambassador's residence of the kind put on as a consolation prize for those too junior to have earned a seat at the King's palace banquet. A secondary event it might be, but it would still be a glittering black-tie affair. Nigel would be working as well, and not just as a sideline. Even so, given the president's unusually light schedule, he would find time enough to accompany Jane on a few sightseeing and shopping expeditions, and for a few romantic dinners.

He'd already checked in at the *Post*. Elsa had greeted him warmly, perhaps hoping that he might find time for another late-night toasted-cheese sandwich - until she found out that he had a girlfriend in tow. Duncan was, as usual, coldly formal. He had initially balked at paying for the trip but relented when Nigel hinted at a 'blockbuster' story that required his presence in London. Duncan was mildly irritated when Nigel told him about Jane, only mollified when told that she was also on a working trip.

"What kind of story is it, anyway?" Duncan had demanded to know.

"You'll find out when I write it," Nigel had replied insolently, but promised 'one big fat scoop'.

Deprived of further details, Duncan had given his assent to the trip on humanitarian grounds, agreeing that, after nearly three months away, Nigel was entitled to visit his children. "But none of your fancy hotels and Mayfair dinners, laddie. We're running a tight ship at the *Pos*t these days. And this mysterious scoop of yours better live up to your inflated billing."

After that, despite the injunction about expenses, Duncan and Nigel lunched at the Savoy Grill. It was Nigel who was grilled, but even after two glasses of wine - his limit that day as he would be driving later - he gave nothing away, leaving Duncan to complain that he'd been asked to 'buy a pig in a poke'. The editor's mood failed to improve when Nigel said he'd have to leave lunch early to pick up his kids. While he could admire Nigel's devotion to his paternal duties, he still felt moved to complain that it was hardly compatible with working on the 'scoop of the century'.

"Seeing the kids is a higher form of duty," Nigel responded. "I desperately want to see them, of course, and besides, if Sarah found out I'd been in London and hadn't taken the trouble, there would be hell to pay." Duncan, a devoted father himself, could only concede the point.

Nigel had rented a car, the only way he could conveniently get to Jack's preparatory school, St Edmund's, which was located a few miles west of London near Windsor, and to Ellie's, conveniently just a few miles away near Reading. His plan was to pick them both up in turn and take them out to an early dinner, with a surprise theatre visit to follow. Nigel had never approved of Jack's school. For all the accolades it had received from the education community, he found St Edmund's altogether too steeped in Church, King and Country, a moth-eaten mantra that to Nigel only served to maintain the nonsense, observed since the infamous Tudor divorce, that the monarch still served as God's representative in England. The school was housed in the former home of some duke or other, a rambling Victorian pile with modern glass-walled wings bolted incongruously onto each side, respectively a science laboratory and music centre. Each extension had cost millions. *'No wonder the bloody school fees kept going up,'* Nigel mused. The playing fields at the rear of the school seemed to stretch to the horizon. Somewhere in this vast expanse his son was playing rugby for the school's first team. The game, being played out of season, was an annual fixture against Grayston Hall, a school that St Edmunds regarded as a despised rival in all things, sporting and academic. Arriving twenty minutes after kick-off, Nigel joined a small, raucously animated crowd of parents on the touchline. Jack's team, he learnt, were seven points ahead and dominating the match. Jack was playing at full-back, which required him to catch high downfield kicks, for which task Nigel had trained him with hours of practice in Battersea Park.

"Come on you Blues," he yelled, somewhat self-consciously, drawing stares from some of the spectators, his fellow parents.

Jack acknowledged him with a wave but was immediately called into action to tackle a flying winger. Bundling the boy into touch, conveniently where most of the parents were gathered, Jack drew a rousing cheer.

Nigel tingled with pride. "That's my boy!"

He'd called Sarah two days earlier for permission to pick up the children and take them out for the evening. This had been granted, over Vincent's strong objections. "I'm their bloody father now, not him," he'd protested, earning what he felt was a needless rebuke from his wife: "Stepfather," she'd corrected him. Sarah gave her blessing to Nigel's expedition with her usual admonition: "Just try not to get them into too much trouble."

One of the spectators approached Nigel and introduced himself as Julian, the father of one of Jack's teammates. Nigel failed to catch the hyphenated surname, which sounded like something out of an Evelyn Waugh novel. He was a giant of a man with a basilic stare and bristled with aggression. Nigel introduced himself and pointed to his son. "That's Jack there, and I'm his father."

"Mine's a flanker, somewhere in that pile over there." Julian indicated a collapsed maul. "He's a good player, that lad of yours. I've been watching him. Rock solid under the high ball. Good tackler, too. Someone's been teaching him a thing or two." The appraisal was delivered in the manner of an officer commending a drill sergeant for a smart parade turnout. It turned out that Julian had indeed served in the army.

"That would be me," Nigel said, trying not to sound too prideful. He had taken an instant dislike to the man but felt obliged to put on a polite front in the interest of parental solidarity. "I take it you've played a bit yourself," he said. "And I'd guess from your size you were in the back row."

"Got it in one," Julian said. "And damned good I was. Or could have been. Had to retire early. Knee trouble. Twisted it on an army assault course twenty years ago. I was never the same again. Still bothers me a bit, especially in winter. You played a bit yourself I take it."

"At university. Inside-centre. Haven't played since, though, and I'm far too old now. Anyway, I live in America."

"Oh, well done!" Julian exclaimed, mysteriously. Nigel was unsure whether he was being congratulated for living in exile or whether Jack was being applauded for some exploit on the field of play. Julian had apparently been wondering about Nigel because he suddenly asked, "Aren't you Sarah Harper's ex-husband?"

"Yes, I am."

"Thought so. I've met that new husband of hers. American chap. Banker. Rhymes with wanker, and in his case it fits perfectly. Sometimes comes to school events... Oh, well played that lad! Strictly entre nous, can't say I much care for him. Little man, big mouth. Arrogant. Full of himself." Other than the reference to Vincent's height, the man could have been describing himself. "Typical American if you ask me. They say he might be in line for a cabinet post over there. Treasury, I suppose. Or the Fed. Either way, it's an alarming thought. As if the markets haven't enough to contend with right now."

"You're probably right," Nigel said, making little attempt to sound interested in Julian's economic theories. He'd have loved to tell him that a jail term loomed more likely in Vincent's future than a cabinet post, but merely said. "You're in finance yourself, I take it."

"I'm at a small investment bank. A boutique, some would call it. Wren Capital. Don't suppose you've heard of it. We don't have much to do with your Mr Marchetti, but I know all about him. Oh, yes, often see him on television. Usually spouting nonsense. The man's a shameless self-publicist."

Nigel had no desire to hear more, but Julian was now on a roll. "Last time he was here, he stood right where you are, shouting stupid things, making a complete spectacle of himself. Obviously knows fuck all about the game. Didn't even seem to know you can't pass the ball forward. That didn't hold him back, mind. He just kept yelling his head off, regardless. The man's an idiot, however much money he's made."

At this point Nigel said he wanted to follow the play from a fresh vantage point, an excuse to walk away from this bore. But Julian followed him, still going on about Vincent Marchetti's touchline display of ignorance. Relief came with the half-time whistle. Nigel, followed by a limping Julian, trotted across to the boys, who had formed a huddle, arms linked, heads bowed. St Edmunds were now ahead by fourteen points - two tries, both converted. Jack broke away to greet his father. Nigel hugged him and tousled his hair.

"Good game, but I think you've got their measure. Full-back suits you, as I always said it would."

"Thanks, Dad. Yes, I think we're fitter and faster. But Mr Broughton, our rugby coach, says we should never rest on our laurels."

"Mr Broughton gives sound advice," Nigel said. "When you've got 'em down, grind 'em down, I say." He realized, as he said it, that he sounded like Julian, and amended the advice. "Just don't let them off the hook. A quick try and they're back in the game."

Nearby, Jack's teammates had now broken their huddle and gathered round the coach. "You'd better join them," Nigel said. "I'll see you afterwards. Then we'll pick up Ellie and go out for a meal, just the three of us."

"Smashing! Hamburgers? Please, Dad! We never get them at home. Mum doesn't approve. And chips."

"Hamburger it is," Nigel promised, "and all the chips you can eat." Jack, delighted with the prospect, skipped over to his teammates.

The persistent Julian, having dispatched his own son, sauntered over. "Good lad, that boy of yours. So, Nigel, what is it you do in America? Banking? Oil? Technology?"

"I'm a journalist."

Julian looked a little taken aback. He had no time for journalists. "Not one of those peddlers of fake news, are you?" he said with a humour-free laugh.

"As often as I can," Nigel countered flippantly.

"Who'd you write for, anyway?"

"The *Morning Post*. I'm their White House correspondent."

"Met the main man, have you?"

"Not yet."

"I know he's obnoxious and all that, but I still think he's got some good ideas. Like that wall of his. Can't have the country overrun with Mexicans and other riffraff. Only wish we could build one over here."

"We have one already."

Julian looked puzzled. "We do?"

"Yes, the English Channel." Julian's uncomprehending frown remained in place. "So, Julian, what's your background? Before banking, I mean."

"Ten years in the army. Captain. Green Jackets. No long-term future there, so I found a job in the City. Sadly, my firm's struggling a bit right now, thanks to those stupid fucking traders down on the fifth floor. But I'm still earning big moolah. Mergers and acquisitions, that's my game. Lots of that going on, I can tell you. Take the money while it lasts, that's my motto."

"Very sensible," said Nigel, absently.

"What most people fail to understand is that banks don't know the first thing about money." Julian chuckled at his little aphorism. "When the show is over, which can't be soon enough for me, I think I'll retire to Majorca. Build a house there. I've already got some land. This country is going down the drain if you ask me. Overrun with welfare dodgers, drug gangs, immigrants. It's the beginning of the end."

Nigel wanted to get Julian off this tack. "I know you've met Vincent Marchetti on the touchline here, but any business dealings with him?"

"None. Do you care? I mean he's…"

"… I was just wondering, that's all."

"He's in the hedge fund business. Not my line of country. Perhaps it should have been since he's made a fortune. Your ex must be doing quite well herself. My wife reads that magazine. Beats me what she sees in it. Nothing but ads. Good for profits, of course. She and Vincent must be raking it in if they can afford these school fees. I can hardly afford them myself, and I'm told they'll be going up again next year. Why, when inflation's virtually at zero? Explain that to me."

Nigel admitted that he couldn't. He hadn't heard that the fees were going up, but no doubt Sarah would inform him soon enough. At that moment, the players trotted back onto the pitch, giving Nigel an excuse to get away from the overbearing Julian. "It's been nice talking to you, Julian, but if you don't mind I think I'm going to stand on the other side. I think I'll see more of my lad there."

"Oh, alright," Julian replied sniffily. "Be that way if you like." Nigel was relieved that Julian hadn't said, *"Good idea, I think I'll join you."*

The game ended with St Edmund's winning by 34 points to 24. Jack spent twenty minutes showering and changing and then joined his father at the school entrance. Julian, mercifully, had vanished. They set off in the car to pick up Ellie, whose school was a fifteen-minute drive away.

"Good win," Nigel said, "but in the end a bit closer than I thought it would be."

Jack looked at his father. "A win is a win, though, isn't that what you always said?"

Nigel laughed. "Yes, that's true."

The plan Nigel outlined to Jack was that, after picking up Ellie, they'd head for the Lone Pine Café, where the hamburgers were enormous and the piped rock music deafening. When they pulled into the driveway of Ellie's school, they spotted her outside chatting to classmates. She was in a sulky mood for having been 'torn away' from her friends, but she brightened instantly when informed of their destination.

Nigel drove around the side streets off Piccadilly for twenty minutes searching for a parking space, before settling for a multi-story garage at an exorbitant rate of fifty quid. That was the way things were in London these days, although Washington was not so different. The Lone Pine at Hyde Park Corner was packed as always, and they stood in line for fifteen minutes waiting to get in. But once seated they were served promptly. Three giant cheeseburgers soon appeared, accompanied by bucket-loads of fries, which the children submerged under ketchup from a grubby-looking bottle. The Cokes came in huge paper containers a foot high. They all chuckled at the size of the portions. The children were in heaven, and looked, Nigel thought, angelic. He watched them enjoying the excesses, thinking, *'We're getting to be more like America than America'.*

"How are the burgers?" he asked, pointlessly since they had been half consumed in two bites.

"You're eating one yourself," Jack said, a red and yellow substance running in rivulets down his chin.

"Mine's fine, though I'm not really a burger person." He related his recent American experience with one of them. The children laughed. This one was no smaller. Britain had indeed caught up.

"Is that why you're using a knife and fork?"

"Yes, because I don't want to finish up looking like a Jackson Pollock painting, as you do right now."

"Who's Jackson Pollock?"

"An artist. An abstractionist who splashes paint all over the place." Jack looked bemused. "How's your burger, Ellie?"

"Scrumptious, thanks." Ellie was intent on competing with her brother to see who could finish first.

"I wish you were over here more often, Dad," Jack said dolefully. "Mum doesn't like us eating this kind of food, and Vincent just goes along with whatever she says."

Ellie nodded in vigorous agreement. "She says you're a bad influence."

"Is that the only reason you miss me - because I buy you hamburgers? And, by the way, your mother isn't wrong. This stuff is not good for you. You should eat it only on special occasions."

"Well, *this* is a special occasion," Jack declared, for which Nigel was immensely grateful. "And don't feel bad, Dad, because she says the same thing to Vincent. He eats junk food all the time. And also, he's got terrible table manners. Smacks his lips when he eats. Mum's always telling him off about it."

"Well, I feel much, much better for hearing that."

Ellie changed the subject, as she usually did when the topic under discussion was the 'most boring thing in the world'. "Do you have a girlfriend in America?"

Nigel pretended to be startled. He'd thought about bringing Jane along, but Sarah would probably have made a fuss. "You're not supposed to ask questions like that, young lady. But I do have a special friend, since you ask. Why?"

"Because if we can have two Dads, why can't we have two Mums as well?"

"One day you might, but not just yet."

"So, you're here on your own?"

"No. I have my friend here with me. One day I hope you'll get to meet her."

Ellie wasted no time getting to the nub of the matter. "And she's your girlfriend?" The 'girl' was stressed.

"Yes."

"And you live together?"

"No, but we live quite close to each other."

"If you like her, why don't you live with her?"

"Because we've only known each other a couple of months."

"Is she rich?" Jack asked.

"No. Not that it matters. Money isn't everything, you know."

"Mum seems to think so," Jack stated bluntly. "And Vincent. That's all they ever seem to talk about."

"Well, I happen to disagree with them."

"Can we tell her that?" Jack asked.

"She already knows what I think."

Jack stopped talking to make a concentrated effort to get the second half of his hamburger into his mouth in one go, failing spectacularly. Why are you here, anyway? Is it because President Jameson's in town?"

"Yes. I'm helping to cover the visit for my paper."

"Vincent says the president's a good man," Jack said, looking at his father for confirmation. "Some kids at school think so, too. What do you think, Dad?"

Nigel laughed. "Well, to be perfectly honest. I'm not keen on him myself. But I'm not paid to approve what he does, just *report* what he does." It occurred to him that he sounded like Graham Welbeck. "Whether I like what he says or does is neither here nor there. He's who Americans voted for. He does his job as he sees fit, but so do I and sometimes, when I don't like what he says or does, I say so in my articles."

Jack wanted to know more. "I've heard Mummy and Vincent talking about it. Vincent says President Jameson is his friend. He also says you'd do anything to hurt him."

"Hurt the president or your father?"

"I don't know. The president, I suppose. But we know that you and Vincent don't like each other."

"Now, who told you that?"

"Well, it's obvious, Dad. I've heard him call you names. Mummy sometimes tells him to shut up. Last week I heard him say he was going to... I can't say it because he used a bad word."

"Yes, you can. If you're quoting someone it's okay. What did he say?"

"He said he was going to, um, fuck you up. What did he mean by that? And how will he, you know, do what he said. And what can he stop you from doing?"

"I've no idea," Nigel said, knowing the answer only too well. Inwardly, he was seething. If Vincent saw his paternal role as a perpetual campaign to discredit their natural father, he could at least do it without resorting to threatening and crude language in front of the kids. In that vein, Nigel's thoughts turned to Samantha Jameson's secret plan to destroy her husband, and how it might inflict collateral damage on Vincent Marchetti. The sooner Samantha let loose whatever dogs of war she had on a leash the better. He fumed silently as he sucked through a straw his inexhaustible Coke.

"Why do you look so angry?" asked Jack, looking at his father with an expression of puzzled concern.

"Do I? Sorry, Jack. I'm not angry. I was just miles away. Forgot something I was supposed to do, that's all." The time had come to turn the conversation to the more pleasant job in hand. "Now I want you both to eat up, because after this I have a special treat in store." He enjoyed watching their faces freeze in the act of chewing. "First, though, we'll have ice cream, or cake, or whatever it is you want for pudding, and then... wait for it... we're going... to the theatre."

"To see what?" Ellie demanded to know. Unlike her brother, she was always braced for disappointment.

"*The Wizard.*"

The children squealed in unison. "Wow!" cried Ellie, suddenly impressed.

"Yippee," yelled Jack.

"Yes, I've received special permission from your mother to keep you out late because you're both off school tomorrow. After theatre, I'll drop you both off at home." For the first time in weeks, Nigel felt more like a man of action than a mere spectator.

* * *

Winfield House, the United States ambassador's London residence in Regents Park, was a vast red-brick structure in the Georgian style. It had once been the home of Barbara Hutton, the Woolworth heiress, and one-time wife of Cary Grant. She had donated it to the nation - to America, that is, not Britain - for one dollar. The surrounding twelve acres - the second largest garden in London after Buckingham Palace, he'd read - gave the place the appearance of a country house, although the impression was undermined by the nearby roar of London's traffic. The perimeter was patrolled day and night, as it was this night, only with three times as many guards.

The party to which Nigel and Jane had been invited would be in the 'tent room', an annex that resembled an oversized orangery. Nigel had rented a tuxedo from Moss Bross for the occasion. Jane had bought what she'd be wearing, a lovely backless black dress from a fancy store on Bond Street. "My treat," Nigel declared when she blanched at the price. After seeing her emerge from the changing room, he would have paid anything. As they were changing for dinner, he thought she looked ravishing. She reciprocated by telling him he looked dashing.

"The last time I felt this excited," she gushed, "was prom night at high school."

"Pity the King won't be there," he said. "You might have got to meet him."

"And the president."

"I wouldn't want to meet *him*."

"Whyever not. You earn a living writing about him."

"Well, I'll probably meet him anyway one of these days, if only at a briefing."

Nigel had foolishly prepared for the evening by sharing two lunchtime bottles of claret with Duncan. "Not your best idea of the day," was Jane's comment as he arrived back at the hotel looking, she thought, slightly the worse for wear. "I think a pot of coffee is in order." She'd ordered two from room service.

They took a taxi to Winfield House. The Marylebone traffic was so snarled that they walked the last hundred yards. Around the gated entrance there seemed to be more security guards than guests. The short walk along the tree-lined driveway to the house was pleasant enough in the balmy weather, the romantic ambience dispelled only by the presence of yet more gun-toting policemen and, it seemed, an entire division of the United States Marine Corps.

"This place is better protected than the White House," Nigel observed. "And POTUS isn't even going to be here." Nigel's thoughts turned to Samantha, who at this moment, a mile or so to the west, was probably sitting across from a king and a prime minister, valiantly keeping up appearances with empty dinner-table conversation, occasionally smiling winsomely at her husband, the man she intended to destroy.

"I expect the police are out in force because they knew you were coming," Jane said, squeezing his arm affectionately.

"What's the form tonight, anyway? Is there a sit-down dinner?"

"No, it's a reception, not a dinner. There will be a buffet, though."

And a bar, I hope," he said ominously.

I hope there'll be dancing, too. I can hear a band already."

Nigel flinched. Never very adept on the dance floor, to put it gently, he was far from keen on the prospect of proving it.

"Thank God it's not a sit-down. With my luck, I'd have been stuck between two ancient diplomats with acute hearing problems. Or, worse, two Republican grand dames telling me how proud they are of what this fabulous president is doing for the country, not believing a word of it."

"Don't be such a cynic, darling. In any event, you'll have to talk to them whether you're sitting or standing."

"Standing is always better. You can walk away."

Nigel's words, Jane thought, were a little slurred. She began to fret. "Just how much *did* you drink at lunchtime? Quite a bit would be my guess. You sound as fuzzy as you look."

"I drank no more than I usually do with Duncan."

"That, my darling, is precisely what's worrying me."

"Have no fear, I'll be perfectly fine. Think of lunch as a dress rehearsal."

They strolled up to the grand house in the company of several other couples, all equally dressed up for the occasion. The house was ablaze with lights, the marine band playing American show tunes.

"Quite a place isn't it," Nigel said. "You have to make campaign donations in the millions to get this posting." He recalled that the Ambassador, Bunny Stephens, a Philadelphia pharmaceutical tycoon in a former life, had gone well beyond the normal bounds of financial propriety to merit his appointment. In short, like most of his predecessors he'd bought his way into the post.

"Can you imagine what this place would be worth on the open market?"

"Tens of millions I imagine," Jane said, not much interested in this line of conversation.

Scores of millions, Nigel thought. Perhaps hundreds of millions.

A United States marine, impeccably turned out in red and blue, ushered them inside with white-gloved hands. The band was now into a medley of Rodgers and Hammerstein. Not that anyone was listening. The mood in the 'tent', packed with the cream of Anglo-American society, struck Nigel as somewhat feverish. Earlier in the day, the president, at Buckingham Palace, had committed a faux pas by pushing in front of the King and here, under the hardly less ornate chandeliers of Winfield House, the chattering classes were chattering about it. Dozens of guests had spilled out onto a terrace, where conversation was easier, nervously watched from various points in the garden by guards discreetly disguised as flunkeys.

As they entered the building, Nigel turned to Jane and kissed her on the cheek. "Amid all this glitter and gloss, you are by far the most eye-catching figure here." He meant it, too.

She stood back and appraised him in return. "And you my sweet boy are looking very debonair yourself."

A waiter approached with a tray of welcoming drinks. Nigel picked up a flute of champagne. Jane took a glass of mineral water. "I may have to mingle tonight, so I'm going to pace myself. I suggest you do the same, especially as you've had a head start."

She spotted a group of State Department colleagues past and present. "I should report in. I hope you don't mind, honey. I'll catch up with you as soon as I can. Promise."

"You go right ahead, darling" Nigel said. "I'm going to the bar. Maybe I can get a proper drink there."

Nigel ordered an Irish whiskey and turned to survey the crowd, elbows on the bar. He heard a familiar voice behind him ordering a glass of mineral water. "Well, look what the cat dragged in," the voice said. Nigel swung round to find himself face-to-face with Vincent Marchetti. He was dressed, Nigel observed with ill-disguised distaste, in a bizarre, rather lurid outfit: trews, waistcoat and bow tie all coordinated in the check of some Scottish clan or another, probably unknown in Scotland.

"Hello, Vincent. What an unpleasant surprise. Where's Sarah?"

"Busy working the room. She's always working, even when she's not. But I don't have to tell you that."

"And very good at it she is, too," Nigel said. "I like to think I taught her everything she knows."

"Then at least she came out of the marriage with something."

"Other than two fine children. By the way, I had a lovely time with them yesterday. They're delightful company when the mood takes them."

"I think I can take some of the credit for that," Vincent proclaimed. "Not that I'll get any from you."

"You can make that no credit at all." Five minutes into the evening and Nigel's hackles were already rising. "Vincent, you have an unerring knack of turning any pleasant encounter into an unpleasant confrontation. I can't decide whether it's your natural manner or merely professional posturing. I'm inclined to the former." It didn't occur to him that he had fired the first shots, as he usually did.

Before Vincent could deliver a riposte, Sarah suddenly appeared. Protectively, she grabbed her husband's arm. "Hello, darling. Having fun? Oh, Nigel! I'm surprised to see you here. Were you invited or did you gatecrash, as you usually do?"

"I'm here, as it happens, as the guest of a guest."

"Oh, really. And who, pray tell, would be so daring as to risk going to a grand event like this with you? And where is she? I presume it's a 'she'."

"It is. Her name's Jane. She's around here somewhere, catching up with a few colleagues."

"Colleagues? What does she do, this Jane?"

"She works at the State Department. On the Middle East desk. She's an analyst."

"And are you two…?" Sarah had adopted an absurdly coquettish look, leaving the question unfinished.

"We're good friends, if that's what you were about to ask."

"May we at least know her surname?" Vincent asked.

"Hockley. Why do you ask?" Nigel sensed danger.

"Just curious, that's all."

Sarah pursed her lips in a superior manner, as if the name had somehow lowered the tone. "Well, perhaps we'll bump into her before the evening ends."

"Perhaps you will."

"The children tell me you had a…"

She was interrupted by an elderly British gentleman, tipsy in the grand manner of the lifelong drinker, who inserted himself into the conversation to announce himself as Sir something-or-other, a retired something-or-other at the Foreign Office. Vincent took him to one side, to rescue his wife, leaving Sarah and Nigel to talk about the children.

"The kids obviously had fun yesterday," Sarah resumed. She managed to sound disappointed. "Most of all, they seemed to be thrilled with the hamburgers. I don't like them eating junk food, as you know. But I suppose I ought to be grateful that you dropped them off at the house in one piece."

"Two pieces, in fact. And their happy faces were, to me, all the thanks I needed."

"Well, they certainly…"

Another interloper had appeared. Jane. Replicating Sarah's gesture, she grabbed Nigel's arm. "I'm sorry, honey, I couldn't get away... Oh, am I interrupting something?"

"Sarah, I'd like you to meet Jane Hockley. Jane, meet Sarah, the former Mrs Harper, in case you were thinking she was my older sister."

"He will have his little jokes," Sarah said, looking at Jane with an exaggerated look of exasperation. It quickly turned to one of appraisal. It was reciprocated in full measure. "I hear you work for the State Department, Jane. How interesting. And how, may I ask, did you two meet?"

"In New York," Jane said. "In a bar."

"A sleazy bar of course," Nigel cut in, knowing that Sarah would later be reviewing the situation with Vincent. *'He picked her up in a bar, for God's sake. How typical!'*

Jane laughed to break the tension. "They're the only kind I ever go to. I just love sleazy bars. And sleazy men."

"Well, you've certainly found one."

Jane, already tired of the banter - which was no such thing - and the tension - which was very real - pretended to spot an acquaintance across the room and waved gaily. "I do apologize, er, Sarah, but I've just seen someone I simply must talk to. It was nice meeting you." Turning to leave, she pecked Nigel on the cheek and shot him a look that involved both eyebrows being raised. She and Nigel would be having an interesting late-night discussion, too.

Vincent was still trying to disengage himself from the former Foreign Office mandarin, who was refusing to budge. Nigel heard 'Suez' mentioned once or twice. The old man seemed to be explaining that he was referring to the political crisis of the Fifties. Vincent was probably wondering whether the canal might ever come up for sale. "It spelled the end of Britain as a world power," the man from the FO was saying. "And you Americans took great delight in it. That's gratitude for you. And after all our countries had been through together in the war. I can remember a time when…"

Nigel was happy to let Vincent stew, and since he'd already tired of Sarah's regal put-downs, he too made his excuses. "Sorry, Sarah, but I've also just seen someone I need to talk to." With that he melted into the crowd, leaving his former wife seething that she should be abandoned in such a way, and left moreover with the task of extricating her husband from the clutches of His Majesty's Foreign Office.

"God, I thought the man would never shut up," Vincent told Sarah, after finally shaking him off. "What a bore. And I have to say, you Brits are never grateful to us Americans for pulling your chestnuts out of the fire."

Sarah shrugged. "It was all a long time ago, Vincent, dear. And besides, you're confusing me with someone who gives a fuck. Now, will you be a dear heart and hold my drink. I simply must find a ladies' room."

Vincent, seeing that her glass was empty, went to the bar to refill it. "I'll be here at the bar when you get back."

Nigel was already there, as if he had been waiting for him. "Oh, well done, Vincent, you finally got free of Mr Gladstone. Or was he Lord Salisbury?"

Vincent gave him a blank look.

"Former British prime ministers," Nigel felt the need to explain. "About the same vintage as your charming companion from the FO."

"I know who they are," Vincent snapped. "You contemptuous superior English types seem to think we Americans don't know anything."

"When it comes to history, other than your own, that's usually the case. It's why we find it so amusing that your man in the White House – and he's not the first, to be fair - wants to spend all that money defending countries he's never heard of."

"And what makes you such an expert on American foreign policy?"

"I suppose I did pick up a few things reading history at Oxford."

"Oh, you do like to bandy that about, don't you? But then I suppose it allows you to turn your nose up at lesser mortals like me who could only manage advanced degrees in economics."

"Ah, yes, the dismal science. And those who study it, in my experience, almost invariably prove it."

"I can assure you that I'm far from dismal - as your former wife would be the first to tell you."

"If I made your kind of money, I don't suppose I'd be dismal either." A quiet inner voice told Nigel he should quit while he was behind, but judgement had fled to brutish beasts, and he couldn't stop himself. Nor, if the truth be known, did he wish to stop, an alternative, much louder voice egging him on. "And much of it made by dubious means, I've no doubt."

"Exactly what do you mean by that?"

"I mean trading on information not freely available to the investing public. That's not my idea of an honourable occupation. But that *is* how the stock market works isn't it? You Insiders pile in first, leaving poor Joe Public to get in when it's too late. And then you hide the proceeds offshore. I dare say that goes for your pals in the military establishment as well. Oh, I know what goes on, believe me. But then, doesn't everybody."

"Exactly what are you getting at?" Vincent repeated, his face turning scarlet. "I don't like your insinuations."

Belatedly, Nigel realized that he'd gone too far. He'd mentioned nothing specific, but he'd said too much at the wrong time to the wrong man. Repeated warnings to mind his tongue should have put him on his guard, but it was too late for palliative discretion now. All he could was to beat a hasty retreat, as at Dunkirk; get most of the army off the beaches if not all of it.

"Oh, don't go getting on your high horse, Vincent. I'm only repeating what everyone knows. You Wall Street professionals somehow always have the inside track on everything before it happens." Now he regretted repeating the word 'inside' and saw that Vincent had picked up on it.

Vincent was now looking thunderous. "I'd be very careful, if I were you. If you're trying to imply that my business dealings are anything but legal, you'd be well advised to watch your tongue. And your pen. Otherwise, you may find yourself on the receiving end of a communication from my lawyers. I don't issue such threats lightly, I can tell you, and my attorneys are not the kind of men you'd wish to trifle with."

Nigel looked helplessly round the room for a potential source of rescue. Where the hell was Jane when he needed her? Or even Sarah. Better still, that tiresome old drunk from the Foreign Office.

"I don't think I've said anything I haven't read in the papers." The Dunkirk moment had arrived. "But if I've given offence, any offence at all, it was unintended, and I apologize unreservedly." An apology from Nigel Harper being a rare event, Vincent was initially startled. "What do you say we call a truce?" Nigel continued. "This is far too pleasant an occasion to be spoilt by a quarrel."

But Nigel had hit a raw nerve and Vincent, he noticed, was looking almost as alarmed as he was angry, and in no mood to be mollified by belated proforma apologies. "Your apology is noted but not accepted. And let me warn you again in case you didn't hear me the first time: if anything in your shitty newspaper so much as hints that my business dealings are anything but above board, I'll react swiftly and decisively. You can't possibly imagine how much legal firepower I have at my disposal. I could go nuclear."

"You sound like a Russian general," Nigel quipped, desperate to lighten the situation, but as usual only darkening it.

"My God, you really are a prize asshole."

Now the Foreign Office man really did ride to the rescue. "Still here, you chaps, and in the very same spot. Now, where was I when I…"

Nigel and Vincent glowered at each other for a moment and then stalked off in opposite directions, leaving the FO man looking bewildered.

* * *

In the taxi back to the hotel, Nigel was withdrawn, lost in thought.

"What's the matter?" Jane asked. "You didn't enjoy the party? Or have you been over-served, as you like to say?"

"I've been over-served alright. I've also been indiscreet." His voice was hoarse, and little more than a whisper.

"You'd better tell me what happened," she said.

Reluctantly, he told her about his exchanges with Vincent. He had told Jane very little about Samantha's Maryland revelations, only enough to alert her that 'something big' was brewing. As much as he would have liked to tell her the whole story, all he could do was dance around the periphery of it.

"The thing is, I know some bad stuff that's going on at a high level in government, financial stuff. This is based on information given to me in confidence. I wish I could say more, but I can't. I'm sorry."

"So far, I understand perfectly," Jane said.

"Good. But here's the problem. Vincent Marchetti – you just met him – is somehow deeply involved. Worse, I've implied that I know about it."

"How is he involved?"

"I can't say more."

"Oh, I see. It seems that you're perfectly prepared to tell him things that you're not willing to tell me."

"I'm sorry."

"Just how far did you go?"

"Far enough to piss him off."

"What I meant was, how specific were you?"

"Not specific at all. I spoke only in generalizations, but he gathered that I knew everything and was referring to something he'd done. He threatened to set his lawyers onto me."

"That sounds serious."

"It would be if it happened."

"You don't think it will?"

"No, because it will be in Mr Marchetti's interest to let this sleeping dog lie. He may do something else, though, only I've no idea what."

"All I can say is, what on earth were you thinking?" Jane was now ready to explode. "And to him of all people! You know he hates you. You know he has powerful friends. You know he can't wait to get at you. All this you know, yet you can't resist baiting him. Normally, it would be none of my business, the nasty things you two have to say to each other, but in this case I'm not so sure. I feel as if I'm being slowly sucked in."

"I know, I know," Nigel said. "And yes, I'm a prize idiot."

"I can't disagree. And since he doesn't drink, tomorrow morning he's not going to forget what you said. You, on the other hand…"

"I'm not going to forget it either." Nigel looked abject. "But you're right. I've been a fool."

"I'd say," she agreed again, this time rather too emphatically for his liking.

"Well, now that it's done, what do you suggest I do?" His tone was plaintive.

"I've no idea. Nothing. That would be my advice, at least until we've taken some professional advice." Jane was as decisive and commanding as he had ever seen her. "Anything else would probably only make matters worse. All we can hope is that Mr Marchetti does the same – keeps shtum - though from everything you've ever told me about him, doing nothing isn't exactly his style."

"I suppose I ought to alert Samantha…"

"You'll do no such thing." Jane's tone was scolding. "Look, I'm not privy to what's going on, and God knows I've no wish to be, but my advice stands. Just shut up. To be honest, I'm sorry that you've told me as much as you have. Your only hope is that the whole episode blows over. And if Mr Marchetti really has been up to something illegal, you're probably right: there's probably no incentive for him to take this any further."

"That's true," Nigel said, his mood suddenly brightening. Then he suffered a relapse. "But I've still been an idiot."

"Yes, you have, but don't keep repeating it. I'm getting bored."

"Thank you, my sweet, for your sage advice. You're always so reassuring." The words were slurred, 'reassuring' acquiring two or three additional syllables.

"You certainly know how to fuck up a nice evening," was all she said in conclusion, as the taxi pulled up outside their hotel.

* * *

In their room, he undressed and showered and then, still wet, fell into bed. Within seconds he was fast asleep, snoring loudly. Not so dashing now, Jane was thinking. Confirming with a shake of his shoulders that he really was out for the count, she crept out of the room. She went downstairs in the lift and crossed the deserted lobby to the pavement outside. She took out her phone and dialled.

"Hey, babe, what's doing?" cried Fran, chipper as always. "Are you two having a great time over there?"

"Well, we were until…"

Fran picked up on the hesitant tone. "Uh, oh. I smell something not quite right. What's happened?"

"I'm not sure. It may be nothing…"

"I'm sorry, you'll have to explain."

"I'm outside our hotel on the sidewalk. We've just got back from the reception at Winfield House. Well, how shall I put this…? Nigel, bless him, had a little too much to drink."

"What else is new?"

"What's new is that he may have committed a little faux pas."

"Well, that doesn't surprise me either," Fran said breezily. "What's he done, vomited down the cleavage of the Ambassador's wife? Punched a policeman?"

"Perhaps worse," Jane said in a sombre tone. "It's something to do with the Samantha Jameson business. Look, I have no idea what's going on. He's hardly told me anything. But here's the thing: it seems he may have said something to someone else."

Fran was now on full alert, her tone serious. "Oh dear. Who?"

"Vincent Marchetti, his ex-wife's boyfriend."

"Oh, Lordy. Not him. I mean, of all people..."

"Just what I said. Anyway, it seems they got into an argument of sorts and Nigel made some remarks. Something about insider trading. Apparently, Marchetti blew his top. Threatened to call his lawyers." There was no response at the other end of the phone. "Fran? Hello? Are you still there? Hello?"

Fran finally spoke. "How bad was it? I mean, just how much did he say?"

Jane repeated, as far as she could recall, what Nigel had told her.

"What else did he tell you?"

"About what's going on? Nothing. As I said, I'm completely in the dark. What can *you* tell me?"

"Nothing. And, believe me, for you it's better that way. I've just one question: were they alone? I know it was a party, of course, but did anyone else hear his remarks?"

"I don't think so. Someone could have overheard him, of course."

Another brief silence followed, and then Fran spoke. "I'm not saying this to make you feel better, but it may not be as serious as it seems. Nigel's been stupid, I'll grant you that, but what he said sounds sufficiently vague not to justify a legal response. Look, Marchetti has no way of knowing what Nigel knows, or if he knows anything at all. And if he's the only one who heard the remarks, that limits the damage. There's not enough here for Marchetti's lawyers to get their fangs into. And would he want them to draw blood anyway? I think not. That's my opinion, anyway. Of course, I'm no lawyer."

Jane's sigh of relief was audible. "I'm so glad I called you, Fran. I knew you'd put things into perspective. For a while, I was in something of a panic."

"Panic is what we need to avoid at all costs. Panic is like alcohol: it feeds indiscretion. Where's your jerk of a boyfriend now?"

"He's up in the room, sound asleep. But please don't tell him I called you. I told him in no uncertain terms that he should tell no one, so I'm breaking my own rule. I just thought you ought to know."

"I'm glad you called. Who else would he tell anyway?"

"He was thinking of telling Samantha Jameson. I'm not sure why."

"He shouldn't do that. On no account should he do that. The poor woman has enough on her plate already. I've got company here, so I can't say more right now."

"I'd like to know what's at risk here. For me, if not for him."

"All I can tell you is that we're working on a story, and the situation is delicately poised and highly sensitive. I can't tell you how sensitive. Look, I wish I could say more, but too much has been said already."

"Look, Fran, I'm not demanding to know what's going on. I'm not even asking. All I know is that Nigel's in a bit of a state about it. Distraught, in fact."

"And so he deserves to be, the idiot. Want my advice, dear girl? Forget about tonight's incident. The more I think about it, the less dangerous it seems. I hope to God I'm right. Anyway, what's done is done. Try to enjoy the rest of the trip. See the sights. Go shopping. Have great sex. And when you get back, I'll hear Nigel's confession personally. I usually prescribe a little self-flagellation, although in this case I may flog him myself."

"It was the booze doing the talking," Jane mused, stating the obvious.

"I know. Look, do me and everyone else a favour and just make sure he stays sober for the rest of the trip. And if there's the slightest chance of him running into Marchetti again, keep him away. Shoot him in the knee if you have to."

"Don't worry," Jane said. "Until we're on the plane home I'm going to keep him under close supervision. Goodnight, Fran. Sorry to have troubled you. And thank you."

* * * * *

Chapter 14

Samantha Jameson sat at her desk in her East Wing office signing letters and routine documents, killing time before her eleven-clock appointment with Marty Ginsberg, her personal attorney. Rosalie Burgess, her principal private secretary, hovered behind her, methodically placing papers on the desk for signature. After signing the last one, Samantha eased back in her chair and gazed out of the window, watching Washington go about its business - as much as could be seen of it from there.

Rosalie interrupted her thoughts. "Will there by anything else, Mrs Jameson?"

Samantha shook her head. "That'll be all, thanks, Rosalie. Just send Mr Ginsberg in as soon as he arrives."

"Don't bother, I'm already here." Marty was standing in the doorway.

"Come in Marty, come on in. A sight for sore eyes."

Rosalie left, gently closing the door behind her.

Marty, who had a one-man practice in Washington, had been Samantha's personal attorney for ten years. He was in his late sixties, short and stocky, with a shock of grey curly hair that had not been cut for some months. He looked, as always, somewhat dishevelled, more Jewish academic than high-powered celebrity lawyer. His tie was loosened, his tan suit rumpled, his shoes scuffed. He carried a battered briefcase that had seen the inside of many a courtroom. This he placed on the corner of the desk, as if staking a territorial claim.

"You seem a little out of breath, Marty," Samantha said. "Perhaps, finally, you'll give up those cigars."

Marty collapsed into a chair with a loud exhalation. "I've given up everything else. Surely a man in his later years is entitled to retain a few residual vices. But thanks for the advice."

"I'm always accepting yours, so perhaps for once you'll take mine."

"It's not the occasional cigar that puts my health at risk," he said wearily. "It's all the running around I do on behalf of clients who then have the nerve to tell me I'm overdoing it. You're my third appointment today. But since your call sounded urgent, I've made sure you're the last." He opened the briefcase and took out a yellow legal pad. "Anyway, here I am, at your disposal for the rest of the day."

"Coffee?"

"That would hit the spot. Black, no sugar."

Samantha had given up coffee. Life was stressful enough without regular infusions of caffeine. She buzzed Rosalie with an order for one.

"You're a gem, Marty. I don't know how I'd manage without you. And I really do appreciate the house calls. Not many lawyers offer such a service."

"In your case, my dear Mrs Jameson, it's a privilege as well as a duty. Not many lawyers get to represent the first lady of the land. And after ten years as your attorney, making a house call is the least I can do. How was your trip to London? I watched some of it on television."

"Exhausting, but then these visits always are. There were some diverting interludes. The demonstrators were kept at bay, although the rain probably helped more than the police. The president isn't popular over there, as you've no doubt gathered."

"You met the King, of course. How was he?"

"Delightful, but as inscrutable as ever. Who knows what goes on behind that perpetually smiling pudding of a face. He only seems to become animated when someone mentions global warming. Fortunately, he and I share that passion. Otherwise, I'm not sure what we'd have found to talk about. And, of course, I got to sleep in the Palace."

"And how was that? Magnificent?"

"Draughty. And in need of refurbishment."

"Well, now that you're back in what we laughingly call civilization, what's on the agenda today? The divorce? You're not revising your will again?"

"Neither. I need to talk to you about that other matter, the one we discussed last time we met."

"Oh, dear, that again."

"Well, I need to make some decisions. And since we last spoke, I've received more information than I knew at the time. It will shock even you."

"In that case, wouldn't we have been better off meeting in my office than here?"

"Are you suggesting that this one may be bugged?"

Marty smiled. "Well, there *have* been instances of meetings in the White House being recorded. We lost a president that way, as I recall."

"No loss, in my opinion. But this isn't the Oval Office, so I think we're safe enough."

"I hope you're right."

Marty removed a ball-point pen from his inside pocket and started clicking it, a habit he had acquired when nervous, and for some reason he was now nervous. "So, what's this new information?"

Samantha beckoned Marty to a small round mahogany table. She was about to respond to the question when Rosalie arrived with his coffee.

"We don't want to be disturbed," Samantha told her, somewhat curtly. "And please postpone my three o'clock with Senator Fordham's wife. Ask if we can reschedule for tomorrow. I'm free all day, as it happens."

As Rosalie closed the door behind her, Samantha instinctively leaned closer to her attorney. Reflexively, he did the same, until they were inches apart. She spoke in a low voice. "As you'll recall from our last meeting, I have reason to believe that my husband, along with certain other high-ranking political figures, is involved in certain illegal financial market activities."

"Yes, I remember. You were uncertain what to do about it."

"I was. But now I have far more compelling evidence."

"Tell me about it."

"I will. But first let me recap what's happened since we last spoke. I told you about the evidence I'd acquired. Well, since then I've since discovered that these illegal activities go well beyond anything I'd imagined, and on a scale that might take even *your* breath away."

Marty automatically scribbled the date and time on his yellow pad. Below that, underlined, he wrote a subject heading: 'Illegal Financial Activities'.

"Would you care to describe this new evidence?"

"There are several aspects..." Samantha paused to think about what order to put them in. "I mentioned that I'd found evidence of an offshore bank account. Well, it's now clear that it was set up to receive the proceeds from a wide-ranging scheme of illicit trading, money-laundering and tax evasion."

"And you now have documentary proof of this?"

"Yes."

"From what source, may I ask?"

"I hired a team of investigators. The documentation is part of the report they've given me. An interim report, I might add."

Marty's eyebrows rose in alarm. "What kind of investigators?"

"A firm called Kwest. They've provided ample proof to confirm my initial suspicions. You know them?"

"Yes, I've had dealings with them from time to time. They're the best in the business, no doubt about that. And, more importantly, they know how to keep secrets. But let's get back to them in a moment. First, let me ask you about these alleged offences. Over what period did they take place?"

"About two years, maybe more. The Kwest investigation is ongoing. It's all quite complex and I'm not sure I understand everything, but the amounts involved are quite staggering."

"How staggering?"

"Hundreds of millions of dollars."

"Is that all." Marty's tone was ironic. Seeing her surprised reaction, he adopted a more solemn one. "So, we can proceed on the assumption that the evidence of your husband's involvement is unimpeachable." He smiled. "I suppose, in the circumstances, I might have used a more appropriate word."

Samantha smiled too, but her manner quickly turned serious again. "I'd say the evidence is not only compelling. I'd say it's irrefutable."

"I hate to ask, but I know you'll understand why I must: were you yourself, directly or indirectly, knowingly or unknowingly, involved in this illegal enterprise?"

"None of the above." Her tone was emphatic, verging on the indignant. She hesitated for a moment before adding, "Unless, of course, accounts have been opened in my name without my knowledge. But I've no reason to suppose that. Let me put it this way: I haven't knowingly signed anything that would implicate me. I always make a point of reading everything that leaves this desk over my signature. Unlike some I could mention..."

"How many people are aware of all this, other than Kwest and me?"

"I've told no one." She surprised herself by how easily the lie tripped off the tongue.

"Good. Let's keep it that way."

"I have, though, *alluded* to it."

"Oh, dear." Marty sighed audibly. "To whom and in what form?"

"My friend Frank Hoffman, the White House press secretary, and Fran Powell, my senior communications adviser. Oh, and one other, a British journalist named Nigel Harper. All conversational."

"A journalist! Oy vey!" Marty gave the impression of a man about to fall out of his chair. "In God's name why?"

"Yes, I know. Look, I took a risk, I admit, but it's a calculated one. I'll need a journalist so that I can control the narrative when the time comes. He was digging around in certain aspects of my private life, and I couldn't be sure what would come out. I needed him to back off, so I promised him an even bigger story."

"The bigger story being your husband's financial crimes?"

"Yes. But it's more complicated than that."

"It had better be. But let me get to that later. I'm more than a little shocked that you've told a reporter. Do you know him?"

"Not until recently, but I'm certain he can be trusted. I haven't mentioned any names, to him or the other two." This, too, was skirting the truth, and she tried hard not to blush as she spoke the words.

Marty now looked angry. "I'd rather you hadn't said anything to anyone, least of all to a reporter. You should have called me first."

"I know. But I think the situation is under control. Two of the three are dear friends of long-standing."

"It's the reporter I'm concerned about. A Brit, you say. Who is he?"

"He works for a London paper called the *Post*. He's become a friend of Fran Powell's. He has an incentive not to write anything. If he does, I'll simply deny everything."

Marty shook his head. "What kind of incentive?"

"If the story should break, my thinking was that we'd need a friend in the media, someone other than a famous big-shot American reporter who'd set off a competitive media stampede."

"Is the story going to break?" he asked pointedly.

Samantha turned coy. "I'll get to that, too. I have a plan. Meanwhile, I'm confident that the situation is manageable."

"From your mouth to God's ears - and only He can know what damage you may have done already. From now on tell nobody anything. And I mean nobody. I can't stress strongly enough the need to keep the lid on this until we've worked out what's to be done… if anything."

"I get the message, Marty." Samantha was contrite and irritated at the same time. "I'm sorry, but this has all been rather stressful. I'm sitting on a powder-keg knowing it could blow up at any moment. I had my own peace of mind to consider as well as my plan. But not another word from now on. Cross my heart and hope to die."

"In my case," Marty joked, "that would be neither valid nor appropriate. I want to talk about your plan, whatever that is, but first I'd like to know how the documents that aroused your suspicion came into your possession. You haven't told me your source."

Relieved to have Marty's anticipated reprimand out of the way, Samantha relaxed a little. "There *was* no source. I found them."

"Found them! Where? In a coffee shop? In a taxi?"

"No, in the Oval Office."

Marty groaned. "This story gets curiouser and curiouser. And riskier and riskier. But tell me more."

"About three months ago, a friend of the president's - someone I've met socially once or twice - stopped by the Oval Office to see him. I'd just left after a short meeting with my husband... as they all are these days."

"Were they alone, or were others present?"

"Just the two of them."

"And this meeting with the friend was a social rather than formal occasion?"

"Probably both. He's an old college friend of my husband's. Also, as I now know, his business partner - the business being what we've just been talking about."

"How do you know what they discussed if you'd left the room?"

"Because I left my purse on the desk, and when I went back in to get it, they shut up immediately."

"They could have been talking man-talk, locker-room stuff."

"I don't think so. They looked terribly serious. Almost conspiratorial."

"That," Marty observed," could apply to many conversations in the Oval Office."

"True, but it looked too serious for locker-room talk. Voices were raised."

"Who is this friend?"

"His name is Vincent Marchetti. He's a hedge fund tycoon. A very successful one, I believe."

"I've heard of him."

"And what have you heard?"

"Nothing that would persuade me to invite him for dinner, but that's neither here nor there. He's well known in financial circles. A potential member of the cabinet - or so I've heard said."

"Then you'll probably know that he's an oily little creep or, as our British friends would say, a thoroughly nasty piece of work."

"Your assessment may be accurate, but for the sake of good order let's try to avoid personal opinions. They tend to be prejudicial. So, you heard nothing of what they were discussing."

"Nothing at all. The Oval Office door was closed. I was in the adjoining office, chatting to my husband's principal secretary, Rose Parkin."

"And what happened next?"

"Marchetti left and Parkin went in to call my husband away to a meeting, so he left as well."

"And then."

"On an impulse, which I can't explain, I went back into the Oval Office. The first thing I noticed was that someone had left a buff-coloured envelope on the sofa where Marchetti had been sitting. I picked it up, as any good housewife would, and was about to place it on the desk; then I noticed the logo of a Cayman Islands bank. That piqued my interest…"

"Was the envelope sealed?"

"No, it had been opened."

"And you decided to take a look inside…"

"Yes."

Marty gave her another disapproving look. "Do you make it a regular habit to examine documents you find lying around in the Oval Office?"

"Not at all."

"And what did you find inside?"

"There were three single sheets of paper. One was a bank statement from Cayman Islands Bank International. It contained details of several deposits. What struck me was the amount at the bottom - nearly two hundred million dollars."

"And the other two documents…?"

"The second was a typewritten list. Twelve names were on it. Surnames. In my husband's case, just his initials. There was no letterhead, but at the top someone had scribbled 'Cayman Group.' And next to each name was a figure, which I took to be a dollar amount. The smallest was twenty million, the biggest, next to my husband's initials was fifty million."

"And the third document...?"

"A deposit slip from the Cayman bank for several million dollars. I forget the exact amount."

"And would you care to give me the names on the list?"

"My husband's. And five prominent politicians: Senators Charles Pitman of New Mexico and William Curtis of Arizona, and three congressmen: Branson of Pennsylvania, Darling of Wyoming, and Hedges of Florida. All Republicans, of course. I've met both senators, but only briefly at official events."

"That's only six names. Who were the others?"

"Rickenbacker and Arnold, both high-ranking generals, and four others I haven't been able to identify. That's twelve in all."

"And you assumed that these three documents were connected?"

"It was obvious. The figure at the bottom of the bank statement matched the one at the bottom of the list of names. The receipt, dated a week earlier, was for a recent transaction - March of this year, I seem to recall. It matched a figure on one of the entries on the statement."

"And then what did you do?"

"I photo-copied all three pages."

"Where?"

"In an administrative area, in the room where the copiers are."

"Did you make them yourself, or ask someone else to do it?"

"I did it myself."

"And then?"

"I put the originals back in the envelope, went back into the Oval Office and left the envelope exactly where I'd found it."

"On the sofa?

"Yes."

"And these photocopies, where are they now?"

"In a bank vault."

Marty scribbled more notes. As he was writing, Samantha rose and buzzed Rosalie to bring more coffee. He put down his pad and pen. "I'll need to see them, of course. And anything else you've acquired since."

"Yes, of course," Samantha said solemnly. "Tell me, Marty, could I be legally compromised for doing what I did?"

"Well, removing documents from the Oval Office is potentially a serious matter, but since no one apparently knows what you did, let's not concern ourselves with that for now. My working assumption for the time being is that no one knows anything except you, Hoffman, Powell, the reporter and Kwest... and now me. Is that correct?"

"Yes."

"Any chance Parkin, or others, observed what you were doing?"

"Parkin wasn't there. Others were but none of them paid me the slightest attention. I'm a familiar figure there."

"Let's talk about Kwest. You told them about these papers and presumably gave them copies, and then you commissioned them to investigate further."

"Yes."

"How? By telephone, e-mail, letter?"

"None of the above. I had lunch with the chief executive. Someone gave me his name. I can't remember who."

"Someone who may be curious to know why you asked..."

"Oh, dear, another misstep."

"I know Robert Palladino. He, at least, can be trusted. He can't afford not to be in his line of work. And what have Kwest found since then?"

"Oh, a good deal more than what I found. For example, one large transaction in the shares of a well-known defence company, United Aerospace Industries. It had been executed in the name of one of Vincent Marchetti's investment companies. The stock subsequently rose sharply, they told me."

"One random transaction doesn't represent a pattern."

"No. But Kwest found much more. They unearthed - don't ask me how - an unmistakable pattern of insider trading involving several other companies. The investigation, as I said, is still in progress. They also delved into the Cayman account. It was set up several years ago."

"Before your husband was president?"

"Yes, but there was considerable activity after that. The bank was evidently used as a vehicle for receiving the trading proceeds. A few transactions were routed through other offshore companies. One, I remember, was in Gibraltar, another in Cyprus. Kwest has written all this up in a preliminary report. You'll need to see it, I suppose."

"Of course. I take it that's also in the bank vault. Is everything in the bank vault?"

"Yes."

"You didn't think to bring any documents to this meeting?"

"No. Sorry. I thought about it, but I'm being ultra-cautious."

"Well, that's a step in the right direction... I need to see all of it, as soon as possible."

"I'll get them over to you right away."

"To be on the safe side, I suggest you bring them yourself. What, by the way, was Palladino's take on all this?"

"I had lunch with him two days ago. His opinion is that there's more than enough to justify both civil and criminal proceedings. But that's beyond my expertise... something we'll presumably need to discuss."

"Where did you have lunch?"

"Somewhere very discreet if that's what you're getting at. A suburban coffee shop in Virginia."

"So, to summarize, it seems we have enough evidence to implicate the president in a scheme that contravenes United States securities laws, which, if it were to become public knowledge, would end his presidency. He'd have to resign, or face impeachment, or prosecution."

"Yes, I imagine so."

From the expression on Samantha's face, Marty concluded that she would relish any one of the three. He gave her a searching look. "Now, about this plan you mentioned; let's talk about that. The first question is what you intend to do with this information. Is the object of the exercise - your so-called plan - to take the evidence public and expose the president of the United States as a crook?" Samantha was suddenly trembling, he noticed. He patted her hand reassuringly. "You can speak openly to me. Remember, we're covered by lawyer-client privilege."

"You and my therapist..." She giggled nervously, attempting to release the tension.

Marty ignored the remark. "Just tell me what your thinking is, and then I'll decide whether it makes sense."

"I was rather hoping you'd tell me what I *can* do. Or, rather, *should* do."

Marty looked uncomfortable. "I'm not sure I know enough yet to give advice."

Samantha faced him squarely. "Before I say anything, Marty, I need to understand something. What's my legal exposure? I'm not sure where the law stands. Two questions: First, am I'm legally obliged to report evidence of wrongdoing? Second, could I be at risk of being charged as an accessory after the fact, or even as an accomplice?"

"Sounds like you've already been doing some research." Marty stood up and ambled over to the window. For two minutes he said nothing; then he returned to the table. His expression was grave. "My initial response - as inadequate as it may strike you - is that I'd be guessing. It's no time for guesswork. Your situation involves an arcane area of the law, one in which I'm far from expert. You need the advice of specialists in the field. I'm sorry if you think that's passing the buck, but it's sound advice."

"Do you have someone in mind?"

"I'm thinking of a large New York firm with experience dealing with this kind of case. Also, one that deals regularly with the US Attorney's office for the Southern District, which is where most big market trading scams end up. I happen to know the chief prosecutor, and I can tell you he's not a man to trifle with. Whatever we decide you should do, we'll have to be damned sure of our ground."

"I was hoping for more from you, to be honest. No disrespect intended…"

"None taken. But you should never trust instant reactions, not even mine. I'll need to do some reading on this, but in the first instance you're probably safe. The law as it stands doesn't require you to report a crime. In the second instance, I think you're in the clear, since you can reasonably argue that you didn't know what was going on. But there may be potential danger in both positions. I can't go beyond that without expert and up-to-date advice."

"Where would you get that?"

"There are several firms that specialize in this area."

"Let me put it another way, then. Which one would you least like to come up against in a courtroom?"

Marty didn't have to think for long about that. "Kraft, Slade & Bradwell. I know them well. Like Kwest, they're the best at what they do - as I've discovered to my disadvantage on more than one occasion."

"Strangely enough," Samantha said, "Bob Palladino came up with the same name. Well, perhaps not so strange... Can you arrange a meeting?"

"I'll call them as soon as I've gone over the Kwest file. How's your schedule over the next few days?"

"Relatively light. But I'll try to clear my diary. Right now, nothing's more important than this, looking after my own interests."

"I agree. But what does that mean, exactly? You've still told me nothing about the plan you referred to." Waiting for the response, Marty feared the worst. The worst was duly confirmed.

"I intend, subject to legal advice, to use the information in my possession to bring about, one way or another, an end to Martin Jameson's presidency." She told him of her planned course of action.

Marty was momentarily lost for words. In all the years he had known her, he had never seen her demonstrate such single-minded resolve or venom. He found it frightening to behold. When he finally spoke, it was in a grave tone. "All I can say, Samantha Jameson, is that you seem to have acquired some very dangerous ambitions."

"Yes, I know," she said, matching his gravity. "Believe me, I know."

* * *

Four days later they flew to New York. Arriving in Manhattan half an hour earlier than expected, they went to a coffee shop on Madison Avenue, a block away from the offices of Kraft, Slade & Bardwell. Marty, having scrutinized the documents since their first meeting, had been shocked to the core. Shock was followed by disgust. The president - his client's husband - was a crook; of that there could be little doubt. Of everything else, including what to do about it, he was far from certain.

Manhattan was sweltering in the mid-summer sunshine. The streets were crowded, the chorus of honking car horns unceasing. It all struck Marty as manic - and he was a New Yorker born and bred. He had relocated his business to Washington twenty-five years earlier, but his New York roots were deep. He still owned a home in Brooklyn Heights, where most of his relatives still lived. "Oy, this place gets crazier by the year…"

"I know what you mean about New York," Samantha said. "But I love the place. At least it's alive, so much going on, so much diverse energy. Washington's dead. It's a city with a one-track mind."

Marty reluctantly agreed while paying the bill. He looked as unkempt as ever and was still lugging the battered briefcase. Samantha was impressed that he hadn't bothered, as she had, to dress for the occasion.

"Ready to face the music?"

"No, but it has to be done," she said, with the resignation of someone embarked on an enterprise that could only end, whatever direction it might take, in sordid headlines. But that made her the more determined to hasten the day of reckoning. "I'm a little nervous, I can tell you. Make that terrified. All this is way out of my comfort zone."

"You and me both," Marty said, consolingly.

"That doesn't sound like the Marty Ginsberg I know."

"Why shouldn't I be nervous? Thanks to you, Mrs Jameson, I'm the recipient of the most explosive set of documents I've ever seen - and I've seen quite a few in my time. We're about to enter secret discussions with one of the top securities law firms in the country, as a result of which you may decide to bring down the President of the United States. Nothing like this has happened to me before. This beats Watergate and Iran-Contra hands down. I'm just a nice Jewish boy from Brooklyn. All I ever wanted was to get through law school, earn enough to look after a wife, a couple of kids and my parents - and a little left over for Israel."

"You may be a nice Jewish boy from Brooklyn, Marty, but you also happen to be one of the best in your profession. Coming third in class at Harvard Law School is no mean achievement. Since then, you've won some of the most famous cases in legal history. So, don't give me this nice Jewish boy stuff. How *is* Brooklyn, by the way?"

"Still Brooklyn, but a little more gentrified than I remember. All the better for it, they tell me, but I'm not so sure."

"And Rebecca? Your wife was ill for a while, wasn't she? Is she better?"

"Rebecca's fine now. In the clear - God and Sloan Kettering willing. She thinks I spend far too much time in DC. She's right. The two boys are out of university now, so she thinks we should spend more time together. Neither of the boys are lawyers, by the way. They both went into banking."

"It could have been worse," Samantha said, laughing. "They could have gone into politics."

"It doesn't bear thinking about." Marty checked his watch. "Time to go, young lady. And let's not refer to your intentions while we're in there. This is all about your immediate legal exposure. Nothing else."

The reception desk was on the forty-fifth floor of a glass midtown skyscraper, with spectacular views over the East River, and beyond that the borough of Queens. The wood-panelled walls were dominated by two large rocky landscapes from the Hudson River school, though waiting visitors were more inclined to watch the planes landing and taking off at La Guardia, marvelling at the frequency. The firm also occupied the floors above and below, all three connected by an ornate spiral staircase. The receptionist, a prim, well turned-out lady in her sixties, ushered Marty and Samantha to a plush sofa and went back to her desk to call Simon Jenkins, the man they had come to see. He was one of the firm's senior partners, an acknowledged expert in securities law, especially insider trading, in which he was regarded as something of a guru.

Jenkins appeared in the lobby dead on the stroke of eleven, the time of their appointment. He was tall, dark-haired and, for a man who spent most of his time in conference rooms and courts, unusually bronzed. The son of English immigrants, he looked and sounded more like a London barrister than a New York lawyer. He was as fastidious in his dress as in his timekeeping, the creases in his trousers razor edged, his jacket beautifully cut to the contours of his torso. The shirt was white, of course, the collar starched, the tie calculated to be at once bold and conservative. Jenkins, like Marty, had attended Harvard Law School, though by the time he studied there Marty was already a tutor. Simon liked to say that Marty had taught him everything he knew about the law. He was in his mid-forties, Samantha guessed.

"Good to see you again Marty," Simon said effusively, extending a hand. "It's been quite a while. The last time, we were on opposing sides, and you won."

"At least two years, I've worked out. Simon, allow me to introduce Samantha Jameson."

"Good morning, Mrs Jameson. "It's a pleasure and a rare privilege to meet the first lady of the United States."

Samantha noted the firm handshake. "Please call me Samantha, at least in the office."

"Done."

Guiding them through a set of wide glass doors, he immediately turned right into a large conference room with windowless walls panelled in the same fruitwood tones as the lobby. It was dominated by a long mahogany table with satin-wood trim, and cushioned chairs in a Chippendale design. On the walls were more, smaller Hudson Valley landscapes, the river wending its way through mist shrouded mountains. The old-world décor struck Samantha as resolutely out of keeping with the surrounding acres of glass.

Simon read her mind. "This room is an oasis, where the partners, and important clients, can get together to relax and chat in private. So much more discreet than those aquariums, with everyone peering in, trying to figure out what's going on. Please take a seat. Coffee? Tea? Danish?"

All three were declined.

As soon as they had sat down, they had to spring up to greet a newcomer, a younger man, perhaps not yet forty, tall with blond curly hair and an engaging smile. "This is Clyde Barron," Simon said. "He's a partner here; our youngest, as a matter of fact, and our resident expert in laws protecting whistle-blowers."

"I was once a whistle-blower myself," said Clyde, apparently feeling obliged to explain his background. "Before I went into law I was employed as an accountant at a big consumer goods company in New Jersey. After a while, I came across some serious financial irregularities. When I brought them to the attention of management, they fired me. That's when the law beckoned. I managed to get into Yale."

"Harvard and Yale at the same table," Marty said, grinning. "How on earth do you guys manage to work together?"

"It's sometimes difficult," Simon said, laughing, "and often impossible. But somehow, we make it work. So, to business..."

Simon Jenkins, Samantha was pleased to observe, was someone who liked to keep polite conversation to a minimum, which, given his eye-popping hourly fee, was all to the good so far as she was concerned. He took a seat at the end of the table, obviously intent on chairing the meeting.

"Marty, I understand we'll be joined later by Robert Palladino."

"That's right," Marty said, checking his notebook for names. "And two others: Susan Archer, ex-Price Waterhouse, and Veronica Kingston, or Ronnie, as he called her, both former SEC enforcement investigators who specialize in insider trading. Between them they've been involved in dozens of these cases in recent years. They've been working together on this one."

Simon nodded with apparent approval, though it was hard to tell. He had been involved in a few such cases himself and knew Palladino well. "So, let's get started. Marty, I've read the documents you sent me, including the Kwest report. Very thorough, as one might expect. Also, on the face of it, very damning. Mrs Jameson, I understand that you have concerns about your legal obligations and potential liabilities. Is that correct?"

"Yes, it's why we're here."

"Quite so. But before we start, I don't intend to ask you any questions about your intentions in this matter. That may become relevant, but for now let's just stick to the narrow legal issues... if that's alright with you."

"It is," said Samantha, feeling rather relieved that her intentions were off the table.

"The good news, if I may blow the firm's trumpet, is that we have considerable experience with cases of this kind. None involving the White House, of course. The bad news is that this is one of the more arcane areas of the law. It's also one that's constantly evolving, especially since the Dodd-Frank legislation. Nothing seems black and white anymore. I should warn you in advance that you'll probably be asking a great many straightforward questions and getting rather complicated answers in return. I apologize in advance."

Samantha responded crisply. "Duly noted. What I need to know above all, Simon, is whether my actions so far have put me in any kind of personal legal jeopardy."

Simon pondered his response for several seconds. "Let me first ask you this: are you familiar with the definition of insider trading?"

"Broadly speaking, yes. But I'd like to hear it from - forgive me - the horse's mouth."

"Well, insider trading is essentially taking advantage - making money or avoiding losses - using information about a publicly listed company which has not yet been made available to the public. That's illegal under US securities law. By material, I mean information sufficiently important to lead to a change in the value of the company's stock, whether up or down. For example, let's say you were to buy a company's shares based on a tip from someone working for the company that it's about to announce a huge rise in earnings, or an acquisition, or being acquired itself. The tipster would automatically break the law. You, as the recipient of that information would, potentially, be just as guilty as the informant. Do you understand?"

"Perfectly," said Samantha, waiting for the 'buts' to arrive.

"So far, so simple," Simon continued. "But from that point of reference, things start to get a bit more complicated. There's nothing to stop insiders trading shares of the company they work for, of course, provided what they know has already been made public, either through a corporate press release or a filing with the SEC. In those instances, everything would be above board. But if they acted before the release or the filing, it wouldn't be. As for trading tip-offs, we could have a lengthy debate about what constitutes a tip, and whether the information is material, because many more issues come into play. But that, in a nutshell, is what largely defines the term insider trading."

"So far, it's all clear," Samantha said, smiling, but feeling rather patronized.

"Good. Now, forgive me for asking this, and I'm sure Marty has already asked you, but have you to the best of your knowledge ever used privileged inside information about a company to make a profit, or to avoid a loss, either by trading in its securities, or asking someone else to trade? I'm talking in general, but that includes this case."

"Never."

"And as a standard follow-up question, have you ever allowed your husband to use your name on any such transactions?"

"Knowingly, never."

"And in the matter under discussion here, have you ever, again to the best of your knowledge, ever benefitted, directly or indirectly, from his allegedly illicit activities?"

"Again, not knowingly."

"We won't, if you don't mind, get into money-laundering or tax evasion issues, which are even more complex. Suffice to say that financial institutions which suspect that something shady is taking place are now required by law to report it to the relevant authorities. This is done through a device called a SAR. That's short for Suspicious Activity Report. It does what it says on the label. You, of course, are not a financial institution, so…"

At that point, a commotion at the door announced the arrival of the team from Kwest. Robert Palladino, a large, powerfully built man with dark wavy hair tinged with grey, appeared. Filling the room, he made a beeline for Samantha and kissed her extended hand. His subordinates, Sue Archer and Ronnie Kingston, emerged from his shadow to introduce themselves. Both were in their thirties, Sue tall and trim, Ronnie shorter and overweight. Both wore glasses and, Samantha thought, looked suitably geeky.

Simon beckoned them to join the meeting. "How's business, Robert?"

"Almost as lucrative as yours, I dare say, Simon, which seems unfair, considering that we have to do all the legwork."

"Brains always win over brawn," Simon retorted with a grin that Robert suspected masked a hidden feeling of superiority. But that was a fact of life for anonymous private investigators, who could never hope to occupy the same lofty pedestal as lawyers. "As we seem to have reached a natural break in the proceedings, does anyone need coffee? Show of hands please." No hands went up. "Good, then let's press on."

Marty jumped in. "Robert, you've produced a small mountain of paper on this case, so why don't you take us through the highlights." Robert, with a wave of the hand, deferred to Sue.

"We started," Sue intoned flatly, and slightly nervously, "with the papers that Mrs Jameson provided. Those were revealing, but not quite revealing enough. Working from there, though, we discovered more, much more, and so complex that this may not be the time or place to present it in detail. Anyway, it's all in our preliminary report, which I understand has been distributed to this group."

"It has been," Simon confirmed. "For which many thanks. But for the purposes of this meeting, please give us a summary."

"What we've discovered shows a clear pattern of insider trading over the course of two or three years. It also reveals the existence of an intricate network of financial pipelines established for channeling the funds to several accounts, but one in particular: I refer to a Cayman Islands bank account, which is registered in the names of twelve members of an investment group that informally calls itself the Cayman Club."

Simon interrupted again. "Could you give us some examples of how this worked?"

"Sure. We found that some of the funds being funnelled into the Cayman account originated with various foreign-registered companies. In one instance, it was the sales agent for an Italian armaments company, which received kickbacks for purchases from US firms with government contracts. The Cayman Club, so-called, seems to have simultaneously negotiated an agency agreement giving it a share of those kickbacks. Again, the proceeds were routed through to the Cayman account. We've listed the names on that account in our report. They are all, I can confirm, American citizens."

Simon broke in again. "Yes, we have the names. How many other offshore companies are involved?"

"We've found four so far. We may still find more. It's painstaking work, as you'll appreciate. And it's not just the Cayman Islands bank that's been receiving funds; the group seems to have bank accounts in Panama and Gibraltar - both typical offshore banking venues." Sue looked across the table at her colleague. "Ronnie, can you take it from here?"

Ronnie, also nervous, took a sip of water. "There's a great deal of money involved, but they're not making it just from kickbacks. Much of it comes from playing the stock market, all based as far as we can tell on inside information. Much of it is related to pending government defence contracts. These transactions were all cleverly dispersed at different times and at different investment firms to avoid detection. Disguising stock market activity is a difficult proposition in this computer age, but we're getting the hang of it. The SEC enforcement unit where I once worked examined billions of data entries to identify unusual trading volumes in shares of companies ahead of public announcements. After that, the SEC's market abuse team would track which investment firms were trading and, where possible, on whose behalf. Then there was, still is, the Analysis and Detection Center, which has experts in quantitative analysis, high-frequency trading, index arbitraging, and so on. Those ADC guys are all mathematical geniuses. They tend to sweep up, using advanced methodologies, whatever the other departments might have missed."

Simon broke in again. "Just to be clear - and this is largely for the benefit of Samantha - your report confirms that the Cayman Group is trading on inside information, channelling the proceeds through certain offshore investment funds, and then through other foreign companies set up for the purpose of laundering money and evading taxes. Is that it?"

"Exactly," Ronnie replied matter-of-factly. "But of late, meaning over the last few weeks, the group seems to have put the brakes on certain investment houses. We don't know why. Perhaps they felt they were pushing their luck and found some alternative vehicle. We discovered, for example, an obscure outfit run by a couple of Harvard dropouts - twin brothers, actually - who seem to have developed a state-of-the-art ATS, probably designed to evade SEC detection."

"What's an ATS?" Samantha asked.

"It's short for Algorithmic Trading Strategy. Nowadays, high-speed ATS trading accounts for two-thirds of all transactions in US equities. Most of the trades are in large blocks, using sophisticated mathematical trading models that track market trends and other financial data. This makes it harder to track who's buying or selling what, although the SEC's surveillance technology eventually catches up. Well, some of it, but by no means everything."

Samantha was finding all this both fascinating and confusing. There were just too many dots to connect to produce a clear picture. Marty tapped her gently on the arm, as if to say, *'A lot of this is Greek to me, too.'* And some if it was. But the gist of it seemed clear enough.

Sue offered the next insight. "Then there's the problem of how you channel the sheer volume of profits to the individuals concerned. There's a limit to the number of phony accounts that can be used without risking the attention of the regulators here in the United States." Sue proceeded to launch into an explanation of how it was done but after fifteen minutes of largely unfathomable exposition, Marty decided to call a halt to this part of the meeting. There were just too many intricate facts to absorb at one sitting, many of them surplus to the purposes of the meeting.

"In summary," Marty said, interrupting Sue in full flow, and using words that he had heard from Samantha herself, "the evidence of all this, in the case of the Cayman Island account, is compelling if not to say irrefutable."

"Irrefutable will do nicely," Sue said. "No question about it. We have it all here in black and white." She tapped a thick file, which she hadn't opened, lying on the desk in front of her.

"I think that'll do for now, Sue," said Simon, rather abruptly. "Thank you. And thanks to you, and your whole team for a job well done. I'm conscious that Mrs Jameson has another meeting to go to shortly, so she and I will need a few minutes to wrap things up here. So, Robert, if you'll excuse us, and with our heartfelt thanks…"

Robert, looking slightly miffed, was heading for the door when Simon stopped him. "But before you go, can you stick around for a bit? You and I need to put our heads together, to see in totality what we've got here; go over the fine details."

Robert nodded and directly addressed Samantha, his client. "If I can be of any more help, Mrs Jameson, please call me. Same goes for you, Marty."

"I will," Marty said. "And probably soon."

"Thanks, Robert," Samantha said.

Simon showed them out. When he returned, Marty said, "That was a fascinating overview, but as usual the devil is in the details." He looked at Simon. "Having heard what you've just heard, and what you've read, let me ask you where you think that leaves Mrs Jameson's legal obligations."

It was Clyde who spoke first. "Just two fundamental questions, Mrs Jameson, just for the record. First, have you ever purchased, or been given, or traded in the shares of any of the companies under scrutiny here."

"I've already answered that. No." Samantha sounded testy. '*I'm not the one who's been playing games here.*'

"And one more question: am I right in inferring that you haven't discussed this with your husband, either directly or indirectly?"

"That is correct," she said, adding, "So far."

"Forgive me," Simon said, "but I'm given to understand there is a degree of - how shall I put it - distance between the two of you."

"Yes, you're safe in assuming that, though I'm not sure why it's relevant."

"It may not be. It might be, though, if any of the incriminating documents had been acquired by illegal means, or if certain official confidences had been breached. Either of those might - and I say only might - tend to complicate matters in a court of law."

Samantha, assuming that Simon was unaware of where the original documents had been found, shuddered at the phrase "court of law". It made her want to hear definitive answers to basic questions. "What I want to understand, the reason I'm here, is exactly what I'm obliged to do about what I've discovered, and to which Kwest has added. Should I have called, or should I now be calling the SEC, or whoever one is supposed to call in these cases?"

Simon took over. "If you were a corporate insider - a director, senior executive or key employee - then you would be obliged to report such activities. But you're not, so the same rules don't apply. You haven't traded on tips, or on anything that you've discovered by accident. And since, as I'm given to understand, your name doesn't appear on any of your husband's accounts you can defend yourself against any possible charges by contending that you had no control over them, or indeed no knowledge of them." He paused.

Samantha filled the space. "I think I hear another 'but' coming..."

"I'm afraid so. While everything I've just said is true in law, real life is such that the longer you know about what's been going on, the more difficult it could be for you to claim that you are not an accessory. For example, signing a joint tax return when you know the source of the income is illegal would itself be illegal; you would be exposed if your husband filed a joint return that concealed from the Internal Revenue Service certain taxable gains from illicit sources."

"What about the other question, the misprision of a felony?" Marty asked.

"Misprision?" Samantha was unfamiliar with the word. It sounded ugly.

"Ah, yes, professor," Simon said, tugging an imaginary forelock. "You're referring to failure to report a felony. Under Federal law, failure to report is not an offence for an individual. American jurisprudence has traditionally shied away from sanctions for such omissions. This doesn't apply to financial institutions which, under recent banking legislation, are required to file reports of suspicious activity – the SARS I referred to earlier. But for individuals, the law is clear: you cannot easily be prosecuted for not reporting a financial crime. I underline 'easily'; prosecutions have been known. But the courts have traditionally required evidence of active concealment rather than passive failure to report. In other words, a prosecutor would need to show that you actively conspired to conceal a crime as opposed to having failed to report it. I should also add that this does not apply when an individual - such as a government or banking officer - has a statutory duty to report a crime. In your case, Samantha, I don't think that applies. Meanwhile, I should add, by way of warning, that the courts seem to be increasingly less lenient on the issue of non-reporting. That makes it a somewhat grey area."

"Oh, God, you and your grey areas," Samantha said, by now completely bewildered.

"Grey areas, my dear, are why we lawyers earn what we do. So, while you're generally not obliged to notify the authorities, there are some exceptions. It could be argued by a prosecutor that by not reporting a financial crime committed by your husband you benefitted from it, raising the question of whether your inaction shaded into concealment. It means, again only in theory, that you might be charged, depending on the circumstances, with acting as an accessory after the fact. Again, I'm not sure that applies in your case."

Samantha had now graduated from bewildered to frightened. Bracing herself, she spoke firmly. "Let's get to the bottom line here: what do you think I should do? And this time, if you don't mind, with no 'ifs' or 'buts'. What I'm hearing is that I'm not legally obliged to report what I know. Morally, we'll leave aside."

If Samantha had expected Simon to deliver a resounding final opinion, she was about to be disappointed.

"We'll need to do more diligence on this," Simon said. "While failure to report isn't necessarily an offence, as I've explained, there are certain risks in not doing so. In my opinion, knowing what I've learnt so far, you should seriously consider taking the initiative."

"Meaning what?"

"Meaning that you avoid the grey areas we've talked about to avoid any suggestion of concealment. Consider, for example, what your position would be if all this all became public at some future time and then the authorities discovered that you had known it all along and did nothing. You might then come under serious scrutiny."

Samantha pondered this. "I'll have to think about that. Well, Marty will."

Apparently, the meeting was now over, as Simon had stood up. Everyone followed suit. Marty said to Simon, "Will you get back to me?"

"As soon as I can. I need to study the documents again first. And I need to think further about some of the points of law I've touched on. I'm not sure what's going to change, but I'd just like to have a full picture."

In the elevator, even though they were alone, Samantha said nothing. Marty seemed likewise lost in thought. Stepping outside the building into the bright Manhattan sunshine, and the cacophony of traffic noise, Samantha looked at him.

"What do *you* think I should do, Marty? And I'm asking you not so much as a lawyer than as a friend."

"I'll tell you what I'm thinking. An hour ago, I'd been hoping to advise you to keep your discoveries to yourself."

"And now?"

He paused before answering. "Now I think, on balance, that it's probably time to start singing like the proverbial canary. But it's your choice."

"And my plan?"

"I think the less I know about your plan the better."

* * * * *

Chapter 15

In the White House press room, Nigel distractedly flipped through the morning newspapers while waiting for a briefing to start. He found little of interest in any of them. The dog days had arrived. Political activity in Washington had been largely suspended for the summer break, most Beltway professionals having fled for shoreline resorts, leaving the city to indifferent residents and exuberant tourists. The press room, as humid as ever, exuded a listless air. One reporter was idly throwing spitballs at an electric fan. Another was playing with a yo-yo, a toy that had been out of fashion long before Nigel had been born. Expecting the briefing to be uneventful, Frank had left the chore in the uncertain hands of his deputy, Nick Charles, who always seemed daunted by the task, his responses from the podium rarely extending beyond "No comment" or "I'll have to refer".

Other professional quarters in the city were just as languid. The deserted offices of the Capitol and Senate Building were echo-chambers, the occupants scattered from Maine to Hawaii. President Jameson had left to play golf at his Florida campus. No one seemed to know where his wife was, but then it was unlikely that even he knew. Across the inner suburbs, the poor sat rheumy-eyed on the stoops of rundown tract houses, idly watching the world go by. Only the tourists seemed animated, oblivious to the mid-summer heat, marvelling at monuments which in their marbled splendour reassured them that everything must be well with the Grand Old Republic.

Nigel's cell phone buzzed.

"Mr Harper? Nigel Harper?" The voice was that of an older woman, soft but assertive, with a trace of a southern accent.

"Yes, Harper speaking."

"This is Maeve Carpenter, Senator Curtis's executive assistant. That's Senator William Curtis of Arizona."

"Yes?" Nigel was suddenly alert. How had she got his number? Not that it was a secret, but he sensed that it meant trouble, and he had a good idea what kind.

"I'm calling for the senator. He was wondering, Mr Harper, whether you might, at your earliest convenience, stop by for a chat."

"What about?" Nigel asked, a slight crack in his voice.

Senior senators were not in the habit of calling reporters in for a 'chat' for no special reason, least of all foreign reporters whom they had never met. Putting two and two together, Nigel could think of only one reason: his recent run-in with Vincent Marchetti. Curtis was a member of the Senate Defense Committee, which meant that he and Vincent almost certainly knew each other well. If so, Nigel supposed, Marchetti may well have called the senator to warn him that trouble might be brewing. It might also mean, Nigel surmised, that Curtis was one of the three senators on Samantha's Cayman list. Then again, perhaps he was allowing his imagination to run wild, and the invitation had a more innocent explanation, though what it might be Nigel couldn't begin to imagine.

"He didn't tell me what it's regarding," Maeve said unhelpfully. An unlikely excuse, Nigel thought. Senior secretaries in the higher reaches of government were supposed to know everything, and in his experience usually did. "When does he want to do this?"

"He said to tell you whatever time is suitable for you."

She had said 'time', Nigel noted, rather than 'day', which he took to mean this day. He asked the question.

"Today would be perfect," said Maeve.

He thought about making up some excuse - that he was about to catch a plane - but then decided that the sooner he knew what this was about the better. "How about this afternoon, say at three?"

"Give me a moment, Mr Harper, while I check his diary."

While Maeve was doing that - or pretending to - Nigel could hear through the phone raised voices in the background. One of them seemed to be that of the senator himself. "Tell that sonofabitch I want him here, in my fucking office, and I mean NOW!" It occurred to Nigel that he might be the 'sonofabitch' in question, and considered changing the appointment to another day, but Maeve was already back on the line.

"Sorry about that," she said, which could have meant an apology for the delay or for the senatorial expletives. "We've all been rushed off our feet today, believe it or not. The senator says three o'clock would be just fine. His office is room 302 in the Dirksen Senate Office Building. I presume you know how to get here."

"I'm sure I'll have no trouble finding it," Nigel told her, and then regretted that he had just given away the fact that he had never been there before.

"I'm sure you won't," said Maeve, adding helpfully. "Big white building. You can't miss it. I look forward to seeing you then." She hung up.

As Nigel pocketed his phone, Sonny stuck his head over the partition. "Hey, buddy boy, fancy a beer later. It's been a while." In fact, it had been several weeks.

"I may need one," Nigel said dolefully.

"Oh, why's that?"

"I just had a call from Senator Curtis. Completely out of the blue. He wants to see me. Today."

"Curtis of Arizona? I'm surprised he's even heard of you. Or the *Post*. What does he want to see you about?"

"Beats me." Nigel was not about to confess his London misstep to Sonny. "His secretary said he'd like to chat, that's all."

"Chat, my ass! He wants something. They always do. Maybe he has some message he wants to send to the British government. He can't use the ambassador. If he wanted a British back channel, I'd have thought it more likely he'd have called the BBC man, or Reuters… no offence, old chap."

"What should I know about Curtis?"

Sonny grinned. "A smooth operator, and one powerful dude. Ranking member on the Defense Appropriations Committee; an early backer of the President's election campaign; one of his most reliable allies on the Hill. I'm not sure whether you should be feeling honoured or scared."

"Scared sounds more likely. You've had dealings with him?"

"Oh, yes. I once interviewed him during an election campaign. After we'd run the story, he called my editor to claim that I'd misrepresented what he'd said. It was bullshit. I had him on tape. He also said I'd been hostile, which was also bullshit. He hates the media. But then, given the party he represents, that goes without saying. He's like the rest of them on the Hill, happy to use us when it suits their purpose, outraged when we don't go along with the crap they're peddling. My guess is he's got an angle. Maybe wants to explain why we're selling arms to some corrupt dictator who uses them to kill his own people… something like that."

"You're probably right," Nigel said, but convinced otherwise.

"I've only one piece of advice: watch your step. Oh, and before you leave his office, check to make sure you've still got your wallet."

"He can take it as far as I'm concerned. It's empty."

"He'd take it anyway. So, how about that beer, then?"

"I'm seeing Curtis at three. Maybe I'll catch up with you later."

"I'll be around, but only till six. My wife has invited a few neighbours round for a barbecue. Maybe you'd like to join us…"

"Another time, maybe… ah, the briefing's about to start."

Only a scattering of reporters had bothered to show up, each wondering why the White House would have a briefing when there was nothing much to report.

"Maybe they've got a surprise in store for us," Nigel said to the Reuters man on the way in.

"Nah, we'd have heard something," the Reuters man said. "And Frank wouldn't have left Nervous Nick to fuck it up." Nick looked ill at ease even when in private conversations, convinced that a reporter's sole mission in life was to trip him up. At the podium, he thought they were collectively out to ambush him. "I think Frank likes to give him a run-out from time to time, just for practice. Suits me. These sessions remind me of religious instruction classes at school, with some vicar droning on for an hour while we all sat there doing our homework."

"I hope it wasn't my dad."

"He was a vicar?"

"Yes. Can't you tell from my ecclesiastical manner?"

"Frankly, no. Ah, here comes Nick now, trying not to look terrified. He's late. Probably had to change his pants."

A few inevitable questions were asked by two or three reporters from farm-belt papers, who always sat together at the back of the room to confer, as if in a caucus, before earnestly asking the kind of questions that no one else in the room understood, much less cared about. Apparently, American dairy farmers were suffering some form of economic hardship about which an indifferent administration was doing nothing. A bemused Nick, perspiring freely, hands trembling, predictably parried each question with the stock 'I'll-have-to-get-back-to-you' responses. Nigel noticed that heads were nodding and eyelids drooping. He was not far off joining them.

Listening to the deputy press secretary's stumbling monologue, he found his attention wandering. He was thinking of the man who normally stood at the podium, Frank Hoffman, who handled the reporters with such effortless aplomb. Since the dinner in Maryland two weeks earlier, Nigel had revised his opinion of him. He'd found him bright and cultured, a man of varied interests, and entertaining company. Samantha, it was clear, trusted him implicitly. But Nigel reflected that Samantha must trust him as well, or she wouldn't have invited him to join such a select group. And an odd group it was, a cabal of political saboteurs preparing to light fuses for an explosion, which, like the shot in Sarajevo, would be heard around the world. Nigel wasn't really a member of it, merely a 'useful idiot', more exploited than honoured. But who was exploiting whom was always debatable in these situations, and either way it would be worth it for the scoop of a lifetime.

Even before the call from Curtis's secretary, he had been fretting about the London incident, Marchetti's veiled threats. Time tends to heal personal embarrassments by persuading the memory that whatever had happened couldn't be nearly as bad as it first seemed. Nigel had fallen into that trap. But following the call from the senator's office, the greater his recurring dread of the potential repercussions, convinced that the senator's urgent summons must be one of them. What else could it be? The senator was a key player in government defence spending, so it was almost certain that Vincent had alerted him to their encounter in London, and Curtis would want to find out exactly what Nigel knew. For his part, Nigel had already decided that whatever the outcome of the meeting, he would confess his sin to Samantha. The punishment, he presumed, would be his summary banishment from her presence as a high security risk and a traitor to the cause.

All these thoughts were still spinning through his mind as he navigated his way to the Dirksen Senate Office Building through the throngs of visitors sauntering about in every direction. When he arrived, dead on time, even the heavily armed guards seemed lethargic, and he had no trouble clearing the security checks. One of the senator's aides, Peter Schmidt, a tall young man with a flat, mid-western accent and a very serious manner was waiting for him in the lobby. Room 302 was in fact a whole suite of offices. In the vestibule, half a dozen young women were tapping on computer keyboards and answering telephones, often managing to do both at the same time. No summer break for them, apparently. They were all young, Nigel noticed, and every single one good-looking, presumably a reflection of the senator's essential hiring prerequisites. Schmidt unsmilingly handed him over to Maeve Carpenter, who managed a smile that must have involved the painful rearrangement of rarely used facial muscles. A small, dumpy, plain woman in her late fifties, her hair was tied at the back into a matronly bun. In this buzzing hive of activity, she was unquestionably the queen bee.

"Ah, Mr Harper!" she said tonelessly. "We spoke on the telephone. Thank you for coming in at such short notice." Nigel read her severe manner as an ominous sign. "The senator has a visitor in there right now, but he'll be free shortly. May I offer you a cup of coffee?"

He declined the coffee, and Maeve directed him to a seat on a hard bench obviously designed for short-term occupancy. From an adjoining table he picked up a copy of the *Congressional Record*, the only reading material available. A couple of secretaries, bored with whatever they were doing, looked up occasionally to eye him curiously, perhaps intrigued by his accent; the senator from Arizona probably didn't get to entertain many British visitors.

Maeve's 'shortly' turned out to be twenty minutes. She was on the verge of apologizing for the third time when Curtis finally emerged from his inner office, accompanied by an earlier visitor who looked none too happy; probably, Nigel guessed, the 'sonofabitch' he had overheard the senator shouting at. Whatever it was the visitor had done to incur senatorial anger, he was sent on his way with a laugh, a firm handshake, and a hearty slap on the back. Not that such gestures meant anything other than to remind visitors who wielded the power in this place. The visitor managed a wan smile and slunk away.

Senator Curtis, a tall, lean man with thinning black hair, was immaculately dressed in a striped dark-blue suit. The office was warm but the senator, Nigel noticed, was not perspiring. Still wearing his institutional smile, Curtis turned to Nigel and gave him the same hail-fellow treatment he had used in seeing off his previous visitor. "Glad to see you, my boy. Come in, come in. This place is a madhouse today. Summer madness, you might say. I should be back home on my ranch by now, getting some well-earned rest and recreation. No rest for the wicked, they say. Forgive me for keeping you waiting."

The tone was affable enough, but beady probing eyes bore into Nigel's. He felt like an antelope that had strayed from the herd and was being evaluated by a ravenous lion.

"I could always come back another time," Nigel said, hoping the offer would be taken up, knowing that it wouldn't be.

"Not at all," gushed Curtis. "Not at all. Wouldn't hear of it. Tell the truth, it's pretty much always like this around here. Isn't that right, Maeve?"

Maeve confirmed as much with a resigned roll of the eyes, again without the faintest trace of a smile. "You got that right, Senator. And today's not even the worst of them. No sir, not by any means."

Nigel was being steered into the inner sanctum by a firm hand to the small of his back. Never having been in a senator's office before, he found this one much as he had always imagined - a large, wood-panelled room, impersonally decorated, presumably to convey an impression of business-like efficiency. Its focal point was a large, uncluttered desk. Behind it lay a wing-backed chair and behind that a credenza with nothing on it but a bronze sculpture of a cowboy roping a steer, and a large silver tray crowded with bottles of expensive whisky and crystal glasses. On the opposite side of the room, a buttoned leather sofa large enough to seat four took up a quarter of it. On the walls were a few framed documents and photographs, most of them attesting to the substantial and varied accomplishments of William Alban Curtis: college degrees and citations for meritorious service to the United States Army, the Senate and the State of Arizona. One photograph showed a much younger Curtis, probably in his twenties, in a marine officer's uniform in a tropical setting receiving a medal from a general whose face Nigel recognized. From a potted biography of Curtis that Nigel had read half an hour earlier, he learnt that he had won an award for valour during the siege of Khe Sanh.

"How about a drink?" The senator was beaming. "As you can see, I've got a great selection of single malts here. I'm told you like a malt." Nigel found that last remark mildly unnerving, but he had no hesitation in accepting the offer. A drink was just what he needed right now. "I'd be delighted to join you, Senator."

"You like peaty or not?"

"Preferably not." Nigel was about to ask if the senator had Irish whiskey but thought better of it.

"I have an eighteen-year-old Macallan, will that do?"

"That would be perfect."

Curtis half-filled two exquisite cut-glass tumblers and handed one to Nigel. "Cheers." He saw Nigel admiring the glass. "My late father once told me: 'Son, never drink expensive whisky out of a cheap glass', and I've always followed that advice. They say it makes no difference to the taste, but I beg to differ."

Curtis was now steering Nigel to the giant sofa. He parked himself at one end and Nigel at the other. They were at least five feet apart, but to Nigel it still seemed too close for comfort.

"This old sofa here could tell some tales," Curtis said, patting it affectionately. "Seen more acts of congress than the House Ways and Means Committee, if you know what I mean." Nigel knew exactly what he meant and forced a laugh. The senator winked, pleased with his well-practised joke. "We call it the casting couch."

"Does that mean, Senator, I'm auditioning for something?" Nigel punned.

"Yes, in a manner of speaking." Curtis put his glass on a table and inhaled deeply as if preparing himself for the ordeal of imparting bad news. "I hope you don't mind me calling you Nigel, by the way. We like to be informal around here. Makes for a friendlier atmosphere, I find."

"Nigel is fine. It is, after all, my name." Curtis ignored the intended drollery. He didn't invite Nigel to call him Bill, let alone William.

"Well, Nigel, let me talk plainly." Curtis hesitated, pursing his lips. "It has recently come to my attention, I won't say how, that you've... how shall I say this... made reference to certain financial activities which may not have been entirely above board." The senator had adopted a grave expression. "I'm told that these alleged activities involve companies in the defence industry. Now, as ranking member of the Defense Appropriations Committee, I'd say that would bring the situation directly into my purview. Wouldn't you agree?"

Nigel gulped involuntarily, and then tried to disguise it with a clearing of the throat.

The senator didn't wait for a response. "Up here on the Hill, in every department of the government, we must take any reports of financial impropriety very seriously. You can understand why, I'm sure."

"Yes, of course."

"Well now, Nigel, let me ask you this: are you, in a professional capacity, looking into such a matter? If so, I'd sure like to know what you've heard, and where you heard it."

'*So, here it is,*' Nigel was thinking, '*Marchetti's pay-back*'. He had suspected from the moment Maeve called that it was why he had been summoned, but the senator's direct approach still caught him off-guard. He had to think for a moment about how to respond. His decision was to brazen it out. The whisky helped. "Whatever gave you that idea, Senator Curtis? Or perhaps I should say *who* gave you that idea."

"Now, let's not be coy about this. Taking a leaf out of your journalistic rulebook, I can't name my source."

"Well, Senator, I couldn't name mine either. But since I'm not working on a story like that there *is* no source."

"Let's just say, then, that my information is that you've been overheard making comments about possible financial irregularities relating to the award of government defence contracts, and implied that illicit trading has taken place in the shares of those companies. I'm talking about insider trading. That's a term with which you're familiar, I take it."

Nigel gulped again. "I am, sir."

"Now, tell me, is what I've just said an accurate interpretation of what happened or not? If not, perhaps you'd be so kind as to tell me exactly what you *did* say. Or, if you prefer, what you meant."

"I can't, Senator. Not because I won't, you understand, but because I didn't say what I'm alleged to have said. Nor, I should add, am I working on such a story. Given that neither is true, I'd be curious to know how you came to be informed that they are."

The senator pretended to inspect his well-manicured nails. He was still smiling. "Let me get this straight, Nigel. What you're telling me is that my information is utterly incorrect."

"Yes," said Nigel. "Utterly. Either given in error... or perhaps with malicious intent."

"Malicious intent!" the senator cried, his voice rising. "Now, there's an interesting phrase."

"And I use it advisedly," Nigel said boldly, the whisky now giving him a warm feeling of confidence. "Because, if the statement from your informant is untrue, it follows that it was made mistakenly or deliberately."

Curtis fixed Nigel with a searching and patently skeptical stare. "Now, tell me, can you think of anyone who would be motivated to do a thing like that?"

Nigel presented a straight bat. "Senator, I can't."

The senator's eyes narrowed, to reinforce the impression of grave concern. "The only reason I'm asking, and the reason I invited you here today, is that a man in my position would have to be seriously concerned if something illegal was going on right under his nose. For the sake of national security, you understand, but also for his personal credibility." Curtis was now in full oratorical flow in the Senate's fulsome tradition of righteous indignation. "As ranking member of my committee, I'm acutely conscious of the sensitivity that surrounds the awarding of defence contracts, and I for one am determined to see that the process is irreproachable. These contracts, as you know, can often involve billions of dollars of taxpayers' money. Any abuse of public trust would undermine the integrity of our system, our very democracy. That would be a matter of some gravity. Integrity goes to the very core of why we're here in Washington. It's what the good citizens of this country sent us here to uphold. They are entitled to know that the process works."

"Amen to that," Nigel said, somewhat flippantly, before biting his lip.

"My point here, Nigel, is that if there has been any abuse, I would want to be the first to know about it, not read about it in your paper. You understand what I'm saying?"

"Perfectly, Senator. But I can only repeat what I said: I've absolutely no interest in this subject. I cover the White House. Scandals, financial or otherwise, I leave to others. Now those others may be up to something, but not me."

"Well, I'm mighty glad to hear it, Nigel. I'd always want to be informed if you heard anything of that nature. Those of us who proudly work here, day and night, in the public interest, have a duty of care in these matters. And let me tell you, we take that duty very seriously. My fellow-citizens, especially the good people of Arizona who elected me, would expect nothing less." The senator's smile had faded and with it the tone became menacing, or so it seemed to Nigel. "Now, young man, have I made myself clear?"

"You have, Senator. As clear as the beautiful crystal I'm holding in my hand."

Curtis exhaled a patently manufactured sigh of relief. "Well, my friend, I can't tell you how glad I am to hear it, and I mean that sincerely. Nothing, and I mean nothing, is as important to me as the protection of this country and its ideals." The senator was now into his election stump speech. "The American people I represent in this great institution of ours are entitled to know if the system has been corrupted, to know if some bad apple had betrayed that trust. And they'd want to be sure that the culprit had been caught and suffered the full consequences mandated by law. And I can assure you that justice would be swift and harsh. Now, I'll be the first to admit that bad apples do show up from time to time, as they do in any enterprise. That, my friend, is why we must be constantly vigilant."

"Yes, Senator, I see that. I applaud the sentiment."

Senator Curtis, still acting the part, pretended to relax. "That's my little speech over and done with. Now what say you we just sit here a spell and enjoy our whisky. How about another?" Nigel automatically offered his glass for a refill, though he would rather the meeting had ended there and then. "Speaking of whisky, Nigel, do you happen to be of Scottish descent? Like our president, as it so happens."

"Afraid not. English through and through, actually. Most of my family are from Suffolk. That's a county in East Anglia - the flat bit on the eastern side of the country. It's where some of the earliest English settlers came from. Including, I might add, some of my own ancestors."

"I know the area well."

"Really! How?"

"I used to fly out of American air bases in Cambridgeshire." The last syllable was pronounced 'shyer'. "On our way to Vietnam. That was a long time ago, mind. Before you were born."

"There are still a few American bases in the area. Some go back to the Second World War. Our chaps still fly from them, too."

"Ah, yes, the Royal Air Force. I've always been a great admirer We didn't have them along with us in Vietnam - for reasons best left unsaid - but what a grand contribution they made to winning the Second World War. Saved Britain, no doubt about it. Saved Europe, too." This declaration was followed by an odd non sequitur. "Are you a religious man, Nigel? I'm a Lutheran myself, thanks to a German grandmother."

"I'm Church of England. Or as you would say, Episcopalian. As a matter of fact, my father was a man of the cloth. A vicar. Recently retired. A lifetime of dealing with sinners must have been exhausting." Nigel laughed. It wasn't reciprocated.

"Now, that's quite a coincidence because my own father was a church elder. Well, I'll be doggoned." The senator seemed genuinely pleased. "I don't get to church as often as I'd like these days, but I'm proud to endorse Christian values and I try to live by them. They're a beacon of hope in a troubled and increasingly godless world."

Nigel smiled at the banalities but could think of no sensible way to respond, least of all admit that he himself was among the godless. Having finished his drink, he now worried that Curtis might offer him another. But the senator was looking at his watch. Evidently, on this inspiring note, the meeting was over.

But not quite.

"Remind me, Nigel, how long have you been here? In the United States, I mean."

Nigel tried to sound casual under the baleful patrician stare. "A few months now. It seems longer. I suppose that must mean I'm settling in."

"Time sure does fly. You got that right. And let me tell you as one who knows: the older you get the faster it flies. I hope you're having fun, Nigel. It's important to have fun while you're still young. Take it from an old man."

As trite as Nigel found these observations, he nodded energetically as if he'd just been privileged to hear words of Socratic wisdom. "I'll try to remember that, Senator."

"By the way, I met your predecessor, Graham. A few times. Helluva guy. A journalist of great integrity. See, there's that word again. Integrity. Now, if only the rest of the media would take a leaf out of his book, instead of stirring up trouble all the time, attacking our institutions, belittling our elected representatives. Worst of all our duly elected president. And when he fights back, he's accused of being a demagogue, a threat to democracy, a threat to free speech. I tell you…"

Nigel's instinct, every fibre of his being, urged a brutal reply, but he held back. What purpose would it serve? He was desperate to leave, but Curtis would excuse him in his own good time, and not before. Polite chit-chat, for once, seemed the best response. "Graham, since you mention him, is now happily enjoying the delights of retirement in Florida."

"A fine state, Florida," the senator mused, with a blank, unfocused look. "Went big for our party at the last election. Against all poll projections, too. Just shows that you can't believe anything the polls predict these days. They're all biased against us anyway. My own state is rock-solid Republican, of course, and even more so with Martin Jameson in the White House."

The senator, Nigel observed, probably saw every state less as a geographical entity than as a political one, either a GOP stronghold or an enemy position to be overrun.

"You enjoy covering politics, I'm guessing," the senator said, again apropos of nothing.

"Yes. It's been my job for many years. At Westminster, of course. But I'll be doing the same thing here - once I get the hang of things. You have a very different system from ours, of course, and it'll take some getting used to."

"You strike me as a man who can cope with change, with adversity, take anything that's thrown at him and come back fighting."

"I like to think so, Senator. We journalists take a lot of flak."

"Yes," the senator agreed, "and much of it richly deserved, I'd say."

Nigel didn't respond. The priority now was not to win points but to get out of there. But Senator Curtis had had other ideas.

"Tell me, Nigel, what kind of visa do we give you foreign media people these days?"

Another question out of the blue, and one that had Nigel wondering where it could be heading. He didn't like the first answer that came to mind.

"I'm only asking because I'm curious," the senator added. "Is it a special visa? Do you have indefinite leave to stay, or whatever the wording is…?"

"I'm on something called an 'I' visa. That's a special classification for foreign media representatives on assignment. It's valid for as long as the assignment lasts - subject to review."

"And in your case, how long will that be."

"I'm here for four years, although the arrangement is somewhat open-ended."

"Four years! Is that so?"

"Why do you ask?"

"I told you, no special reason. But it so happens that immigration is high on this administration's agenda, and I like to keep abreast of these matters. Not that you look like a terrorist or an undesirable." The senator laughed at his own witticism, Nigel laughing nervously along with him. "Hell, you don't look remotely Mexican. And now I know you're not a Muslim."

'Bloody racist,' Nigel was thinking, *'and how typical of this whole rotten administration.'*

Finally, and much to Nigel's relief, the senator got up from the sofa. Nigel rose too, thinking he was about to be dismissed, but Curtis had only walked over to his credenza to fetch the bottle. He came back, sat down again, and refilled Nigel's glass. But not his own, Nigel noticed.

"Hey, I'm told you've already got yourself a little lady here."

"How on earth would you know that?" Nigel knew the answer. His concern was now becoming acute. He took out a handkerchief to wipe a perspiring brow.

"Oh, we senators have our sources, you know."

"Well, yes, I am seeing a lady. But I've only known her a few weeks, so I'm not sure how serious it is. Pretty serious, I think. You'd have to ask her." Nigel laughed nervously.

"American girl, is she?" If Curtis knew about Jane, he'd also know that she was American. He might just be showing off, but Nigel had no option but to go along with the interrogation. "Yes. She's from Pennsylvania."

"Now there's another fine state. Went heavily for us in the last election, too - yet another result the pollsters got wrong. But good for you, my friend. I believe you were married once." *'Marchetti had been busy.'*

"Yes, I'm divorced."

"I've had three wives myself. Two divorces." You probably know that I nearly lost my current wife, Loretta, a year or so back. Cancer. But she's fine now, I'm happy to report. California girl. Beautiful. Irreplaceable." The Senator adopted a soulful look, and for a moment Nigel thought he might be about to cry. "And what does this lady friend of yours do for a living, if I may ask?"

Nigel's nose hairs were tickling now. "She works at the State Department. Analyst. Specializes in the Middle East."

"Ah, she must be a clever woman. And mighty busy these days, I mean given everything that's going on over there right now."

"Inordinately busy - as she sees fit to tell me every day."

"Well, there's a great deal to be done there. Our president is working day and night to find a solution - which is more than his lazy predecessor ever did. I happen to believe that Israel is a staunch ally of ours. None better, in fact. Except, perhaps, your own country. We must do everything in our power to support them. Shifting the capital to Jerusalem was a good start, I'd say."

"The Palestinians wouldn't agree," Nigel said, surprised by his boldness.

"That only tells me it was a good move. Any decision the Palestinians don't like is a good decision, as far as I'm concerned.

Those people are terrorists, nothing more. Bad people. Always were and always will be. What did you say her name was, your friend?"

"I didn't. But it's Jane." Nigel withheld the surname. Not that it mattered. Curtis, if he chose to, could easily find out who she was. And Nigel believed he'd be doing exactly that. His mood darkened. What the hell was he supposed to tell Jane?

Curtis suddenly rose again from the sofa with a groan. "Oh Lord, these old bones of mine creak a little these days. Too much college football. The knees have gone. But I can still ride a horse with the best of 'em."

Nigel stood as well. The interview, or whatever it was he had just been subjected to, was finally over. An avuncular senatorial arm snaked around his shoulder, a gesture Nigel had seen in many a Hollywood movie about politics - and the arm usually belonging to one of the villains of the piece.

"Well now, it's been a real pleasure talking with you, Nigel. But before you leave, a word of advice: if there's anything you should ever need in the line of duty, just pick up the telephone. I'll always take your call. If I'm not here, you can always leave a message with Maeve. She's been my gatekeeper for twenty-five years now, bless her, and you can tell her anything, no matter how sensitive. She's a real honey when you get to know her."

'Honey' was the last word Nigel would have associated with Maeve Carpenter, even if she was Queen Bee. "That's good to know, Senator. And thanks for the offer. Oh, and thanks for the drink."

"I'd be happy to continue our conversation, but I really do need to get back to work. The enemies of the United States never sleep, so neither can the United States." The draped arm was abruptly removed. They shook hands. "So long for now," said Curtis, "and be sure to stay in touch now, y'hear."

Nigel left the building in something of a daze, convinced that he'd just been quietly and deftly strong-armed into keeping his mouth shut or suffer certain consequences if he didn't. The questions about his visa, the enquiries about Jane, hadn't been idle chatter but calculated threats. He now had no doubt at all that Vincent Marchetti and the senator from Arizona had marked him as a target. A warning shot had been fired across his bows. The next one, he was certain, would be aimed amidships.

What to do next? He was pondering that very question as he crossed a street against a light and was startled by a loud screech of brakes. A taxi driver was yelling obscenities at him. "Hey, asshole, if it's suicide you have in mind, go do it someplace else."

"Sorry."

On the walk back to the White House he called Sonny to tell him that drinks would have to keep for another time.

"How did it go with Curtis?" Sonny wanted to know.

"It's a bit complicated," said Nigel. "I'll tell you when I next see you." *'But preferably not any time soon.'*

Back in the press room, he called Fran.

She picked up right away. "Okay, Nigel, what have you done now? Do I need to sit down?"

He gave her a brief account of the meeting with Curtis. "How about meeting me for a coffee? I could use someone to talk to. Someone friendly."

"I don't know if I qualify," Fran said, but agreed to meet him. She suggested a coffee bar near the White House. Nigel knew the place. "I'll see you there in an hour."

* * *

"Obviously Marchetti tipped off Curtis," Fran said, stirring her cappuccino. "And my guess - well it seems perfectly clear - is that Cutis is up to something. By the way, just to make you feel even better, I'm pretty sure he's on Samantha's list."

"You told me you didn't know who was on the list."

"I don't. But I think I remember hearing his name mentioned. I may be wrong. But given your encounters with those two gentlemen, I think it's time we came clean with Samantha. I haven't told her about you shooting your mouth of at Marchetti in London, but now I think she should know. Especially given his appetite for mischief."

"I agree. Do you think she'll be angry?"

"She won't be angry... she'll be fucking apoplectic."

"What's to be done in the meantime?"

"By you, nothing. You've done enough damage already. Just sit tight and leave the talking to me. Understood?"

"Yes, ma'am," he said, saluting.

"I'll play it cool, of course, tell her that your conversation with Marchetti was all a bit vague. But Curtis is another matter. Still, let's not start getting paranoid. Curtis was fishing. They can't be sure what you know, or even that you know anything. But one thing is clear: the longer Samantha waits to break this thing open, the more likely they'll figure out what she's up to. They're clever bastards, and once they've worked out that something's going on they'll be utterly ruthless in finding out what. But I think Curtis has made a tactical mistake."

"Why do you say that?"

"Because now he's shown his hand. He's revealed that he and Marchetti are in touch. He's also revealed that he's worried. That wasn't cool."

Nigel felt better.

"But you'll need to be prepared for bad things to happen."

"Bad things?"

"If they think you've stumbled on to something they'll almost certainly make further moves to find out what it is."

"What kind of moves? What can they do?"

"I don't want to sound melodramatic, but you'll probably be watched."

"Watched?"

"Yes, as in put under observation, placed under surveillance, call it what you will. You've seen the movies. You know how it works."

"You mean I should be looking out for men sitting in parked cars at the end of the street, that kind of thing?"

"Well, it happens in real life, too. Let's not kid ourselves. This is no squabble between neighbours over a boundary fence. Our mutual friend is talking about taking down the most powerful man in the world. What stakes could be higher than that."

"I thought you were relaxed about the Marchetti thing. You seem to have changed your tune."

"Your little session with Curtis has changed that. It could, for all I know, be about to change everything."

"You're not making me feel any better." Nigel sounded plaintive.

Fran's rejoinder was sharp. "I'm not in the business of making you feel better. Truth be told, I want you to feel worse. Maybe that way you'll be more careful. You need to wise up, fast. These people have a long reach and finely-honed survival instincts. I know it's a cliché, but they're men who'll stop at nothing."

"If you're trying to scare the shit out of me, you're succeeding."

"That's exactly what I'm trying to do. You knew from the start what you were getting into. You can still get out of it. Just say the word, and you can walk away from all this right now."

Nigel was angry now. "I didn't know what the fuck I was getting into. I got conned into it, apparently by you. And there's no question of my walking away."

"That may no longer be your decision. And let me remind you that you're the one who started digging around in search of a scandal, creeping around in search of some Mata Hari of your own fantasy, with grand fucking ideas about becoming a media hero, winning yourself a Pulitzer Prize. And you're the one who screwed up by shooting your mouth off at a cocktail party. Think about it, Nigel, this is a shitstorm of your own making."

"Okay, okay, I get the message. "Where's Samantha now?"

"On a horse farm, somewhere in upstate New York. Anna's with her. I'm not looking forward to telling her about the Curtis meeting, since I'm the one who's going to get an earful. I'm just glad I'll be doing it by telephone."

"If I'm going to be watched, what do you think I should do about it?"

"I've no idea. Chances are you won't even know they're there. Your best bet would be to get out of town, better still out of the country. Sounds like a western movie, doesn't it."

"Sounds like I could be deported before then anyway. Why else would he be asking about my fucking visa?"

"I wouldn't put it past him to try. But we do still have something called due process." She tried to think of something to alleviate Nigel's pain. "Let's not sink into despair, my friend. That way lies madness. And remember, you have one thing going for you..."

"What's that?"

"They don't yet know what you know. They're just probing. Short of bumping you off - just joking, by the way - if they moved overtly against you, they'd run the risk of your blowing the whistle. Senator fucking Curtis can huff and puff all he wants, but he's got nothing on you. Yet."

"Well, there is nothing. Yet."

"One more thing. Perhaps you shouldn't see Jane for a while, at least until this thing cools down. Or explodes. But I know you're not going to take that advice either."

"You're right. What's Jane got to do with this anyway?" Even before the question left his lips, he knew the answer.

"If you're going to be investigated, the chances are that she will be, too. But again, I don't want to over-dramatize the situation."

"What a bloody mess."

"Look, I'll talk to Samantha. Maybe this Curtis thing will get her to move faster."

"And what should I do in the meantime?" Nigel sounded helpless, as indeed he was.

"Go home and suffer in silence. It's no more than you deserve."

"And not contact Jane, is that what you're saying?"

"I can't tell you what to do. All I'm saying is that the less exposure she has to this situation, the better off she'll be. That's an opinion, not an instruction. You might also consider getting yourself a lawyer."

"Now I know I'm in America."

Fran didn't laugh. "Serves you right. You've gone from useful idiot to village idiot, all because you can't hold your liquor." She thought that remark sounded harsh and softened it. "Look, we've all done it. Even me. But for now, go home, or back to work, or whatever it is you need to do to keep yourself together."

Fran stood up, air-kissed him on both cheeks, and left without another word.

* * *

Nigel took a taxi to Jane's apartment. As a precaution he asked the driver to drop him off at the end of the street. He walked around the block, pausing every now and then to see if he could spot men in raincoats or blurred faces in car windows, unable to decide whether he felt afraid or ridiculous. In either event, the coast seemed clear. Perhaps he *had* seen too many movies. He was starting to feel as though he was in one.

Jane was doing something in the kitchen. "You're home early."

"Hello, darling. What are you up to? I thought we were going out to dinner."

"Yes, we are. I'm just pottering." As he kissed her, she noticed his hangdog expression. "You look sad. Has something happened?"

"Sit down for a moment. I need to tell you something."

He told her a great deal more than something. He took her through his golf course conversation with Samantha Jameson. He told her of his conversation with Curtis, even mentioning that the senator had made a point of asking about her. He finished with Fran's advice that they refrain from seeing each other for a while.

Jane was shocked. Then shock turned to anger. "This thing is scary. It could turn out worse than nasty; it could be deadly. I don't mind telling you, Nigel, you've got me rattled. If there's an end in sight, the sooner we get there the better."

He could offer no comfort. "The end is in Samantha Jameson's hands. It's her move."

"Where is she now?"

"Horse-riding, somewhere upstate New York."

"That doesn't get us anywhere."

"No. But my guess is that something will break soon. I just don't know what."

Jane suddenly felt ashamed of expressing her fears. "I'm not going to cower in my apartment like some criminal on the run. This isn't Putin's Russia. You're not going to be murdered with a poison-tipped umbrella. As for not seeing each other, to hell with that. You and I have a dinner date tonight and I for one intend to keep it."

"Brava!" he cried, brightening. "Luigi's it is." Checking his phone, he saw a 'missed call' message. Fran. He called her back.

"What are you doing tomorrow?" she said.

"We have nothing planned. By the way, I've just told Jane pretty much everything."

"Well, you'll be relieved to hear that I have no comment."

"You were asking about tomorrow…."

"We're meeting Samantha. Usual routine. I'll pick you up at eight."

"You've spoken to her?" His voice quivered as he said it.

"Yes. I hung up twenty minutes ago. I brought her up to date, from your indiscretion in London to the Curtis business."

"And how did she respond?" His voice was now almost a croak.

"She responded the way you'd have expected: she was livid. She threw a plate at the wall. I heard the crash over the telephone. By now she may have destroyed a whole dinner service. I can confirm, by the way, that Curtis is on the list."

"Well, that comes as no surprise."

"Anyway, Samantha cooled down long enough to tell me the game is now on."

"We're heading to Maryland tomorrow, I presume."

"No. Virginia. To a fancy horse farm owned by friends of Samantha. It's an hour's drive from your place - or so my computer tells me. I've only ever been there by helicopter."

"No golf?"

"No, but perhaps you'd care to bring jodhpurs. Do you ride?"

"No. I have a love-hate relationship with horses. I love them, they hate me."

"Don't tell Samantha that. Oh, and one more thing, you're to bring Jane."

"Really! There's a surprise."

"We seem to be living in a world of surprises. Samantha thought it only fair to bring her into the picture. Don't tell her you've already done it. It also means, of course, that she's not going to send you packing. That, if you ask me, is a classic case of keeping friends close but enemies closer… but be ready to duck if you see her with a plate in her hand."

"I'm no enemy," Nigel protested.

"No, Nigel, you're far more dangerous than that. You're a careless friend."

* * * * *

Chapter 16

Fresh from a late morning ride and a bracing shower, Samantha Jameson emerged onto the front porch of the grand white colonial mansion to await the arrival of her three guests. They would be showing up within minutes, her Secret Service agents had reported, and she thought it would be a nice gesture to greet them at the door. She was dressed in the familiar preppy ensemble of slacks, blouse and angora sweater. Minutes later, Fran's car rounded the bend in the drive and came to a rather abrupt halt, scattering gravel.

Fran was dressed casually in jeans and a denim shirt. Jane, eager to make a good impression, had opted for an eerily similar look to that of her hostess. Nigel, who cared little about his appearance, wore cargo pants and a casual denim shirt. He worried that he might look a little foolish in an outfit more suited to a man half his age, but Jane had assured him he looked 'cool' - whatever that meant. He was also wearing the now patented look of a schoolboy outside the headmaster's office awaiting punishment.

"What a beautiful place," Jane exclaimed, examining the mansion in front of them. "It's like something from one of those 'America the Beautiful' books."

Fran echoed her friend's opinion. "And the property stretches for thousands of acres." Then she lowered her voice to a whisper. "Wonder what you need to do to get to afford all this?"

"Cheat or steal, I imagine," Nigel muttered behind her, though neither she nor anyone else heard him, which was just as well.

Samantha greeted Fran with a prolonged hug, accompanied by a chorus of welcoming whinnies from the nearby stable block. "I decided to get my morning ride in before you got here. "Obviously you found the place alright."

"No problems at all. Once we left the highway, though, the roads were somewhat winding. At one point I thought we'd gone round in a full circle."

"You probably had. No signs of… er… trouble on the way?"

'Trouble! What kind of trouble?' Nigel found the question slightly unnerving, but then feeling unnerved was his natural condition of late.

Fran gave irritated voice to the thought. "Well, we weren't chased or shot at, if that's what you mean."

Samantha laughed. "Knowing you, Fran, you probably drove like James Bond in that Aston Martin being pursued by enemy agents."

Fran still looked peeved. "I'm glad you think this is a joking matter, Samantha. I've been feeling a little on edge lately."

"Come on, Fran, let's not lose our sense of humour. Anyway, you're all here now, safe and sound, and that's all that matters."

Samantha turned and beamed at the newcomer hovering behind Fran. "And you must be Jane. I've heard so much about you over the years. I can't think why we've never met. Well, we have now, so welcome to my favourite hideaway." Jane offered her hand and was surprised when Samantha ignored it and leaned over to kiss her on both cheeks. The first lady was clearly in an ebullient mood, almost carefree. Or was it all a show of bravado, Nigel found himself silently thinking.

"It's certainly isolated," Jane said, as they entered the house. "I can see why you love it."

Nigel, skulking in the background, felt that he was being given the cold shoulder. Under the circumstances, that suited him just fine, but then Samantha suddenly turned, as if remembering something, and offered him her hand. "I'm so sorry, Nigel, I wasn't trying to ignore you. Please forgive my bad manners."

Nigel was momentarily lost for words, another common occurrence these days.

Fran, as observant as ever, jumped in to defuse what she thought was about to be an awkward moment. "Nigel's feeling a little nervous this morning, Samantha, mostly about seeing you. He thinks he's in the doghouse. Isn't that right, Nigel?"

Nigel did indeed have a hangdog expression.

"Well, I'm not going to start throwing the crockery," Samantha said breezily. "Not here anyway, it's far too expensive for that." Everyone laughed nervously. "But perhaps, Nigel, you could use a drink." Samantha grinned as she said it before turning serious and making a second apology. "I'm sorry, that remark was unworthy."

"You've every right to be angry," said Nigel, glumly. "I can't begin to tell you how sorry I am about my…"

"Fuck-up," said Samantha, completing the sentence with another laugh. "I'll admit I was angry when Fran told me about it, but I'm perfectly calm now. Look, we've all been under pressure lately and

I'm all too aware that I'm the cause of it." Her expression abruptly turned serious. "What you did, Nigel, could have placed me in a difficult position, but I've been thinking about it since, and decided that it might have happened to any of us. Who knows, perhaps it has." Samantha's attitude, Nigel thought, was beyond reasonable, verging on the saintly. "So, let's just put the incident behind us. But from this point on we can't afford any more distractions that might undermine our purpose."

Nigel, having expected a severe dressing-down, or worse, looked relieved. "I can only say again, Samantha, how sorry I am. It won't happen again, believe me."

"Well, now we've got that unpleasant duty out of the way, let's not stand here on the doorstep chattering. Come in, all of you, and prepare to be impressed."

They were. The house was beautifully appointed in the Federal style, the décor clearly the work of someone of great wealth and impeccable taste. Nigel's first thought was that it looked like a spread from *Architectural Digest*. His eye was immediately drawn to a large painting above the drawing room fireplace, a portrait of a lady, which he guessed was a John Singer Sargent. On closer inspection this was confirmed by the artist's signature. The huge hearth was flanked by two plush beige sofas facing a coffee table piled high with art books. The floor was covered by two huge complementary Serapis of a certain age. The furnishings were all mahogany, walnut and burl, dominated by a ceiling-high chest of drawers under a curved pediment, each piece in pristine condition and highly polished. No reproductions here, Nigel guessed; this stuff was the genuine article and no doubt of inestimable value. French doors at the rear of the room opened on to a large verandah, which looked over a stunning walled rose garden in the English style. Beyond lay the soft undulating Virginia countryside, rolling westward to an uncluttered horizon. Gazing at the view, Nigel tried to imagine how it must have looked during the Civil War; he pictured a genteel southern family, all bonnets and gaiters, drinking mint juleps, and in the distance a Confederate Army snaking through the hills, trailing dust, heading north to meet the hated 'bluebellies' on the Potomac.

"I adore this place," Samantha declared, taking Nigel's arm in a gesture that he took as confirmation of his rehabilitation. "I saw you admiring the art, Nigel. Quite a collection isn't it. In the library there are two pieces by Monsieur Degas - jockeys, as you'd expect - and there's also a Stubbs." Samantha guessed what Nigel was thinking. "The house belongs to my friends, the Barrs. They're so rich that I'm almost tempted to disapprove, but that would be rank hypocrisy on my part. Patrick Barr is one of this country's most successful horse-breeders." Nigel confessed that he knew nothing of the Barrs, or the equestrian milieu. "What a pity. He's a genius with horses. Once trained a Kentucky Derby winner. Some years back he adopted me; thought I was a rider of great promise. Perhaps I was, although I could never hope to get anywhere near his class. He and his wife are away in Europe just now, on the Grand Equestrian Tour – Ascot, Longchamps and the rest - so I have the place all to myself. Fully staffed, too. It's all quite stunning, inside and outside."

Nigel could only agree.

Everyone gravitated to the huge kitchen, which looked as though it belonged in a French chateau, with copper pots and saucepans hanging by the dozen from a gantry along one wall. In the middle, a vast granite center island was as big as Nigel's living room. Today, it was covered by papers, stacked in neat piles. Rosalie Burgess, Samantha's personal assistant, was in the process of packing them into boxes. "Hi, everybody," she said. "Don't mind me, I'll be leaving soon."

"Legal documents," Samantha explained. "Having spent days poring over them I now know enough to sound intelligent. Or, as my lawyers would say, enough to be dangerous." Nigel was dying to sneak a look at them. Samantha, guessing as much, wagged a finger. "Now then, there will be no peeking." She laughed at his startled look. "Not that this situation is about legal issues. There's far more at stake here than that." She scanned the faces of the other two ladies, but they were too absorbed exploring the kitchen, with regular gasps of astonishment, to hear her.

"I agree with you," Nigel chipped in earnestly, grateful for any opportunity to inveigle his way back into her good graces. "My own experience of lawyers - thankfully limited - is that they can never see the forest for the trees."

"Mine can't seem to see the trees for the leaves."

Nigel laughed sympathetically. The first lady was in an expansive mood, he was happy to see, but also wondering why.

At that moment, as if from nowhere, Frank Hoffman materialized. Evidently, he had stayed overnight. "Hello, everyone. Well, here we are again. Same cast, same script, but a brilliant new location." He spotted Jane. "Ah, and a new cast member." He introduced himself as 'your boyfriend's nemesis' but said it with a genuinely friendly smile.

Jane returned it in kind. "I've heard nothing but good things about you, Mr Hoffman, and not just from Nigel."

"I'm delighted to hear that," he said, kissing her hand gallantly, "although I don't believe a word of it. I'm delighted to see that Nigel's taste in women is exemplary, if in nothing else." Jane couldn't decide whether the remark was complimentary or misogynistic but in the interest of good cheer she happily settled for the former.

"Drinks anyone?" Frank said, rubbing his hands in anticipation. "I know it's a little early, but I've been up since the crack of dawn." He went over to a floor-to-ceiling wine cooler at the far end of the kitchen and stood for a moment, not for the first time, admiring the serried rows of bottles. He pulled out a couple for closer inspection. "Quite a collection they have here, an oenophile's wet dream."

When everyone settled for white wine, Frank selected a Chassagne Montrachet. Then he hesitated, looking at Samantha as if for permission. "Are you sure the Barrs won't mind us drinking their best stuff?"

"It's considerate of you to ask, Frank," she said, "but I doubt there's anything here *but* the best stuff."

"You could sell some of these at auction for thousands. God knows what's in the cellar... I presume there *is* a wine cellar."

Samantha confirmed it. "And quite an extensive one. I'll take you on a tour later if you like."

Frank filled glasses. Nigel, still playing the penitent, said, "I'll have mineral water, if you don't mind."

Samantha jumped in with feigned vehemence. "Frank may not mind, but I do. It's a little late to be joining the temperance movement don't you think?" Everyone laughed.

Nigel reddened. "Well, I suppose, just to be sociable..."

After handing out the drinks, Frank put on a blue and white striped apron. Samantha had given the kitchen staff the day off, on the grounds that their presence would inhibit free discussion. "I'm doing the cooking as well as the bartending," Frank explained, brandishing a large knife with mock menace. "Don't worry, Nigel, I'm not going to use it on you... much as I'm tempted to."

Nigel was finding the banter tiresome, but he opted to grin and bear it, hoping that it would soon run its course.

"That's all we'd need," Fran said, with a convincing look of horror, "another tabloid headline: *'White House Aide Slays British Journalist in First Lady's Secret Hideaway.'*"

"That's one scoop Nigel Harper wouldn't get to write," Frank joked, enjoying the badinage.

"Now, that's enough!" said Jane, magisterially, surprising herself with the force of her intervention. She took Nigel's arm. "I mean, can't you see how much the poor man's suffering already?"

"Well said, Jane," Samantha declared. "And now, let me propose a toast. To love, friendship and loyalty... in honour of which I hereby declare a permanent cease-fire."

"I'll drink to that," Nigel said gratefully, proposing a toast of his own: "And to Samantha Jameson... and to a happy resolution of all your..." he paused to search for the word "... challenges."

"And America's," Fran added.

"Amen," someone muttered, completing the benediction.

Frank took Nigel's arm and led him toward the verandah. "Fancy a breath of fresh air, before I become a slave in the kitchen?"

"Sure, I'd like that."

Once out of earshot of the rest, Frank resurrected the forbidden subject. "I hope you don't think I was giving you a hard time in there because I'm mad at you. I would have been... I was... but it's not my place to be objectionable. Take that as an apology under the terms of the disarmament treaty."

"No apology needed but accepted anyway."

"The only reason I brought it up again was to tell you, by way of consolation, that I came this close to doing the same thing." He demonstrated how close with finger and thumb. "And aimed at the same target, our mutual friend Marchetti. I use the word 'friend' sardonically."

"Oh? When did that happen?"

"A few weeks ago, Marion and I invited Vincent and Sarah Marchetti for dinner. The evening was a disaster. At one point I thought I was going to deck the bastard. He's socially inadequate and politically obnoxious. Worse, he's a closet anti-Semite. At one point I had to go to the kitchen to recover my poise. Thankfully, they didn't hang around long after that. Marion and I were glad to see the back of them."

"I've had the same experience several times," Nigel said, with a grim smile.

"What on earth happened to your former wife? I can't imagine she was always like that."

"She wasn't. But she's changed beyond all recognition."

"Marchetti's influence, I suppose."

"He hasn't helped, but sadly she was changing even before she met him. He just came in and completed the job. They deserve each other."

"Well, they're off my guest list, and I'm equally certain I'm off theirs. But enough of them. I hear the esteemed senator from Arizona gave you a good working over."

"He tried hard to be subtle about it, but yes. Well, maybe not so subtle."

"Subtlety isn't one of his more obvious virtues, unless we're talking snake-like cunning."

"There were no overt threats, just hints. He asked me about my visa, for example. That can't have been just idle curiosity. Then he asked about Jane - where she worked, what she did. I think he just wanted to let me know that he knew all about us."

"You gave him her name?"

"There seemed no point in concealing it. He can find out easily enough who she is."

"True. The man has connections everywhere. Calls in on the president at least once a week. I've never been invited to sit in, so I've no idea what they talk about. Well, now I do."

Frank produced a half-full bottle of Montrachet from his apron pocket and refilled their glasses. "Changing the subject, any idea what new sensations we might be exposed to this evening?"

"I'd have thought you'd know better than I would."

"I don't. But with Samantha I've learnt always to be ready for a surprise or two. There's one revelation that I know you'll personally find interesting - a minor one in the wider scheme of things - but I'll say no more for now. I should get back to slaving over a hot stove. I think you're going to like what I've prepared. Beef Wellington. Calls for a decent claret, don't you think, old chap?"

"I'd say so. And it seems there are plenty to choose from."

* * *

As evening approached, Frank was still busy in the kitchen, manfully juggling several simmering containers. The others took their places for dinner at one end of a long and handsome Federal mahogany dining table. Samantha took up position at the head of it, with Fran and Frank on her right, Nigel and Jane on her left. Rosalie had left with her precious cargo of documents, with parting instructions from Samantha: "Rosalie dear, please try not to get caught speeding. Or, God forbid, get involved in an accident. Can you imagine this stuff falling into the hands of the local police?" She imitated a gruff station desk sergeant: *"Hey captain, get a look at this. Not sure what we've got here, but it sure looks interesting."* Everyone had laughed nervously.

The only other 'outsiders' present were Samantha's two secret service agents, stationed outside the house. Frank had earlier provided them with sandwiches and coffee.

In the middle of the table stood a vast bowl of salad, dressed with a special mustard sauce from Frank's own 'special recipe' which in fact he had cut out of the *Washington Post* Lifestyle section. He enjoyed dabbling in the kitchen, and it showed, although this evening, flitting in and out of the dining room with salvers and dishes, he looked harassed. He asked Nigel to light the candles in the two large silver candelabra flanking the salad bowl. As soon as the last of the salvers had been delivered, he sat down at the table himself.

"My word, that was a good workout," he said, inviting a compliment.

Samantha delivered it on cue. "Well done, Frank, you're a master." She raised a glass. To our esteemed chef, Frank Hoffman, whose culinary talents are exceeded only by his wit and charm." Glasses were raised all round.

Nigel contributing an archaic sounding "Hear, hear."

Half an hour later, Samantha glanced round the table to make sure that the main course had been consumed. Then, rising from her chair, she lightly tapped her glass with a spoon. "If I may crave your attention, dear friends, I've a few announcements to make... as no doubt many of you anticipated."

Frank, sitting on her right, let out an artificial groan. She looked at him. "Well, you wouldn't have expected anything else, would you, Frank? To begin with..." She paused to look at him again. "Shall I tell them, Frank, or do you want the privilege? I don't want you thinking I'm usurping your role as press secretary."

"Go right ahead, Mrs Jameson. You're the mistress of ceremonies this evening."

Samantha thanked him with a slight bow. "The first thing you should know, everyone - and you're the first to be told - is that

Frank's days as White House press secretary are coming to an end. He'll be resigning. That's a loss - not to me, as I have my own staff - but to the government... and the country. A lone voice of reason amid a chorus of bilious and mind-numbing discordance."

Nigel, eyebrows raised, glanced across at Frank, who returned the look with a shrug, as if to say, "Told you it was minor."

"It won't be announced just yet," Samantha continued. "Frank hasn't even written his resignation letter. That will happen in the next few days. Do you wish to elaborate, Frank?"

Frank remained seated as he spoke. "Thank you, Samantha, for those kind words. By way of explanation, I'll add only this: two years working in an asylum is time enough for anyone intent on preserving their sanity." Encouraged by the sympathetic smiles that greeted this remark, he decided to say more. "The plain fact is that I find myself - as I have for some time - increasingly at odds with this president. Not just with his policies, such as they are, but with the increasingly extreme views that now seem to inform every executive utterance. He manifestly cares nothing for the underprivileged in our society. He's a closet racist. He's a congenital liar. I'm a lifelong Republican, but the GOP we used to know has sold its soul to the devil. It has been taken over by people determined to drag this country back to less enlightened times. I'm unable in all conscience go on delivering that message. Standing at that podium in the press room I often feel..." He paused to search for the right word..."tainted." His voice turned even more solemn for a concluding remark. "The sooner this administration is history the better off America will be. And the rest of the world. I won't be putting all this in my resignation letter, of course, but that's how I feel."

Nigel was about to applaud but thinking better of it delivered a valediction. "Frank, I'm as sorry to hear of your decision as I am proud of you for making it. It can't have been easy for you these past two years. I salute you." He raised his glass.

"And I'm proud to second that," Fran said. She had long known of Frank's unhappiness, and while she had not been expecting this development, she was far from surprised.

Samantha, who had sat down for Frank's peroration, now stood up again. "I heartily endorse everything Frank just said. Excusing this administration's policies while secretly reviling them can't have been easy for a man of his integrity and intelligence. He now joins the ever-lengthening procession of defectors from this White House.

Sadly, shamefully, the old political virtues of compromise and consensus are now considered irredeemably old-fashioned. Political debate has been reduced to shouting insults. America is divided as never before - the more so because of the scandalous behaviour of elected representatives who claim they wish to unite us."

Frank looked across at Nigel. "There you are, Mr Harper, you have your first scoop."

"Scoop?"

"Yes, my resignation. I'll be happy to leak the news through the *Post*. Call it an appetizer for the feast to come."

"Delighted," said Nigel. "How do you want it handled?"

"I'm not so vain as to believe that the resignation of a press secretary is front-page news, but before I hand in my letter, which will be in the next couple of days, I suggest you write a piece speculating about my reasons. You can quote high-level government sources... but I don't need to tell you how to write the goddamned story. The White House will know it came from me, but who cares? If you like, we can work on it together, just to make sure the tone is right. If that's okay with you."

"That sounds fine," Nigel said. "How do you think the president will respond?"

"The same way he has to all the previous resignations. He'll be angry, not because he regrets it, but because he hadn't seen it coming. Resignations offend his ego, just as leaks feed his paranoia. So, he'll go on Fox News and tell them he was about to fire me anyway; say I was incompetent and disloyal; and that he's well rid of me. None of which, by the way, will bother me one bit." He addressed Nigel directly. "You'll come under scrutiny, though, and not only by the dishonourable gentleman from Arizona. Your colleagues in the press room - most of whom have known me far better and longer than you have - will be curious to know how you came to break the story.

Nigel put on his best Churchillian glower of defiance. "Fuck 'em all. Just let me know when you want to work on it."

"Attaboy! We can start this evening if you like. After dinner."

Nigel nodded.

For a while they all concentrated on eating, the conversation mostly about what Frank would be doing with his new-found leisure time, a subject to which he had given little thought. "I might do some travelling; Marion would like that. Me too, for that matter. Maybe do some teaching. Or writing. Perhaps the *Post* would like to engage me as a pundit."

"We could do a lot worse," Nigel said.

And then Samantha was tapping her glass again. "And so, to my second announcement..." Her expression had turned sad. "Frank's not the only one who's been making decisions. After a great deal of soul-searching, Anna Litovka and I have mutually agreed to end our relationship. 'Suspended' might be a better word, since, God willing, we'll be able to restore it at some future date. But for now, it seems the wisest course." There were intakes of breath around the table, including one from Fran, who had failed to see this one coming either. "We're both terribly sad, as you can imagine, and it wasn't a decision we took lightly. But given everything else that's going on, I think it's for the best. Especially in view of what I intend to do next… but I'll get to that shortly. The point is, I could hardly claim the moral high ground if it became known that I was having a secret extra-marital affair, even if my husband spends hardly less time with his mistresses than he does on the golf course. And it would only muddy the waters. It's the only sensible course of action, and I'm taking it while there's still time, and while the tabloids are still barking up the wrong tree." She looked directly at Nigel with a thin smile.

"I'm so sorry, Samantha," Fran said, reaching over to take her hand. "We all liked her very much."

"Let's continue to use the present tense, if you don't mind."

"How has Anna taken it?" It was Jane speaking, an event rare enough to turn heads.

"She'll be fine. She grasped the situation right away." Samantha turned to Nigel. "So, Mr Harper, I'm afraid there will be no sensational revelations about Anastasia Litovka, sultry KGB agent, working her wicked voluptuous wiles to get close to the President. Sorry."

"Under the circumstances," Nigel declared with feeling, "I'm more than happy to abandon the story. And that, I should add, comes from the heart."

"I'm relieved to know that you have one," Frank quipped.

Samantha continued. "There's one more thing I'd like to say about Anna. Rumours that she's an agent of the Kremlin are sheer nonsense. Not because she told me - although she did - or because the idea is laughable…"

Samantha held the punchline in check for a moment. "The reason I know she wasn't spying for Russia is because she was spying for America." Looks were exchanged across the table. "Yes, for a very short time she was what I think the Agency would call an 'asset'. Not a terribly important one, nor a terribly good one, as she'd be the first to admit. The Langley people recognized that soon enough and dropped her. Why did she do it? Because she was desperate to show that she was a true American. I knew about her CIA link long before she told me, by the way. It may surprise you to know that I have my own sources in the intelligence community. The Agency once tried to recruit me when I was young and living in Paris. But I had no interest, and I dare say no more talent for the job than she did."

The audience, taking all this in, fell silent. It was Frank who finally spoke. "May I be so impertinent as to remind you all that dinner, unlike revenge, is a dish best served hot. Samantha, you've already given us much to digest intellectually, but may we now take a few moments to digest a few things anatomically? Like my fabulous dessert."

"Of course," Samantha said. "Forgive me. I should have waited until the meal was over."

"It's delicious," pronounced Jane. Everyone agreed vigorously.

"And more yet to savour," Frank said. He turned to Nigel. "You'll be delighted to learn, my dear fellow, that I've brought some truly rancid French cheeses. Just for you. Can't stand the stuff myself."

"You seem to know all my weaknesses," Nigel said.

"I doubt that very much. Perhaps Jane will tell me later."

"How much time do you have?" Jane said perkily.

The rest of the meal was consumed in relative silence, broken only by small talk about the ingredients and how they had been prepared, a topic of some interest to Jane who, more than anyone at the table, welcomed the break from alarming disclosures.

Frank went to the kitchen to fetch another bottle of wine. Fran followed him, ostensibly to help. "Can we expect any more revelations tonight?" she whispered in his ear.

"I've no idea," he said, with a shrug. "You know the woman better than I do."

She didn't believe him and said so. "I had no idea about the break-up with Anna. Did you? And as for that throwaway line about the CIA... I mean, who would have guessed?"

"I didn't know about it either. But what else can I say, my dear Fran, except perhaps to echo Margo Channing in *All About Eve:* 'Fasten your seatbelts, it's going to be a bumpy night.'" Fran's eyes rolled skyward. Frank fussed with the cheeseboard, arranging the crackers in neat rows. "Would you mind taking this in? But mind how you go, because some of this stuff is already trying to make its escape."

Nigel, the lone cheese-eater, eagerly loaded his plate. Fran tasted the époisses, one of the would-be escapees, and turned up her nose in disgust. "Ugh! How can you eat this stuff?"

Nigel pretended to be offended. "I adore you Americans, but when it comes to cheese, your ignorance is profound. I suppose you'd prefer those plastic orange slices you call cheese, and which I think of as ceiling tiles. Frankly, I'm innately suspicious of any country that can't be bothered to produce a decent cheese."

"That's rich," Fran responded, "coming from the citizen of a country with national dishes called 'bubble and squeak' and 'toad-in-the-hole'."

"Not to forget 'bangers and mash'," Frank put in. "You Brits must really hate your food to give them such unappetizing names."

"Now, now, children," Samantha said in her best matronly manner, "I was always taught that it's impolite to fight at the dinner table." Then, with a quiet cough, she mentioned that she had more to report. "The good news, you'll be relieved to learn, is that there's not much more. The bad news is that I've saved the worst for last, though some of you may think it's the other way around."

Frank, leaning into Fran, whispered, "Fasten those seatbelts."

"As some of you already know, if only in the vaguest terms, I've discovered that my husband, and several of his political cronies, have been engaged in some very shady financial dealings. I can now tell you that I've acquired substantial documentary evidence of it. I'm talking insider trading, money laundering and tax evasion, all processed through an offshore bank account in the Cayman Islands. The amounts involved are big. All this I know from a team of investigators I hired for the purpose. They're still looking into the matter as I speak, but to date they've uncovered irrefutable evidence... and no doubt there's more to come. I've fully briefed my personal attorney - under privilege, of course - and certain other lawyers who are expert in the field of financial crimes. The consensus is that the case against my husband is watertight. I'll spare you the sordid details. I don't want to send you all to sleep..."

"No chance of that," Nigel interjected, drawing a sharp look from Jane.

"So, what happens next?" Frank asked.

"Good question. But I'm not yet sure I know the answer. I thought you might help me decide."

"You must report the crimes," Frank said flatly. "Isn't that the law?" Nigel was surprised that Frank didn't know of The Plan.

"I can understand why you think so," Samantha said. "But no, it's not the law. And what wife would readily turn in a husband, the father of her children, to face serious criminal charges that might send him to jail for the rest of his life?"

"I understand that but…"

"Let me finish, Frank, because I've been seriously considering an alternative course of action. You're right. I should, if only for reasons of personal safety, report what I've discovered to the authorities. I could do that anonymously. That's essentially what my lawyers seem to be recommending. But consider this: if I go to the SEC and hand over the evidence I've acquired, the result would be a White House scandal that would rank with the worst of them. The president would almost certainly be forced to resign. Or be impeached. He might face other criminal proceedings. Well deserved, you may be thinking, and I don't disagree. But think of the devastating effect on the country. The chaos would last for months on end." She paused to let all this sink in. "Which is why I'm weighing up another option that would avoid all that turmoil. It might also mean a legal risk for me - or so my lawyers have warned - but it's one that I'm willing to take." Samantha paused again, this time to take a sip of wine. "I apologize for being so long-winded, but I'm trying to summarize all this as best I can."

"You're doing an excellent job," Frank interjected. "Take your time, Samantha. You have all night and a captive audience."

At that precise moment, the grandfather clock in the hall struck nine. Samantha smiled. "Ah, a perfectly timed reminder to get on with it." She waited for the chimes to finish before continuing. "My alternative plan is to bring about the same political result, but without the mess. In the interest of full disclosure, I suppose I should mention that it would also help me to achieve certain personal objectives, but in this case, my interests and those of the nation conveniently converge. There are times when doing the wrong thing produces the right result. This, I believe, is one of those times."

She now had a rapt audience, like theatregoers at the preview of a mystery play with a familiar plot except for an ending that the author has kept secret. "I've pretty much decided on this course of action. The country needs to be rid of this president, and I wish to be rid of my husband. My plan will achieve both ends. It is my intention to confront him with the incriminating evidence and offer him a deal: my silence for his departure. But here's the crux of it: I won't insist he resign. He must merely announce that he's decided not to run for a second term. At the same time, he'll grant me an uncontested divorce, the timing of which we'll negotiate, though perhaps not until his term ends."

There was a stunned silence. Nigel, who had known most of this, started to raise a hand, but a sharp nudge in the ribs from Jane brought it down again.

"Just let me finish," Samantha said, "and then you can ask questions. I know what you're thinking: my plan sounds too fantastic to take in. Well, I can hardly believe it myself. Nor, frankly, can I predict the consequences. But if my husband accepts my offer, he gets to leave office with his dignity, and that of his office, intact. The country will be spared the chaos, and all the other consequences. Now, you may also be asking yourselves, 'What if he doesn't play ball and rejects my deal out of hand.' It's possible. If that should happen, I'm prepared to go to the authorities with the evidence. Now, if I were in his position, I know which option I'd choose. Of course, I'm *not* him. And as you all know, he's nothing if not unpredictable."

Nigel's hand was hovering again. This time Jane rather noisily pinned it to the table, sensing that Samantha had not yet finished.

"I can guess what you're about to ask, Nigel, but bear with me for two more minutes. I want to address the potential flaw, the immediate danger, as I see it: he decides to fight back. I've no idea how, but he has an army of lawyers who'll be only too pleased to tell him how. But my instinct tells me he won't. If he allows me to unleash the dogs of war, as it were, then the consequences will be terrible. For him especially, but also for others.

"In my proposal, he gets to serve out the remaining sixteen months of his term. Yes, I know that gives him ample time to inflict yet more damage on the country, but he'll be a lame duck. My guess is that even his loyal Republican flunkies in Congress will start jumping ship. That's what rats do, isn't it? My plan ends his presidency with a whimper rather than a bang. But since the bang is unthinkable, it's a better option. So, that, in a nutshell, is my plan. There is, in fact, *only* the nutshell. The equation is very simple: if he turns me down, I turn him in."

Samantha gently dabbed her brow and took a sip of water. She had now finished. "Well, everyone, now it's your turn. Fire away." She scanned the table for reactions. Understandably, no one leapt at the chance to volunteer the first opinion.

It was, perhaps inevitably, Nigel who spoke up. "I'll put in my ten bobs' worth, or I should say, ten cent's worth." He started to rise, but thinking that might seem portentous, promptly sat down again. He looked thoughtful.

"Go ahead, Nigel," Samantha said. "I'd love to hear an informed viewpoint."

Nigel had been privy to the plan but spoke as if he had just heard it for the first time. "To be honest, I'm gobsmacked. That, by the way, is a popular English word for astonished."

"Ah, a typical English response," Samantha commented. "Earthy but non-committal."

Undeterred, Nigel continued. "Tactically, it's a clever plan but I'm in no position to judge its legal merits. Practically, it seems to presume a great deal, above all that your husband will go quietly. Given his nature, I'd say that qualifies as a long shot."

"I agree, but then I didn't say the plan was risk-free. What would you do if you were him?"

"Well, to echo your earlier comment, I'm not him. But I'd go for it in a shot. You're offering him a clean exit, the chance to avoid the kind of humiliation Nixon suffered. Also - and please don't misunderstand me - even losing a job and a wife sounds a bloody sight less daunting than the prospect of thirty years in the slammer." Samantha smiled, and started to speak, but Nigel had one more thing to add. "Another thought occurs to me. Who's to say he's even decided to run for a second term? He hasn't said that he will, and I've read somewhere that he's in two minds about it."

"Baloney. Let me assure you that he wants a second term. He's had a taste of power and likes it. Never mind the negative opinion polls. He never believes them anyway, unless they show him well ahead." Samantha kept Nigel on the hook. "But what, given what you've just heard, and whatever your misgivings, is your public verdict, as opposed to your private opinion?"

Nigel dabbed his lips with his napkin and topped up his glass. "Since we're talking of odds, I'd say your plan has a sporting chance. But the situation is unprecedented, so I'm shooting in the dark."

"Thank you." Samantha turned to her right. "Frank, you're looking pensive."

Frank stroked his chin thoughtfully to illustrate the fact. "I'm in no position to evaluate your legal risk, Samantha, your lawyers will have to call that one. Everything else depends entirely on the president's reaction. He's a vain man, and not always in touch with reality. I'm betting his first response will be something like 'Go ahead and try, see where it gets you'. His second, of course, will be to call in his lawyers. They'll tell him what he wants to hear. My guess is that they'll circle the wagons."

"Even when they learn the extent of the evidence against him?"

"All fake, they'll try to claim."

"But that won't wash. It's not just a matter of my word against his. I've got a paper trail a mile long."

"The flaw in your plan, as I see it, is that it depends on the response of a man whose judgement is driven entirely by ego and who has no moral compass to guide him. The narcissism makes him think he's invincible. His first impulse will be to counterattack, and he's vindictive enough to try anything." Frank watched Samantha's face register disappointment. "Look, all I'm saying is that any plan which relies on a madman to act rationally is, almost by definition, problematic. We all know how he gets when someone crosses him. And you're double-crossing him."

Samantha sighed. "You're right, Frank, as usual. But my only other option, other than doing nothing, is to go to the SEC. Their investigation would involve hundreds of people. There would be leaks. The media would have a field day. All that turmoil would run for months, perhaps years. I can't bear to think about it."

"He wouldn't care about that."

"He would if it meant thirty years in the slammer."

"Maybe…"

Samantha turned to Fran.

Fran was, as usual, decisive. "I hate to disagree with these gentlemen, but you won't be surprised that I do. Yes, he'll be shocked at first, but then, after he's thought about it a bit, and cursed a great deal, he'll be terrified. Yes, he may let his legal dogs off the leash, but their room for maneuver is restricted by the sheer weight of evidence. Then, I think, they'll follow the line of least resistance: tell him to accept your offer while it's on the table. I'm no lawyer, but I can't think what choice they have. So, my verdict is unequivocal: go for it." Samantha smiled, grateful to her closest aide for her down-to-earth approach to everything. "I do have one question though," Fran said, as an afterthought. "What happens to the rest of those shit-bags, his partners-in-crime. If the boss caves, they all get off scot-free."

"Yes, I'm afraid that's a price I'll have to pay. It's galling, I agree, but at least their scam will come to an abrupt halt, since I imagine they'd wind everything up to cover their tracks."

"In other words, cash in."

"Yes. But I can't let my husband off the legal hook and then go after his accomplices, as much as I'd like to."

Frank jumped in. "It wouldn't surprise me if they're already winding the thing up. If so, we may have Nigel's little outburst to thank. Who knows, it could turn out to have been a blessing in disguise."

"Very heavily disguised," Nigel said, quoting Churchill.

"I don't think so, Frank," Samantha replied. "My investigators would have reported any winding up."

She suddenly turned her attention to the only person at the table who hadn't yet spoken. "Jane, you've been awfully quiet. You're an analyst. Why don't you exercise your powers and analyze this?"

Jane, taken by surprise, shifted nervously in her seat. Nigel squeezed her arm encouragingly.

"Frankly," Jane began, a little hesitantly, "I'm a bit overwhelmed. I'm also, with respect, a little disturbed."

"In what way," asked Samantha.

"Well, here am I, a relatively low-level government employee, sitting in a secret meeting with the first lady of the land and two senior White House executives, plotting how to bring down a lawfully elected president. He may be a shit. No argument there. He may even be a crook. I'm prepared to believe that, too, although it remains to be seen. But what we're talking about here verges on - forgive me Samantha - a coup. A bloodless coup, yes, but one that involves methods that even your own your lawyers seem to find questionable." She waited for a reaction, but since no one spoke, she moved to her concluding comment. "I heartily applaud the end, but my conscience is nagging me about the means. In short, I'm debating with myself whether two wrongs make a right, and so far not coming up with any kind of resolution. Meanwhile, I can only feel uncomfortable. I'm sorry, Samantha, but you asked for my opinion."

Jane's remarks were greeted with a stunned silence. Even Samantha seemed lost for words. Nigel looked at Jane with an expression of mingled awe and pride, but quickly recovered in an attempt to break the ice. "Jane, darling, I haven't heard you say that much in one go since we first met."

Everyone laughed except Jane, who was flashing Nigel one of those looks that deliver metaphorical daggers.

Samantha had listened to Jane as intently as she had to the others. Time now, she decided, to sum up the case for the prosecution. Or was it for the defence?

"Thank you Jane. Your opinion is noted. It's also respected. But I'd argue that this isn't a coup. Look, I'm not attempting to overthrow the government, or democracy. I'm trying to rescue both. And I'm not deposing our leader, I'm giving him a choice. I've wrestled with my own conscience on this point, believe me. I haven't slept for weeks. But now my mind is clear. The fact remains, whatever the ethical pros and cons, that I have compelling evidence from neutral and reliable sources that the President of the United States has engaged in criminal acts. Impeachable acts. He's shamed himself and his office. My conspiracy is nothing to the one that he's contrived. He's acted solely in his own interests, whereas I'm thinking only of the country's interests. Leave aside my personal interest in the matter, or not, as you see fit, and tell me that I'm wrong to want a solution that averts an even greater threat to our democracy. After that, whichever way this thing goes, history will be the judge."

"Except that, if you plan works, there won't be any history," Frank pointed out. "None of this will ever come to light."

"True, but history has a habit of eventually revealing what wasn't apparent at the time."

"Ah, I hear a memoir coming," Frank said, attempting to lighten the mood. "Perhaps Nigel here will ghost it for you."

"I'd love to," Nigel said. "But meanwhile, I have a question for the here and now: exactly when do you intend to, er, pull the trigger? Produce the fabled 'smoking gun'."

Samantha smiled. "Not an analogy I'd have used, Nigel, but as usual you get to the heart of the matter. The answer is: as soon as possible. That means very soon, with or without the approval of my legal advisers."

"How will this happen? I mean, how will it be staged, if that's the right word?"

"'Staged' will do if it's drama you're looking for. I plan to confront my husband next Wednesday. The stage will be a golf course in Florida. *His* golf course, just to add poignancy to tension. Funnily enough, we've hardly ever played together, so my invitation will be the first shock."

"Why on the golf course?" Nigel asked, but then remembered his own golf date with Samantha.

"Because out on there I can be sure we won't be bugged or distracted. It'll be just the two of us."

"G-Day…" muttered Nigel.

"Is that wise?" Fran asked, with a mock look of concern. "I mean, he'll have a golf club in his hands."

"So will I," Samantha replied, forcing a laugh. "Besides, there will be secret service agents all over the place. He's hardly likely to assault me in front of witnesses."

Jane, suddenly feeling that she might have been too critical in her remarks, now saw an opportunity to redress the balance. "All I can say, Mrs Jameson, is that for all the doubts and concerns I just expressed, you make a compelling case. I'm still uncertain, but I apologize for the 'coup' remark. A poor choice of words. Whatever my reservations – which I'll no doubt work out - I can only hope that you come up with a result that benefits the country and you. I truly mean that."

Nigel looked at her again with the same blend of admiration and surprise as before.

Samantha thanked her. "No apologies needed, my dear girl. You spoke your mind, which is what I asked for. And you're entitled to have your misgivings. God knows, I've had them in spades. Samantha yawned and stretched her arms. "I think that's enough for one evening, I really do. I don't know about the rest of you but I for one am ready to call it a day." She rose heavily from the table. "Stay up all night if you like. I know I've given you plenty to think about. We can talk more over breakfast if you can stand it. So, goodnight to you all."

With that, she swept from the room.

After Samantha had gone to bed, Fran and Jane settled into a sofa to chat. The atmosphere was tense. Frank poured two stiff brandies and invited Nigel to join him on the verandah again. Taking two cigars from his pocket, he offered one to Nigel.

"I didn't know you smoked," said Nigel, who in London had enjoyed an occasional Havana. There were no Havanas to be had in the United States, of course, all imports from Cuba still sanctioned. Frank's cigars were from Dominica.

"I rarely smoke," Frank said, lighting up with vigorous puffs. "But at times of stress I find it helps, and I'd say tonight qualifies on that count."

A full moon in a cloudless sky cast a luminous glow over the distant hills, threw stark shadows across the verandah. Frank gazed up at the panoply of irreproachable stars. "If only things down here on earth could be that clear."

"Perhaps it's a portent," Nigel said, contentedly exhaling smoke rings.

"How so," asked Frank.

"On Wednesday, all will be revealed - one way or the other."

"We shall see..."

"You sound skeptical."

"Who wouldn't be? This is a unique situation. And I use 'unique' advisedly. When did a sitting president face a threat to his tenure from a first lady? Oh, some may have tried to persuade their husbands to quit - Mrs Lincoln, for one - but none succeeded, so far as anyone knows."

"Think she'll pull it off?"

"The short answer is, I don't know. But I've learnt over the years never to underestimate that lady's resolve. Let me just say this: if anyone can pull it off, she can."

"I still can't believe what I've just heard, and I'd already heard most of it."

"Yeah, quite a story isn't it. And it'll become *your* story in the editorial sense. Think what a hero you're going to be when it breaks. You'll be the toast of Fleet Street. The world over, at least in the newsrooms."

"You know, Frank, I was thinking about that on the way over here, but I find myself less and less concerned with the personal glory than about the political result. And most of all about Samantha's well-being - if that doesn't sound too self-righteous."

"It sounds as self-righteous as hell. What happened to the stone-hearted, crusading, career journalist?"

"I must be getting soft in my middle years."

"You're becoming a mensch, my boy."

"Mensch?"

"That's a Jewish word for a proper human being."

Nigel, puffing contentedly, accepted the compliment with a grin. "What do you think you'll do next, Frank? To earn a living, I mean. I presume you still *need* to earn a living."

"I don't. Not that I'm fabulously wealthy, but I'm comfortably off. Between you and me, I've inherited from a couple of aunts, and Marion has a trust fund that's never been touched. I'll do *something*, but first I need a break. And my dear long-suffering wife, bless her, could use a little more attention from me than she's been getting these past few years."

"Does she know about any of this?"

"Nothing. Or next to nothing. She knows I'm resigning, of course, but not the rest of it, least of all Samantha's story. I chose to keep it that way, at least for now. She suspects something's going on, of course, and I may have dropped a few vague hints, but she's smart enough not to ask for more."

"How long have you two been married?"

"Fifteen years next month. Never thought I'd do it. Get married, that is. Nor did my friends. I was what they used to call a 'confirmed bachelor'. Turned out to be the best thing I ever did." Catching Nigel's quizzical look, he added, "You know, of course, that many people think I'm a closet-dweller."

"I heard rumours. Are you? Not that I care."

"Between us, I did once experience a brief period of sexual ambivalence. That was long ago. But I just didn't turn far enough in that direction. That I was unmarried, and celibate, had nothing to do with it. I just never met a woman I thought of as a potential wife. And then I met Marion. Met her at a cinema festival in New York, We hit it off right from the start. Soulmates, you might say - in movie tastes and much else besides. I've had no regrets since. Not one. My wife's a gem and I love her madly. Funny, but I don't think I've ever spoken to anyone about this. Must be that full moon over there. Speaking of romance, how about you and Jane? Any plans?"

"Not right now. I like her very much. After her performance tonight, I may even fall in love. But then, I may have been in love already."

"Well, good for you," Frank said with genuine enthusiasm. "I like her. She's obviously a woman with a keen mind to go with those more visible assets."

"Yes, I'm a lucky man."

"I'd say so," Frank said, conspicuously failing to mention that she might also be a lucky woman.

"I've been meaning to ask you something, Frank."

"What about?"

"If, or perhaps I should say when, we come to write this story, how are we going to control what the president says about deciding not to run? He'll issue some bullshit about having set the nation on the right course, refer to advancing years, or family issues, but we'll be writing the story before he makes his announcement."

"I'm sure Samantha will discuss that with him. I know she wants to control the narrative from end to end, and that includes all matters of disclosure. She's been very clear on that point. It'll be part of the deal."

"The point is," Nigel persisted, "that we don't want to find ourselves reporting one thing and then having him come out and say something different. Something we weren't expecting. We'd look foolish. And as you pointed out earlier, he's nothing if not unpredictable."

"Forget the 'we'," Frank said, grinning. "It's going to be your byline on the story, not mine. You're the only one who'll look foolish."

"Bastard!" Nigel laughed nervously. Then he took a new tack. "By the way, there's something else I've been meaning to bring up. I've been thinking about my editor, Duncan Erskine. At some point, I've got to bring him up to speed. I can't just spring this on him, call him an hour before the print run and say, "By the way, Duncan, I'm about to file an exclusive story that the president of the United States won't be running for re-election.' As it is, he'll have a hundred questions - about the background, documentary evidence, sources, and what have you. I don't have a press secretary's luxury of responding with, 'No comment' or 'I'll have to get back to you.'"

"What are you asking me exactly?"

"I'd like, at an appropriate time, to get him over here."

"For what specific purpose?"

"Look, this is a story in which the editor of the paper ought to be personally involved. The minute I tell him what's going on he'll insist on being engaged anyway. He's a bright man, and an honest one, and he's been around the news business a long time. His input could be valuable in any number of ways. If he's going to be all over it, perhaps it's better that he's all over it over here. I mean, working with us."

Frank thought about it for a minute. "Sounds reasonable, but I'd like to run it by Samantha in the morning. I think she needs to approve any further additions to the inner circle."

"Fair enough. Just thought I'd mention it."

"Well, I'm glad you did. Now, before anything else, why don't we go inside and start working on my resignation story."

Stubbing out their cigars, they went indoors. The other two ladies had already retired for the night. Bleary-eyed, the men finished writing the piece just as the sun began to rise.

* * * * *

Chapter 17

Like his man in Washington, Duncan Erskine religiously observed an early-morning ritual of combing through the other dailies to make sure the *Post* hadn't missed any important stories. It rarely had, and this morning he finished the chore satisfied with the paper's performance. He could only hope that the *Post*'s readers would be just as happy with the result. In truth, there was little going on to be happy, or unhappy, about. At least not in Britain. With Parliament in recess and Whitehall virtually evacuated, Fleet Street was well into the annual news hiatus known as the 'silly season'. Real domestic news was hard to find, which was why even the *Post*, always aspiring to appeal to the serious-minded, fell back on filling the inside pages with summer trivia. Buckingham Palace garden parties were a summer staple. So were contrived holiday snaps of prominent political figures cavorting in Mediterranean resorts, some wearing silly hats, baggy shorts and loud shirts, desperate to convey the impression that they were just like normal people enjoying a well-deserved summer break. Even the prime minister had stooped to being photographed, face laughably contorted, licking an ice cream on an Italian beach. Why, Duncan wondered, did these supposedly serious men and women seem to think that such pictures were appealing when they were clearly quite the opposite?

"Does he honestly think this revolting image might get him some votes?" he asked Elsa, who at that moment had appeared in his office with coffee and muffins. "Our PM looks revolting even when he's not eating ice cream," was her sensible response.

"I've always hated this time of year," Duncan said grumpily. "There's little enough going on, and so much of it utterly stupid. Look at this." He held up the front page of one of the tabloids. It was devoted to the antics of a man who had foolishly tried to replicate an attempted wartime escape from a German castle by flying off a bridge in a home-made glider made from packing paper and wooden struts and had broken both legs on landing. "I can't think why my esteemed Fleet Street colleagues bother running this kind of stuff. The world is mad enough already."

Elsa disagreed. "I think our readers need a little light relief from politics, scandals and disasters. Better a few silly stories like these than page after page of how the politicians have fucked up the economy, or how the world will soon be coming to an end because the polar icecaps are melting."

Duncan grunted, whether by way of contradiction or disgust she couldn't tell.

Elsa went back to her desk to answer the telephone. She reappeared moments later. "Lord Goodfriend wants a word."

"Well, put him through, for Pete's sake," Duncan said irritably.

"He's not on the line. He's on his way over. Says he'll be here in ten minutes."

"Damn! What could he possibly want? Must be something serious."

"He didn't say."

"Well, don't just stand there, help me clean this place up."

Elsa scooped up a pile of crumpled newspapers from Duncan's desk and dumped them into a filing cabinet. Then she rounded up several stray coffee mugs that had been nurturing staphylococcus cultures for weeks. Duncan found a tie in a drawer and grabbed a jacket that had been draped over the back of his chair. Trying to put them on simultaneously, he failed at both. "Elsa, help me with this bloody thing - and tell those slobs out there to tidy up their desks, too. We might as well look like an efficient, well-ordered newsroom even if it's only for temporary public display."

Elsa spread the word but was greeted with contemptuous grins. These she happily returned. A few juniors deigned to clear their desktops, only to receive disapproving looks from colleagues. Most journalists found it hard to work without desktop disorder, even in an increasingly paper-less age.

The desultory clean-up had scarcely been completed when the Dark Lord - as His Lordship was known in the newsroom - appeared. Stepping out of a lift he looked, as some wag observed, like a malign monster emerging from a cave for an evening's hunting. Duncan hurried over to greet him. "Lord Goodfriend, this is a rare honour."

The proprietor scowled at the implied criticism of his prolonged absences. "I just happened to be in the neighbourhood. Not catching you at a bad time, am I?"

"Not at all. It's a quiet day, as you can imagine."

"I'd like a word in private," Lord Goodfriend said, having taken note of the inquisitive looks across the newsroom. "Why don't we use the conference room?" *'More layoffs?'* was the unasked question behind them.

"May I offer you a coffee? Tea?"

"Nothing, thanks. My doctor keeps telling me to cut down on the caffeine. I think that's what all doctors do when they can't find anything wrong: lecture you about your - what's the phrase? - lifestyle choices. Cut down on this, eliminate that. No smoking. No drinking. Live like a monk. Then, of course, after years of lecturing, they finally discover something wrong with you and don't seem to have a clue what to do."

"You look well enough to me, Lord Goodfriend," Duncan said, noting the suntan and the taut skin - the latter, he suspected, having been surgically enhanced.

"And I *feel* perfectly well, thank you. I think that's what the quacks find baffling. Annoys the hell out of them when you don't do anything they've told you to do and yet still feel fine. But that's enough about me. Let's talk about the paper. This place. How's it all going? I mean since the redundancies were announced, how's morale holding up?"

"Pretty well, I think, but any more layoffs and that could change in a hurry."

"I think we're done with them for now. But who knows? We can only wait and see how the figures look. Circulation seems to have stalled again."

"That in itself is encouraging," Duncan said, keen to turn a negative into a positive.

"Arresting a decline isn't what I like to hear. We won't make money by being in a holding pattern. Still, I suppose it could be worse. And at least we're all in the same crowded, leaky boat. Bloody social media is killing us. Killing our brains as well if you ask me. But it's not the circulation that bothers me so much as the advertising revenue. That's been in reverse for three months now. The classifieds are down to two columns these days."

"But as you pointed out, Lord Goodfriend, every paper on the Street has the same problem." This was uttered with no more conviction than repetition deserved.

"Yes, yes, yes, so we all keep telling ourselves, but it'll be no consolation if this ship goes down that the rest of the fleet has foundered as well." Lord Goodfriend suddenly chuckled, a rare event. "Incidentally, I was amused by those pictures of the PM grappling with an ice cream. Like a strip cartoon. Made me laugh all the way over here. We should run more of that kind of thing. Gives the readers some light relief from all the doom and gloom." Duncan, recalling Elsa's comment, responded with a cross between a laugh and a snort.

"What's so funny?"

"That's pretty much what my PA was saying just before you arrived."

"Well, that only goes to show she has the right instincts. Promote the girl at once."

"I did. She's now called senior executive assistant. What next? Senior assistant executive." Lord Goodfriend was unamused. Duncan knew that the staff found their managing editor dour but compared to the proprietor he was funnier than Coco the Clown. The proprietor, Duncan now noticed, had suddenly gone quiet, apparently thinking about what to say next. Duncan decided to help him out. "Was there a specific reason for your visit?" He quickly added, "As welcome as they always are."

"As it happens, there *is* something. How's our new man in Washington doing? I ask because I haven't seen anything of great note from Mr Harper since we sent him there. Supposed to liven up the file, wasn't he? When's he going to start doing it?"

Like most editors whose reporters are under attack, Duncan reflexively took up a defensive position. "Well, it *is* the summer, and Washington, like Westminster, takes a long break, regardless of what's going on in the world. And he's still getting his feet under the table. He's only been there three months, you know."

Lord Goodfriend adopted a familiar frown, which to Duncan could only spell trouble. Whatever the owner had on his mind, he seemed to be having trouble coming out with it. "By the way," he said, "it's been brought to my attention that he's been stirring things up a bit."

"Oh, in what way?" Duncan was now concerned.

"As I understand it, he seems to be working on some kind of financial scandal. Insider trading, or some such thing. US defence stocks being traded before government contracts have been announced."

"Oh, really? Well, that's news to me - no pun intended. Where's all this coming from?"

"I can't disclose my source, as you of all people will understand, but it seems that your man was at some cocktail party here in London recently making certain remarks of a potentially slanderous nature to one of the guests. An American. I don't have all the details, but Harper was apparently inebriated. I'm told that's par for the course - which, by the way, I didn't know. Anyway, the story seems to have travelled back to Washington. You know how fast these things get around these days. The real point, though, is that my source is well connected in DC, and it seems that certain senior people over there took umbrage. I gather from your blank look that none of this has been brought to your attention."

"No, it hasn't. But I appreciate your telling me. Do you want me to investigate?"

"Well, investigate may be too strong a word. But when you next speak to Mr Harper you might ask him to explain himself."

"I'll make a point of it. But my first reaction is that remarks overheard at cocktail parties are notoriously inaccurate and usually misinterpreted. Chinese whispers, and all that, alcohol induced."

"You're right. And I'm not after a full-blown enquiry. It's probably a storm in a teacup. But, as I said, it did travel across the pond, and to high-level quarters. As high as they go, if you get my drift."

"I do."

"All I can say is this: if your Mr Harper thinks he's on to something, I'd sooner read about it in the paper than hear it on the grapevine. He hasn't filed such a story, I take it."

"No. Nor has anyone else."

"Well, if there's anything in it - which I agree may be uncertain - no doubt he will. Meanwhile, you might advise him to write a bloody story and keep his trap shut."

"I will."

"There's one more thing I might add. My source is associated with companies that spend a great deal of money advertising in this paper and he went to great lengths to point that out. We can't afford to lose important advertisers. But dammit, I've said too much already. Now you'll no doubt work out who I'm talking about."

Duncan had been thinking about it but failed to come up with an answer. "As it happens, I'd been planning to call Nigel this afternoon. I'll have a word."

"Yes, you do that."

"You want me to report back on what he has to say?"

"Only if you think it's necessary. Meanwhile I'm going to enjoy a well-earned holiday and don't want to be disturbed unless you think I need to be."

There being nothing further to be said on the subject, Duncan moved on to other matters. "Did you get to meet President Jameson when he was in town?"

"No. I left the day he arrived - purely by coincidence, I should add. But I did catch up with him, briefly, a couple of weeks back."

"How was his mood? I mean, is he going for a second term. It's now just a year and a half away, and not so much as a hint."

"I'm surprised you should ask. There's no question he'll run. Why on earth wouldn't he? Ask your new man in Washington, he'll tell you."

"I must say Jameson seems as buoyant and aggressive as ever. But then fools are rarely assailed by doubts." Duncan bit his lip, aware that Lord Goodfriend and Jameson met regularly.

"Well, you won't catch me agreeing with you there, much less in public. But Jameson and I are not as close as you seem to think. Yes, I make a point of seeing him, but only for the sake of the franchise. The truth is - and this isn't for publication - I've never much cared for him personally. And I've grave doubts on several levels about his suitability for the office. I wonder sometimes whether he's quite all there. But that's also strictly off the record - even if millions of others think so, too. Perhaps that'll make you feel better about writing some of those unusually harsh editorials you've been writing about him of late."

Duncan responded to what he took to be criticism of the paper's stance. "Yes, we have been hard on him, but no more than many. Frankly, the man invites ridicule. Every time he speaks he puts his foot in his mouth. 'Foot-and-mouth disease, the reporters call it."

"Well, I can't argue the point. And even if I wanted to I wouldn't since I always give my editors a free hand. Always within reason, of course." He saw the concerned look on Duncan's face. "Don't look so alarmed, old chap. That's not about to change. I made that promise when I bought the paper, and I'm sticking to it. I'm not Rupert Murdoch, you know."

"You can't know how much better that makes me feel, Lord Goodfriend."

"That I don't interfere, or that I'm not Rupert Murdoch?" The question was accompanied by another rare smile.

"Frankly, both."

His Lordship rose wearily from his chair. He'd said what he'd come to say and heard what he wished to know. "Anything else you want to talk about while I'm here?"

"Well. Nothing and everything, but nothing specific." Duncan had thought of a great many things, but he'd been given no time to prepare, and being unprepared for a conversation with Lord Goodfriend was never a good idea.

"In that case, I'll be off. I'm speaking at a forum at the London School of Economics this afternoon. We're supposed to be talking about Britain's allegedly failing foreign policy. Frankly, I wasn't even aware that we had a policy, failed or otherwise. And, sadly, who listens to Britain these days, anyway? Why they've asked me to do this thing, I can't imagine, since I know next to nothing about the subject. But there we are… After that I'm off to France. I'll be gone three weeks, barring emergencies."

"Well, enjoy it."

"You really must come out one of these days," Lord Goodfriend said, as he had done a dozen times before, without result. "And bring a lady friend, if you have one." Duncan watched the proprietor closely to see if he had glanced at Elsa, but the proprietor's face was impassive. "And be sure to bring some tennis gear. I can't meddle in your sacred editorial process, but I'd be delighted to thrash you on the tennis court as compensation."

"I'd be honoured," Duncan said, more obsequiously than he'd intended.

"And when I get back, we really must have lunch at my club." This was another standing invitation that never sat down.

"I look forward to it, Lord Goodfriend. Meanwhile, good luck with the foreign policy forum. I'm sure you'll have some useful intelligence to impart."

Lord Goodfriend snorted. "Well, I must be on my way."

Striding through the newsroom, he looked neither left nor right. When he reached the elevators, someone had thoughtfully detained one for him.

Duncan headed back to his office and called Elsa in. "Remind me, after lunch, to call your pal Nigel Harper."

"He's no pal of mine," said Elsa, rather emphatically, he thought.

Duncan knew better than to ask if something had happened between her and Nigel. More to the point, he couldn't be bothered. His affair with Elsa had cooled off in recent weeks, and part of him was quietly relieved that it might be nearing the end of its course.

He hoped that Elsa might be feeling the same way, suspecting that she probably was.

* * *

Nigel arrived at the White House press room that morning to find the troll-like Sonny lying in wait with yet another invitation to meet for a drink. "Hey, what's happening, Sir Nigel, my good fellow?"

Nigel found Sonny's mingling of British and American argot more annoying than engaging. "You haven't been around for a while."

"Well, things are rather quiet around here. We seem to be approaching the dog days of summer. As usual, come the fourth of July everything grinds to a halt in this town. How's that other situation, by the way? Anything doing?" Sonny's nonchalance seemed a little too studied.

"Oh, and what situation is that?" Nigel asked disingenuously.

"You know, the one we talked about." Sonny glanced around furtively.

Nigel didn't. "Oh, that! I've no idea. Haven't given it much thought, to be honest."

"I suppose I ought to be relieved. Lost interest, have you?"

"Too many dead ends, too few sources, too much like hard work. I've decided that you were right: no one seems to care."

"You've changed your tune, I must say."

"Yes, I suppose so. Look, why don't I fill you in later. Maybe at Slattery's."

Nigel had no intention of discussing 'that other situation', either in the press room or the bar, but Sonny was nothing if not persistent. He would have to tell him *something,* anything that would take the subject off the man's agenda.

"You're on," said Sonny, and much to Nigel's relief, he wandered away.

Nigel's cell phone buzzed. It was Duncan.

"Duncan here, laddie. Got a minute?"

"For you, Duncan, all the time in the world." Nigel had been meaning to call his managing editor all morning and felt slightly put out that Duncan had beaten him to it. "What's on your mind?"

Duncan got to the point directly. "I had a visit this morning from Lord Goodfriend. He showed up in the newsroom unexpectedly."

"Must be bad news," said Nigel casually, knowing that he might not like what he was about to hear. "And how is our all powerful proprietor?"

"In good form. About to decamp to the South of France, thank God. The good news is that he doesn't foresee the need for more layoffs."

"That's good to hear. And the bad news?"

"I'm not sure it *is* bad news, but he mentioned an incident… something you allegedly said to someone at a cocktail party when you were last here. Ring any bells?"

Nigel groaned inaudibly. Before answering, he looked around the press room to make sure that he couldn't be overheard, and that Sonny was nowhere in earshot. But three other reporters were huddled only a few paces away.

"Nigel, are you there? Nigel…?"

"I'm still here, but if you don't mind, I'll call you right back. Give me ten minutes." Nigel left the White House and headed for Dupont Circle, which was directly across the street and had a small park in the middle. He found an unoccupied bench and called Duncan back.

"Dare I ask," Duncan said, "what the hell's going on? What is it that I should know that you haven't bothered to tell me and which I first get to hear from the proprietor?"

"I've been trying to call you, Nigel fibbed.

"Well, I haven't been anywhere, laddie."

"I know. But I got tied up on a story, which, by the way, I did mention when I was in town."

"In passing. You were a little short on details."

"Probably because I didn't have any. Since then, things have been moving quickly. You know how it is."

"I don't know how it is. That's the point. What story? What things? If you can spare the time, your editor would like to be brought into the picture."

"Fair enough. There have been some developments… but perhaps I should start from the very beginning."

"That's a very good place to start, as the song goes."

"It's quite a story, but you'll be the judge of that... and how we should approach it when the time comes."

Nigel recounted the whole saga: his discovery of the first lady's infidelity; his Faustian deal to hold on that story in return for a bigger one; Samantha Jameson's golf-course revelations; his run-in with Vincent; and, finally, his meeting with Senator Curtis. Duncan, unusually restrained, failed to interrupt once, and when Nigel had finished, he failed to say anything for several seconds. Nigel deduced that his editor was silently weighing up whether he believed every word of it, or none of it all. Finally, he spoke. "You were right on one thing. It *is* quite a story."

"And all of it true," said Nigel, as if sensing Duncan's doubts.

"Well, I would hope so. And where, exactly, do things stand now?"

"Were you taking notes?" Nigel asked in a concerned tone.

"Of course. Otherwise, I might not credit what I've just heard."

"Well, just make sure you keep them in a safe place. And for God's sake not so much as a hint to Elsa."

"You're hardly in a position to presume to lecture me about being careful. So, to repeat my question, laddie, where exactly does it stand? When is all this going to break? I should say if it breaks."

"I can't answer that until Samantha Jameson meets her husband. Then we'll have to wait for his response. Whatever it is, the *Post* gets the story first."

Duncan was again silent for a moment, gathering his thoughts. Then came the questions, not about the story itself but about the *Post*'s role. "Why us? Why a British newspaper most Americans have never heard of? Or, for that matter, a British paper Americans *have* heard of. It doesn't make sense. Why not an American outlet? Why not the *Washington Post?*"

Nigel explained Samantha's rationale for picking London's *Post*. Even as he spoke, he found it as unconvincing as ever, and was certain that Duncan would too, although he remained as certain as he could be that there was no hidden agenda.

Duncan found it equally strange. "I'm at a loss what else to say. In all my years as a journalist, this may be the strangest situation I've ever been in. I'm not sure what to believe. Or more to the point, who to believe."

"You might start by believing me. I haven't made any of this up. I'm sharing with you what I've been told, and who told me. The president's wife and two senior White House officials. My sources are nothing if not copper-bottomed."

"One might even say gold-plated," Duncan conceded but sounding less impressed than miffed. "I just wish you'd taken me into your confidence from the start - especially at the point where you decided not to report one story in exchange for a bigger one. If this were to go pear-shaped, laddie, you'd have a lot to answer for. And at least then I'd have been better prepared for Lord Goodfriend. As it is, he must have left my office thinking I've no fucking idea what's going on. In this instance, he'd have been right." Nigel was disconcerted that Duncan seemed more concerned about appearing foolish in the proprietor's eyes than in the potential for putting the *Post* on the map with the scoop of the decade. "You're supposed to trust your editor, you know…" Duncan was saying.

Nigel apologized again. "As I said, I really was going to call you this morning, but I had to wait for permission from Samantha to bring you in on it. Frank Hoffman cleared it with her only last night. He's the White House press secretary."

"Yes, I know who he is, for God's sake. Look, I'm not complaining about not being told last night, I'm complaining that you didn't tell me right from the start, when it began to gather momentum." Having recovered from the shock of Nigel's revelations, Duncan was now in managing editor mode. "How, may I ask, is this whole thing supposed to be choreographed? And when does the balloon go up, or whatever clichéd metaphor you want to use?"

"It's a moveable feast, Duncan, but here's how it looks. To kick things off, I'll be filing a story in the next day or so about Frank Hoffman's resignation. That will also be a *Post* exclusive."

"A relatively minor one," Duncan sniffed.

"But a significant one, nevertheless. And the media here will be furious. I've already written the piece and I'll send it over shortly, probably today. Frank has already approved it."

"Oh, is Frank Hoffman your editor now? And here was I foolishly thinking it was me."

"Don't be daft. He was the source of the story, so the least I could do was make sure it struck the right tone."

"Maybe… why did he resign anyway? And I'm not referring to what the bullshit public version will say. What has he told you in private?"

"Nothing scandalous. He's just had enough. Can't stand his boss anymore. Can't go along with his policies. Says the White House is in chaos. We know that, of course. More to the point, he's always been a close friend of Samantha Jameson, and is even closer now. Naturally, the piece I've written won't mention any of that."

"What will it say, then?"

"The usual bullshit, as you called it. Who cares, anyway? The point is that it will break first in the *Post*."

"If Hoffman can't stand the man or his policies, why did he take the bloody job in the first place?"

"It seemed like a good idea at the time, is all he said. By the way, the president has no idea this is coming. That makes it an even better story."

"My taking this job also seemed like a good idea at the time," Duncan said sourly. "Now, I'm beginning to wonder. But never mind Frank Hoffman, he's just a supporting player. What about the main event? When's that likely to happen?"

"Samantha intends to confront her husband next week. In Florida. On the golf course, for security reasons. Says she'll tell him everything she knows. What happens after that depends entirely on how he reacts. Until we know that we can't prepare the story. We should write two versions: one that he's not going to run again, for reasons yet to be disclosed; the other that he and others have been caught with their hands in the cookie jar and that anything could happen."

"I know which one I'd prefer to write."

"You and me both… but that's out of our control."

"If she goes public," Duncan put in, managing to sound as skeptical as ever, "we won't have our exclusive."

"I don't know about that. The choreography gets a little trickier, it's true. An announcement that he won't run for a second term would be a less dramatic story than a full-blown scandal, but it's still one hell of a beat, wouldn't you say?"

"Yes, I'd have to say so," Duncan said, sounding as if he were making a concession. "What's the betting in your little group, your 'Gang of Five'… it sounds like an Enid Blyton story."

"That he'll cave."

"And they're confident of that?" The tone was still skeptical.

"No. His lawyers will muddy the waters, for sure. Who knows what kind of defence they'll come up with."

"I'm trying to think what their options are. What their legal obligations are. I don't come up with an immediate answer."

"That goes for all of us." From Duncan's responses, as studiously questioning as they were, Nigel sensed his editor was subtly shifting from incredulous to intrigued. "Whichever way it goes, it will be a *Post* exclusive. That's the clear understanding I have with Samantha."

"Oh, it's Samantha, is it? How very cozy! And you trust her to keep her word?"

"Yes."

"You have nothing in writing, of course..."

"How could there be?"

"True." Duncan switched back to incredulous. "This 'Gang of Five', it's quite a coterie of Shakespearian plotters, isn't it. I've never been a conspiracy theorist myself, but I may have to change my tune. Magic circle! Conspiracy! Blackmail! Frankly, it all sounds too far-fetched for my less than febrile imagination."

"Imagine how I felt when all this came up."

Duncan couldn't be bothered to think about that; he was too busy weighing up the odds of any of it happening, and what might go wrong. "Explain to me again exactly what happens if the president plays hardball, which, by the way, I'm guessing is the likeliest scenario. Who does she call first? The *Post*, or the SEC? I could see complications arising..."

"I can't answer that."

Duncan said nothing for a moment. Then he delivered his verdict, which was no verdict at all. "I need some time to think about all this. Frankly, I'm still trying to take it all in. From any other source, I'd be reluctant to believe a bloody word of it, but even you can't have been drunk for the entire three months you've been there."

The jibe hit home. "That's a low fucking blow, Duncan, even for you."

"Okay, okay, I withdraw the remark. And even I admit that your sources are... what was the phrase?"

"Gold-plated, I think we agreed."

"To be perfectly honest, I'm not quite sure what to do next," Duncan said. "I'm never comfortable with uncertainty, especially when I'm a mere bystander, relying on others, and in this case when they're three thousand miles away. Right now, I'm feeling distinctly surplus to requirements. It's not my favourite position."

Nigel replied crisply. "I think the answer is that you become *essential* to requirements. Get yourself involved by catching a plane to Washington. Right now. Help me put this story together. We don't know which one we'll be writing, or exactly when, but what I do know is that the *Post*'s managing editor deserves to be in the thick of it. How can you not be for such a momentous event?"

"Flattery will get you nowhere. You're one major pain in the arse. You've just told me a story that I'm still trying hard to swallow, and now you want to drag me into it. I'm guessing you want someone to blame if it goes wrong."

"Not at all, fuck you very much." Nigel was angry. "Here is precisely where you belong, in my considered opinion, but if I've got to 'drag you into it', as you put it, then don't fucking bother. I'll take care of everything and just keep you informed as best I can. But take a moment to think about it: do you want to be a helpless observer or an active participant? I know which I'd choose."

"Just as reporters must trust their editor, an editor must trust his reporters. But on this occasion, you're right - I should be there."

"Good. Now, get over here pronto. That's a request, by the way, not an order. You'll meet the players, including Samantha Jameson herself. Then you can make up your own mind about her - about everything. If you're still unhappy after that, you'll know what to do."

"Which will be, in a word, nothing."

"You're right, but as things stand - and knowing Samantha Jameson as I do - nothing seems to me the least likely outcome."

Duncan had no response to that. He switched from editor to executive. "First, I need to think about what to tell Lord Goodfriend. He won't be as tolerant of being blind-sided as I've been. And the old goat will be intensely curious if I suddenly take off for Washington."

Nigel was taken aback that yet again his managing editor's focus seemed to be more on handling the proprietor than the story. "I leave the corporate politics to you, Duncan. Frankly, I think they're peripheral. Also, please remember that I've taken a vow of silence, to which you are so far the only approved exception. If you tell His Lordship what's going on, he'll blab to his friends in high places. He wouldn't be able to help himself. The story will be round the world in minutes. Goodbye scoop."

"You make a good point. What do you suggest I tell him meanwhile?"

"For what it's worth, tell him nothing. Fill him in at the last possible moment, meaning just before we go to press. He won't know you've kept him in the dark. This was a breaking story, you'll explain, and it happens to be true."

"Agreed. You never cease to amaze me, Nigel Harper. Meanwhile, it sounds as though I'll be seeing you in the next day or so."

"Tomorrow. Please. This thing could..."

"Yes, yes, I know, break wide open at any time. Just how hot is it over there, by the way?"

"Are you referring to politics or the weather?"

"The weather."

"Hot as hell right now... but not as hot as this story."

"You've got that right, laddie - or at least I hope so. And if you're wrong, there'll be hell to pay - and even hotter in the place where we'd both end up."

* * *

Nigel met Sonny at Slattery's that afternoon but stayed only long enough to reaffirm with a straight face that he had nothing new to report. Then, after two beers, with an excuse that he was meeting Jane for dinner - which was true - he headed home. He stopped on the way to buy two bottles of wine. Jane hadn't called him since the meeting in Virginia, which he found surprising, especially as he had left her three voice messages. Instead of going straight to his own apartment, he went to hers. It was close to six by the time he got there. She would normally be home by now. He pushed the front door buzzer. She let him in without a word.

Immediately he noticed that she had been crying. Her eyes were red. Mascara had trickled down one cheek.

"What on earth's wrong?" He put a consoling arm around her shoulders, expecting to hear about a death in the family.

"I've been fired."

"Fired!?"

"Yes, fired. As in dismissed, sacked, terminated." She was beyond crying now. She was furious.

"What happened? The government doesn't fire people."

"This government does. It just fired me."

"For what reason?"

"Only one reason I can think of."

"I can't imagine what that would be."

"Try harder."

"Senator Curtis? You think so?"

"Who else, for God's sake? You think your meeting with him and my dismissal were pure coincidence?"

"No, I don't. What did they tell you?"

"I was called into the Deputy Secretary of State's office just before lunchtime. He told me that my work had been falling off lately. Also, he said, the Department was scaling back in accordance with the president's election pledge to trim down the Federal government. It's all nonsense, of course. The same man told me in London just weeks ago what a great job I'd been doing." Nigel remembered her telling him that at the now infamous London party.

"What are you going to do about it?"

"What can I do? I'm just a staffer, junior enough for them to get rid of me without generating bad headlines."

"You should call a lawyer. I'm not up with the rules over here, but surely you can't be fired without cause, least of all by the government. You're too young to play the age card, but you could play the feminist card."

Jane tried to make light of the situation, forcing a smile. "And spend a fortune on legal fees? You know what? For some time, I've been saying I needed a break. Now I've got one."

"A rather longer one than you'd anticipated." Nigel didn't mean to sound flippant, but Jane seemed oblivious. "I'm so sorry. This is all my fault."

"Yes, you could say that…" Her tone was unforgiving. "… and Samantha Jameson's."

"It's hardly her fault."

"Yes, it is. This whole thing began when you got yourself drawn into this mad scheme of hers. You seem very taken by the woman I've noticed."

"Don't tell me you're jealous."

"Hardly, given what we now know about her. Don't get me wrong: I like and admire the woman. I can even applaud what she's trying to do. But she does seem to be leading you and your associates, or whatever you call them, a merry dance. And what if it should all go horribly wrong? What then?"

"I think you're being unfair to her. It wasn't her that shot her mouth off at a cocktail party, it was me. I've apologized to her for that, and I now apologize to you. I was a fool."

"Oh, don't start that again. The self-flagellation scars have barely healed." Jane adopted a slightly more conciliatory tone. "Look, the fact is that dirty tricks are the stock-in-trade of this town. I'm not the first victim, and I won't be the last. What's done is done. But the fact remains that I'm now suddenly and unexpectedly out of work."

"The real villain here," Nigel said, ruminating, "isn't me, or Samantha Jameson. It's Senator William fucking Curtis. And I was the target, not you. You're just collateral damage. Next thing we know, I'll find myself being interviewed by the Department of Immigration and Naturalization, then put on a plane."

"I wouldn't put anything past him, but I think that's a stretch."

"I'm not so sure. If they can get at you, they can certainly get at me. Hell, I wonder if they bugged our phones." Getting no response, Nigel went to the kitchen to open one of the bottles. "Red or white?"

"Right now, I don't care."

He selected an expensive white and pulled a cork. "This has all come full circle, hasn't it. Marchetti reports our little spat to Martin Jameson; Jameson contacts Curtis; he makes a call to the Secretary of State; you're fired. By the way, Marchetti also contacted my proprietor. He in turn spoke to my editor. So, now we've suddenly got the White House, the United States Senate and the bloody House of Lords involved. Not to mention Wall Street. That's quite an accomplishment."

"Not one that I'd boast about."

"No. This thing is getting out of hand."

Jane shivered. "You could say that. And if you don't think it scares me, think again."

"That makes two of us, my beloved. Fran was right: she warned me not to underestimate these people. Speaking of Fran, have you told her yet?"

"No. And it's a duty I'd happily relinquish. She'll go off the deep end."

"She'll tell Samantha, of course, and perhaps that could help you find…"

"Samantha Jameson's help I can do without, thank you very much."

He filled two glasses almost to the brim. They started drinking without bothering to raise the customary toast. He gently guided Jane to the dining room table and sat her down, placed himself next to her. "Then what *are* you going to do find a job?"

Jane suddenly looked despondent again. "I've no idea. There won't be another one for me in government."

"There's the private sector…"

"How many employers in the private sector do you think need a Middle East analyst?"

"Oil companies, I would have thought."

"Possibly. But finding an organization in need of my peculiar talents will be a challenge. I'm not exactly a prize catch, you know. And who can tell how far Curtis's reach extends." Jane didn't seem too keen to pursue that line of thought any further. "Thanks for the wine, by the way."

"Call it a peace offering..."

"... from my own kitchen, very generous of you."

"What do you say we stay home tonight? Get rat-arsed. Or spend all night fucking? Or both..."

Jane managed to laugh. "All night, huh? The last time you said that you were asleep before midnight."

"Are you impugning my manhood?"

"No, your capacity for alcohol... but let's not go there."

Now it was Nigel's turn to laugh. "Still, it was worth the old college try."

Nigel kissed her, holding her close. She submitted easily enough but without enthusiasm. It had been a trying day, one that would reshape the rest of her life. Sex was the last thing on her mind.

Nigel, sensing it, pulled away.

"I'm sorry," Jane said, "but losing one's job tends to be something of a passion-killer."

"Oh, I nearly forgot to tell you," Nigel said, changing the subject. "Duncan Erskine, my managing editor is coming over. He's going to be joining our little group."

"How very nice for both of you," Jane said, not much caring.

Nigel tried another tack. "Meanwhile, let's decide before anything else whether we're hungry or horny."

"To be honest, I'm neither."

"Then let's stay in and watch television. I think an old black and white film is called for. We both need to empty our heads."

"Not *Brief Encounter*," she joked mirthlessly.

* * *

Duncan was just preparing to leave the office when he caught sight of a caption on the television in his office, tuned as usual to BBC news. He turned the sound up. "Hey, Elsa, come on in and listen to this." Elsa stood next to him and watched the screen. Ivan Brand was the commentator. *"... and the press secretary's rumoured resignation, as reported today in a London newspaper, the* Morning Post, *but not yet confirmed by the White House, is the latest in a series of departures from this administration. We are expecting a formal statement shortly. Meanwhile, there had been no prior indication that Mr Hoffman's resignation was imminent, but American political observers haven't been short of speculation, ranging from his failure to endorse the president's social programme with sufficient enthusiasm to reports that..."*

"I'm so glad they mentioned the *Post*," Elsa said, beaming with pride. "Good old Nigel."

Duncan was grinning, too. "Yes, good old Nigel indeed. Brilliant publicity. Your friend has finally earned his keep. I told you he'd start making things happen..."

Elsa snorted. "That wasn't what you were saying a week ago. 'What on earth is he doing over there?' you were asking. Speaking of Washington, I think you should get going. You know how the traffic can be getting through Knightsbridge."

Duncan felt a strange reluctance to tear himself away from the television.

"... and yesterday's briefing was conducted by Mr Hoffman's deputy, who declined to comment on the Post *story, or answer reporters' questions. So, the mystery remains: did Mr Hoffman resign or was he pushed...?'*

"You're right, I'd better be off," said Duncan, leaving Mr Brand to his speculations. "Keep the place going while I'm gone," he instructed Elsa. In the interest of office decorum, they shook hands.

"Well, if you can't give *me* a hug," Elsa said, "at least give Nigel a big one from me." But he was already halfway across the newsroom and didn't hear her.

Nigel was shaving when Duncan called from the car. "I'm on my way, laddie. You certainly scored a direct hit with the Hoffman story." He sounded exultant. "The British media have jumped all over it. Everyone covered their backs by attributing it to the *Post*. I'm surprised the story got so much play over here. What are the Americans saying? I bet they're still wondering how they were scooped by a British paper."

Nigel replied with becoming modesty. "Look, this is no big deal compared with some other stories I could mention. He's just the press secretary. He'll be replaced by tomorrow, if he hasn't been already."

"Yes, but *he's* not the story. The real story is the relentless march of White House defections. There was his third chief of staff a few weeks ago; his national security adviser last month; and before that the chief counsel, his fourth in two years. It's abundantly clear that no one with an independent streak survives for long in this White House. That's the story. Have you seen Hoffman since it broke?"

"No, he's gone to ground, as he said he would, but the story's just been confirmed."

"By whom?"

"A reporter I know just called to tell me that Frank's resignation letter has gone in. Security guards have already escorted him off the premises. Jameson's a vindictive bastard. We can ask Frank what happened when you get here. Until then, I'll file a story on his formal departure. While I've got you, have you by chance spoken to Lord Goodfriend?"

"I called to tell him that I was going to Washington without telling him why. Gave him some cock-and-bull story about organizing coverage for the primary season. He seemed to buy it."

"Did he happen to mention the Marchetti incident again?"

"No. He's probably forgotten about it."

"I doubt that. But right now, he may be too busy cavorting with that French mistress of his. I know I would be. Where are you now, by the way?"

"In a taxi on Cromwell Road. The traffic's a nightmare, as Elsa would say, but I left a margin for mishaps. By the way, you needn't meet me at the airport."

Nigel had not thought of doing so but said, "Of course I'll be there. Even managing editors are due some measure of respect."

"Not that I've noticed..."

"I've booked us a table for dinner tonight. It won't match up to the Savoy Grill, but apart from the ghastly Wild West décor I think you'll like it."

"Wild West décor! In Washington! What's it called?"

"The *Happy Heifer*. It's a steak house. Graham Welbeck, of all people, introduced me to it."

"Do I have to wear a Stetson? I don't have one."

"Now, you in a Stetson I would pay to see. Just don't wear a deerstalker, or a tam-o'-shanter."

"What else are you getting me into?"

"A giant rib-eye steak to start with. After that, time will tell. Is there anything else?"

"No, I'll see you in twelve hours, or whatever."

"Have a good flight."

"It'll give me a chance to do some research on what first ladies have got up to through the ages."

"Good idea. I've been doing a little research myself. We'll compare notes over dinner."

"I'm looking forward to it… I think."

"It'll be a blast," Nigel said, adding, "one way or the other."

* * * * *

Chapter 18

In the crowded arrivals hall at Dulles International, Nigel waited for Duncan with diminishing patience and rising concern. Why was it that whenever he met someone at an airport, they were always among the last to come through? His anxiety was heightened by seeing dozens of arriving passengers streaming past him with British Airways tags on their luggage. Could there be another BA flight? He checked the arrivals display board, but it showed only one. So, where the hell could the idiot have got to?

Nigel's imagination started to get the better of him. Could Duncan have been bundled off to some stark windowless office in the bowels of the terminal to be interrogated by agents about his reasons for entering the United States? The name 'Curtis' kept popping into his head. Was it possible that the senator had somehow learned that Duncan was coming and put in a telephone call to stop him entering the country? The notion was absurd, Nigel concluded. Or was it? Curtis had already demonstrated to Nigel's satisfaction that the Arizona senator had a long reach, so perhaps the idea was not so far-fetched. Standing in plain sight, he suddenly felt vulnerable. He edged behind a pillar, a vantage point from which he could scan the terminal for sinister-looking men in suits with bulges in their pockets without being spotted himself. The idea that he could hide in an airport arrivals hall was absurd, but lurking made him feel better all the same.

Finally, to his immense relief, he spotted Duncan, a lone gawky figure in a crumpled tan suit that looked as if it hadn't seen action since college days. Nigel waved, but Duncan, distracted, ignored him, and would have walked straight past if Nigel had not dashed over and grabbed his arm.

"Oh, hello," Duncan said absently. "I was lost in thought. Sorry to keep you waiting. As usual, my bag was the last one to come out. Happens to me all the time."

"I'm mighty relieved," Nigel said, and meant it. "For a moment I was starting to think the worst."

"I had to wait forty minutes for my bag. I was the only passenger left at the carousel. I was about to report it as lost. And then I had to stand in line for half an hour to have my passport checked. Then, to cap everything, an officious customs man made me open my bag and took everything out. That took another twenty minutes."

"Don't laugh, but I was starting to think you'd been escorted off somewhere to be interrogated."

"Interrogated! What an extraordinary idea. For what reason?"

"I don't know... as a warning."

"That sounds altogether too dramatic to merit a serious response. Warning? What is it I'm supposed to have done?"

"Associated with me, for a start."

"Dear God, you've become a paranoiac."

"Have I? These things have been known to happen - people being grabbed, classified as undesirable, put on the next flight back to wherever they came from."

Duncan scoffed at the idea. "You're in a country where conspiracy theory is now a cottage industry, but it grieves me that you've apparently joined it."

"Laugh all you like," Nigel said solemnly, "but recent events have really rattled my cage."

"I can see that." Duncan held out both hands. "Look, no handcuffs. We're free to go."

"Then let's get the hell out of here - and the sooner the better."

Nigel led his managing editor out to the taxi rank, looking nervously from left to right.

Duncan noticed. "My God, they really have got to you, haven't they? This is the United States; people don't just disappear, never to be seen again. It happens in Bruce Willis movies, but not in real life."

"I'm not so sure. The situation in which I find myself has become something of a personal ordeal, I don't mind telling you."

"Evidently," said Duncan, unsympathetically. He relented a little when Nigel told him about Jane's abrupt dismissal.

"That," Nigel offered, "was no coincidence."

"Well, tell me more about it later. Meanwhile, I appreciate your taking the trouble to meet me, laddie. Are you well... other than suffering from an acute case of paranoia?"

Nigel laughed mirthlessly. "Physically, never been better. Mentally, never been worse. You may think I'm being neurotic, but we face some testing and possibly dangerous days ahead."

"Dangerous?"

"Yes, dangerous. When powerful people smell rats, it's not usually good news for the rats."

"You're being melodramatic again," Duncan said sharply. "It doesn't become you, laddie. This isn't the cynical, hard-bitten newsman I know... or thought I knew. You need to get a grip. If what you say is going to happen in the next day or so really does happen - and forgive me if I still have my doubts - then we'll need to maintain our critical faculties in good working order. Panic attacks won't help us make objective judgements."

"I'm not the first to suffer. You read *All the President's Men,* perhaps even saw the film."

"Both, as it happens. Why?"

"You remember the scene in the film where Bob Woodward meets 'Deep Throat' in an underground parking lot?"

"Yes, of course."

"Then you'll recall that when Woodward leaves the parking lot, he's convinced he's being followed. It's dark, the streets are deserted, and he breaks into a trot, while the creepy soundtrack music winds us up. Well, I've been getting that same queasy feeling. I've relived that scene several times in the past few days - sleeping and waking."

Duncan was ready with a rebuttal. "But you'll also recall that Woodward wasn't being followed. Or watched. Not then, or at any other time. It was all in his imagination. In other words, he succumbed to the same paranoia that you're now exhibiting."

If Duncan had meant to sound reassuring, Nigel's look told him he had failed.

Meanwhile, Nigel had hailed a taxi. He directed the driver to the Hotel Washington, where he had booked Duncan a room. The solid old Beaux-Arts edifice, within hailing distance of the White House, had once been a popular rendezvous for politicians and lobbyists but in recent years, despite an extensive refurbishment, had fallen out of favour with the Beltway crowd and was now more favoured by tourists than Washington insiders.

"A bit pricey, isn't it?" Duncan observed, as vigilant as ever about preserving Lord Goodfriend's profit margins. "Somewhere more modest would have been just fine."

Nigel smiled. "I could have put you in the Capitol, where I first stayed, but then I wouldn't have heard the last of it. Anyway, by this time next week, provided everything goes according to plan, no one will be pestering you about your expenses."

"From your mouth to God's ears, as my Jewish friends would say. Speaking of the plan, what's the order of business?"

Nigel glanced at the driver in the mirror, before raising a finger to his lips. "We can't be too careful." Duncan rolled his eyes. "We'll chat about it over dinner this evening. Tomorrow, or within the next day or so, we'll head out to Frank's place in Maryland. You'll get to meet him and Fran... and in due course the lady in question. I imagine we'll be holed up there for a couple of nights while we develop a strategy for handling the story. Or stories."

"Or wonder why we embarked on this venture in the first place."

"O, ye of little faith."

"I practise my faith in the kirk, not in the newsroom. Where will the lady in question be in the meantime?"

"She'll be down in Florida, with you-know-who and, one way or another, making history."

"Or making a fool of herself."

"I don't think so. If she means business, as I'm firmly convinced that she does, then something will have to give. Either way, we'll get our story."

"And if nothing happens? What if he resists and she folds?"

"Then I'll look like an idiot, you'll have had a wasted trip, and you'll have to decide whether I should be fired or committed to an institution for the insane. But I'd say the prospect of nothing happening down there is unlikely."

"We shall see." Duncan pursed his lips, to convey doubt, and then fell into silent contemplation, as did his backseat companion.

Having just spent nine hours at 35,000 feet going over the situation, covering the entire range of possible outcomes, some of them barely plausible, Duncan still nursed certain misgivings about the whole enterprise. Nothing about it, including the potential immensity of the outcome, matched anything he had ever experienced in his career as a journalist. For a start, everything was far too dependent on the actions of a woman about whom he knew precious little, and the reactions of a man he knew to be entirely driven by ego, and it occurred to him that one of them, and perhaps both, might be deranged. All that aside, Nigel's display of nerves had unsettled him. Gazing out the window as the drab Washington suburbs slid by, he began to question his own state of mind. Were his doubts about the story those of a trained newsman, or merely a manifestation of stage fright? Given what was at stake, he was forced to admit that he and Nigel could be putting themselves at risk, but what kind of risk he was unable to define. The potential for embarrassment was clear, but was there also - as Nigel seemed convinced - something much sinister at play? To that question he had no answer. Men of significant power rarely relinquished it without a fight, as any reading of history could testify, and in this case the chief protagonist, in addition to being patently unstable, had demonstrated disturbing signs of an authoritarian mindset. Perhaps, then, he had been unduly dismissive of his colleague's angst. He preferred, though, to take a coldly professional view, that of a journalist who had a duty of care to question everything about the story. Any story. The reality was that Duncan, in approaching this editorial adventure, was a man caught in two minds, neither of which provided convenient answers.

During the long airborne hours, he had read up on a history of first ladies, trying to find an instance of one determined to destroy her husband's presidency. As he had suspected, he found nothing remotely close to what Samantha Jameson was contemplating. Most of them had been dutiful wives. Some had, behind the scenes, nagged and hectored their husbands to influence policy, and so relentlessly that, if their influence been publicly known, they might have earned recognition as co-presidents. Eleanor Roosevelt and Nancy Reagan were frequently cited as typical examples. Neither of them, though, would have dreamt of sabotaging their husband's reputation, much less of ending his presidency. Jackie Kennedy could have chosen to demolish her husband's carefully cultivated Camelot myth by exposing his serial philandering, but she adored him too much for that, and so, under Papa Joe Kennedy's baleful influence - or, as some claimed, the lure of the family fortune - she kept her counsel and had come to be admired for it. All of which put Samantha Jameson in a category of her own. Could she pull it off, this mad scheme of hers to unseat a president, and without revealing the reason?

Duncan had certain reservations about the purity of her motive, but never having met the woman, or indeed read much about her, he was in no position to make a character judgement. Her husband was a different matter. His character was all too plain to see, on display every day on page and screen, analyzed to monotonous excess by pundits and psychologists. She might be resolute - and he was prepared to concede that her motives were worthy - but no one would calculate that he was the kind of man to be driven from office without a struggle, whatever the cost. President Jameson had at his disposal the considerable power of his office, the entire apparatus of government, and an army of clever lawyers who owed their living to him. On the other hand, Duncan felt obliged to admit, his will might be drastically diluted in the face of evidence that might send him to prison. The vital lacuna in weighing the merits of her charges, and his likely reaction to them, was that he, Duncan, had yet to see any evidence to corroborate them. Neither, apparently, had Nigel. This worried him above all else. He broke his silence to raise that very question when the White House came into view.

"Ah, the wolf's lair," cried Nigel, pointing to the familiar building ahead of them. Then, in a hushed tone, almost a whisper, he said, "To answer your question, I haven't seen any documents. The lady in question" - another glance in the driver's mirror - "has pretty much outlined what's in them, and I find no reason not to believe her. I can't imagine she's making this whole thing up."

"Unless," Duncan replied, "she has an agenda that we don't know about. Where are these documents, anyway?"

"Locked in a safe deposit box at her bank, she told me. By now, though, her lawyer may have them. He'll be covered by client privilege."

"Very convenient. But it would be a good sign if her lawyer had them."

"Oh, why is that?"

"Because while she might deceive her friends, or even journalists like us, she wouldn't lie to her lawyer. Who is her lawyer, anyway?"

"I've no idea, but she says he's the best there is."

"He'll need to be, is all I can say."

"Look, Duncan, she's under no illusion about the magnitude of what she's about to do, or about the personal consequences if she gets it wrong. She's been... ah, we're here."

The taxi had pulled up to the curb directly outside the hotel entrance. Nigel paid the driver and was about to open the door when he spotted two men, one of whom was the last person in town he would wish to run into. Senator William Curtis had just emerged from the lobby with a man of similar age and bearing, who on closer inspection became identifiable as Pitman, the senator whom Nigel had met on his first day in town. Graham Welbeck's friend. Nigel ducked back into the taxi and closed the door. Duncan, already halfway out on the other side, was hauled back in by a tug on his jacket, banging is head on the door frame.

"Damn. That hurt. What on earth are you doing?"

"See those two men over there?" Nigel pointed at them. "The taller one is Senator William Curtis. I've told you about him. The other is Charles Pitman, the senator from New Mexico. I've met him just once. I don't want to meet either of them, and if we get out of the cab right now that's exactly what will happen."

Annoyingly, the two senators had stopped for a chat. Neither of them looked happy. Both were clearly animated. Curtis was gesticulating angrily. Their discussion went on in this vein for several minutes.

Duncan peered at them through the window. "So that's Curtis. You're right, he's a slick-looking devil. They both are."

The taxi driver turned impatiently to face his passengers. "Are you guys planning to stay here for the rest of the afternoon? I turned the meter off. Sitting here is costing me money."

"Give us a minute or two," Nigel commanded. "Meanwhile, you can put the meter back on."

Several minutes later, Curtis and Pitman finished their conversation and strode off in opposite directions. Nigel waited until they were a safe distance away and then paid the driver, adding a generous tip.

As they got out of the taxi, Duncan said, "My God, you weren't kidding, this really is like some television thriller. And I thought you said politicians didn't frequent this hotel anymore."

"Well, obviously I was misinformed. We'll just have to be careful."

"How are we supposed to do that? Wear Groucho Marx face masks?"

Nigel had no answer. Compensating for bumping Duncan's head, he carried his editor's solitary piece of luggage, which was surprisingly light and compact. "Not planning on staying long, then."

"For as long as it takes." As well as his bag, Duncan's tone suggested that he thought this would not be very long at all.

At the reception desk, Nigel suggested that Duncan head upstairs, freshen up, and then meet him in the lobby bar.

"Give me half an hour," Duncan said. "I still stink of aircraft. I'd like to take a shower and change."

After watching his managing editor enter the elevator, Nigel wandered over to the bar. Before entering, he checked out the other patrons. They all seemed to be tourists. He took a stool at the bar. The place was busy but far from crowded.

Duncan came down thirty minutes later, as promised. He had changed into dress slacks and a polo shirt with a dragon-like logo on the chest, maybe the Loch Ness monster, Nigel thought. He had never seen his managing editor, normally a stickler for appearance, dressed so casually. He looked like a tourist himself, which was no bad thing, all the better in the cause of anonymity. Nigel had thought about taking him to Slattery's, but that would have risked running into Sonny and their exposure to relentless questioning. Besides, Duncan was fastidious to a fault about what he drank and where he drank it and Slattery's would have failed the test on both counts. They took a small window table from where they could see the hotel entrance. Duncan, sensing that Nigel was even more nervous now, mentioned it in a tone laced with sarcasm. "Should we be seen in public like this? I mean, you've already spotted one of our supposed protagonists. There could be more. Wouldn't we be safer talking in my room? Of course, you'd probably claim it was bugged."

Even as he said it, he took the precaution of looking round the bar, as if half expecting to see a man pretending to read a newspaper, as they did in the movies. Paranoia, apparently, was contagious. As it happened, there *was* a man across the bar reading a newspaper, but he seemed to be making no attempt to peer over the top of it.

"I'm not sure we're safe anywhere," said Nigel, somewhat dramatically. "But then I suppose if they're determined to find us, find us they will. There's nothing to be done about it. We can't skulk in the shadows."

Duncan didn't bother to ask who the 'they' might be. "So, where exactly are we in this... situation, or whatever we're calling it?" He spoke in a voice low enough that Nigel had to lean across the table to hear him.

"The situation is that our lady will be confronting her husband tomorrow. In Florida. Out on the golf course, for security reasons." *'Our lady,'* he mused, sounded vaguely religious, like Our Lady of Sorrows. This one would need to perform a miracle as well, he thought, extending the analogy beyond its useful life. "What happens after that, your guess is as good as mine. You enjoy a flutter on the horses, Duncan, for all your Presbyterian impulses. So, tell me this: which horse do you fancy in the three o'clock."

Three o'clock was the appointed hour of Samantha's golf course showdown.

"Well, since we're in the racing vernacular, I fancy the man will pip the woman at the post."

"Why?"

"Because, and let's drop the racing analogies, he's going to react badly. What else can he do? No one likes to be blackmailed, least of all by his own spouse. And who gives up the most powerful position in the Free World without a fight? Certainly not this man. He'll find a way to retain power and discredit her, you mark my words."

"Nixon resigned when he was found out."

"But only when he realized the game was up. By then his impeachment was all but inevitable. Up to that point, he'd fought back right to the end. He had nothing left. And by then, of course, he'd secured the promise of a presidential pardon from his designated successor."

"She isn't demanding that he resign, remember, just that he declines to run again. That's a big difference. I know which decision I'd take if I were facing the prospect of a lifetime in the slammer."

"A lifetime?"

"Well, thirty or forty years. Some Wall Street crooks have been given that kind of sentence. Over here they treat financial crimes more seriously than murder. Swindling people out of their hard-earned savings is a bigger threat to the capitalist system than some idiot chopping his wife up."

Duncan, like one of those sniffer dogs he had just seen at the airport, returned to the matter of the evidence. "Until I see something in print, I'm not making any judgements. For a start, those mysterious documents I've heard so much about... alleged documents. Who's the source, anyway?"

"I don't know. We'll ask. And we'll ask to see them."

"Believe me, I'll be demanding to see them, not asking. How can we proceed without seeing them?"

"Why does it matter? If the president announces he won't run again, we'll know that the evidence was real, even if we haven't seen it with our own eyes."

"True enough. But I'd want to see them anyway. And, by the way, I'm not sure a decision not to run would warrant my presence here. Now, if she were to blow the whistle, and all hell broke loose, that would be an entirely different matter."

"But since we can't predict which way it will go, let's just call your presence here a judicious precaution. And either way, it's still one hell of a story. You'll be on hand when history is made. You'll be a part of it, think of it that way."

Duncan went quiet, obviously thinking of other questions. "This is out of nowhere, but I've just thought of something: if she *were* to blow the whistle, could he pardon himself? My understanding is that, under the constitution, he has the power to do that. Nixon thought about doing it, I seem to remember reading."

"Can Jameson do that even if he's under criminal investigation?"

"Well, I'm no expert in American constitutional matters, so I can't answer that. But what if he could?"

"It would be an admission of guilt."

"He wouldn't have to specify why he's doing it. It could be a blanket pardon, covering all crimes and misdemeanours committed while in office. At least that's my understanding."

"You may be right, I don't know either, but it would arouse great public curiosity. The media would immediately go on a scavenger hunt. Congress, too. And sooner or later, someone just might dig up the truth. And his wife might just be pissed off enough to save them all the trouble, which would produce the result she wants anyway, by costing him the next election."

"You make a good point, laddie."

Nigel always found it hard to work out what Duncan was thinking behind the droll manner, the public display of diffidence, the apparent pendular swings in viewpoint from one utterance to the next. "Whatever happens," he said, "think about the impact. You could start with the change in the political landscape. The presidential election - every election - would be thrown into doubt. New figures would emerge from both sides of the aisle to take his place; there might be a complete reversal of Jameson's policies; and think about the impact of a change in American leadership on the rest of the world... the list goes on. Whatever story we end up writing, the short one or the long one, the consequences will keep people talking for weeks. And think of the personal glory. I know you're a man who shuns the limelight, but you'll be a media hero. Editor of the Year, for sure. Lord Goodfriend would be so thrilled that you might even finish up running the whole company. God knows, his kids couldn't."

"The glory will be yours, not mine," said Duncan. He grinned. "Boy, I've underestimated you, Nigel Harper. Your reputation for ruthless ambition is apparently well deserved. And for you, there's also that personal angle, isn't there, I mean bringing down Mr Marchetti and poking a stick in your ex-wife's eye."

"The personal stuff has nothing to do with it," Nigel protested, but not too strongly. "As much as I dislike what they stand for, I'm thinking of the kids. I wouldn't want them to be embarrassed by watching television and seeing their father in handcuffs. As for the accolades, what self-respecting journalist doesn't like to bask in the admiration of his peers?"

"*Direach a 'tarraing asda*," said Duncan, mystifyingly. "That, laddie, is Scottish Gaelic for 'just kidding'. In other words, I'm just winding you up."

"Well, I wouldn't want you to break a lifetime habit."

"Seriously, though, if any of this happens, you'll have done a remarkable job. You're just months into the job and here you are hobnobbing with the first lady and two senior White House officials like old primary school pals and pissing off senior senators." He sat back in his seat with a self-congratulatory grin. "It just goes to show that my instincts were right: you *are* the man for the job."

"Ah, so you *are* preparing to take credit," said Nigel, paying him back in kind. "Now that's more the Duncan I know."

"Or think you know. I still say the real Duncan is someone who ought to have had more sense than getting himself into a situation like this."

"I can't keep up with your mood swings, Duncan. You're something of a schizophrenic. One minute you're ready to take the next plane home, and then you're ready to reel in the scoop of the year. One minute, I'm an idiot, the next I'm a hero. Make up your fucking mind."

Duncan had to concede the point and did so with a swaying head movement and a sheepish grin. "Touché, my friend."

Nigel patted his hand. "Want my prediction? This time next week, as a change from editing your words, you'll be eating them. Until then, getting down to present logistics - and since jet lag will soon be catching up with you - I've made an early reservation for dinner. Why don't we get the hell out of here now, stop by the office for half an hour, just to show the flag, and then head over to the *Happy Heifer*."

"You're in sole charge of this expedition. I can only follow your lead… God help me."

"He's one of my high-level contacts, too, you know."

"I can well believe it."

Suddenly Nigel looked perplexed. "I've just realized that Pitman might show up there. He's apparently a regular. That's where I first met him, introduced by Graham Welbeck, of all people."

"If that worries you, then we can go somewhere else."

For a moment, Nigel thought about doing just that, but quickly decided the risk was worth taking. "Fuck it. And what if we *do* meet him? I can handle it. And if what I think is going to happen really does happen, he's the one who ought to be skulking in the shadows."

"Well said," cried Duncan, apparently re-invigorated. "So, let's go out and face the enemy head on."

* * *

After dinner, Nigel hailed a taxi and dropped Duncan off at his hotel. "Let's meet at the office at nine," he suggested.

Duncan agreed. He was so tired he would have agreed to anything, and the Happy Heifer, as expected, had not been to his taste; he had not so much eaten a steak so much as wrestled it to the ground.

Nigel continued his journey to Georgetown, directing the driver to Jane's address.

On the way, he fell to thinking about their domestic arrangement. He was these days spending more time in her flat, and her bed, than in his own, and more of his clothes now hung in her closet than in his. Perhaps he would bring up that point this very evening, with a view to changing the inconvenience of living in two locations to the convenience of living in one. It would also eliminate a considerable expense, something worth considering now that she was unemployed. Moving in together made perfect sense to him, and for more reasons than those of economy. He suddenly remembered what his father had once told him when he mentioned that he was moving in with Sarah in order to save paying double rent. "Companies merge, Nigel, but people marry."

How Jane would respond to a 'merger' proposal he hardly dared to guess. For a start, she placed great value on her independence. He braced himself for the prospect of being turned down. And while their relationship had grown into something more than mere friendship, how much more he was hard pressed to say. Was he in love with the girl? He supposed so. But was she in love with him? He thought so. But the word 'love' in his mind lacked adequate definition and in others had always aroused his suspicion. He thought of Prince Charles' now infamous phrase: "Whatever that means." The word was swarmed about with sentimental baggage, largely inflicted by poets, and of late by pop singers. It triggered his retrospective ambivalence about his early days with Sarah. They had fallen in love in a brilliant flash of ardour, but then fallen out of it in a sordid unravelling. Now they despised each other. Could such a thing happen again? Or, would this new relationship, to quote his favourite American author, "forever wed his unutterable visions to her perishable breath"? He had no answer. For now, forever would have to wait. He knew that he wished to spend as much time with her as possible. And she, as far as he could tell, felt the same way. Not that they had ever even alluded to the matter, much less discussed it.

Any hopes of discussing their future living arrangements were dashed when he reached Jane's, as Fran, not Jane, opened the door. *Damn the woman! She has an uncanny knack of showing up at the wrong times.*

"Why hello," he lied cheerily, "what a pleasant surprise."

Fran, always astute in matters of the heart, if not always her own, immediately assumed the role of a guest who had outstayed their welcome. "Don't worry, Nigel, I'll be leaving soon. Hello yourself, by the way."

"Don't leave on my behalf," he said, hoping she would do exactly that.

Jane appeared, greeting him with a hug and a kiss, accompanied by an apologetic rolling of eyes. Observing their show of spontaneous affection, Fran adopted her den-mother look. "I can't tell you how happy I am to see you two so contented, so much in effortless harmony with each other. It's a beautiful thing to behold, let me tell you."

"That's rich coming from you," Jane said. "Why, only a couple of weeks ago, sitting on this very sofa, you were telling me not to rush into things." Nigel shot Fran a look that asked, '*Whose side are you on anyway?*' He knew the answer, of course.

Fran looked more aggrieved than embarrassed. "I don't remember saying any such thing. Anyway, girl, much water has flowed under the bridge since then… as is plain to see." As she said it, her grin extended from ear to ear.

But Jane was in no mood to let her off the hook. "Let me remind you, Miss Powell, what you were saying just a few weeks back. You described Nigel as an 'unknown quantity' and that was the mildest of your descriptions. 'I like him,' you said, 'but I don't know him, and nor do you.' That's what you said."

Fran turned to face Nigel with an indignant expression. "I've simply no recollection of saying any such thing." Then, turning to Jane, and speaking as if Nigel wasn't there, as adults sometimes do when speaking of their children, she said, "Since then, he's kind of grown on me - as, quite clearly, he has on you. You two have become genuine soul mates."

"Whereas, Fran, you and I may soon be cell mates," Nigel quipped, rather pleased with his riposte.

"More likely you'll be deported."

"Don't even mention the word. It has been on my mind ever since the Curtis meeting."

"There is, of course, one obvious way round the problem, Nigel," Fran said with a coquettish look.

"Oh, and what would that be?"

"Marry the girl, of course. Then you'd be sure to qualify for an American passport. No more deportation worries."

Jane, flustered, and more than a little irritated, broke in. "I think this conversation has gone quite far enough. At the risk of sounding rude, Nigel will decide when or if to ask me, and my response would be based on a great many factors, none of which, I should stress, would include helping him become an American citizen."

But Fran was now in full flow. "At least you two might consider moving in together, especially now that one of you is unemployed. And all this running back and forth to each other's apartment must be getting tedious. I can't help but notice, looking around, that Nigel's stuff is everywhere. I see two toothbrushes on the bathroom shelf, not to mention the after-shave."

'Good for Fran,' Nigel was now thinking in a sudden change of heart. *'She's done half my job for me.'* "We haven't even discussed it," he said, "and with the greatest respect, it's not something I want to talk about in front of you, or, anyone else for that matter."

Jane nodded to confirm that she shared the sentiment.

Fran, her matchmaking done, her welcome overstayed, reached for her duffel bag. "Now, having stirred the simmering pot, I'll take my leave of you." No voices were raised in objection, she noted. At the door she turned to address Nigel. "I nearly forgot to ask. Did your editor chap, Jock whatever-his-name is, arrive safely?"

"Duncan. Yes, he's here, and happily ensconced in the Hotel Washington. He's probably fast asleep, or perhaps busy writing alternative leads for stories yet to come. For some strange reason he's looking forward to meeting you, Fran."

"Well, there could only be one reason - you've told him what an intelligent and engaging person I am." And then, with a blown kiss to them both, she left, gently closing the door behind her.

Jane turned to Nigel with an apologetic look. "I'm sorry about that."

"About what?"

"All that stuff about you and me… how I doubted that you were good enough for me… all that talk about us moving in together. I want you to know that I didn't put her up it."

"I believe you."

"I could stir a few pots of my own… the things I could tell you about my friend."

Nigel coughed nervously. "But since the subject *has* come up…"

"Which one?"

"Our moving in together. That woman must be a witch. Coming over here, I was thinking of raising that very subject. And I promise you, scout's honour" - he gave Baden-Powell's three fingered salute - "that she and I have never discussed it either."

"I believe you, too," said Jane, saying nothing further, waiting for Nigel to continue the discussion, or, as she expected, change the subject.

He continued the discussion. "Look," he said, suddenly looking slightly uncomfortable, "I'm not pushing you for an answer right now. We don't even have to talk about it if you'd prefer not to… but maybe it is something to think about. Cards on the table? I happen to think it's a good idea."

Jane sat down on the sofa. She looked, Nigel thought, rather pensive, almost nervous. He placed himself next to her. "What are you thinking right now… first reaction?"

She spoke softly and evenly. "My reaction is that she may be right. We do seem to get along well, and you do seem to spend more time here than at your place." She broke off, thinking about what to say next. "And while economy is a secondary issue, I do suddenly find myself without the means to support myself. Mind you, I'm not in immediate financial distress. I have a little something put aside from a trust fund. An old aunt of mine…"

Look, I don't want to pressure you. God knows we've got plenty to think about."

She said, "This place would be a bit cramped for two people. We'd need something bigger."

Nigel perked up. "Do I take that as a provisional 'yes'."

"A provisional yes to what?"

"Moving in together. So far, the only objection you've raised is the size of the apartment. If we get a bigger one, that goes away. Are there other factors you'd want to think about?"

Jane laughed. "Only one that I can think of... your slovenly domestic habits. You seem to like living in disorder. I don't."

"I can change. And I'm pretty handy with a vacuum cleaner."

"Then I suppose we ought at least to thank my friend for breaking the ice." Jane suddenly looked sheepish. "And I've a confession to make."

Nigel feared what was coming. "Oh, what's that?"

"I've already spoken to my landlord. It just so happens he's got a two-bedroom apartment, similar to this one, coming up next month. It's just two blocks from here."

"That can only mean one thing," Nigel replied, relieved. "This was meant to happen."

"I don't know about that... which doesn't mean it shouldn't happen."

"So, it seems we have a deal."

"Not if you're going to make it sound like a business transaction."

"I'm sorry. That's the last thing I'd call it."

They embraced warmly, though rather perfunctorily, as a long-married couple might. Reserve seemed more appropriate to the occasion than unrestrained joy. In Jane's case, it was because she didn't want to give the impression that their moving in together was something she had been desperate to achieve... but also because she had flour on her apron. "I was baking an apple pie," she explained.

Nigel could now hardly contain himself, flour or no flour. "This, darling, calls for a celebration." He went to the kitchen to open a bottle of red wine. While opening it, he reverted to practical matters. "There's a small question of the unexpired time left on our respective leases," he said, pouring two glasses of an expensive champagne instead, which was much more appropriate to the occasion.

"My landlord says it won't be a problem."

"You've already talked to him about that, too?"

"Just this morning, as a matter of fact."

"Well, you've obviously been thinking this through. And here I was concerned that I'd have to use all my renowned wiles and charms to talk you into it. You're something of a dark horse."

"Actually, in case you hadn't noticed, I'm not that dark, and I'm certainly not a horse."

Laughing, they sealed the deal with another kiss, this one more passionate than the last. Jane, Nigel was pleased to notice, had shed a small tear.

* * *

"Congratulations are in order," Nigel declared the following morning, over breakfast with Duncan at the hotel. He told him his news. Duncan looked slightly disappointed; he had expected something quite different.

"Well, well," he said. "You're full of surprises these days. And when am I going to meet this gorgeous creature of yours, as I've no doubt she is?"

"I was thinking lunchtime today. We've nothing else on."

"Other than the biggest news story in a decade. But why not? I'm anxious to meet this lion-taming temptress."

"I'll call her right now. She's rather keen to meet you herself."

"She is? She doesn't know me from Adam."

"She's heard me cursing you after some of our livelier telephone calls. Anyway, thanks to Senator Curtis, she's got nothing better to do right now."

Duncan, looking down at his plate, abruptly changed the subject. "You know the trouble with breakfasts here? Americans can't do proper bacon. Take these pancakes: they're too, I'm looking for the word, permeable. Soggy. I prefer them a bit more solid, English style. Nor do raspberries and bacon on the same plate much appeal to me, either." He pushed his full plate aside. "In the absence of kippers and porridge, I think I'll have the scrambled eggs. They'll go with my mindset."

"Just don't ask for HP sauce," Nigel advised. "They'd think you were trying to order a computer. This is ketchup country."

"Isn't today, what do you call it? D-Day? Down in Florida, I mean. Shouldn't we be getting our heads together to…"

"To do what, exactly?"

"I'd have thought it obvious."

"We already have our plans in place. This afternoon, after lunch, we'll head out to Maryland. Fran Powell will pick us up at Jane's at four, if that's alright with you. Frank is already out there. The Jamesons won't be playing their game - golf, that is - until three. I wouldn't expect a call from Samantha until this evening."

Duncan shrugged. "This is your show, laddie. All I'm saying, to quote Mr Dickens, is that 'Barkis is willin'."

Duncan's mobile buzzed. "Lord Goodfriend," he said, looking at the screen, and then at Nigel. "What can he possibly want? He's supposed to be down on the Riviera."

Duncan took the call. "Lord Goodfriend, good morning, sir. What can I do for you? Yes, I'm in Washington. Got in yesterday afternoon. Yes, I'm having breakfast with him as we speak. Yes, we're working on an interesting story. Yes, the Hoffman resignation was a splendid scoop. I'll be sure to tell him." Duncan said nothing for two minutes, listening to what Nigel heard as a Teutonic rumble. "Yes, of course I'll keep you informed. No, I felt that a trip by the managing editor to the biggest news market in the world was somewhat overdue. I haven't been here for two years, and there's an election coming up soon. I know it's eighteen months away, but these things require careful planning, and I wanted to get myself up to speed with the political situation here. Yes, the weather's lovely here, too. Even hotter than in France, I dare say." Duncan screwed up his face for Nigel's benefit. "No, I haven't heard anything on the Marchetti thing. Yes, a storm in a teacup, I agree. Yes, in a few days, I hope. Goodbye. And do enjoy your holiday.

"What did he want?" Nigel asked anxiously.

"To know what I'm doing here. Or, as he put it, what I'm *really* doing here. He smells something, I'm sure. But then he always does, even when there's nothing to smell. Oh, and he asked again about the Marchetti thing."

"Fuck."

"Don't panic. It was only in passing. I did tell him that we were working on something interesting but didn't say what."

"He didn't ask?"

"Yes, of course he did. But I didn't tell him, and he didn't press the point. You heard me: I told him I was just checking out the political climate, staying in touch."

"Was that wise? When you report the real reason you're here, he'll remember that you didn't tell him."

"I'll handle that when the time comes. What's today? Wednesday, isn't it? Not his weekly call, then, but I'm not going to lose sleep over it."

"By the way, who's running the ship back home?"

"Charlie Wood. Who else?" Charlie was the *Post*'s news editor, always a good man in a crisis, Duncan observed. "He's a steady Eddie. These days he runs the show most of the time anyway. I may be admiral of the fleet, if you like, but he commands the flagship. Hardy to my Nelson."

"I didn't know you were so well versed in naval protocol."

"I'm not. My ancestors were all army men. Argyll and Sutherland Highlanders."

"You're a lowlander."

"Yes, but there wasn't a regiment called the Argyll and Sutherland Lowlanders."

"Your father served?"

"A Presbyterian minister! Hardly. No, as a born-again pacifist, and a saver of souls, as opposed to a destroyer of souls, he broke with the family tradition. As, of course, have I."

"Oh? In what way?"

"First, by not joining the army. Second, by not taking up clerical orders. Third, and worse, by going down to that doomed city of Gomorrah we call London."

Nigel was beginning to worry all over again during this small talk, but about what he couldn't quite pin down. The elation generated by his domestic news had now subsided. Duncan looked a little concerned, too, despite his insouciant manner of a minute earlier. "Look, His Lordship is no fool. I'm sure he's worked out that something's cooking, but clearly he's no idea what. I'll fill him in when the time comes… whenever that may be."

"It could be sooner than you think."

"Which means that I'll be no less surprised than he will. When we know we've got something more tangible, when Samantha has, as you put it, lit the touch paper, then I'll call. But not before. If I tell him what's going on and then nothing happens, I'll look like a fool. Besides, I don't want our scoop - your scoop - to be scooped by our own proprietor. He's known for flapping his lips as well as his ears. I'll manage the situation. I could, of course, remind you that you kept your managing editor in the dark for weeks. So, I'm just following your lead. Now, you were going to call that girlfriend of yours. I think I could use a pleasant diversion."

"Maybe I should add Fran to the lunch party. That way we can go straight to Maryland from the restaurant. By the way, you should bring an overnight bag."

"What exactly does Jane know? I don't want to spend the entire lunch on tenterhooks, terrified of saying the wrong thing. I hate all this subterfuge."

"She knows some of it, but not much. But I suggest we stay away from business over lunch, or at least this business."

"Good thinking. And now, I think I could use that walk. I'll just go up and fetch my bag. I did bring one suitable for an overnight stay."

"We're having lunch in Georgetown, so I suggest we take a leisurely stroll there. We can go via the tourist spots if you're interested. We can chat along the way."

It was Nigel who first spotted the man following them. He had fallen slightly behind Duncan, whose idea of a brisk walk meant an Olympic 400-metre heat. Nigel thought he recognized the stalker but failed to put a name to the face. Then, as the man drew closer, he realized that it was Schmidt, the administrative assistant from Curtis's office.

Nigel trotted to catch up with Duncan. "Don't look round, but we're being tailed."

Duncan turned anyway, pretending to take in the views up and down the National Mall. He saw nothing to cause him concern. "There you go again with the cloak-and-dagger stuff. There are thousands of people here, half of them walking in our direction."

"But only one that I recognized," Nigel said. Even Duncan had to admit that this might constitute reasonable grounds for suspicion. "The man in the suit with a rolled-up newspaper."

"I see him. Doesn't look terribly sinister. Who is he?"

"His name's Schmidt. He's one of Senator Curtis's administrative aides."

At Nigel's suggestion, they left the pathway and wandered over to a bench and sat down. That way the man would either turn away or walk right past them. The bench had just been vacated by a couple with two children eating ice creams, leaving a dripping pink residue on the seat. Duncan, with evident distaste, wiped it off with a tissue. They sat and waited for the man to walk past, but he was heading straight for them. Moments later, he was standing in front of them. "Nigel Harper, isn't it?"

"Yes."

"I thought so. Schmidt. Senator Curtis's office. We met there briefly, if you remember, the other day. Quite a coincidence bumping into you like this."

"Yes, isn't it," said Nigel in a breezy tone. He wondered what was coming next. "Oh, this is my friend, er, Jock." Schmidt and 'Jock' shook hands.

"Beautiful day for a walk," Schmidt gushed. "Washington looks brilliant in the sunshine, don't you think? I just had to get out of the office. It's stifling in there. And still manic. It's bad enough I have to work during the summer season but cooped up in that madhouse makes it worse."

"I can only imagine," Nigel said sympathetically. "That's why Jock and I decided to take a stroll, enjoy the weather and the sights. Jock's from Edinburgh. He's never been to DC before."

"Well, Jock, I wish you a pleasant stay in our wonderful capital," Schmidt said pleasantly, but giving Duncan a lingering look, which Nigel interpreted as a sizing up. Perhaps Schmidt was pondering whether these two Brits were romantically attached. Or perhaps trying to determine whether 'Jock' was another person who needed to be watched. The conversation, such as it was, quickly dried up.

Schmidt checked his watch. "Well, I guess I'd better be getting back. There's a heap of work on my desk, believe it or not. And you know my boss. He has no time for shirkers. Even now, I bet he's asking where I am. Good to see you again, Mr Harper. And good meeting you, Jock. Enjoy your stay." Schmidt turned and walked back the way he had come.

Nigel turned to Duncan. "I did warn you we might be watched."

Duncan seemed more concerned about his newly acquired appellation. "Jock!?"

"It was a spur-of-the-moment thing."

Do I look like a Jock?"

"You *are* a Jock. But more to the point, do you really think that running into him was a coincidence?"

"I'd say so. A chance meeting, nothing more."

"I disagree."

"On what grounds?"

"I don't believe in coincidences. Not this kind, anyway."

"Then explain this," Duncan said, in the manner of a barrister making a telling point in court. "If he was tailing us, why on earth would he walk over for a chat?"

"That's easy. Once he knew we'd spotted him he figured that coming over to talk to us would allay suspicion. That's what I think happened. It's exactly what I would have done."

"Okay, Sherlock, then explain something else to me. Why would the senator, who's presumably a smart cookie, have you tailed by someone you might recognize? That wouldn't make sense. If he wanted you followed, he'd have hired a professional, a private eye, or at least someone you didn't know."

These were plausible explanations, Nigel had to admit. But he remained unsatisfied and uneasy. "You may be right, but I think we ought to take a taxi the rest of the way."

Duncan could only shake his head. His Washington protégé had either spent too much time in the sun or had been reading too many cheap thrillers. Clearly, he was becoming delusional. But as Duncan climbed into the taxi, Nigel noticed that he paused to look over his shoulder.

Schmidt was nowhere to be seen. But who, Nigel asked, was that man in a dark suit, standing under a tree, apparently watching them? Just then a woman came over and kissed him and they walked away, arm in arm. Duncan, roaring with laughter, got into the taxi.

They both failed to spot the man, fifty yards away, taking photographs of them before they drove off.

* * * * *

Chapter 19

The clamorous ring tone of the telephone in Frank Hoffman's kitchen made them all jump. Frank got up from the dining room table, where he and the other three guests had just finished dinner, to take the call. He moved tentatively, as if dreading what he was about to hear. In truth, he was.

The others remained seated at the table. The wine had flowed freely, but each of them was stone cold sober. They exchanged anxious glances. Fran, who had been pouring coffee, froze in mid-movement, like someone caught in a cocktail party snapshot. From the dining room, they could hear Frank's muffled voice but little of what he was saying. Not that he seemed to be doing much of the talking; for the next five minutes he said hardly a word, frustrating the eavesdroppers.

Then, abruptly, he wrapped up the call. "Are you sure you're alright, Samantha? Good, I'm mighty relieved to hear it. Yes, I'm sure you are. Yes, until tomorrow then. Thank you. And God bless you. Yes, I know you don't, but God bless you anyway."

Replacing the receiver, Frank returned to the table and sat down with a prolonged sigh, whether from relief or disappointment the others couldn't tell. His face was taut, like that of a man who'd just heard bad news about the health of a friend. For a minute - it seemed much longer - he said nothing, his head bowed as if in prayer. The other three watched him intently, hoping for the best, fearing the worst, but unwilling to ask. The man seemed close to crying. And then he really was crying, they noticed, a single tear trailing down his cheek. Finally, he looked up, unsmiling, and then, in the manner of a judge on the bench, announced the verdict.

"She's done it. She's really done it."

This pronouncement was followed by another interminable silence, his and theirs, as they absorbed the momentous news.

Fran, impatient as ever, broke it. "Well, Frank, are you going to tell us what happened, or do we have to sit here all fucking night and work it out for ourselves?"

Suddenly, his face brightened, his whole being suddenly transformed. "She's done it," he repeated. "The man is going. I can hardly believe it." He seemed to be about to lapse into catatonia again, but then said, "I'm sorry. I don't know about you, but I find those four simple words almost too much for me to take in."

Nigel, robotically, repeated Frank's words: "The man is going. I can't believe it either."

Duncan and Fran opened their mouths as if preparing to say something, but nothing emerged, and so they closed them again. Yet another silence followed, this one even more oppressive than the first two. Then, as if woken from a trance, Frank shook his head, as if clearing his sinuses, realizing that they were waiting for him to provide more details - the gory details, as Fran would have said.

"Forgive me again," he mumbled. "I needed a few moments to collect my thoughts." Rather self-consciously he rose from his chair and placed his hands on the back of it as if gripping the lectern in the White House briefing room. He coughed, as if what he was about to say needed a clear throat as well as a clear head. "That was Samantha," he began, pointlessly.

"Well, we know *that*," said Fran, irritably. "But what did she have to say?"

"Here's the situation, and I'm telling you just as she relayed it to me." He paused yet again as if to collect his thoughts, or perhaps for dramatic effect. "This afternoon, President and Mrs Jameson went out to play a round of golf. They didn't get past the first hole. Samantha laid it all on him, chapter and verse: the investigation - she didn't mention whose - the documentary evidence, her demands… in short, everything. To make sure he was under no illusion about how much she knew, she mentioned a couple of names and dates and even gave him details of certain transactions." Frank took a sip from a glass of whisky, which Nigel had considerately pushed across the table. "Thanks for that," he muttered.

"And what was his reaction?" asked Fran, in an exasperated tone.

"For a minute, Samantha said, he was speechless. Visibly shaken. Then, of course, he hit back. He demanded to know how she'd found out and who had collected the 'supposed evidence', as he called it. Then he claimed it was probably fake. Well, you'd expect that from him, wouldn't you. She assured him that it was genuine beyond a shadow of doubt, and that she had more than enough to satisfy a federal prosecutor or congressional committee. The kind of material, she told him, that could lead to prosecution or impeachment, or both."

Frank paused to take a large draft of whisky. "That's when she told him how he might avoid both, spelled out her terms and conditions. You know what those are, so I don't have to repeat them."

"And then...?" Fran demanded to know, eager to push the narrative along.

"I'm getting to that, "Frank replied testily. "At first, Samantha said, he sneered. Told her she wouldn't dare. She warned him not to underestimate her. Then, she said, came the inevitable show of bravado. He demanded to see the evidence. Claimed that someone out to get him must have made it all up. He would launch an investigation to find the culprit. She told him that, on advice of counsel, she wasn't prepared to show him anything, that an investigation would be pissing in the wind - or words to that effect."

Frank hesitated again, presenting Nigel with an opportunity to ask the crucial question. "And how did he respond to that little lot?"

"He went through what Samantha called four distinct phases: denial, excuse, pleading and threat. The documents must be clever fakes, he repeated. But then he changed tack, gave her some cock and bull story about how he'd long suspected that something might be going on but insisted that he hadn't been involved. Then, when she told him that kind of nonsense wouldn't wash, he resorted to pleading: asked her to consider the impact it would have on the family and the country. Finally, when none of that worked, he reminded her of the power of his office, how he had all the resources at his disposal to make her life difficult. In other words, he was all over the place - understandably, given what she'd just told him, and the implications for his presidency."

Frank now seemed visibly weary, as Nigel had noticed he sometimes did when speaking from the press room podium, but exhaling a deep sigh, he carried on. "Apparently, the conversation became more and more heated. It became a shouting match. This went on for over an hour, back and forth, no quarter given. Then, she said, he just seemed to capitulate. 'Crumble' was the word she used. At one point she thought he was going to cry. His last words to her were, 'I guess you win this round.' That, she inferred, meant the fight was by no means over. Oh, and then, as he was stalking back to the house, she topped it all off by demanding a divorce. At that point, she said, he looked like a man who'd been told by his doctor that he had only three months to live; in political terms, you can make it eighteen months."

Nigel and Duncan again exchanged glances, both already working out in their heads how they would write the story, or at least trying to imagine the headline and the lead sentence.

Frank was now ready to sum up. "So, here's the bottom line, folks: the chances are that President Martin Jameson will shortly be volunteering to become a lame duck. That will depend, of course, on what his lawyers have to say. They could kibosh the whole deal - although Samantha can't think how they can do it without exposing him. Neither can I."

Nigel cut in. "They're clever bastards, though, and as unscrupulous as he is. I imagine they'll look to drag out the negotiations for as long as possible."

"They would, given the chance, but he's under a strict deadline. She made that abundantly clear."

"How long a deadline?"

"Seventy-two hours. Non-negotiable."

"And if his lawyers do come up with a plausible defence strategy, what then?"

"Then the deal's off. She made that clear, too."

Frank, his task completed, pulled his chair back and sat down heavily. "I think I've covered everything. Now all we can do is wait. Questions?"

Fran spoke first. "Not a question, but what a moment that must have been. I can't imagine how she felt. She's one gutsy woman, I tell you. So, we'll know what happens next in three days... now two."

Frank nodded. "That's the deal."

Nigel went next. "Can we talk about the lawyers for a bit? You must know them all, Frank. How do *you* think they'll react?"

Frank shrugged. "In truth, I don't know them all, and none of them that well. They're all relatively new. The chief White House counsel has been in the job a month. He also has private lawyers I've never met, including a bunch of sharp characters in New York. So, to answer your question, I've no idea how they'll react. I imagine they'd feel comfortable advising him to defend himself against undocumented accusations, but if they were convinced that she had material evidence, I can't imagine what they'd do, or what they could do. They can hardly go to court, that would have the same result as her blowing the whistle. They're in what you might call a Catch 22 situation."

"I presume, nevertheless, that they'll still demand to see the documents," Duncan put in, speaking for the first time. "How could they mount any kind of defence without seeing them?"

"I don't know. I'm not a lawyer."

"But would she be prepared to hand them over, the documents, at least some of them?"

"Again, I've no idea. The point here, I think, is that she couldn't be forced to reveal anything except through a legal order from a judge, which is the last thing they'd want. Then it would be in the public domain."

Duncan again. "What other options does he have?"

"If you mean non-legal options, I can't think of any. He's already agreed to her terms, at least in principle."

"Principle isn't a word I'd normally associate with this president," said Duncan, flippantly.

"I meant it only in the narrow legal sense."

Nigel took over the interrogation. "Let's assume that he does capitulate; what should Duncan and I be doing? I'm thinking about logistics and timing."

"No idea. Ask me again in two days. By then we'll know which bomb you'll be detonating, Little Boy or Fat Man."

Fran looked puzzled. "What?"

"Those were the names given to the two atom bombs we dropped on Japan. Come to think of it, those terms seem to fit the present situation perfectly. But I'm sure Samantha will have more to say on matters of disclosure and timing. By the way, I forgot to mention that, barring unexpected developments, she'll be joining us here tomorrow."

Nigel persisted. "All I'm saying is that we need time to prepare."

"You're a journalist. You should be used to working under deadline pressure."

"Fair point."

"And how much preparation do you need? If it's Little Boy, you can tell the story in a short headline and a few crisp paragraphs. I could dictate them myself, right now. If it's Fat Man, there will be more to do… but I don't think it'll come to that."

Nigel mumbled his response. "I was just hoping for something more tangible."

Frank now seemed slightly exasperated himself. "Well, I can't give you anything tangible. Nor can Samantha. All I can say is that she's managing the process. I know you're anxious to realize a return on your investment, but if it's getting scooped you're worrying about, I'm sure she'll honour whatever commitments she's made to you. Of that, I haven't the slightest doubt."

"It's not her promise that I'm worried about. My concern is that we could be scooped by *him*. He could launch a pre-emptive strike."

"She wouldn't allow it. She's made it clear that she will control the narrative. Anyway, why would he do that?"

"Well, we know he's an obsessive tweeter."

"The last thing he'll want to do is risk getting her pissed… in the American sense, that is. She's already made clear that she won't tolerate any funny business. Of course, there's always the unexpected."

"Like what?" Nigel sounded genuinely alarmed.

"If I knew that, they wouldn't be unexpected would they," Frank said, sourly. "Look, we can talk about all this until we're blue in the face. I'm already halfway there. But let's do this tomorrow when Samantha herself is here. There's no point in our debating problems that don't yet exist and can't be predicted. It may be frustrating, but you'll just have to be patient a little longer."

Nigel still looked far from satisfied, but now Duncan piped up, ignoring Frank's admonition that little more need be said. "Getting back to his lawyers, Frank, what do you think their legal options are? Your best guess."

"Limited, I'd say. Or, to put it more succinctly: who the fuck knows? They have their own positions to consider; whatever they do, they'll want to cover their backs. I'm less worried about them, strange as it may seem - and to Nigel's point - than about him. He has a tenuous acquaintance with reality so that makes him hard to predict, whatever his lawyers tell him. Meanwhile, our working assumption should be, based on Samantha's account, that he'll see sense and announce that he's not going to run again. And that, my friends, is still one hell of a story."

Duncan spoke again, predictably returning to the matter of the documents. "What happens to the documentary evidence? I'm only asking because I'm curious."

"We can only hope that they'll never see the light of day. In legal terms, you could say that they don't exist. They'll only exist if he forces her hand. In that event they'd become exhibits in a courtroom. I don't know what else to tell you. I'm not a lawyer, neither am I an astrologer."

Now, Duncan had taken over from Nigel. "Let me ask you about this Kwest outfit. They know everything. Are they safe? Who's to say Jameson won't try and persuade them, with a hefty incentive, to deny all knowledge of the case?"

"Jameson has no idea they're involved."

"He could find out."

"Unlikely. Even if he did, I can't imagine any amount of cash would induce Kwest to risk going out of business, which is what would happen. The firm has a highly lucrative business delving into secrets… and keeping them. The only way Kwest would give up its files would be in response to a subpoena, and that, God willing, isn't going to happen."

Duncan came up with a startling new angle. "All this assumes, of course, that some of this stuff hasn't been secretly recorded on White House tapes."

"Dear God, the crazy things you journos come up with…"

"I'm just asking. And there's a precedent."

"Well, I happen to know for a fact that there *are* no such tapes." Frank seemed emphatic. "Just don't ask me how I know."

Apparently satisfied for now about questions of evidence, Duncan went back to editorial management issues. "Let's say he does go gentle into that good night - still a big if in my mind - what reason will he give for not running again?"

"You could make up any reason yourself: he's completed the task of restoring America to greatness; he's decided to put family first; unexpected health problems; time to hand the reigns to a younger man… take your pick. He's already closer to seventy than sixty, so voluntary retirement doesn't sound entirely implausible."

"His medical records are a matter of public record," Nigel offered.

"Yes, and he had a clean bill of health just six months ago. But these things can change. Only a few months ago he suffered a health 'incident'. I can't tell you what happened because I don't know. It was hushed up. The media never got wind of it. Whatever it was, he was laid up for a week. The official version - put out by me, by the way - was that he'd taken a brief and well-deserved break at Camp David. In fact, he was in Walter Reed hospital."

"Whatever reason he comes up with," Duncan said, "I doubt that it will stop the *New York Times* and the *Washington Post* from looking into it. They'll smell a rat for sure."

"I agree. They'll dig away for a few weeks. But when they find nothing, they'll get bored and move on. The political fall-out will keep them occupied instead."

Duncan, still struggling to grasp the import of everything he had heard, asked, "So, what can we usefully do here and now, pending more definitive news?"

Frank responded decisively. "First thing after dinner, the three of us will draft a few lead paragraphs for both versions of the story." He turned to Fran. "You've been uncharacteristically quiet, young lady. Do you have anything to contribute?"

Fran bristled at what she perceived as Frank's patronizing tone. "Not if I'm considered a fucking afterthought," she snapped. "But perhaps you think the best way this 'young lady' can make herself useful is by keeping busy in the kitchen."

Nigel galloped to the rescue, knightly armour glistening. "I for one greatly value your opinion, Fran. Meanwhile, someone - anyone but you, Fran - might think about making some coffee, and plenty of it. This could be a late night."

"Now that I've made my point," said Fran, standing, "I'll be perfectly happy to make the coffee." She rose from the table for that purpose.

I apologize, Fran," Frank said sheepishly. "I didn't mean…"

"Forget it, Frank. But one more demeaning remark like that and I may just give you a good hard kick in the balls."

* * *

Even before Frank, in an apparent act of penance, had cleared the table, Nigel was pecking at his laptop, Duncan peering over his shoulder.

"I'm starting with the Little Boy version," Nigel explained, as Duncan peered over his shoulder at a blank screen. He wrote a headline, reading it out in a voice loud enough for everyone to hear. *"President Jameson Will Not Seek Second Term - Report."*

"Okay so far," Frank called out from the kitchen. "But I hope there's more…"

"Only a fool criticizes a job half done," Nigel replied chirpily, and continued typing.

"President Martin Jameson has decided not to run for a second term, the Morning Post *has learned from authoritative Washington sources."*

"I don't like that word 'authoritative'," Duncan cut in. "It suggests the president himself is the source."

"Point taken." Nigel erased the word. "What do you suggest instead?"

"I'd use 'senior administration sources', or 'sources close to the White House'... that could be anyone."

"Agreed," Frank yelled from the kitchen, loading the dishwasher.

"Also," Duncan added, "there's no need to be so definitive. 'Has decided' leaves us no wriggle room. How about 'is believed to be close to deciding', or something vague like that."

"Another fair point," said Nigel, rewriting the sentence.

"In a startling development that will rock American politics to the core, President Martin R. Jameson is close to deciding not to run for a second term, the Morning Post *has learnt from senior sources close to the White House."*

The tapping continued.

"There was no immediate comment from the White House, but the president is said to believe that his age, 68, might be a burden in what is likely to be a long and bruising election campaign. If he were to run, he would be one of the oldest presidential candidates in history and, if re-elected, one of the oldest sitting presidents. Family concerns were another factor, these same sources mentioned. The president and his wife have reportedly been estranged for some time, and rumours of an impending legal separation have not been denied. Also prominent in the president's thinking may be his poor standing in the opinion polls, which in recent months have consistently shown him running ten points behind all three of the front-running Democratic candidates. Given that his nomination is far from assured, many figures on the liberal wing of the Republican Party expect, and may encourage, a serious convention challenge by a more mainstream rival."

"Keep going, laddie" said Duncan, quietly attempting to assert his editorial authority.

"If that were to happen, Republican leaders in Congress - whose enthusiastic support for Martin Jameson has been unwavering - would suddenly find themselves confronting issues that they would otherwise have wished to avoid, first and foremost, the matter of the party's future political direction under a new, and at present unknown, candidate. Vice-President Edmund Mears would almost certainly throw his hat into the ring, but his unquestioning support for many of President Jameson's more controversial positions on

social issues such as immigration and health care would give a more centrist opponent considerable ammunition. Moreover, in the last election, the former Governor of Missouri had proved to be a poor campaigner."

"We'd squirt in a lot of background stuff at that point," said Nigel, cracking his knuckles. "And, of course, we'll need to be ready to follow up with reactions and quotes and analysis."

"We've already got the president's obituary on file," Duncan offered. "That'll be a useful source. I'll dig it out later - no pun intended."

"At some point, we ought to mention family matters," said Nigel, the father of two, representing his class. "I'm thinking not only of the main news, but of the impending divorce. Remind me how old the children are."

"Three in their thirties from two previous wives," Frank said, emerging from the kitchen, wiping his hands on a dish towel. "Not children. With Samantha he has another two, a boy of seventeen, a girl of fifteen. Hardly children, either. Do you have a view, Fran?" Frank was anxious to bring her into the discussion to make amends for his earlier offense.

Fran was grateful for the opportunity to offer an opinion. "If the president uses family issues as a factor in his decision, the younger children will be part of the story, but I don't think we need to walk on eggshells. As teenagers they spend half the day on social media or watching television. Their classmates will tell them what's going on anyway. I think they'll be fine."

"I notice you didn't mention newspapers," Nigel complained.

"Kids don't read newspapers."

"The *Post* has a website," Duncan reminded them both, "in case you've forgotten. And a bloody good one it is, too."

"I'm sure it is," Fran replied. "But how many Americans read it? How many Brits, for that matter."

"After this news gets out, maybe millions," Duncan offered brightly, relishing the thought.

The ad hoc editorial conference continued well into the night. Nigel kept tapping, changing a word here, adding a sentence there, prompted from time to time by Duncan or Frank. By eleven, he had written two or three main stories and a couple of sidebars. He had also written an alternative piece, the one he secretly hoped would be the one they would be running. *"President Martin Jameson, several other high-ranking elected politicians and senior military figures, made fortunes from a secret offshore investment fund that exploited insider trading, money laundering and other illegal acts, according to secret documents seen by the* Post.*"*

Since the *Post* had not seen any documents yet, Nigel could write no more. Duncan, meanwhile, had composed a long editorial excoriating the presidency of Martin Jameson, under the heading *"America Should Collectively Sigh with Relief"*.

After reading all the articles, with mutual declarations of approval, Frank decided to call it a night. "If no one has any objections, I'm going to turn in early. I'm reading a book about Lincoln - how he rounded up his political enemies, put them all in his cabinet, and formed a coherent government. It's riveting stuff. This president ought to have followed his lead… he compares himself with the man often enough."

Fran stayed the course until well after midnight, then even she - usually the last to succumb - nodded off on the sofa. An hour later, waking up with a start, she headed upstairs, leaving Nigel, umbilically attached to the laptop, and Duncan, hovering over him, defying the onset of jet lag, still debating the kind of editorial nuances that only journalists get excited about.

The clock in the hall struck three before even they ran out of steam and inspiration. Essential background material could safely be left to lesser editorial mortals in London. "When and if the time comes," Duncan noted cautiously.

Nigel suggested a brief, refreshing stroll in the garden, now illuminated by an almost full moon in a cloudless, star-filled sky. Duncan declined the offer of a cigar, but watched, fascinated, as Nigel lit his with much vigorous puffing. Like all former smokers, Duncan was now a fervent anti-smoker. "Those blasted things will kill you, even if this story doesn't."

"One of these a month won't do me any harm. But you're right, this story could do the trick in one day." Duncan obviously had something on his mind. "What are you thinking?" Nigel asked.

"Just that this whole business is a bit… I don't know the word for it… bizarre. What do you make of it now that events seem to have been set in motion? I mean, I can't help wondering if all this is real."

"I'm not sure what you mean."

"It means that here we have a sitting president - apparently a crook - being blackmailed by his wife into leaving office, a wife who, as I understand it, removed allegedly incriminating documents from the Oval Office. That, by the way, may in itself be a criminal offence."

"Your point being?"

"That I just can't get rid of a nagging feeling that all this seems to be falling into place rather too neatly. I keep waiting for another shoe to drop."

"What are you suggesting?" Nigel sounded surprised, perhaps even a little affronted, although in weaker moments he had entertained similar thoughts. "You think this whole thing is an elaborate set-up? A con? Or what? And if so, to what end?"

"I'm not suggesting anything, only that it all sounds a bit... again, I can't reach the word I'm looking for... convenient."

"We'll find out soon enough," was all Nigel could manage.

"What if this thing goes in a direction none of us has anticipated?"

"Like what?"

"Well, we know this president is erratic. Here's a nightmare scenario: we go out on a limb with the story that he won't run for a second term and then for some reason he changes his mind. Worse, it turns out that the incriminating documents are not quite as conclusive as they've been described to us. I haven't seen them. Nor have you. What if it turns out that they don't even exist?"

"I agree we're taking a risk, but I'd say it's a calculated one."

"And what is that calculation?"

"That Samantha Jameson is neither a flake nor a liar. It's also what I happen to believe."

"She's also the most enigmatic first lady of recent times. Quite inscrutable, from everything I've read about her. Your proverbial woman of mystery..."

"Well, I've met her three times," Nigel responded, "and I've found nothing inscrutable about her. On the contrary, she strikes me as open and straightforward, perhaps to a fault."

"All I'm saying is that if this extraordinary proposition of hers goes pear-shaped, we'll both look like idiots. We'll be done for. Both of us. I'd have to resign. You, too. Lord Goodfriend would insist on it, I'm afraid. Neither of us would ever work in journalism again."

Nigel thought carefully about his response. "I admit I've had my own reservations from time to time, but if it does all go terribly wrong - if we really have been led up the garden path - then three very senior public figures will go down with us."

"Frank's already gone down."

"Voluntarily."

Duncan still looked pensive. Finding nothing more to say about Samantha Jameson's motives or honesty, he contradicted himself as was his habit. "On the other hand, here we are, you and I, secretly hoping that it's all true, that it goes public, and the president is prosecuted. What a story that would be. It would run for months. Years even."

"But you don't believe that will happen. You've said so."

"I'm not sure what's going to happen, to be perfectly honest. I'd prefer a full-blown scandal, of course, but I wouldn't say that to anyone around here except you. And tell me you haven't had the same unworthy thought."

"I have," Nigel admitted, making it sound like a confession.

Duncan, while continuing to fret that everything depended on the word of a woman he had yet to meet, let alone evaluate, came up with another possible scenario. "You know, I've also had another thought. Who's to say that Jameson won't respond to his wife's threat with one of his own. Two can play at her game."

"What would he use to threaten her?"

"He could threaten to expose his wife as an adulteress - a lesbian one at that - and one who may have put national security at risk."

"Apparently, he doesn't know about Anna. I'm not sure, at this stage, that she'd care if he did."

"He might find out - stick investigators on to her. You found out."

"Well, I suppose anything's possible. But you can't compare the two offences. Financial corruption is criminal, adultery merely - for want of a better word - reprehensible."

"All I'm saying is that he could put the shoe on the other foot, offer *her* a deal to keep quiet. He's worth a fortune, after all."

"So is she. Apparently, she's worth millions."

"He's worth billions."

"Yeah, billions in debt."

"He'd have no problem raising the cash."

Nigel, acting for the defence, thought about his next response. "I just can't see it happening. She's not in this for the money. She's on a mission. You raise some valid points, but I think you may be suffering a case of what theatre people call first-night nerves."

"You're damned right I am. Someone around here needs to."

"If you're feeling that nervous, you can raise all this directly with her. Face-to-face. Tomorrow."

"I probably will. Right now, though, my nagging concern is that we're all too ready to believe everything we've been told. I'm not saying she's making it up, or even exaggerating, but we're newsmen; we're trained to take nothing at face value. Isn't that what defines our noble profession? And ask yourself this: are you being entirely objective here? You've become somewhat infatuated with the woman, I've noticed."

Nigel bridled at that last remark. "I like her, that's true. I also admire her pluck. But I don't think that's affected my judgement. I've also thought about it, long and hard, excluding no possibilities, and my objective evaluation is that she's telling the truth. Why? Because if she's telling us porkies, she'd be found out soon enough. Frankly, Duncan, telling me that my judgement may have become clouded because I'm besotted with her is a low blow."

"It's not a low blow, it's aimed straight at your head. Or perhaps, rather, at your heart..."

"Let's just look at the facts. There are the documents she found..."

"Which we haven't seen..."

"And then there are the results of the Kwest investigation. I can't say how they'd hold up in a court of law, but apparently Kwest has come up with some really damaging stuff. If she's making things up, then so is Kwest. How fucking likely is that?"

"I hate to be a bore but when do we get to see all this evidence?"

Back to that again, Nigel was thinking. "If the president goes quietly, they'll be irrelevant."

"I'd want to see them anyway."

"Why?"

"Because, as you said, they are the entire justification for Samantha Jameson's actions. We should insist on seeing them - or at least some of them."

"Well, we can always ask."

"Look, if I sound doubtful, it's because I'm paid to be. So are you. Until I've seen something on paper, I'll feel uncomfortable with the story. Call me a pedant, if you like. Meanwhile, all I've got to go on is the testimony of two people I met for the first time today, and the principal source of this story, whom I've yet to meet."

"I thought we'd agreed that they're solid sources: gold-plated, you called them. They're not our usual anonymous Grub Street tipsters. I mean, how much fucking credibility do you require other than two senior White House officials?" A quarrel seemed to be looming. "Let's think about it overnight," Nigel said, through a deep yawn.

"If we're asleep, we can't have thoughts," Duncan said, pedantically. "Only dreams, or in this case perhaps, nightmares."

Even Nigel, the notorious night owl was suddenly feeling weary, but he was keen to wrap up the conversation on a positive note. "I happen to think the woman has played with a straight bat. If I'm wrong, then she's fooled both of us - and a great many others besides. If our sources are trying to pull the wool over our eyes, all I can say is that they're bloody good actors. We're sticking our necks out here, but I happen to think, objectively, that Samantha Jameson is the real deal. You can make your own call when you meet her tomorrow, maybe get to see some of the evidence. Then you can make an informed decision on what we should do."

"If I'm still personally unconvinced, what will you do?"

"You're the managing editor of the paper, Duncan, and my boss. Whatever you decide, I'll accept."

Nigel expected a sarcastic riposte, something like "that would be a first" but Duncan had fallen into a contemplative silence. He scanned the twinkling bay with a dreamy faraway look.

"What are you thinking about now?" Nigel enquired.

"I'm thinking, laddie, how that stretch of moonlit water brings back memories of a lake near my childhood home, where I used to swim and fish for trout. And where, during my last idyllic summer at home, I courted a local village beauty. Mary Jean Ferguson was her name. What a cracker. I lost my virginity to her. Life was so much simpler back then. Less cynical, less… I don't know… less brutal."

"That's a sentimental side to you I've never seen before."

"Yes, I'm well aware that you think of me as a hard-nosed prick, but I can be as nostalgic as the next man."

"That's good to know. But the life you're leading now is a damn sight more exciting and more challenging than the one you'd have spent by yon bonnie banks and braes. You surprise me, mooning over a lost love I bet you can scarcely recall, and wouldn't recognize if she walked out here right now. What happened to her, anyway, the puir wee lassie?"

"I can still see her face quite clearly… and other parts I won't mention. As for what happened: well, I went off to university and became a media titan, if you'll pardon the immodesty, and she married a local accountant. She has four children now, I hear. Still lives in Biggar. They were carefree days, is all I'm saying..."

"And you'd swap that life for this one? Come on..."

"No, of course I wouldn't. I'm just reminiscing, that's all."

"Speaking of wee lassies," Nigel said, catching the suddenly wistful mood, "I wish Jane were here. What did you think of her, anyway?"

"I liked her. A woman of quiet strength. Easily underestimated. Why she allowed herself to get tangled up with a scoundrel like you, I can't begin to fathom. You've already cost her a promising career."

Nigel looked suitably penitent. "I know, I know... let's just hope this little adventure doesn't cost me mine."

"Or, far more importantly, mine," said Duncan, still gazing absently across the loch called Chesapeake Bay. "But I guess we'll find out soon enough." He stretched and stifled a yawn of his own. "Meanwhile, laddie, I think it's going to be goodnight from me."

Nigel reluctantly stubbed out his half-smoked cigar. "And from me, too."

* * *

Samantha had hoped to avoid making a grand entrance, but even as she emerged from her car, four expectant faces were peering at her from the front window. She looked composed, as she always did, but also weary, as well she might. The last forty-eight hours had been grueling, both mentally and physically. Someone with less resilience might have suffered worse. Following her out of the car came the dedicated Rosalie, as business-like as ever, and as usual carrying a box of papers. The driver, from the Secret Service detail, planted himself a few yards down the drive, assuming the familiar agent's stance, poised for trouble. A second one was already in position at the gate.

Having half-expected, and dreaded, a celebratory round of applause, Samantha was relieved to find the mood in the house introspective, almost gloomy. It matched her own. The spectators thought she looked like someone at the end of an impossibly long tether. It was not far from the truth.

Frank welcomed her on the front porch with a silent and extended embrace, tears welling in his eyes.

"How's Marion?" Samantha enquired, disengaging. "She hasn't been well of late, you mentioned."

Frank could only marvel that Samantha, at a time like this, could be thinking of his wife. "She's fine," he said, ushering her through the front door. "It was just a chest infection - the kind that doesn't want to go away. But I think she's got it licked now. She sends her love, of course. More to the point, Samantha, how are you? You look worn out."

"I am. But I also feel strangely exhilarated. More than anything, though, I'm just relieved. Also, a little surprised. Make that shocked. In the end, my encounter on the golf course went so much to plan that it was almost an anti-climax. That worries me. Or should. But right now, just about everything worries me. I can't relax until this whole thing is over. I'd be crazy if I did. I'd kill for a cup of coffee, by the way."

"It's already perking," said Fran, who had been waiting her turn for a hug.

Nigel and Duncan were greeted more formally with handshakes. "And you must be the redoubtable Duncan Erskine."

"I am indeed," Duncan said, looking almost bashful, "although I'm not so sure about the redoubtable."

"Oh, don't be so modest, Mr Erskine. Everyone knows that you're *un homme serieux*."

"It's a pleasure to meet you, too, Mrs Jameson." He had been about to say, 'an honour' but felt at the last moment that it would have sounded a mite too servile… and perhaps a mite too premature. "I understand you've had a trying time of it."

"Not as trying as others found it," Samantha shot back with a conspiratorial chuckle. "Ah, the gang's all here, I see."

"We few; we happy few, we band of brothers…" Nigel intoned.

"… and sisters," Fran added on cue, handing Samantha a mug of coffee. "How about you, Rosalie, need a coffee?"

Rosalie nodded. "Strong and black, please. But let me help you in the kitchen." Rosalie followed Fran inside. Their hands, Nigel noticed, brushed lightly on the way, and not accidentally. Fran and Rosalie, it seemed, had become more than just colleagues. Nigel smiled at the thought.

"Meanwhile, if you'll excuse me," Samantha announced, "I'll take a few minutes to freshen up." She headed upstairs.

Nigel eyed the box Rosalie had placed on the dining table. Some of the infamous documents, he surmised. Duncan was looking at it, too, and with the same thought. But Rosalie was watching like a museum guard watching over a priceless artefact. Even if she hadn't, Frank was alert to the danger.

He picked up the box. "I trust you both, of course, but I think removing temptation is the best way to avoid it." He and the box followed Samantha upstairs.

About twenty minutes later she came back down. "I feel so much better now... and some lunch would complete the transformation."

"Nearly ready," Fran announced from the kitchen, where, between many touches and whispered exchanges, she and Rosalie were preparing cold cuts and a salad bowl.

When they were all seated on the terrace - except Rosalie, who had diplomatically found an errand to run - Frank opened the conversation he had been saving for this moment. "So, tell us, Samantha, how was it, your showdown on the first tee? Now to be known, perhaps, as the OK Corral."

"Bloody awful," she replied, "but at least not bloody bloody. In the end, it was almost a non-event. Well, not quite... but that part is over. And now, not to be overly theatrical, my fate, and that of the nation, if I may be so presumptuous, lies in the hands of others."

"I gave everyone a straightforward summary of events," Frank told her. "Pretty much what you told me on the phone last night. Is there anything you'd like to add, or feel you want to add?"

"Nothing I can think of. Now we can only await the outcome of clandestine meetings of gentlemen with pale faces, sharp suits and a penchant for sycophancy - and, I hope, an elemental sense of fear."

"What does your instinct tell you?"

"My instinct is strangely inert right now. Despite the hours I've spent with lawyers, I've no feel for the legal aspects of this thing, either from my husband's perspective or my own. I can tell you that my lawyer - an old friend, by the way - is terrified. So, I dare say, are the president's. At least I hope so. But you know how lawyers are... 'On the one hand this, on the other hand that'..."

Duncan seized the opening. "That's why they say you should always hire a one-armed lawyer."

Samantha laughed along with the others.

"On a more serious note," Duncan said, "exactly what has your lawyer been telling you? Forgive me if I'm asking questions which you've already answered, but I arrived late to the party."

"You're forgiven. Their considered advice - that's lawyers, plural - is that I should have gone straight to the authorities. What else would they say? And who's to say they're wrong. It would have been by far the most sensible thing to do."

"What was their collective verdict?"

"They said, collectively, 'on your head be it'. We are, of course, covered by attorney-client privilege."

"May I ask *why* you decided to ignore them," Duncan said, bravely. "I mean, especially if it entailed a degree of personal risk." He thought he knew the answer but wanted to hear it from the horse's mouth.

Samantha sighed wearily. "Everyone here's heard it already, so I'll be brief. Whether I've done the right thing time alone will tell, and you'll be the judge of that. I can only say that I've been guided by my conscience. The risk, as far as I understand it, is that I could be charged with concealing a crime, or somehow with being an accessory. It's a question, I'm told, of misprision - failure to report a crime. On that point, the law is far from clear, and could only be decided on the whim of a judge. I haven't done anything for personal gain, which apparently works in my favour. I've already explained why I haven't gone to the authorities - the endless chaos that would result if I did. I'm not sure that answers your question, Duncan, but it's the best I can do."

"It does," Duncan said, suddenly thinking how utterly convincing she sounded. He looked across at Nigel, an earlier convert, who had been watching his editor carefully to see how far he was prepared to go with this line of questioning. What he wanted to hear more about, as they all did, was the president's apparent capitulation, and whether it would stick. He was about to raise it when Frank beat him to it.

"You say the president seemed to give up, just like that." Frank snapped his fingers to illustrate the point.

"Not quite that fast, but much faster than I'd anticipated. I'd expected him to push back right from the start. That's his normal reaction to bad news. We've seen it on television many times. He did resist at first, but it was… I don't know… half-hearted. And then something just seemed to break, like someone with a delayed reaction after taking a drug. It was rather unnerving to watch. He's usually got an answer for everything - as I'm sure you've noticed - but he was virtually speechless. That changed as we talked. He reverted to form, throwing out insults and threats. Not very pleasant, but nothing I hadn't seen before. Anyway, after an hour of ranting, he stalked off."

"And now, twenty-four hours later, when he's had time to think it over and no doubt consulted with his lawyers, what do you think will happen?" Frank involuntarily leaned forward with an expectant look, but the answer was disappointing.

"The simple truth? I've no idea. He's not a man who likes to be crossed. But if he knows what's good for him, he'll recognize the futility of his position. I'm hoping his lawyers will tell him just that. They'll demand to see the documents, I'm sure, but my lawyer would have to agree to that, and I don't think that's likely to happen. Only a judge or a public prosecutor could demand to see them, and if it gets to that stage then... well, you know the rest."

Frank replied in a solicitous tone. "He stalked off the golf course, you said. Did you see him after that? And if so, what was his demeanour?"

"I saw him briefly before I left, but he was already on the phone. He looked surly, as you'd expect. When he caught me listening, he ushered me out and slammed the door shut. Then, I left the house and returned to Washington. I may be clutching at straws here, but he struck me as a beaten man trying very hard not to sound like one. His parting words were, 'You may think you've fucked me over, bitch, but you've also fucked the nation.' I'm sure he genuinely believes that I'm depriving the United States of a great president, a true man of destiny, one who, if given the chance, would alter the course of history. That, by the way, is a chance I'm perfectly willing to take."

The last line produced an outburst of ironic laughter.

Nigel spoke next. "There will be no written agreement..."

"Certainly not, for obvious reasons."

"... in which case, when will we know that he's going to do what you've demanded?"

"To satisfy my terms he first needs to send a letter to the Republican Party stating that he won't accept their nomination for a second term. That will be released to the media - after the *Post* has already reported it, of course." Her smile was benevolent.

"And when do you think we can do that?" Nigel asked. "I mean, is there a timetable?"

"Yes. He can't drag this out. I've given him three days to get back to me. Now two. He knows that if he tries to stall, or changes his mind, I'll be forced to act. I left him in no doubt that I would."

Nigel nodded. "I understand. But if you'll forgive me for belaboring the point, Duncan and I are concerned about timing. If we went with the story and then he changed his mind, we'd be hung out to dry."

"Spoken like a true newsman. But this thing will be resolved, one way or the other, within my deadline. Assuming he doesn't change his mind, or try any other tricks, I'll be managing the disclosure process, from the publication of the story - via the *Post*, of course - to the communication to the Party leadership. If, between those events, he tried to renege on the deal, I'd go public, it's as simple as that. And then you'd be printing an even juicier story." Samantha smiled. "I know you'd much prefer to write about a full-blown financial scandal, and I don't blame you, but we'll cross the bridge when - I should say if - we come to it."

"In either event," Duncan interjected boldly, "we'd like a chance to examine the incriminating documents."

Samantha's look seemed to convey her doubt that any such thing would happen. "I'm not sure about that…"

Duncan, having set out his stall, started selling his wares. "With respect, this entire story hinges on those documents: the ones you, er, found, and the evidence your investigators have since come up with. They're material to the credibility of the story, whichever one we go with. Nigel and I would like to see them. That's not to impugn your integrity, you understand, Mrs Jameson, but we have an editorial duty of care. On the other hand..."

"Now you're beginning to sound like a one-armed lawyer yourself, Mr Erskine."

"That may be the worst insult I've ever received," Duncan shot back, blunting his tone with a nervous laugh. "The point is, with the greatest respect, that seeing the evidence is no more than routine editorial procedure. You're trusting Nigel and me to be an essential part of this process, and we're sticking our necks out, so I don't think we're asking too much."

Samantha looked thoughtful for a moment before answering. "Understand, please, that I'm not sure of my legal position here. Right now, the entire file is lodged in a safe in my attorney's office, and that as far as I'm concerned is where it's going to stay. I doubt that he'd allow you to see them, even if I asked."

"I understand why," Duncan said. "But I have to ask. And forgive me, I'm still asking."

Samantha suddenly stood up, looking slightly put out. "Alright, Duncan. I'm going to show you a couple of documents - the three I found in the Oval Office. They're photocopies of photocopies, but I assume they'll suffice for your purpose." She went upstairs and came back down with three sheets of paper. "These should be in the safe with the others, so you can look but not have. One is a bank account statement, which you can see from the letterhead, was issued by a Cayman Island bank. That one, I think, speaks for itself. The second is a list of names. There's no letterhead on that one but the amount at the bottom is the same, which I'm sure you'll agree can't be a coincidence. You'll recognize most of the names. The other paper is just a deposit slip. Look them over by all means, here and now, and then give them back to me. I'm not trying to impugn your integrity either, Mr Erskine, but if any of these documents were to fall into unfriendly hands, I couldn't guarantee the consequences, for me especially."

Duncan was too busy examining them to respond. Then, after a few minutes, he handed them to Nigel, who ran his eye over all three and handed them back to Samantha.

"Does that convince you?" she asked Duncan.

"They certainly look genuine."

"Well, they are. I didn't forge them I assure you. I'm not that desperate. And then, of course, there's the Kwest file."

"It's just that seeing the evidence in cold print... well, it makes everything more tangible."

"Good. Then let's hear no more about it... except to say this: if my husband does what I'm demanding, publicly, that will surely demonstrate that he believes the documents exist even if he hasn't seen them. I've given him enough details - names and transaction - that he can be in no doubt that they're authentic."

"You make a valid point," said Duncan, apparently satisfied that the dead horse had been sufficiently flogged to move on.

"Thank you, Mrs Jameson," Nigel chipped in, feeling that a deferential gesture was in order.

"Samantha," she corrected him. "Especially since you now know *all* my secrets." She smiled in anticipation of what she was about to say. "We all have our appointed roles in this drama. I think I've played mine for all it's worth. Now it's your turn to provide the final act, as it were. Naturally I'd like to see what you write before anything goes out."

Nigel gave Duncan an enquiring look, but Duncan merely nodded.

"I'll show you what we've written so far," Nigel said brightly, leaving the table to fetch his laptop. "I've written up a few lead paragraphs. Both versions. It's still a work in progress, you understand…." He pushed the laptop across the table. "These are the essentials of the story; the rest will be largely boilerplate - background, reactions and so on. Speaking of which, we'll need a statement from you, Samantha."

"I'll dictate one right now, if you like." She turned the laptop around and Nigel waited, fingers poised over the keyboard.

"At long last," she dictated, "the country is rid of a vile and dangerous would-be despot, and America can get back to some semblance of its normal, decent, civilized self…."

Nigel had kept up with the dictation but stopped after the word dangerous. "Is that, er, really what you want to say? I don't think…"

Samantha interrupted him with a mischievous cackle. "Ha, I really had you going there for a moment."

Everyone else laughed, too.

"Now for the real thing. 'The president has acted in the best interests of his family and of the nation, both of which he has served to the best of his ability. The president can now look forward to enjoying a long and, as far as I'm concerned, a well-deserved retirement when his term expires.' There, will that do? For the first version, that is. For the second… well, I'll have no immediate comment and probably none after that."

"Short, if not so sweet," Nigel remarked with a grin, noting the "well-deserved retirement" jibe.

"And for now, you two, I'd say your job is close to being finished," Samantha said. "That must be the easiest money you've ever earned."

They all laughed again, even Duncan.

"Meanwhile," Samantha said with a handclap, "let's enjoy lunch and an afternoon of invigorating conversation about other interesting topics."

Nigel and Duncan left the Maryland house early the next morning. There was little more they could do there, and they felt physically isolated from the editorial process that would now have to be set in motion. Samantha's dinner conversation had produced no end of useful colour, all of it on 'deep background'. She candidly answered many questions of a deeply personal nature, often offering more than they had asked for. Nigel took no notes, since in his experience, interviewees always talked more freely when they were not being recorded. The real loosener, though, was the wine, which Samantha consumed in volumes that matched theirs.

She saw them off with comradely embraces and a promise that, "Frank will call you the minute something breaks." She had approved the final story drafts with only cosmetic changes. They were ready to go, just as soon as the presidential surrender was confirmed.

"There's the small matter of the upcoming long weekend," Frank observed before they left, drawing blank stares from the two Brits. "It's the Fourth of July holiday weekend. It's one that we colonials take very seriously, thanks to you limeys. I mention it because it's relevant to the timing of your story."

"How so?" Nigel asked.

"Because, my red-coated, royalist friend, for the next four days this country will be out of commission, and in some cases out of its tree. Not the ideal time to be delivering a scoop unless it's an ice cream. If you break the story at the start of the long weekend, no one on this side of the pond will remember who broke it first."

"What do you suggest?"

"For maximum impact wait until Sunday evening. I've cleared it with Samantha. She agrees."

Although nervous about any suggestion of delay, however slight, Duncan and Nigel agreed that Frank's idea made sense.

* * *

Back in Washington, Nigel and Duncan went straight to the *Post*'s N Street office. Joe Hart, the junior reporter, had left for his summer vacation, but they summoned him back to be ready to man the telephones, though without telling him why. Strangely, he didn't ask. They set to work on the editorial logistics. Nigel would remain in Washington to file the copy already written, adding or amending as the situation developed. Duncan was in two minds about returning to London to oversee matters of presentation: space allocation, page layouts, photographs. But after some debate with himself he decided that his deputy could do all that in his sleep. Duncan had already written the editorial. He would stay, if only to watch the fun, but also because he wanted to be present when history was being made.

At some point between now and then he would have to brief Lord Goodfriend. His Lordship, alerted by Duncan's sudden dash to Washington, already suspected that something was in the works. "I'm not a man who likes surprises," Duncan had often heard him say. For this one, though, His Lordship might make an exception. At the right time - but not just yet - Bill Palmer would be briefed and would join Nigel in Washington to work on reactions from political leaders, many of whom Bill knew. He would also be better than Nigel at writing political analytical follow-ups. Duncan's presence had inevitably aroused Bill's suspicions, too, but Duncan and Nigel had agreed - given Bill's penchant for blabbing in bars - to keep him in the dark for the time being. There would be hell to pay for that later, Nigel was thinking.

Now, all that remained was to wait for the go-ahead call from Frank.

The Frank Hoffman resignation story had been a minor scoop, and while London cared little about yet another White House resignation, Washington did. Nigel had already become something of a celebrity in the White House press room, with much backslapping and numerous invites to drinks. But the congratulations, he knew, were salted with suspicion. How had a Brit, a White House neophyte, trumped everyone on the departure of a man some of them had known for many years? Mercifully, Sonny had been on vacation when the story ran. He telephoned the next day, but Nigel failed to return the call; Sonny would have too many questions that Nigel was reluctant to answer.

After handing in his formal resignation letter, Frank had instantly become persona non grata at the White House. Conscientious objectors were considered traitors in wartime, and this government took the same view of them in peacetime. Frank's resignation letter had been bland to the point of rudeness. There had been not so much as a hint of criticism of the president, or the government, but Frank was a defector, whatever the reasons. He had first, as a courtesy, called Martin Jameson in Florida, but the call had been given short shrift. In fact, the president had hung up on him. The president's shock had quickly turned to anger, his calls to the White House counsel laced with expletives. A short time later, two assistants had appeared in Frank's office, accompanied by two security guards, to order him to clear out his desk and vacate the premises. He had already cleared out most of his personal effects anyway. The guards then escorted him, cardboard box in hand, from the building. The White House press office issued a curt statement, written by Frank's deputy, confirming the resignation, with none of the usual homilies thanking him for his services to the nation.

Two days later, the now former press secretary made the call that Nigel and Duncan had been waiting for. Yes, he had spoken to Samantha. "You're cleared for take-off. Little Boy."

"Roger that," Nigel said, going along with the aviation nomenclature.

"I'm sorry if that disappoints you."

"Not at all," Nigel said, truly grateful that the ball was now finally in his court.

* * *

In London, the *Post* was going to print as most respectable citizens were thinking of turning in for the night. In Washington, five hours behind, people were preparing evening meals.

The story was carried on the *Post*'s front page, of course, but without the normal tabloid devices, such as a box marked 'Exclusive' or 'Breaking News'. Duncan thought them rather vulgar, unworthy of a serious newspaper, better suited to interviews with film stars or models. No, the story stood on its own two sturdy legs. Inside the paper, two pages were devoted to the various ancillary details: what the president's action would mean for the American political situation; a list of names of who might replace him as the Republican Party's nominee; what his legacy would be. Duncan's leader, of which he was inordinately proud, would be held for the next day's paper.

Even as the paper rolled off the presses, the *Post*'s website was being updated, scooping the paper by several hours. It could not be helped in the electronic age, when print took an increasingly secondary role. Anyway, there was no point in holding back the on-line version, since all the papers routinely picked up the early editions to make sure no stories had been missed. Night editors around the city were duly shocked by what they read, and reporters in Washington and London were soon being called to arms. This was easier said than done in Washington, where most of them were attending the last rites of the Fourth of July celebrations, under a burning sun in backyards and on patios.

The Associated Press and Reuters ran with the story immediately, careful to attribute it to the *Post* in case it turned out to be nonsense - which most journalists were initially inclined to believe, even if the *Post*'s sourcing sounded definitive.

In Washington, several thousand telephones had started ringing at once, several thousand answering voices registering shock and disbelief. Some editors - those lucky enough to reach their reporters - demanded an explanation. Sonny, hunched over a barbecue, and well on the way to not caring much about anything after a beery afternoon, was one of them. "Find out what the fuck's going on, and then call to tell me it's total shit. And if it's not, explain to me how some crappy London paper no American has ever heard of can get a fucking story like that before the rest of us. Before the *Washington Post*, for Chrissakes."

"It probably is shit," Sonny fibbed, though as certain as he knew that the sun would shortly be setting that the story was genuine. Hanging up the phone, he laughed his head off, startling his wife as she was handing out steaks and hamburgers. "Well, I'll be damned," he said out loud to no one in particular. "That clever, devious bastard."

"I think we're going to need more hamburgers," his wife was saying, wondering why her husband seemed to be laughing at nothing.

Television talk show hosts wasted no time abandoning planned topics for the next day's breakfast programmes. Some news executives were busy changing programming schedules, anticipating the approaching hurricane of punditry.

In Republican circles, where the story was potentially a game-changer, disbelief was mingled with anger. If the story was true, why had the party leaders not been informed? They soon would be. For Democrats, disbelief was mingled with joy that the beast had been slain. Why or how was hardly important. Telephone calls were being made to every state, where senators and congressmen had given no more thought to a political upheaval than they had to a Russian missile strike. Some, of course, had been expecting the news. Senator Curtis, for one, in his ranch outside Tucson, ignoring the presence of four dozen members of his extended family, and desperately trying to reach, without much success, his co-conspirators.

President Jameson himself, in Florida, had been on the golf course. Ironically, he was about to tee off at the same hole where he had been first informed of the revelations that created the media frenzy about to envelop him, wrecking his administration, and his legacy. He was partnered by three of his lawyers, a lugubrious trio, which the president had dubbed his 'three stooges'. An assistant press secretary, a young woman who had never met her ultimate boss, seemed understandably overwhelmed by the task of informing him of the *Post* story. She had expected an outright denial. "It's fake news, what else, so go back to the party"- and was shocked to be told that a press statement was, at this very moment, being prepared by the office of the White House counsel. Meanwhile, she was advised, she should avoid taking any calls from reporters - or anyone else. Clambering back into the golf cart in which she had driven there, she left the scene close to tears, now utterly convinced that the story was true. She was far from alone; among the staffers still gathered around a pool, the atmosphere had quickly degenerated from carefree to bewildered and was now heading for devastated.

A handful of senior White House lawyers already knew the truth, of course, but they wouldn't be talking. Not now. Not ever. The attorneys had spent two days and two nights closeted with the president, who had described his predicament in sordid and embarrassing detail. Several exculpating strategies had been considered, but each in turn had been rejected as at best impractical and at worst illegal. To a man, the lawyers had agreed that if Samantha's claims were validated by evidence, then the game truly was up.

At the Barr horse farm, Samantha, informed by Fran that the story was out, smiled in satisfaction. She had exacted her revenge in full measure - on her husband, on the more extreme elements of the Republican Party, and on the American media. An evening ride was in order.

At eleven o'clock the following morning, the chief White House counsel accompanied the acting press secretary to a press conference in the briefing room. The place was packed, although the representative of the London *Morning Post*, now the talk of the town, was conspicuously absent. "Probably too embarrassed to show his face," the Reuters man opined. Few disagreed with him.

The lawyer did all the talking, or rather the reading, which was from a prepared text. No questions would be allowed, he announced before starting. "In response to media speculation, the president confirms that he has been considering whether to allow his name to be placed in nomination as the Republican Party's candidate for a second term in office. While no decision has yet been made, over the next few days the president will be consulting with his wife, his advisors and the Republican Party's congressional leadership. No further statement will be issued until these consultations have run their course. Meanwhile, the White House will have no further comment."

The statement might as well have said "the published story is true." The reporters scattered, like chaff in a wind, and now the Washington rumour mill would be churning in earnest.

The following Sunday evening, a haggard-looking president ended all speculation in a brief television address.

"Good evening, my fellow Americans. I'm taking this opportunity to address you tonight in response to recent media speculation about my political future as well as my marital status. Tonight, I can confirm that for some time I've been considering both questions, the first in consultation with my senior advisers and the Republican Party's congressional leadership, the second with my wife and family. Throughout these discussions, my principal consideration was - as it always has been - how I could best continue to serve the American people and the national interest. Accordingly, I am announcing tonight that I will neither seek nor accept the nomination of my Party as its candidate for the next presidential election. I have so informed the Party leadership. I am also announcing, with a heavy heart, that my wife and I will be separating. These decisions have been reached only after much soul-searching, but also with a clear head.

"The programmes and measures that my administration has set in motion to restore this country to the greatness it deserves should, I've decided, be placed in the hands of a new Republican candidate who will be, as I expect, the head of a new Republican administration. My health is fine, but I believe that for a man of my years the stresses of a partisan re-election campaign, as well as my domestic situation, would only serve to distract me from those duties. For the past two years or more, I have been proud to serve the American people. I have set in motion a broad range of policies which I firmly believe will restore America's economic vitality and pre-eminent place as the leader and inspiration of the Free World. In these matters, and others, we have ended the drift and complacency that characterized previous administrations, which had sapped this country of its confidence and its energy.

"I am proud to say that there are unmistakable signs that these policies are working. The United States now enjoys full employment, rising industrial production, low inflation and record low interest rates. America is on the move again. There is still much to do, of course, and for what remains of my term, the responsibilities and duties of this great office will continue to receive my full attention. I owe you, the American people, nothing less, and you should demand no less of your elected president. It has been an honour to lead this great nation, and the Republican Party, which has served this country so well throughout its history. It will remain my honour and privilege to continue the good work during the remainder of my term. Thank you, my fellow citizens, and goodnight. And may God bless these United States of America."

Throughout Washington, telephones immediately began to ring all over again. Cell phones could be heard buzzing in restaurants and bars, patrons hastily settling bills and leaving. In summer homes across the country, members of Congress began to pack bags for a swift return to the capital. The Senate majority leader, Milt O'Donnell, cruising on his yacht in Chesapeake Bay, ordered the captain to head back to shore. He had been briefed by the president, of course, but only two days earlier, and there had been no mention of the marital issue. That, he surmised, had the potential for a public relations disaster in the Bible Belt, even though the president's misogynistic utterances and rumours of infidelity had for years been conveniently overlooked.

"There's one thing I don't get," O'Donnell told an aide as they skimmed back to port. "If the president is suddenly feeling his age, and the office is fucking up his marriage, why didn't he just resign? Or at least tell us what he was thinking."

The aide shrugged. "I don't know, Senator, but I guess we've now got a busy couple of years ahead of us."

"You got that right."

Meanwhile, the president's criminal accomplices had been busy, too. Funds in the Cayman Island account were being withdrawn at an unseemly rate, a process that would continue until the account could be closed. A dozen offshore asset-free companies had also been liquidated. But much more needed to be done - and was being done - to cover tracks which, if discovered, would lead inexorably to Federal penitentiaries. This was no damage limitation exercise; it was a panic-stricken capitulation.

In a white-walled, red-tiled mansion in Beaulieu-sur-Mer, Vincent Marchetti could only follow events from his poolside lounger with a growing sense of alarm and foreboding. He contrived as best he could to hide the truth from Sarah, although her curiosity was aroused by the time he seemed to be spending on the telephone, and she sensed his change of mood. She grilled him relentlessly, but to no avail. By way of explanation, he told her that he still had some 'cleaning up' to do after his resignation from various enterprises, and for that reason would have to cut short their vacation, or at least his, and get back to New York. If she failed to connect any of Vincent's preoccupations with the president's announcement, she was no less curious about it. Vincent had insisted that he had known nothing of the president's decision before the White House broadcast and reinforced the claim by complaining that none of his calls to the president had been returned. Sarah seemed far from convinced but frustrating as it was, she could do nothing.

* * *

Nigel, anxious to avoid a grilling by his peers, had stayed away from the White House press room. In truth, though, he was more worried about being summoned by White House lawyers demanding to know his source. It also occurred to him that, if he did show up, he might find that his press credentials had been withdrawn. He sent his junior reporter to attend the next two briefings but watched them on television in case there were unexpected developments. Watching the deputy press secretary's hapless performances, Nigel noted with satisfaction that the poor man seemed even more bemused by the sudden turn of events than his audience. No one at the White House had advised him what to say, least of all the president himself, who remained in Florida, apparently still closeted with his advisers.

Nigel didn't go to the office, either, as several local television crews had set up camp outside, hoping for an interview. They lost interest after being informed that the object of their interest had taken a short holiday. A couple of well-known news presenters called to suggest lunch. Oprah Winfrey's producers called with an invitation to appear on her confessional sofa. A Fox News pundit, known for his close friendship with the president, intimated on air that Nigel Harper might be on the Kremlin's payroll, that Putin himself might somehow have engineered the president's downfall. Many of his viewers believed him, but only those inclined to believe anything he said, even when it was arrant nonsense.

After an absence of two weeks, Nigel returned to the White House press room. He was immediately collared by questioning colleagues wanting to find out, chapter and verse, how he had managed to humiliate them. He didn't make the mistake of confusing his sudden celebrity with popularity. Journalists might pretend to admire the editorial triumphs of others but only with barely concealed pangs of jealousy and resentment. That was true in spades of the Washington press corps. Who the hell was this louche newcomer, they asked themselves, this typically bibulous Fleet Street hack, to be beating them at their own game on their home turf? And not just once, which could be put down to dumb luck, but twice in the space of a few days. Who could he possibly know deep in the White House establishment that they did not? The first scoop could only have come from Frank Hoffman, that much was clear, but the second, far more significant one, concerned a president who hated the media and hunted down leakers with all the subtlety of a seasoned KGB officer looking for traitors. The president himself couldn't have been the source, or surely it would have come out on Fox News, not from some obscure British broadsheet. Frank Hoffman was earmarked as the culprit, but he was nowhere to be found, not even at his Maryland hideaway, and calls to his telephone went straight to voicemail.

None of the ever-expanding ripples of speculation reached the ears of Samantha Jameson. Following her husband's address, she had issued a brief statement of her own, but one that merely emphasized that she understood and supported her husband's decision not to run. In it, she resolutely declined to comment on the state of their marriage, which she said was a private matter to be worked out between them. After that, she too had not so much faded into the background as vanished altogether. She was in fact staying at the Barr horse farm in Virginia.

Watching the president's broadcast with Duncan and Jane, Nigel had been unable to shake off a gnawing concern, echoing that of his managing director, that Martin R. Jameson might yet pull a clever stunt. "Perhaps you were right, Duncan, this has all been too easy."

Duncan, in one of his odd role reversals, was now the more sanguine of the two. "It's all over. He's made his statement, so he can hardly reverse it now. And if he did, we'd get another bite of the cake. For now, just let me say well done, laddie. Thanks to you, the *Post* is the talk of the city. Two cities… and, I dare say, a great many others."

Elsa called Nigel to offer her congratulations, as proud as if they were an old married couple. "I always knew you'd be a winner, my darlin'. Good luck to you. And don't let that crafty old haggis-muncher take all the credit."

"I won't," Nigel said. "But to be fair, he's been singing my praises to anyone who'll listen. Thanks for calling, by the way, which means more to me than I can say." In fact, at that moment it meant very little as he was suffering from a monumental hangover. That, and an attack of the editorial equivalent of post-partum depression.

"Well, I must say, as our conquering hero, you don't sound too cheerful," she told him. "What's up, my love? You were the one who set this all up. You alone deserve the credit. I'd have thought you'd be in a mood to celebrate. Over here we're all well chuffed. But perhaps the explanation is that you *have* been celebrating." Elsa, as always, knew the score.

After the call, Nigel sank back into a reflective mood that even Jane had failed to lift. He was a realist. His fame would be fleeting, his exclusives soon forgotten. In the heyday of newspapers, scoops might linger in the memory for days, if not weeks. In the new electronic world of instant electronic communication, they lasted minutes. Long before the *Post* had arrived on their doorsteps, readers the world over would have seen the headline on hand-held devices or lap-top computers or television screens, most of them blissfully unaware of the origin of the story. His byline had been on it in print, and on the website, but only journalists paid attention to bylines these days.

The American media had quickly caught up. Within seconds of the story appearing on the *Post*'s website, every on-line news outlet in the country had carried it, few bothering to credit the *Post*. Discouragingly, even many of the *Post*'s loyal readers - people whose profiles classed them as intelligent and sophisticated - would later be unable to identify the paper as the source.

All this Nigel explained to Jane, who was becoming a little concerned about his inexplicable melancholia.

"If you're going be so down about all this, I have a suggestion. Why don't we just go to bed, right now, and stay there for the rest of the day. At least we'd be doing something useful."

"I've got to call Bill Palmer. We're still busy working on all the follow-up stuff."

"What a flimsy excuse. Why don't you text him just to say that you might be a little late?"

Nigel sent the text, paraphrasing Dorothy Parker: "Too fucking busy and too busy fucking." Bill, he knew, would understand.

* * * * *

Chapter 20

President Jameson's broadcast reduced the Beltway's chattering classes to a state of bemused inarticulacy. But not for long. Politics, like nature, abhors a vacuum, and Washington's unaccustomed void was rapidly filled with speculation ranging from intelligent conjecture to the more extreme realms of conspiracy theory.

Much of it owed more to imagination than to reason, but if little of it collided with the truth, some of it came closer than anyone realized. One hypothesis was that Samantha Jameson had engineered the whole thing. According to this line of thought, she had hated living in the White House, despised her husband, and had never taken the trouble to conceal either. It stood to reason, then, that she had presented him with a spousal ultimatum. That much, as far as it went, was obvious, but it had no farther to travel than that since the president had announced that they had agreed to separate - the one aspect of his address that had surprised no one. Some observers noted that his wife seemed to have gone to ground, leading them to conclude that she had indeed been behind his decision, but since her public appearances had been sparse throughout her husband's tenure, she was doing no more than acting in character. More mystifying had been the president's references to waning health and advancing years. His last medical check six months earlier had given him a clean bill of health. 'Excellent for a man his age', the report had said, so what had changed since then? Had he since been diagnosed with a serious illness? If so, why keep it a secret? As for the reference to age, many observers pointed out that he was five years younger than his opponent at the previous election, a man who was now openly campaigning to become his successor.

As one well-followed newspaper columnist expressed it, this was a story with all the elements of a mystery play except the last act. Journalists are never keen on stories that can't be explained, and the lacuna in this one cast them in a bad light. If there was a hidden reason why the president had decided not to run again - an almost universal assumption - they were supposed to dig it out, but there had already been more digging going on than during the excavations for the city's Metro, and without so much as a clue to buried treasure. Television pundits, required to fill the ether for hours on end, as usual expounded eloquent opinions, but few found anything illuminating to say. Some editors in desperation commissioned psychologists to trawl through the history of the president's utterances, hoping to discover motivational clues. Some even claimed to have found them, although none sounded convincing. Others hired medical specialists to look for signs of mental deterioration - invoking the memory of Ronald Reagan, who had lapsed into dementia shortly after completing his second term and had probably been suffering from it while still in office - but few prognoses, psychological or medical, offered much more than regurgitated jargon.

In the end, Washington, politicians and media mavens alike, had no choice but to embrace a banal consensus: that while the president's action might be rooted in a motive unrelated to anything in his formal statement, the true reason remained unfathomable and was likely to remain so at least for the foreseeable future, if not forever.

Admitting defeat, journalists quickly turned from hunting the causes of the president's announcement to analyzing the effects, specifically what they saw as a radically changed political landscape. At least they could now indulge in well-reasoned speculation. Clichés were hurriedly dusted off. "The entire political paradigm has changed," the commentariat solemnly intoned, resurrecting a word that had been battered to death in an earlier decade. But then the paradigm always changed when a sitting president was reduced in status from strutting potentate to lame duck, the status to which Martin Jameson had now been reduced.

Republicans on the Hill quickly graduated from mystified to offended: Jameson had let them all down, and shame on him for doing it. A sitting president adored by his party, as well as a substantial portion of the electorate, owed them a second term, especially as he had seemed a virtual shoo-in for re-election. The party leadership had been expecting no less. They could only conclude now that he simply hadn't cared. Why else would he have not given the party grandees the slightest inkling of what he was about to do? For that alone, he would not readily be forgiven. Not that it mattered now.

No less shocked by the president's decision than the rest of Washington were his partners-in-crime. Shock gave way to confusion, though, when he told them that the entire Cayman Island enterprise would have to be terminated - and quickly - to avoid the risk of detection. Something had happened, obviously, but he had declined to tell them what. "Let's just say that it has been brought to my attention that if we don't wind this thing up, we may find ourselves in some jeopardy." With that mysterious remark, which the president refused to amplify, confusion gave way in turn to panic. Had some clever investigative journalist discovered something? If so, how? Had someone in their inner circle talked carelessly at a dinner party? Or, worse, had there been a deliberate leak? If it had been accidental, the finger of suspicion pointed to the president himself, who even his friends acknowledged was a boastful man and an inveterate blabber, and one with a lifelong record of embarrassing gaffes. He denied having done any such thing, of course, and in such vociferous terms that suspicion promptly shifted to a handful of senior congressional staff members who might have been aware of what their superiors had been up to. One who had been nursing a secret grudge, perhaps, or someone who had suddenly fallen prey to an attack of morality. Curtis reckoned it might have been one of their financial advisors. "No way," Vincent Marchetti had protested, adding an echo of Robert Palladino of Kwest: "We earn our living keeping secrets."

In the end, no real effort was made to find the culprit, and for one overriding reason: the more questions asked, the greater the danger of attracting attention from the media... or regulators. Instead, measures were taken to guarantee the silence of several aides by awarding them generous bonuses, in return for which they were required to sign new legally binding and wide-ranging non-disclosure agreements. None of them objected. Not even Maeve Carpenter, who rarely missed an opportunity to boast to friends that she knew "where all the bodies are buried" and to a few had even revealed their location.

Whatever the reasons behind the president's winding-up order, the Cayman Island bank account would now be emptied - in stages to avoid the impression of panic - and various ancillary companies shut down. Vincent Marchetti was put in charge of all of it.

A month after the president's broadcast, Senator Curtis announced unexpectedly that he would not be contesting his Senate seat at the next election. The formal statement from his press office cited medical advice, reminding constituents that he had suffered a mild stroke a few years earlier. True, he had since defended his seat with no ill effects, but the senator could reasonably claim that the rigours of a re-election campaign, followed by another five years in office, would at best be medically inadvisable and at worst might prove fatal. The senator also pointed out, even more irrefutably, that he was not getting any younger, although at seventy-two he was no more than middle-aged by Senate standards. His third wife, thirty years his junior, told a Tucson newspaper that spending what she called his twilight years on their beloved ranch was the best palliative medicine she could think of, and spoke of "riding off into the sunset".

Soon afterwards, Senator Pitman followed suit, insisting that the seat he had held for four terms ought now to be contested by a younger candidate. The oleaginous people-wrangler from New Mexico had just turned sixty-nine, and though he looked considerably younger, and seemed in rude health, few reporters thought to question his decision. Nor did any of them find it odd that such close and long-time political allies as Curtis and Pitman - the two most prominent congressional advocates of increased military spending - had decided to withdraw from public life at the same time. A handful of Democrats on the Hill wondered about it but were soon too busy celebrating the opportunity to fill the pending vacancies on two key congressional committees.

The three congressmen in the Cayman group said nothing. Likewise, the two high-ranking generals on Samantha's list. They would ride out the storm, on the grounds that, with the winding up of the Cayman group, there was no reason to expect a meteorological event of any kind.

Samantha Jameson extended Kwest's contract by a month, with a brief to monitor the status of the Cayman Islands bank account. Hardly had the ink dried on it than Kwest's investigators reported a series of large withdrawals. A few weeks later, Robert Palladino called Samantha personally to inform her that the account had been closed.

"It seems the chickens have flown the coop," he reported.

"I'd rather they had come home to roost," she replied wistfully.

"Me, too," said Robert, a lifelong Democrat, and no admirer of his client's husband. "So, what next?"

"Case closed," Samantha replied emphatically. "And let me take this opportunity, Robert, to thank you for all your meticulous and dedicated work: a job well done and efficiently accomplished. You've done the nation a great service. It's just too bad that the nation will never know how great."

"We were well paid for it," Robert replied, rather cynically, she thought. "Truth to tell, it was also a secret pleasure."

"Well, enjoy the pleasure by all means, but preserve the secret."

"You can be assured of it, Samantha. It was one of the more disturbing cases I've been involved in. Some of my senior associates are still astonished, not so much by what they found, but who they found."

"All the more reason for my gratitude," said Samantha, "which I hope you'll convey to them."

"Any time you should require our services again, you only have to call."

"With all due respect, I hope we'll never be doing business again. By the way, what measures have you taken to protect the documents? Forgive me for asking, but… well, I know you understand my sensitivity on that point."

"They're in my personal safe: our report, all internal memos and notes. At some appropriate time, I hope they'll be destroyed… but I'll await your instructions on that."

"And I'll be awaiting instructions from my lawyer. They won't be needed for my memoirs, I can assure you."

"Oh, why is that?" Robert asked, knowing the answer, but wanting to hear it.

"Because, my friend, for reasons I'm sure I don't have to explain, I don't intend to write them."

"That's a pity," said Robert. "I don't normally read political memoirs, but for yours I would happily have stood in line for a signed copy."

"You have my signature already - on a contract," she said, laughing.

Any satisfaction Samantha felt that the miscreants had been thwarted was diluted by regret that they would be walking away with their ill-gotten gains intact. But there was nothing she could do about that, not without opening one of Marty Ginsburg's cans of worms.

Marty, in any event, had other cans to open, notably the Jameson divorce settlement. The papers he drew up cited irreconcilable differences. That was closer to the truth in this case than in most of the others he had handled; not that it mattered, since the divorce would be uncontested. Against his advice, Samantha refused to take her husband to the metaphorical cleaners. As it was, she would be receiving more money than she could spend in a lifetime. There would, though, be a trust fund set up to put the children through college. "I don't need his money, Marty, and even if I did, I wouldn't want it. It's tainted."

"Tainted or not," he insisted, "you've earned it." When she still objected, he won her over with a more telling point: "Your husband made a fortune from criminal activities, so why don't you add an amount to the settlement to be distributed to your favourite charities?"

Samantha agreed on the spot. "I should have thought of that myself. Marty, you're a clever man."

"Not so clever as to have believed for one moment that you'd pull this whole thing off... and against my advice and of many others. Frankly, I still worry about it. I can't explain why."

"I can't think why, either. But keep worrying, Marty, and I'll happily keep paying you for it."

Marty had no response to that.

Days later, a press release from the first lady's office announced that she and the children would be moving out of the White House residence within days. The news was hardly controversial since most people assumed that she already had. She had rented a house in the Sheridan-Kalorama district, the capital's most exclusive residential enclave, where several former presidents had lived in the past. One of her husband's predecessors, whose wife Samantha considered a close friend, still did.

In New York, Vincent Marchetti would have been incandescent about Nigel Harper's new-found media celebrity, but he was far too occupied covering his tracks, which ranged over three continents. If he was grateful for one thing it was that Sarah had failed to ask more questions about the president's startling announcement. She had asked him one day what he thought of it, but he silenced her by claiming that he had been told nothing. Up to a point, it was true.

"Well, if *you* don't know why he did it," she told him huffily, "then I'm sure *I* don't. And now that it's history, I'm not sure I want to know." That last comment seemed to suggest that she might suspect that something fishy had been going on and for that reason had decided not to press the matter further.

Her curiosity finally found its voice a few weeks later when he casually informed her over breakfast that he had resigned as chief executive of all his main investment funds and would be giving up several other board positions. Sarah, startled, saw this development as a potential threat to their lifestyle. "What the hell's going on,

Vincent? This doesn't make sense to me; it's your life's work we're talking about. Maybe there *is* something I ought to know that you're not telling me. Does it have something to do with your friend in the White House?"

"Not at all," he said, lying easily. "Why on earth would you think that?"

"Because, my sweet, ever since his address you've seemed... I'm not sure what the word is... preoccupied... on edge... short-tempered... in case you hadn't thought I'd noticed."

He fobbed her off with excuses about having become 'stretched too thin'. To placate her, he threw in that his retreat would give him more time with her and the children. "There comes a time in every man's life when he needs to get his priorities right," he proclaimed portentously, and, as far as she could tell, sincerely. "You and the children must come first - that's my new priority." He failed to mention something that had been bothering him for some time: a London journalist renowned for unearthing financial scandals had been making discreet enquiries about his tangled financial affairs; relinquishing his corporate offices and adopting a lower profile might discourage any further probing. That would prove to be the case. "Anyway, our financial status will in no way be compromised," he reassured his wife. My wealth remains intact. I just won't be adding to it for a while, that's all."

"But what on earth are you going to do with yourself?"

"We can do some travelling. India, maybe. You've always wanted to go there. Broaden our minds. We can take the children along and broaden theirs."

"I do have a job, you know," Sarah reminded him, curtly. "Nor can the children skip school, not with exams coming up. The school wouldn't allow it, anyway."

"That wouldn't be a problem, not with all those generous donations we've made over the years. They've even named the new music center after us. We might also focus on our art collection. There's a David Hockney I've had my eye on coming up for sale."

"I can't stand Hockney. Paints like a schoolboy... acts like one, too. Now, a Monet would be another matter."

"That would even be out of my league. We could also think about buying that property in France we've talked about. Languedoc would be my choice." Then he added, to her astonishment, "We could even consider getting married."

Sarah, spoiling the moment, said rather airily, "Yes, we could... and maybe we should."

"Well, that's not quite the enthusiastic response I'd expected."

"Take it as a yes," she said, but with no more feeling than her first response. "And, if I might say so, it's not before time."

Sarah remained unconvinced by Vincent's sudden enthusiasm for family life, much less his sudden embrace of culture. In fact, she found it downright odd. Which is why, weeks later, when the political storm across the Atlantic had subsided, she returned to the issue of the president's decision. She had been reading an article in a weekend supplement noting that the president's demeanour seemed to have changed from arrogant to reasonable, verging on humble. He seemed a new man, the article said. "His decision didn't make sense to me at the time and the more I think about it, the less sense it makes."

"Your guess is as good as mine," said Vincent. Omertà still ruled.

"But have you spoken to him? I mean, you two used to be so close. I'd have thought he'd have called you with an explanation. The real reason, that is. I don't for one moment believe the ones he gave. Nor, it seems, does anyone else."

"If there was something else, I'm sure he'd have called me... but we're not as close as we used to be."

"Have *you* called *him*?"

"Yes, but he hasn't got back to me." The lies still tripped out easily. "He's been rather busy of late, I'm sure, what with that bitch of a wife demanding a divorce."

Sarah flinched at the gender slur but said nothing. "And what about your friend Frank Hoffman? He must know the whole story. Have you spoken to him at all?"

"I'm not sure we're still on speaking terms." This was his most accurate observation of the evening.

"What a shame," was all she said. "I quite liked them."

In the absence of useful intelligence from her husband, Sarah could only follow the story in the media. She silently considered the various speculative theories doing the rounds, but none rang true. She was certain that her partner knew more than he was telling her. She even wondered whether he might somehow be involved. But at that point, her curiosity faded. Best not to know, she decided. She was, of course, aware that her former husband had broken the story, and had tried to reach him several times, not so much to offer her congratulations as to grill him for the 'inside dope' that Vincent had signally failed to provide, but Nigel hadn't seen fit to return her calls. Belatedly, she realized why: her message that the kids were okay and doing well had nullified the only reason he ever called her back. Annoyingly, he was calling *them* regularly these days; they seemed excited about it. "We've been invited to visit him in America next year," they reported. "Well, I'm not so sure about that," she told them.

In one last attempt to elicit a response she left a new message with Nigel that *MODE* magazine would like to interview him, and with a hefty fee attached, but even that failed to elicit a response. Where the hell had the wretched man got to?

* * *

Arizona was the answer.

He and Jane had gone out west to fulfil his lifelong dream of riding a trail in the Grand Canyon. The ambition seemed, on the face of it, out of character: he was afraid of horses, hated the Great Outdoors, and was hardly in peak physical condition. But the prospect of trying something new and challenging had excited him, and Jane had found a travel agency that offered 'executive tours' that would require minimum physical effort in return for maximum expenditure. And so off they went. He was also keen, 'since we'll be in the neighborhood', to play a few blackjack tables in nearby Las Vegas. Jane dismissed the side trip to Vegas as "hardly in keeping with our plan to commune with nature". Nigel countered that it would provide another welcome distraction from the enervating political drama they had just lived through.

Nigel had left Bill Palmer in charge of the Washington office. Astonished by his colleague's triumph, Bill was also miffed that he had been left out of the loop, even though he had contributed to Nigel's early 'research'. And even after the great scoop, he had been given little information about how it had been accomplished. But he enjoyed his return to DC 'batting cleanup', as he put it, and kept Nigel regularly informed with dispatches from the front, hoping to be repaid with some inside dope in return. Washington, he reported, may have been evacuated for the summer but it was still rampant with rumours. He mentioned a few, but none that Nigel had not heard already. One was that the president had quit because he would otherwise have been exposed by 'his buddy in the Kremlin' over some shady commercial deal they had been cooking up together, which Putin had apparently killed after hearing disparaging remarks the president had made about him at a NATO summit.

"You know, the Putin thing could explain everything," Bill declared. He didn't believe that for one moment but said it in the hope of receiving some reciprocal intelligence. He would be disappointed.

"I'd like to tell you more, Bill, but sources are sacred. You know that."

Another caller was Duncan. Bill had reported that their managing editor was milking the scoop for all it was worth, causing Nigel to worry that his editor might be tempted to break their solemn vow of silence. He would not shoot his mouth off at a cocktail party - Nigel had that market cornered - but he might try to earn merit points by dropping a few hints to Lord Goodfriend, the last person to be entrusted with such secrets. Yes, Duncan said, he had indeed spoken to His Lordship. And, yes, he had asked who their sources were. But no, he had not told him any more than what they had agreed: that the story had come from a high-level government source - and been confirmed by a second. Lord Goodfriend knew enough about the business not to ask for names, merely observing grumpily that, "You'd think the owner of the bloody newspaper would be allowed to know where its bloody news comes from."

One afternoon, just as Nigel and Jane were descending, precariously, on horseback into the bowels of a deep canyon, at the bottom of which a white-water torrent raged, Duncan rang again. Much to the annoyance of their guides, Nigel dismounted to take the call. "This had better be good," he told his managing editor. Duncan said he was calling to report that Nigel should expect a call from the proprietor, congratulating him on his scoop. "But be on your guard, because he'll try to wheedle the names of the sources out of you. Just thought I'd give you a heads up."

"Thanks for the warning," Nigel replied. "I'll tell him only what we agreed."

"Nothing more," Duncan admonished. He also had news of a personal nature. "Oh, I thought you also ought to know something else: Elsa and I have ended our relationship. It was my decision. I must say she took it very well."

"I'm sorry to hear that. But I'm glad it ended in a civilized manner."

"Well, not entirely. Elsa quit. Left the company yesterday." Nigel asked for more details, but Duncan promised to reveal all when Nigel was back from his vacation. Duncan had one more bulletin. "Caroline and I are getting back together - trying to make another go of it, as they say."

Nigel offered his congratulations. "Funny, isn't it, how one's whole world can change in the course of a few weeks."

Bill Palmer, on his next call, filled in the details of the Elsa story that Duncan had left out. "It was Elsa, not Duncan, who ended the affair," he reported. "I have that on good authority. She'd met a wealthy foreign exchange trader at Xanadu, a trendy Mayfair nightclub frequented by City high-fliers, and after a third or fourth date he'd proposed, and she'd accepted." Elsa, he added, had already flown out to join her intended, someone named Rupert, for an Adriatic cruise on a fully crewed sixty-foot yacht.

Elsa confirmed Bill's version in a postcard to Nigel, inviting him and Jane to the wedding on a Greek Island neither of them had ever heard of. The concluding sentence made Nigel chuckle: *'Just remember, my sweet man, you had every chance.'*

Romance was in the air in Washington, too. Fran called Jane to report that she and Rosalie would be moving in together. "I'm certain, my darling girl, that this is the real thing. I'm over the moon. We'll probably get married." Jane promised to arrange a celebratory dinner as soon as she and Nigel returned from vacation.

Even Frank Hoffman telephoned, anxious to report on the 'fallout' from the president's announcement. "Washington's confusion is a joy to behold," he chortled. "Talk about headless chickens. I don't think I've ever been quite so entertained. But it's also a bit nerve-wracking. I have this recurring dream that I'll wake up one morning and read in the *Washington Post* that they've worked it all out." He also mentioned that he and Marion had booked an Atlantic crossing on a cruise liner and would be away for five weeks on a tour of European museums and art galleries. "You and Jane should feel free to use the Maryland house while we're away. I've already alerted the housekeeper." Nigel thanked him and said they might just take him up on the offer.

Jane was in a thoughtful mood that evening. They were sitting around a campfire, eating a gourmet meal prepared by their guides. "We go away for just a few days," she said, distractedly poking at the fire with a stick, "and all these people call to say they're changing their lives."

"Feeling left out, are we?" Nigel asked in mock pity.

"Not at all. I've experienced a few life-changing events of my own in recent months. Thanks to you, honeybun," - he hated the expression - "I've wrecked my career and acquired a man."

"A fair exchange, wouldn't you say? Are you ready for more?"

"More what?"

"Changes."

"That depends on what you have in mind."

"I've been thinking... maybe we should give up this 'living in sin' - as my father would call it – and go for something more respectable. What do you say?"

She laughed nervously. "I'd say the desert heat has gone to your head."

"On the contrary, I'd say the desert air has cleared it."

"Is that a proposal I just heard?"

"What else could it have been?"

"I must say this is all very sudden ..."

"Is that your only response?" He was watching her anxiously, but the flickering shadows from the campfire distorted her expression. An empathetic owl hooted mournfully nearby.

She was quietly enjoying his discomfiture. "No, it means only that I'll need time to think about it."

He looked crestfallen. "How much time?"

"Oh, about ten seconds." She counted them off, pretending to look grim, but revelling in the suspense.

"And what's the decision?"

"Considering all the damning evidence: that we've known each other for only a few months; that you've yet to lift a finger to help with the housework; that you're an irrecoverable slob; that your mood changes from one hour to the next... it's a conditional yes."

"Conditional? On what?"

"That you get down on bended knee and offer a ring. I'm old-fashioned that way."

"I'm afraid I didn't bring a ring."

"So, this is a sudden impulse?"

"An impulse, yes, but not a whim."

"What's the difference?"

"I don't know since you ask. But I *have* given the matter considerable thought."

"Well, I'll settle for a bended knee."

He rose awkwardly from his canvas director's chair and lowered himself to one knee, disturbing a log that sent up a shower of sparks. "A metaphor for the fire of my passion," he joked.

"But in reality, only more evidence of your clumsiness."

"I just can't win," he said.

"I think you just did," she replied, laughing.

And with that, under a star-filled Arizona sky, he plighted his troth.

* * * * *

CHAPTER 21

The former first lady intended to spend what remained of the summer at the Barr horse farm. Anna would come out from New York on Friday evenings - she was working at a private language school on the East Side - but otherwise Samantha had only the stable girls and two housekeepers for company. She was not lonely. She enjoyed the seclusion. Fran Powell would call every other day, insisting on keeping her former boss in touch with Washington's current preoccupations. These included the activities of the new first lady, based on information provided by Fran's own successor with whom she had struck up a friendship during the post-election handover.

In truth, after three years of freedom, Samantha was far from enthralled by what went on in the White House, or elsewhere in Washington, but Fran's accounts, replete with gossipy asides, were as entertaining as they were informative. Especially, as they now involved the Democrats, newly in power but already out of favour.

"You don't work for me now," Samantha had reminded her, but Fran said it was a duty of love, not an obligation.

Fran herself was now working as the communications director for a recently formed political think tank, which sought to promote the old-fashioned notion that politics ought to return to the middle ground. Reading between the lines of what appeared on its website, it was about restoring the art of compromise and consensus but with a decidedly liberal bias.

One morning late in August, after an invigorating cross-country ride, Samantha handed her mount to one of the stable girls and checked her cell phone. Among the many messages left, only one caught her eye. The caller was a veteran Republican senator, Claude Hansen of Ohio. She had met him once or twice, but only to exchange pleasantries at political gatherings. She couldn't imagine why he would be calling her, least of all in August, with Congress still on its summer break.

Hansen had once been revered in the GOP as a power broker and kingmaker, as a conciliator who cultivated friends across an ever widening and increasingly acrimonious political divide. Since the

GOP's shameful submission to the so-called Tea Party and other elements of the alt-right, and the accession to the White House of the crude rabble-rouser who had represented, and in many cases, formed their views, Hansen had been reduced to operating at the political margins. Though respected by some party colleagues as a man of integrity, he was increasingly dismissed as an irrelevance. Samantha recalled a courtly, rotund man in his early seventies, with snow white hair and an expansive Mark Twain moustache. He was a mid-westerner born and bred but tended to speak in the fulsome oratorical tradition of the Deep South.

The message asked Samantha to call him at her earliest convenience. Curious, and vaguely uneasy, she telephoned him from the stable yard. His wife Martha answered. The senator was at home, she said, but was busy in the hothouse tending to "his beloved orchids".

"I do hope you're well, Mrs Jameson," Martha suddenly said, solicitously, the accent betraying her genuine Southern roots. "I was deeply sorry to hear about your marital troubles, my dear. I do hope most of them are behind you now."

"Thank you, Mrs Hansen. I'm just fine. Really. I'm just glad it's all over. It has been something of an ordeal, but now that it's over, and everything's out in the open, I feel a profound sense of relief. Now, we can both move on."

Martha didn't ask where the 'moving on' was likely to take her. "I'm sure glad to hear it. Now, if you'll please hold, I'll fetch my husband... if he hasn't expired from the heat. It's ninety in the shade today, and in that blessed greenhouse of his it must be over a hundred."

After a minute or two, the senator came on the line. He sounded slightly out of breath. "Good morning, Mrs Jameson. Thank you for getting back to me so promptly. How's the weather down there in DC? We're sweltering in a heatwave here in southern Ohio."

"I'm in Virginia, Senator, and the weather here is divine. Warm but not oppressive. I've just been out riding. I'm never happier, you know, than when I'm astride a horse with the breeze in my hair."

"Good, good... that sounds delightful. I'm glad to hear from Martha that you're in such good form after your recent... adventures. Have I caught you at an inconvenient moment?"

"Not at all, Senator."

"I apologize for having kept you hanging on. I'm trying to save some ailing dendrobiums. Are you familiar with orchids?"

"I'm afraid not, Senator. I find them beautiful beyond words, but my ignorance on the subject is profound."

"What a pity. Orchids are my passion in life. After politics, of course. These days I seem to have more success with the former than with the latter. But you know, orchids and politicians have a great deal in common."

Samantha fell for it. "Oh? In what way?"

"They're both parasites, both need a lot of heat to thrive, and both have a sordid history of driving men mad."

Samantha laughed. "I know exactly what you mean."

"Again, Mrs Jameson, I appreciate your returning my call so promptly."

"My pleasure, Senator. I might say my duty: you are, after all, one of the GOP's most revered elder statesmen."

"Elder certainly, but no longer revered. As for statesman, well that's a word that seems to belong to a different century. We live in changing times, politically speaking - and I'm sorry to say, not altogether for the better."

"I hope you're wrong, Senator. If there's anything the world needs right now, it's statesmen. I've always been an admirer of yours. You're a quiet voice of reason in a world going mad. As a lifelong Republican, it grieves me to say that the Party, as it presently functions, contributes little to the cause of sanity."

"I couldn't agree more, my dear. This so-called Grand Old Party of ours isn't so grand anymore. Some of my colleagues - I won't mention names - seem intent on taking us into the kind of dark places where dangerous monsters are known to dwell… if I may be permitted a rhetorical flourish."

"Speaking of monsters, have you spoken to my husband lately?"

"No. We have nothing to say to each other. Anyway, he stopped taking my calls, so I stopped making them. Most of the time I'd get put through to his latest chief of staff, or even some lesser functionary."

"Why am I surprised?"

"It really doesn't matter, my dear. He's out of office now. And that brings me to the reason for my call…" The senator hesitated. "There's a matter of some importance I'd like to discuss with you."

Samantha was now fully alert, wondering what might be coming next. She responded with contrived perkiness. "Fire away, Senator. I'm all ears. And please call me Samantha. Since I'm no longer a first lady in anything but title, I think a degree of informality is appropriate."

"And you, Samantha, must call me Claude. Now, the first thing on my mind is how you're coping. I mean, really coping. Your husband's announcement took the entire country by surprise, including me, incidentally. It's not often that I'm caught off-guard, I can tell you, but I nearly fell over, and for a man of my brittle bones that could have had serious consequences. So, how are you?"

"I'm doing just fine, Senator. But thank you for asking. Times have been difficult these past two years, but I think the worst is over, as I was telling your wife. I certainly hope so."

"And your - er - domestic situation, has that been resolved to your satisfaction? I'm not prying, you understand, just concerned."

"I understand perfectly. Our marriage had been troubled for some time. The fact is, we found out that we increasingly had little in common. I sometimes wonder whether we ever did... but that's a whole different story. The situation had become intolerable. I realized I was living a lie. My husband was living a lie, too, but he seemed more comfortable with it than I was. So, now I'm living in a beautiful home in Sheridan-Kalorama, enjoying my children and my new-found freedom... but I don't want to bore you with all that."

"I'm far from bored, Samantha, I'm genuinely concerned. Let me just say that if you ever feel you need someone to confide in, a shoulder to cry on - for whatever reason - I'm always available, and I mean that sincerely."

"That's most thoughtful of you, Senator... Claude."

"Well, we live in strange times, when kindness and courtesy are considered old-fashioned virtues."

"Many of us have recognized the problem, Senator, believe me. Even some in what remains of the Republican Party, or at least the one that we remember."

"A declining number of us, I'd have to say. We're always too busy shouting at each other." This was followed by an awkward silence, which Samantha assumed was the senator working out how to broach the reason for his call. She expected an opening statement that would set the scene and he duly delivered it. "I can only assume that his decision not to run again was something you and he had been discussing for some time..." He was probing, she guessed. He in turn noted the pause before she replied.

"No, Senator Hansen... Claude, I had no idea until a few days before his broadcast." She felt bad that the lie tripped so easily off the tongue. "But as you know, my husband is a man driven by sudden and often inexplicable impulses. This, I can only suppose, was one of them."

"Yes, of course," the senator said, not bothering to disguise his skeptical tone. "Well, I dare say it's all for the best... both for you *and* the country. Mind you, despite my differences with him, I feel no sense of joy in a Republican president giving up office. I'm speaking as a senator in a state that gave this president a sizeable majority... and me, I should add, an uncomfortably smaller one."

"I'm sure the good people of Ohio will reverse that the next time out."

"If there is a next time."

"I hope there will be, and I mean that sincerely. The Senate would be a poorer place without you." Samantha had indeed meant every word of it, but she was also tiring of the small talk. "But you mentioned, Senator, that there was something you wanted to speak to me about."

"There is, but it's not something I wish to discuss on the telephone. I'm rather hoping we can meet face-to-face. Perhaps for lunch. It so happens I'm going to be in Washington next week. How's your calendar? And I apologize, dear lady, for interrupting your vacation. You've certainly earned one. And if it's not convenient I'll understand."

"I'd be delighted to have lunch, Senator. In fact, I'd regard it as a high point of my vacation." This was laying it on a bit thick, but she knew that he responded to florid language.

"You flatter me, Madam. But thank you. How about next Wednesday?"

"I'll have to check my diary, but from memory I'm free that day. Where?"

"Let me find a restaurant in the DC area and get back to you. I'd prefer somewhere discreet, perhaps somewhere out in the suburbs. Washington may look empty right now but there are still a great many prying eyes around. I'll ask my secretary to find a suitable venue and then have her call you, if that's alright."

"That'll be fine," said Samantha. She was now intensely curious. "Are you going to give me a clue as to what we'll be talking about? I mean, is this something I need to prepare for?"

"No preparation needed," the senator replied, lightly. "Let's just say that I have an interest in your future as well as your present and would like to offer the benefit of my wisdom. Dispensing wisdom is something I'm good at, or so my grandchildren tell me... and I've got more of those than I can sometimes remember."

Since he was obviously not prepared to say more, Samantha ended the conversation. "I'll wait for your secretary's call. Goodbye, Senator Hansen... Claude, and thank you for calling."

* * *

The lunch venue selected by Hansen's secretary was a small Italian restaurant wedged between a hardware store and a dry cleaner in a strip mall in one of the city's drearier blue-collar northwestern suburbs. "Casual dress, of course," the secretary had stressed, "and I mean casual." Some form of disguise was presumably what she really meant. Fellow diners might recognize the unmistakable figure of the senator, but Samantha followed her instructions to the letter with an unflattering ensemble of scruffy denim pants and a checked shirt. She also wore, despite the heat, a well-scuffed leather bomber jacket, borrowed from one of the stable girls. It smelled of horses, she realized on the way over. She wore no make-up, and her hair was tied back into a rather severe bun. She might, she decided, easily be taken for a harried housewife on a shopping errand. She drove herself to the restaurant, without her security detail, although someone had probably followed her anyway.

The senator had arrived ahead of her. At first, she failed to spot him. The interior of the restaurant was gloomy, and he had taken a corner table partly obscured by a potted palm with large plastic leaves coated in grease to which a layer of dust had adhered. He in turn failed to recognize her until she had almost reached the table.

"So much easier, isn't it, to dress down than to dress up," she said by way of apology for her appearance. He had observed the injunction to dress casually only to the extent of discarding a tie, in favour of an open collar from which, she noticed, a cluster of grey chest hairs struggled to escape.

"How on earth did you find this place?" Samantha asked, shaking his hand vigorously and her head questioningly. "Even my sat-nav had a hard time getting me here."

"Thank my secretary's daughter, who apparently lives somewhere near here. Her advice, by the way, was to ignore the ambience and enjoy the food. Based on the décor, we can only hope she's right. I ordered a bottle of red wine, by the way. A Barolo. Happens to be a favourite of mine. I hope you'll like it, too."

"I adore Barolo. Unfortunately, I drove myself here. But I suppose I can have one glass."

She scrutinized the senator as he half-filled her glass. Then he raised his own. "A toast, Madam. Here's to you, Samantha Jameson, and a bright new future - for you, and for the Republican Party. May it emerge from the darkness."

She amended the toast. "Here's to a bright future for a new and improved Republican Party - if that doesn't make it sound too much like washing power."

The senator amended her amendment. "Not to a new Republican Party, perhaps, but a speedy return to the old one."

"So, tell me, Senator (since this was apparently a business meeting, Samantha decided to stay in a more formal mode of conversation) do you think the party we know, and once loved, still has a future? There are those who believe it has now been seriously, perhaps even fatally, compromised by extremists, and by the previous president."

"That view may be a bit extreme, my dear. Yes, the political landscape looks bleak for the moderate right, which is why we must change our ways. Get back closer to the mainstream. And I'm confident we can. If we don't, then it won't just be the party that's in trouble but the country. Democracy itself."

"The Democrats ought by right to sweep the board next time out."

"Ah, yes, the dear old Democrats. Well, they're in a tangle as well. It always seems to happen whenever they're on the brink of a long period in power, I shed no tears for them. But whichever party is in power, we need a healthy national debate. We need two healthy political parties, and I mean two parties that can talk to each other. Civilly. Disagree without resorting to shouting in the language of the street. That's the way our democracy always worked. No wonder the voters are disillusioned with politicians. All of us. The truth is, I sometimes verge on the disillusioned myself."

Samantha was wondering where this was going. "I hope, Senator, you don't think my domestic misfortunes will contribute to the GOP losing the White House next time around."

The senator smiled impishly. "Oh, they've already been forgotten. But I would argue that your husband's strange decision not to run did the Republican Party a service, even if it doesn't know it yet."

"How so?" Certain now that the senator had been holding something back, she was ready to hear what it was.

"Your husband's departure in my opinion was a blessing in disguise. I'm hardly alone in that view among my Republican colleagues in Congress, even if few can summon the courage to say so. Those who've stayed silent are the puppets of the alt right extremists who installed your husband to dance at the end of their strings. That's not necessarily the way I express it in my speeches, of course, although I've come darned close from time to time."

"I know. I've read some of them."

The senator smoothed the checkered tablecloth, which she interpreted as a symbolic gesture to prepare the placing of cards on the table. "Your husband's presidency will, I believe, be seen by historians as an aberration, brought about by a collective nervous breakdown of the electorate. But we're supposed to learn from history, not repeat it. What concerns me now is how we prevent it happening again. Now that we find ourselves out of power, we have that opportunity."

"And how do you think it can be achieved?"

"In order to win the next election, we need a fresh approach. A 'kinder, gentler' approach, as one of our former Republican presidents put it. When the time comes, we need to run a ticket drawn from the moderate wing. By that I mean a ticket with traditional conservative values but humane policies. A ticket free of ideological dogma. A ticket that will acknowledge, not despise, the changing face of America. Thanks to you, we have a chance to put together such a ticket."

"Thanks to me? It was my husband's decision not to run again, not mine."

Senator Hanson displayed a knowing smile. "Come, come, Samantha, I think we're both aware that there was more to his decision than that."

"What do you mean exactly?" *Here come the cards,* she was thinking.

The Senator grinned gnomically. "Let me just say that I know more about the reason behind your husband's action than you might think."

Samantha suddenly looked alarmed. "And how, may I ask, do you know that? I should say, why do you think that?"

"How I know isn't important. Let me say this: I was aware some time ago that your husband, and others - all Republicans, I'm afraid

- were up to no good; that sooner or later one of them would be caught with a hand in the cookie jar. I'm only grateful that you were the one who entered the kitchen when that moment arrived."

"I really don't know what to say…"

"I honestly don't either, Samantha, so perhaps I should avoid saying it. And in case you were afraid that I'd be subjecting you to some form of interrogation, I'm not. Nor am I going to embarrass you by asking. What matters is the outcome. Suffice to say that, by doing what you did, you prevented a scandal that might have destroyed this democracy of ours, and at considerable risk to yourself. For that alone, I applaud you - as I applaud you for much else besides."

Samantha saw no option but to end the innocent charade. "I don't suppose there's any point in my demanding to know how you found out."

"None whatever."

"And how many others know what you know?"

"Very few."

"Define 'very few'."

"Me and, as far as I know, just four others. They are all close associates of mine. They are people who can be trusted, so please don't worry that any of this will leak out."

"But I *do* worry, Senator. I *must* worry. And after what you've just told me I'll be even more worried. If you only knew what…"

"I do know, my dear, I do know." He patted her hand. "Believe me, I know. But let's not dwell on it. You have your secrets and I have mine. Let's leave it at that. I won't mention the matter again. What's important now is that the Republican Party, the real GOP, moves on."

"I couldn't agree more."

"Good. Because that brings me to the point of our meeting, the reason we're sitting in a rather dreary café in the back of beyond." Waving away a lurking waiter, the senator leaned across the table with an earnest look and cleared his throat nervously. He spoke in a voice so soft she strained to hear it. "I've been meaning to ask you something, and I'm now going to put it to you plainly, while looking you right in the eye." He paused, as if having second thoughts, before proceeding. "How would you feel about running for office?"

Samantha's reaction was less than impressive. "I'm sorry?"

"You heard me correctly."

"Run? For what office?"

"Vice-President. On the next Republican ticket." The senator sat back in his seat, content to wait for her response. *'No one buys anything after hearing the first pitch,'* he was thinking, *'but the next move is hers'.*

Her mouth was agape. Several agonizingly elongated seconds passed before she could respond. "Are you serious, Senator?"

"Perfectly serious."

"Senator, I'm lost for words, I don't mind telling you. I've no idea what to say. You're talking about a prospective vice-president of the United States."

"Yes. That's what, by tradition, a running mate becomes if his or her party wins."

"I'm still speechless..."

The senator smiled again. "I'm quite adept at rendering people speechless, my dear. It's a skill one develops over a lifetime in politics. It often comes in handy I've found." The smile receded. "But on this occasion, I'd appreciate a reply. I'm not looking for a definitive reply but an instinctive reaction. From the gut, not the brain." He could tell, though, that she was organizing her thoughts, trying to put her response into some semblance of order.

"Aside from anything else, Senator, I've never run for public office - not so much as a charity board."

"That's not a constitutional requirement. You of all people should know that. To cite an obvious example, your former husband had never run for anything in his life. Then, out of the blue, as it were, he was sitting in the Oval Office. I still find it hard to believe."

She had walked into that one. "Unfortunately for the country, and to its everlasting shame."

She's stalling, he thought.

But then she spoke again, this time calmly and deliberately. "You mentioned I'd be number two on the ticket. Does that mean you have someone in mind for the first spot?"

'Not only has she not said no,' he was thinking, *'but she's asking the right questions.'* "Yes. We're thinking of Senator Martin Leach of Minnesota. You know him?"

"Not really. We've met a few times."

"And...?"

"I liked him. A charming man. And, as far as I can tell, a decent one."

"Do you like his political views as well?"

"He's a moderate. That's in his favour. As I understand it, a balanced budget man in the Republican tradition but a liberal on social issues. The alt-right despises him, but that's another point in his favour. I haven't a clue about his foreign policy views. I imagine you don't get to conduct much international diplomacy in Minnesota."

"Well observed. Yes, on domestic issues he's a middle-of-the-roader. Some would say - and have said - he's a bit wishy-washy. Others have found him boring. They're not wrong. But boring is not such a terrible thing in the present febrile climate. In international affairs he would be a neophyte, but then so are most incoming presidents, including most of the recent ones. I know he's wary of China, perhaps even a bit hawkish by his standards, but there would be no danger of him starting a shooting war on a minor issue. He's a facilitator, not a sabre-rattler."

"I know very little else about his personal life."

"I can give you a potted version. He's fifty-five. A family man, married for twenty-nine years to his college sweetheart. Three kids, all at university. None busted for drug-peddling that I know of. No hint of family scandals of any kind. No extra-marital affairs, I'm certain of that." The senator took note of Samantha's downward glance as he said it. "Of course, you never can tell, can you."

"Religion?"

"Is that important?"

"Just curious."

"He's Episcopalian. A regular churchgoer, I believe."

"That would make two of us on the same ticket."

"That's not an obstacle. While it doesn't contribute to the more inclusive GOP we're hoping to create, your gender takes care of that."

Samantha smiled. "I'm not a churchgoer, I should tell you. I'm an agnostic, flirting with atheism."

The senator's sly look returned. "And are you flirting with anything else?"

Samantha reddened. "Like what? Danger?"

"That might be one way of putting it."

Knowing exactly what he was getting at, Samantha looked none too pleased. "If you're referring to my private life, Senator Hansen, I'd like to keep it that way."

"Something to hide?"

"Nothing that I'm not entitled to hide." Samantha was starting to bristle, he could tell.

"I'm not prying, you understand, but…"

"But what? Just explain to me, Senator, the difference between having something to hide and having a desire for privacy. When do they not amount to one and the same thing?" Samantha recognized as she said it that she had almost spat out the words. The senator clearly knew something and knew that she knew he knew - Nigel Harper's Washington Lie - so why did he not just come out and say so?

He had the same thought. "Let me speak openly, Samantha, because I'm far too old to be dancing around the issues. And you deserve better. The truth is - sad as it may be - that when you run for office, your private life no longer qualifies as private. I happen to know all about your Russian lady-friend in New York. It's of interest to me for one reason only: if you *were* to go on the national ticket, the rest of the world would have to know about her, too. If you don't disclose these things voluntarily, they'll only come out in the wash."

"How, may I ask out of curiosity, did you find out about her?"

"While we were doing our background check. We're required to investigate anyone being considered for public office. Corporate lawyers call it due diligence. It comes with the territory, I'm afraid."

"That only tells me the 'when' and the 'why'. I asked about the 'how'."

"I'd rather not get into the specifics of that, if you don't mind. As our friends in the media would say, I don't reveal my sources."

"This merging of the personal and the political, it's not - I don't know - seemly. Or relevant."

Senator Hansen shrugged. "I couldn't agree more. But then I don't make the rules. In some recent cases, those rules were carelessly overlooked and see what happened. When the truth emerges, as it always does, the candidate always ends up looking devious. Like it or not, the public is convinced that all politicians have something to hide - and all too often they're right. To be fair, they're entitled to know whether the candidates are what they claim to be. In any event, it's the way things are done - how they've always been done."

"Even so, I'm still an adulteress."

"True enough, although the word sounds rather biblical these days."

Samantha took a sip of wine, silently wishing she had come with a driver so that she could drink herself into a state of disbelief. "Not to the evangelicals, it doesn't."

"Also true. But they are not the entire party."

"Even so, what makes you think the GOP, as it now presents itself to voters, could nominate a ticket that included an adulterous lesbian atheist? And that's before we come to the question of winning an election with such a ticket."

Her blunt challenge failed to rattle him. "It won't be easy, I agree, but I can't see why not. In the words of Mr Dylan, 'the times they are a'changin'. Even an old Republican fossil like me can see that." She laughed at the reference to someone who probably didn't appear on Senator Hansen's list of favourite entertainers.

"They seem to be changing, all right, but in many respects for the worse."

"Let's not concern ourselves for now with the narrow issue of how we convert a few million voters in Middle America. Let's take instead a broader perspective, a world view. The world is a very different place from what it was fifty years ago, and by and large for the better. Consider this, Samantha. When I was growing up - long before most of today's voters were born - the South was segregated. Russia was a Soviet Empire hell-bent on destroying us, China a vast rural backwater, which is the way most of us thought it would always be, like some immutable law of nature. But in the second half of my lifetime everything changed. Segregation was overcome, the Soviet Union collapsed, and China is now a world power. I can only presume that the world will keep changing in myriad unforeseen ways. We must try to ensure that it changes for the better. That means putting people in power who understand that, not the people who want to take us back decades."

"Who can argue with that?" Samantha said. "And if we don't face those challenges head-on, we're all lost. The planet, not just America. I'm thinking of climate change, which of course my husband denies is happening." Her reply drew a satisfied smile from the man across the table.

"And guess what? Change, when it happens, isn't always so bad - and this is an old fogey talking. Who would have thought, fifty years ago, even twenty-five, that America would have an African American president? Not even this supposedly wise old bird, I confess. But did the skies fall in when we had a black man in the Oval Office? Did the world cease to spin on its axis? Were whites slaughtered on the streets, as some of my colleagues from the southern states seemed to think they would be?"

"And the issues of my sexuality...?"

"Well, things have changed in that regard, too. Some of us, and that includes me, have learnt a great a deal over the years."

"Not yet changed enough," she said. "And I'm not referring to you personally, Senator."

Senator Hansen put on his well-practiced earnest look. "You probably don't know this, Samantha, so I'll tell you. I have a gay daughter. Ellen, my eldest. She came out - as we now say - soon after she left college. It was a very brave thing for her to do, and more so then than now. I admired her for it. I love her not a scintilla less for it. Her partner is the nicest person you could wish to meet, and now part of the family. I look at it this way: if my daughter is happy, then I'm happy. What else is there to be said or done? I might not have thought that way twenty years ago, and I'm pretty sure I didn't. The point is, we must all shed our old prejudices and push for a more enlightened age, rather than being pulled into it kicking and screaming. A woman in the White House? Why not? It's about time. Your gender represents fifty percent of the population. A lesbian? Gays are probably ten percent of the population, maybe more. All voters, by the way. Britain has already had three female leaders. We're not even close to having a first - much less if she happens to be a Republican. We need to get rid of all these, these... shibboleths. And I'm speaking here as a lifelong Lutheran."

Samantha would have liked to stand and applaud. "Bravo, Senator. Clearly, you are a New Age man, and far from typical of your generation or your class, much less your party, at least in its present condition."

"Perhaps it means I'm in the wrong party. Certainly, some of my senatorial colleagues seem to think so."

"Well, shame on them." Samantha, now recovered from the initial shock of his proposition, returned to it, replacing philosophical virtues with practical realities. "I take it you've discussed all this with Senator Leach?"

"I have. At some length. I told him I'd be meeting you."

"Does that mean he approves of me? And does he know about my husband's financial crimes? Or my sexuality?"

"Yes to the first. No, to the second, of course. Yes, to the third."

"And he's still in favour of having me on the ticket?"

"Not yet. You haven't even met. But let me put it this way: we reviewed a list of eight possible running mates - not a short list, you understand, but a kicking-around thing. We had already eliminated some names and replaced them with others. Of the eight names we finished up with he immediately deleted five. Yours remained. We agreed that the remaining three were, and remain, viable candidates."

"And the other two names?"

"I can't tell you. I'm sure you understand why."

"Perfectly. May I ask what qualities, apart from gender, sexual orientation and progressive politics, convinced you that I'm worthy of such an honour? Surely not my temperament. I can be quite sensitive, you know. And sometimes quite volatile. I've been known to throw crockery."

"What you call volatility, I prefer to call spirit. Either way, it's an easy question to answer. I'll start with two: integrity and courage. Your actions as first lady demonstrated both. I'll add intelligence and empathy: you plainly possess both. These are virtues singularly lacking in some of our recent candidates. And presidents. I've done my homework, Samantha. As well as your virtues I know your faults. I don't consider them insurmountable. Nobody's perfect."

"Voters these days seem to think their politicians should be."

"That thesis was contradicted by your husband's election, wouldn't you say?"

"A fair point, but there will always be aberrations. My husband was one of them, as history will show. But I will be an aberration, too?" She realized as she spoke that he might think she was fishing for compliments.

"Not at all, unless you're trying to tell me something that I've missed."

"You seem to know everything already, Senator. Supposing I were to express an interest in this bold venture of yours, what would happen next?"

"Ah, now we're getting down to cases. First and foremost, you must consider carefully - and I mean carefully - what I've said. I realize that I've sprung it on you, and I wasn't expecting a yes response. In fact, I was expecting a no. So, after a decent interval, you'll indicate that you're at least willing to have your candidacy considered. Second, assuming you are, I'd need to talk to Senator Leach. So would you. The two of you would have to meet, more than once, to see whether you could get along; find out what, if any, differences of opinion you had on key issues. Also, to establish whether there was a personal chemistry. Third, we'd have to conduct a more thorough background check on you. And I mean thorough. If there are, forgive me, any other skeletons lurking in your closet, you'd have to be prepared to see them come clattering out onto the floor. That, of course, would include your liaison with Anna. Have there been any other lovers, by the way?"

"None, sadly. Until Anna, I'd been living a life of celibacy for years - and that included the latter years of my marriage."

"I see…" Senator Hansen said, looking embarrassed. "Anyway, after we'd examined your life in forensic detail - and found nothing disqualifying - a great many other things would happen. It's a gruelling process, as you know, and not for the faint of heart. But until we've cleared the first hurdle, your expression of interest, there's no point in discussing any of that. The Republican Party leaders would have to be quietly consulted, of course, on the Hill and elsewhere. I should also point out that I'm no longer as influential as I once was. A great many other voices would need to be heard. In short, this won't happen just because I'm in favour of it, not by a long chalk. The extreme wing of the party will, of course, fight like furies to prevent it. Oh, and other candidates may well throw their hats into the ring."

"Do you know of any who might?"

"Oh, I've heard up to a dozen names mentioned. At the last election, there were six candidates in the Republican debate. They soon fell apart. Even you might wilt under the pressure. It happens to the best. One false note, a slip of the tongue and - poof - you'd be gone. That's how it is in this age of social media. Before then, of course, there would be the primaries. Mr Leach would have to emerge a clear winner, or failing that, at least among a handful of front-runners. The primaries are an endless process, in diverse states, some of them somewhat, shall we say, rustic, and all of them highly unpredictable. This whole enterprise is unpredictable. To be perfectly honest, this whole idea is a long shot. There, have I managed to put you off the idea yet?"

"No, at least not for the reasons you mentioned, Senator. And, believe me, I understand what lies ahead. Remember, I've seen the process at first hand. Other than that, I'm not sure what else to say."

"You've already said it."

"What?"

"I asked if I'd put you off and you said no. That's a start. But seriously, you need some time to think this over, carefully and thoughtfully. And may I say, at the risk of sounding corny, with due humility."

"This has all been so unexpected, Senator, I'm still not sure…" Her voice tailed off. "How long do I have to consider a response."

"Oh, a few months. But not too many. The election process proper won't start for another three years. But the sooner we start it the better. Forgive the expression, but we need to start selling you at an early stage. To the party first, and then to the voters."

Samantha could think of nothing else to ask or say. She'd been tempted, at several points, to quash the whole mad idea before it took root. Dismiss it out of hand. But something had stopped her. She couldn't have defined what that was, but it was something buried deep in her soul. There would be time to haul it out later, in a quieter, private moment. Meanwhile, she owed the senator at least the courtesy of agreeing to do some hard thinking. She looked across at him. Was he serious? Or had this entire exercise been nothing but a fishing expedition? And if so, to what end? The senior senator from Ohio didn't strike her as the kind of man to play games, although in Washington one could never tell. Finally, she asked: "What do you think the prospects are for a Republican victory next time round?"

"A good question. Depends on how this administration performs. How the world economy performs. What certain despots do to upset the American applecart. Before anything else happens, in my opinion, the Republican Party needs to be thoroughly disinfected. Let me be brutally frank, and to mix metaphors, there will be a mountain to climb in the first instance. But who can tell where the country, the world, will be in three years' time? I can't. Before then - and here I'm thinking out loud - we might find you a congressional seat to contest. There are two in Connecticut coming up, and you were born and bred in that state."

"I hadn't even thought of that."

"Your husband won without being an elected politician, but I wouldn't want that to be a template."

"Anything else?"

"Not than I can think of, least of all anticipate. A British prime minister, Harold Macmillan, was once asked what he feared most about political life. Do you know what he said? 'Events, dear boy, events.' He himself fell from power due to unforeseen events some years later. All I'm saying, my dear, is that any political campaign, no matter how impressive, no matter how in keeping with the zeitgeist, is an obstacle course, and for any number of reasons other than the quality of the ticket." The senator fell silent. He beckoned a waiter. "You know, Samantha, we've been sitting here for at least half an hour and we've yet to order something to eat. I don't know about you, but I'm starving."

"Me, too," Samantha said. It wasn't true. At that moment, eating was the last thing on her mind.

* * * * *

Chapter 22

Frank, recently returned from an extended European trip with Marion, sent out six invitations for an 'anniversary' dinner at his Maryland house. The invitees were Samantha, Nigel, Jane, Fran and Rosalie, plus a mystery guest. Marion would be doing the cooking, he mentioned, as if that might be an inducement to accept.

"What's the occasion?" Nigel asked.

"A celebration of sorts," Frank told him. In fact, dinner was Samantha's idea. Apart from the joy of seeing you all again, she'd like to thank you all for your support, these past few years."

Fran and Rosalie agreed to drive Nigel and Jane. They would all stay overnight.

Labor Day, marking the end of summer, had come and gone. As usual, the weather had seemed to change overnight. There was now an unmistakable though not yet unpleasant nip in the air. A few trees were already shedding leaves. Chesapeake Bay was roiled by whitecaps.

The four guests were greeted at the door by Marion. Nigel and Jane had never met her. She was dark-haired, pretty and petite, just as Nigel had imagined her. She and Frank had enjoyed a wonderful time in Europe, she gushed, and could hardly stop talking about the 'forgotten glamour' of an ocean voyage. She recommended the others think about doing the same thing. "Takes a little longer than flying, of course, but that's the whole point… so much more civilized, relaxing."

"Unless you hit an iceberg," said Nigel, raising no laughs. He had a primal fear of water - especially when it was pitch black and two miles deep.

From the staircase, Samantha made her entrance. Like the others, she had dressed for the occasion. She wore a clinging blue silk cocktail dress that showed off her figure and enough of her shapely legs to draw attention to them. She was in a carefree mood, so different from the anguished woman they had once known. It also helped that she seemed to have gained a few pounds, which everyone agreed was a positive. Except Marion, who watched her own diet to the point of obsession. "It's a constant struggle, isn't it," she remarked, although Nigel, without saying so, thought she needed to put on weight rather than lose it.

Nigel asked Frank about the mystery guest, expecting the pronoun to offer a clue. "They'll be here soon," Frank said, wise to that old trick. "All I'll say is that it's someone most of you have already met."

Marion was about to summon everyone to dinner when the doorbell rang. Samantha virtually leapt out of her seat to answer it. Expectant faces turned in unison. They could hear the newcomer offering profuse apologies in a light Slavic accent, which all but one recognized as that of Anna Litovka. Anna entered the dining room smiling demurely, like one of Tolstoy's duchesses at a Moscow society ball. Everyone stood, grinning.

"I'm sorry to be so late but my flight took off an hour late," Anna explained. She had just flown in from New York. "Is always the same in evening rush hour, especially at that awful La Guardia."

Nigel introduced her to Jane. "So nice to meet you at last, Jane. You look lovely." Jane smiled, instantly signalling her approval of the woman she had long been dying to meet. "I'm delighted to meet you, too, Anna. Nigel has told me so much about you... all good, I should add."

Ethel, the housekeeper, who'd been busy helping Marion in the kitchen, now appeared with the food and began serving, while Frank battled with the cork of a French white wine. "Time to switch to screw-tops," he muttered. "And I never thought I'd hear myself saying that."

Marion looked on with a look of feigned exasperation. "I spend all afternoon in the kitchen while all he's required to do is open a bottle and he can't even do that. And, of course, he leaves it as usual to the last minute. Men!" Her chiding was gentle and affectionate. She and Frank were hardly a typical American couple, but they were happy to play the part, as if putting on a stage act. Nigel decided that he liked them both very much.

Once the main course had been consumed, Samantha tinkled her glass with a spoon and rose from her chair - now a familiar routine.

"Oh, God, not another round of revelations," Nigel cried, feigning horror.

Samantha stared at him in mock revulsion. "Yes, as a matter of fact there are. Just a few, if I may crave your attention for just a few moments."

An expectant hush descended on the table. She had their full attention. Even Frank was listening, having successfully opened not one bottle but two.

"First, let me welcome back into the fold my little lost lamb Anna. We are now together again. And publicly. No more hiding. No more denials. No more pretence." Nigel knew intuitively that this was a warm-up announcement. So did Jane, who glanced across the table at him with a quizzical look that said, *"Whatever next?"* Samantha remained standing and looked directly at Nigel. She smiled, as if just for him. "Yes, I'm afraid there's more."

"I had a bet with myself that there would be," he said.

"Well, you've won." She paused before continuing. "In recent weeks, I've been engaged in conversations with several senior figures in the Republican Party, among them Senator Claude Hansen of Ohio and Senator Martin Leach of Minnesota. I should say, rather, senior figures in the liberal wing of the Party; the other side would be horrified if they knew. Here's the point: they think I should consider running for public office. I've been thinking about it very seriously."

Frank had adopted one of his stagey incredulous looks. "Don't tell me you're thinking of running for town clerk in Greenwich, Connecticut."

"Something a little more ambitious than that. The people I'm talking to want the Republican Party to contest the next presidential election with a new-look ticket. A moderate ticket. Even a liberal ticket." She paused to enjoy watching the guests trying to work out what was coming next. And once more she didn't disappoint. "I've been asked to consider joining that ticket as Senator Leach's running mate. After a great deal of thought - and, I have to say, considerable misgivings - I've decided to accept the invitation, or at least start the process. Hansen's thinking, frankly, is that Leach's nomination is a long-shot, and even if it happened, our winning the election an even longer one. But we agreed that something must be done to stem the conservative tide that has overwhelmed the party in recent years. There are signs that it's already receding. And if nothing else, running a moderate ticket would be good practice for the next time around. Well, that's it. I wanted to run it by you, to ask your views, since you're my unofficial advisors and close friends."

Astonished looks were exchanged across the table. Frank Hoffman's wasn't one of them, Nigel noticed.

Samantha, suddenly remembering, had one more thing to add. "Before then, I'll probably run for a Congressional seat in Connecticut. This would give me some experience in elected office, and of running a campaign. There's a seat about to be vacated, the 4th Congressional District, which happens to include Greenwich, my hometown. See, Frank, you were very close. There, that's all I have to say."

Frank rose to speak. "Let me offer my... congratulations... I think that's the right word."

"But not necessarily the first one you first thought of."

"No, but that's not one I'd care to mention."

"Then I thank you for not mentioning it."

"You never cease to amaze me, Samantha," said Frank. "You've made yet another incredibly brave decision. The question in my mind is whether it's a wise one. Either way it goes without saying that you'd be a great credit to your party and your country, and I'll happily drink to that." He raised a glass, which triggered the others to do the same, turning it into a salute.

Samantha acknowledged them with a nod and then turned back to Frank. "Your toast is appreciated, but there was a 'but' coming. What's the 'but'?"

"The 'but' is that it's fraught with risk. Not just political risk; I'm thinking of the possible effect on your health..."

"My health is perfectly fine," Samantha broke in. "I've never felt better. My doctors confirm it."

"Here's my concern: you'll be entering a brutal gladiatorial arena. Stronger men than you have tried and failed."

"But no stronger women."

"Two, in fact, and look what happened to them."

"What actually happened to them, Frank? They lost, that's all. They lost, and then disappeared. That's politics: someone wins, and so someone also has to lose. I'm prepared for that eventuality. In fact, I rather expect it."

"Then why do it?"

"Because, Frank, I want to make a point."

"The point being...?"

"That the reactionary forces can't have everything their own way; that there are decent people out there who disagree with them and want their voices heard."

"The alt-right's voices would be heard, too, believe me. You'll be totally exposed to public scrutiny. Your life - every bit of it - will be laid bare for all to see. You hate the limelight. You've said so yourself. Many times."

"I know, but I didn't have a cause that I believed in. Now I do. Not just to become the first female vice-president, and the first gay one, but to put the democratic process back on track. It has been derailed, as we all know, and we're all living in fear of the possible consequences."

"That speaks to my point," Frank said. "The extremists won't take your candidacy lying down. They'll do everything in their power to bring you down, and they have considerable power - not just in Washington but out there in the heartlands. Those loonies are everywhere, and some of them are armed and dangerous. They're well organized and have a lust for revenge, even for blood. I for one would fear for your safety. Yes, sympathetic crowds may egg you on, but it's the hostile ones I'd be afraid of. To be honest, I think you've done enough for your country already, without putting yourself in harm's way."

"I'm grateful for your concern for my welfare," Samantha replied evenly. "But before we get carried away, let me stress that until this thing takes more shape it's just an idea. It may never become a plan. For a start, Leach needs to survive the primaries and emerge as the clear front-runner. If he doesn't, then the nomination may go to the convention. If that happened, no one could predict the result. In short, all this may come to nothing. And, given the country's present mood, it probably will. In fact, you might say the whole thing is so far from guaranteed as to be improbable. Leach is a moderate, and that's a dirty word in GOP circles these days. And I'm a… well there's a dirty word for that, too." Samantha took a fortifying sip from a glass of water. "But this isn't something I need to do, and, frankly, it hadn't occurred to me until I had lunch with Senator Hansen. But now I'm thinking that it's something I *want* to do." Samantha sat down. "Now, as Frank used to say, I'll be happy to take questions."

All eyes turned to Nigel. "First, Samantha, let me say that your brilliant talent for making remarkable and startling revelations remains undiminished. I couldn't have been more staggered if you'd told us that you were taking holy orders."

"That, under the circumstances, would be an extremely improbable event," she said with a grin, casting a glance at Anna, sitting next to her.

"Second, I agree with Frank. As much as your candidacy would be a great thing for the country, as well as your party, you've been through a great deal already. I'm no expert on your political system but as far as I can see, a presidential campaign is a marathon, a Darwinian struggle for the survival of the fittest. Are you sure you're up to it? Not just physically, but mentally. Like Frank, I'm only asking for reasons of personal concern."

"I think I'm very much up for it," Samantha said, sounding slightly peeved, as if the matter were above debate. "But we'll find out soon enough. Physically, I feel well. Mentally, I'm in a good place, as we say nowadays. I also have this new-found urge to serve the country, as foolish or naïve as that may strike you."

"I think you've done that already," Frank repeated. "I mean, served your country."

"I agree," Marion said, speaking for the first time. Privately, she was appalled at the prospect of Samantha being lashed by gale-force political winds. Personal winds, too. She already sensed an approaching storm.

"Third," Nigel continued regardless, "it seems to me - and please forgive my blunt language - that while your gender may bring electoral advantage, your sexuality may cancel it out. I'm assuming that your liaison with Anna will have become public knowledge by then. That will cost you votes out in the Bible Belt. There's still a lot of hate and bigotry out there; much of it, I should mention, stirred up by the previous administration, not to mention by this Supreme Court, which has become nothing but a political tool of the Republican Right."

Samantha pretended to be offended by the idea that the American electorate could still harbour such prejudices, but of course she knew better. "They'll just have to get over it," she said off-handedly, as if such a thing was not only possible but a foregone conclusion. "If they can't, then we'll have to re-examine afresh what kind of country we're living in. And, as a candidate, I want to be a catalyst for real change. If that sounds quixotic, then so be it." Nigel, Samantha could tell, looked doubtful. "Look, we've had Catholic presidents, once considered unelectable. We've had divorced presidents which was not supposed to happen either. More recently, we've had a black president, unthinkable a decade earlier. With respect, Nigel, you're view of the electorate fails to recognize that we Americans, if not the gun toting loonies, have caught up with the times.

"The gun-toting loonies, as you call them, are a very large minority," Nigel countered. "One that managed to get your husband elected in close to a landslide. His jaundiced view of the world not only reflected theirs but also made it respectable. They're all still out there, just waiting for an excuse to vent their anger. And they have guns. Not only that, but you'll probably be up against a candidate who will be financed by them. Several of them are waiting in the wings as we speak."

"Yes, yes, I know all that," Samantha said testily. "But we still need, more than ever, to appeal to those better angels of our nature that one of our presidents - a mid-western Republican, by the way - referred to a century and a half ago. We must shift the political debate to a higher level. Focus on issues that matter to ordinary, hard-working, struggling Americans. Someone must have the courage to step up and win them over without reverting to demagoguery. It's called moral leadership, even if it's in a losing cause."

Frank, ever the pragmatist, though still doubtful about the whole enterprise, wanted to move the conversation on from issues of morality to questions of practicality. "What do you need from us, Samantha?"

"Ah, I'm glad you asked, Frank. Should the time arrive - assuming I get to contest the Connecticut seat - I'd hope you'd consider becoming my communications director. Yes, I know you and Marion are enjoying your retirement" - she looked enquiringly, perhaps pleadingly, at Marion - "but I can't think of a better man, or none that I could trust implicitly."

Frank looked at his wife, who shrugged in resignation but said nothing. "Naturally, I'm honoured to be asked, Samantha, but Marion and I will have to discuss it first. She may well have other ideas." Marion still said nothing but managed a thin smile.

"Fair enough. I'm not asking for instant decisions here. I'm just going through some of my options."

"I'll also be debating it with myself," Frank added. "This wouldn't be just a campaign job. If you were to win, you'd want me back in the White House. For at least four years. Possibly eight. Frankly, I'm just not sure it's something I want to do, however worthy the cause. And just think how old I'd be by then."

"I understand," Samantha said. "But let me stress again, this is just me thinking out loud." She looked next at Fran. "And you, my dear friend, I'd like you to consider being Frank's deputy." She knew that Fran and Frank had experienced moments of creative tension but that, she thought, would only make them a better team. "Again, just something to think about."

Fran was deeply affected. "I'm not sure how to respond… except to say that I'd have to talk it over with Frank. And, of course, my Rosalie here."

Rosalie reached over and squeezed Fran's hand. "You'll do it, I've no doubt about that. I'd also have no objection."

"Well," said Fran, "that's because you haven't had a chance to think it through."

"True enough. But whither thou goest…"

Fran, tears welling, leaned over and gave her a hug.

But Samantha had not yet finished. She turned to Nigel. "I'll need someone to write press releases and take care of the media. I'd offer you the post of press relations manager. Reporting to Frank. You two seem to have buried the hatchet - and not in each other."

Nigel said nothing but shook his head. This was all a bit too much to take in so quickly. He felt as if he, and the others, were being swept along by a sudden violent gust of wind.

"I'll also need someone to analyze polling and other data. How about you, Jane? I think you'd be perfect for running the campaign research programme. Not your usual line of country, I admit, but we'd recruit some seasoned professionals to help you."

Jane glanced again at Nigel, sharing his disbelief.

"And last but by no means least, Rosalie, I've got you down as my personal assistant, as you are now. There, I think that covers it for now."

No voices were raised, not even to ask questions.

Then, after an interval, Frank responded. "On reflection, I'd be honoured to serve in your campaign, Samantha, and in your administration… but only if Marion is okay with it. I might yet change my mind, even if she doesn't do it for me."

"Since when did you start asking *my* permission," Marion said with a wry smile.

"I'm suppose I'm asking right now, aren't I?"

Frank's response seemed to embolden Nigel. "I'm also honoured to be asked, Samantha, so don't get me wrong when I ask an obvious question: have you considered whether I'm remotely qualified for such a job. In case you hadn't noticed, I'm not a native of this land. It seems to me you'll need someone who knows his way around the political scene here. I'm not one of those."

Samantha laughed. "If you don't know your way around Washington right now, you soon will. As for your nationality, I'd say that's as irrelevant as my sexuality."

"The point is," Nigel persisted, "that I…"

"The point is," Samantha interrupted, "that I wish to have around me a team of people I trust. People I can work with. Perhaps more importantly, people I genuinely like."

"I'll have to give it some serious thought," said Nigel.

"You all must," said Samantha. "I don't want anyone jumping into this. It will be a rough ride, no doubt about that."

Jane, not for the first time, had the most penetrating observation. "I'm sitting here, Samantha, realizing that I don't even know what your politics are. Progressive, that much is clear, but progressive is a relative word. What kind of platform will you run on?"

"How about 'Make America Decent Again'?"

"Perfect," cried Nigel, turning to give Jane an admiring glance.

Jane hadn't finished her point. "Some might say you're running for the wrong party, that you're a Democrat in sheep's clothing."

"I probably am. But it's not the Democrats who approached me."

"What if they had?"

"I've always been a Republican, and I'm not going to switch now. Anyway, it's the GOP that needs purging."

"I've never trusted the Republicans," the putative press relations manager put in, as if to announce yet another disqualification. But he knew, in his gut and in his heart, that he would do it. He would do it for her. They all would.

Frank didn't know that. "Well, that's a bloody good start," he shot back affecting an English accent. "Five minutes into the campaign and already we have a subversive in our midst."

But it was Marion who made the most decisive intervention of the evening. "All this is very well, ladies and gentlemen, but if I may say so a little speculative. Meanwhile, I've baked a delightful home-made tarte tatin if anyone's interested. And especially for you, Nigel, there's again some rancid cheese to follow."

"You won't be getting such treats on the rubber chicken circuit," Samantha saw fit to mention.

* * * * *

EPILOGUE

Four Years Later

On a cold, blustery January day in Washington, the president-elect faced the Chief Justice of the United States and raised a hand to take the oath of office. There was no Bible involved because the oath was being affirmed rather than sworn - one of several unprecedented acts in this unusual and once almost unimaginable inauguration ceremony: "I do solemnly affirm that I will faithfully execute the Office of the President of the United States…"

The ceremony, in accordance with recent custom, was performed on a raised platform erected on the western porch of the United States Capitol. Witnessed by the great and the good of American politics, among them four of the new president's predecessors. A fifth, Martin Jameson, had declined to attend, citing ill-health, although he seemed fit enough when photographed playing a round of golf the next day.

On the Capitol steps below the stand were several rows of lesser dignitaries, including Nigel Harper and his wife Jane, Frank and Marion Hoffman, and newlyweds Fran and Rosalie Powell. "The Crazy Gang," as Nigel called them, after a famous British wartime comedy troupe that his grandfather often used to talk about. The six of them stood in silent reflection, each shedding a tear. Once united in adversity, they would soon be parting in nostalgia, to be fully exercised later in the day at a valedictory lunch, which, in keeping with the mood, Nigel had insisted that it be held at a frowzy downtown restaurant called the *Happy Heifer*. "It's for old times' sake," Nigel added in response to the horrified looks of the others.

Behind them a vast throng stretched along the National Mall to a horizon punctured by the obelisk of the Washington Monument. Few spectators could hear the oath being recited, but a respectful hush had descended in observance of this quadrennial reaffirmation of American democracy. The unnatural silence was broken only by the sound of flags being slapped against metal poles by the bone-chilling northerly wind, or a screech from a low-flying seagull. A moment later, a ripple of applause from the platform confirmed that the oath had been taken, and there arose a prolonged and exuberant round of cheering. The noise had barely subsided when the newly sworn president advanced to the podium to address the nation to an even noisier welcome.

How very different an occasion it might have been, Nigel was thinking, his mind racing back to the shocking act of violence in Philadelphia that had changed the direction of the campaign, and perhaps the course of history.

It had followed an all too familiar pattern: a peaceable public event sickeningly shattered by a misfit with a concealed firearm and a consuming resentment. That it had happened in the so-called City of Brotherly Love merely added bitter irony to gross insult. The Republican team had gone there, two months before Election Day for the first of what was intended to be a series of joint appearances, in the hope that the poor personal approval ratings of Senator Richard Leach would be boosted by the presence of his popular running mate, Congresswoman Samantha Farnsworth. A dense and congenial audience had gathered in front of Independence Hall for the occasion, women outnumbering men by a significant margin. The senator had just completed a rambling stump speech, in which the loudest cheer was reserved for the moment he invited his running mate to join him on the platform. He was about to shake her hand when there were three loud bangs, followed soon after by a fourth. Witnesses later recalled the sounds 'like firecrackers going off', the inadequacy of the words an echo of those that had described several such incidents in the past.

What followed was the usual chaos of incomprehension. Television viewers had the best view, and watched stupefied as the senator collapsed, with a glazed look of disbelief, one hand half raised as if in supplication. Samantha, momentarily stunned, remained standing for a moment before being thrown to the floor by a quick-thinking Secret Service agent. Viewers noticed a spattering of blood on her dress, giving rise to a rumour that she had also been hit. The assailant, a leather-clad young man in his twenties described as a homeless drifter with a history of mental illness, had meanwhile been wrestled to the ground by bystanders, but not before he'd somehow wriggled free to turn the gun on himself.

Of the three bullets that struck the senator, the first entered his chest, the second grazed his head, and the third went through his left shoulder. Samantha was promptly hustled away to the nearest hospital as a precaution. It would be an hour before a news bulletin confirmed that she had escaped unharmed.

The senator's wounds were not fatal. Miraculously, the bullet in his chest had missed vital organs. The shoulder would heal in time. The head wound, which had given the main cause for concern, proved to be superficial. At a hastily convened press conference, doctors opined that he was expected to make a full recovery, but only after several months of recuperation. In answer to a question, they declared that he would not be returning to the campaign trail any time soon.

Until then, most commentators had been calling the election result a foregone conclusion: an emphatic if not overwhelming win for the Democrats. Both sides had earned unstinting praise for running a decent campaign, mercifully free of the snarling invective that had marred recent presidential contests, but Senator Leach had proved to be an uninspired orator. Nor had he performed well in the debates, at times looking befuddled by an opponent skilled in the dark arts of the wounding riposte and the well-aimed put-down. His running mate by contrast had come across as empathetic and eloquent, both on the stump and in debate. But vice-presidential candidates tend to be reduced to little more than ciphers, perhaps reflecting the perceived secondary importance of the office.

Philadelphia, like Dallas, had now given the lie to that.

Up to that point, the rhetorical shortcomings of the ticket's senior partner had proved too great a burden to tip the scales to the Republicans, and in the South and Midwest Samantha's sexuality had proved to be unhelpful, if not as ruinously so as might have been anticipated. Philadelphia changed all that. Senator Leach withdrew from the race, and by agreement between the parties, campaigning was suspended for a week. Congress declined to postpone the election, on the grounds that it had never happened before. In the tradition of the circus, after a high-wire act had gone wrong, the show would go on.

The Republican National Committee, after hastily polling its 160-odd members, decided that Samantha Farnsworth would now head the ticket, with a new running mate to be approved as quickly as possible. Party functionaries set to work on a short list.

"Democracy must always prevail over violence," Samantha declared, a week after Philadelphia, "and to that end we have a duty to carry on. And carry on we shall."

In keeping with the times, she had considered selecting as her running mate a person of colour, or even another woman, but in the end settled for - indeed insisted on - someone who would require no prolonged vetting and, more importantly, given her relative lack of experience, someone who would bring to the contest - and the vice-presidency - proven integrity, reassuring solidity, and a deep knowledge of the legislative process. The candidate she turned to was ideal on all three counts: her friend and mentor, the senior statesman from Ohio, Senator Claude Hansen.

Inevitably, the shooting generated a wave of sympathy for the opposition party. Hansen's calming, avuncular presence did the rest. In a curious inversion of traditional party positions - and to the fury of the party's right wing - Samantha had been presciently vocal in demanding draconian reforms of the gun control laws. Her opponent, the White House incumbent, shared her views, but he had done nothing to further the cause during his four years in office. She enjoyed the additional benefit of having come perilously close to being a victim of gun crime herself. Swing voters who had doubted the stricken candidate's leadership abilities now flocked to the Republican nominee in large numbers. Women, according to various polls, made up the largest component.

And so, weeks after the tumult of the campaign had receded, and the votes had been counted, it was Samantha Farnsworth who stepped forward to take the oath of office on this cold January morning.

"... and will to the best of my ability, preserve, protect and defend the Constitution of the United States."

"Congratulations, Madam President," said a beaming Chief Justice, stressing the second word, mindful that he was the first in history to address a president in that form.

After a band had played a rollicking version of *Hail to the Chief,* President Samantha Farnsworth kissed Anna Litovka on both cheeks and stepped forward to address the nation.

In a speech later widely praised as both wise and magnanimous, she outlined a vision of a more tolerant, considerate and inclusive America, one that would become a model for the world to admire and emulate. Right-wing watchwords fell like apples in autumn. The ideals would be easier said than accomplished, of course. But the crowd sensed that this president might be more capable than her recent predecessors in converting platitudes into policy and roared its approval.

Nigel had never doubted her determination, but this was a new, confident, assertive Samantha, someone who really might change the world, despite his deep-seated reservations about her party, and the prospect of a severe reaction from its more extreme element.

She also looked, he thought, more radiant than ever.

"Quite a speech," said a tearful Frank Hoffman, turning to Nigel when it was over. "And quite a moment. I can't believe what I just heard. But now, I really can look forward to that well-earned retirement I've been talking about." He meant it, too. "I've had enough," he'd told Samantha, turning down an offer to be her press secretary, and several other administrative posts she had mentioned. "I'm sorry, truly I am, but you need someone younger and someone more in tune with the zeitgeist than this old warrior. But I'll always be there for you, Samantha, you know that. Any time."

She refrained from arguing that a man in his fifties hardly qualified as an 'old warrior', or that if he was 'always there' for her, he would have accepted her offer. But she let it go, recognizing that he was determined to fade from the scene. "You'll always be a welcome visitor to the Farnsworth White House," she had said, embracing him warmly. "I'll be needing all the help I can get. And if it's free, so much the better."

Fran Powell had needed no persuasion to accept a role as the administration's senior communications strategist. "Suddenly, the world looks a different place," she gushed, "and I want to be there to see the transformation completed, while the world is still listening."

Samantha had also expressed her gratitude to Nigel, who had turned down a role in the campaign but had made occasional literary contributions to it. She hadn't offered him a post in the administration, nor had he expected it. And now, with two toddlers to raise, his priorities now lay elsewhere. He needed a change of pace, and perhaps a change of scenery, and had been feeling homesick of late. He was much too fond of the *Post* to entertain offers from rivals, of which he had turned down several over the years. Then, a few days after the inauguration, he'd received a call from the chief executive of the news division of a British television company. Would he consider joining the group as its chief political correspondent? The job would be based in London. The salary mentioned was more than he'd ever earned, and more than double his current one.

He consulted Jane, who, without a moment's hesitation, urged him to take the offer. He hadn't needed any persuading himself.

Even Duncan Erskine, sorry as he was to be losing his protégé, thought that he should take it. "I told you six years ago - in the Savoy Grill, if you remember - that there would be a bidding war for your services. Good luck to you, I say. You deserve it, laddie."

What Duncan failed to mention was that he'd shortly be leaving the *Post*, too, for the top job in a well-known publishing house.

A month later, as Nigel and Jane were finishing the packing, ready to catch the redeye to London, she described the move as a "return to normalcy".

"Normality," he corrected her.

"Yes, I suppose I'll have to learn a whole new language," she said.

"Well, I had to."

"Meanwhile," she said, closing the last bag with a gratifying click, "since we'll have nothing much to do for the next seven hours, we might give some thought to where we'd like to live."

"Ah, I'm glad you mentioned it," he said brightly. "I forgot to tell you: Duncan is selling his flat, but he's offered it to us on a temporary basis. It's small, but there are two bedrooms."

"Still a little tight for four, though, wouldn't you say?"

"The kids won't take up too much room, darling. It will do for a month or so, while we're looking for something permanent."

"Also, isn't it in Chelsea? Wouldn't that be a little too close to your ex for comfort - not to mention you-know-who?"

"She and Vincent have parted company."

"You didn't mention that."

"Sorry. Anyway, she's now living in a sprawling mansion in Hampstead. Shacked up with some French cosmetics mogul - or so I've been told."

"Well, good for her."

"And even better for me."

"I wouldn't bet on it."

"Ah, I hear the doorbell. Must be our limo." He yelled at the girls, playing in the yard. "Come in, Sam. You too, Fran. It's time to go."

ABOUT THE AUTHOR

John Jessop was born on 20 May 1942 in Amersham, Buckinghamshire. He spent most of his early professional life at Reuters, first as a financial journalist and then as a marketing executive. He subsequently became a celebrated figure in the financial information industry, which specialises in distributing news and market data to banks and investment firms. He wrote about that experience, and the history of the business, in *Tales from the South Pier*. This is his first novel. A dual British and American citizen, he currently lives in Surrey, England with his wife Martha.

Milton Keynes UK
Ingram Content Group UK Ltd.
UKHW041851050924
447857UK00018B/217/J

9 781835 630631